THE BEST
WAR
STORIES
EVER TOLD

THE BEST
WAR
STORIES
EVER TOLD

EDITED BY
STEPHEN BRENNAN

Skyhorse Publishing

Skyhorse Publishing books may be purchased in bulk at special discounts for sales promotion, corporate gifts, fund-raising, or educational purposes. Special editions can also be created to specifications. For details, contact the Special Sales Department, Skyhorse Publishing, 307 West 36th Street, 11th Floor, New York, NY 10018 or info@skyhorsepublishing.com.

Skyhorse® and Skyhorse Publishing® are registered trademarks of Skyhorse Publishing, Inc.®, a Delaware corporation.

www.skyhorsepublishing.com

10 9 8 7 6 5 4 3 2 1

Library of Congress Cataloging-in-Publication Data is available on file.
ISBN: 978-1-61608-433-2

Printed in the United States of America

CONTENTS

THE RAGE OF ACHILLES

HOMER

Thus, then, did the Achaeans arm by their ships round you, O son of Peleus, who were hungering for battle; while the Trojans over against them armed upon the rise of the plain.

Meanwhile Jove from the top of many-delled Olympus, bade Themis gather the gods in council, whereon she went about and called them to the house of Jove. There was not a river absent except Oceanus, nor a single one of the nymphs that haunt fair groves, or springs of rivers and meadows of green grass. When they reached the house of cloud-compelling Jove, they took their seats in the arcades of polished marble which Vulcan with his consummate skill had made for father Jove.

In such wise, therefore, did they gather in the house of Jove. Neptune also, lord of the earthquake, obeyed the call of the goddess, and came up out of the sea to join them. There, sitting in the midst of them, he asked what Jove's purpose might be. "Why," said he, "wielder of the lightning, have you called the gods in council? Are you considering some matter that concerns the Trojans and Achaeans- for the blaze of battle is on the point of being kindled between them?"

And Jove answered, "You know my purpose, shaker of earth, and wherefore I have called you hither. I take thought for them even in their destruction. For my own part I shall stay here seated on Mt. Olympus and look on in peace, but do you others go about among Trojans and Achaeans, and help either side as you may be severally disposed. If Achilles fights the Trojans without hindrance they will make no stand against him; they have ever trembled at the sight of him, and now that he is roused to such fury about his comrade, he will override fate itself and storm their city."

Thus spoke Jove and gave the word for war, whereon the gods took their several sides and went into battle. Juno, Pallas Minerva, earth-encircling Neptune, Mercury bringer of good luck and excellent in all cunning-all these joined the host that came from the ships; with them also came Vulcan in all his glory, limping, but yet with his thin legs plying lustily under him. Mars of gleaming helmet joined the Trojans, and with him Apollo of locks unshorn, and the archer goddess Diana, Leto, Xanthus, and laughter-loving Venus.

So long as the gods held themselves aloof from mortal warriors the Achaeans were triumphant, for Achilles who had long refused to fight was now with them. There was not a Trojan but his limbs failed him for fear as he beheld the fleet son of Peleus all glorious in his armour, and looking like Mars himself. When, however, the Olympians came to take their part among men, forthwith uprose strong Strife, rouser of hosts, and Minerva raised her loud voice, now standing by the deep trench that ran outside the wall, and now shouting with all her might upon the shore of the sounding sea. Mars also bellowed out upon the other side, dark as some black thunder-cloud, and called on the Trojans at the top of his voice, now from the acropolis, and now speeding up the side of the river Simois till he came to the hill Callicolone.

Thus did the gods spur on both hosts to fight, and rouse fierce contention also among themselves. The sire of gods and men thundered from heaven above, while from beneath Neptune shook the vast earth, and bade the high hills tremble. The spurs and crests of many-fountained Ida quaked, as also the city of the Trojans and the ships of the Achaeans. Hades, king of the realms below, was struck with fear; he sprang panic-stricken from his throne and cried aloud in terror lest Neptune, lord of the earthquake, should crack the ground over his head, and lay bare his mouldy mansions to the sight of mortals and immortals-mansions so ghastly grim that even the gods shudder to think of them. Such was the uproar as the gods came together in battle. Apollo with his arrows took his stand to face King Neptune, while Minerva took hers against the god of war; the archer-goddess Diana with her golden arrows, sister of far-darting Apollo, stood to face Juno; Mercury the lusty bringer of good luck faced Leto, while the mighty eddying river whom men can Scamander, but gods Xanthus, matched himself against Vulcan.

The gods, then, were thus ranged against one another. But the heart of Achilles was set on meeting Hector son of Priam, for it was with his blood that he longed above all things else to glut the stubborn lord of battle. Meanwhile Apollo set Aeneas on to attack the son of Peleus, and put courage into his heart, speaking with the voice of Lycaon son of Priam. In his likeness therefore, he said to Aeneas, "Aeneas, counsellor of the Trojans, where are now the brave words with which you vaunted over your wine before the Trojan princes, saying that you would fight Achilles son of Peleus in single combat?"

And Aeneas answered, "Why do you thus bid me fight the proud son of Peleus, when I am in no mind to do so? Were I to face him now, it would not be for the first time. His spear has already put me to Right from Ida, when he attacked our cattle and sacked Lyrnessus and Pedasus; Jove indeed saved me in that he vouchsafed me strength to fly, else had the fallen by the hands of Achilles and Minerva, who went before him to protect him and urged him to fall upon the Lelegae and Trojans. No man may fight Achilles, for one of the gods is always with him as his guardian angel, and even were it not so, his weapon flies ever straight, and fails not to pierce the flesh of him who is against him; if heaven would let me fight him on even terms he should not soon overcome me, though he boasts that he is made of bronze."

Then said King Apollo, son to Jove, "Nay, hero, pray to the ever-living gods, for men say that you were born of Jove's daughter Venus, whereas Achilles is son to a goddess of inferior rank. Venus is child to Jove, while Thetis is but daughter to the old man of the sea. Bring, therefore, your spear to bear upon him, and let him not scare you with his taunts and menaces."

As he spoke he put courage into the heart of the shepherd of his people, and he strode in full armour among the ranks of the foremost fighters. Nor did the son of Anchises escape the notice of white-armed Juno, as he went forth into the throng to meet Achilles. She called the gods about her, and said, "Look to it, you two, Neptune and Minerva, and consider how this shall be; Phoebus Apollo has been sending Aeneas clad in full armour to fight Achilles. Shall we turn him back at once, or shall one of us stand by Achilles and endow him with strength so that his heart fail not, and he may learn that the chiefs of the immortals are on his side, while the others who have all along been defending the Trojans are but vain helpers? Let us all come down from Olympus and join in the fight, that this day he may take no hurt at the hands of the Trojans. Hereafter let him suffer whatever fate may have spun out for him when he was begotten and his mother bore him. If Achilles be not thus assured by the voice of a god, he may come to fear presently when one of us meets him in battle, for the gods are terrible if they are seen face to face."

Neptune lord of the earthquake answered her saying, "Juno, restrain your fury; it is not well; I am not in favour of forcing the other gods to fight us, for the advantage is too greatly on our own side; let us take our places on some hill out of the beaten track, and let mortals fight it out among themselves. If Mars or Phoebus Apollo begin fighting, or keep Achilles in check so that he cannot fight, we too, will at once raise the cry of battle, and in that case they will soon leave the field and go back vanquished to Olympus among the other gods."

With these words the dark-haired god led the way to the high earth-barrow of Hercules, built round solid masonry, and made by the Trojans and Pallas Minerva for him fly to when the sea-monster was chasing him from the shore on to the plain. Here Neptune and those that were with him took their seats, wrapped in a thick cloud of darkness; but the other gods seated themselves on the brow of Callicolone round you, O Phoebus, and Mars the waster of cities.

Thus did the gods sit apart and form their plans, but neither side was willing to begin battle with the other, and Jove from his seat on high was in command over them all. Meanwhile the whole plain was alive with men and horses, and blazing with the gleam of armour. The earth rang again under the tramp of their feet as they rushed towards each other, and two champions, by far the foremost of them all, met between the hosts to fight- to wit, Aeneas son of Anchises, and noble Achilles.

Aeneas was first to stride forward in attack, his doughty helmet tossing defiance as he came on. He held his strong shield before his breast, and brandished his bronze spear. The son of Peleus from the other side sprang forth to meet him, fike some fierce lion that the whole country-side has met to hunt and kill- at first he bodes no ill, but when some daring youth has struck him with a spear, he crouches openmouthed, his jaws foam, he roars with fury, he lashes his tail from side to side about his ribs and loins, and glares as he springs straight before him, to find out whether he is to slay, or be slain among the foremost of his foes- even with such fury did Achilles bum to spring upon Aeneas.

When they were now close up with one another Achilles was first to speak. "Aeneas," said he, "why do you stand thus out before the host to fight me? Is it that you hope to reign over the Trojans in the seat of Priam? Nay, though you kill me Priam will not hand his kingdom over to you. He is a man of sound judgement, and he has sons of his own. Or have the Trojans been allotting you a demesne of passing richness, fair with orchard lawns and corn lands, if you should slay me? This you shall hardly do. I have discomfited you once already. Have you forgotten how when you were alone I chased you from your herds helter-skelter down the slopes of Ida? You did not turn round to look behind you; you took refuge in Lyrnessus, but I attacked the city, and with the help of Minerva and father Jove I sacked it and carried its women into captivity, though Jove and the other gods rescued you. You think they will protect you now, but they will not do so; therefore I say go back into the host, and do not face me, or you will rue it. Even a fool may be wise after the event."

Then Aeneas answered, "Son of Peleus, think not that your words can scare me as though I were a child. I too, if I will, can brag and talk unseemly. We know one another's race and parentage as matters of common fame, though neither have you ever seen my parents nor I yours. Men say that you are son to noble Peleus, and that your mother is Thetis, fair-haired daughter of the sea. I have noble Anchises for my father, and Venus for my mother; the parents of one or other of us shall this day mourn a son, for it will be more than silly talk that shall part us when the fight is over. Learn, then, my lineage if you will- and it is known to many.

"In the beginning Dardanus was the son of Jove, and founded Dardania, for Ilius was not yet stablished on the plain for men to dwell in, and her people still abode on the spurs of many-fountained Ida. Dardanus had a son, king Erichthonius, who was wealthiest of all men living; he had three thousand mares that fed by the water-meadows, they and their foals with them. Boreas was enamoured of them as they were feeding, and covered them in the semblance of a dark-maned stallion. Twelve filly foals did they conceive and bear him, and these, as they sped over the rich plain, would go bounding on over the ripe ears of corn and not break them; or again when they would disport themselves on the broad back of Ocean they could gallop on the crest of a breaker.

Erichthonius begat Tros, king of the Trojans, and Tros had three noble sons, Ilus, Assaracus, and Ganymede who was comeliest of mortal men; wherefore the gods carried him off to be Jove's cupbearer, for his beauty's sake, that he might dwell among the immortals. Ilus begat Laomedon, and Laomedon begat Tithonus, Priam, Lampus, Clytius, and Hiketaon of the stock of Mars. But Assaracus was father to Capys, and Capys to Anchises, who was my father, while Hector is son to Priam.

"Such do I declare my blood and lineage, but as for valour, Jove gives it or takes it as he will, for he is lord of all. And now let there be no more of this prating in mid-battle as though we were children. We could fling taunts without end at one another; a hundred-oared galley would not hold them. The tongue can run all whithers and talk all wise; it can go here and there, and as a man says, so shall he be gainsaid. What is the use of our bandying hard like women who when they fall foul of one another go out and wrangle in the streets, one half true and the other lies, as rage inspires them? No words of yours shall turn me now that I am fain to fight- therefore let us make trial of one another with our spears."

As he spoke he drove his spear at the great and terrible shield of Achilles, which rang out as the point struck it. The son of Peleus held the shield before him with his strong hand, and he was afraid, for he deemed that Aeneas's spear would go through it quite easily, not reflecting that the god's glorious gifts were little likely to yield before the blows of mortal men; and indeed Aeneas's spear did not pierce the shield, for the layer of gold, gift of the god, stayed the point. It went through two layers, but the god had made the shield in five, two of bronze, the two innermost ones of tin, and one of gold; it was in this that the spear was stayed.

Achilles in his turn threw, and struck the round shield of Aeneas at the very edge, where the bronze was thinnest; the spear of Pelian ash went clean through, and the shield rang under the blow; Aeneas was afraid, and crouched backwards, holding the shield away from him; the spear, however, flew over his back, and stuck quivering in the ground, after having gone through both circles of the sheltering shield. Aeneas though he had avoided the spear, stood still, blinded with fear and grief because the weapon had gone so near him; then Achilles sprang furiously upon him, with a cry as of death and with his keen blade drawn, and Aeneas seized a great stone, so huge that two men, as men now are, would be unable to lift it, but Aeneas wielded it quite easily.

Aeneas would then have struck Achilles as he was springing towards him, either on the helmet, or on the shield that covered him, and Achilles would have closed with him and despatched him with his sword, had not Neptune lord of the earthquake been quick to mark, and said forthwith to the immortals, "Alas, I am sorry for great Aeneas, who will now go down to the house of Hades, vanquished by the son of Peleus. Fool that he was to give ear to the counsel of Apollo. Apollo will never save him from destruction. Why should this man suffer when he is guiltless, to no purpose, and in another's quarrel? Has he not at all times offered acceptable sacrifice to the gods that dwell in heaven? Let us then snatch him from death's jaws, lest the son of Saturn be angry should Achilles slay him. It is fated, moreover, that he should escape, and that the race of Dardanus, whom Jove loved above all the sons born to him of mortal women, shall not perish utterly without seed or sign. For now indeed has Jove hated the blood of Priam, while Aeneas shall reign over the Trojans, he and his children's children that shall be born hereafter."

Then answered Juno, "Earth-shaker, look to this matter yourself, and consider concerning Aeneas, whether you will save him, or suffer him, brave though he be, to fall by the hand of Achilles son of Peleus. For of a truth we two, I and Pallas Minerva, have sworn full many a time before all the immortals, that never would we shield Trojans from destruction, not even when all Troy is burning in the flames that the Achaeans shall kindle."

When earth-encircling Neptune heard this he went into the battle amid the clash of spears, and came to the place where Achilles and Aeneas were. Forthwith he shed a darkness before the eyes of the son of Peleus, drew the bronze-headed ashen spear from the shield of Aeneas, and laid it at the feet of Achilles. Then he lifted Aeneas on high from off the earth and hurried him away. Over the heads of many a band of warriors both horse and foot did he soar as the god's hand sped him, till he came to the very fringe of the battle where the Cauconians were arming themselves for fight. Neptune, shaker of the earth, then came near to him and said, Aeneas, what god has egged you on to this folly in fighting the son of Peleus, who is both a mightier man of valour and more beloved of heaven than you are? Give way before him whensoever you meet him, lest you go down to the house of Hades even though fate would have it otherwise. When Achilles is dead you may then fight among the foremost undaunted, for none other of the Achaeans shall slay you."

The god left him when he had given him these instructions, and at once removed the darkness from before the eyes of Achilles, who opened them wide indeed and said in great anger, "Alas! what marvel am I now beholding? Here is my spear upon the ground, but I see not him whom I meant to kill when I hurled it. Of a truth Aeneas also must be under heaven's protection, although I had thought his boasting was idle. Let him go hang; he will be in no mood to fight me further, seeing how narrowly he has missed being killed. I will now give my orders to the Danaans and attack some other of the Trojans."

He sprang forward along the line and cheered his men on as he did so. "Let not the Trojans," he cried, "keep you at arm's length, Achaeans, but go for them and fight them man for man. However valiant I may be, I cannot give chase to so many and fight all of them. Even Mars, who is an immortal, or Minerva, would shrink from flinging himself into the jaws of such a fight and laying about him; nevertheless, so far as in me lies I will show no slackness of hand or foot nor want of endurance, not even for a moment; I will utterly break their ranks, and woe to the Trojan who shall venture within reach of my spear."

Thus did he exhort them. Meanwhile Hector called upon the Trojans and declared that he would fight Achilles. "Be not afraid, proud Trojans," said he, "to face the son of Peleus; I could fight gods myself if the battle were one of words only, but they would be more than a match for me, if we had to use our spears. Even so the deed of Achilles will fall somewhat short of his word; he will do in part, and the other part he will clip short. I will go up against him though his hands be as fire- though his hands be fire and his strength iron."

Thus urged the Trojans lifted up their spears against the Achaeans, and raised the cry of battle as they flung themselves into the midst of their ranks. But Phoebus Apollo came up to Hector and said, "Hector, on no account must you challenge Achilles to single combat; keep a lookout for him while you are under cover of the others and away from the thick of the fight, otherwise he will either hit you with a spear or cut you down at close quarters."

Thus he spoke, and Hector drew back within the crowd, for he was afraid when he heard what the god had said to him. Achilles then sprang upon the Trojans with a terrible cry, clothed in valour as with a garment. First he killed Iphition son of Otrynteus, a leader of much people whom a naiad nymph had borne to Otrynteus waster of cities, in the land of Hyde under the snowy heights of Mt. Tmolus. Achilles struck him full on the head as he was coming on towards him, and split it clean in two; whereon he fell heavily to the ground and Achilles vaunted over him saying, "You he low, son of Otrynteus, mighty hero; your death is here, but your lineage is on the Gygaean lake where your father's estate lies, by Hyllus, rich in fish, and the eddying waters of Hermus."

Thus did he vaunt, but darkness closed the eyes of the other. The chariots of the Achaeans cut him up as their wheels passed over him in the front of the battle, and after him Achilles killed Demoleon, a valiant man of war and son to Antenor. He struck him on the temple through his bronze-cheeked helmet. The helmet did not stay the spear, but it went right on, crushing the bone so that the brain inside was shed in all directions, and his lust of fighting was ended. Then he struck Hippodamas in the midriff as he was springing down from his chariot in front of him, and trying to escape. He breathed his last, bellowing like a bull bellows when young men are dragging him to offer him in sacrifice to the King of Helice, and the heart of the earth-shaker is glad; even so did he bellow as he lay dying. Achilles then went in pursuit of Polydorus son of Priam, whom his father had always forbidden to fight because he was the youngest of his sons, the one he loved best, and the fastest runner. He, in his folly and showing off the fleetness of his feet, was rushing about among front ranks until he lost his life, for Achilles struck him in the middle of the back as he was darting past him: he struck him just at the golden fastenings of his belt and where the two pieces of the double breastplate overlapped. The point of the spear pierced him through and came out by the navel, whereon he fell groaning on to his knees and a cloud of darkness overshadowed him as he sank holding his entrails in his hands.

When Hector saw his brother Polydorus with his entrails in his hands and sinking down upon the ground, a mist came over his eyes, and he could not bear to keep longer at a distance; he therefore poised his spear and darted towards Achilles like a flame of fire. When Achilles saw him he bounded forward and vaunted saying, "This is he that has wounded my heart most deeply and has slain my beloved comrade. Not for long shall we two quail before one another on the highways of war."

He looked fiercely on Hector and said, "Draw near, that you may meet your doom the sooner." Hector feared him not and answered, "Son of Peleus, think not that your words can scare me as though I were a child; I too if I will can brag and talk unseemly; I know that you are a mighty warrior, mightier by far than I, nevertheless the issue lies in the the lap of heaven whether I, worse man though I be, may not slay you with my spear, for this too has been found keen ere now."

He hurled his spear as he spoke, but Minerva breathed upon it, and though she breathed but very lightly she turned it back from going towards Achilles, so that it returned to Hector and lay at his feet in front of him. Achilles then sprang furiously on him with a loud cry, bent on killing him, but Apollo caught him up easily as a god can, and hid him in a thick darkness. Thrice did Achilles spring towards him spear in hand, and thrice did he waste his blow upon the air. When he rushed forward for the fourth time as though he were a god, he shouted aloud saying, "Hound, this time too you have escaped death- but of a truth it came exceedingly near you. Phoebus Apollo, to whom it seems you pray before you go into battle, has again saved you; but if I too have any friend among the gods I will surely make an end of you when I come across you at some other time. Now, however, I will pursue and overtake other Trojans."

On this he struck Dryops with his spear, about the middle of his neck, and he fell headlong at his feet. There he let him lie and stayed Demouchus son of Philetor, a man both brave and of great stature, by hitting him on the knee with a spear; then he smote him with his sword and killed him. After this he sprang on Laogonus and Dardanus, sons of Bias, and threw them from their chariot, the one with a blow from a thrown spear, while the other he cut down in hand-to-hand fight. There was also Tros the son of Alastor- he came up to Achilles and clasped his knees in the hope that he would spare him and not kill him but let him go, because they were both of the same age. Fool, he might have known that he should not prevail with him, for the man was in no mood for pity or forbearance but was in grim earnest. Therefore when Tros laid hold of his knees and sought a hearing for his prayers, Achilles drove his sword into his liver, and the liver came rolling out, while his bosom was all covered with the black blood that welled from the wound. Thus did death close his eyes as he lay lifeless.

Achilles then went up to Mulius and struck him on the ear with a spear, and the bronze spear-head came right out at the other ear. He also struck Echeclus son of Agenor on the head with his sword, which became warm with the blood, while death and stern fate closed the eyes of Echeclus. Next in order the bronze point of his spear wounded Deucalion in the fore-arm where the sinews of the elbow are united, whereon he waited Achilles' onset with his arm hanging down and death staring him in the face. Achilles cut his head off with a blow from his sword and flung it helmet and all away from him, and the marrow came oozing out of his backbone as he lay. He then went in pursuit of Rhigmus, noble son of Peires, who had come from fertile Thrace, and struck him through the middle with a spear which fixed itself in his belly, so that he fell headlong from his chariot. He also speared Areithous squire to Rhigmus in the back as he was turning his horses in flight, and thrust him from his chariot, while the horses were struck with panic.

As a fire raging in some mountain glen after long drought- and the dense forest is in a blaze, while the wind carries great tongues of fire in every direction- even so furiously did Achilles rage, wielding his spear as though he were a god, and giving chase to those whom he would slay, till the dark earth ran with blood. Or as one who yokes broad-browed oxen that they may tread barley in a threshing-floor-and it is soon bruised small under the feet of the lowing cattle-even so did the horses of Achilles trample on the shields and bodies of the slain. The axle underneath and the railing that ran round the car were bespattered with clots of blood thrown up by the horses' hoofs, and from the tyres of the wheels; but the son of Peleus pressed on to win still further glory, and his hands were bedrabbled with gore.

THE WOODEN HORSE
AND THE SACK OF TROY

QUINTUS OF SMYRNA

When at last the Greek soldiers had worked to utter weariness around the walls of Troy without bringing the war to an end, then it was that Calchas called a meeting of the princes. By the promptings of Apollo, he had an expert knowledge of the flights of birds, the stars, and all the other signs that exist for men through the will of the gods. When they had come together, he spoke to them like this:

"Work no more at war, settled down beside the walls, but contrive some other contrivance in your minds, and a trick which will profit the soldiers and ourselves. I assure you that yesterday I personally saw a sign here: a hawk was chasing a dove. She, hard pressed, went down into a hole in a rock. The hawk was extremely angry and waited for a very long time close to the hole, but she kept out of his way. Then, still full of terrible anger, he hid under a bush. She rushed out in her folly, thinking that he was gone. The exultant hawk then brought a cruel death to the wretched dove. So now let us not attempt any longer to sack the city of Troy by force, but see if trickery and contrivance may perhaps accomplish something."

So he spoke, but none of the princes was able to devise in his mind anything to save them from miserable fighting, although they tried to discover a means. Only Odysseus, the son of Laertes, in his wisdom had an idea, and he spoke out to Calchas:

"My friend, greatly honored by the heavenly gods, if it is really fated that the brave soldiers of Greece sack Priam's town by trickery, we will make a horse, and we Greek princes will gladly go into it as an ambush. The soldiers must go away to Tenedos with the ships, and they must all set fire to their barracks, so the Trojans will pour out fearlessly into the plain, when they have seen this from the city. One courageous man, whom no one among the Trojans knows, should stay behind outside of the horse, steeling his soldier's heart. He must cower under the well-built horse and pretend that he has escaped the proud might of the Greeks, who had been strongly desirous of sacrificing him on behalf of their return. 'This horse they made for Pallas Athena, who was angry on account of the Trojan soldiers.' He must stick to this story during their long questioning until, stubborn though they are, they believe him and take the wretched fellow at once into the city. This is necessary so that he may make for us a grim sign for war. For the men on Tenedos, he should quickly raise a bright torch, and he should urge the men in the great horse to come out, when the sons of Troy are in carefree sleep."

So he spoke, and they all approved. Above all, Calchas marveled at him and at the way he had suggested to the Greeks a contrivance and good trick, which was going to protect the Greeks' victory and be a great disaster for the Trojans. He spoke, therefore, among the brave princes:

"Spend no more time now contriving another trick in your minds, my friends, but be persuaded by brave Odysseus. The idea that he has suggested in his wisdom will not turn out to be useless, because the gods are already accomplishing the Greeks' wish, and signs that will lead to something are appearing in various places: Zeus's thunders, accompanied by lightning, are roaring loudly through the air on high; birds are darting by the troops on the right and shrieking with loud voices. We must not stay for a long time around the city now. Necessity has breathed great boldness into the Trojans, which rouses even a worthless man to war. Then it is that men are strongest in fighting, when they stake their lives and are careless of painful death. So now the sons of Troy are fighting fearlessly around their city, and their hearts are in a real frenzy."

When he had said this, Achilles' sturdy son said to him:

"Calchas, strong men fight their enemies face to face. Those whose minds are harried by fear, worthless men, shun their enemy and fight inside from their walls. Let us not now, therefore, think up any trick or any other contrivance. It is proper for princes to show themselves men in battle and with the spear. Courageous men are better in a fight."

When he had said this, strong Odysseus Laertesson said to him:

"Stouthearted child of fearless Achilles, you have made all these statements as befits a noble and brave man, courageously putting your trust in your hands. But not even the fearless strength of your mighty father had the power to sack Priam's wealthy city, nor have we, even though we have fought very hard. Come, let us, in accordance with Calchas' suggestions, proceed quickly to our swift ships and construct a horse, using the hands of Epeius, who is far the best among the Greeks in carpentry. Athena taught him his trade."

So he spoke, and all the princes were persuaded by him, except brave Neoptolemus. Odysseus did not win over Philoctetes either, whose noble mind was set on deeds of strength. These two were still not sated with wretched war. They were planning to continue the fight in the field, and they gave orders to their own soldiers to bring to the vast wall all the things that prosper fighting in battles. They hoped to sack the strong citadel, because both of them had come to the conflict through plans of the gods. And they would soon have accomplished all that their spirits desired, except that Zeus in the upper sky grew indignant at them; so he made the earth quiver under the Greeks' feet and shook all the air above them, too, and threw a mighty thunderbolt in front of the heroes. All Dardania resounded from it. Their brave thoughts were quickly converted to fear. They quite forgot their strength and splendid might and, even against their will, gave their allegiance to famous Calchas. They came to the ships along with the other Greeks, marveling at the prophet, who, they said, was descended from Zeus—from Zeus or Apollo—and they obeyed him in everything.

When the shining stars were moving in their course around the heaven, all gleaming everywhere, and man forgot his trouble, then it was that Athena left the high dwelling place of the blessed ones and came to the ships and the army. She looked in every way like a tender girl, and she stood over the head of Epeius, dear to Ares, in a dream. She ordered him to make the wooden horse and said that, while he was busy with it, she would work with him herself and stand close beside him, encouraging him in his work. When he heard the goddess' speech, he leapt from carefree sleep with exultation in his heart. He knew she was a deathless divine god, and he had no other thought in his heart, but he kept his mind constantly on the wonderful work, and his shrewd skill possessed his thoughts.

When the Dawn came, after pushing the thick shadows aside into outer darkness, and a sparkling gleam came through the air, then it was that Epeius told his divine dream among the eager Greeks, what he had seen, what he had heard. And they felt the greatest pleasure as they listened. Then the sons of Atreus sent swift men to go into the flourishing glens of wooded Ida. They assailed the fir trees in the forest, felling the tall trees. The valleys re-echoed roundabout as the trees were struck. Long ridges in the high mountains were robbed of their forest; a whole valley was revealed, no longer so well-liked by wild animals as before. The felled trees were withering, missing the force of the wind. The Greeks cut these up with their axes and carried them quickly from the wooded mountain to the shores of the Hellespont. Men and mules alike put their hearts into the work. The soldiers were extremely busy, serving Epeius on every side. Some cut timbers with the saw and measured off planks; some with their axes trimmed off branches from the logs that were still unsawed. Every man found something to work at and was busy. Epeius made the feet and legs of the wooden horse and then the belly. Above this he fastened the back and flanks, a throat in front, and on top of the lofty neck he fitted a mane that moved as though it were real. He put on a shaggy head and a flowing tail, ears, transparent eyes, and everything else with which a horse is equipped. The holy work grew just as if it were a living horse, because the goddess had given to the man a splendid skill. With the inspiration provided by Pallas Athena, everything was finished in three days. The great army of the Greeks were delighted with it and marveled how spirit and speed of foot had been worked out in wood and how it looked as if it were neighing. Then Epeius offered up a prayer on behalf of the huge horse, stretching out his hands to tireless Tritonian Athena:

"Listen, O goddess great of soul, keep safe me and your horse."

So he spoke, and the goddess, wise Athena, listened to him, and she made what he had created an object of wonder to all men upon the earth, those who saw it, and those who heard about it thereafter.

While the Greeks were enjoying the sight of Epeius' work, and the frightened Trojans were staying inside their walls, avoiding death and pitiless doom, then it was that proud Zeus left the other gods and went to the streams of Ocean and the caverns of Tethys. With his departure, strife fell upon the immortals. In their agitation, their spirits were divided two ways. They mounted upon the blasts of the winds and were soon carried from heaven to earth, and the air roared as they passed. They went to the river Xanthus and took up positions opposite each other, some favoring the Greeks, some the Trojans, and a yearning for battle fell upon their hearts. Along with them those gods were gathered who had received as their portion the wide sea. Some of the gods in their anger were eager to destroy the crafty horse along with the ships, others wanted to destroy lovely Ilios. But wily Fate restrained them and turned the mind of the blessed ones to conflict. Ares began the fighting by leaping against Athena, and then the rest fell upon one another. Their divine golden armor rang loudly as they moved. The broad sea roared in answer, and the dark earth trembled beneath the immortals' feet. All of them at once raised a loud cry, and the terrible din reached all the way to broad heaven and as far as the abyss of proud Hades. The Titans far below were terrified. From around them came groans from all of lofty Ida, the noisy streams of her ever-flowing rivers, the long ravines, the ships of the Greeks, and the famous city of Priam. Human beings, however, felt no fear. Through the will of the gods themselves, they were not even aware of the divine quarrel.

The gods were now breaking off with their hands peaks from Mt. Ida and throwing them at one another. But the peaks were easily scattered here and there like grains of sand, broken into bits about the gods' invincible frames. All this did not remain hidden from the noble mind of Zeus at the ends of the earth. He left Oceanus' streams at once and went up into the broad heaven. Eurus and Boreas together with Zephyrus and Notus carried him. Bright Iris brought them under the marvelous yoke of the everlasting chariot that divine Aeon had made of indestructible adamant with his tireless hands. He reached the great ridge of Olympus. In his anger, he made all the air shake beneath him. Thunder and lightning roared loudly on all sides. Thunderbolts poured out thick and fast to earth. The air was ablaze beyond telling. Terror fell upon the hearts of the immortals. The limbs of all trembled, immortal though they were. Glorious Themis, terrified for them, leapt like a thought through the clouds and soon reached them. (She alone had stayed out of the painful conflict.) She spoke to them like this to check them from fighting:

"Hold back from this noisy tumult. It is not right, when Zeus is angry, for creatures who are forever to quarrel for the sake of short-lived men. You will all soon be made to disappear, because he will crush all the mountains into one mass up there to use against you and will not spare either his sons or his daughters. He will cover you all alike with a vast mound of earth. There will be no way for you to escape into the light, but wretched darkness around you will always keep you in."

So she spoke, and they were persuaded, fearing Zeus's attack. They checked their conflict, cast away their anger, and arranged harmonious friendship. Some of them returned to heaven, some went into the sea, and some stayed on the earth.

Then the shrewd planner Odysseus, the son of Laertes, spoke to the brave Greeks:

"Glorious Greek commanders, stout of heart, now give proof, when I want it, who among you are wonderfully strong and noble. For the task assigned us by necessity is certainly upon us. Let us give our thoughts to fighting and go into the polished horse, to find an end to hideous war. This will be the better way, if by trickery and cruel cunning we sack the great city for whose sake we came here and have suffered many pains, far away from the land we love. Now put into your hearts noble courage and strength. Many a man forced by harsh necessity in battle has put boldness into his spirit and killed a better man, when he was by nature inferior. Boldness gives one a much better spirit. It is boldness more than anything else that is a glory to men. Come, you princes, prepare a good ambush. You others go to the holy city of Tenedos and stay there, until the enemy drag us to the town, imagining that they are bringing a gift to Athena. Let some brave young man whom the Trojans don't know well stand close by the horse, steeling his heart. He must take very great care of all that I said before, and have no other thought in mind, so that what we Greeks are doing will not be revealed to the Trojans."

So he spoke. The others were afraid, but the famous man Sinon answered him. He was about to perform a really great deed, and the vast army marveled at him and his ready spirit. He spoke among them:

"Odysseus and all you excellent sons of the Greeks, I will carry out this task in answer to your desires, if they actually torture me and decide to throw me alive into the fire. This is my spirit's pleasure: to bring to the Greeks the great glory that they desire, whether I die at the hands of our enemies or escape."

So he spoke, boldly, and the Greeks were greatly pleased. And one among them said:

"What great courage a god has given this man today. He was not coura- geous before. A supernatural power is urging him on to become a mischief for all the Trojans or for ourselves. Now I think the cruel war doubtless will soon reach its destructive end."

So one of the warlike Greeks in the army spoke. Then Nestor, on the other side, spoke encouragingly among them:

"Now, my dear children, you need your strength and noble courage. For now the gods are bringing into our hands the end of labor and the noble victory we desire. Come, proceed courageously into the vast horse. Courage brings great glory to men. How I wish I still had in my limbs such great strength as when Jason, Aeson's son, was summoning the princes to go into the swift ship Argo. I was planning to be the first of the princes to go down into her, but godlike Pelias checked me against my will. As things are, lamentable old age comes upon me. But even so, like a young man in his prime, I will go boldly down into the horse. Boldness gives courage and glory."

When he had said this, the son of brown-haired Achilles said to him:

"Nestor, in intelligence you are the best of all men, but pitiless old age has you in its grip, and, much as you want to participate in the work of war, your strength is not unimpaired. You, therefore, must go to the shores of Tenedos. We young men, who still have not had our fill of battle, will go into the ambush. You, sir, ordered it so, and this also suits our own wishes."

So he spoke, and Nestor Neleusson came close to him and kissed both of his hands and his head as well, because he undertook to go first into the huge horse and ordered the older man to stay outside with the other Greeks, revealing thus his eagerness for the work of war. And he spoke to Neoptolemus, who was longing for battle:

"In strength and sensible speech you are a true son of your famous father, godlike Achilles. I have hopes that the Greeks will sack Priam's famous city by your hands. Although late and after labor, great glory will be ours, who have endured many grim pains in fighting. Pains the gods put before men's feet, but good things far away, and they put labor in between. Because of this, the way to wretched trouble is easy for men, while the way to glory is difficult, until a man forces his way through the painful labor."

So he spoke, and Achilles' famous son answered him:

"Sir, I hope that in answer to our prayers we achieve the hopes of your heart. This is far the better way. But if the gods will otherwise, so be that, too. I should wish to die gloriously in war rather than acquire the great disgrace of running away from Troy."

With these words, he put upon his shoulders the immortal armor of his father. The best of the heroes, all whose spirit was bold, were quick to arm themselves, too. Now in answer to my question, tell me, Muses, accurately and one by one, all those who went down into the vast horse. You put all song in my heart, before the down was spread over my cheeks. I was pasturing my fine sheep in the plains of Smyrna, three times as far from the Hermus as one can hear a man shouting. It was by a temple of Artemis, in the garden of Zeus the Deliverer, on a hill neither particularly low nor very high.

First of all there went down into the hollow horse Achilles' son Neoptolemus, and with him sturdy Menelaus, Odysseus, Sthenelus, and godlike Diomedes. Philoctetes went and Anticlus and Menestheus, and with them spirited Thoas, brown-haired Polypoetes, Aias, Eurypylus, and godlike Thrasymedes. Meriones went, too, and Idomeneus, distinguished men both, and with them Podalirius of the good ashen spear, and Eurymachus, godlike Teucer and stout-hearted Ialmenus, Thalpius, Antimachus, and the stubborn fighter Leonteus. With them went godlike Eumelus, Euryalus, Demophoon, Amphimachus, and sturdy Agapenor, and also Acamas, and Meges, son of sturdy Phyleus. All the others, too, who were outstandingly excellent went down into it—all whom the polished horse could contain within it. The last man to go down among them was glorious Epeius, the man who had actually made the horse. He knew in his spirit how to open up the horse's doors and how to close them. For this reason, he went in the last of all. Then he drew inside the ladders on which they had mounted, and, after he had closed everything very carefully, he sat down there beside the bolt. All the heroes sat there in silence, just halfway between victory and death.

When the others had burned the quarters in which they had formerly slept, they sailed in their ships over the wide sea. In command of them, two strong-minded men were giving orders, Nestor and the warrior Agamemnon. They had wanted to go down inside the horse too, but the Greeks checked them, so that they might stay with the ships and give orders to the army. Men proceed to a task much better when lords are in charge. On this account, they stayed outside of the horse, most excellent men though they were. They quickly reached the shores of Tenedos, threw the anchors down in deep water, and speedily disembarked. They fastened the cables to the shore and remained there at ease, waiting for the desired torch to shine.

The men in the horse were close to the enemy, sometimes doubtless expecting to die, and sometimes expecting to destroy the sacred city. These were their expectations as Dawn came upon them.

The Trojans noticed the smoke still rising swiftly through the air on the shores of the Hellespont. They did not, of course, see the ships that had brought them terrible destruction from Greece. All of them ran joyfully onto the beach, first putting on their armor, because fear still enveloped their spirits. They noticed the polished horse, and they naturally stood around it and marveled that so very great a thing had been made. Then they noticed the luckless Sinon close by. They surrounded him in a circle and asked questions about the Greeks from every side. First they questioned him with soft words, but then they used terrible threats and continued for a long time to employ great violence on the crafty man. But he was steadfast as a rock, and his body was clothed in firmness. At last they cut his ears off and his nose as well, using every sort of maltreatment to make him say truthfully where the Greeks had gone with their ships and what the horse really had inside it. But his heart was full of courage, and he showed no concern for the hideous outrage, but his spirit bore up under the blows and even when he was painfully tortured with fire, for Hera inspired him with great strength. And such were the things he said among them, his mind full of guile:

"The Greeks have run away over the sea with their ships, worn out by the long war and their troubles. On the advice of Calchas, they built the horse for wise Athena Tritogeneia, in order to avoid the goddess' wrath, since she is extremely angry because of the Trojans. At the suggestion of Odysseus, they planned destruction for me for the sake of their return. They were going to kill me by the roaring ocean as an offering to the divinities of the sea. But I found out about it, quickly escaped from the cruel libations and offerings of barley meal, and threw myself at the feet of the horse, through the plans of the immortals. They were forced to leave me there, although they didn't want to, out of fear of great Zeus's strong-minded daughter."

So he spoke in his cunning, and his spirit was not exhausted by his pains. It is characteristic of a strong man to endure harsh necessity. Some of the Trojans in the army believed him, while others said that he was a wily deceiver, and Laocoon's plan, of course, appealed to them: he spoke sensibly and said this was a terrible trick devised by the Greeks. He urged them all to set fire to the horse immediately and find out if the wooden horse concealed anything.

They would have obeyed him and escaped destruction, if Athena Tritogeneia, extremely angry at him, the Trojans, and the city, had not shaken the earth miraculously under Laocoon's feet. Fear fell upon him at once, and a trembling shattered the strength of the proud man's limbs. Black night poured over his head, and a loathsome pain fell upon his eyelids, and the man's eyes under his shaggy brows were thrown into disorder. The pupils were pierced with terrible pains and agitated right from their roots, and his eyeballs rolled with all this internal distress. The awful anguish reached even to the membranes and base of the brain. His eyes were at times bright and suffused with blood, at times they had a blind glare of severe pain. There was frequently a discharge from them, like the water mixed with snow that flows sometimes from a rough rock in the mountains. He was like a madman, saw everything double, and groaned dreadfully. Yet he kept giving his orders to the Trojans and disregarded his misery. Then the divine goddess deprived him of his eyesight, and his eyes stood out white under his eyebrows as a result of the destructive blood.

The people groaned around him, pitying the man they loved and fearing Athena, the immortal goddess who drives off the booty, lest in his folly he had committed some wrong against her. Their own thoughts, too, were turned toward terrible destruction, because they had outraged the body of wretched Sinon, hoping in their hearts that he would tell the whole truth. And so with good will they led him into the Trojan city, pitying him very belatedly. At the same time they all got together and quickly threw a rope around the huge horse, fastening it from above. Able Epeius had put smooth-running wooden wheels under its great feet, so that it might follow the young men to the citadel, dragged by the hands of the Trojans. They were all dragging at it, applying their strength as a group. Just as men work hard to drag a ship into the noisy sea, and the strong rollers groan under the friction, and the keel squeaks terribly as it goes sliding down into the swell of the sea; so they were working hard all together dragging Epeius' work into their town for their own ruin. They put around it a splendid decoration of lavish garlands, and they put garlands on their own heads. The flutes sounded loudly, as the men called to one another. Enyo laughed when she saw this harsh end to the war, and up above Hera rejoiced, and Athena was glad at it. When they reached the city, they broke down battlements of the great town and brought in the ruinous horse. The Trojan women shouted, and they all stood around the horse and looked with wonder at the great work of Epeius. Their ruin was hidden within it.

Laocoon still stood firm and urged his companions to destroy the horse with blazing fire. But they were not persuaded at all, because they were afraid of the rebuke of the immortals. The goddess, proud Athena, had another still more abominable plan, this one directed against Laocoon's luckless sons. There was somewhere under a rocky crag a dark cavern where mortals could not go. Terrible wild animals of the deadly stock of Typhon still lived in it. It was in a cleft of the island in the sea off Troy that people call Calydna. The goddess roused mighty dragons from this cave and called them to Troy. Set into quick motion by the goddess, they made the island quake terribly. The sea roared as they moved, and the waves parted before them. While they rushed along, they flicked their tongues dreadfully, and the creatures of the sea shuddered. The nymphs, daughters of Xanthus and Simois, groaned loudly, and on Olympus Cyprian Aphrodite was filled with sorrow.

They came quickly to the spot where the goddess had ordered, whetting their teeth on their grim jaws, preparing ruin for the luckless boys. Cowardly flight came upon the Trojans, when they saw the terrible monsters in the town. Not a one of the men, not even if he had been fearless before, ventured to stand his ground. Absolute terror possessed them all, as they tried to get away from the beasts. There, too, the women wailed in anguish. Some women doubtless forgot their children in their own efforts to get away from a loathsome doom. As her people rushed away, Troy groaned roundabout. Many persons, as they hurried into one place, had the skin torn from their limbs. They packed the streets, cowering down everywhere.

Laocoon was left apart, alone with his sons. Destructive Doom and the goddess bound them fast. The dragons seized both the sons in their deadly jaws, frightened of death and stretching out their hands to their dear father, but he had no strength to protect them. The Trojans, watching from a distance, wept with wonder in their hearts. When the snakes had zealously carried out Athena's command, so hostile to the Trojans, they both disappeared underground. There is still a marker indicating where they entered Apollo's shrine in holy Pergamum. In front of this shrine, the sons of Troy gathered together and built a cenotaph for Laocoon's sons, mercilessly killed, and their father shed upon it tears from his blind eyes. Their mother, wailing about the cenotaph, raised many a cry over it, expecting something else still worse. She groaned for her husband, ruined by his folly, and was afraid of the blessed ones' wrath. Just as in a shadowy glen a nightingale, filled with great misery, wails around her ravaged nest, when a grim snake has destroyed in its strong jaws her stillhelpless young before they had their full power of song and so brought pain to the mother bird, and she, grieved beyond telling, wails with many a cry around her empty home; so this mother groaned over the hideous fate of her sons and wailed around their empty tomb. She had, too, the other terrible disaster of her blinded husband.

So she kept up a lament for her dead sons and her husband—the sons dead, the husband with no share in the sunlight. The Trojans, however, were busy with sacrifices to the gods, pouring libations of choice wine, because their hearts were convinced that they would escape from the heavy might of wretched war. But the sacrifices would not burn, and the flame of the fire went out, as though a roaring storm of rain had swooped down from above. Bloodstained smoke rose up from the sacrifices, and all the thigh pieces fell quivering to the ground. The altars collapsed, and the libations turned to blood. Tears flowed from the statues of the gods, the temples became wet with gore, groans came from unexpected places, the high circling walls shook, and the towers gave loud roars, as if they were in pain. The bars of the gates opened automatically with terrible shrieks, and night birds moaned dismally in answer and gave desolate cries. All the stars above the city that gods had built were covered with a mist, even though the sky was bright and cloudless. The laurels by the temple of Phoebus Apollo withered, although they had previously been most flourishing. Wolves and fierce jackals howled inside the gates. A thousand other portents appeared, bringing ruin to the Trojans and their city. But no troublesome fear came into the Trojans' hearts, as they saw all the troublesome portents in the city. Fates drove all of them out of their minds, so that they might meet their doom at the banquet table and be destroyed by the Greeks.

Only one person kept a firm heart and an intelligent mind: Cassandra. No word of hers had ever gone unfulfilled; what she said was always true, but through some fate she was always heard without profit, so that griefs might come to the Trojans. When she saw the grisly portents in the town, all leading swiftly to one conclusion, she gave a loud cry, just like a lioness which an eager hunter has stabbed or shot in the woods, and her heart rages within her from pain, and she runs roaring everywhere on the high mountains, and her strength is beyond holding; so Cassandra's prophetic heart was frantic within her. She went from the hall, and her hair poured about her silver shoulders and down her back. Her eyes glared terribly, and her neck quivered like a tree in the wind. With a deep groan the noble girl cried out:

"My miserable people, now we are for the dark. Our city is full of fire and blood and hideous doom. Everywhere the immortals are showing portents full of tears, and ultimate doom is before our feet. You poor fools, you do not understand at all your evil fate, but all of you alike are rejoicing, still acting senselessly regarding what has your complete destruction hidden within *it*. You pay no attention to me, no matter how much I tell you, because the Furies are filled with anger because of Helen and her dreadful marriage, and the pitiless Dooms are darting everywhere through the citadel. At a banquet full of pains, you eat your last feast, food defiled with evil gore, and you are already setting foot on the road used by ghosts."

And one of them, sneering at her, made this pernicious speech:

"Daughter of Priam, why do your mad tongue and your folly command you to speak this windy nonsense? No pure, maidenly modesty clothes you, but a fatal madness possesses you. So every human being always dishonors you for talking so much. Go and make your evil predictions to the Greeks, or to yourself. An even more painful trouble awaits you than disrespectful Laocoon's. Because it isn't right to destroy in one's folly the dear gifts of the immortals."

So one of the Trojans spoke in the town. Others, also, blamed the girl in the same way, and said her talk was unsuitable. This was, of course, because ruin and the terrible might of Fate had taken their stand close to the Trojans. They jeered at her, with no thought of destruction, and diverted her from the vast horse. She was bent on shattering all the wood or burning it up with blazing fire. And so she had taken from the hearth a stick of pine that was still burning, and with it she rushed on. She carried in her other hand a double ax and was making her way toward the grim horse, so that the Trojans might see clearly the ambush that would bring them sorrow. But they threw the fire and the destructive iron far from her hands and carelessly set about their feast—a grim one, for their last night was truly coming upon them.

The Greeks inside the horse were delighted when they heard the noise of the men banqueting in Troy and paying no attention to Cassandra. They marveled at her themselves—at how she had been endowed with an unerring knowledge of the purpose and plan of the Greeks.

And Cassandra, just as a leopard runs harried in the mountains, one which dogs and hard-working herdsmen chase swiftly, and the leopard, her heart full of savagery, draws back under their pressure, although she keeps turning upon them; so Cassandra ran away from the vast horse, her heart full of grief for the slaughter of the Trojans. She expected a really great disaster.

* * * * *

So the trojans were feasting in the citadel, and among them was the loud music of flute and pipe alike. Everywhere there was song and dancing and a confused noise of banqueters, such as accompanies banqueting and wine. Many a man there, taking a full goblet in his hands, drank with carefree heart. Their wits grew heavy within them, their eyes rolled. Word after word came from their lips, as they babbled brokenly. The furniture in the halls and the building itself seemed to them to be in motion, and they thought that everything in the town was turning every way. A mist came over their eyes. The vision and the intelligence of men are impaired by strong drink when it is taken in quantity and reaches the mind. This is the sort of thing a man said, his head heavy with wine:

"The Greeks certainly brought a great army here to no purpose. The wretches did not carry out all the plans they had in mind, but they just rushed away from our city like foolish children or women."

So one of the Trojans spoke, his wits in the grip of wine. Poor fool, he did not notice the ruin at his doors.

When they had sated themselves with abundant wine and food, and sleep held men everywhere through the town, then it was that Sinon lifted up the shining torch, showing the Greeks the blaze of fire. He had a thousand worries in his heart, afraid that the powerful Trojans might see him and everything be quickly revealed. But they were in their beds, sleeping their last sleep, weighed down by much strong drink. When the Greeks saw the signal, they made ready to sail in their ships from Tenedos.

Sinon himself came close to the horse. He called softly, very softly, so that no one among the Trojans might hear him, but only the Greek officers. They were so eager to be at the work of war that sleep had completely flown from them. And so the men in the horse heard Sinon, and all inclined their ears toward Odysseus. He urged them to go out of the horse quietly and fearlessly. They obeyed his summons to battle and were zealous to move on out of the horse to the ground. But he was wise enough to check them all in their eagerness, and then with his swift hands he personally opened the sides of the wooden horse here and there, working very quietly under the direction of Epeius of the good ashen spear. He raised himself a little above the openings and peered around in all directions to see if any Trojan was awake anywhere. Just as when a wolf, his heart struck by the pain of hunger, comes down from the mountains with a great longing for food and approaches a wide sheepfold and then, avoiding the men and dogs who are eager to guard the sheep, walks unhindered over the fence of the fold; so Odysseus came down from the horse. The other mighty kings of the Greeks followed him, filing down the ladders that Epeius had made as ways for the sturdy princes to enter and leave the horse. They went down along them then, some from one exit, others from another, like bold wasps which a woodcutter disturbs, and they all pour out from the branch with angry spirits, when they hear the noise; so they poured eagerly from the horse into the splendid citadel of Troy, their hearts pounding in their breasts.

They were soon at work killing the enemy, and meanwhile the others were rowing at sea, and the ships moved quickly over the great expanse. Thetis directed their way and sent a breeze after them, and the minds of the Greeks were cheered. They soon reached the shores of the Hellespont, where they halted their ships again. They skillfully collected all the gear that ships always carry, disembarked at once, and hurried toward Troy, making no noise, just like sheep hurrying to the fold from a woodland meadow in an autumn night; so without a sound they moved quickly to the city of the Trojans, all of them eager to help their princes. Just as wolves in a terrible frenzy of hunger attack a sheepfold in the high wooded mountains, when the hard-working shepherd is asleep, and in the darkness they destroy one sheep after another inside the enclosure, and everywhere roundabout there is death and blood; so the Greek leaders filled Troy with blood and corpses, and a terrible destruction began, even though still more of the Greeks were outside.

But when quite all of them had reached the walls of Troy, then they eagerly and steadily poured into Priam's town, breathing the might of war. They found the whole citadel full of battle and corpses, and everywhere in the unhappy town they found buildings being cruelly burned with fire. Their hearts were greatly pleased, and they themselves rushed upon the Trojans with evil thoughts. Ares was raging among them along with Enyo, goddess of groaning. Everywhere the dark blood flowed, and the earth grew wet, as the Trojans and their foreign allies were destroyed. Some of them, mastered by chill death, lay in their blood in the citadel. Others fell on top of them, breathing out their strength. Others again, holding their entrails clutched in their hands, were wandering piteously in the houses. Some, with both their feet cut off, crawled among the corpses, shrieking terribly. Many who had been eager to fight lay in the dust with their hands cut off and their heads as well. Others were struck as they fled, the spears piercing their backs and going straight through to their breasts, or reaching their waists above their genitals, where the spearpoint of tireless Ares is most full of anguish. Everywhere through the town a wretched howling of dogs arose, and the pitiable groaning of wounded men, and all the rooms were filled with noise beyond telling.

There was, too, the sad wailing of women. They were like cranes when they see an eagle swooping from above through the air. They have no bold courage in their hearts, but merely chirp loudly in their fear of the eagle, the sacred bird. So the Trojan women were wailing loudly on all sides, some rising up from their beds, some leaping to the ground. They had no concern now for proper dress in their misery, but roamed about after throwing a single garment around them. Some did not stop to take even a veil or a long cloak; in their fear of the attacking enemy, their hearts pounded, they were shackled by helplessness, and, poor creatures, they concealed their nakedness only with their swift hands. Some in their misery were pulling the hair from their heads, beating their breasts with their hands, and groaning loudly. Still others ventured to face the enemy turmoil and forgot their fear in their eagerness to help their husbands and children who were being killed; necessity gave them boldness.

The wailing roused from sleep the children, whose tender spirit had never yet known cares. One after another they breathed their last. Some lay there who had seen their doom simultaneously with their dreams. Grim Fates took delight in the piteous deaths. The Trojans were killed by the thousands, like pigs in the home of a rich man who is preparing a great feast for his people. The wine still left in the mixing bowls became mixed with grisly gore. There was no one who would have kept his cruel iron free from slaughter, not even if he was a complete weakling. The Trojans were being destroyed just as sheep are killed by jackals or by wolves, when excessive heat comes on at midday, and the flocks gather all close together in a shady place, waiting for the shepherd who has gone to the house with milk, and the wild beasts attack them, fill their capacious bellies, and lap up the black blood, staying to destroy the whole flock and fashion an evil feast for the wretched shepherd; so the Greeks in Priam's town attacked the Trojans in their last battle and killed one man after another. Not a Trojan was left unwounded, every man's limbs were spattered and black with streams of blood.

The Greeks did not escape unwounded from the conflict either. Some were hit with goblets, some with tables, some with sticks of wood that were still burning on the hearth. Some died pierced by spits on which hot chitterlings had doubtless been left still sizzling in the warmth of the strong fire. Others, again, writhed in their blood from blows of hatchets and swift battle-axes. Some had their fingers cut from their hands when they threw their hands upon a sword, hoping to keep off a loathsome death. Many a man doubtless hit a comrade with a stone in the confusion and mixed his skull with his brain. Like wild beasts wounded at a shepherd's fold in the country, they raged cruelly in the ghastly night, as their anger was roused. In their great desire for war, they rushed about Priam's palace and routed enemies from everywhere. Many of the Greeks were killed with spears too, because all of the Trojans who were quick enough to lift a sword or a long spear in their hands destroyed enemies, even though they were heavy with wine. A great glare rose up through the city, because many of the Greeks held bright flares in their hands, so that they could clearly distinguish friend from foe in the conflict.

Then the soldier Coroebus, son of famous Mygdon, came against Diomedes, Tydeus' son, in the turmoil, and Diomedes pierced him with his spear through the hollow throat, where are the quick ways of drink and food. He found his black doom on the spear and fell among the black blood and the heaps of other corpses. Poor fool, he got no good of the marriage for which he had come the day before to Priam's town, with the promise to thrust the Greeks from Troy. The god did not fulfill his hope, for the Fates sent doom upon him first. With him Tydeus' son killed Eurydamas, who came against him. He was a spear fighter and a son-in-law of Antenor, who had the highest pre-eminence among the Trojans for his sensible spirit. There, too, Tydeus' son met Ilioneus, an elder of the people, and drew his terrible sword against him. The limbs of Ilioneus' aged body completely collapsed. He held out both his trembling hands, with one grasping the swift sword, and with the other taking hold of the murderous hero's knees. And Tydeus' son, rushing into battle though he was, whether because he put off his anger, or at the bidding of some god, held his sword away from the old man for a little, so that he might say something, beseeching the swift and mighty man. Ilioneus, in the grip of loathsome fear, quickly gave a miserable cry:

"I beseech you, whoever you are of the sturdy Greeks, have respect for my arms, as I fall before you, and stop your harsh anger. A man wins great glory, if he kills a man who is young and strong. But if you kill an old man, no praise of your strength will follow you. Turn your hands, therefore, away from me and against the young men, hoping some day to reach an old age like mine."

In answer to his words, the son of mighty Tydeus said to him:

"Sir, I hope to reach a good old age, but while my strength is still growing I will not spare any enemy of my person. I will send them all to Hades. He is a good man who defends himself against an enemy."

With these words, the fearful man drove his deadly sword through Ilioneus' throat and directed it to where the doom of life is swiftest for mortals, and the terrible paths of the blood lie. And so a terrible doom shattered Ilioneus, destroyed by Tydeusson's hands. Diomedes continued to slaughter Trojans, rushing up through the citadel and raging terribly in his strength. He killed noble Abas, and he hit with his long spear the son of Perimnestus, famous Eurycoon. And Aias killed Amphimedon, Agamemnon killed Damastorson, Idomeneus killed Mimas, and Meges killed Deiopites.

Achilles' son, for his part, destroyed with his invincible spear glorious Pammon and struck Polites as he attacked, and with them he killed Antiphonus, all of them alike sons of Priam. As glorious Agenor came against him in the conflict, he cut him down. He dispatched one hero after another. Everywhere there was apparent the black doom of dying men. Wearing his father's strength, he eagerly butchered all whom he met. His mind was filled with evil thoughts when he came upon the enemy king himself beside the altar of Zeus of the courtyard. When Priam saw Achilles' son, he recognized at once who he was, and he felt no fear, because in his heart he was himself longing to join his sons in death. And so, in his eagerness to die, he said to him:

"Stouthearted son of the good soldier Achilles, kill me in my misery and feel no pity for me. Personally, after such great and such terrible sufferings, I have no desire to look upon the light of the all-seeing sun. I want to die now, along with my sons, and quite forget my dismal troubles and the hideous confusion of war. I wish your father had killed me before I saw Ilios in flames, killed me when I brought him the ransom for dead Hector, my son whose life your father took. But the Fates, I suppose, spun it this way. Sate your mighty heart in my slaughter, so that I may forget my sorrows."

In reply to him, Achilles' mighty son said:

"Sir, you command a man who is ready and eager. I will not leave you who are my enemy among the living, for nothing is dearer to men than life."

So speaking, he cut off the old man's grey head, easily, just as if someone were reaping an ear of grain from a dry field in the season of warm summer. The head, with a deep moan, rolled a considerable distance away from the rest of the body. And so he lay in the black blood and gore of the other men, Priam, once renowned for wealth and noble birth and numerous children. Glory does not for long increase for human beings, but disgrace comes on unexpectedly. Yet, while doom overtook Priam, he did forget all his troubles.

The Greeks of the swift horses also threw Astyanax from a high tower. In their anger at Hector, who had caused troubles for them when he was alive, they snatched his dear child from its mother's arms and took its life. They hated Hector's stock, and they threw the boy down from the high wall, just a baby, with no knowledge yet of the conflict of war. Just as wolves in need of food cut off a calf from its mother and her milky udders and evilly drive it over an echoing cliff, and the cow, moaning for its dear calf, runs here and there with loud laments, and later another evil comes upon her, when the cow herself is snatched by lions; so hostile men took, along with the other captive women, noble Eëtion's daughter Andromache, wild with grief for her son and crying out dreadfully. She, Andromache of the fair ankles, when she thought of the terrible slaughter of her son, her husband, and her father, wanted to die. It is better for royal persons to die in war than to serve their inferiors. With deep grief in her heart, she uttered this sad cry:

"You Greeks, come now and throw my body quickly down from the dreadful wall, or down from crags, or into the fire, for my troubles are truly beyond telling. Achilles, Peleus' son, killed my noble father in holy Thebe, and in Troy my famous husband, who was to me absolutely everything that my heart desired. He left to me in our halls a son, still small, in whom I took infinite pride, for whom I had many hopes. An evil and monstrous doom has cheated me of him. And so take from me quickly in my sorrow a life with so much misery. Don't bring me to your homes along with those your spears have won. My spirit finds no pleasure any longer in being with humankind, because a supernatural power has destroyed my family. Besides my other hateful sufferings, a terrible pain awaits me if I am left alone and without the Trojans."

So she spoke in her desire to be dead and buried. It does not befit those persons to remain alive whose great glory has been swallowed up by disgrace, for it is a terrible thing to be looked down upon by others. But the Greeks, much against her will, dragged her forcibly away to the day of slavery.

Men were losing their lives in various other houses, and very melancholy cries arose in them, but not in the halls of Antenor, because the Greeks remembered his charming hospitality. He had previously entertained as his guests in the town godlike Menelaus and Odysseus, when they came together, and he had kept them safe. Out of kindness to him, the excellent sons of the Greeks spared his life and left his property unharmed, showing regard both for all-seeing Themis and for a man who had befriended them.

Then it was that the brave son of noble Anchises, after much courageous labor with his spear about the city of Priam, child of gods, and after having taken the life of many, gave up hope in his heart of looking any longer upon his strongly fortified city. And when he saw that the grim hands of the enemy had set fire to the citadel, that people were dying in great numbers, that vast treasure as well was being destroyed, that wives with their children were being dragged from their homes, he made plans to escape from the great disaster. Just as when on the deep sea a man controlling the rudder of a ship skillfully avoids wind and wave that rush at him from every quarter in the hateful season of winter, and then his hand and his spirit alike grow weary, and when the ship, breaking up, begins to sink, he abandons his rudder and transfers to a small skiff, no longer giving his concern to the merchant ship; so the brave son of wise Anchises left to the enemy his city, blazing with sheets of fire. He snatched his son and his father and took them with him. With his strong hands, he set his father, suffering from the many miseries of old age, on his broad shoulders; the boy he allowed to walk and, holding him by his soft hand, led him away from the noisy fighting. The little boy was frightened by the deeds of destructive turmoil and had to hang clinging to him, with tears flowing on his tender cheeks. Aeneas leapt with swift feet over many dead bodies, and many, too, he trampled on in the darkness without meaning to. His mother, Cyprian Aphrodite, led the way, carefully saving from the terrible disaster her grandson, son, and husband. As Aeneas rushed on, the fire yielded everywhere beneath his feet, the blasts of raging flame parted, and the spears and arrows of men which the Greeks hurled at him in the cruel battle all fell fruitless on the ground. Then it was that Calchas gave a great shout to hold the army back:

"Stop hurling your cruel arrows and destructive spears at mighty Aeneas. It is decreed for him by the splendid plan of the gods to go from Xanthus to the broad stream of Tiber. There he shall fashion a sacred city, an object of wonder for future generations, and he shall himself be lord of a widespread people. The stock born from him shall thereafter rule all the way from the rising to the setting sun. Moreover, it is decreed for him to take a place among the immortals, because he is the son of fair-haired Aphrodite. And let us, in any case, keep our hands away from this man, because in preference to gold and all his other possessions, things that preserve a man when he goes as an exile to a foreign land, in preference to all this, he has chosen his father and his son. A single night has revealed to us a son marvelously kind to his old father, a noble father marvelously kind to his son."

So he spoke, and they all listened to him and looked upon Aeneas as a god. He was quickly gone from his city to the place where his busy feet carried him, while the Greeks continued the sack of the splendid citadel of Troy.

Then it was that Menelaus killed with his cruel sword Deiphobus, having found the luckless wretch drowsing by Helen's bed. (She had run and hid in the house.) As the blood poured out, Menelaus rejoiced at the killing and spoke like this:

"You dog, this day I have given you a painful death. The divine Dawn will not find you still alive among the Trojans, even if you are proud to be the son-in-law of Zeus, the loud thunderer. Black destruction has found you, overcome pitilessly in the halls of my wife. How I wish that before now cursed Alexander had come against me in battle, and I had taken his life away too; my sorrow would then have been easier to bear. But by now he has paid all the penalties he owed and has gone underneath the chill darkness. It is now clear, too, that my wife was not to bring you any profit. Sinful men do not ever escape pure Themis.

She watches them night and day, and she flits everywhere through the sky over the races of men, punishing along with Zeus those who participate in evil deeds."

When he had said this, he continued his merciless destruction of the enemy. The jealous spirit within him was raging and grew steadily more impassioned. His bold mind was full of evil intentions toward the Trojans, intentions that now the goddess, revered Justice, executed. The Trojans had been the first to do wrong in connection with Helen, they had been the first to break their oaths—wicked men, because in their minds' transgressions they completely forgot the black blood and the other rites of the immortals. For this reason, the Furies created sorrows for them thereafter. And this is why, of course, some of them died in front of the wall, and others inside the city while enjoying themselves with feasting and with their fair-haired wives.

At last, in the innermost parts of the house, Menelaus found his wife. She was fearful of this attack by the firm-minded husband of her youth. When he caught sight of her, he was planning to kill her in the jealousy of his mind, but lovely Aphrodite restrained his strength, knocked the sword from his hand, and checked his attack. She removed his black jealousy from him and roused sweet desire in his heart and eyes. An unexpected amazement came upon him, and when he saw Helen's conspicuous beauty, he could no longer bring himself to strike her neck with his sword. He stood like a dead tree on a wooded mountain, which neither the swift blasts of Boreas nor of Notas can shake as they rush through the air upon it; so he stood for a long time, lost in wonder. His strength was shattered as he looked upon his wife, and he immediately forgot all the wrongs she had done to him and to their marriage bed. Everything was effaced by the goddess Cyprian Aphrodite, the goddess who conquers the mind of all immortals and mortal men. Even so, however, he lifted his swift sword again from the ground and charged upon his wife. But his mind within was planning other things as he rushed at her: he was, of course, beguiling the Greeks with a trick. And then his brother Agamemnon held him back, for all his zeal, and with gentle words gave him much earnest advice, because he was afraid that all they had done might become useless:

"You have gone far enough, Menelaus, angry though you are. It isn't proper to kill the wife of your youth, for whose sake we endured many sorrows and made evil plans against Priam. Helen is not to blame, as you think, but Paris, who forgot Zeus, the god of guest and host, and forgot what he owed your table. A supernatural power has therefore brought him to painful punishment."

So he spoke, and Menelaus was prompt to obey him. The gods then covered glorious Troy in dark clouds and mourned for it, except for fair-haired Tritonian Athena and Hera. Their minds were filled with exultation when they saw the famous city of goddescended Priam being sacked. But no, not even wise Athena Tritogeneia herself was wholly tearless when within her temple Aias, the strong son of Oileus, defiled Cassandra. He was a man deranged in mind and spirit, and the goddess afterward cast upon him a terrible disaster and punished him for the outrage. She did not look upon his disgraceful deed, but shame and anger enveloped her. She turned her grim eyes to her high temple, the divine image resounded, and the floor of the temple shook vigorously. But Aias did not stop his hideous outrage, because Cyprian Aphrodite had infatuated his mind.

All over the town, tall buildings were falling down on every side, and a choking dust mingled with the smoke. A terrible noise arose, and the streets quaked. Aeneas' home was burning, and all the rooms of Antimachus' house. The great city height was ablaze around lovely Pergamus, the shrine of Apollo, the holy temple of Tritonian Athena, and the altar of Zeus of the Courtyard. The lovely rooms of Priam's grandsons were burning up, and the whole city was being completely destroyed.

As for the Trojans, some fell beneath the sons of the Greeks, some were killed by the ghastly fire and their own homes, which became at once their evil death and their tomb; others drove swords through their own throats, when they saw fire at the door along with the enemy. Still others killed their wives and children and then, completing a monstrous deed forced upon them by necessity, fell dead upon them. One man, thinking the enemy was fighting far off, quickly took up a jar from the fire and was planning to go for water. But he was heavy with wine, and a Greek, anticipating him, struck him with a spear and took away his life. He fell inside his house, and the empty water jar fell down beside him. A burning beam fell upon another while he was running through his great hall and brought quick death as it crashed upon him. Many women, too, who had hurried off in wretched flight, remembered their dear children whom they had left in bed at home. Running back at once, they were killed along with the children, when the buildings fell upon them. Horses and dogs were rushing in terror through the city, running from the force of the hideous fire. With their feet they trampled upon men who had been killed and frequently brought death to the living by crushing them. Shrieks resounded through the city. One young man was rushing through the flames as he spoke, and pitiless doom destroyed those inside. Various were the ways of cruel death that carried men off. The blaze rose up into the divine sky, and a brightness beyond telling spread abroad. The neighboring peoples saw it, all the way to the high peaks of the Idaean hills, Samothrace, and the island of Tenedos. And a man on shipboard out at sea said:

"The strong-minded Greeks have done a deed beyond telling, after their many toils for Helen of the glancing eyes. All Troy, vastly rich before, is now being consumed with fire, and no god defended them, for all their longing. Irresistible Fate looks upon all the works of men, and many things that have been undistinguished and inconspicuous she makes famous, and lofty things she brings low. Very often good comes out of evil, and out of good comes evil, as our miserable life keeps changing."

So some man spoke, as he looked from a distance on the brightness beyond telling. Painful anguish still held the Trojans, but the Greeks were spreading confusion through the town. Just as the blustering gales when they have been roused drive the boundless sea wildly, when opposite to Arcturus, star of evil winds, the Altar rises into the starry threshold, turned to the murky south wind, and at its rising many ships are overwhelmed in the sea and sunk as the winds increase; like them the sons of the Greeks were sacking lofty Ilios, and it was burning in the vast fire. Just as a mountain covered with dense woods burns quickly when fire is roused by the winds, and the tall hills roar, and all the wild creatures are in pitiful distress in it, as they are driven in circles through the forest by the force of the fire; so the Trojans were being killed in the town. No one of the heavenly ones protected them, because the Fates had set their high nets around them everywhere, those nets which no mortal has ever escaped.

And then Aethra, mother of great Theseus, met in the city Demophoon and the stubborn fighter Acamas. She was eager to meet some Greek, and one of the blessed gods had led her and brought her face to face with them. She had been running in terror from the fighting and the fire. When in the bright glare they saw the build and size of the woman, they thought she was the godlike wife of Priam, son of gods. Immediately and enthusiastically, they laid hands on her, eager to take her to the Greeks. But she gave a terrible cry and said:

"You glorious sons of the warlike Greeks, don't take me to your ships by dragging me away like an enemy. I make no boast of Trojan stock, but I am of good Greek blood and very famous too. Pittheus begot me in Troezen, and glorious Aegeus took me in marriage, and from me was born a famous son: Theseus. Please, by great Zeus and your happy parents, if the sons of noble Theseus have really come here with the Atreussons, show me to his dear sons in the army. I think they are of the same age as you. They are eager to see me, and my heart will have relief if I see them alive and both of them princes."

So she spoke, and as they listened they remembered their father: all that he had done in connection with Helen, and how her brothers, Castor and Polydeuces, sons of Zeus the thunderer, had in other days sacked Aphidnae, while they were themselves still babies, and their nurses had hidden them away from the fighting. And they remembered illustrious Aethra and all she had suffered under the hardships of slavery, when she became at once the mother-in-law and the maidservant of divine Helen. They were so delighted they could hardly speak. And then excellent Demophoon spoke in answer to her eager request:

"Well, the gods are quick to fulfill the wish of your heart. You see in us the sons of your noble son. We'll lift you in our loving arms and carry you to the ships, and we'll gladly bring you to the holy soil of Greece, the very place where before you were a queen."

When he had said this, the mother of his great father flung her arms about him and pressed him to her, and she kissed his broad shoulders, his head and chest, and his bearded cheeks. Then she kissed Acamas in the same way, and sweet tears flowed down from their eyes as they wept. Just as when people spread a report about the death of a man who has been in foreign lands, and he returns to his home from somewhere, and his sons cry with great joy at the sight of him, and he in his turn weeps himself in his halls on his sons' shoulders, and around the house there hovers a mournful cry of men who are sweetly wailing; so as they wept there arose a lamentation that was pleasant to hear,

And then it was, I fancy, men say that Laodice, daughter of long-suffering Priam, lifted her arms to the sky, praying to the tireless blessed ones that the earth might swallow her before she put her hand to slavish tasks. And one of the gods heard her and immediately caused the great earth to break beneath her. At the request of the god, the earth received the glorious girl within the hollow gulf, as Troy was being destroyed.

Men say that because of Troy, too, long-robed Electra herself hid her body in mist and clouds and left the chorus of the other Pleiades, who are her sisters. They rise in a troop into heaven, visible to toiling mortals, but she alone hides ever unseen, because the holy city of her noble son Dardanus fell in ruins. Not even Zeus himself, most high, brought her any help from heaven, because even the might of great Zeus yields to the Fates. This destruction, I fancy, was probably brought about by the good purpose of the gods and by the Fates themselves.

The Greeks, meanwhile, were still stirring up their spirit against the Trojans everywhere in the citadel, and Eris, goddess of strife, held in her hands the conclusion of the conflict.

DAVID SLEW GOLIATH

THE KING JAMES BIBLE

Now the Philistines gathered together their armies to battle, and were gathered together at Shochoh, which belongeth to Judah, and pitched between Shochoh and Azekah, in Ephes-dammim. And Saul and the men of Israel were gathered together, and pitched by the valley of Elah, and set the battle in array against the Philistines. And the Philistines stood on a mountain on the one side, and Israel stood on a mountain on the other side: and there was a valley between them.

And there went out a champion out of the camp of the Philistines, named Goliath, of Gath, whose height was six cubits and a span. And he had an helmet of brass upon his head, and he was armed with a coat of mail; and the weight of the coat was five thousand shekels of brass. And he had greaves of brass upon his legs, and a target of brass between his shoulders. And the staff of his spear was like a weaver's beam; and his spear's head weighed six hundred shekels of iron:, and one bearing a shield went before him.

And he stood and cried unto the armies of Israel, and said unto them, Why are ye come out to set your battle in array? am not I a Philistine, and ye servants to Saul? choose you a man for you, and let him come down to me. If he be able to fight with me, and to kill me, then will we be your servants: but if I prevail against him, and kill him, then shall ye be our servants, and serve us. And the Philistine said, I defy the armies of Israel this day; give me a man, that we may fight together.

When Saul and all Israel heard those words of the Philistine, they were dismayed, and greatly afraid.

Now David was the son of that Ephrathite of Beth-lehem-judah, whose name was Jesse; and he had eight sons: and the man went among men for an old man in the days of Saul. And the three eldest sons of Jesse went and followed Saul to the battle: and the names of his three sons that went to the battle were Eliab the firstborn, and next unto him Abinadab, and the third Shammah. And David was the youngest: and the three eldest followed Saul. But David went and returned from Saul to feed his father's sheep at Beth-lehem.

And the Philistine drew near morning and evening, and presented himself forty days. And Jesse said unto David his son, Take now for thy brethren an ephah of this parched corn, and these ten loaves, and run to the camp to thy brethren; And carry these ten cheeses unto the captain of their thousand, and look how thy brethren fare, and take their pledge.

Now Saul, and they, and all the men of Israel, were in the valley of Elah, fighting with the Philistines. And David rose up early in the morning, and left the sheep with a keeper, and took, and went, as Jesse had commanded him; and he came to the trench, as the host was going forth to the fight, and shouted for the battle. For Israel and the Philistines had put the battle in array, army against army. And David left his carriage in the hand of the keeper of the carriage, and ran into the army, and came and saluted his brethren. And as he talked with them, behold, there came up the champion, the Philistine of Gath, Goliath by name, out of the armies of the Philistines, and spake according to the same words: and David heard them.

And all the men of Israel, when they saw the man, fled from him, and were sore afraid. And the men of Israel said, Have ye seen this man that is come up? surely to defy Israel is he come up: and it shall be, that the man who killeth him, the king will enrich him with great riches, and will give him his daughter, and make his father's house free in Israel.

And David spake to the men that stood by him, saying, What shall be done to the man that killeth this Philistine, and taketh away the reproach from Israel? for who is this uncircumcised Philistine, that he should defy the armies of the living God?

And the people answered him after this manner, saying, So shall it be done to the man that killeth him.

And Eliab his eldest brother heard when he spake unto the men; and Eliab's anger was kindled against David, and he said, Why camest thou down hither? and with whom hast thou left those few sheep in the wilderness? I know thy pride, and the naughtiness of thine heart; and thou art come down that thou mightest see the battle.

And David said, What have I now done? Is there not a cause? And he turned from him toward another, and spake after the same manner: and the people answered him again after the former manner. And when the words were heard which David spake, they rehearsed them before Saul: and he sent for him.

And David said to Saul, Let no man's heart fail because of him; thy servant will go and fight with this Philistine.

And Saul said to David, Thou art not able to go against him: for thou art but a youth, and he a man of war from his youth.

And David said unto Saul, Thy servant kept his father's sheep, and there came a lion, and a bear, and took a lamb out of the flock: And I went out after him, and smote him, and delivered it out of his mouth: and when he arose against me, I caught him by his beard, and smote him, and slew him. Thy servant slew both the lion and the bear: and this uncircumcised Philistine shall be as one of them, seeing he hath defied the armies of the living God. David said moreover, The Lord that delivered me out of the paw of the lion, and out of the paw of the bear, He will deliver me out of the hand of this Philistine. And Saul said unto David, Go, and the Lord be with thee.

And Saul armed David with his armour, and he put an helmet of brass upon his head; also he armed him with a coat of mail. And David girded his sword upon his armour, and he assayed to go; for he had not proved it. And David said unto Saul, I cannot go with these; for I have not proved them. And David put them off him.

And he took his staff in his hand, and chose him five smooth stones out of the brook, and put them in a shepherd's bag which he had, even in a scrip; and his sling was in his hand: and he drew near to the Philistine.

And the Philistine came on and drew near unto David; and the man that bare the shield went before him. And when the Philistine looked about, and saw David, he disdained him: for he was but a youth, and ruddy, and of a fair countenance.

And the Philistine said unto David, Am I a dog, that thou comest to me with staves? And the Philistine cursed David by his gods. And the Philistine said to David, Come to me, and I will give thy flesh unto the fowls of the air, and to the beasts of the field.

Then said David to the Philistine, Thou comest to me with a sword, with a spear, and with a shield: but I come to thee in the name of the Lord of hosts, the God of the armies of Israel, whom thou hast defied. This day will the Lord deliver thee into mine hand; and I will smite thee, and take thine head from thee and I will give the carcases of the host of the Philistines this day unto the fowls of the air, and to the wild beasts of the earth; that all the earth may know that there is a God in Israel. And all this assembly shall know that the Lord saveth not with sword and spear: for the battle is the Lord's, and He will give you into our hands.

And it came to pass, when the Philistine arose, and came and drew nigh to meet David, that David hasted, and ran toward the army to meet the Philistine. And David put his hand in his bag, and took thence a stone, and slang it, and smote the Philistine in his forehead, that the stone sunk into his forehead; and he fell upon his face to the earth.

So David prevailed over the Philistine with a sling and with a stone, and smote the Philistine, and slew him; but there was no sword in the hand of David. Therefore David ran, and stood upon the Philistine, and took his sword, and drew it out of the sheath thereof, and slew him, and cut off his head therewith. And when the Philistines saw their champion was dead, they fled.

And the men of Israel and of Judah arose, and shouted, and pursued the Philistines, until thou come to the valley, and to the gates of Ekron. And the wounded of the Philistines fell down by the way to Shaaraim, even unto Gath, and unto Ekron. And the children of Israel returned from chasing after the Philistines, and they spoiled their tents. And David took the head of the Philistine, and brought it to Jerusalem; but he put his armour in his tent.

And when Saul saw David go forth against the Philistine, he said unto Abner the captain of the host, Abner, whose son is this youth? And Abner said, As thy soul liveth, O king, I cannot tell. And the king said, Inquire thou whose son the stripling is.

And as David returned from the slaughter of the Philistine Abner took him, and brought him before Saul with the head of the Philistine in his hand. And Saul said to him, Whose son art thou, thou young man? And David answered, I am the son of thy servant Jesse the Bethlehemite.

THE BATTLE OF CANNAE

LIVY

Whilst time was thus being wasted in disputes instead of deliberation, Hannibal withdrew the bulk of his army, who had been standing most of the day in order of battle, into camp. He sent his Numidians, however, across the river to attack the parties who were getting water for the smaller camp. They had hardly gained the opposite bank when with their shouting and uproar they sent the crowd flying in wild disorder, and galloping on as far as the outpost in front of the rampart, they nearly reached the gates of the camp. It was looked upon as such an insult for a Roman camp to be actually terrorised by irregular auxiliaries that one thing, and one thing alone, held back the Romans from instantly crossing the river and forming their battle line—the supreme command that day rested with Paulus.

The following day Varro, whose turn it now was, without any consultation with his colleague, exhibited the signal for battle and led his forces drawn up for action across the river. Paulus followed, for though he disapproved of the measure, he was bound to support it. After crossing, they strengthened their line with the force in the smaller camp and completed their formation. On the right, which was nearest to the river, the Roman cavalry were posted, then came the infantry; on the extreme left were the cavalry of the allies, their infantry were between them and the Roman legions. The javelin men with the rest of the light-armed auxiliaries formed the front line. The consuls took their stations on the wings, Terentius Varro on the left, Aemilius Paulus on the right.

As soon as it grew light Hannibal sent forward the Balearics and the other light infantry. He then crossed the river in person and as each division was brought across he assigned it its place in the line. The Gaulish and Spanish horse he posted near the bank on the left wing in front of the Roman cavalry; the right wing was assigned to the Numidian troopers. The centre consisted of a strong force of infantry, the Gauls and Spaniards in the middle, the Africans at either end of them. You might fancy that the Africans were for the most part a body of Romans from the way they were armed, they were so completely equipped with the arms, some of which they had taken at the Trebia, but the most part at Trasumennus. The Gauls and Spaniards had shields almost of the same shape; their swords were totally different, those of the Gauls being very long and without a point, the Spaniard, accustomed to thrust more than to cut, had a short handy sword, pointed like a dagger. These nations, more than any other, inspired terror by the vastness of their stature and their frightful appearance: the Gauls were naked above the waist, the Spaniards had taken up their position wearing white tunics embroidered with purple, of dazzling brilliancy. The total number of infantry in the field was 40,000, and there were 10,000. cavalry. Hasdrubal was in command of the left wing, Maharbal of the right; Hannibal himself with his brother Mago commanded the centre. It was a great convenience to both armies that the sun shone obliquely on them, whether it was that they had purposely so placed themselves, or whether it happened by accident, since the Romans faced the north, the Carthaginians the South. The wind, called by the inhabitants the Vulturnus, was against the Romans, and blew great clouds of dust into their faces, making it impossible for them to see in front of them.

When the battle shout was raised the auxiliaries ran forward, and the battle began with the light infantry. Then the Gauls and Spaniards on the left engaged the Roman cavalry on the right; the battle was not at all like a cavalry fight, for there was no room for manoeuvering, the river on the one side and the infantry on the other hemming them in, compelled them to fight face to face. Each side tried to force their way straight forward, till at last the horses were standing in a closely pressed mass, and the riders seized their opponents and tried to drag them from their horses. It had become mainly a struggle of infantry, fierce but short, and the Roman cavalry was repulsed and fled. Just as this battle of the cavalry was finished, the infantry became engaged, and as long as the Gauls and Spaniards kept their ranks unbroken, both sides were equally matched in strength and courage. At length after long and repeated efforts the Romans closed up their ranks, echeloned their front, and by the sheer weight of their deep column bore down the division of the enemy which was stationed in front of Hannibal's line, and was too thin and weak to resist the pressure. Without a moment's pause they followed up their broken and hastily retreating foe till they took to headlong flight. Cutting their way through the mass of fugitives, who offered no resistance, they penetrated as far as the Africans who were stationed on both wings, somewhat further back than the Gauls and Spaniards who had formed the advanced centre. As the latter fell back the whole front became level, and as they continued to give ground it became concave and crescent-shaped, the Africans at either end forming the horns. As the Romans rushed on incautiously between them, they were enfiladed by the two wings, which extended and closed round them in the rear. On this, the Romans, who had fought one battle to no purpose, left the Gauls and Spaniards, whose rear they had been slaughtering, and commenced a fresh struggle with the Africans. The contest was a very one-sided one, for not only were they hemmed in on all sides, but wearied with the previous fighting they were meeting fresh and vigorous opponents.

By this time the Roman left wing, where the allied cavalry were fronting the Numidians, had become engaged, but the fighting was slack at first owing to a Carthaginian stratagem. About 500 Numidians, carrying, besides their usual arms and missiles, swords concealed under their coats of mail, rode out from their own line with their shields slung behind their backs *as* though they were deserters, and suddenly leaped from their horses and flung their shields and javelins at the feet of their enemy. They were received into their ranks, conducted to the rear, and ordered to remain quiet. While the battle was spreading to the various parts of the field they re mained quiet, but when the eyes and minds of all were wholly taken up with the fighting they seized the large Roman shields which were lying everywhere amongst the heaps of slain and commenced a furious attack upon the rear of the Roman line. Slashing away at backs and hips, the, made a great slaughter and a still greater panic and confusion. Amidst the rout and panic in one part of the field and the obstinate but hopeless struggle in the other, Hasdrubal, who was in command of that arm, withdrew some Numidians from the centre of the right wing, where the fighting was feebly kept up, and sent them in pursuit of the fugitives, and at the same time sent the Spanish and Gaulish horse to the aid of the Africans, who were by this time more wearied by slaughter than by fighting.

Paulus was on the other side of the field. In spite of his having been seriously wounded at the commencement of the action by a bullet from a sling, he frequently encountered Hannibal with a compact body of troops, and in several places restored the battle. The Roman cavalry formed a bodyguard round him, but at last, as he became too weak to manage his horse, they all dismounted. It is stated that when some one reported to Hannibal that the consul had ordered his men to fight on foot, he remarked, "I would rather he handed them over to me bound hand and foot." Now that the victory of the enemy was no longer doubtful this struggle of the dismounted cavalry was such as might be expected when men preferred to die where they stood rather than flee, and the victors, furious at them for delaying the victory, butchered without mercy those whom they could not dislodge. They did, however, repulse a few survivors exhausted with their exertions and their wounds. All were at last scattered, and those who could regained their horses for flight. Cn. Lentulus, a military tribune, saw, as he rode by, the consul covered with blood sitting on a boulder. "Lucius Æmilius," he said, "the one man whom the gods must hold guiltless of this day's disaster, take this horse while you have still some strength left, and I can lift you into the saddle and keep by your side to protect you. Do not make this day of battle still more fatal by a consul's death, there are enough tears and mourning without that." The consul replied: "Long may you live to do brave deeds, Cornelius, but do not waste in useless pity the few moments left in which to escape from the hands of the enemy. Go, announce publicly to the senate that they must fortify Rome and make its defence strong before the victorious enemy approaches, and tell Q. Fabius privately that I have ever remembered his precepts in life and in death. Suffer me to breathe my last among my slaughtered soldiers, let me not have to defend myself again when I am no longer consul, or appear as the accuser of my colleague and protect my own innocence by throwing the guilt on another." During this conversation a crowd of fugitives came suddenly upon them, followed by the enemy, who, not knowing who the consul was, overwhelmed him with a shower of missiles. Lentulus escaped on horseback in the rush.

Then there was flight in all directions; 7000 men escaped to the smaller camp, 10,000 to the larger, and about 2000 to the village of Cannae. These latter were at once surrounded by Carthalo and his cavalry, as the village was quite unfortified. The other consul, who either by accident or design had not joined any of these bodies of fugitives, escaped with about fifty cavalry to Venusia; 45,500 infantry, 2700 cavalry—almost an equal proportion of Romans and allies—are said to have been killed. Amongst the number were both the quaestors attached to the consuls, L. Atilius and L, Furius Bibulcus, twenty-nine military tribunes, several ex-consuls, ex-praetors, and ex-ædiles (amongst them are included Cn. Servilius Geminus and M. Minucius, who was Master of the Horse the previous year and, some years before that, consul), and in addition to these, eighty men who had either been senators or filled offices qualifying them for election to the senate and who had volunteered for service with the legions. The prisoners taken in the battle are stated to have amounted to 3000 infantry and 1500 cavalry.

Such was the battle of Cannae, a battle as famous as the disastrous one at the Allia; not so serious in its results, owing to the inaction of the enemy, but more serious and more horrible in view of the slaughter of the army. For the flight at the Allia saved the army though it lost the City, whereas at Cannae hardly fifty men shared the consul's flight, nearly the whole army met their death in company with the other consul. As those who had taken refuge in the two camps were only a defenceless crowd without any leaders, the men in the larger camp sent a message to the others asking them to cross over to them at night when the enemy, tired after the battle and the feasting in honour of their victory, would be buried in sleep. Then they would go in one body to Canusium. Some rejected the proposal with scorn. "Why," they asked, "cannot those who sent the message come themselves, since they are quite as able to join us as we to join them? Because, of course, all the country between us is scoured by the enemy and they prefer to expose other people to that deadly peril rather than themselves." Others did not disapprove of the proposal, but they lacked courage to carry it out.

P. Sempronius Tuditanus protested against this cowardice. "Would you," he asked, "rather be taken prisoners by a most avaricious and ruthless foe and a price put upon your heads and your value assessed after you have been asked whether you are a Roman citizen or a Latin ally, in order that another may win honour from your misery and disgrace? Certainly not, if you are really the fellow-countrymen of L. Æmilius, who chose a noble death rather than a life of degradation, and of all the brave men who are lying in heaps around him. But, before daylight overtakes us and the enemy gathers in larger force to bar our path, let us cut our way through the men who in disorder and confusion are clamouring at our gates. Good swords and brave hearts make a way through enemies, however densely they are massed. If you march shoulder to shoulder you will scatter this loose and disorganised force as easily as if nothing opposed you. Come then with me, all you who want to preserve yourselves and the State." With these words he drew his sword, and with his men in close formation marched through the very midst of the enemy. When the Numidians hurled their javelins on the right, the unprotected side, they transferred their shields to their right arms, and so got clear away to the larger camp. As many as 600 escaped on this occasion, and after another large body had joined them they at once left the camp and came through safely to Canusium. This action on the part of defeated men was due to the impulse of natural courage or of accident rather than to any concerted plan of their own or any one's generalship.

Hannibal's officers all surrounded him and congratulated him on his victory, and urged that after such a magnificent success he should allow himself and his exhausted men to rest for the remainder of the day and the following night. Maharbal, however, the commandant of the cavalry, thought that they ought not to lose a moment. "That you may know," he said to Hannibal, "what has been gained by this battle I prophesy that in five days you will be feasting as victor in the Capitol. Follow me; I will go in advance with the cavalry; they will know that you are come before they know that you are coming." To Hannibal the victory seemed too great and too joyous for him to realise all at once. He told Maharbal that he commended his zeal, but he needed time to think out his plans. Maharbal replied: "The gods have not given all their gifts to one man. You know how to win victory, Hannibal, you do not know how to use it." That day's delay is believed to have saved the City and the empire.

The next day, as soon as it grew light, they set about gathering the spoils on the field and viewing the carnage, which was a ghastly sight even for an enemy. There all those thousands of Romans were lying, infantry and cavalry indiscriminately as chance had brought them together in the battle or the flight. Some covered with blood raised themselves from amongst the dead around them, tortured by their wounds which were nipped by the cold of the morning, and were promptly put an end to by the enemy. Some they found lying with their thighs and knees gashed but still alive; these bared their throats and necks and bade them drain what blood they still had left. Some were discovered with their heads buried in the earth, they had evidently suffocated themselves by making holes in the ground and heaping the soil over their faces. What attracted the attention of all was a Numidian who was dragged alive from under a dead Roman lying across him; his ears and nose were torn, for the Roman with hands too powerless to grasp his weapon had, in his mad rage, torn his enemy with his teeth, and while doing so expired.

After most of the day had been spent in collecting the spoils, Hannibal led his men to the attack on the smaller camp and commenced operations by throwing up a breastwork to cut off their water supply from the river. As, however, all the defenders were exhausted by toil and want of sleep, as well as by wounds, the surrender was effected sooner than he had anticipated. They agreed to give up their arms and horses, and to pay For each Roman three hundred "chariot pieces," for each ally two hundred, *and* for each officer's servant one hundred, on condition that after the money was paid they should be allowed to depart with one garment apiece. Then they admitted the enemy into the camp and were all placed under guard, the Romans and the allies separately.

Whilst time was being spent there, all those in the larger camp, who bad sufficient strength and courage, to the number of 4000 infantry and 200 cavalry, made their escape to Canusium, some in a body, others straggling through the fields, which was quite as safe a thing to do. Those who were wounded and those who had been afraid to venture surrendered the camp on the same terms as had been agreed upon in the other camp. An immense amount of booty was secured, and the whole of it was made over to the troops with the exception of the horses and prisoners and whatever silver there might be. Most of this was on the trappings of the horses, for they used very little silver plate at table, at all events when on a Campaign.

Hannibal then ordered the bodies of his own soldiers to be collected for burial; it is said that there were as many as 8000 of his best troops. Some authors state that he also had a search made for the body of the Roman consul, which he buried.

THE PASS AT
THERMOPYLAE

CHARLOTTE YONGE

"Stranger, bear this message to the Spartans, that we lie here
obedient to their laws."

There was trembling in Greece. "The Great King," as the Greeks called the chief potentate of the East, whose domains stretched from the Indian Caucasus to the AEgaeus, from the Caspian to the Red Sea, was marshalling his forces against the little free states that nestled amid the rocks and gulfs of the Eastern Mediterranean. Already had his might devoured the cherished colonies of the Greeks on the eastern shore of the Archipelago, and every traitor to home institutions found a ready asylum at that des court, and tried to revenge his own wrongs by whispering incitements to invasion. "All people, nations, and languages," was the commencement of the decrees of that monarch's court; and it was scarcely a vain boast, for his satraps ruled over subject kingdoms, and among his tributary nations he counted the Chaldean, with his learning and old civilization, and the steadfast Jew, the skilful Phoenician, the learned Egyptian, the wild freebooting Arab of the desert, the dark-skinned Ethiopian, and over all these ruled the keen-witted, active native Persian race, the conquerors of all the rest, and led by a chosen band proudly called the Immortal. His many capitals—Babylon the great, Susa, Persepolis, and the like were names of dreamy splendour to the Greeks, described now and then by Ionians from Asia Minor who had carried their tribute to the king's own feet, or by courtier slaves who had escaped with difficulty from being all too serviceable at the tyrannic court. And the lord of this enormous empire was about to launch his countless host against the little cluster of states the whole of which together would hardly equal one province of the huge Asiatic realm! Moreover, it was a war not only on the men, but on their gods. The Persians were zealous adorers of the sun and of fire; they abhorred the idol-worship of the Greeks, and defiled and plundered every temple that fell in their way. Death and desolation were almost the best that could be looked for at such hands; slavery and torture from cruelly barbarous masters would only too surely be the lot of numbers should their land fall a prey to the conquerors.

True it was that ten years back the former Great King had sent his best troops to be signally defeated upon the coast of Attica; but the losses at Marathon had but stimulated the Persian lust of conquest, and the new king Xerxes was gathering together such myriads of men as should crush the Greeks and overrun their country by mere force of numbers.

The muster-place was at Sardis, and there Greek spies had seen the multitudes assembling and the state and magnificence of the king's attendants. Envoys had come from him to demand earth and water from each state in Greece, as emblems that land and sea were his; but each state was resolved to be free, and only Thessaly, that which lay first in his path, consented to yield the token of subjugation. A council was held at the Isthmus of corinth, and attended by deputies from all the states of Greece, to consider the best means of defence. The ships of the enemy would coast round the shores of the Aegean Sea, the land army would cross the Hellespont on abridge of boats lashed together, and march southwards into Greece. The only hope of averting the danger lay in defending such passages as, from the nature of the ground, were so narrow that only a few persons could fight hand to hand at once, so that courage would be of more avail than numbers.

The first of these passes was called Tempe, and a body of troops was sent to guard it; but they found that this was useless and impossible, and came back again. The next was at Thermopylae. Look in your map of the Archipelago, or Aegean Sea, as it was then called, for the great island of Negropont, or by its old name, Euboea. It looks like a piece broken off from the coast, and to the north is shaped like the head of a bird, with the beak running into a gulf, that would fit over it, upon the mainland, and between the island and the coast is an exceedingly narrow strait. The Persian army would have to march round the edge of the gulf. They could not cut straight across the country, because the ridge of mountains called, Ceta rose up and barred their way. Indeed, the woods, rocks, and precipices came down so near the seashore that in two places there was only room for one single wheel track between the steeps and the impassable morass that formed the border of the gulf on its south side. These two very narrow places were called the gates of the pass, and were about a mile apart. There was a little more width left in the intervening space; but in this there were a number of springs of warm mineral water, salt and sulphurous, which were used for the sick to bathe in, and thus the place was called Thermopylae, or the Hot Gates. A wall had once been built across the westernmost of these narrow places, when the Thessalians and Phocians, who lived on either side of it, had been at war with one another; but it had been allowed to go to decay, since the Phocians had found out that there was a very steep, narrow mountain path along the bed of a torrent by which it was possible to cross from one territory to the other without going round this marshy coast road.

This was therefore an excellent place to defend. The Greek ships were all drawn up on the farther side of Euboea to prevent the Persian vessel from getting into the strait and landing men beyond the pass, and a division of the army was sent off to guard the Hot Gates. The council at the Isthmus did not know of the mountain pathway, and thought that all would be safe as long as the Persians were kept out of the coast path.

The troops sent for this purpose were from different cities, and amountsed to about 4,000, who were to keep the pass against two millions. The leader of them was Leonidas, who had newly become one of the two kings of Sparta, the city that above all in Greece trained its sons to be hardy soldiers dreading death infinitely less than shame. Leonidas had already made his mind that the expedition would probably be his death, perhaps because a prophecy had been given at the Temple at Delphi that Sparta should be saved by the death of one of her kings of the race of Hercules. He was allowed by law to take with him

300 men, and these he chose most carefully, not merely for their strength and courage, but selecting those where had sons, so that no family might be altogether destroyed. These Spartans with their helots or slaves, made up his own share of the numbers, but all the army was under his generalship. It is even said that the 300 celebrated their own funeral rites before they set out, lest they should be deprived of them by the enemy, since, as we have already seen, it was the Greek belief that the spirits of the dead found no rest till their obsequies had been performed. Such preparations did not daunt the spirits of Leonidas and his men; and his wife, Gorgo, was not a woman to be faint-hearted or hole him back. Long before, when she was a very little girl, a word of hers saved her father from listening to a traitorous message from the King of Persia; and every Spartan lady was bred up to be able to say to those she best loved that they must come home from battle "with the shield or on it"—either carrying it victoriously or borne upon it as a corpse.

When Leonidas came to Thermopylae, the Phocians told him of the mountain path through the chestnut woods of Mount Ceta, and begged to have the privilege of guarding it on a spot high up on the mountain side, assuring him that it was very hard to find at the other end, and that there was every probability that the enemy would never discover it. He consented, and encamping around the warm springs, caused the broken wall to be repaired and made ready to meet the foe.

The Persian army were seen covering the whole country like locusts, and the hearts of some of the southern Greeks in the pass began to sink. Their homes in the Peloponnesus were comparatively secure: had they not better fall back and reserve themselves to defend the Isthmus of Corinth? Buti Leonidas, though Sparta was safe below the Isthmus, had no intention of abandoning his northern allies, and kept the other Peloponnesians to their posts, only sending messengers for further help.

Presently a Persian on horseback rode up to reconnoitre the pass. He could not see over the wall, but in front of it and on the ramparts he saw the Spartans, some of them engaged in active sports, and others in combing their long hair. He rode back to the king, and told him what he had seen. "Now, Xerxes had in his camp an exiled Spartan prince, named Demartus, who had become a traitor to his country, and was serving as counsellor to the enemy. Xerxes sent for him, and asked whether his countrymen were to be thus employed instead of fleeing away; but Demartus made answer that a hard fight was no doubt in preparation, and that it was custom of the Spartans to array their hair with especial care when they were about to enter upon any great peril. Xerxes would, however, not believe that so petty a force could intend to resist him, and waited four days, probably expecting his fleet to assist him; but as it did not appear, the attack was made.

The Greeks, stronger men and more heavily armed, were far better able to fight to advantage than the Persians with their short spears and wicker shields, and beat them off with great ease. It is said, that Xerxes three times "leapt off his throne in despair at the sight of his troops being driven backwards; and thus for two days it seemed as easy to force a way through the Spartans as through the rocks themselves. Nay, how could slavish troops, dragged from home to spread the victories of an ambitious king, fight like freemen who felt that their strokes were to defend their homes and children?

But on that evening a wretched man, named Ephialtes, crept into the Persian camp, and offered, for a great sum of money, to show the mountain path that would enable the enemy to take the brave defenders in the rear. A Persian general, named Hydarnes, was sent off at nightfall with a detach-ment to secure this passage, and was guided through the thick forests that clothed the hillside. In the stillness of the air, at daybreak, the Phocian guards of the path were startled by the crackling of the chestnut leaves under the tread of many feet. They started up, but a shower of arrows was discharged on them, and forgetting all save the present alarm, they fled to a higher part of the mountain, and the enemy, without waiting to pursue them, began to descend.

As day dawned, morning light showed the watchers of the Grecian camp below a glittering and shimmering in the torrent bed where the shaggy forests opened; but it was not the sparkle of water, but the shine of gilded helmets and the gleaming of silvered spears! Moreover, a Cimmerian crept over to the wall from the Persian camp with tidings that the path had been betrayed; that the enemy were climbing it, and would come down beyond the Eastern Gate. Still, the way was rugged and circuitous, the Persians would hardly descend before midday, and there was ample time for the Greeks to escape before they could thus be shut in by the enemy.

There was a short council held over the morning sacrifice. Megistias, the seer, on inspecting the entrails of the slain victim, declared, as well he might, that their appearance boded disaster. Him Leonidas ordered to retire, but he refused, though he sent home his only son. There was no disgrace to an ordinary tone of mind in leaving a post that could not be held, and Leonidas recommended all the allied troops under his command to march away while yet the way was open. As to himself and his Spartans! they had made up their minds to die at their post, and there could be little doubt that the example of such a resolution would do more to save Greece than their best efforts could ever do if they were careful to reserve themselves for another occasion.

All the allies consented to retreat, except the eighty men who came from Mycæne and the 700 Thespians, who declared that they would not desert Leonidas. There were also 400 Thebans who remained; and thus the whole number that stayed with Leonidas to confront two million of enemies were fourteen hundred warriors, besides the helots or attendants on the 300 Spartans, whose number is not known, but there was probably at least dpi to each. Leonidas had two kinsmen in the camp, like himself claiming the blood of Hercules, and he tried to save them by giving them letters and messages to Sparta; but one answered that "he had come to fight, not to carry letters," and the other that "his deeds would tell all that Sparta wished to know." Another Spartan, named Dienices, when told that the enemy's archers were so numerous that their arrows darkened the sun replied, "So much the better: we shall fight in the shade." Two of the 300 had been sent to a neighbouring village, suffering severely from a complaint, in the eyes. One of them, called Eurytus, put on his armour, and commanded his helot to lead him to his place in the ranks; the other, called Aristodemus, was so overpowered with illness that he allowed himself to be carried away with the retreating allies. It was still early in the day when all were gone, and Leonidas gave the word to his men to take their last meal. "To-night," he said, "we shall sup with Pluto."

Hitherto he had stood on the defensive, and had husbanded the lives of his men; but he now desired to make as great a slaughter as possible, so as to inspire the enemy with dread of the Grecian name. He therefore marched out beyond the wall, without waiting to be attacked, and the battle began. The Persian captains went behind their wretched troops and scourged them on to the fight with whips! Poor wretches! they were driven on to be slaughtered, pierced with the Greek spears, hurled into the sea, or trampled into the mud of the morass; but their inexhaustible numbers told at length. The spears of the Greeks broke under hard service, and their swords alone remained; they began to fall, and Leonidas himself was among the first of the slain. Hotter than ever was the fight over his corpse, and two Persian princes, brothers of Xerxes, were there killed; but at length word was brought that Hydarnes was over the pass, and that the few remaining men were thus enclosed on all sides. The Spartans and Thespians made their way to a little hillock within the wall, resolved to let this be the place of their last stand but the hearts of the Thebans failed them, and they came towards the Persians holding out their hands in entreaty for mercy. Quarter was given to them, but they were all branded with the king's mark as untrustworthy deserters. The helots probably at this time escaped into the mountains while the small desperate band stood side by side on the hill still fighting to the last, some with swords, others with daggers, others even with their hands and teeth, till not one living man remained amongst them when the sun went down. There was only a mound of slain, bristled over with arrows.

Twenty thousand Persians had died before that handful of men! Xerxes asked Demaratus if there were many more at Sparta like these, and was told there were 8,000. It must have been with a somewhat failing heart that he invited his courtiers from the fleet to see what he had done to the men who dared to oppose him, and showed them the head and arm of Leonidas set up upon a cross; but he took care that all his own slain, except 1,000, should first be put out of sight. The body of the brave king was buried where he fell, as were those of the other dead. Much envied were they by the unhappy Aristodemus, who found himself called by no name but the "Coward," and was shunned by all his fellow-citizens. No one would give him fire or water, and after a year of misery he redeemed his honour by perishing in the forefront of the battle of Plataea, which was the last blow that drove the Persians ingloriously from Greece.

HORATIUS AT THE BRIDGE

LIVY

By this time the Tarquins had fled to Lars Porsena, king of Clusium. There, with advice and entreaties, they besought him not to suffer them, who were descended from the Etrurians and of the same blood and name, to live in exile and poverty; and advised him not to let this practice of expelling kings to pass unpunished. Liberty, they declared, had charms enough in itself; and unless kings defended their crowns with as much vigour as the people pursued their liberty, the highest must be reduced to a level with the lowest; there would be nothing exalted, nothing distinguished above the rest; hence there must be an end of regal government, the most beautiful institution both among gods and men. Porsena, thinking it would be an honour to the Tuscans that there should be a king at Rome, especially one of the Etrurian nation, marched towards Rome with an army. Never before had such terror seized the Senate, so powerful was the state of Clusium at the time, and so great the renown of Porsena. Nor did they only dread their enemies, but even their own citizens, lest the common people, though excess of fear should, by receiving the Tarquins into the city, accept peace even though purchased with slavery. Many concessions were therefore granted to the people by the Senate during that period. Their attention, in the first place, was directed to the markets, and persons were sent, some to the Volscians, others to Cumse, to buy up corn. The privilege of selling salt, because it was farmed at a high rate, was also taken into the hands of the government, and withdrawn from private individuals; and the people were freed from port-duties and taxes, in order that the rich, who could bear the burden, should contribute; the poor paid tax enough if they educated their children. This indulgent care of the fathers accordingly kept the whole state in such concord amid the subsequent severities of the siege and famine, that the highest as well as the lowest abhorred the name of king; nor was any individual afterwards so popular by intriguing practices as the whole Senate was by their excellent government.

Some parts of the city seemed secured by the walls, others by the River Tiber. The Sublician Bridge well-nigh afforded a passage to the enemy, had there not been one man, Horatius Codes (fortunately Rome had on that day such a defender) who, happening to be posted on guard at the bridge, when he saw the Janiculum taken by a sudden assault and the enemy pouring down thence at full speed, and that his own party, in terror and confusion, were abandoning their arms and ranks, laying hold of them one by one, standing in their way and appealing to the faith of gods and men, he declared that their flight would avail them nothing if they deserted their post; if they passed the bridge, there would soon be more of the enemy in the Palatium and Capitol than in the Janiculum. For that reason he charged them to demolish the bridge, by sword, by fire, or by any means whatever; declaring that he would stand the shock of the enemy as far as could be done by one man. He then advanced to the first entrance of the bridge, and being easily distinguished among those who showed their backs in retreating, faced about to engage the foe hand to hand, and by his surprising bravery he terrified the enemy. Two indeed remained with him from a sense of shame: Sp. Lartius and T, Herminius, men eminent for their birth, and renowned for their gallant exploits. With them he for a short time stood the first storm of the danger, and the severest brunt of the battle. But as they who demolished the bridge called upon them to retire, he obliged them also to withdraw to a place of safety on a small portion of the bridge that was still left. Then casting his stern eyes toward the officers of the Etrurians in a threatening manner, he now challenged, them singly, and then reproached them, slaves of haughty tyrants who, regardless of their own freedom, came to oppress the liberty of others. They hesitated for a time, looking round one at the other, to begin the fight; shame then put the army in motion, and a shout being raised, they hurled weapons from all sides at their single adversary; and when they all stuck in his upraised shield, and he with no less obstinacy kept possession of the bridge, they endeavoured to thrust him down from it by one push, when the crash of the falling bridge was heard, and at the same time a shout of the Romans raised for joy at having completed their purpose, checked their ardour with sudden panic. Then said Cocles: "Holy Father Tiber, I pray thee, receive these arms, and this thy soldier, in thy propitious stream." Armed as he was, he leaped into the Tiber, and amid showers of darts, swam across safe to his party, having dared an act which is likely to obtain with posterity more fame than credit. The state was grateful for such valour; a statue was erected to him in the comitium, and as much land given to him as he could plough in one day. The zeal of private individuals was also conspicuous among his public honours. For amid the great scarcity, each contributed something, according to his supply, depriving himself of his own support.

JOSHUA CONQUEST OF JERICHO

THE KING JAMES BIBLE

Now after the death of Moses the servant of the Lord it came to pass, that the Lord spake unto Joshua the son of Nun, Moses' minister, saying, Moses my servant is dead; now therefore arise, go over this Jordan, thou, and all this people, unto the land which I do give to them, even to the children of Israel. Every place that the sole of your foot shall tread upon, that have I given unto you, as I said unto Moses. From the wilderness and this Lebanon even unto the great river, the river Euphrates, all the land of the Hittites, and unto the great sea toward the going down of the sun, shall be your coast. There shall not any man be able to stand before thee all the days of thy life: as I was with Moses, so I will be with thee: I will not fail thee, nor forsake thee. Be strong and of a good courage: for unto this people shalt thou divide for an inheritance the land, which I sware unto their fathers to give them. Only be thou strong and very courageous, that thou mayest observe to do according to all the law, which Moses my servant commanded thee: turn not from it to the right hand or to the left, that thou mayest prosper whithersoever thou goest. Have not I commanded thee? Be strong and of a good courage; be not afraid, neither be thou dismayed: for the Lord thy God is with thee whithersoever thou goest.

Then Joshua commanded the officers of the people, saying, Pass through the host, and command the people, saying, Prepare you victuals; for within three days ye shall pass over this Jordan, to go in to possess the land, which the Lord your God giveth you to possess it.

And they answered Joshua, saying, All that thou commandest us we will do, and whithersoever thou sendest us, we will go.

And Joshua the son of Nun sent out of Shittim two men to spy secretly, saying, Go view the land, even Jericho. And they went, and came into an harlot's house, named Rahab, and lodged there.

And it was told the King of Jericho, saying, Behold, there came men in hither to night of the children of Israel to search out the country. And the King of Jericho sent unto Rahab, saying, Bring forth the men that are come to thee, which are entered into thine house: for they be come to search out all the country.

And the woman took the two men, and hid them, and said thus, There came men unto me, but I wist not whence they were: And it came to pass about the time of shutting of the gate, when it was dark, that the men went out: whither the men went I wot not: pursue after them quickly; for ye shall over-take them. But she had brought them up to the roof of the house, and hid them with the stalks of flax, which she had laid in order upon the roof. And the men pursued after them the way to Jordan unto the fords; and as soon as they which pursued after them were gone out, they shut the gate.

And before they were laid down, she came up unto them upon the roof; And she said unto the men, I know that the Lord hath given you the land, and that your terror is fallen upon us, and that all the inhabitants of the land faint because of you. For we have heard how the Lord dried up the water of the Red Sea for you, when ye came out of Egypt; and what ye did unto the two kings of the Amorites, that were on the other side Jordan, Sihon and Og, whom ye utterly destroyed. And as soon as we had heard these things, our hearts did melt, neither did there remain any more courage in any man, because of you: for the Lord your God, He is God in heaven above, and in earth beneath. Now therefore, I pray you, swear unto me by the Lord, since I have shewed you kindness, that ye will also shew kindness unto my father's house, and give me a true token: And that ye will save alive my father, and my mother, and my brethren, and my sisters, and all that they have, and deliver our lives from death.

And the men answered her, Our life for yours, if ye utter not this our business. And it shall be, when the Lord hath given us the land, that we will deal kindly and truly with thee.

Then she let them down by a cord through the window: for her house was upon the town wall, and she dwelt upon the wall. And she said unto them, Get you to the mountain, lest the pursuers meet you; and hide yourselves there three days, until the pursuers be returned: and afterward may ye go your way.

And the men said unto her, We will be blameless of this thine oath which thou hast made us swear. Behold, when we come into the land, thou shalt bind this line of scarlet thread in the window which thou didst let us down by: and thou shalt bring thy father, and thy mother, and thy brethren, and all thy father's household, home unto thee. And it shall be, that whoso ever shall go out of the doors of thy house into the street, his blood shall be upon his head, and we will be guiltless: and whosoever shall be with thee in the house, his blood shall be on our head, if any hand be upon him. And if thou utter this our business, then we will be quit of thine oath which thou hast made us to swear.

And she said, According unto your words, so be it. And she sent them away, and they departed: and she bound the scarlet line in the window.

And they went, and came unto the mountain, and abode there three days, until the pursuers were returned: and the pursuers sought them throughout all the way, but found them not. So the two men returned, and descended from the mountain, and passed over, and came to Joshua the son of Nun, and told him all things that befell them: And they said unto oshua, Truly the Lord hath delivered into our hands all the land; for even all the inhabitants of the country do faint because of us.

And Joshua rose early, in the morning; and they removed from Shittim, and came to Jordan, he and all the children of Israel, and lodged there before they passed over.

And Joshua spake unto the priests, saying, Take up the ark of the covenant, and pass over before the people. And they took up the ark of the covenant, and went before the people.

And the Lord said unto Joshua, This day will I begin to magnify thee in the sight of all Israel, that they may know that, as I was with Moses, so I will be with thee. And thou shalt command the priests that bear the ark of the covenant, saying, When ye are come to the brink of the water of Jordan, ye shall stand still in Jordan. And Joshua said unto the children of Israel, Come hither, and hear the words of the Lord your God. And Joshua said, Hereby ye shall know that the living God is among you, and that He will without fail drive out from before you the Canaanites, and the Hittites, and the Hivites, and the Perizzites, and the Girgashites, and the Amorites, and the Jebusites. Behold, the ark of the covenant of the Lord of all the earth passeth over before you into Jordan. Now therefore take you twelve men out of the tribes of Israel, out of every tribe a man. And it shall come to pass, as soon as the soles of the feet of the priests that bear the ark of the Lord, the Lord of all the earth, shall rest in the waters of Jordan, that the waters of Jordan shall be cut off from the waters that come down from above; and they shall stand upon an heap.

And it came to pass, when the people removed from their tents, to pass over Jordan, and the priests bearing the ark of the covenant before the people; And as they that bare the ark were come unto Jordan, and the feet of the priests that bare the ark were dipped in the brim of the water, (for Jordan overfloweth all his banks all the time of harvest), that the waters which came down from above stood and rose up upon an heap very far from the city Adam, that is beside Zaretan: and those that came down toward the sea of the plain, even the salt sea, failed, and were cut off: and the people passed over right against Jericho. And the priests that bare the ark of the covenant of the Lord stood firm on dry ground in the midst of Jordan, and all the Israelites passed over on dry ground, until all the people were passed clean over Jordan.

About forty thousand prepared for war passed over before the Lord unto battle, to the plains of Jericho.

On that day the Lord magnified Joshua in the sight of all Israel; and they feared him, as they feared Moses all the days of his life.

And it came to pass, when Joshua was by Jericho, that he lifted up his eyes and looked, and, behold, there stood a man over against him with his sword drawn in his hand: and Joshua went unto him, and said unto him, Art thou for us, or for our adversaries?

And he said, Nay; but as captain of the host of the Lord am I now come.

And Joshua fell on his face to the earth, and did worship, and said unto him, What saith my lord unto his servant? And the captain of the Lord's host said unto Joshua, Loose thy shoe from off thy foot; for the place whereon thou standest is holy. And Joshua did so.

Now Jericho was straitly shut up because of the children of Israel: none went out, and none came in.

And the Lord said unto Joshua, See, I have given into thine hand Jericho, and the king thereof, and the mighty men of valour. And ye shall compass the city, all ye men of war, and go round about the city once. Thus shalt thou do six days. And seven priests shall bear before the ark seven trumpets of rams' horns: and the seventh day ye shall compass the city seven times, and the priests shall blow with the trumpets. And it shall come to pass, that when they make a long blast with the ram's horn, and when ye hear the sound of the trumpet, all the people shall shout with a great shout; and the wall of the city shall fall down flat, and the people shall ascend up every man straight before him.

And Joshua the son of Nun called the priests, and said unto them, Take up the ark of the covenant, and let seven priests bear seven trumpets of rams' horns before the ark of the Lord. And he said unto the people, Pass on, and compass the city, and let him that is armed pass on before the ark of the Lord.

And it came to pass, when Joshua had spoken unto the people, that the seven priests bearing the seven trumpets of rams' horns passed on before the Lord, and blew with the trumpets: and the ark of the covenant of the Lord followed them. And the armed men went before the priests that blew with the trumpets, and the rearward came after the ark, the priests going on, and blowing with the trumpets. And Joshua had commanded the people, saying, Ye shall not shout, nor make any noise with your voice, neither shall any word proceed out of your mouth, until the day I bid you shout; then shall ye shout. So the ark of the Lord compassed the city, going about it once: and they came into the camp, and lodged in the camp.

And Joshua rose early in the morning, and the priests took up the ark of the Lord. And seven priests bearing seven trumpets of rams' horns before the ark of the Lord went on continually, and blew with the trumpets: and the armed men went before them; but the rearward came after the ark of the Lord, the priests going on, and blowing the trumpets.

And the second day they compassed the city once, and returned into the camp: so they did six clays.

And it came to pass on the seventh day, that they rose early about the dawning of the day, and compassed the city after the same manner seven times: only on that day they compassed the city seven times. And it came to pass at the seventh time, when the priests blew with the trumpets, Joshua said unto the people, Shout; for the Lord hath given you the city. And the city shall be accursed, even it, and all that are therein, to the Lord: only Rahab the harlot shall live, she and all that are with her in the house, because she hid the messengers that we sent. And ye, in any wise keep yourselves from the accursed thing, lest ye make yourselves accursed, when ye take of the accursed thing, and make the camp of Israel a curse, and trouble it. But all the silver, and gold, and vessels of brass and iron, are consecrated unto the Lord: they shall come into the treasury of the Lord.

So the people shouted when the priests blew with the trumpets: and it came to pass, when the people heard the sound of the trumpet, and the people shouted with a great shout, that the wall fell down flat, so that the people went up into the city, every man straight before him, and they took the city. And they utterly destroyed all that was in the city, both man and woman, young and old, and ox, and sheep, and ass, with the edge of the sword.

But Joshua had said unto the two men that had spied out the country, Go into the harlot's house, and bring out thence the woman, and all that she hath, as ye sware unto her.

And the young men that were spies went in, and brought out Rahab, and her father, and her mother, and her brethren, and all that she had; and they brought out all her kindred, and left them without the camp of Israel.

And they burnt the city with fire, and all that was therein: only the silver, and the gold, and the vessels of brass and of iron, they put into the treasury of the house of the Lord.

And Joshua saved Rahab the harlot alive, and her father's household, and all that she had; and she dwelleth in Israel even unto this day; because- she hid the messengers, which Joshua sent to spy out Jericho.

And Joshua adjured them at that time, saying, Cursed be the man before the Lord, that riseth up and buildeth this city Jericho: he shall lay the foundation thereof in his firstborn, and in his youngest son shall he set up the gates of it.

So the Lord was with Joshua; and his fame was noised throughout all the country.

CAESAR INVADES BRITAIN

JULIUS CAESAR

During the short part of summer which remained, Cæsar, although in these countries, as all Gaul lies toward the north, the winters are early, neverthe-less resolved to proceed into Britain, because he discovered that in almost all the wars with the Gauls succors had been furnished to our enemy from that coun-try; and even if the time of year should be insufficient for carrying on the war, yet he thought it would be of great service to him if he only entered the island, and saw into the character of the people, and got knowledge of their localities, harbors, and landing-places, all which were for the most part unknown to the Gauls. For neither does anyone except merchants generally go thither, nor even to them was any portion of it known, except the sea-coast and those parts which are opposite to Gaul. Therefore, after having called up to him the merchants from all parts, he could learn neither what was the size of the island, nor what or how numerous were the nations which inhabited it, nor what system of war they followed, nor what customs they used, nor what harbors were convenient for a great number of large ships.

He sends before him Caius Volusenus with a ship of war, to acquire a knowledge of these particulars before he in person should make a descent into the island, as he was convinced that this was a judicious measure. He commissioned him to thoroughly examine into all matters, and then return to him as soon as possible. He himself proceeds to the Morini with all his forces. He orders ships from all parts of the neighboring countries, and the fleet which the preceding summer he had built for the war with the Veneti, to assemble in this place. In the meantime, his purpose having been discovered, and reported to the Britons by merchants, ambassadors come to him from several states of the island, to promise that they will give hostages, and submit to the government of the Roman people. Having given them an audience, he after promising liberally, and exhorting them to continue in that purpose, sends them back to their own country, and [dispatches] with them Commius, whom, upon subduing the Atrebates, he had created king there, a man whose courage and conduct he esteemed, and who he thought would be faithful to him, and whose influence ranked highly in those countries. He orders him to visit as many states as he could, and persuade them to embrace the protection of the Roman people, and apprize them that he would shortly come thither. Volusenus, having viewed the localities as far as means could be afforded one who dared not leave his ship and trust himself to barbarians, returns to Cæsar on the fifth day, and reports what he had there observed.

While Cæsar remains in these parts for the purpose of procuring ships, ambassadors come to him from a great portion of the Morini, to plead their excuse respecting their conduct on the late occasion; alleging that it was as men uncivilized, and as those who were unacquainted with our custom, that they had made war upon the Roman people, and promising to perform what he should command. Cæsar, thinking that this had happened fortunately enough for him, because he neither wished to leave an enemy behind him, nor had an opportunity for carrying on a war, by reason of the time of year, nor considered that employment in such trifling matters was to be preferred to his enterprise on Britain, imposes a large number of hostages; and when these were brought, he received them to his protection. Having collected together, and provided about eighty transport ships, as many as he thought necessary for conveying over two legions, he assigned such [ships] of war as he had besides to the quæstor, his lieutenants, and officers of cavalry. There were in addition to these eighteen ships of burden which were prevented, eight miles from that place, by winds, from being able to reach the same port. These he distributed among the horse; the rest of the army, he delivered to Q. Titurius Sabinus and L. Aurunculeius Cotta, his lieutenants, to lead into the territories of the Menapii and those cantons of the Morini from which ambassadors had not come to him. He ordered P. Sulpicius Rufus, his lieutenant, to hold possession of the harbor, with such a garrison as he thought sufficient.

These matters being arranged, finding the weather favorable for his voyage, he set sail about the third watch, and ordered the horse to march forward to the further port, and there embark and follow him. As this was performed rather tardily by them, he himself reached Britain with the first squadron of ships, about the fourth hour of the day, and there saw the forces of the enemy drawn up in arms on all the hills. The nature of the place was this: the sea was confined by mountains so close to it that a dart could be thrown from their summit upon the shore. Considering this by no means a fit place for disembarking, he remained at anchor till the ninth hour, for the other ships to arrive there. Having in the meantime assembled the lieutenants and military tribunes, he told them both what he had learned from Volusenus, and what he wished to be done; and enjoined them (as the principle of military matters, and especially as maritime affairs, which have a precipitate and uncertain action, required) that all things should be performed by them at a nod and at the instant. Having dismissed them, meeting both with wind and tide favorable at the same time, the signal being given and the anchor weighed, he advanced about seven miles from that place, and stationed his fleet over against an open and level shore.

But the barbarians, upon perceiving the design of the Romans, sent forward their cavalry and charioteers, a class of warriors of whom it is their practice to make great use in their battles, and following with the rest of their forces, endeavored to prevent our men landing. In this was the greatest difficulty, for the following reasons, namely, because our ships, on account of their great size, could be stationed only in deep water; and our soldiers, in places unknown to them, with their hands embarrassed, oppressed with a large and heavy weight of armor, had at the same time to leap from the ships, stand amid the waves, and encounter the enemy; whereas they, either on dry ground, or advancing a little way into the water, free in all their limbs, in places thoroughly known to them, could confidendy throw their weapons and spur on their horses, which were accustomed to this kind of service. Dismayed by these circumstances and altogether untrained in this mode of battle, our men did not all exert the same vigor and eagerness which they had been wont to exert in engagements on dry ground.

When Cæsar observed this, he ordered the ships of war, the appearance of which was somewhat strange to the barbarians and the motion more ready for service, to be withdrawn a little from the transport vessels, and to be propelled by their oars, and be stationed toward the open flank of the enemy, and the enemy to be beaten off and driven away, with slings, arrows, and engines: which plan was of great service to our men; for the barbarians being startled by the form of our ships and the motions of our oars and the nature of our engines, which was strange to them, stopped, and shortly after retreated a little. And while our men were hesitating (whether they should advance to the shore), chiefly on account of the depth of the sea, he who carried the eagle of the tenth legion, after supplicating the gods that the matter might turn out favorably to the legion, exclaimed, "Leap, fellow soldiers, unless you wish to betray your eagle to the enemy. I, for my part, will perform my duty to the commonwealth and my general." When he had said this with a loud voice, he leaped from the ship and proceeded to bear the eagle toward the enemy. Then our men, exhorting one another that so great a disgrace should not be incurred, all leaped from the ship. When those in the nearest vessels saw them, they speedily followed and approached the enemy.

The battle was maintained vigorously on both sides. Our men, however, as they could neither keep their ranks, nor get firm footing, nor follow their standards, and as one from one ship and another from another assembled around whatever standards they met, were thrown into great confusion. But the enemy, who were acquainted with all the shallows, when from the shore they saw any coming from a ship one by one, spurred on their horses, and attacked them while embarrassed; many surrounded a few, others threw their weapons upon our collected forces on their exposed flank. When Cæsar observed this, he ordered the boats of the ships of war and the spy sloops to be filled with soldiers, and sent them up to the succor of those whom he had observed in distress. Our men, as soon as they made good their footing on dry ground, and all their comrades had joined them, made an attack upon the enemy, and put them to flight, but could not pursue them very far, because the horse had not been able to maintain their course at sea and reach the island. This alone was wanting to Cæsar's accustomed success.

The enemy being thus vanquished in battle, as soon as they recovered after their flight, instandy sent ambassadors to Cæsar to negotiate about peace. They promised to give hostages and perform what he should command. Together with these ambassadors came Commius the Altrebatian, who, as I have above said, had been sent by Cæsar into Britain. Him they had seized upon when leaving his ship, although in the character of ambassador he bore the general's commission to them, and thrown into chains: then after the battle was fought, they sent him back, and in suing for peace cast the blame of that act upon the common people, and entreated that it might be pardoned on account of their indiscretion. Cæsar, complaining, that after they had sued for peace, and had voluntarily sent ambassadors into the continent for that purpose, they had made war without a reason, said that he would pardon their indiscretion, and imposed hostages, a part of whom they gave immediately; the rest they said they would give in a few days, since they were sent for from remote places. In the meantime they ordered their people to return to the country parts, and the chiefs assembled from all quarters, and proceeded to surrender themselves and their states to Cæsar.

A peace being established by these proceedings four days after we had come into Britain, the eighteen ships, to which reference has been made above, and which conveyed the cavalry, set sail from the upper port with a gentle gale, when, however, they were approaching Britain and were seen from the camp, so great a storm suddenly arose that none of them could maintain their course at sea; and some were taken back to the same port from which they had started;—others, to their great danger, were driven to the lower part of the island, nearer to the west; which, however, after having cast anchor, as they were getting filled with water, put out to sea through necessity in a stormy night, and made for the continent.

It happened that night to be full moon, which usually occasions very high tides in that ocean; and that circumstance was unknown to our men. Thus, at the same time, the tide began to fill the ships of war which Cæsar had provided to convey over his army, and which he had drawn up on the strand; and the storm began to dash the ships of burden which were riding at anchor against each other; nor was any means afforded our men of either managing them or of rendering any service. A great many ships having been wrecked, inasmuch as the rest, having lost their cables, anchors, and other tackling, were unfit for sailing, a great confusion, as would necessarily happen, arose throughout the army; for there were no other ships in which they could be conveyed back, and all things which are of service in repairing vessels were wanting, and, corn for the winter had not been provided in those places, because it was understood by all that they would certainly winter in Gaul.

On discovering these things the chiefs of Britain, who had come up after the battle was fought to peiform those conditions which Cæsar had imposed, held a conference, when they perceived that cavalry. and ships, and corn were wanting to the Romans, and discovered the small number of our soldiers from the small extent of the camp (which, too, was on this account more limited than ordinary, because Cæsar had conveyed over his legions without baggage), and thought that the best plan was to renew the war, and cut off our men from corn and provisions and protract the affair till winter; because they felt confident, that, if they were vanquished or cut off from a return, no one would afterward pass over into Britain for the purpose of making war. Therefore, again entering into a conspiracy, they began to depart from the camp by degrees and secretly bring up their people from the country parts.

But Cæsar, although he had not as yet discovered their measures, yet, both from what had occurred to his ships, and from the circumstance that they had neglected to give the promised hostages, suspected that the thing would come to pass which really did happen. He therefore provided remedies against all contingencies; for he daily conveyed corn from the country parts into the camp, used the timber and brass of such ships as were most seriously damaged for repairing the rest, and ordered whatever things besides were necessary for this object to be brought to him from the continent. And thus, since that business was executed by the soldiers with the greatest energy, he effected that, after the loss of twelve ships, a voyage could be made well enough in the rest.

While these things are being transacted, one legion had been sent to forage, according to custom, and no suspicion of war had arisen as yet, and some of the people remained in the country parts, others went backward and forward to the camp, they who were on duty at the gates of the camp reported to Cæsar that a greater dust than was usual was seen in that direction in which the legion had marched. Cæsar, suspecting that which was [really the case],—that some new enterprise was undertaken by the barbarians, ordered the two cohorts which were on duty, to march into that quarter with him, and two other cohorts to relieve them on duty; the rest to be armed and follow him immediately. When he had advanced some little way from the camp, he saw that his men were overpowered by the enemy and scarcely able to stand their ground, and that, the legion being crowded together, weapons were being cast on them from all sides. For as all the corn was reaped in every part with the exception of one, the enemy, suspecting that our men would repair to that, had concealed themselves in the woods during the night. Then attacking them suddenly, scattered as they were, and when they had laid aside their arms, and were engaged in reaping, they killed a small number, threw the rest into confusion, and surrounded them with their cavalry and chariots.

Their mode of fighting with their chariots is this: firstly, they drive about in all directions and throw their weapons and generally break the ranks of the enemy with the very dread of their horses and the noise of their wheels; and when they have worked themselves in between the troops of horse, leap from their chariots and engage on foot. The charioteers in the meantime withdraw some little distance from the battle, and so place themselves with the chariots that, if their masters are overpowered by the number of the enemy, they may have a ready retreat to their own troops. Thus they display in battle the speed of horse, [together with] the firmness of infantry; and by daily practice and exercise attain to such expertness that they are accustomed, even on a declining and steep place, to check their horses at full speed, and manage and turn them in an instant and run along the pole, and stand on the yoke, and thence betake themselves with the greatest celerity to their chariots again.

Under these circumstances, our men being dismayed by the novelty of this mode of battle, Cæsar most seasonably brought assistance; for upon his arrival the enemy paused, and our men recovered from their fear; upon which thinking the time unfavorable for provoking the enemy and coming to an action, he kept himself in his own quarter, and, a short time having intervened, drew back the legions into the camp. While these things are going on, and all our men engaged, the rest of the Britons, who were in the fields, departed. Storms then set in for several successive days, which both confined our men to the camp and hindered the enemy from attacking us. In the meantime the barbarians dispatched messengers to all parts, and reported to their people the small number of our soldiers, and how good an opportunity was given for obtaining spoil and for liberating themselves forever, if they should only drive the Romans from their camp. Having by these means speedily got together a large force of infantry and of cavalry, they came up to the camp.

Although Cæsar anticipated that the same thing which had happened on former occasions would then occur—that, if the enemy were routed, they would escape from danger by their speed; still, having got about thirty horse, which Commius the Atrebatian, of whom mention has been made, had brought over with him [from Gaul], he drew up the legions in order of battle before the camp. When the action commenced, the enemy were unable to sustain the attack of our men long, and turned their backs; our men pursued them as far as their speed and strength permitted, and slew a great number of them; then, having destroyed and burned everything far and wide, they retreated to their camp.

The same day, ambassadors sent by the enemy came to Cæsar to negotiate a peace. Cæsar doubled the number of hostages which he had before demanded; and ordered that they should be brought over to the continent, because, since the time of the equinox was near, he did not consider that, with his ships out of repair, the voyage ought to be deferred till winter. Having met with favorable weather, he set sail a little after midnight, and all his fleet arrived safe at the continent, except two of the ships of burden which could not make the same port which the other ships did, and were carried a little lower down.

When our soldiers, about 300 in number, had been drawn out of these two ships, and were marching to the camp, the Morini, whom Cæsar, when setting forth for Britain, had left in a state of peace, excited by the hope of spoil, at first surrounded them with a small number of men, and ordered them to lay down their arms, if they did not wish to be slain; afterward however, when they, forming a circle, stood on their defense, a shout was raised and about 6000 of the enemy soon assembled; which being reported, Cæsar sent all the cavalry in the camp as a relief to his men. In the meantime our soldiers sustained the attack of the enemy, and fought most valiantly for more than four hours, and, receiving but few wounds themselves, slew several of them. But after our cavalry came in sight, the enemy, throwing away their arms, turned their backs, and a great number of them were killed.

The day following Cæsar sent Labienus, his lieutenant, with those legions which he had brought back from Britain, against the Morini, who had revolted; who, as they had no place to which they might retreat, on account of the drying up of their marshes (which they had availed themselves of as a place of refuge the preceding year), almost all fell into the power of Labienus. In the meantime Cæsar's lieutenants, Q. Titurius and L. Cotta, who had led the legions into the territories of the Menapii, having laid waste all their lands, cut down their corn and burned their houses, returned to Caesar because the Menapii had all concealed themselves in their thickest woods. Caesar fixed the winter quarters of all the legions among the Belgæ. Thither only two British states sent hostages; the rest omitted to do so. For these successes, a thanksgiving of twenty days was decreed by the senate upon receiving Caesar's letter.

THE WARRIOR ANGLO-SAXONS

CHARLES OMAN

In their weapons and their manner of fighting, the bands of Angles, Jutes, and Saxons who overran Britain were more nearly similar to the Franks than to the German tribes who wandered south. In blood and language, however, they were more akin to the Lombards than to the Franks; but two or three hundred years spent by the Danube had changed the Lombard warriors and their military customs, till they had grown very unlike their old neighbours on the Elbe from whom they had parted in the third or fourth century. The Angles and Saxons, even more than the Franks, were in the sixth century a nation of foot-soldiery, rarely provided with any defensive armour save a light shield. They had been in comparatively slight contact with the empire, though they had made occasional piratical descents on the east coast of Britain even before the year 300, and though one "ala Saxonum" appears among the barbarian auxiliaries of the *Notitia*

The arms and appearance of the war-bands which followed Hengist or Cerdic across the North Sea can best be gathered from the evidence of the countless Anglo-Saxon graves which have been excavated of late years. We must trust the Fairford or Ossengal cemeteries rather than the literary evidence of Bede or the *Beowulf,* which are excellent for the seventh and eighth centuries, but cannot be relied upon for the fifth and sixth. Arms and armour had been profoundly modified in the interval.

It is clear that none save kings and great chiefs among the first English war-bands wore defensive armour, which is never found in early graves. The warriors went out to war in their tunics, with undefended head and breast, and bearing the broad shield of linden tree alone. This was a round convex target like that of the Franks, bound with iron at the rim, and furnished with a large projecting iron boss. Often it seems to have been strengthened by a covering of stout leather.

Of the offensive arms of the old English the spear was the most prominent: they were in this respect still in the stage which Tacitus had described four centuries back. The most usual form of the weapon had a lozenge-shaped head, ranging from ten up to eighteen or even twenty inches in length. Barbed, leaf-shaped, and triangular spear-heads are occasionally found, but all of them are far less common than the lozenge-headed type. The shaft was usually ash, fastened to the head by rivets: it seems to have averaged about six feet in length. The sword appears to have been a less universally employed weapon than the spear; the usual form of it was broad, double-edged, and acutely pointed. It had very short cross-pieces, which only projected slightly beyond the blade, and a very small pommel. In length it varied from two and a half to three feet. As an alternative for the sword the old English often used in early times the broad two-edged dagger eighteen inches long, resembling the scramasax of the Franks, which they called *seax,* and associated with the Saxon name. The axe, the typical weapon of the Frank, was rare in England, but the few specimens that have been found are generally of the Frankish type, *i.e.* they are light missile weapons with a curved blade, more of the type of the tomahawk than of the heavy two-handed Danish axe of a later day.

The organisation of the English conquerors of Britain differed from that of the other Teutonic invaders of the empire in several ways. They were not a single race following its hereditary king like the Ostrogoths, nor were they, like the Franks, a mass of small, closely-related tribes welded together and dominated by the autocratic will of the chief who had united them. They were not of such heterogeneous race as the so-called Visigothic conquerors of Spain, nor, on the other hand, so homogeneous as the Lombards of Italy. The Ostrogoths and Lombards were nations on the march; the Franks and Visigoths were at least the subjects of one king. But the old English were war-bands of many kindred tribes, who in their first raids may have obeyed a single pirate-king like Hengist or Aella, but who dropped apart on settlement into many small states, as did the Danes four centuries after. The first kings of the Heptarchy were not the old heads of entire races, but mere *heretogas,* leaders in time of war, who took the regal name after having subdued a district, and lotted it out among their followers. No continental Teutonic State started under such beginnings: the nearest parallel that we can point out is the time when the Lombards, after the death of King Cleph, abode for ten years without a king, and pushed their fortunes under thirty independent dukes. But this lasted but a few years in Italy: in Britain it was more than four hundred years before the Danish peril led to a union of the Heptarchic States.

The old English kingdoms were founded after desperate struggles with the Romano-Britons, who did not submit and stave off slaughter like their equals in Gaul or Spain, but fought valiantly against the scattered attacks of the invaders. If a mighty host commanded by one great king like Alaric or Theodoric had thrown itself upon Britain in the fifth century, the provincials would certainly have submitted: they would have saved their lives, and probably have imposed their tongue and their religion upon the conquerors within a few generations. But instead of one Theodoric there came to Britain a swarm of war-bands, who only united when a specially strong chief was forthcoming, and soon fell apart. The Romano-Britons were often able to hold the invaders back for a space, sometimes to beat them off entirely. Even after the Saxons had gained a firm footing on the eastern coast, they were unable to advance far inland for two generations. Hence it came to pass that in its early stages the conquest was not a matter of submission under terms, such as always happened on the Continent, but a gradual pressure of the Romano-Britons towards the West and NorthIn the first stage of the conquest, therefore, the English kingdoms were almost wholly Teutonic, and the survival of the Celtic element small; yet it is certain that some men of the old race still remained on the soil as *laets* and many more as slaves. The realm of Kent or Sussex or Essex would be composed of a *heretoga* who had become permanent and adopted the title of king, of his personal oath-bound followers or gesiths, and of other freemen, some of noble blood *(eorls),* some of simple blood *(ceorls).* Below them were the non-Teutonic element—a few laets and many more slaves. The kingdom of Kent as it appears in the laws of King Aethelbert (**a.d.** 600) still preserves the character of the days of the first conquest. Having attained its full limits in a few years, and being cut off from further expansion into Celtic Britain, its condition has become stereotyped. In such a state the army consisted of the whole free population, and was a homogeneous Teutonic body, very unlike a contemporary Visigothic or Frankish host. The simple freemen (ceorls) have a very important position in the State: they possess slaves of their own the fine for violating their domicile is half that paid for violating an "eorl's tun"in the same way to put one of them in bonds is a high crime and misdemeanour Laets of various standing exist, but evidently the free Teuton is the backbone of the community. The king's dependants are but slightly mentioned, nor does the word *gesith* occur in the code, though it is found in the additions made to the Kentish law by Wihtraed ninety years later.

But the later and larger English kingdoms were of a somewhat different cast. The picture of Wessex which we get in Ini's Code, a production of about the year 700, gives us a less simple and a less Teutonic realm than that of Aethelbert. Even before the coming of Augustine and the introduction of Christianity, the English had begun to admit the Romano-Britons to terms. After a victorious campaign the cities were still sacked and burned, but the Celtic country-folk were no longer reduced to slavery or at the best to laethood, but were granted an independent, though an inferior, status as freemen. The laws of lni speak of Welsh subjects of the king owning a half-hide or even a whole hide of land They even serve in his retinue: the horse-wealh who rides on his errands is specially mentioned and King Cynewulf had a Welshman among his gesiths we are reminded at once of the Frankish king and his Gallo-Roman *antrustions* on the other side of ,the Channel But something more is to be noted in the Wessex of 700. Society seems to be growing more feudal, and the nobility of service is already asserting itself over the old eorl-blood. We find riot merely slaves and Welshmen, but English ceorls under a *hlaford* or lord, to whom they owe suit and service. If they try to shirk their duty to him, heavy fines are imposed on them. We are tempted to infer that a large proportion of ceorls were now either the vassals of lords or the tribute-paying tenants on royal demesne land The king has *geneats* or landholding tenants, who are so rich that they are *twelve-hynde* and own estates even so large as sixty hides But the most important thing to notice is that the king's *comitatus* seems to have superseded the old eorl-kin as the aristocracy of the land. The "gesithcund man owning land "is the most important person of whom the code takes cognisance, after king and ealdorman.

Probably the greater part of the old noble families had already commended themselves to the sovereign, and entered the ranks of his sworn companions. The actual name of the thegn only once appears instead of that of gesith, but the thegnhood itself is evidently in existence. There still exist, however, certain members of the *comitatus* who have not yet become proprietors of the soil. The "gesithcund men not owning land"—inferior members of the war-band who got but bed and board and weed and war-horse from the king—are valued at double a ceorl's price.

Military service is required from ceorl as well as gesith. When the call to arms is heard, the landed gesith who neglects it is to forfeit his estate and pay *fyrdwite* to the extent of a hundred and twenty shillings. The landless gesith pays eighty for such disobedience, the "ceorlish man "thirty shillings.

One clause in the code is very important as giving the first indication of the fact that armour is growing common. A man weighed down by a great fine, it says, may pay part of it by surrendering his byrnie [mail-shirt] and sword at a valuation. Comparing this with the almost contemporary law of the Ripuarian Franks, we note that Ini says nothing about the helm and the *bainbergce*, whose price is settled under similar circumstances by the continental code Apparently, therefore, the byrnie was much more common than the helm in A.D. 700.

From whence did the old English learn the use of their mail-shirt? No doubt it was already known to them ere they left Saxony and Jutland, though few but kings can have possessed it at that early time. Conceivably armour may have been got from the Britons. If we can be sure that the Gododin poems are fair reproductions of early originals, and were not wholly rewritten, with new surroundings, five hundred years later, we must hold that the use of armour no less than that of the war-horse survived for some time in Britain as a legacy from the Romans. A poem that claims a sixth-century origin speaks of the "loricated legions "of the half-mythical Arthur: another praises at length the battle-steeds of Geraint, "whose hoofs were red with the blood of those who fell in the thick of the melee. "Helm and corslet are mentioned almost as regularly as shield and spear There is no antecedent improbability in believing that such legacies from their old masters lingered on among the Celts of Britain, as they certainly did among the Celts of Gaul. Perhaps the Cymry taught the use of mail to the Englishmen, as the Gallo-Roman taught it to the Frank. If so, the use of these remnants of the old civilisation must have been mainly confined to Eastern Britain. The wilder tribes of Wales, as we find them in the later centuries, were neither wearers of armour nor combatants on horseback. The loss of the plain-land of Loegria, and the gradual decay of all culture among the mountains of the West, may account for the disappearance of the war-horse, and even for that of the mail.

But, on the whole, it is more probable the use of mail came to England from the Franks rather than from the Celts. The invaders seemed to have borrowed nothing save a few dozen words of daily speech from the tribes whom they drove westward.

It is noticeable, too, that mail begins to grow common in England almost at the same moment when we saw it coming into ordinary use on the other side of the Channel.

The Saxon helm, however, was certainly not borrowed from the Franks. Though the crested helm of late-Roman type, such as Merovingian warriors wore, is not unknown in English illustrated MSS., yet the national headpiece was the boar-helm mentioned so frequently in the *Beowulf*. A single specimen of it has been preserved—that dug up at Benty Grange in Derbyshire by Mr. Bateman. This headpiece was composed of an iron framework filled up with plates of horn secured by silver rivets. On its summit was an iron boar with bronze eyes.Another form of helm was destitute of the boar ornament, and consisted merely of a framework of bronze overlaid with leather and topped by a circular knob and ring. Such was the specimen dug up on Leckhampton Hill above Cheltenham in 1844. It is probable that the composite headpiece of iron blended with horn or leather is the early form of the Saxon helm, but that by the seventh or eighth century the whole structure was solid metal. This at least we should gather from the *Beowulf,* where "the white helm with its decoration of silver forged by the metal-smith, surrounded by costly chains,the "defence wrought with the image of the boar, furnished with cheek guards, decked with gold, bright and hardened in the fire"must surely refer to polished metal, not to the less showy and less efficient helmet of composite material. Unfortunately, in Christian times burial in full armour ceased, so that the later helms are only preserved to us in literary descriptions or in illuminated manuscripts. Many seem to have been plain conical headpieces, quite unlike the classical shapes; others, again, resemble the crested Frankish helm of which we have already spoken.

Both head armour and body armour appear so perpetually in the *Beowulf* that we should be tempted to believe that they must have been universal in eighth-century England. But in fact the writer of the epic is using the poet's licence in making his heroes so rich and splendid. Just as Homer paints Achilles wearing arms of impossible beauty and artistic decoration, so the author of the

Beowulf lavishes on his warriors a wealth that the real monarchs of the eighth century were far from owning.

Helm and byrnie were still confined to princes and ealdormen and great thegns.

Unmolested for several centuries in their new island home, and waging war only on each other or on the constantly receding Celt, the English retained the old Teutonic war customs long after their continental neighbours had begun to modify them. They never learned, like the Franks, to fight on horseback; though their chiefs rode as far as the battlefield, they dismounted for the battle. Even in the eleventh century they still were so unaccustomed to act as cavalry that they failed as lamentably when they essayed it as did Swiatoslafs Russians before Dorostolon. One isolated passage in the *Beowulf* speaks of a king's war-horse "which never failed in the front when the slain were falling." But we have no other indication of the use of the charger in the actual battle; perhaps the poet may have been taking the same licence as Homer when he makes Greek kings fight from the chariot, or perchance he is under some continental influence. It is at any rate certain that—in spite of some pictures in English MS. copied from foreign originals, the horse was normally used for locomotion, but not for the charge.

Nor had the old English learned much of the art of fortification: they allowed even the mighty Roman walls of London and Chester to moulder away. At best they stockaded strong positions. The Anglo-Saxon Chronicle tells us that Bamborough, the Bernician capital, was first strengthened with a hedge, and later by a regular wall; but the evidence is late, and Bede tells us that when in 651 Penda the Mercian beset it, he strove to burn his way in, by heaping combustibles against the defences—a fact which seems to suggest that they were still wooden. The plan, we read, must have succeeded but for the miraculous wind raised by the prayers of St. Aidan, which turned back the flames into the besiegers' faces. If an actual stone wall was built across the narrow isthmus of the rock of Bamborough, it was a very unusually solid piece of work for old English engineers to take in hand.

Hence it came that the wars of the English in the sixth, seventh, and eighth centuries were so spasmodic and inconsequent. Edwin or Penda or Offa took the field at the head of a comparatively small force of well-armed *gesiths,* backed by the rude and half-armed levies of the countryside. The strength of their kingdoms could be mustered for a single battle or a short campaign; but even if victory was won, there was no means of holding down the conquered foe.

The king of the vanquished tribe might for the nonce own himself his conqueror's man and contract to pay him tribute, but there was nothing to prevent him from rebelling the moment that he felt strong enough. To make the conquest permanent, one of two things was needed—colonisation of the district that had been subdued, or the establishment of garrisons in fortified places within it. But the English were never wont to colonise the lands of their own kinsmen, though they would settle readily enough on Welsh soil. Fortifications they were not wont to build, and garrisons could not be found when there was no permanent military force. No great warrior king arose to modify the primitive warlike customs of the English till the days of Alfred and Edward the Elder. Hence all the battles and conquests of a Penda or an Offa were of little avail: when the conqueror died, his empire died with him, and each subject State resumed its autonomy.

The Anglo-Saxon battle was a simple thing enough. There is no mention of sleight or cunning in tactics: the armies faced each other on some convenient hillside, ranged in the shield-wall, *i.e.* in close line, but not so closely packed that spears could not be lightly hurled or swords swung. The king would take the centre, with his banner flying above his head, and his well-armed gesiths around him. On each side the levies of the shires would stand. After hurling their spears at each other (the bow was little used in war), the hosts would close and "hack and hew at each other over the war-linden," *i.e.* over the lines of shields, till one side or the other gave way. When victory was achieved, the conqueror thought rather of plundering the richest valleys in his adversary's realm than of seizing the strategical points in it. Systematic conquest never came within the scope of the invader's thoughts: at the best he would make the vanquished his tributaries.

THE BATTLE OF CRESSY

JEAN FROISSART

HOW THE KING OF ENGLAND CAME OVER THE SEA AGAIN,
AND RODE WITH HIS ARMY IN THREE BATTALIONS THROUGH NORMANDY.

The king of England had heard how certain of his men were sore constrained in the castle of Aiguillon, where the Duke of Normandy and the lords of France had laid their siege. Then the king caused a great navy of ships to be ready in the haven of Southampton, and caused all manner of men of war to draw thither about the feast of St. John the Baptist in the year of our Lord God MCCCXLV.

Then the king rode to Southampton, and there tarried for wind: then he entered into his ships, and the Prince of Wales with him, and the Lord Godfrey Harcourt; and all other lords, earls, barons, and knights with all their companies.

Now I shall name you certain of the lords that went over with King Edward in that journey. First, Edward his eldest son, Prince of Wales, who was then of the age of sixteen years or thereabout; the Earls of Hereford, Northampton, Arundel, Cornwall, Warwick, Huntingdon, Suffolk, and Oxford. And of barons, the Lord Mortimer, who was afterwards Earl of March; the Lords John, Louis, and Roger Beauchamp, and the Lord Reginald Cobham; of lords, the Lords Mowbray, Roos, Lucy, Felton, Bradeston, Multon, Leyburn, Mauley, Basset, Barlett, and Willoughby, with divers other lords; and of knights bachelors there was Sir John Chandos, Sir Fulk Fitzwarren, Sir Peter and Sir James Audley, Sir Roger Vertuall, Sir Bartholomew Burghersh and Sir Richard Pembridge, with divers others that I cannot name.

When the king arrived in the Hogue he issued out of his ships, and the first foot that he set on the ground he fell so rudely that the blood burst out of his nose: the knights that were about him took him up, and said, "Sir, for God's sake enter again into your ship, and come not a-land this day; for this is but an evil sign for us."

Then the king answered quickly and said, "Wherefore? this is a good token for me, for the land desireth to have me." Of the which answer all his men were right joyful.

So that day and night the king lodged on the sands, and in the meantime discharged the ships of their horses and other baggages. There the king made two marshals of his host: the one the Lord Godfrey Harcourt, and the other the Earl of Warwick; and the Earl of Arundel, Constable. And he ordained that the Earl of Huntingdon should guard the fleet of ships with a hundred men-of-arms and four hundred archers. And also he ordained three battalions, one to go on his right hand, closing to the seaside, and the other on his left hand, and the king himself in the midst, and every night to lodge all in one camp.

Thus they set forth as they were ordained, and they that went by the sea took all the ships that they found in their ways; and they went forth so long, what by sea and what by land, that they came to a good port and to a good town called Barfleur, the which was won instantly; for they within gave up for fear of death. Howbeit, for all that, the town was robbed, and much gold and silver there found, and rich jewels: there was found so much riches that the boys and servants of the host set no store by good furred gowns.

They made all the men of the town to issue out and to go into the ships, because they would not suffer them to remain behind them for fear of rebelling again.

After the town of Barfleur was thus taken and robbed, without burning, then they spread abroad in the country, and did what they listed: for there was none to resist them. At last they came to a great and a rich town called

Cherbourg: the town they won, and robbed it, and burnt part thereof, but into the castle they could not come, it was so strong and well furnished with men of war: then they passed forth and came to Montebourg, and took it, and robbed and burnt it clean.

In this manner they burnt many other towns in that country, and won so much riches that it was marvel to reckon it. It was hard to think the great riches that there was won, in clothes specially: cloth would there have been sold good cheap, if there had been any buyers.

Then the king went towards Caen, and took it; and the Englishmen were lords of the town three days, and won great riches, the which they sent by barques and barges to St. Sauveur, by the river of Estreham, a two leagues thence, where all their navy lay.

HOW SIR GODFREY HARCOURT FOUGHT WITH THEM
OF AMIENS BEFORE PARIS.

Thus the king of England ordered his business, being in the town of Caen, and sent into England his navy of ships charged with clothes, jewels, vessels of gold and silver and other riches; and of prisoners more than sixty knights and three hundred burgesses.

Then he departed from the town of Caen and rode in the same order as he did before, burning and wasting the country; and took the way to Evreux and so passed by it. Then they entered into the country of Evreux, and burnt and pillaged all except the good walled towns and castles, to which the king made no assault, because of sparing his people and his artillery.

Then the Englishmen passed by Rouen, and went to Gisors, where was a strong castle: they burnt the town, and then they burnt Vernon and all the country about Rouen and Pont de l'Arche, and came to Nantes and to Meulan and wasted all the country about; and passed by the strong castle of Roulleboise; and in every place along the river of Seine they found the bridges broken.

At last they came to Poissy, and found the bridge broken, but the arches and joists lay in the river. The king lay there a five days, and in the mean season the bridge was made good, to pass the host without peril.

The English marshals ran abroad almost as far as Paris, and burnt St. Germain-en-Laye, and Montjoye and St. Cloud, and Boulogne near Paris, and Bourg la Reine: and they of Paris were not well assured of their own safety, for Paris was not then walled.

Then King Philip of France removed to St. Denis, and before he went, caused all the pent-houses in Paris to be pulled down. And at St. Denis were already come the king of Bohemia, the Lord John of Hainault, the Duke of Lorraine, the Earl of Flanders, the Earl of Blois, and many other great lords and knights, ready to serve the French king.

When the people of Paris saw their king depart, they came to him and kneeled down and said, "Ah! Sir and noble king, what will ye do, that ye leave thus this noble city of Paris?"

The king said, "My good people, doubt ye not, the Englishmen will approach you no nearer than they be."

"Why so, Sir?" said they, "they be within these two leagues; and as soon as they know of your departing, they will come and assail us, and we be not able to defend ourselves against them: Sir, tarry here still and help to defend your good city of Paris."

"Speak no more," said the king, "for I will go to St. Denis, to my men of war: for I will encounter the Englishmen, and fight against them, whatsoever may come thereof."

The king of England was then at Poissy, and lodged in the nunnery there, and kept there the feast of Our Lady in August, and sat in his robes of scarlet furred with ermine; and after that feast he went forth in order as they were before.

The Lord Godfrey Harcourt rode out on the one side with five hundred men-of-arms and thirteen hundred archers; and by adventure he encountered a great number of burgesses of Amiens a-horseback, who were riding by the king's commandment to Paris. They were quickly assailed, and they defended themselves valiantly, for they were a great number and well armed: there were four knights of Amiens who were their captains.

This skirmish lasted long: at the first meeting many were overthrown on both parts, but finally the burgesses were taken and nigh all slain, and the Englishmen took all their carriages and harness. They were well stuffed with riches, for they were going to the French king well appointed because they had not seen him for a great season before. There were slain in the field a twelve hundred.

Then the king of England entered into the country of Beauvoisin, burning and wasting the plain country; and lodged at a fair abbey and a rich called St. Messien, near to Beauvais. There the king tarried a night, and in the morning departed; and when he was on his way he looked behind him and saw the abbey afire. He caused instantly twenty to be hanged of them that set the fire there: for he had commanded before on pain of death none to violate any church nor to burn any abbey.

Then they came to Airaines and there lodged; for there the king was minded to lie a day or two, to take advice how he might pass the river of Somme; for it was necessary for him to pass the river, as ye shall hear afterwards.

HOW THE FRENCH KING FOLLOWED THE KING OF
ENGLAND IN THE COUNTRY OF BEAUVAIS.

Now let us speak of King Philip, who was at St. Denis and his people about him, and they daily increased. Then on a day he departed, and rode so long that he came to Coppigny du Guise, a three leagues from Amiens, and there he tarried.

The king of England being at Airaines wist not where to pass the river of Somme, the which was large and deep, and all the bridges were broken and the passages well guarded. Then at the king's commandment his two marshals with a thousand men-of-arms and two thousand archers went along the river to find some passage, and passed by Lompre and came to the bridge of Remy, the which was well guarded with a great number of knights and squires and men of the country.

The Englishmen alighted afoot, and assailed the Frenchmen from the morning till it was noon; but the bridge was so well fortified and defended, that the Englishmen departed without winning anything.

Then they went to a great town called Fontaines, on the river of Somme, the which was clean robbed and burnt, for it was not walled. Then they went to another town called Long, in Ponthieu; they could not win the bridge, it was so well kept and defended. Then they departed and went to Pecquigny, and found the town, the bridge, and the castle so well fortified, that it was not a likely place to cross there.

The French king had so well defended the passages, to the intent that the king of England should not pass the river of Somme to fight with him at his advantage, or else he meant to famish him there.

When these two marshals had essayed in all places to find passage, and could find none, they returned again to the king, and showed how they could find no passage in no place. The same night the French king came to Amiens with more than a hundred thousand men.

The king of England was right pensive, and the next morning heard mass before the sunrising, and then dislodged: and every man followed the marshals' banners. And so they rode into the country of Vimieu, approaching to the good town of Abbeville; and found a town thereby, whereunto was come much people of the country, trusting to a little fort that was there; but the Englishmen anon won it, and all they that were within were slain, and many taken of the town and of the country. The king took his lodging in a great hospital that was there.

The same day the French king departed from Amiens and came to Airaines about noon; and the Englishmen had departed thence in the morning. The Frenchmen found there a great provision that the Englishmen had left behind them, because they departed in haste: there they found flesh ready on the spits, bread and pasties in the ovens, wine in tuns and barrels, and the tables ready laid. There the French king lodged, and tarried for his lords.

That night the king of England was lodged at Oisemont. At night when the two marshals were returned, who had that day overrun the country to the gates of Abbeville and to St. Valery, and made a great skirmish there, the king assembled together his council, and made to be brought before him certain prisoners of the country.

The king right courteously demanded of them if there were any among them that knew any passage below Abbeville, that he and his host might pass over the river of Somme: if he would show him thereof, he should be quit of his ransom, and twenty more of his company for his sake.

There was a varlet called Gobyn a Grace, who stepped forth and said to the king, "Sir, I promise you, on the jeopardy of my head, I shall bring you to such a place, where ye and all your host shall pass the river of Somme without peril. There be certain places in the passage that ye shall pass twelve men afront, two times between day and night; ye shall not go in the water to the knees; but when the time cometh, the river then waxeth so great that no man can pass: but when the tide is gone, the which is two times between day and night, then the river is so low that it may be passed without danger, both a-horse-back and afoot. The passage is hard in the bottom with white stones so that all your baggage-train may go safely: therefore the passage is called Blanchetaque. If ye make ready to depart betimes ye may be there by the sunrising." i The king said, "If this be true that ye say, I quit thee thy ransom, and all thy company, and moreover shall give thee a hundred nobles in money." Then the king commanded every man to be ready, at the sound of the trumpet, to depart.

OF THE BATTLE OF BLANCHETAQUE, BETWEEN THE KING OF ENGLAND AND SIR GODEMAR DU FAY.

The king of England slept not much that night, for at midnight he arose and sounded his trumpet: then instantly they made ready carriages and all things. And at the breaking of the day they departed from the town of Oise-mont, and rode after the guiding of Gobyn a Grace, so that they came by the sunrising to Blanchetaque; but then the tide was up so that they might not pass. So the king tarried there till it was six o'clock; then the ebb came.

The French king had his scouts in the country, who brought him word of the demeanour of the Englishmen. Then he thought to shut in the king of England between

Abbeville and the river of Somme, and so to fight with him at his pleasure.

And when he was at Amiens he had ordained a great baron of Normandy, called Sir Godemar du Fay, to go and keep the passage of Blanchetaque, where the Englishmen must pass, or else in none other place. He had with him a thousand men-of-arms and six thousand afoot, with the Genoese. So they went by St. Ricquier in Ponthieu, and from thence to Crotoy, where the passage lay. And also he had with him a great number of men of the country, so that there were a twelve thousand men, one and other.

When the English host was come thither, Sir Godemar du Fay arranged all his company to defend the passage. The king of England stayed not for all that; but when the tide was gone, he commanded his marshals to enter into the water in the name of God and St. George. Then they that were hardy and courageous entered on both sides, and many a man was overthrown. There were some of the Frenchmen of Artois and Picardy that were as glad to tilt in the water as on the dry land. The Frenchmen defended so well the passage while the Englishmen were issuing out of the water that they had much to do: the Genoese did them much trouble with their crossbows.

On the other side the archers of England shot so wholly together that the Frenchmen were fain to give place to the Englishmen. There was a sore battle, and many a noble feat of arms done on both sides: finally the Englishmen passed over and assembled together in the field; the king and the prince passed, and all the lords; then the Frenchmen kept no order, but departed, he that might best.

When Sir Godemar saw that discomfiture, he fled and saved himself. Some fled to Abbeville and some to St Ricquiers; they that were there afoot could not flee, so that there were slain a great number of them: the chase endured more than a great league.

But when as yet all the Englishmen were not passed over the river, certain scouts of the king of Bohemia and of Sir John of Hainault came on them that were behind and took certain horses and carriages, and slew divers before they could take the passage.

The French king the same morning was departed from Airaines, trusting to have found the Englishmen between him and the river of Somme; but when he heard how that Sir Godemar du Fay and his company were discomfited, he tarried in the field, and demanded of his marshals what was best to do.

They said, "Sir, ye cannot pass the river but at the bridge of Abbeville, for the tide is come in at Blanche-taque." Then he returned, and lodged at Abbeville.

The king of England when he was past the river he thanked God; and so rode forth in like manner as he did before. Then he called Gobyn a Grace, and did quit him his ransom, and all his company; and gave him a hundred nobles in money and a good horse.

And so the king rode forth fair and easily, and his marshals rode to Crotoy on the seaside, and burnt the town, and found in the haven many ships and barques charged with wines of Ponthieu, pertaining to the merchants of Saintonge and la Rochelle: they brought the best thereof to the king's host.

Then one of the marshals rode to the gates of Abbeville and from thence to St. Ricquier, and afterwards to the town of Rue St. Esprit. This was on a Friday, and both battalions of the marshals returned to the king's host about noon; and so lodged all together near to Cressy in Ponthieu.

The king of England was well informed how the French king followed after him to fight: then he said to his company, "Let us take here some plot of ground, for we will go no further till we have seen our enemies. I have good cause here to abide them, for I am on the right heritage of the queen my mother, the which land was given to her at her marriage: I will challenge it of mine adversary Philip of Valois."

And because that he had not the eighth part in number of men as the French king had, therefore he commanded his marshals to choose a plot of ground somewhat for his advantage; and so they did, and thither the king and his host went.

Then he sent his scouts to Abbeville, to see if the French king drew that day into the field or not. They went forth and returned again, and said how they could see no appearance of his coming. Then every man took their lodging for that day, and to be ready in the morning at the sound of the trumpet, in the same place.

Thus on Friday the French king tarried still in Abbeville, waiting for his company; and sent his two marshals to ride out to see the dealing of the Englishmen; and at night they, returned, and said how the Englishmen were lodged in the fields.

That night the French king made a supper to all the chief lords that were there with him; and after supper the king desired them to be friends each to other. The king looked for the Earl of Savoy, who should come to him with a thousand spears; for he had received wages for a three-months of them, at Troyes in Champaigne.

OF THE ORDER OF THE ENGLISHMEN AT CRESSY, AND HOW THEY MADE THREE BATTALIONS AFOOT.

On the Friday, as I said before, the king of England lay in the fields; for the country was plentiful of wines and other victual, and if need had been they had provision following in carts and other carriages.

That night the king made a supper to all his chief lords of his host, and made them good cheer. And when they were all departed to take their rest, then the king entered into his oratory, and kneeled down before the altar, praying God devoutly that if he fought the next day, he might achieve the day's work to his honour.

Then about midnight he laid him down to rest; and in the morning he rose betimes, and heard mass, and the prince his son with him; and the most part of his company confessed and had absolution.

And after the mass said, he commanded every man to be armed and to draw to the field, to the same place before appointed. Then the king caused a park to be made, by the wood-side behind his host; and there they set all carts and carriages, and within the park were all their horses, for every man was afoot; and into this park there was but one entry.

Then he ordained the battalions. In the first was the young Prince of Wales; with him the Earls of Warwick and Stafford, the Lord Godfrey Harcourt, Sir Reginald Cobham, Sir Thomas Holland, the Lord Stafford, the Lord Mauley, the Lord Delawarr, Sir John Chandos, Sir Bartholomew Burghersh, Sir Robert Neville, the Lord Thomas Clifford, the Lord Bourchier, the Lord Latimer, and divers other knights and squires that I cannot name: they were an eight hundred men-of-arms and two thousand archers, and a thousand of others, with the Welshmen. Every lord drew to the field appointed, under his own banner and pennon.

In the second battalion was the Earl of Northampton, the Earl of Arundel, the Lord Roos, the Lord Lygo, the Lord Willoughby, the Lord Basset, the Lord St. Amand, Sir Louis Tufton, the Lord Multon, the Lord Lascelles, and divers others, about an eight hundred men-of-arms and twelve hundred archers.

The king had the third battalion; he had seven hundred men-of-arms, and two thousand archers.

Then the king leapt on a horse, with a white rod in his hand, one of his marshals on the one hand and the other on the other hand: he rode from rank to rank, desiring every man to take heed that day to his right and honour. He spake it so sweetly, and with so good countenance and merry cheer, that all such as were discomfited took courage in the saying and hearing of him.

And when he had thus visited all his battalions, it was then nine of the day: then he caused every man to eat and drink a little: and so they did at their leisure. And afterward they again set in order their battalions: then every man lay down on the earth, and by him his steel cap and bow, to be the more fresher when their enemies should come.

THE ORDER OF THE FRENCHMEN AT CRESSY, AND HOW THEY BEHELD THE DEMEANOUR OF THE ENGLISHMEN.

This Saturday the French king rose betimes, and heard mass in Abbeville in his lodging in the abbey of St. Peter: and he departed after the sunrising.

When he was out of the town two leagues, approaching toward his enemies, some of his lords said to him, "Sir, it were good that ye set in order your battalions, and let all your footmen pass somewhat on before, that they be not troubled with the horsemen."

Then the king sent four knights, the Lord Moyne of Bastleburg, the Lord of Noyers, the Lord of Beaujeu, and the Lord d'Aubigny, to ride to view the English host: and so they rode so near that they might well see part of their dealing. The Englishmen saw them well, and knew well how they were come thither to view them; they let them alone, and made no countenance toward them, and let them return as they came.

And when the French king saw these four knights return again, he tarried till they came to him, and said, "Sirs, what tidings?"

These four knights each of them looked on other, for there was none would speak before his companion: finally the king said to Moyne, who pertained to the king of Bohemia, and had done in his days so much that he was reputed for one of the valiantest knights of the world, "Sir, speak you."

Then he said, "Sir, I shall speak, since it pleaseth you, under the correction of my fellows. Sir, we have ridden and seen the behaving of your enemies; know ye for truth they are halted in three battalions, abiding for you. Sir, I will counsel you, as for my part, saving your displeasure, that you and all your company rest here and lodge for this night; for before they of your company that be behind be come hither, and before your battalions be set in good order, it will be very late, and your people be weary and out of array; and ye shall find your enemies fresh and ready to receive you. Early in the morning ye may order your battalions at more leisure, and advise concerning your enemies at more deliberation, and regard well what way ye will assail them; for, Sir, surely they will abide you."

Then the king commanded that it should be so done. Then his two marshals rode one before, another behind, saying to every banner," Tarry and abide here, in the name of God and St. Denis."

They that were foremost tarried, but they that were behind would not tarry, but rode forth, and said how they would in no wise abide till they were as far forward as the foremost. And when those before saw them come on behind, then they rode forward again, so that the king nor his marshals could not rule them.

So they rode without order or good array till they came in sight of their enemies. And as soon as the foremost saw them they recoiled aback without good array; whereof those behind had marvel, and were abashed, and thought that the foremost company had been fighting. Then they might have had leisure and room to have gone forward, if they had listed. Some went forward and some abode still: the common soldiers, of whom all the roads between Abbeville and Cressy were full, when they saw that they were near to their enemies, they took their swords and cried: "Down with them! let us slay them all!"

There was no man, though he were present at that day's work, that could imagine or show the truth of the evil order that was among the French party: and yet they were a marvellous great number. That which I write in this book I learned it specially of the Englishmen, who well beheld their dealing; and also certain knights of Sir John of Hainault's, who was always about King Philip, showed me all they knew.

OF THE PATTLE OF CRESSY, BETWEEN THE KING
OF ENGLAND AND THE FRENCH KING.

The Englishmen, who were in three battalions, lying on the ground to rest them, as soon as they saw the Frenchmen approach, they rose upon their feet fair and easily, without any haste, and arranged their battalions.

The first was the prince's battalion: the archers there stood in the manner of a harrow, and the men-of-arms at the rear of the battalion. The Earl of Northampton and the Earl of Arundel were on a wing in good order, ready to support the prince's battalion, if need were.

The lords and knights of France came not to the assembly together in good order, for some came before and some came after, in such haste and evil order that one of them did trouble another.

When the French king saw the Englishmen, his blood changed, and he said to his marshals, "Make the Genoese go on before and begin the battle in the name of God and St. Denis."

There were of the Genoese crossbows about a fifteen thousand, but they were so weary of going a six leagues afoot that day armed with their crossbows, that they said to their constables, "We be not well ordered to fight this day, for we be not in the condition to do any great deed of arms; we have more need of rest." These words came to the Earl of Alencon, who said, "A man is well off to be burdened with such a sort of rascals, to be faint and fail now at most need!"

Also at the same time there fell a great rain, and an eclipse of the sun, with a terrible thunder, and before the rain there came flying over both armies a great number of crows, for fear of the tempest coming. Then anon the air began to wax clear, and the sun to shine fair and bright; the which was right in the Frenchmen's eyes and on the Englishmen's backs.

When the Genoese were assembled together and began to approach, they made a great leap and cry, to abash the Englishmen; but they stood still and stirred not for all that. Then the Genoese again the second time made another leap and a fell cry, and stepped forward a little; and the Englishmen removed not one foot; thirdly again they leapt and cried and went forward till they came within shot; then they shot fiercely with their crossbows,

Then the English archers stepped forth one pace, and let fly their arrows so wholly together and so thick that it seemed snow. When the Genoese felt the arrows piercing through heads, arms and breasts, many of them cast down their crossbows, and did cut their strings, and returned discomfited.

When the French king saw them fly away, he said, "Slay these rascals, for they will let and trouble us without reason." Then ye should have seen the men-of-arms dash in among them, and kill a great number of them.

And ever still the Englishmen shot where they saw thickest press; the sharp arrows ran into the men-of-arms and into their horses, and many fell, horse and man, among the Genoese; and when they were down they could not rise again, the press was so thick that one overthrew another.

And also among the Englishmen there were certain rascal's that went afoot, with great knives; and they went in among the men-of-arms, and slew and murdered many as they lay on the ground, both earls, barons, knights and squires; whereof the king of England was afterwards displeased, for he had rather they had been taken prisoners.

The valiant king of Bohemia, called Charles of Luxembourg, son to the noble Emperor Henry of Luxembourg, for all that he was nigh blind, when he understood the order of the battle, he said to them about him, "Where is the Lord Charles my son?"

His men said, "Sir, we cannot tell; we think he be fighting."

Then he said," Sirs, ye are my men, my companions and friends in this day's work. I require you, bring me so far forward that I may strike one stroke with my sword."

They said they would do his commandment; and to the intent that they should not lose him in the press, they tied all their reins of their bridles each to other, and set the king in front to accomplish his desire, and so they went on their enemies.

The Lord Charles of Bohemia his son, who wrote himself king of Bohemia, and bore the arms, came in good order to the battle; but when he saw that the matter went awry on their side, he departed, I cannot tell you which way.

The king his father was so far forward that he struck a stroke with his sword, yea, and more than four, and fought valiantly. And so did his company; and they adventured themselves so forward that they were there all slain; and the next day they were found in the place, about the king, and all their horses tied each to other.

The Earl of Alencon came to the battle in right good order, and fought with the Englishmen; and the Earl of Flanders also on his part: these two lords with their companies coasted past the English archers, and came to the prince's battalion, and there fought valiantly for a long time. The French king would fain have come thither, when he saw their banners, but there was a great hedge of archers before him.

The same day the French king had given a great black courser to Sir John of Hainault, and Sir John of Hainault made the Lord John de Fusselles to ride on him, and to bear his banner. The same horse took the bridle in the teeth, and brought him through all the outposts of the Englishmen; and as he would have returned again he fell into a great ditch, and was sore hurt, and had there been dead if his page had not been there, who followed him through all the battalions, and saw where his master lay in the ditch; he had none other hindrance but for his horse, for the Englishmen would not issue out of their battalions for taking of any prisoner. Then the page alighted and raised up his master; then went not back again the same way' that they came; there was too many in his way.

This battle, fought between La Broyes and Cressy this Saturday, was right cruel and fell, and many a feat of arms was done that came not to my knowledge. In the night divers knights and squires lost their masters, and sometimes came on the Englishmen, who received them in such wise that they were ever nigh slain, for there was none taken to mercy nor to ransom, for so the Englishmen were determined.

In the morning, the day of the battle, certain Frenchmen and Germans perforce broke through the archers of the prince's battalion, and came and fought with the men-of-arms hand to hand. Then the second battalion of the Englishmen came to succour the prince's battalion, the which was time, for they had then much ado; and those with the prince sent a messenger to the king, who was on a little windmill hill.

Then the knight said to the king, "Sir, the Earl of Warwick and the Earl of Stafford, Sir Reginald Cobham, and other such as be about the prince your son, are fiercely fought withal, and are sore handled: wherefore they desire you that you and your battalion will come and aid them, for if the Frenchmen increase, as they doubt they will, your son and they shall have much ado."

Then the king said, "Is my son dead, or hurt, or on the earth felled?"

"No, Sir," said the knight, "but he is hardly matched; wherefore he hath need of your aid."

"Well," said the king, "return to him and to them that sent you hither, and say to them that they send no more to me, whatever adventure befalleth, as long as my son is alive; and also say to them, that they suffer him this day to win his spurs, for if God be pleased, I will that this day's work be his, and the honour thereof, and to them that be about him."

Then the knight returned again to them, and showed the king's words, the which greatly encouraged them; and they repented in that they had sent to the king as they did.

Sir Godfrey Harcourt would gladly that the Earl of Harcourt his brother might have been saved; for he heard say, by them that saw his banner, how that he was there in the field on the French side; but Sir Godfrey could not come to him betimes, for he was slain before he could come at him, and so was also the Earl of Aumale his nephew.

In another place the Earl of Alengon and the Earl of Flanders fought valiantly, every lord under his own banner; but finally they could not. resist against the puissance of the Englishmen, and so there they were also slain, and divers other knights and squires.

Also the Earl Louis of Blois, nephew to the French king, and the Duke of Lorraine, fought under their own banners; but at last they were closed in among a company of Englishmen and Welshmen, and there were slain for all their prowess. Also there was slain the Earl of Auxerre, the Earl of St. Pol, and many others.

In the evening the French king had left about him no more than a three-score persons, one and other, whereof one was Sir John of Hainault, who had remounted the king once, for his horse was slain with an arrow.

Then he said to the king, "Sir, depart hence, for it is time; lose not yourself wilfully; if ye have loss at this time, ye shall recover it again another season." And so he took the king's horse by the bridle, and led him away, in a manner perforce.

Then the king rode till he came to the castle of La Broyes: the gate was closed because it was by that time dark.

Then the king called the captain, who came to the walls, and said, "Who is it that calleth there this time of night?"

Then the king said, "Open your gate quickly, for this is the fortune of France."

The captain knew then that it was, the king, and opened the gate and let down the bridge. Then the king entered; and he had with him but five barons, Sir John of Hainault, Sir Charles of Montmorency, the Lord of Beaujeu, the Lord d'Aubigny, and the Lord of Mountfort. The king would not tarry there, but drank, and departed thence about midnight, and so rode by such guides as knew the country till he came in the morning to Amiens, and there he rested.

This Saturday the Englishmen never departed from their battalions for chasing of any man, but still kept their field, and ever defended themselves against all such as came to assail them. This battle ended about evensong time.

HOW THE NEXT DAY AFTER THE BATTLE THE ENGLISHMEN DISCOMFITED DIVERS FRENCHMEN.

On this Saturday when the night was come, and the Englishmen heard no more noise of the Frenchmen, then they reputed themselves to have the victory, and the Frenchmen to be discomfited, slain, and fled away.

Then they made great fires, and lighted up torches and candles because it was very dark. Then the king came down from the little hill where he stood, and all that day till then his helm came never upon his head.

Then he went, with all his battalion, to his son the prince, and embraced him in his arms and kissed him, and said, "Fair son, God give you good perseverance; ye are my good son, thus ye have acquitted you nobly, ye are worthy to guard a realm." The prince inclined himself to the earth, honouring the king his father.

This night they thanked God for their good adventure, and made no boast thereof; for the king would have that no man should be proud or make boast, but every man humbly to thank God.

On the Sunday in the morning there was such a mist, that a man might not see the breadth of an acre of land from him. Then there departed from the host, by the commandment of the king and marshals, five hundred spears and two thousand archers, to see if they might see any Frenchmen gathered again together in any place.

The same morning, out of Abbeville and St. Ricquier in Ponthieu, the common soldiers of Rouen and of Beauvais issued out of their towns, not knowing of the discomfiture the day before; they met with the Englishmen weening they had been Frenchmen. And when the Englishmen saw them they set on them freshly, and there was a sore battle; but at last the Frenchmen fled, and kept no order. There were slain in the roads and in hedges and bushes more than seven thousand; and if the day had been clear, there had never a one scaped.

Afterwards another company of Frenchmen were met by the Englishmen—the Archbishop of Rouen and the Great Prior of France, who also knew nothing of the discomfiture the day before, for they heard that the French king should have fought the same Sunday, and they were going to join him. When they met with the Englishmen there was a great battle, for they were a great number; but they could not endure against the Englishmen, they were nigh all slain; few scaped; the two lords were slain.

This morning the Englishmen met with divers Frenchmen that had lost their way on the Saturday, and had lain all night in the fields, and wist not where the king was, nor the captains. They were all slain, as many as were met with; and it was showed me, that of the common soldiers and men afoot of the cities and good towns of France, there were slain four times as many as were slain on the Saturday in the great battle.

HOW THE NEXT DAY AFTER THE BATTLE OF CRESSY, THEY THAT WERE DEAD WERE NUMBERED BY THE ENGLISHMEN.

The same Sunday, as the king of England came from mass, such as had been sent forth returned, and showed the king what they had seen and done, and said, "Sir, we think surely there is now no more appearance of any of our enemies."

Then the king sent to search how many were slain, and what they were. Sir Reginald Cobham and Sir Richard Stafford, with the heralds, went to search the field and country; they visited all them that were slain, and rode all day in the fields, and returned again to the host as the king was going to supper. They made just report of that they had seen, and said how there were eleven great princes dead, fourscore lords with banners, twelve hundred knights, and more than thirty thousand others.

The Englishmen still kept their field all the night, and on the Monday in the morning the king prepared to depart. The king caused the dead bodies of the great lords to be taken up and conveyed to the abbey of Montenay, and there buried in holy ground; and made a cry in the country to grant truce for three days, to the intent that they of the country might search the field of Cressy to bury the dead bodies.

Then the king went forth, and came before the town of Montreuil by the sea, and his marshals ran toward Hesdin. The next day they rode toward Boulogne, and came to the town of Wissant; there the king and the prince lodged, and tarried there a day to refresh his men; and on the Wednesday the king came before the strong town of Calais.

HENRY V BEFORE
THE BATTLE

WILLIAM SHAKESPEARE

*T*he English camp.
Enter GLOUCESTER, BEDFORD, EXETER, ERPINGHAM, with all his
host: SALISBURY and WESTMORELAND

GLOUCESTER
Where is the king? BEDFORD
The king himself is rode to view their battle. WESTMORELAND
Of fighting men they have full three score thousand. EXETER
There's five to one; besides, they all are fresh. SALISBURY
God's arm strike with us! 'tis a fearful odds.

God be wi' you, princes all; I'll to my charge:
If we no more meet till we meet in heaven,
Then, joyfully, my noble Lord of Bedford,
My dear Lord Gloucester, and my good Lord Exeter,
And my kind kinsman, warriors all, adieu!
BEDFORD
Farewell, good Salisbury; and good luck go with thee! EXETER
Farewell, kind lord; fight valiantly to-day: And yet I do thee wrong to mind thee of it, For thou art framed of the firm truth of valour.

Exit SALISBURY

BEDFORD
He is full of valour as of kindness; Princely in both.
Enter the KING
WESTMORELAND
O that we now had here
But one ten thousand of those men in England
That do no work to-day!
KING HENRY V
What's he that wishes so?
My cousin Westmoreland? No, my fair cousin:
If we are mark'd to die, we are enow
To do our country loss; and if to live,
The fewer men, the greater share of honour.
God's will! I pray thee, wish not one man more.
By Jove, I am not covetous for gold,
Nor care I who doth feed upon my cost;
It yearns me not if men my garments wear;
Such outward things dwell not in my desires:
But if it be a sin to covet honour,
I am the most offending soul alive.
No, faith, my coz, wish not a man from England:
God's peace! I would not lose so great an honour
As one man more, methinks, would share from me
For the best hope I have. 0, do not wish one more!
Rather proclaim it, Westmoreland, through my host,

That he which hath no stomach to this fight,
Let him depart; his passport shall be made
And crowns for convoy put into his purse:
We would not die in that man's company
That fears his fellowship to die with us.
This day is called the feast of Crispian:
He that outlives this day, and comes safe home,
Will stand a tip-toe when the day is named,
And rouse him at the name of Crispian.
He that shall live this day, and see old age,
Will yearly on the vigil feast his neighbours,
And say To-morrow is Saint Crispian:'
Then will he strip his sleeve and show his scars.
And say These wounds I had on Crispin's day.'
Old men forget: yet all shall be forgot,
But he'll remember with advantages
What feats he did that day: then shall our names.
Familiar in his mouth as household words
Harry the king, Bedford and Exeter,
Warwick and Talbot, Salisbury and Gloucester,
Be in their flowing cups freshly remember'd.
This story shall the good man teach his son;
And Crispin Crispian shall ne'er go by,
From this day to the ending of the world,
But we in it shall be remember'd;
We few, we happy few, we band of brothers;
For he to-day that sheds his blood with me
Shall be my brother; be he ne'er so vile,
This day shall gentle his condition:
And gentlemen in England now a-bed
Shall think themselves accursed they were not here,
And hold their manhoods cheap whiles any speaks
That fought with us upon Saint Crispin's day.

Re-enter SALISBURY

SALISBURY

My sovereign lord, bestow yourself with speed: The French are bravely in their battles set, And will with all expedience charge on us. KING HENRY V

All things are ready, if our minds be so. WESTMORELAND

Perish the man whose mind is backward now! KING HENRY V

Thou dost not wish more help from England, coz? WESTMORELAND

God's will! my liege, would you and I alone, Without more help, could fight this royal battle! KING HENRY V

Why, now thou hast unwish'd five thousand men; Which likes me better than to wish us one. You know your places: God be with you all!

Enter MONTJOY

MONTJOY

Once more I come to know of thee, King Harry,

If for thy ransom thou wilt now compound,

Before thy most assured overthrow:

For certainly thou art so near the gulf,

Thou needs must be englutted. Besides, in mercy,

The constable desires thee thou wilt mind

Thy followers of repentance; that their souls

May make a peaceful and a sweet retire

From off these fields, where, wretches, their poor bodies

Must lie and fester.

KING HENRY V

Who hath sent thee now?

MONTJOY

The Constable of France. KING HENRY V

I pray thee, bear my former answer back:

Bid them achieve me and then sell my bones.

Good God! why should they mock poor fellows thus?

The man that once did sell the lion's skin

While the beast lived, was killed with hunting him.

A many of our bodies shall no doubt

Find native graves; upon the which, I trust,

Shall witness live in brass of this day's work:

And those that leave their valiant bones in France,

Dying like men, though buried in your dunghills,

They shall be famed; for there the sun shall greet them,

And draw their honours reeking up to heaven;

Leaving their earthly parts to choke your clime,
The smell whereof shall breed a plague in France.
Mark then abounding valour in our English,
That being dead, like to the bullet's grazing,
Break out into a second course of mischief,
Killing in relapse of mortality.
Let me speak proudly: tell the constable

We are but warriors for the working-day; Our gayness and our gilt are all besmirch'd With rainy marching in the painful field; There's not a piece of feather in our host—Good argument, I hope, we will not fly—And time hath worn us into slovenry: But, by the mass, our hearts are in the trim; And my poor soldiers tell me, yet ere night They'll be in fresher robes, or they will pluck The gay new coats o'er the French soldiers' heads And turn them out of service. If they do this,—As, if God please, they shall,—my ransom then Will soon be levied. Herald, save thou thy labour; Come thou no more for ransom, gentle herald: They shall have none, I swear, but these my joints; Which if they have as I will leave 'em them, Shall yield them little, tell the constable. MONTJOY

I shall, King Harry. And so fare thee well: Thou never shalt hear herald any more.

Exit

KING HENRY V
I fear thou'lt once more come again for ransom.

Enter YORK

YORK
My lord, most humbly on my knee I beg The leading of the van. KING HENRY V

Take it, brave York. Now, soldiers, march away: And how thou pleasest, God, dispose the day!

Exeunt

THE BATTLE
OF HASTINGS, 1066 A.D.

CHARLES OMAN

As the last great example of an endeavour to use the old infantry tactics of the Teutonic races against the now fully-developed cavalry of feudalism, we have to describe the battle of Hastings, a field which has been fought over by modern critics almost as fiercely as by the armies of Harold Godwineson and William the Bastard.

About the political and military antecedents of the engagement we have no need to speak at length. Suffice it to say that the final defeat of the old English thegnhood was immediately preceded by its most striking victory. In the summer of 1066 the newly-chosen King Harold was forced to watch two enemies at once. The Norman Duke William had openly protested against the election that had taken place in January, and was known to be gathering a great army and fleet at St. Valery. Harold knew him well, and judged him a most formidable enemy; he had called out the available naval strength of his realm, and a strong squadron was waiting all through June, July, and August, ranging between the Isle of Wight and Dover, ready to dispute the passage of the Channel. At the same time the earls and sheriffs had been warned to have the land forces of the realm ready for mobilisation, and the king with his housecarles lay by the coast in Sussex waiting for news. Duke William came not, for many a week; his host took long to gather, and when his ships were ready, August turned out a month of persistent storm and northerly winds, unsuited for the sailing of a great armament.

Meanwhile there was danger from the North also. King Harold's rebel brother, Earl Tostig, had been hovering off the coast with a small squadron, and had made a descent on the Humber in May, only to be driven away by the Northumbrian Earl Edwin. But Tostig had leagued himself with Harald Hardrada, the warlike and greedy King of Norway, and a Norse invasion was a possibility, though it seemed a less immediate danger than the Norman threat to the South Coast. September had arrived before either of the perils materialised.

By a most unlucky chance the crisis came just when the English fleet had run out of provisions, after keeping the sea for three months. On September 8, Harold ordered it round to London to revictual, and to refit, for it had suffered in the hard weather. It was to resume its cruising as soon as possible. Seven days later came the news that a Norwegian fleet of three hundred sail had appeared off the Yorkshire coast, and had ravaged Cleveland and taken Scarborough. Harold was compelled to commit the guard of the Channel to the winds, which had hitherto served him well, and to fly north with his housecarles to face Hardrada's invasion. On his way he got the disastrous message that the two Earls Edwin of Northumbria and-Morkar of Mercia had been beaten in a pitched battle at Fulford, in front of York (September 20), and that the city was treating for surrender. Pressing on with all possible speed, the English king arrived at York in time to prevent this disaster, and the same afternoon he brought the Norsemen to action at Stamford Bridge on the Derwent, seven miles from the city. Here he inflicted on them an absolutely crushing defeat— Hardrada was slain, so was the rebel Earl Tostig, and the invading host was so nearly exterminated that the survivors fled on only twenty-four ships, though they had brought three hundred into the Humber.

The details of the fight are absolutely lost—we cannot unfortunately accept one word of the spirited narrative of the *Heimskringla,* for all the statements in it that can be tested are obviously incorrect. Harold *may* have offered his rebel brother pardon and an earldom, and have promised his Norse ally no more than the famous "seven feet of English earth, since his stature is greater than that of other men." The Vikings *may* have fought for long hours in their shieldring, and have failed at evening only, when their king had been slain by a chance arrow. But we cannot trust a saga which says that Morkar was King Harold Godwineson's brother, and fell at Fulford; that Earl Waltheof (then a child) took part in the fight, and that the English army was mostly composed of cavalry and archers. The whole tale of the *Heimskringla* reads like a version of the battle of Hastings transported to Stamford Bridge by some incredible error. The one detail about it recorded in the Anglo-Saxon Chronicle, namely, that the fighting included a desperate defence of a bridge against the pursuing English, does *not* appear in the Norse narrative at all. We can only be sure that both sides must have fought on foot in the old fashion of Viking and Englishman, "hewing at each other across the war-linden" till the beaten army was well-nigh annihilated.

Meanwhile, on September 28—two days after Stamford Bridge—William of Normandy had landed at Pevensey, unhindered either by the English fleet, which was refitting at London, or by the king's army, which had gone north to repel the Norwegians. The invaders began to waste the land, and met with little resistance, since the king and his chosen warriors were absent. Only at Romney, as we are told, did the landsfolk stand to their arms and beat off the raiders.

Meanwhile, the news of William's landing was rapidly brought to Harold at York, and reached him—as we are told—at the very moment when he was celebrating by a banquet his victory over the Northmen. The king received the message on October 1 or October 2: he immediately hurried southward to London with all the speed that he could make. The victorious army of Stamford Bridge was with him, and the North Country levies of Edwin and Morkar were directed to follow as fast as they were able. Harold reached London on the 7th or 8th of October, and stayed there a few days to gather in the fyrd of the neighbouring shires of the South Midlands. On the 11th he marched forth from the city to face Duke William, though his army was still incomplete. The slack or treacherous earls of the North had not yet brought up their contingents, and the men of the western shires had not been granted time enough to reach the mustering place. But Harold's heart had been stirred by the reports of the cruel ravaging of Kent and Sussex by the Normans, and he was resolved to put his cause to the arbitrament of battle as quickly as possible, though the delay of a few days would per haps have doubled his army. A rapid march of two days brought him to the outskirts of the Andredsweald, within touch of the district on which William had for the last fortnight been exercising his cruelty.

Harold took up his position at the point where the road from London to Hastings first leaves the woods, and comes forth into the open land of the coast. The chosen ground was the lonely hill above the marshy bottom of Senlac, on which the ruins of Battle Abbey stand, but then marked to the chronicler only by "the hoar apple tree" on its ridge, just as Ashdown had been marked two centuries before by its aged thorn.

The Senlac position consists of a hill some 1100 yards long and 150 yards broad, joined to the main bulk of the Wealden Hills by a sort of narrow isthmus with steep descents on either side. The road from London to Hastings crosses the isthmus, bisects the hill at its highest point, and then sinks down into the valley, to climb again the opposite ridge of Telham Hill. The latter is considerably the higher of the two, reaching 441 feet above the sea-level, while Harold's hill is but 275 at its summit. The English hill has a fairly gentle slope towards the south, the side which looked towards the enemy, but on the north the fall on either side of the isthmus is so steep as to be almost precipitous. The summit of the position, where it is crosse by the road, is the highest point. Here it was that King Harold fixed his two banners, the Dragon of Wessex, and his own standard of the Fighting Mar The position was very probably one that had served before for some army of an older century, for we learn from the best authorities that there la about it, especially on its rear, ancient banks and ditches, in some place-scarped to a precipitous slope. Perhaps it may have been the camp of some part of Alfred's army in 893-894, when, posted in the east end of the Andredsweald, between the Danish fleet which had come ashore at Lymne and the other host which had camped at Middleton, he endeavoured fror his central position to restrain their ravages in Kent and Sussex. No place indeed could have been more suited for a force observing newly-landed foes. It covers the only road from London which then pierced the Andredsweald, and was so close to its edge that the defenders could seek shelter in the impenetrable woods if they wished to avoid a battle.

The hill above the Senlac bottom, therefore, being the obvious positio to take, for an army whose tactics compelled it to stand upon the defensive, Harold determined to offer battle there. We need not believe the authorities who tell us that the King had been thinking of delivering a night attack upon the Normans, if he should chance to find them scattered abroad on their plundering, or keeping an inefficient lookout. It was most unlikely that he should dream of groping in the dark through eight miles of rolling ground, to assault a camp whose position and arrangements must have been unknown. His army had marched hard from London, had apparently only reached Senlac at nightfall, and must have been tired out. Moreover, Harold knew William's capacities as a general, and could not have thought it likely that he would be caught unprepared. It must have seemed to him a much more possible event that the Norman might refuse to attack the strong Senlac position, and offer battle in the open and nearer the sea. It was probably in anticipation of some such chance that Harold ordered his fleet, which had run back into the mouth of the Thames in very poor order some four weeks back, to refit itself and sail round the North Foreland, to threaten the Norman vessels now drawn ashore under the cover of a wooden castle at Hastings. He can scarcely have thought it likely that William would retire over seas on the news of his approach, so the bringing up of the fleet must have been intended either to cut off the Norman retreat in. the event of a great English victory on land, or to so molest the invader's stranded vessels that he would be forced to return to the shore in order to defend them.

The English position is said by one narrator of the battle to have been entrenched. According to Wace, the latest and the most diffuse of our authorities, Harold ordered his men to rear a fence of plaited woodwork from the timber of the forest which lay close at their backs. But the earlier chroniclers, without exception, speak only of the shield-wall of the English, of their dense mass covering the crest of the hill, and of relics of ancient fortifications, the *antiquus agger* and *frequentia fossarum,* and *fovea magna* mentioned above. There is nothing inconceivable in the idea of Harold's having used the old Danish device of palisading a camp, save that he had arrived only on the preceding night, and that his army was weary. In the morning hours of October 14 little could have been done, though between daybreak and the arrival of the Norman host there were certainly three long hours. But it is difficult to suppose that if any serious entrenching had been carried out, the earlier Norman narrators of the fight would have refrained from mentioning it, since the more formidable the obstacles opposed to him, the more notable and creditable would have been the triumph of their duke. And the Bayeux Tapestry, which (despite all destructive criticism) remains a primary authority for the battle, appears to show no traces of any breastwork covering the English front. Probably Wace, writing from oral tradition ninety years after the battle, had heard something of the *frequentia fossarum* mentioned by William of Poictiers, and the *agger* described by Orderic, and translated them into new entrenchments, which he described as works of the best military type of his day.

From end to end of the crest of the hill the English host was ranged in one great solid mass. Probably its line extended from the high road, which crosses the summit nearer to its eastern than to its western side, for some 200 yards to the left, as far as the head of the small steep combe (with a rivulet at its bottom) which lies 200 yards to the due east of the modern parish church; while on the other, or western, side of the high road, the battle-front was much longer, running from the road as far as the upper banks of the other ravine (with a forked brook flowing out of it from two sources) which forms the western flank of the hill. From the road to this ravine there must have been a front of 800 or 850 yards. Harold's two standards were, as we know, set up on the spot which was afterwards marked by the high altar of Battle Abbey. His standing-place must there fore have been in the left-centre rather than in the absolute middle-front of the line. But the spot was dictated by the lie of the ground—here is the actual highest point of the hill, 275 feet above sea-level, while the greater part of the position is along the 250 feet contour. It was the obvious place for the planting of standards to be visible all around, and a commander standing by them could look down from a slight vantage-ground on the whole front of his host.;

In this array, the English centre being slightly curved forward, its flank slightly curved back, the army looked to the Normans more like a circular mass than a deployed line. Although the Northumbrian and West-country levies were still missing, the army must have numbered many thousands, for the fyrd of south and central England was present in full force, and stirred to great wrath by the ravages of the Normans. It is impossible to guess at the strength of the host: the figures of the chroniclers, which sometimes swell up to hundreds of thousands, are wholly useless. As the position was about 1100 yards long, and the space required by a single warrior swinging his axe or hurling his javelin was some three feet, the front rank must have been at least some eleven hundred or twelve hundred strong. The hilltop was completely covered by the English, whose spear-shafts appeared to the Normans like a wood, so that they cannot have been a mere thin line: if they were some eight or ten deep, the total must have reached ten or eleven thousand men. Of these the smaller part must have been com posed of the fully-armed warriors, the king's housecarles, the thegn-hood, and the wealthier and better-equipped freemen, the class owning some five, hides of land. The rudely-armed levies of the fyrd must have constituted the great bulk of the army: they bore, as the Bayeux Tapestry shows, the most miscellaneous arms—swords, javelins, clubs, axes, a few bows, and probably even rude instruments of husbandry turned to warlike uses. Their only defensive armour was the round or kite-shaped shield: body and head were clothed only in the tunic and cap of everyday wear.

In their battle array we know that the well-armed housecarles—perhaps two thousand chosen and veteran troops—were grouped in the centre around the king and the royal standards. The fyrd, divided no doubt according to its shires, was ranged on either flank. Presumably the thegns and other fully-armed men formed its front ranks, while the peasantry stood behind and backed them up, though at first only able to hurl their weapons at the advancing foe over the heads of their more fully-equipped fellows.

We must now turn to the Normans. Duke William had undertaken his expedition not as the mere feudal head of the barons of Normandy, but rather as the managing director of a great joint-stock company for the conquest of England, in which not only his own subjects, but hundreds of adventurers, poor and rich, from all parts of western Europe had taken shares. At the assembly of Lillebonne the Norman baronage had refused in their corporate capacity to undertake the vindication of their duke's claims on England. But all, or nearly all, of them had consented to serve under him as volunteers, bringing not merely their usual feudal contingent, but as many men as they could get together. In return they were to receive the spoils of the island kingdom if the enterprise went well. On similar terms William had accepted offers of help from all quarters: knights and sergeants flocked in, ready, "some for land and some for pence," to back his claim. It seems that, though the native Normans were the core of the invading army, yet the strangers considerably outnumbered them on the muster-rolls. Great nobles like Eustace Count of Boulogne, the Breton Count Alan Fergant, and Haimar of Thouars were ready to risk their lives and resources on the chance of an ample profit. French, Bretons, Flemings, Angevins, knights from the more distant regions of Aquitaine and Loth-aringia, even—if Guy of Amiens speaks truly—stray fighting men from among the Norman conquerors of Naples and Sicily, joined the host.

Many months had been spent in the building of a fleet at the mouth of the Dive. Its numbers, exaggerated to absurd figures by many chroniclers, may possibly have reached the six hundred and ninety-six vessels given to the duke by the most moderate estimate. What was the total of the warriors which it carried is as uncertain as its own numbers. If any analogies may be drawn from contemporary hosts, the cavalry must have formed a very heavy proportion of the whole. In continental armies the foot-soldiery were so despised that an experienced general devoted all his attention to increasing the numbers of his horse.

If we guess that there may have been three thousand or even four thousand mounted men, and eight thousand or nine thousand foot-soldiers, we are going as far as probability carries us, and must confess that our estimate is wholly arbitrary. The most modest figure given by the chroniclers is sixty thousand fighting men; but, considering their utter inability to realise the meaning of high numbers, we are dealing liberally with them if we allow a fifth of that estimate.

After landing at Pevensey on September 28, William had moved to Hastings and built a wooden castle there for the protection of his fleet. It was then in his power to have moved on London unopposed, for Harold was only starting on his march from York. But the duke had resolved to fight near his base, and spent the fortnight which was at his disposal in the systematic harrying of Kent and Sussex. When his scouts told him that Harold was at hand, and had pitched his camp by Senlac hill, he saw that his purpose was attained; he would be able to fight at his own chosen moment, and at only a few miles' distance from his ships. At daybreak on the morning of October 14, William bade his host get in array, and marched over the eight miles of rolling ground which separate Hastings and Senlac. When they reached the summit of the hill at Telham, the English position came in sight, on the opposite hill, not much more than a mile away.

On seeing the hour of conflict at hand, the duke and his knights drew on their mail-shirts, which, to avoid fatigue, they had not yet assumed, and the host was arrayed in battle order. The form which William had chosen was that of three parallel corps, each containing infantry and cavalry. The centre was composed of the native contingents of Normandy; the left mainly of Bretons and men from Maine and Anjou; the right, of French and Flemings. But there seem to have been some Normans in the flanking divisions also. The duke himself, as was natural, took command in the centre, the wings fell respectively to the Breton Count Alan Fergant and to Eustace of Boulogne: with the latter was associated Roger of Montgomery, a great Norman baron.

In each division there were three lines: the first was composed of bowmen mixed with arbalesters: the second was composed of foot-soldiery armed not with missile weapons but with pike and sword. Most of them seem to have worn mail-shirts, unlike the infantry of the English fyrd. In the rear was the really important section of the army, the mailed knights. We may presume that William intended to harass and thin the English masses with his archery, to attack them seriously with his heavy infantry, who might perhaps succeed in getting to close quarters and engaging the enemy hand to hand; but evidently the crushing blow was to be given by the great force of horsemen who formed the third line of each division.

The Normans deployed on the slopes of Telham, and then began their advance over the rough valley which separated them from the English position.

When they came within range, the archery opened upon the English, and not without effect; at first there must have been little reply to the showers of arrows, since Harold had but very few bowmen in his ranks. The shield-wall, moreover, can have given but a partial protection, though it no doubt served its purpose to some extent. When, however, the Normans advanced farther up the slope, they were received with a furious discharge of missiles of every kind, javelins, lances, taper-axes, and even—if William of Poictiers is to be trusted—rude weapons more appropriate to the neolithic age than to the eleventh century, great stones bound to wooden handles and launched in the same manner that was used for the casting-axe. The archers were apparently swept back by the storm of missiles, but the heavy armed foot pushed up to the front of the English line and got to hand-to-hand fighting with Harold's men. They could, however, make not the least impression on the defenders, and were perhaps already recoiling when William ordered up his cavalry. The horsemen rode up the slope already strewn with corpses, and dashed into the fight. Foremost among them was a minstrel named Taillefer, who galloped forward cheering on his comrades, and playing like a *jougleur* with his sword, which he kept casting into the air and then catching again. He burst right through the shield-wall and into the English line, where he was slain after cutting down several opponents. Behind him came the whole Norman knighthood, chanting their battle-song, and pressing their horses up the slope as hard as they could ride. The foot-soldiery dropped back—through the intervals between the three divisions, as we may suppose—and the duke's cavalry dashed against the long front of the shield-wall, whose front rank men they may have swept down by their mere impetus. Into the English mass, however, they could not break: there was a fearful crash, and a wild interchange of blows, but the line did not yield at any point. Nay, more, the assailants were ere long abashed by the fierce resistance that they met; the English axes cut through shield and mail, lopping off limbs and felling even horses to the ground. Never had the continental horsemen met such infantry before. After a space the Bretons and Angevins of the left wing felt their hearts fail, and recoiled down the hill in wild disorder, many men unhorsed and overthrown in the marshy bottom at the foot of the slope. All along the line the onset wavered, and the greater part of the host gave back, though the centre and right did not fly in wild disorder like the Bretons. A rumour ran along the front that the duke had fallen, and William had to bare his head and to ride down the ranks, crying that he lived, and would yet win the day, before he could check the retreat of his warriors. His brother Odo aided him to rally the waverers, and the greater part of the host was soon restored to order.

As it chanced, the rout of the Norman left wing was destined to bring nothing but profit to William. A great mass of the shire-levies on the English right, when they saw the Bretons flying, came pouring after them down the hill. They had forgotten that their sole chance of victory lay in keeping their front firm till the whole strength of the assailant should be exhausted. It was mad to pursue when two-thirds of the hostile army was intact, and its spirit still unbroken. Seeing the tumultuous crowd rushing after the flying, Bretons, William wheeled his centre and threw it upon the flank of the pursuers. Caught in disorder, with their ranks broken and scattered, the rash peasantry were ridden down in a few moments. Their light shields, swords, and javelins availed them nothing against the rush of the Norman horse, and the whole horde, to the number of several thousands, were cut to pieces. The great bulk of the English host, however, had not followed the routed Bretons, and the duke saw that his day's work was but begun. Forming up his disordered squadrons, he ordered a second general attack on the line. Then followed an encounter even more fierce than the first. It would appear that the fortune of the Normans was somewhat better in this than in the earlier struggle: one or two temporary breaches were made in the English mass, probably in the places where it had been weakened by the rash onset of the shire-levies an hour before. Gyrth and Leofwine, Harold's two brothers, fell in the forefront of the fight, the former by William's own hand, if we may trust one good contemporary authority. Yet, on the whole, the duke had got little profit by his assault: the English had suffered severe loss, but their long line of shields and axes still crowned the slope, and their cries of "Out! out!" and "Holy Cross!" still rang forth in undaunted tones.

A sudden inspiration then came to William, suggested by the disaster which had befallen the English right in the first conflict. He determined to try the expedient of a feigned flight, a stratagem not unknown to Bretons and Normans of earlier ages. By his orders a considerable portion of the assailants suddenly wheeled about and retired in seeming disorder. The English thought, with more excuse on this occasion than on the last, that the enemy was indeed routed, and for the second time a great body of them broke the line and rushed after the retreating squadrons. When they were well on their way down the slope, William repeated his former procedure. The intact portion of his host fell upon the flanks of the pursuers, while those who had simulated flight faced about and attacked them in front. The result was again a foregone conclusion: the disordered men of the fyrd were hewn to pieces, and few or none of them escaped back to their comrades on the height. But the slaughter in this period of the fight did not fall wholly on the English; a part of the Norman troops who had carried out the false flight suffered some loss by falling into a deep ditch,—perhaps the remains of old entrenchments, perhaps the "rhine" which drained the Senlac bottom,—and were there smothered or trodden down by the comrades who rode over them. But the loss at this point must have been insignificant compared with that of the English.

Harold's host was now much thinned and somewhat shaken, but, in spite of the disasters which had befallen them, they drew together their thinned ranks, and continued the fight. The struggle was still destined to endure for many hours, for the most daring onsets of the Norman chivalry could not yet burst into the serried mass around the standards. The bands which had been cut to pieces were mere shire-levies, and the well-armed housecarles had refused to break their ranks, and still formed a solid core for the remainder of the host.

The fourth act of the battle consisted of a series of vigorous assaults by the duke's horsemen, alternating with volleys of arrows poured in during the intervals between the charges. The Saxon mass was subjected to exactly the same trial which befell the British squares in the battle of Waterloo—incessant charges by a gallant cavalry mixed with a destructive hail of missiles. Nothing could be more maddening than such an ordeal to the infantry-soldier, rooted to the spot by the necessities of his formation. The situation was frightful: the ranks were filled with wounded men unable to retire to the rear through the dense mass of their comrades, unable even to sink to the ground for the hideous press. The enemy was now attacking on both flanks: shields and mail had been riven: the supply of missile spears had given out: the English could but stand passive, waiting for the night or for the utter exhaustion of the enemy. The cavalry onsets must have been almost a relief compared with the desperate waiting betwee the acts, while the arrow-shower kept beating in on the thinning host. We have indications that, in spite of the disasters of the noon, some of the English made yet a third sally to beat off the archery. Individuals worked to frenzy by the weary standing still, seem to have occasionally burst out of the line to swing axe or sword freely in the open and meet a certain death. But the mass held firm—"a strange manner of battle," says William of Poictiers, "where the one side works by constant motion and ceaseless charges, while the other can but endure passively as it stands fixed to the sod. The Norman arrow and sword worked on: in the English ranks the only movement was the dropping of the dead: the living stood motionless." Desperate as was their plight, the English still held out till evening; though William himself led charge after charge against them, and had three horses killed beneath him, they could not be scattered while their king still survived and their standards still stood upright. It was finally the arrow rather than the sword that settled the day: the duke is said to have bade his archers shoot not point-blank, but with a high trajectory, so that the shafts fell all over the English host, and not merely on its front ranks. One of these chance shafts struck Harold in the eye and gave him a mortal wound. The arrow-shower, combined with the news of the king's fall, at last broke up the English host: after a hundred ineffective charges, a band of Norman knights burst into the midst of the mass, hewed Harold to pieces as he lay wounded at the foot of his banners, and cut down both the Dragon of Wessex and the Fighting Man.

The remnant of the English were now at last constrained to give ground: the few thousands—it may rather have been the few hundreds—who still clung to the crest of the bloodstained hill turned their backs to the foe and sought shelter in the friendly forest in their rear. Some fled on foot through the trees, some seized the horses of the thegns and housecarles from the camp and rode off upon them. But even in retreat they took some vengeance on the conquerors. The Normans, following in disorder, swept down the steep slope at the back of the hill, scarped like a glacis and impassable for horsemen,—the back defence, as we have conjectured, of some ancient camp of other days. Many of the knights, in the confused evening light, plunged down this trap, lost their footing, and lay floundering, man and horse, in the ravine at the bottom. Turning back, the last of the English swept down on them and cut them to pieces before resuming their flight. The Normans thought for a moment that succours had arrived to join the English—and, indeed, Edwin and Morkar's Northern levies were long overdue. The duke himself had to rally them, and to silence the fainthearted counsels of Eustace of Boulogne, who bade him draw back when the victory was won. When the Normans came on more cautiously, following, no doubt, the line of the isthmus and not plunging down the slopes, the last of the English melted away into the forest and disappeared. The hard day's work was done.

The stationary tactics of the phalanx of axemen had failed decisively before William's combination of archers and cavalry, in spite of the fact that the ground had been favourable to the defensive. The exhibition of desperate courage on the part of the English had only served to increase the number of the slain. Of all the chiefs of the army, only Esegar the Staller and Leofric, Abbot of Bourne, are recorded to have escaped, and both of them were dangerously wounded. The king and his brothers, the stubborn housecarles, and the whole thegnhood of Southern England had perished on the field. The English loss was never calculated; practically it amounted to the entire army. Nor is it possible to guess that of the Normans: one chronicle gives twelve thousand,—the figure is absurd, and the authority is not a good or a trustworthy one for English history. But whatever was the relative slaughter on the two sides, the lesson of the battle was unmistakable. The best of infantry, armed only with weapons for close fight and destitute of cavalry support, were absolutely helpless before a capable general who knew how to combine the horseman and the archer. The knights, if unsupported by the bowmen, might have surged for ever against the impregnable shield-wall. The archers, unsupported by the knights, could easily have been driven off the field by a general charge. United by the skilful hand of William, they were invincible.

THE DEATH OF MONTEZUMA

WILLIAM PRESCOTT

The palace of Axayacatl, in which the Spaniards were quartered, was, as the reader may remember, a vast, irregular pile of stone buildings, having but one floor, except in the centre, where another story was added, consisting of a suite of apartments which rose like turrets on the main building of the edifice. A vast area stretched around, encompassed by a stone wall of no great height. This was supported by towers or bulwarks at certain intervals, which gave it some degree of strength, not, indeed, as compared with European fortifications, but sufficient to resist the rude battering enginery of the Indians. The parapet had been pierced here and there with embrasures for the artillery, which consisted of thirteen guns; and smaller apertures were made in other parts for the convenience of the arquebusiers. The Spanish forces found accommodations within the great building; but the numerous body of Tlascalan auxiliaries could have had no other shelter than what was afforded by barracks or sheds hastily constructed for the purpose in the spacious court-yard. Most of them, probably, bivouacked under the open sky, in a climate milder than that to which they were accustomed among the rude hills of their native land. Thus crowded into a small and compact compass, the whole army could be assembled at a moment's notice; and, as the Spanish commander was careful to enforce the strictest discipline and vigilance, it was scarcely possible that he could be taken by surprise. No sooner, therefore, did the trumpet call to arms, as the approach of the enemy was announced, than every soldier was at his post, the cavalry mounted, the artillery-men at their guns, and the archers and arquebusiers stationed so as to give the assailants a warm reception.

On they came, with the companies, or irregular masses, into which the multitude was divided, rushing forward each in its own dense column, with many a gay banner displayed, and many a bright gleam of light reflected from helmet, arrow, and spear-head, as they were tossed about in their disorderly array. As they drew near the inclosure, the Aztecs set up a hideous yell, or rather that shrill whistle used in fight by the nations of Anahuac, which rose far above the sound of shell and atabal, and their other rude instruments of warlike melody. They followed this by a tempest of missiles;—stones, darts, and arrows,—which fell thick as rain on the besieged, while volleys of the same kind descended from the crowded terraces in the neighborhood.

The Spaniards waited until the foremost column had arrived within the best distance for giving effect to their fire, when a general discharge of artillery and arquebuses swept the ranks of the assailants, and mowed them down by hundreds. The Mexicans were familiar with the report of these formidable engines, as they had been harmlessly discharged on some holiday festival; but never till now had they witnessed their murderous power. They stood aghast for a moment, as with bewildered looks they staggered under the fury of the fire; but, soon rallying, the bold barbarians uttered a piercing cry, and rushed forward over the prostrate bodies of their comrades. A second and third volley checked their career, and threw them into disorder, but still they pressed on, letting off clouds of arrows; while their comrades on the roofs of the houses took more deliberate aim at the combatants in the court-yard. The Mexicans were particularly expert in the use of the sling; and the stones which they hurled from their elevated positions on the heads of their enemies did even greater execution than the arrows. They glanced, indeed, from the mail-covered bodies of the cavaliers, and from those who were sheltered under the cotton panoply, or *escaupil*. But some of the soldiers, especially the veterans of Cortes, and many of their Indian allies, had but slight defences, and suffered greatly under this stony tempest.

The Aztecs, meanwhile, had advanced close under the walls of the intrenchment; their ranks broken and disordered, and their limbs mangled by the unintermitting fire of the Christians. But they still pressed on, under the very muzzle of the guns. They endeavored to scale the parapet, which, from its moderate height, was in itself a work of no great difficulty. But the moment they showed their heads above the rampart, they were shot down by the unerring marksmen within, or stretched on the ground by a blow of a Tlascalan *maquahuitl*. Nothing daunted, others soon appeared to take the place of the fallen, and strove, by raising themselves on the writhing bodies of their dying comrades, or by fixing their spears in the crevices of the wall, to surmount the barrier. But the attempt proved equally vain.

Defeated here, they tried to effect a breach in the parapet by battering it with heavy pieces of timber. The works were not constructed on those scientific principles by which one part is made to overlook and protect another. The besiegers, therefore, might operate at their pleasure, with but little molestation from the garrison within, whose guns could not be brought into a position to bear on them, and who could mount no part of their own works for their defence, without exposing their persons to the missiles of the whole besieging army. The parapet, however, proved too strong for the efforts of the assailants. In their despair they endeavored to set the Christian quarters on fire, shooting burning arrows into them, and climbing up so as to dart their firebrands through the embrasures. The principal edifice was of stone. But the temporary defences of the Indian allies, and other parts of the exterior works, were of wood. Several of these took fire, and the flames spread rapidly among the light, combustible materials. This was a disaster for which the besieged were wholly unprepared. They had little water, scarcely enough for their own consumption. They endeavored to extinguish the flames by heaping on earth. But in vain. Fortunately the great building was of materials which defied the destroying element. But the fire raged in some of the outworks, connected with the parapet, with a fury which could only be checked by throwing down a part of the wall itself, thus laying open a formidable breach. This, by the general's order, was speedily protected by a battery of heavy guns, and a file of arquebusiers, who kept up an incessant volley through the opening on the assailants.

The fight now raged with fury on both sides. The walls around the palace belched forth an unintermitting sheet of flames and smoke. The groans of the wounded and dying were lost in the fiercer battle-cries of the combatants, the roar of the artillery, the sharper rattle of the musketry, and the hissing sound of

Indian missiles. It was the conflict of the European with the American; of civilized man with the barbarian; of the science of the one with the rude weapons and warfare of the other. And as the ancient walls of Tenochtitlan shook under the thunders of the artillery,—it announced that the white man, the destroyer, had set his foot within her precincts.

Night at length came, and drew her friendly mantle over the contest. The Aztec seldom fought by night. It brought little repose, however, to the Spaniards, in hourly expectation of an assault; and they found abundant occupation in restoring the breaches in their defences, and in repairing their battered armor. The beleaguering host lay on their arms through the night, giving token of their presence, now and then, by sending a stone or shaft over the battlements, or by a solitary cry of defiance from some warrior more determined than the rest, till all other sounds were lost in the vague, indistinct murmurs which float upon the air in the neighborhood of a vast assembly.

The ferocity shown by the Mexicans seems to have been a thing for which Cortes was wholly unprepared. His past experience, his uninter- rupted career of victory with a much feebler force at his command, had led him to underrate the military efficiency, if not the valor, of the Indians. The apparent facility, with which the Mexicans had acquiesced in the out- rages on their sovereign and themselves, had led him to hold their courage, in particular, too lightly. He could not believe the present assault to be any thing more than a temporary ebullition of the populace, which would soon waste itself by its own fury. And he proposed, on the following day, to sally out and inflict such chastisement on his foes as should bring them to their senses, and show who was master in the capital.

With early dawn, the Spaniards were up and under arms; but not I before their enemies had given evidence of their hostility by the random 1 missiles, which, from time to time, were sent into the inclosure. As the grey light of morning advanced, it showed the besieging army far from being diminished in numbers, filling up the great square and neighboring avenues in more dense array than on the preceding evening. Instead of a confused, disorderly rabble, it had the appearance of something like a regular force, with its battalions distributed under their respective banners, the devices of which showed a contribution from the principal cities and districts in the Valley. High above the rest was conspicuous the ancient standard of Mexico, with its well known cognizance, an eagle pouncing on an ocelot, emblazoned on a rich mantle of feather-work. Here and there priests might be seen mingling in the ranks of the besiegers, and, with frantic gestures, animating them to avenge their insulted deities.

The greater part of the enemy had little clothing save the *maxtlatl*, or sash round the loins. They were variously armed, with long spears tipped with copper, or flint, or sometimes merely pointed and hardened in the fire. Some were provided with slings, and others with darts having two or three points, with long strings attached to them, by which, when discharged, they could be torn away again from the body of the wounded. This was a formidable weapon, much dreaded by the Spaniards. Those of a higher order wielded the terrible *maquahuitl*, with its sharp and brittle blades of obsidian. Amidst the motley bands of warriors, were seen many whose showy dress and air of authority intimated persons of high military consequence. Their breasts were protected by plates of metal, over which was thrown the gay surcoat of feather-work. They wore casques resembling, in their form, the head of some wild and ferocious animal, crested with bristly hair, or overshadowed by tall and graceful plumes of many a brilliant color. Some few were decorated with the red fillet bound round the hair, having tufts of cotton attached to it, which denoted by their number that of the victories they had won, and their own preeminent rank among the warriors of the nation. The motley assembly plainly showed that priest, warrior, and citizen had all united to swell the tumult.

Before the sun had shot his beams into the Castilian quarters, the enemy were in motion, evidently preparing to renew the assault of the preceding day. The Spanish commander determined to anticipate them by a vigorous sortie, for which he had already made the necessary dispositions. A general discharge of ordnance and musketry sent death far and wide into the enemy's ranks, and, before they had time to recover from their confusion, the gates were thrown open, and Cortes, sallying out at the head of his cavalry, supported by a large body of infantry and several thousand Tlascalans, rode at full gallop against them. Taken thus by surprise, it was scarcely possible to offer much resistance. Those who did were trampled down under the horses feet, cut to pieces with the broadswords, or pierced with the lances of the riders. The infantry followed up the blow, and the rout for the moment was general.

But the Aztecs fled only to take refuge behind a barricade, or strong work of timber and earth, which had been thrown across the great street through which they were pursued. Rallying on the other sid they made a gallant stand, and poured in turn a volley of their light weapons on the Spaniards, who, saluted with a storm of missiles at the same time, from the terraces of the houses, were checked in their career, and thrown into some disorder.

Cortes, thus impeded, ordered up a few pieces of heavy ordnance, which soon swept away the barricades, and cleared a passage for the army. But it had lost the momentum acquired in its rapid advance. The enemy had time to rally and to meet the Spaniards on more equal terms. They were attacked in flank, too, as they advanced, by fresh battalions, who swarmed in from the adjoining streets and lanes. The canals were alive with boats filled with warriors, who, with their formidable darts searched every crevice or weak place in the armor of proof, and made havoc on the unprotected foodies of the Tlascalans. By repeated and vigorous charges, the Spaniards succeeded in driving the Indians before them; though many, with a desperation which showed they loved vengeance better than life, sought to embarrass the movements of their horses by clinging to their legs, or, more Successfully strove to pull the riders from their saddles. And woe to the unfortunate cavalier who was thus dismounted to be despatched by the brutal *maquahuitl,* or to be dragged on board a canoe to the bloody altar of sacrifice!

But the greatest annoyance which the Spaniards endured was from the missiles from the *azoteas,* consisting often of large stones, hurled with a force that would tumble the stoutest rider from his saddle. Galled in the extreme by these discharges, against which even their shields afforded no adequate protection, Cortes ordered fire to be set to the buildings. This was no very difficult matter, since, although chiefly of stone, they were filled with mats, cane-work, and other combustible materials, which were soon in a blaze. But the buildings stood separated from one another by canals and drawbridges, so that the flames did not easily communicate to the neighboring edifices. Hence, the labor of the Spaniards was incalculably increased, and their progress in the work of destruction—fortunately for the city—was comparatively slow. They did not relax their efforts, however, till several hundred houses had been consumed, and the miseries of a conflagration, in which the wretched inmates perished equally with the defenders, were added to the other horrors of the scene.

The day was now far spent. The Spaniards had been everywhere victorious. But the enemy, though driven back on every point, still kept the field. When broken by the furious charges of the cavalry, he soon rallied behind the temporary defences, which, at different intervals, had been thrown across the streets, and, facing about, renewed the fight with undiminished courage, till the sweeping away of the barriers by the cannon of the assailants left a free passage for the movements of their horse. Thus the action was a succession of rallying and retreating, in which both parties suffered much, although the loss inflicted on the Indians was probably tenfold greater than that of the Spaniards. But the Aztecs could better afford the loss of a hundred lives than their antagonists that of one. And, while the Spaniards showed an array broken, and obviously thinned in numbers, the Mexican army, swelled by the tributary levies which flowed in upon it from the neighboring streets, exhibited, with all its losses, no sign of diminution. At length, sated with carnage, and exhausted by toil and hunger, the Spanish commander drew off his men, and sounded a retreat.

On his way back to his quarters, he beheld his friend, the secretary Duero, in a street adjoining, unhorsed, and hotly engaged with a body of Mexicans, against whom he was desperately defending himself with his poniard. Cortes, roused at the sight, shouted his war-cry, and, dashing into the midst of the enemy, scattered them like chaff by the fury of his onset; then, recovering his friend's horse, he enabled him to remount, and the two cavaliers, striking their spurs into their steeds, burst through their opponents and joined the main body of the army. Such displays of generous gallantry were not uncommon in these engagements, which called forth more feats of personal adventure than battles with antagonists better skilled in the science of war. The chivalrous bearing of the general was emulated in full measure by Sandoval, De Leon, Olid, Alvarado, Ordaz, and his other brave companions, who won such glory under the eye of their leader, as prepared the way for the independent commands which after-wards placed provinces and kingdoms at their disposal.

The undaunted Aztecs hung on the rear of their retreating foes, annoying them at every step by fresh flights of stones and arrows; and, when the Span-iards had reentered their fortress, the Indian host encamped around it, showing the same dogged resolution as on the preceding evening. Though true to their ancient habits of inaction during the night, they broke the stillness of the hour by insulting cries and menaces, which reached the ears of the besieged. "The gods have delivered you, at last, into our hands," they said; "Huitzilopotchli has long cried for his victims. The stone sacrifice *is* ready. The knives are sharpened. The wild beasts in the palace are roaring for their offal. And the cages," they added, taunting the Tlascalans with their leanness, "are waiting for the false sons of Anahuac, who are to be fattened for the festival!" These dismal menaces, which sounded fearfully in the ears of the besieged, who understood too well their import, were mingled with piteous lamentations for their sovereign, whom they called on the Spaniards to deliver up to them.

Cortes suffered much from a severe wound which he had received in the hand in the late action. But the anguish of his mind must have been still greater, as he brooded over the dark prospect before him. He had mistaken the character of the Mexicans. Their long and patient endurance had been a violence to their natural temper, which, as their whole history proves, was arrogant and ferocious beyond that of most of the races of Anahuac. The restraint, which, in deference to their monarch, more than to their own fears, they had so long put on their natures, being once removed, their passions burst forth with accumulated violence. The Spaniards had encountered in the Tlascalan an open enemy, who had no grievance to complain of, no wrong to redress. He fought under the vague apprehension only of some coming evil to his country. But the Aztec, hitherto the proud lord of the land, was goaded by insult and injury, till he reached that pitch of self-devotion, which made life cheap, in comparison with revenge. Armed thus with the energy of despair, the savage is almost a match for the civilized man; and a whole nation, moved to its depths by a common feel- ing, which swallows up all selfish considerations of personal interest and safety, becomes, whatever be its resources, like the earthquake and the tornado, the most formidable among the agencies of nature.

Considerations of this kind may have passed through the mind of Cortes, as he reflected on his own impotence to restrain the fury of the Mexicans, and resolved, in despite of his late supercilious treatment of Montezuma, to employ his authority to allay the tumult,—an authority so successfully exerted in behalf of Alvarado, at an earlier stage of the insurrection. He was the more confirmed in his purpose, on the following morning, when the assailants, redoubling their efforts, succeeded in scaling the works in one quarter, and effecting an entrance into the inclosure. It is true, they were met with so resolute a spirit, that not a man, of those who entered, was left alive. But, in the impetuosity of the assault, it seemed, for a few moments, as if the place was to be carried by storm.

Cortes now sent to the Aztec emperor to request his interposition with his subjects in behalf of the Spaniards. But Montezuma was not in the humor to comply. He had remained moodily in his quarters ever since the general's return. Disgusted with the treatment he had received, he had still further cause for mortification in finding himself the ally of those who were the open enemies of his nation. From his apartment he had beheld the tragical scenes in his capital, and seen another, the presumptive heir to his throne, taking the place which he should have occupied at the head of his warriors, and fighting the battles of his country. Distressed by his position, indignant at those who had placed him in it, he coldly answered, "What have I to do with Malinche? I do not wish to hear from him. I desire only to die. To what a state has my willingness to serve him reduced | me!" When urged still further to comply by Olid and father Olmedo, he added, "It is of no use. They will neither believe me, nor the false words and promises of Malinche. You will never leave these walls alive." On being assured, however, that the Spaniards would willingly depart, if a way were opened to them by their enemies, he at length—moved, probably, more by a desire to spare the blood of his subjects, than of the Christians—consented to expostulate with his people.

In order to give the greater effect to his presence, he put on his imperial robes. The *tilmatli*, his mantle of white and blue, flowed over his shoulders, held together by its rich clasp of the green *chalchivitl*. The same precious gem, with emeralds of uncommon size, set in gold, profusely ornamented other parts of his dress. His feet were shod with the golden sandals, and his brows covered by the *copilli*, or Mexican diadem, resembling in form the pontifical tiara. Thus attired, and surrounded by a guard of Spaniards and. several Aztec nobles, and preceded by the golden wand, the symbol of sovereignty, the Indian monarch ascended the central turret of the palace. His presence was instantly recognised by the people, and, as the royal retinue advanced along the battlements, a change, as if by magic, came over the scene. The clang of instruments, the fierce cries of the assailants, were hushed, and a deathlike stillness pervaded the whole assembly, so fiercely agitated, but a few moments before, by the wild tumult of war! Many prostrated themselves on the ground; others bent the knee; and all turned with eager expectation towards the monarch, whom they had been taught to reverence with slavish awe, and from whose countenance they had been wont to turn away as from the intolerable splendors of divinity! Montezuma saw his advantage; and, while he stood thus confronted with his awe-struck people, he seemed to recover all his former authority and confidence, as he. felt himself to be still a king. With a calm voice, easily heard over the silent assembly, he is said by the Castilian writers to have thus addressed them.

"Why do I see my people here in arms against the palace of my fathers? Is it that you think your sovereign a prisoner, and wish to release him? If so, you have acted rightly. But you are mistaken. I am no prisoner. The strangers are my guests. I remain with them only from choice, and can leave them when I list. Have you come to drive them from the city? That is unnecessary. They will depart of their own accord, if you will open a way for them. Return to your homes, then. Lay down your arms. Show your obedience to me who have a right to it. The white men shall go back to their own land; and all shall be well again within the walls of Tenoch-titlan."

As Montezuma announced himself the friend of the detested strangers, a murmur ran through the multitude; a murmur of contempt for the pusillanimous prince who could show himself so insensible to the insults and injuries for which the nation was in arms! The swollen tide of their passions swept away all the barriers of ancient reverence, and, taking a new direction, descended on the head of the unfortunate monarch, so far degenerated from his warlike ancestors. "Base Aztec," they exclaimed, "woman, coward, the white men have made you a woman,—fit only to weave and spin!" These bitter taunts were soon followed by still more hostile demonstrations. A chief, it is said, of high rank, bent a bow or brandished a javelin with an air of defiance against the emperor, when, in an instant, a cloud of stones and arrows descended on the spot where the royal train was gathered. The Spaniards appointed to protect his person had been thrown off their guard by the respectful deportment of the people during their lord's address. They now hastily interposed their bucklers. But it was too late. Montezuma was wounded by three of the missiles, one of which, a stone, fell with such violence on his head, near the temple, as brought him senseless to the ground. The Mexicans, shocked at their own sacrilegious act, experienced a sudden revulsion of feeling, and, setting up a dismal cry, dispersed panic-struck, in different directions. Not one of the multitudinous array remained in the great square before the palace!

The unhappy prince, meanwhile was borne by his attendants to his apartments below. On recovering from the insensibility caused by the blow, the wretchedness of his condition broke upon him. He had tasted the last bitterness of degradation. He had been reviled, rejected, by his people The meanest of the rabble had raised their hands against him. He had nothing more to live for. It was in vain that Cortes and his officers en- deavored to soothe the anguish of his spirit and fill him with better thoughts. He spoke not a word in answer. His wound, though dangerous, might still, with skilful treatment, not prove mortal. But Montezuma refused all the remedies prescribed for it. He tore off the bandages as often as they were applied, maintaining, all the while, the most determined silence. He sat with eyes dejected, brooding over his fallen fortunes, over the image of ancient majesty, and present humiliation. He had survived his honor. But a spark of his ancient spirit seemed to kindle in his bosom, as it was clear he did not mean to survive his disgrace.—From this painful scene the Spanish general and his followers were soon called away by the new dangers which menaced the garrison.

Opposite to the Spanish quarters, at only a few rods' distance, stood the great *teocalli* of Huitzilopotchli. This pyramidal mound, with the sanctuaries that crowned it, rising altogether to the height of near a hundred and fifty feet, afforded an elevated position that completely commanded the palace of Axaya-catl, occupied by the Christians. A body of five or six hundred Mexicans, many of them nobles and warriors of the highest rank, had got possession of the *teo-calli*, whence they discharged such a tempest of arrows on the garrison, that no one could leave his defences for a moment without imminent danger; while the Mexicans, under shelter of the sanctuaries, were entirely covered from the fire of the besieged. It was obviously necessary to dislodge the enemy, if the Spaniards would remain longer in their quarters.

Cortes assigned this service to his chamberlain, Escobar, giving him a hundred men for the purpose, with orders to storm the *teocalli*, and set fire to the sanctuaries. But that officer was thrice repulsed in the attempt, and, after the most desperate efforts, was obliged to return with considerable loss, and without accomplishing his object.

Cortes, who saw the immediate necessity of carrying the place, determined to lead the storming party himself. He was then suffering much from the wound in his left hand, which had disabled it for the present. He made the arm serviceable, however, by fastening his buckler to it, and, thus crippled, sallied out at the head of three hundred chosen cavaliers, and several thousand of his auxiliaries.

In the court-yard of the temple he found a numerous body of Indians prepared to dispute his passage. He briskly charged them, but the flat, smooth stones of the pavement were so slippery, that the horses lost their footing, and many of them fell. Hastily dismounting, they sent back the animals to their quarters, and, renewing the assault, the Spaniards succeeded without much difficulty in dispersing the Indian warriors, and opening a free passage for themselves to the *teocalli*. This building, as the reader may remember, was a huge pyramidal structure, about three hundred feet square at the base. A flight of stone steps on the outside, at one of the angles of the mound, led to a platform, or terraced walk, which passed round the building until it reached a similar flight of stairs directly over the preceding, that conducted to another landing as before. As there were five bodies or divisions of the *teocalli*, it became necessary to pass round its whole extent four times, or nearly a mile, in order to reach the summit, which, it may be recollected, was an open area, crowned only by the two sanctuaries dedicated to the Aztec deities.

Cortes, having cleared a way for the assault, sprang up the lower stairway, followed by Alvarado, Sandoval, Ordaz, and the other gallant cavaliers of his little band, leaving a file of arquebusiers and a strong corps of Indian allies to hold the enemy in check at the foot of the monument. On the first landing, as well as on the several galleries above, and on the summit, the Aztec warriors were drawn up to dispute his passage. From their elevated position they showered down volleys of lighter missiles, together with heavy stones, beams, and burning rafters, which, thundering along the stairway, overturned the ascending Spaniards, and carried desolation through their ranks. The more fortunate, eluding or springing over these obstacles, succeeded in gaining the first terrace; where, throwing themselves on their enemies, they compelled them, after a short resistance, to fall back. The assailants pressed on, effectually supported by a brisk fire of the musketeers from below, which so much galled the Mexicans in their exposed situation, that they were glad to take shelter on the broad summit of the *teocalli.*

Cortes and his comrades were close upon their rear, and the two parties soon found themselves face to face on this aerial battle-field, engaged in mortal combat in presence of the whole city, as well as of the troops in the court-yard, who paused, as if by mutual consent, from their own hostilities, gazing in silent expectation on the issue of those above. The area, though somewhat smaller than the base of the *teocalli,* was large enough to afford a fair field of fight for a thousand combatants. It was paved with broad, flat stones. No impediment occurred over its surface, except the huge sacrificial block, and the temples of stone which rose to the height of forty feet, at the further extremity of the arena. One of these had been consecrated to the Cross. The other was still occupied by the Mexican war-god. The Christian and the Aztec contended for their religions under the very shadow of their respective shrines; while the Indian priests, running to and fro, with their hair wildly streaming over their sable mantles, seemed hovering in mid air, like so many demons of darkness urging on the work of slaughter!

The parties closed with the desperate fury of men who had no hope but in victory. Quarter was neither asked nor given; and to fly was im possible. The edge of the area was unprotected by parapet or battlement. The least slip would be fatal; and the combatants, as they struggled in mortal agony, were sometimes seen to roll over the sheer sides of the precipice together. Cortes himself is said to have had a narrow escape from this dreadful fate. Two warriors, of strong, muscular frames, seized on him, and were dragging him violently towards the brink of the pyramid. Aware of their intention, he struggled with all his force, and, before they could accomplish their purpose, succeeded in tearing himself from their grasp, and hurling one of them over the walls with his own arm! The story is not improbable in itself, for Cortes was a man of uncommon agility and strength. It has been often repeated; but not by contemporary history.

The battle lasted with unintermitting fury for three hours. The number of the enemy was double that of the Christians; and it seemed as if it were a contest which must be determined by numbers and brute force, rather than by superior science. But it was not so. The invulnerable armor of the Spaniard, his sword of matchless temper, and his skill in the use of it, gave him advantages which far outweighed the odds of physical strength and numbers. After doing all that the courage of despair could enable men to do, resistance grew fainter and fainter on the side of the Aztecs. One after another they had fallen. Two or three priests only survived to be led away in triumph by the victors. Every other combatant was stretched a corpse on the bloody arena, or had been hurled from the giddy heights. Yet the loss of the Spaniards was not inconsiderable. It amounted to forty-five of their best men, and nearly all the remainder were more or less injured in the desperate conflict.

The victorious cavaliers now rushed towards the sanctuaries. The lower story was of stone; the two upper were of wood. Penetrating into their recesses, they had the mortification to find the image of the Virgin and the Cross removed. But in the other edifice they still beheld the grim figure of Huitzilo-potchli, with his censer of smoking hearts, and the walls of his oratory reeking with gore,—not improbably of their own countrymen! With shouts of triumph the Christians tore the uncouth monster from his niche, and tumbled him, in the presence of the horror-struck Aztecs, down the steps of the *teocalli*. They then set fire to the accursed building. The flames speedily ran up the slender towers, sending forth an ominous light over city, lake, and valley, to the remotest hut among the mountains. It was the funeral pyre of Paganism, and proclaimed the fall of that sanguinary religion which had so long hung like a dark cloud over the fair regions of Anahuac!

Having accomplished this good work, the Spaniards descended the winding slopes of the *teocalli* with more free and buoyant step, as if conscious that the blessing of Heaven now rested on their arms. They passed through the dusky files of Indian warriors in the court-yard, too much dismayed by the appalling scenes they had witnessed to offer resistance; and reached their own quarters in safety. That very night they followed up the blow by a sortie on the sleeping town, and burned three hundred houses, the horrors of conflagration being made still more impressive by occurring at the hour when the Aztecs, from their own system of warfare, were least prepared for them.

Hoping to find the temper of the natives somewhat subdued by these reverses, Cortes now determined, with his usual policy, to make them a vantage-ground for proposing terms of accommodation. He accordingly invited the enemy to a parley, and, as the principal chiefs, attended by their followers, assembled in the great square, he mounted the turret before occupied by Montezuma, and made signs that he would address them. Marina, as usual, took her place by his side, as his interpreter. The multitude gazed with earnest curiosity on the Indian girl, whose influence with the Spaniards was well known, and whose connection with the general, in particular, had led the Aztecs to designate him by her Mexican name of Malinche. Cortes, speaking through the soft, musical tones of his mistress, told his audience they must now be convinced, that they had nothing further to hope from opposition to the Spaniards. They had seen their gods trampled in the dust, their altars broken, their dwellings burned, their warriors falling on all sides. "All this," continued he, "you have brought on yourselves by your rebellion. Yet for the affection the sovereign, whom you have so unworthily treated, still bears you, I would willingly stay my hand, if you will lay down your arms, and return once more to your obedience. But, if you do not," he concluded, "I will make your city a heap of ruins, and leave not a soul alive to mourn over it!"

But the Spanish commander did not yet comprehend the character of the Aztecs, if he thought to intimidate them by menaces. Calm in their exterior and slow to move, they were the more difficult to pacify when roused; and now that they had been stirred to their inmost depths, it was no human voice that could still the tempest. It may be, however, that Cortes did not so much misconceive the character of the people. He may have felt that an authoritative tone was the only one he could assume with any chance of effect, in his present position, in which milder and more conciliatory language would, by intimating a consciousness of inferiority, have too certainly defeated its own object.

It was true, they answered, he had destroyed their temples, broken in pieces their gods, massacred their countrymen. Many more, doubtless, were yet to fall under their terrible swords. But they were content so long as for every thousand Mexicans they could shed the blood of a single white man! "Look out," they continued, "on our terraces and streets, see them still thronged with warriors as far as your eyes can reach. Our numbers are scarcely diminished by our losses. Yours, on the contrary, are lessening every hour. You are perishing from hunger and sickness. Your provisions and water are falling. You must soon fall into our hands. *The bridges are broken down, and you cannot escape!* There will be too few of you left to glut the vengeance of our Gods!" As they concluded, they sent a volley of arrows over the battlements, which compelled the Spaniards to descend and take refuge in their defences.

The fierce and indomitable spirit of the Aztecs filled the besieged with dismay. All, then, that they had done and suffered, their battles by day, their vigils by night, the perils they had braved, even the victories they had won, were of no avail. It was too evident that they had no longer the spring of ancient superstition to work upon, in the breasts of the natives, who, like some wild beast that has burst the bonds of his keeper, seemed now to swell and exult in the full consciousness of their strength. The annunciation respecting the bridges fell like a knell on the ears of the Christians. All that they had heard was too true,—and they gazed on one another with looks of anxiety and dismay.

The same consequences followed, which sometimes take place among the crew of a shipwrecked vessel. Subordination was lost in the dreadful sense of danger. A spirit of mutiny broke out, especially among the recent levies drawn from the army of Narvaez. They had come into the country from no motive of ambition, but attracted simply by the glowing reports of its opulence, and they had fondly hoped to return in a few months with their pockets well lined with the gold of the Aztec monarch. But how different had been their lot! From the first hour of their landing, they had experienced only trouble and disaster, privations of every description, sufferings unexampled, and they now beheld in perspective a fate yet more appalling. Bitterly did they lament the hour when they left the sunny fields of Cuba for these cannibal regions! And heartily did they curse their own folly in listening to the call of Velasquez, and still more, in embarking under the banner of Cortes!

They now demanded with noisy vehemence to be led instantly from the city, and refused to serve longer in defence of a place where they were cooped up like sheep in the shambles, waiting only to be dragged to slaughter. In all this they were rebuked by the more orderly, soldier-like conduct of the veterans of Cortes. These latter had shared with their general the day of his prosperity, and they were not disposed to desert him in the tempest. It was, indeed, obvious, on a little reflection, that the only chance of safety, in the existing crisis, rested on subordination and union; and that even this chance must be greatly diminished under any other leader than their present one.

Thus pressed by enemies without and by factions within, that leader was found, as usual, true to himself. Circumstances so appalling, as would have paralyzed a common mind, only stimulated his to higher action, and drew forth all its resources. He combined what is most rare, singular coolness and constancy of purpose, with a spirit of enterprise that might well be called romantic. His presence of mind did not now desert him. He calmly surveyed his condition, and weighed the difficulties which surrounded him, before coming to a decision. Independently of the hazard of a retreat in the face of a watchful and desperate foe, it was a deep mortification to surrender up the city, where he had so long lorded it as a master; to abandon the rich treasures which he had secured to himself and his followers; to forego the very means by which he hoped to propitiate the favor of his sovereign, and secure an amnesty for his irregular proceedings. This, he well knew, must, after all, be dependent on success. To fly now was to acknowledge himself further removed from the conquest than ever. What a close was this to a career so auspiciously begun! What a contrast to his magnificent vaunts! What a triumph would it afford to his enemies! The governor of Cuba would be amply revenged.

But, if such humiliating reflections crowded on his mind, the alternative of remaining, in his present crippled condition, seemed yet more desperate. With his men daily diminishing in strength and numbers, their provisions reduced so low that a small daily ration of bread was all the sustenance afforded to the soldier under his extraordinary fatigues, with the breaches every day widening in his feeble fortifications, with his ammunition, in fine, nearly expended, it would be impossible to maintain the place much longer—and none but men of iron constitutions and tempers, like the Spaniards, could have held it out so long—against the enemy. The chief embarrassment was as to the time and manner in which it would be expedient to evacuate the city. The best route seemed to be that of Tlacopan (Tacuba). For the causeway, the most dangerous part of the road, was but two miles long in that direction, and would, therefore, place the fugitives, much sooner than either of the other great avenues, on terra firma. Before his final departure, however, he proposed to make another sally in that direction, in order to reconnoitre the gound, and, at the same time, divert the enemy's attention from his real purpose by a show of active operations.

For some days, his workmen had been employed in constructing a military machine of his own invention. It was called a *manta,* and was contrived somewhat on the principle of the mantelets used in the wars of the Middle Ages. It was, however, more complicated, consisting of a tower made of light beams and planks, having two chambers, one over the other. These were to be filled with musketeers, and the sides were provided with loop-holes, through which a fire could be kept up on the enemy. The great advantage proposed by this contrivance was, to afford a defence to the troops against the missiles hurled from the terraces. These machines, three of which were made, rested on rollers, and were provided with strong ropes, by which they were to be dragged along the streets by the Tlascalan auxiliaries.

The Mexicans gazed with astonishment on this warlike machinery, and, as the rolling fortresses advanced, belching forth fire and smoke from their entrails, the enemy, incapable of making an impression on those within fell back in dismay. By bringing the *mantas* under the walls of the houses, the Spaniards were enabled to fire with effect on the mischievous tenants of the *azoteas*, and when this did not silence them, by letting a ladder, or light drawbridge, fall on the roof from the top of the *manta*, they opened a passage to the terrace, and closed with the combatants hand to hand. They could not, however, thus approach the higher buildings, from which the Indian warriors threw down such heavy masses of stone and timber as dislodged the planks that covered the machines, or, thundering against their sides, shook the frail edifices to their foundation, threatening all within with indiscriminate ruin. Indeed, the success of the experiment was doubtful, when the intervention of a canal put a stop to their further progress.

The Spaniards now found the assertion of their enemies too well confirmed. The bridge which traversed the opening had been demolished; and, although the canals which intersected the city were, in general, of no great width or depth, the removal of the bridges not only impeded the movements of the general's clumsy machines, but effectually disconcerted those of his cavalry. Resolving to abandon the *mantas,* he gave orders to fill up the chasm with stone, timber, and other rubbish drawn from the ruined buildings, and to make a new passage-way for the army. While this labor was going on, the Aztec slingers and archers on the other side of the opening kept up a galling discharge on the Christians, the more defenceless from the nature of their occupation. When the work was completed, and a safe passage secured, the Spanish cavaliers rode briskly against the enemy, who, unable to resist the shock of the steel-clad column, fell back with precipitation to where another canal afforded a similar strong position for defence.

There were no less than seven of these canals, intersecting the great street of Tlacopan, and at every one the same scene was renewed, the Mexicans making a gallant stand, and inflicting some loss, at each, on their persevering antagonists. These operations consumed two days, when, after incredible toil, the Spanish general had the satisfaction to find the line of communication completely reestablished through the whole length of the avenue, and the principal bridges placed under strong detachments of infantry. At this juncture, when he had driven the foe before him to the furthest extremity of the street, where it touches on the causeway, he was informed, that the Mexicans, disheartened by their reverses, desired to open a parley with him respecting the terms of an accommodation, and that their chiefs awaited his return for that purpose at the fortress. Overjoyed at the intelligence, he instantly rode back, attended by Alvarado, Sandoval, and about sixty of the cavaliers, to his quarters.

The Mexicans proposed that he should release the two priests captured in the temple, who might be the bearers of his terms, and serve as agents for conducting the negotiation. They were accordingly sent with the requisite instructions to their countrymen. But they did not return. The whole was an artifice of the enemy, anxious to procure the liberation of their religious leaders, one of whom was their *teoteuctli,* or high-priest, whose presence was indispensable in the probable event of a new coronation.

Cortes, meanwhile, relying on the prospects of a speedy arrangement, was hastily taking some refreshment with his officers, after the fatigues of the day; when he received the alarming tidings, that the enemy were in arms again, with more fury than ever; that they had overpowered the detachments posted under Alvarado at three of the bridges, and were busily occupied in demolishing them. Stung with shame at the facility with which he had been duped by his wily foe, or rather by his own sanguine hopes, Cortes threw himself into the saddle, and, followed by his brave companions, galloped back at full speed to the scene of action. The Mexicans recoiled before the impetuous charge of the Spaniards. The bridges were again restored; and Cortes and his cavalry rode down the whole extent of the great street, driving the enemy, like frightened deer, at the points of their lances. But, before he could return on his steps, he had the mortification to find that the indefatigable foe, gathering from the adjoining lanes and streets, had again closed on his infantry, who, worn down by fatigue, were unable to maintain their position at one of the principal bridges. New swarms of warriors now poured in on all sides, overwhelming the little band of Christian cavaliers with a storm of stones, darts, and arrows, which rattled like hail on their armor and on that of their well-barbed horses. Most of the missiles, indeed, glanced harmless from the good panoplies of steel, or thick quilted cotton, but, now and then, one better aimed penetrated the joints of the harness, and stretched the rider on the ground.

The confusion became greater around the broken bridge. Some of the horsemen were thrown into the canal, and their steeds floundered wildly about without a rider. Cortes himself, at this crisis, did more than any other to cover the retreat of his followers. While the bridge was repairing, he plunged boldly into the midst of the barbarians, striking down an enemy at every vault of his charger, cheering on his own men, and spreading terror through the ranks of his opponents by the well-known sound of his battle-cry. Never did he display greater hardihood, or more freely expose his person, emulating, says an old chronicler, the feats of the Roman Cocles. In this way he stayed the tide of assailants, till the last man had crossed the bridge, when, some of the planks having given way, he was compelled to leap a chasm of full six feet in width, amidst a cloud of missiles, before he could place himself in safety. A report ran through the army that the general was slain. It soon spread through the city, to the great joy of the Mexicans, and reached the fortress, where the besieged were thrown into no less consternation. But, happily for them, it was false. He, indeed, received two severe contusions on the knee, but in other respects remained uninjured. At no time, however, had he been in such extreme danger; and his escape, and that of his companions, was esteemed little less than a miracle. More than one grave historian refers the preservation of the Spaniards to the watchful care of their patron Apostle, St. James, who, in these desperate conflicts, was beheld careering on his milk-white steed at the head of the Christian squadrons, with his sword flashing lightning, while a lady robed in white—supposed to be the Virgin-was distinctly seen by his side, throwing dust in the eyes of the infidel! The fact is attested both by Spaniards and Mexicans,—by the latter after their conversion to Christianity. Surely, never was there a time when the interposition of their tutelar saint was more strongly demanded.

The coming of night dispersed the Indian battalions, which, vanishing like birds of ill omen from the field, left the well-contested pass in possession of the Spaniards. They returned, however, with none of the joyous feelings of conquerors to their citadel, but with slow step and dispirited, with weapons hacked, armor battered, and fainting under the loss of blood, fasting, and fatigue. In this condition they had yet to learn the tidings of a fresh misfortune in the death of Montezuma.

The Indian monarch had rapidly declined, since he had received his injury, sinking, however, quite as much under the anguish of a wounded spirit, as under disease. He continued in the same moody state of insensibility as that already described; holding little communication with those around him, deaf to consolation, obstinately rejecting all medical remedies as well as nourishment. Perceiving his end approach, some of the cavaliers present in the fortress, whom the kindness of his manners had personally attached to him, were anxious to save the soul of the dying prince from the sad doom of those who perish in the darkness of unbelief. They accordingly waited on him, with father Olmedo at their head, and in the most earnest manner implored him to open his eyes to the error of his creed, and consent to be baptized. But Montezuma—whatever may have been suggested to the contrary—seems never to have faltered in his hereditary faith, or to have contemplated becoming an apostate; for surely he merits that name in its most odious application, who, whether Christian or pagan, renounces his religion without conviction of its falsehood. Indeed, it was a too implicit reliance on its oracles, which had led him to give such easy confidence to the Spaniards. His intercourse with them had, doubtless, not sharpened his desire to embrace their communion; and the calamities of his country he might consider as sent by his gods to punish him for his hospitality to those who had desecrated and destroyed their shrine.

When father Olmedo, therefore, kneeling at his side, with the uplifted crucifix, affectionately besought him to embrace the sign of man's redemption, he coldly repulsed the priest, exclaiming, "I have but a few moments to live, and will not at this hour desert the faith of my fathers." One thing, however, seemed to press heavily on Montezuma's mind. This was the fate of his children, especially of three daughters, whom he had by his two wives; for there were certain rites of marriage, which distinguished the lawful wife from the concubine. Calling Cortes to his bedside, he earnestly commended these children to his care, as "the most precious jewels that he could leave him." He besought the general to interest his master, the emperor, in their behalf, and to see that they should not be left destitute, but be allowed some portion of their rightful inheritance. "Your lord will do this," he concluded, "if it were only for the friendly offices I have rendered the Spaniards, and for the love I have shown them,—though it has brought me to this condition! But for this I bear them no ill-will." Such, according to Cortes himself, were the words of the dying monarch. Not long after, on the 30th of June, 1520, he expired in the arms of some of his own nobles, who still remained faithful in their attendance on his person. "Thus," exclaims a native historian, one of his enemies, a Tlascalan, "thus died the unfortunate Montezuma, who had swayed the sceptre with such consummate policy and wisdom; and who was held in greater reverence and awe than any other prince of his lineage, or any, indeed, that ever sat on a throne in this Western World. With him may be said to have terminated the royal line of the Aztecs, and the glory to have passed away from the empire, which under him had reached the zenith of its prosperity." "The tidings of his death," says the old Castilian chronicler, Diaz, "were received with real grief by every cavalier and soldier in the army who had had access to his person; for we all loved him as a father,—and no wonder, seeing how good he was." This simple, but emphatic, testimony to his desert, at such a time, is in itself the best refutation of the suspicions occasionally entertained of his fidelity to the Christians.

It is not easy to depict the portrait of Montezuma in its true colors, since it has been exhibited to us under two aspects, of the most opposite and contradictory character. In the accounts gathered of him by the Spaniards, on coming into the country, he was uniformly represented as bold and warlike, unscrupulous as to the means of gratifying his ambition, hollow and perfidious, the terror of his foes, with a haughty bearing which made him feared even by his own people. They found him, on the contrary, not merely affable and gracious, but disposed to waive all the advantages of his own position, and to place them on a footing with himself; making their wishes his law; gentle even to effeminacy in his deportment, and constant in his friendship,while his whole nation was in arms against them.—Yet these traits, so contradictory, were truly enough drawn. They are to be explained by the extraordinary circumstances of his position.

When Montezuma ascended the throne, he was scarcely twenty-three years of age. Young, and ambitious of extending his empire, he was continually engaged in war, and is said to have been present himself in nine pitched battles. He was greatly renowned for his martial prowess, for he belonged to the *Quachictin,* the highest military order of his nation, and one into which but few even of its sovereigns had been admitted. In later life, he preferred intrigue to violence, as more consonant to his character and priestly education. In this he was as great an adept as any prince of his time, and, by arts not very honorable to himself, succeeded in filching away much of the territory of his royal kinsman of Tezcuco. Severe in the administration of justice, he made important reforms in the arrangement of the tribunals. He introduced other innovations in the royal household, creating new offices, introducing a lavish magnificence and forms of courtly etiquette unknown to his ruder predecessors. He was, in short, most attentive to all that concerned the exterior and pomp of royalty. Stately and decorous, he was careful of his own dignity, and might be said to be as great an "actor of majesty" among the barbarian potentates of the New World, as Louis the Fourteenth was among the polished princes of Europe.

He was deeply tinctured, moreover, with that spirit of bigotry, which threw such a shade over the latter days of the French monarch. He received the Spaniards as the beings predicted by his oracles. The anxious dread, with which he had evaded their proffered visit, was founded on the same feelings which led him so blindly to resign himself to them on their approach. He felt himself rebuked by their superior genius. He at once conceded all that they demanded,—his treasures, his power, even his person. For their sake, he forsook his wonted occupations, his pleasures, his most familiar habits. He might be said to forego his nature; and, as his subjects asserted, to change his sex and become a woman. If we cannot refuse our contempt for the pusillanimity of the Aztec monarch, it should be mitigated by the consideration, that his pusillanimity sprung from his superstition, and that superstition in the savage is the substitute for religious principle in the civilized man.

It is not easy to contemplate the fate of Montezuma without feelings of the strongest compassion;—to see him thus borne along the tide of events beyond his power to avert or control; to see him, like some stately tree, the pride of his own Indian forests, towering aloft in the pomp and majesty of its branches, by its very eminence a mark for the thunderbolt, the first victim of the tempest which was to sweep over its native hills! When the wise king of Tezcuco addressed his royal relative at his coronation, he exclaimed, "Happy the empire, which is now in the meridian of its prosperity, for the sceptre is given to one whom the Almighty has in his keeping; and the nations shall hold him in reverence!" Alas! the subject of this auspicious invocation lived to see his empire melt away like the winter's wreath; to see a strange race drop as it were, from the clouds on his land; to find himself a prisoner in the palace of his fathers, the companion of those who were the enemies of his gods and his people; to be insulted, reviled, trodden in the dust, by the meanest of his subjects, by those who, a few months previous, had trembled at his glance; drawing his last breath in the halls of the stranger,—a lonely outcast in the heart of his own capital! He was the sad victim of destiny,—a destiny as dark and irresistible in its march, as that which broods over the mythic legends of Antiquity!

Montezuma at the time of his death, was about forty-one years old, of which he reigned eighteen. His person and manners have been already described. He left a numerous progeny by his various wives, most of whom, having lost their consideration after the Conquest, fell into obscurity, as they mingled with the mass of the Indian population. Two of them, however, a son and a daughter, who embraced Christianity, became founders of noble houses in Spain. The government, willing to show its gratitude for the large extent of empire derived from their ancestor, conferred on them ample estates and important hereditary honors; and the Counts of Montezuma and Tula, intermarrying with the best blood of Castile, intimated by their names and titles their illustrious descent from the royal dynasty of Mexico.

Montezuma's death was a misfortune to the Spaniards. While he lived, they had a precious pledge in their hands, which, in extremity, they might possibly have turned to account. Now the last link was snapped which connected them with the natives of the country. But independently of interested feelings, Cortes and his officers were much affected by his death from personal considerations, and, when they gazed on the cold remains of the ill-starred monarch, they may have felt a natural compunction, as they contrasted his late flourishing condition with that to which his friendship for them had now reduced him.

The Spanish commander showed all respect for his memory. His body, arrayed in its royal robes, was laid decently on a bier, and borne on the shoulders of his nobles to his subjects in the city. What honors, if any, indeed, were paid to his remains, is uncertain. A sound of wailing, distinctly heard in the western quarters of the capital, was interpreted by the Spaniards into the moans of a funeral procession, as it bore the body to be laid among those of his ancestors, under the princely shades of Chapoltepec. Others state, that it was removed to a burial-place in the city named Copalco and there burnt with the usual solemnities and signs of lamentation by his chiefs, but not without some unworthy insults from the Mexican populace. Whatever be the fact, the people, occupied with the stirring scenes in which they were engaged, were probably not long mindful of the monarch, who had taken no share in their late patriotic movements. Nor is it strange that the very memory of his sepulchre should be effaced in the terrible catastrophe which afterwards overwhelmed the capital, and swept away every landmark from its surface.

THE MASSACRE AT FORT WILLIAM HENRY

JAMES FENIMORE COOPER

Major Heyward found Munro attended only by his daughters. Alice sat upon his knee, parting the gray hairs on the forehead of the old man with her delicate fingers; and whenever he affected to frown on her trifling, appeasing his assumed anger by pressing her ruby lips fondly on his wrinkled brow. Cora was seated nigh them, a calm and amused looker-on; regarding the wayward movements of her more youthful sister with that species of maternal fondness which characterized her love for Alice. Not only the dangers through which they had passed, but those which still impended above them, appeared to be momentarily forgotten, in the soothing indulgence of such a family meeting. It seemed as if they had profited by the short truce, to devote an instant to the purest and best affection; the daughters forgetting their fears, and the veteran his cares, in the security of the moment. Of this scene, Duncan, who, in his eagerness to report his arrival, had entered unannounced, stood many moments an unobserved and a delighted spectator. But the quick and dancing eyes of Alice soon caught a glimpse of his figure reflected from a glass, and she sprang blushing from her father's knee, exclaiming aloud:

"Major Heyward"!

"What of the lad"? demanded her father; "I have sent him to crack a little with the Frenchman. Ha, sir, you are young, and you're nimble! Away with you, ye baggage; as if there were not troubles enough for a soldier, without having his camp filled with such prattling hussies as yourself"!

Alice laughingly followed her sister, who instantly led the way from an apartment where she perceived their presence was no longer desirable. Munro, instead of demanding the result of the young man's mission, paced the room for a few moments, with his hands behind his back, and his head inclined toward the floor, like a man lost in thought. At length he raised his eyes, glistening with a father's fondness, and exclaimed:

"They are a pair of excellent girls, Heyward, and such as any one may boast of".

"You are not now to learn my opinion of your daughters, Colonel Munro".

"True, lad, true", interrupted the impatient old man; "you were about open-ing your mind more fully on that matter the day you got in, but I did not think it becoming in an old soldier to be talking of nuptial blessings and wedding jokes when the enemies of his king were likely to be unbidden guests at the feast. But I was wrong, Duncan, boy, I was wrong there; and I am now ready to hear what you have to say".

"Notwithstanding the pleasure your assurance gives me, dear sir, I have just now, a message from Montcalm—"

"Let the Frenchman and all his host go to the devil, sir"! exclaimed the hasty veteran. "He is not yet master of William Henry, nor shall he ever be, provided Webb proves himself the man he should. No, sir, thank Heaven we are not yet in such a strait that it can be said Munro is too much pressed to discharge the little domestic duties of his own family. Your mother was the only child of my bosom friend, Duncan; and I'll just give you a hearing, though all the knights of St. Louis were in a body at the sally-port, with the French saint at their head, crying to speak a word under favor. A pretty degree of knighthood, sir, is that which can be bought with sugar hogsheads! and then your twopenny marquisates. The thistle is the order for dignity and antiquity; the veritable "nemo me impune lacessit" of chivalry. Ye had ancestors in that degree, Duncan, and they were an ornamnet to the nobles of Scotland".

Heyward, who perceived that his superior took a malicious pleasure in exhibiting his contempt for the message of the French general, was fain to humor a spleen that he knew would be short-lived; he therefore, replied with as much indifference as he could assume on such a subject:

"My request, as you know, sir, went so far as to presume to the honor of being your son".

"Ay, boy, you found words to make yourself very plainly comprehended. But, let me ask ye, sir, have you been as intelligible to the girl"?

"On my honor, no", exclaimed Duncan, warmly; "there would have been an abuse of a confided trust, had I taken advantage of my situation for such a purpose".

"Your notions are those of a gentleman, Major Heyward, and well enough in their place. But Cora Munro is a maiden too discreet, and of a mind too elevated and improved, to need the guardianship even of a father".

"Cora"!

"Ay -Cora! we are talking of your pretensions to Miss Munro, are we not, sir"?

"I -I -I was not conscious of having mentioned her name", said Duncan, stammering.

"And to marry whom, then, did you wish my consent, Major Heyward"? demanded the old soldier, erecting himself in the dignity of offended feeling. "You have another, and not less lovely child".

"Alice"! exclaimed the father, in an astonishment equal to that with which Duncan had just repeated the name of her sister. "Such was the direction of my wishes, sir".

The young man awaited in silence the result of the extraordinary effect produced by a communication, which, as it now appeared, was so unexpected. For several minutes Munro paced the chamber with long and rapid strides, his rigid features working convulsively, and every faculty seemingly absorbed in the musings of his own mind. At length, he paused directly in front of Heyward, and riveting his eyes upon those of the other, he said, with a lip that quivered violently:

"Duncan Heyward, I have loved you for the sake of him whose blood is in your veins; I have loved you for your own good qualities; and I have loved you, because 1 thought you would contribute to the happiness of my child. But all this love would turn to hatred, were I assured that what I so much apprehend is true".

"God forbid that any act or thought of mine should lead to such a change"! exclaimed the young man, whose eye never quailed under the penetrating look it encountered. Without adverting to the impossibility of the other's comprehending those feelings which were hid in his own bosom, Munro suffered himself to be appeased by the unaltered countenance he met, and with a voice sensibly softened, he continued:

"You would be my son, Duncan, and you're ignorant of the history of the man you wish to call your father. Sit ye down, young man, and I will open to you the wounds of a seared heart, in as few words as may be suitable".

By this time, the message of Montcalm was as much forgotten by him who bore it as by the man for whose ears it was intended. Each drew a chair, and while the veteran communed a few moments with his own thoughts, apparently in sadness, the youth suppressed his impatience in a look and attitude of respectful attention. At length, the former spoke:

"You'll know, already, Major Heyward, that my family was both ancient and honorable", commenced the Scotsman; "though it might not altogether be endowed with that amount of wealth that should correspond with its degree. I was, maybe, such an one as yourself when I plighted my faith to Alice Graham, the only child of a neighboring laird of some estate. But the connection was disagreeable to her father, on more accounts than my poverty. I did, therefore, what an honest man should -restored the maiden her troth, and departed the country in the service of my king. I had seen many regions, and had shed much blood in different lands, before duty called me to the islands of the West Indies. There it was my lot to form a connection with one who in time became my wife, and the mother of Cora. She was the daughter of a gentleman of those isles, by a lady whose misfortune it was, if you will", said the old man, proudly, "to be descended, remotely, from that unfortunate class who are so basely enslaved to administer to the wants of a luxurious people. Ay, sir, that is a curse, entailed on Scotland by her unnatural union with a foreign and trading people. But could I find a man among them who would dare to reflect on my child, he should feel the weight of a father's anger! Ha! Major Heyward, you are yourself born at the south, where these unfortunate beings are considered of a race inferior to your own".

"'Tis most unfortunately true, sir", said Duncan, unable any longer to prevent his eyes from sinking to the floor in embarrassment.

"And you cast it on my child as a reproach! You scorn to mingle the blood of the Heywards with one so degraded -lovely and virtuous though she be"? fiercely demanded the jealous parent.

"Heaven protect me from a prejudice so unworthy of my reason"! returned Duncan, at the same time conscious of such a feeling, and that as deeply rooted as if it had been ingrafted in his nature. "The sweetness, the beauty, the witchery of your younger daughter, Colonel Munro, might explain my motives without imputing to me this injustice".

"Ye are right, sir", returned the old man, again changing his tones to those of gentleness, or rather softness; "the girl is the image of what her mother was at her years, and before she had become acquainted with grief. When death deprived me of my wife I returned to Scotland, enriched by the marriage; and, would you think it, Duncan! the suffering angel had remained in the heartless state of celibacy twenty long years, and that for the sake of a man who could forget her! She did more, sir; she overlooked my want of faith, and, all difficulties being now removed, she took me for her husband".

"And became the mother of Alice"? exclaimed Duncan, with an eagerness that might have proved dangerous at a moment when the thoughts of Munro were less occupied that at present.

"She did, indeed", said the old man, "and dearly did she pay for the blessing she bestowed. But she is a saint in heaven, sir; and it ill becomes one whose foot rests on the grave to mourn a lot so blessed. I had her but a single year, though; a short term of happiness for one who had seen her youth fade in hopeless pining".

There was something so commanding in the distress of the old man, that Heyward did not dare to venture a syllable of consolation. Munro sat utterly unconscious of the other's presence, his features exposed and working with the anguish of his regrets, while heavy tears fell from his eyes, and rolled unheeded from his cheeks to the floor. At length he moved, and as if suddenly recovering his recollection; when he arose, and taking a single turn across the room, he approached his companion with an air of military grandeur, and demanded:

"Have you not, Major Heyward, some communication that I should hear from the marquis de Montcalm"?

Duncan started in his turn, and immediately commenced in an embarrassed voice, the half-forgotten message, it is unnecessary to dwell upon the evasive though polite manner with which the French general had eluded every attempt of Heyward to worm from him the purport of the communication he had proposed making, or on the decided, though still polished message, by which he now gave his enemy to understand, that, unless he chose to receive it in person, he should not receive it at all. As Munro listened to the detail of Duncan, the excited feelings of the father gradually gave way before the obligations of his station, and when the other was done, he saw before him nothing but the veteran, swelling with the wounded feelings of a soldier.

"You have said enough, Major Heyward", exclaimed the angry old man; "enough to make a volume of commentary on French civility. Here has this gentleman invited me to a conference, and when I send him a capable substitute, for ye're all that, Duncan, though your years are but few, he answers me with a riddle".

"He may have thought less favorably of the substitue, my dear sir; and you will remember that the invitation, which he now repeats, was to the commandant of the works, and not to his second".

"Well, sir, is not a substitute clothed with all the power and dignity of him who grants the commission? He wishes to confer with Munro! Faith, sir, I have much inclination to indulge the man, if it should only be to let him behold the firm countenance we maintain in spite of his numbers and his summons. There might be not bad policy in such a stroke, young man".

Duncan, who believe it of the last importance that they should speedily come to the contents of the letter borne by the scout, gladly encouraged this idea.

"Without doubt, he could gather no confidence by witnessing our indifference", he said.

"You never said truer word. I could wish, sir, that he would visit the works in open day, and in the form of a storming party; that is the least failing method of proving the countenance of an enemy, and would be far preferable to the battering system he has chosen. The beauty and manliness of warfare has been much deformed, Major Heyward, by the arts of your Monsieur Vauban. Our ancestors were far above such scientific cowardice"!

"It may be very true, sir; but we are now obliged to repel art by art. What is your pleasure in the matter of the interview"?

"I will meet the Frenchman, and that without fear or delay; promptly, sir, as becomes a servant of my royal master. Go, Major Heyward, and give them a flourish of the music; and send out a messenger to let them know who is coming. We will follow with a small guard, for such respect is due to one who holds the honor of his king in keeping; and hark'ee, Duncan", he added, in a half whisper, though they were alone, "it may be prudent to have some aid at hand, in case there should be treachery at the bottom of it all".

The young man availed himself of this order to quit the apartment; and, as the day was fast coming to a close, he hastened without delay, to make the necessary arrangements. A very few minutes only were necessary to parade a few files, and to dispatch an orderly with a flag to announce the approach of the commandant of the fort. When Duncan had done both these, he led the guard to the sally-port, near which he found his superior ready, waiting his appearance. As soon as the usual ceremonials of a military departure were observed, the veteran and his more youthful companion left the fortress, attended by the escort.

They had proceeded only a hundred yards from the works, when the little array which attended the French general to the conference was seen issuing from the hollow way which formed the bed of a brook that ran between the batteries of the besiegers and the fort. From the moment that Munro left his own works to appear in front of his enemy's, his air had been grand, and his step and countenance highly military. The instant he caught a glimpse of the white plume that waved in the hat of Montcalm, his eye lighted, and age no longer appeared to possess any influence over his vast and still muscular person.

"Speak to the boys to be watchful, sir", he said, in an undertone, to Duncan; "and to look well to their flints and steel, for one is never safe with a servant of these Louis's; at the same time, we shall show them the front of men in deep security. You understand me, Major Heyward"!

He was interrupted by the clamor of a drum from the approaching Frenchmen, which was immediately answered, when each party pushed an orderly in advance, bearing a white flag, and the wary Scotsman halted with his guard close at his back. As soon as this slight salutation had passed, Montcalm moved toward them with a quick but graceful step, baring his head to the veteran, and dropping his spotless plume nearly to the earth in courtesy. If the air of Munro was more commanding and manly, it wanted both the ease and insinuating polish of that of the Frenchman. Neither spoke for a few moments, each regarding the other with curious and interested eyes. Then, as became his superior rank and the nature of the interview, Montcalm broke the silence. After uttering the usual words of greeting, he turned to Duncan, and continued, with a smile of recognition, speaking always in French:

"I am rejoiced, monsieur, that you have given us the pleasure of your company on this occasion. There will be no necessity to employ an ordinary interpreter; for, in your hands, I feel the same security as if I spoke your langauge myself".

Duncan acknowledged the compliment, when Montcalm, turning to his guard, which in imitation of that of their enemies, pressed close upon him, continued:

"En arrière, mes enfants -il fait chaud -retirez-vous un peu".

Before Major Heyward would imitate this proof of confidence, he glanced his eyes around the plain, and beheld with uneasiness the numerous dusky groups of savages, who looked out from the margin of the surrounding woods, curious spectators of the interview.

"Monsieur de Montcalm will readily acknowledge the difference in our situation", he said, with some embarrassment, pointing at the same time toward those dangerous foes, who were to be seen in almost every direction, "were we to dismiss our guard, we should stand here at the mercy of our enemies".

"Monsieur, you have the plighted faith of "un gentilhomme Français", for your safety", returned Montcalm, laying his hand impressively on his heart; "it should suffice".

"It shall. Fall back", Duncan added to the officer who led the escort; "fall back, sir, beyond hearing, and wait for orders".

Munro witnessed this movement with manifest uneasiness; nor did he fail to demand an instant explanation.

"Is it not our interest, sir, to betray distrust"? retorted Duncan. "Monsieur de Montcalm pledges his word for our safety, and I have ordered the men to withdraw a little, in order to prove how much we depend on his assurance".

"It may be all right, sir, but I have no overweening reliance on the faith of these marquesses, or marquis, as they call themselves. Their patents of nobility are too common to be certain that they bear the seal of true honor".

"You forget, dear sir, that we confer with an officer, distinguished alike in Europe and America for his deeds. From a soldier of his reputation we can have nothing to apprehend".

The old man made a gesture of resignation, though his rigid features still betrayed his obstinate adherence to a distrust, which he derived from a sort of hereditary contempt of his enemy, rather than from any present signs which might warrant so uncharitable a feeling. Montcalm waited patiently until this little dialogue in demi-voice was ended, when he drew nigher, and opened the subject of their conference.

"I have solicited this interview from your superior, monsieur", he said, "because I believe he will allow himself to be persuaded that he has already done everything which is necessary for the honor of his prince, and will now listen to the admonitions of humanity. I will forever bear testimony that his resistance has been gallant, and was continued as long as there was hope".

When this opening was translated to Munro, he answered with dignity, but with sufficienct courtesy:

"However I may prize such testimony from Monsieur Montcalm, it will be more valuable when it shall be better merited".

The French general smiled, as Duncan gave him the purport of this reply, and observed:

"What is now so freely accorded to approved courage, may be refused to useless obstinacy. Monsieur would wish to see my camp, and witness for himself our numbers, and the impossibility of his resisting them with success"?

"I know that the king of France is well served", returned the unmoved Scotsman, as soon as Duncan ended his translation; "but my own royal master has as many and as faithful troops".

"Though not at hand, fortunately for us", said Montcalm, without waiting, in his ardor, for the interpreter. "There is a destiny in war, to which a brave man knows how to submit with the same courage that he faces his foes".

"Had I been conscious that Monsieur Montcalm was master of the English, I should have spared myself the trouble of so awkward a translation", said the vexed Duncan, dryly; remembering instantly his recent by-play with Munro.

"Your pardon, monsieur", rejoined the Frenchman, suffering a slight color to appear on his dark cheek. "There is a vast difference between understanding and speaking a foreign tongue; you will, therefore, please to assist me still". Then, after a short pause, he added: "These hills afford us every opportunity of reconnoitering your works, messieurs, and I am possibly as well acquainted with their weak condition as you can be yourselves".

"Ask the French general if his glasses can reach to the Hudson", said Munro, proudly; "and if he knows when and where to expect the army of Webb".

"Let General Webb be his own interpreter", returned the politic Montcalm, suddenly extending an open letter toward Munro as he spoke; "you will there learn, monsieur, that his movements are not likely to prove embarrassing to my army".

The veteran seized the offered paper, without waiting for Duncan to translate the speech, and with an eagerness that betrayed how important he deemed its contents. As his eye passed hastily over the words, his countenance changed from its look of military pride to one of deep chagrin; his lip began to quiver; and suffering the paper to fall from his hand, his head dropped upon his chest, like that of a man whose hopes were withered at a single blow. Duncan caught the letter from the ground, and without apology for the liberty he took, he read at a glance its cruel purport. Their common superior, so far from encouraging them to resist, advised a speedy surrender, urging in the plainest language, as a reason, the utter impossibility of his sending a single man to their rescue.

"Here is no deception"! exclaimed Duncan, examining the billet both inside and out; "this is the signature of Webb, and must be the captured letter".

"The man has betrayed me"! Munro at length bitterly exclaimed; "he has brought dishonor to the door of one where disgrace was never before known to dwell, and shame has he heaped heavily on my gray hairs".

"Say not so", cried Duncan; "we are yet masters of the fort, and of our honor. Let us, then, sell our lives at such a rate as shall make our enemies believe the purchase too dear".

"Boy, I thank thee", exclaimed the old man, rousing himself from his stupor; "you have, for once, reminded Munro of his duty. We will go back, and dig our graves behind those ramparts".

"Messieurs", said Montcalm, advancing toward them a step, in generous interest, "you little know Louis de St. Vèran if you believe him capable of profiting by this letter to humble brave men, or to build up a dishonest reputation for himself. Listen to my terms before you leave me".

"What says the Frenchman"? demanded the veteran, sternly; "does he make a merit of having captured a scout, with a note from headquarters? Sir, he had better raise this siege, to go and sit down before Edward if he wishes to frighten his enemy with words".

Duncan explained the other's meaning.

"Monsieur de Montcalm, we will hear you", the veteran added, more calmly, as Duncan ended.

"To retain the fort is now impossible", said his liberal enemy; "it is necessary to the interests of my master that it should be destroyed; but as for yourselves and your brave comrades, there is no privilege dear to a soldier that shall be denied".

"Our colors"? demanded Heyward.

"Carry them to England, and show them to your king".

"Our arms"?

"Keep them; none can use them better".

"Our march; the surrender of the place"?

"Shall all be done in a way most honorable to yourselves".

Duncan now turned to explain these proposals to his commander, who heard him with amazement, and a sensibility that was deeply touched by so unusual and unexpected generosity.

"Go you, Duncan", he said; "go with this marquess, as, indeed, marquess he should be; go to his marquee and arrange it all. I have lived to see two things in my old age that never did I expect to behold. An Englishman afraid to support a friend, and a Frenchman too honest to profit by his advantage".

So saying, the veteran again dropped his head to his chest, and returned slowly toward the fort, exhibiting, by the dejection of his air, to the anxious garrison, a harbinger of evil tidings.

From the shock of this unexpected blow the haughty feelings of Munro never recovered; but from that moment there commenced a change in his determined character, which accompanied him to a speedy grave. Duncan remained to settle the terms of the capitulation. He was seen to re-enter the works during the first watches of the night, and immediately after a private conference with the commandant, to leave them again. It was then openly announced that hostilities must cease -Munro having signed a treaty by which the place was to be yielded to the enemy, with the morning; the garrison to retain their arms, the colors and their baggage, and, consequently, according to military opinion, their honor.

* * * * *

The hostile armies, which lay in the wilds of the Horican, passed the night of the ninth of August, 1757, much in the manner they would, had they encountered on the fairest field of Europe. While the conquered were still, sullen, and dejected, the victors triumphed. But there are limits alike to grief and joy; and long before the watches of the morning came the stillness of those boundless woods was only broken by a gay call from some exulting young Frenchman of the advanced pickets, or a menacing challenge from the fort, which sternly forbade the approach of any hostile footsteps before the stipulated moment. Even these occasional threatening sounds ceased to be heard in that dull hour which precedes the day, at which period a listener might have sought in vain any evidence of the presence of those armed powers that then slumbered on the shores of the "holy lake".

It was during these moments of deep silence that the canvas which concealed the entrance to a spacious marquee in the French encampment was shoved aside, and a man issued from beneath the drapery into the open air. He was enveloped in a cloak that might have been intended as a protection from the chilling damps of the woods, but which served equally well as a mantle to conceal his person. He was permitted to pass the grenadier, who watched over the slumbers of the French commander, without interruption, the man making the usual salute which betokens military deference, as the other passed swiftly through the little city of tents, in the direction of William Henry. Whenever this unknown individual encountered one of the numberless sentinels who crossed his path, his answer was prompt, and, as it appeared, satisfactory; for he was uniformly allowed to proceed without further interrogation.

With the exception of such repeated but brief interruptions, he had moved silently from the center of the camp to its most advanced outposts, when he drew nigh the soldier who held his watch nearest to the works of the enemy. As he approached he was received with the usual challenge:

"Qui vive"?

"France", was the reply. "Le mot d'ordre"?

"La victorie", said the other, drawing so nigh as to be heard in a loud whisper.

"C'est bien", returned the sentinel, throwing his musket from the charge to his shoulder; "vous promenez bien matin, monsieur"!

"Il est nécessaire d'être vigilant, mon enfant", the other observed, dropping a fold of his cloak, and looking the soldier close in the face as he passed him, still continuing his way toward the British fortification. The man started; his arms rattled heavily as he threw them forward in the lowest and most respectful salute; and when he had again recovered his piece, he turned to walk his post, muttering between his teeth:

"Il faut être vigilant, en vérité! je crois que nous avons là, un caporal qui ne dort jamais"!

The officer proceeded, without affecting to hear the words which escaped the sentinel in his surprise; nor did he again pause until he had reached the low strand, and in a somewhat dangerous vicinity to the western water bastion of the fort. The light of an obscure moon was just sufficient to render objects, though dim, perceptible in their outlines. He, therefore, took the precaution to place himself against the trunk of a tree, where he leaned for many minutes, and seemed to contemplate the dark and silent mounds of the English works in profound attention. His gaze at the ramparts was not that of a curious or idle spectator; but his looks wandered from point to point, denoting his knowledge of military usages, and betraying that his search was not unaccompanied by distrust. At length he appeared satisfied; and having cast his eyes impatiently upward toward the summit of the eastern mountain, as if anticipating the approach of the morning, he was in the act of turning on his footsteps, when a light sound on the nearest angle of the bastion caught his ear, and induced him to remain.

Just then a figure was seen to approach the edge of the rampart, where it stood, apparently contemplating in its turn the distant tents of the French encampment. Its head was then turned toward the east, as though equally anxious for the appearance of light, when the form leaned against the mound, and seemed to gaze upon the glassy expanse of the waters, which, like a submarine firmament, glittered with its thousand mimic stars. The melancholy air, the hour, together with the vast frame of the man who thus leaned, musing, against the English ramparts, left no doubt as to his person in the mind of the observant spectator. Delicacy, no less than prudence, now urged him to retire; and he had moved cautiously round the body of the tree for that purpose, when another sound drew his attention, and once more arrested his footsteps. It was a low and almost inaudible movement of the water, and was succeeded by a grating of pebbles one against the other. In a moment he saw a dark form rise, as it were, out of the lake, and steal without further noise to the land, within a few feet of the place where he himself stood. A rifle next slowly rose between his eyes and the watery mirror; but before it could be discharged his own hand was on the lock.

"Hugh"! exclaimed the savage, whose treacherous aim was so singularly and so unexpectedly interrupted.

Without making any reply, the French officer laid his hand on the shoulder of the Indian, and led him in profound silence to a distance from the spot, where their subsequent dialogue might have proved dangerous, and where it seemed that one of them, at least, sought a victim. Then throwing open his cloak, so as to expose his uniform and the cross of St. Louis which was suspended at his breast, Montcalm sternly demanded:

"What means this? Does not my son know that the hatchet is buried between the English and his Canadian Father"?

"What can the Hurons do"? returned the savage, speaking also, though imperfectly, in the French language.

"Not a warrior has a scalp, and the pale faces make friends"!

"Ha, Le Renard Subtil! Methinks this is an excess of zeal for a friend who was so late an enemy! How many suns have set since Le Renard struck the war-post of the English"?

"Where is that sun"? demanded the sullen savage. "Behind the hill; and it is dark and cold. But when he comes again, it will be bright and warm. Le Subtil is the sun of his tribe. There have been clouds, and many mountains between him and his nation; but now he shines and it is a clear sky"!

"That Le Renard has power with his people, I well know", said Montcalm; "for yesterday he hunted for their scalps, and to-day they hear him at the council-fire".

"Magua is a great chief".

"Let him prove it, by teaching his nation how to conduct themselves toward our new friends".

"Why did the chief of the Canadas bring his young men into the woods, and fire his cannon at the earthen house"? demanded the subtle Indian.

"To subdue it. My master owns the land, and your father was ordered to drive off these English squatters. They have consented to go, and now he calls them enemies no longer".

"Tis well. Magua took the hatchet to color it with blood. It is now bright; when it is red, it shall be buried".

"But Magua is pledged not to sully the lilies of France. The enemies of the great king across the salt lake are his enemies; his friends, the friends of the Hurons".

"Friends"! repeated the Indian in scorn. "Let his father give Magua a hand".

Montcalm, who felt that his influence over the warlike tribes he had gathered was to be maintained by concession rather than by power, complied reluctantly with the other's request. The savage placed the fingers of the French commander on a deep scar in his bosom, and then exultingly demanded:

"Does my father know that"?

"What warrior does not? 'Tis where a leaden bullet has cut".

"And this"? continued the Indian, who had turned his naked back to the other, his body being without its usual calico mantle.

"This! -my son has been sadly injured here; who has done this"?

"Magua slept hard in the English wigwams, and the sticks have left their mark", returned the savage, with a hollow laugh, which did not conceal the fierce temper that nearly choked him. Then, recollecting himself, with sudden and native dignity, he added: "Go; teach your young men it is peace. Le Renard Subtil knows how to speak to a Huron warrior".

Without deigning to bestow further words, or to wait for any answer, the savage cast his rifle into the hollow of his arm, and moved silently through the encampment toward the woods where his own tribe was known to lie. Every few yards as he proceeded he was challenged by the sentinels; but he stalked sullenly onward, utterly disregarding the summons of the soldiers, who only spared his life because they knew the air and tread no less than the obstinate daring of an Indian.

Montcalm lingered long and melancholy on the strand where he had been left by his companion, brooding deeply on the temper which his ungovernable ally had just discovered. Already had his fair fame been tarnished by one horrid scene, and in circumstances fearfully resembling those under which he how found himself. As he mused he became keenly sensible of the deep responsibility they assume who disregard the means to attain the end, and of all the danger of setting in motion an engine which it exceeds human power to control. Then shaking off a train of reflections that he accounted a weakness in such a moment of triumph, he retraced his steps toward his tent, giving the order as he passed to make the signal that should arouse the army from its slumbers.

The first tap of the French drums was echoed from the bosom of the fort, and presently the valley was filled with the strains of martial music, rising long, thrilling and lively above the rattling accompaniment. The horns of the victors sounded merry and cheerful flourishes, until the last laggard of the camp was at his post; but the instant the British fifes had blown their shrill signal, they became mute. In the meantime the day had dawned, and when the line of the French army was ready to receive its general, the rays of a brilliant sun were glancing along the glittering array. Then that success, which was already so well known, was officially announced; the favored band who were selected to guard the gates of the fort were detailed, and defiled before their chief; the signal of their approach was given, and all the usual preparations for a change of masters were ordered and executed directly under the guns of the contested works.

A very different scene presented itself within the lines of the Anglo-American army. As soon as the warning signal was given, it exhibited all the signs of a hurried and forced departure. The sullen soldiers shouldered their empty tubes and fell into their places, like men whose blood had been heated by the past contest, and who only desired the opportunity to revenge an indignity which was still wounding to their pride, concealed as it was under the observances of military etiquette.

Women and children ran from place to place, some bearing the scanty remnants of their baggage, and others searching in the ranks for those countenances they looked up to for protection.

Munro appeared among his silent troops firm but dejected. It was evident that the unexpected blow had struck deep into his heart, though he struggled to sustain his misfortune with the port of a man.

Duncan was touched at the quiet and impressive exhibition of his grief. He had discharged his own duty, and he now pressed to the side of the old man, to know in what particular he might serve him.

"My daughters", was the brief but expressive reply.

"Good heavens! are not arrangements already made for their convenience"?

"To-day I am only a soldier, Major Heyward", said the veteran. "All that you see here, claim alike to be my children".

Duncan had heard enough. Without losing one of those moments which had now become so precious, he flew toward the quarters of Munro, in quest of the sisters. He found them on the threshold of the low edifice, already prepared to depart, and surrounded by a clamorous and weeping assemblage of their own sex, that had gathered about the place, with a sort of instinctive consciousness that it was the point most likely to be protected. Though the cheeks of Cora were pale and her countenance anxious, she had lost none of her firmness; but the eyes of Alice were inflamed, and betrayedhow long and bitterly she had wept. They both, however, received the young man with undisguised pleasure; the former, for a novelty, being the first to speak.

"The fort is lost", she said, with a melancholy smile; "though our good name, I trust, remains".

"Tis brighter than ever. But, dearest Miss Munro, it is time to think less of others, and to make some provision for yourself. Military usage -pride -that pride on which you so much value yourself, demands that your father and I should for a little while continue with the troops. Then where to seek a proper protector for you against the confusion and chances of such a scene"?

"None is necessary", returned Cora; "who will dare to injure or insult the daughter of such a father, at a time like this"?

"I would not leave you alone", continued the youth, looking about him in a hurried manner, "for the command of the best regiment in the pay of the king. Remember, our Alice is not gifted with all your firmness, and God only knows the terror she might endure".

"You may be right", Cora replied, smiling again, but far more sadly than before. "Listen! chance has already sent us a friend when he is most needed".

Duncan did listen, and on the instant comprehended her meaning. The low and serious sounds of the sacred music, so well known to the eastern provinces, caught his ear, and instantly drew him to an apartment in an adjacent building, which had already been deserted by its customary tenants. There he found David, pouring out his pious feelings through the only medium in which he ever indulged. Duncan waited, until, by the cessation of the movement of the hand, he believed the strain was ended, when, by touching his shoulder, he drew the attention of the other to himself, and in a few words explained his wishes.

"Even so", replied the single-minded disciple of the King of Israel, when the young man had ended; "I have found much that is comely and melodious in the maidens, and it is fitting that we who have consorted in so much peril, should abide together in peace. I will attend them, when I have completed my morning praise, to which nothing is now wanting but the doxology. Wilt thou bear a part, friend? The meter is common, and the tune "Southwell".

Then, extending the little volume, and giving the pitch of the air anew with considerate attention, David recommenced and finished his strains, with a fixedness of manner that it was not easy to interrupt. Heyward was fain to wait until the verse ws ended; when, seeing David relieving himself from the spectacles, and replacing the book, he continued.

"It will be your duty to see that none dare to approach the ladies with any rude intention, or to offer insult or taunt at the misfortune of their brave father. In this task you will be seconded by the domestics of their household".

"Even so".

"It is possible that the Indians and stragglers of the enemy may intrude, in which case you will remind them of the terms of the capitulation, and threaten to report their conduct to Montcalm. A word will suffice".

"If not, I have that here which shall", returned David, exhibiting his book, with an air in which meekness and confidence were singularly blended. Here are words which, uttered, or rather thundered, with proper emphasis, and in measured time, shall quiet the most unruly temper:

"Why rage the heathen furiously?"

"Enough", said Heyward, interrupting the burst of his musical invocation; "we understand each other; it is time that we should now assume our respective duties".

Gamut cheerfully assented, and together they sought the females. Cora received her new and somewhat extraordinary protector courteously, at least; and even the pallid features of Alice lighted again with some of their native archness as she thanked Heyward for his care. Duncan took occasion to assure them he had done the best that circumstances permitted, and, as he believed, quite enough for the security of their feelings; of danger there was none. He then spoke gladly of his intention to rejoin them the moment he had led the advance a few miles toward the Hudson, and immediately took his leave.

By this time the signal for departure had been given, and the head of the English column was in motion. The sisters started at the sound, and glancing their eyes around, they saw the white uniforms of the French grenadiers, who had already taken possession of the gates of the fort. At that moment an enormous cloud seemed to pass suddenly above their heads, and, looking upward, they discovered that they stood beneath the wide folds of the standard of France.

"Let us go", said Cora; "this is no longer a fit place for the children of an English officer".

Alice clung to the arm of her sister, and together they left the parade, accompanied by the moving throng that surrounded them.

As they passed the gates, the French officers, who had learned their rank, bowed often and low, forbearing, however, to intrude those attentions which they saw, with peculiar tact, might not be agreeable. As every vehicle and each beast of burden was occupied by the sick and wounded, Cora had decided to endure the fatigues of a foot march, rather than interfere with their comforts. Indeed, many a maimed and feeble soldier was compelled to drag his exhausted limbs in the rear of the columns, for the want of the necessary means of conveyance in that wilderness. The whole, however, was in motion; the weak and wounded, groaning and in suffering; their comrades silent and sullen; and the women and children in terror, they knew not of what.

As the confused and timid throng left the protecting mounds of the fort, and issued on the open plain, the whole scene was at once presented to their eyes. At a little distance on the right, and somewhat in the rear, the French army stood to their arms, Montcalm having collected his parties, so soon as his guards had possession of the works. They were attentive but silent observers of the proceedings of the vanquished, failing in none of the stipulated military honors, and offering no taunt or insult, in their success, to their less fortunate foes. Living masses of the English, to the amount, in the whole, of near three thousand, were moving slowly across the plain,toward the common center, and gradually approached each other, as they converged to the point of their march, a vista cut through the lofty trees, where the road to the Hudson entered the forest. Along the sweeping borders of the woods hung a dark cloud of savages, eyeing the passage of their enemies, and hovering at a distance, like vultures who were only kept from swooping on their prey by the presence and restraint of a superior army. A few had straggled among the conquered columns, where they stalked in sullen discontent; attentive, though, as yet, passive observers of the moving multitude.

The advance, with Heyward at its head, had already reached the defile, and was slowly disappearing, when the attention of Cora was drawn to a collection of stragglers by the sounds of contention. A truant provincial was paying the forfeit of his disobedience, by being plundered of those very effects which had caused him to desert his place in the ranks. The man was of powerful frame, and too avaricious to part with his goods without a struggle. Individuals from either party interfered; the one side to prevent and the other to aid in the robbery. Voices grew loud and angry, and a hundred savages appeared, as it were, by magic, where a dozen only had been seen a minute before. It was then that Cora saw the form of Magua gliding among his countrymen, and speaking with his fatal and artful eloquence. The mass of women and children stopped, and hovered together like alarmed and fluttering birds. But the cupidity of the Indian was soon gratified, and the different bodies again moved slowly onward.

The savages now fell back, and seemed content to let their enemies advance without further molestation. But, as the female crowd approached them, the gaudy colors of a shawl attracted the eyes of a wild and untutored Huron. He advanced to seize it without the least hesitation. The woman, more in terror than through love of the ornament, wrapped her child in the coveted article, and folded both more closely to her bosom. Cora was in the act of speaking, with an intent to advise the woman to abandon the trifle, when the savage relinquished his hold of the shawl, and tore the screaming infant from her arms. Abandoning everything to the greedy grasp of those around her, the mother darted, with distraction in her mien, to reclaim her child. The Indian smiled grimly, and extended one hand, in sign of a willingness to exchange, while, with the other, he flourished the babe over his head, holding it by the feet as if to enhance the value of the ransom.

"Here -here -there -all -any -everything"! exclaimed the breathless woman, tearing the lighter articles of dress from her person with ill-directed and trembling fingers; "take all, but give me my babe"!

The savage spurned the worthless rags, and perceiving that the shawl had already become a prize to another, his bantering but sullen smile changing to a gleam of ferocity, he dashed the head of the infant against a rock, and cast its quivering remains to her very feet. For an instant the mother stood, like a statue of despair, looking wildly down at the unseemly object, which had so lately nestled in her bosom and smiled in her face; and then she raised her eyes and countenance toward heaven, as if calling on God to curse the perpetrator of the foul deed. She was spared the sin of such a prayer for, maddened at his disappointment, and excited at the sight of blood, the Huron mercifully drove his tomahawk into her own brain. The mother sank under the blow, and fell, grasping at her child, in death, with the same engrossing love that had caused her to cherish it when living.

At that dangerous moment, Magua placed his hands to his mouth, and raised the fatal and appalling whoop. The scattered Indians started at the well-known cry, as coursers bound at the signal to quit the goal; and directly there arose such a yell along the plain, and through the arches of the wood, as seldom burst from human lips before. They who heard it listened with a curdling horror at the heart, little inferior to that dread which may be expected to attend the blasts of the final summons.

More than two thousand raving savages broke from the forest at the signal, and threw themselves across the fatal plain with instinctive alacrity. We shall not dwell on the revolting horrors that succeeded. Death was everywhere, and in his most terrific and disgusting aspects. Resistance only served to inflame the murderers, who inflicted their furious blows long after their victims were beyond the power of their resentment. The flow of blood might be likened to the outbreaking of a torrent; and as the natives became heated and maddened by the sight, many among them even kneeled to the earth, and drank freely, exultingly, hellishly, of the crimson tide.

The trained bodies of the troops threw themselves quickly into solid masses, endeavoring to awe their assailants by the imposing appearance of a military front. The experiment in some measure succeeded, though far too many suffered their unloaded muskets to be torn from their hands, in the vain hope of appeasing the savages.

In such a scene none had leisure to note the fleeting moments. It might have been ten minutes (it seemed an age) that the sisters had stood riveted to one spot, horror-stricken and nearly helpless. When the first blow was struck, their screaming companions had pressed upon them in a body, rendering flight impossible; and now that fear or death had scattered most, if not all, from around them, they saw no avenue open, but such as conducted to the tomahawks of their foes. On every side arose shrieks, groans, exhortations and curses. At this moment, Alice caught a glimpse of the vast form of her father, moving rapidly across the plain, in the direction of the French army. He was, in truth, proceeding to Montcalm, fearless of every danger, to claim the tardy escort for which he had before conditioned. Fifty glittering axes and barbed spears were offered unheeded at his life, but the savages respected his rank and calmness, even in their fury. The dangerous weapons were brushed aside by the still nervous arm of the veteran, or fell of themselves, after menacing an act that it would seem no one had courage to perform. Fortunately, the vindictive Magua was searching for his victim in the very band the veteran hd just quitted.

"Father -father -we are here"! shrieked Alice, as he passed, at no great distance, without appearing to heed them. "Come to us, father, or we die"!

The cry was repeated, and in terms and tones that might have melted a heart of stone, but it was unanswered. Once, indeed, the old man appeared to catch the sound, for he paused and listened; but Alice had dropped senseless on the earth, and Cora had sunk at her side, hovering in untiring tenderness over her lifeless form. Munro shook his head in disappointment, and proceeded, bent on the high duty of his station.

"Lady", said Gamut, who, helpless and useless as he was, had not yet dreamed of deserting his trust, "it is the jubilee of the devils, and this is not a meet place for Christians to tarry in. Let us up and fly".

"Go", said Cora, still gazing at her unconscious sister; "save thyself. To me thou canst not be of further use".

David comprehended the unyielding character of her resolution, by the simple but expressive gesture that accompanied her words. He gazed for a moment at the dusky forms that were acting their hellish rites on every side of him, and his tall person grew more erect while his chest heaved, and every feature swelled, and seemed to speak with the power of the feelings by which he was governed.

"If the Jewish boy might tame the great spirit of Saul by the sound of his harp, and the words of sacred song, it may not be amiss", he said, "to try the potency of music here".

Then raising his voice to its highest tone, he poured out a strain so powerful as to be heard even amid the din of that bloody field. More than one savage rushed toward them, thinking to rifle the unprotected sisters of their attire, and bear away their scalps; but when they found this strange and unmoved figure riveted to his post, they paused to listen. Astonishment soon changed to admiration, and they passed on to other and less courageous victims, openly expressing their satisfaction at the firmness with which the white warrior sang his death song. Encouraged and deluded by his success, David exerted all his powers to extend what he believed so holy an influence. The unwonted sounds caught the ears of a distant savage, who flew raging from group to group, like one who, scorning to touch the vulgar herd, hunted for some victim more worthy of his renown. It was Magua, who uttered a yell of pleasure when he beheld his ancient prisoners again at his mercy.

"Come", he said, laying his soiled hands on the dress of Cora, "the wigwam of the Huron is still open. Is it not better than this place"?

"Away"! cried Cora, veiling her eyes from his revolting aspect.

The Indian laughed tauntingly, as he held up his reeking hand, and answered: "It is red, but it comes from white veins"!

"Monster! there is blood, oceans of blood, upon thy soul; thy spirit has moved this scene".

"Magua is a great chief"! returned the exulting savage, "will the dark-hair go to his tribe"?

"Never! strike if thou wilt, and complete thy revenge". He hesitated a moment, and then catching the light and senseless form of Alice in his arms, the subtle Indian moved swiftly across the plain toward the woods.

"Hold"! shrieked Cora, following wildly on his footsteps; "release the child! wretch! what is't you do"?

But Magua was deaf to her voice; or, rather, he knew his power, and was determined to maintain it.

"Stay -lady -stay", called Gamut, after the unconscious Cora. "The holy charm is beginning to be felt, and soon shalt thou see this horrid tumult stilled".

Perceiving that, in his turn, he was unheeded, the faithful David followed the distracted sister, raising his voice again in sacred song, and sweeping the air to the measure, with his long arm, in diligent accompaniment, in this manner they traversed the plain, through the flying, the wounded and the dead. The fierce Huron was, at any time, sufficient for himself and the victim that he bore; though Cora would have fallen more than once under the blows of her savage enemies, but for the extraordinary being who stalked in her rear, and who now appeared to the astonished natives gifted with the protecting spirit of madness.

Magua, who knew how to avoid the more pressing dangers, and also to elude pursuit, entered the woods through a low ravine, where he quickly found the Narragansetts, which the travelers had abandoned so shortly before, awaiting his appearance, in custody of a savage as fierce and malign in his expression as himself. Laying Alice on one of the horses, he made a sign to Cora to mount the other.

Notwithstanding the horror excited by the presence of her captor, there was a present relief in escaping from the bloody scene enacting on the plain, to which Cora could not be altogether insensible. She took her seat, and held forth her arms for her sister, with an air of entreaty and love that even the Huron could not deny. Placing Alice, then, on the same animal with Cora, he seized the bridle, and commenced his route by plunging deeper into the forest. David, perceiving that he was left alone, utterly disregarded as a subject too worthless even to destroy, threw his long limb across the saddle of the beast they had deserted, and made such progress in the pursuit as the difficulties of the path permitted.

They soon began to ascend; but as the motion had a tendency to revive the dormant faculties of her sister, the attention of Cora was too much divided between the tenderest solicitude in her behalf, and in listening to the cries which were still too audible on the plain, to note the direction in which they journeyed. When, however, they gained the flattened surface of the mountain-top, and approached the eastern precipice, she recognized the spot to which she had once before been led under the more friendly auspices of the scout. Here Magua suffered them to dismount; and notwithstanding their own captivity, the curiosity which seems inseparable from horror, induced them to gaze at the sickening sight below.

The cruel work was still unchecked. On every side the captured were flying before their relentless persecutors, while the armed columns of the Christian king stood fast in an apathy which has never been explained, and which has left an immovable blot on the otherwise fair escutcheon of their leader. Nor was the sword of death stayed until cupidity got the mastery of revenge. Then, indeed, the shrieks of the wounded, and the yells of their murderers grew less frequent, until, finally, the cries of horror were lost to their ear, or were drowned in the loud, long and piercing whoops of the triumphant savages.

PARTISAN WAR

FAANCIS PARKMAN, JR.

Shirley's grand scheme for cutting New France in twain had come to wreck. There was an element of boyishness in him. He made bold plans without weighing too closely his means of executing them. The year's campaign would in all likelihood have succeeded if he could have acted promptly; if he had had ready to his hand a well-trained and well-officered force, furnished with material of war and means of transportation, and prepared to move as soon as the streams and lakes of New York were open, while those of Canada were still sealed with ice. But timely action was out of his power. The army that should have moved in April was not ready to move till August. Of the nine discordant semi-republics whom he asked to join in the work, three or four refused, some of the others were lukewarm, and all were slow. Even Massachusetts, usually the foremost, failed to get all her men into the field till the season was nearly ended. Having no military establishment, the colonies were forced to improvise a new army for every campaign. Each of them watched its neighbors, or, jealous lest it should do more than its just share, waited for them to begin. Each popular assembly acted under the eye of a frugal constituency, who, having little money, were as chary of it as their descendants are lavish; and most of them were shaken by internal conflicts, more absorbing than the great question on which hung the fate of the continent. Only the four New England colonies were fully earnest for the war, and one, even of these, was ready to use the crisis as a means of extorting concessions from its Governor in return for grants of money and men. When the lagging contingents came together at last, under a commander whom none of them trusted, they were met by strategical difficulties which would have perplexed older soldiers and an abler general; for they were forced to act on the circumference of a vast semicircle, in a labyrinth of forests, without roads, and choked with every kind of obstruction.

Opposed to them was a trained army, well organized and commanded, focused at Montreal, and moving for attack or defence on two radiating lines,—one towards Lake Ontario, and the other towards Lake Champlain,—supported by a martial peasantry, supplied from France with money and material, dependent on no popular vote, having no will but that of its chief, and ready on the instant to strike to right or left as the need required. It was a compact military absolutism confronting a heterogeneous group of industrial democracies, where the force of numbers was neutralized by diffusion and incoherence. A long and dismal apprenticeship waited them before they could hope for success; nor could they ever put forth their full strength without a radical change of political conditions and an awakened consciousness of common interests and a common cause. It was the sense of powerlessness arising from the want of union that, after the fall of Oswego, spread alarm through the northern and middle colonies, and drew these desponding words from William Livingston, of New Jersey: "The colonies are nearly exhausted, and their funds already anticipated by expensive unexecuted projects. Jealous are they of each other; some ill-constituted, others shaken with intestine divisions, and, if I may be allowed the expression, parsimonious even to prodigality. Our assemblies are diffident of their governors, governors despise their assemblies; and both mutually misrepresent each other to the Court of Great Britain." Military measures, he proceeds, demand secrecy and despatch; but when so many divided provinces must agree to join in them, secrecy and despatch are impossible. In conclusion he exclaims: "Canada must be demolished,—*Delenda est Carthago*,—or we are undone." But Loudon was not Scipio, and cis-Atlantic Carthage was to stand for some time longer.

The Earl, in search of a scapegoat for the loss of Oswego, naturally chose Shirley, attacked him savagely, told him that he was of no use in America, and ordered him to go home to England without delay. Shirley, who was then in Boston, answered this indecency with dignity and effect. The chief fault was with Loudon himself, whose late arrival in America had caused a change of command and of plans in the crisis of the campaign. Shirley well knew the weakness of Oswego; and in early spring had sent two engineers to make it defensible, with particular instructions to strengthen Fort Ontario. But they, thinking that the chief danger lay on the west and south, turned all their attention thither, and neglected Ontario till it was too late. Shirley was about to reinforce Oswego with a strong body of troops when the arrival of Abercromby took the control out of his hands and caused ruinous delay. He cannot, however, be acquitted of mismanagement in failing to supply the place with wholesome provisions in the preceding autumn, before the streams were stopped with ice. Hence came the ravages of disease and famine which, before spring, reduced the garrison to a hundred and forty effective men. Yet there can be no doubt that the change of command was a blunder. This is the view of Franklin, who knew Shirley well, and thus speaks of him: "He would in my opinion, if continued in place, have made a much better campaign than that of Loudon, which was frivolous, expensive, and disgraceful to our nation beyond conception. For though Shirley was not bred a soldier, he was sensible and sagacious in himself, and attentive to good advice from others, capable of forming judicious plans, and quick and active in carrying them into execution." He sailed for England in the autumn, disappointed and poor; the bull-headed Duke of Cumberland had been deeply prejudiced against him, and it was only after long waiting that this strenuous champion of British interests was rewarded in his old age with the petty government of the Bahamas.

Loudon had now about ten thousand men at his command, though not all fit for duty. They were posted from Albany to Lake George. The Earl himself was at Fort Edward, while about three thousand of the provincials still lay, under Winslow, at the lake. Montcalm faced them at Ticonderoga, with five thousand three hundred regulars and Canadians, in a position where they could defy three times their number. "The sons of Belial are too strong for me," jocosely wrote Winslow; and he set himself to intrenching his camp; then had the forest cut down for the space of a mile from the lake to the mountains, so that the trees, lying in what he calls a "promiscuous manner," formed an almost impenetrable abatis. An escaped prisoner told him that the French were coming to visit him with fourteen thousand men; but Montcalm thought no more of stirring than Loudon himself; and each stood watching the other, with the lake between them, till the season closed.

Meanwhile the western borders were still ravaged by the tomahawk. New York, New Jersey, Pennsylvania, Maryland, and Virginia all writhed under the infliction. Each had made a chain of blockhouses and wooden forts to cover its frontier, and manned them with disorderly bands, lawless, and almost beyond control. The case was at the worst in Pennsylvania, where the tedious quarrelling of Governor and Assembly, joined to the doggedly pacific attitude of the Quakers, made vigorous defence impossible. Rewards were offered for prisoners and scalps, so bountiful that the hunting of men would have been a profitable vocation, but for the extreme wariness and agility of the game. Some of the forts were well-built stockades; others were almost worthless; but the enemy rarely molested even the feeblest of them, preferring to ravage the lonely and unprotected farms. There were two or three exceptions. A Virginian fort was attacked by a war-party under an officer named Douville, who was killed, and his followers were put to flight. The assailants were more fortunate at a small stockade called Fort Granville, on the juniata. A large body of French and Indians attacked it in August while most of the garrison were absent protecting the farmers at their harvest; they set it on fire, and, in spite of a most gallant resistance by the young lieutenant left in command, took it, and killed all but one of the defenders.

What sort of resistance the Pennsylvanian borderers would have made under political circumstances less adverse may be inferred from an exploit of Colonel John Armstrong, a settler of Cumberland. After the loss of Fort Granville the Governor of the province sent him with three hundred men to attack the Delaware town of Kittanning, a populous nest of savages on the Alleghany, between the two French posts of Duquesne and Venango. Here most of the war-parties were fitted out, and the place was full of stores and munitions furnished by the French. Here, too, lived the redoubted chief called Captain Jacobs, the terror of the English border. Armstrong set out from Fort Shirley, the farthest outpost, on the last of August, and, a week after, was within six miles of the Indian town. By rapid marching and rare good luck, his party had escaped discovery. It was ten o'clock at night, with a bright moon. The guides were perplexed, and knew neither the exact position of the place nor the paths that led to it. The adventurers threaded the forest in single file, over hills and through hollows, bewildered and anxious, stopping to watch and listen. At length they heard in the distance the beating of an Indian drum and the whooping of war-riors in the war-dance. Guided by the sounds, they cautiously moved forward, till those in the front, scrambling down a rocky hill, found themselves on the banks of the Alleghany, about a hundred rods below Kittanning. The moon was near setting; but they could dimly see the town beyond a great intervening field of corn. "At that moment," says Armstrong, "an Indian whistled in a very sin-gular manner, about thirty perches from our front, in the foot of the cornfield." He thought they were discovered; but one Baker, a soldier well versed in Indian ways, told him that it was only some village gallant calling to a young squaw. The party then crouched in the bushes, and kept silent. The moon sank behind the woods, and fires soon glimmered through the field, kindled to drive off mosquitoes by some of the Indians who, as the night was warm, had come out to sleep in the open air. The eastern sky began to redden with the approach of day. Many of the party, spent with a rough march of thirty miles, had fallen asleep. They were now cautiously roused; and Armstrong ordered nearly half of them to make their way along the ridge of a bushy hill that overlooked the town, till they came opposite to it, in order to place it between two fires. Twenty minutes were allowed them for the movement; but they lost their way in the dusk, and reached their station too late. When the time had expired, Armstrong gave the signal to those left with him, who dashed into the cornfield, shooting down the astonished savages or driving them into the village, where they turned and made desperate fight.

It was a cluster of thirty log-cabins, the principal being that of the chief, Jacobs, which was loopholed for musketry, and became the centre of resistance. The fight was hot and stubborn. Armstrong ordered the town to be set on fire, which was done, though not without loss; for the Delawares at this time were commonly armed with rifles, and used them well. Armstrong himself was hit in the shoulder. As the flames rose and the smoke grew thick, a warrior in one of the houses sang his death-song, and a squaw in the same house was heard to cry and scream. Rough voices silenced her, and then the inmates burst out, but were instantly killed. The fire caught the house of Jacobs, who, trying to escape through an opening in the roof, was shot dead. Bands of Indians were gathering beyond the river, firing from the other bank, and even crossing to help their comrades; but the assailants held to their work till the whole place was destroyed. "During the burning of the houses," says Armstrong, "we were agreeably entertained by the quick succession of charged guns, gradually firing off as reached by the fire; but much more so with the vast explosion of sundry bags and large kegs of gunpowder, wherewith almost every house abounded; the prisoners afterwards informing us that the Indians had frequently said they had a sufficient stock of ammunition for ten years' war with the English."

These prisoners were eleven men, women, and children, captured in the border settlements, and now delivered by their countrymen. The day was far spent when the party withdrew, carrying their wounded on Indian horses, and moving perforce with extreme slowness, though expecting an attack every moment. None took place; and they reached the settlements at last, having bought their success with the loss of seventeen killed and thirteen wounded. A medal was given to each officer, not by the Quaker-ridden Assembly, but by the city council of Philadelphia.

The report of this affair made by Dumas, commandant at Fort Duquesne, is worth noting. He says that Attiqué, the French name of Kittanning, was attacked by "le Général Wachinton," with three or four hundred men on horseback; that the Indians gave way; but that five or six Frenchmen who were in the town held the English in check till the fugitives rallied; that Washington and his men then took to flight, and would have been pursued but for the loss of some barrels of gunpowder which chanced to explode during the action. Dumas adds that several large parties are now on the track of the enemy, and he hopes will cut them to pieces. He then asks for a supply of provisions and merchandise to replace those which the Indians of Attiqué had lost by a fire. Like other officers of the day, he would admit nothing but successes in the department under his command.

Vaudreuil wrote singular despatches at this time to the minister at Versailles. He takes credit to himself for the number of war-parties that his officers kept always at work, and fills page after page with details of the *coups* they had struck; how one brought in two English scalps, another three, another one, and another seven. He owns that they committed frightful cruelties, mutilating and sometimes burning their prisoners; but he expresses no regret, and probably felt none, since he declares that the object of this murderous warfare was to punish the English till they longed for peace.

The waters and mountains of Lake George, and not the western borders, were the chief centre of partisan war. Ticonderoga was a hornet's nest, pouring out swarms of savages to infest the highways and byways of the wilderness. The English at Fort William Henry, having few Indians, could not retort in kind; but they kept their scouts and rangers in active movement. What they most coveted was prisoners, as sources of information. One Kennedy, a lieutenant of provincials, with five followers, white and red, made a march of rare audacity, passed all the French posts, took a scalp and two prisoners on the Richelieu, and ourned a magazine of provisions between Montreal and St. John. The party were near famishing on the way back; and Kennedy was brought into Fort William Henry in a state of temporary insanity from starvation. Other provinial officers, Peabody, Hazen, Waterbury, and Miller, won a certain distinction in this adventurous service, though few were so conspicuous as the blunt and Sturdy Israel Putnam. Winslow writes in October that he has just returned from the best "scout" yet made, and that, being a man of strict truth, he may be entirely trusted. Putnam had gone with six followers down Lake George in a whaleboat to a point on the east side, opposite the present village of Hague, hid the boat, crossed northeasterly to Lake Champlain, three miles from the French fort, climbed the mountain that overlooks it, and made a complete reconnoisjiance; then approached it, chased three Frenchmen, who escaped within the lines, climbed the mountain again, and moving westward along the ridge, made a minute survey of every outpost between the fort and Lake George. These aidventures were not always fortunate. On the nineteenth of September Captain Hodges and fifty men were ambushed a few miles from Fort William Henry by thrice their number of Canadians and Indians, and only six escaped. Chus the record stands in the *Letter Book* of Winslow. By visiting the encampments of Ticonderoga, one may learn how the blow was struck.

After much persuasion, much feasting, and much consumption of tobacco and brandy, four hundred Indians, Christians from the Missions and heathen from the far west, were persuaded to go on a grand war-party with the Canadians. Of these last there were a hundred,—a wild crew, bedecked and bedaubed like their Indian companions. Perière, an officer of colony regulars, had nominal command of the whole; and among the leaders of the Canadians was the famous bushfighter, Marin. Bougainville was also of the party. In the evening of the sixteenth they all embarked in canoes at the French advance-post commanded by Contrecœur, near the present steamboat-landing, passed in the gloom under the bare steeps of Rogers Rock, paddled a few hours, landed on the west shore, and sent scouts to reconnoitre. These came back with their reports on the next day, and an Indian crier called the chiefs to council. Bougainville describes them as they stalked gravely to the place of meeting, wrapped in colored blankets, with lances in their hands. The accomplished young aide-de-camp studied his strange companions with an interest not unmixed with disgust. "Of all caprice," he says, "Indian caprice is the most capricious." They were insolent to the French, made rules for them which they did not observe themselves, and compelled the whole party to move when and whither they pleased. Hiding the canoes, and lying close in the forest by day, they all held their nocturnal course southward, by the lofty heights of Black Mountain, and among the islets of the Narrows, till the eighteenth. That night the Indian scouts reported that they had seen the fires of an encampment on the west shore; on which the whole party advanced to the attack, an hour before dawn, filing silently under the dark arches of the forest, the Indians nearly naked, and streaked with their war-paint of vermilion and soot. When they reached the spot, they found only the smouldering fires of a deserted bivouac. Then there was a consultation; ending, after much dispute, with the choice by the Indians of a hundred and ten of their most active warriors to attempt some stroke in the neighborhood of the English fort. Marin joined them with thirty Canadians, and they set out on their errand; while the rest encamped to await the result. At night the adventurers returned, raising the death-cry and firing their guns; somewhat depressed by losses they had suffered, but boasting that they had surprised fifty-three English, and killed or taken all but one. It was a modest and perhaps an involuntary exaggeration. "The very recital of the cruelties they committed on the battle-field is horrible," writes Bougainville. "The ferocity and insolence of these black-souled barbarians makes one shudder. It is an abominable kind of war. The air one breathes is contagious of insensibility and hardness." This was but one of many such parties sent out from Ticon-deroga this year.

Early in September a band of New England rangers came to Winslow's camp, with three prisoners taken within the lines of Ticonderoga. Their captain was Robert Rogers, of New Hampshire,—a strong, well-knit figure, in dress and appearance more woodsman than soldier, with a clear, bold eye, and features that would have been good but for the ungainly proportions of the nose. He had passed his boyhood in the rough surroundings of a frontier village. Growing to manhood, he engaged in some occupation which, he says, led him to frequent journeyings in the wilderness between the French and English settlements, and gave him a good knowledge of both. It taught him also to speak a little French. He does not disclose the nature of this mysterious employment; but there can be little doubt that it was a smuggling trade with Canada. His character leaves much to be desired. He had been charged with forgery, or complicity in it, seems to have had no scruple in matters of business, and after the war was accused of treasonable dealings with the French and Spaniards in the west. He was ambitious and violent, yet able in more ways than one, by no means uneducated, and so skilled in woodcraft, so energetic and resolute, that his services were invaluable. In recounting his own adventures, his style is direct, simple, without boasting, and to all appearance without exaggeration. During the past summer he had raised a band of men, chiefly New Hampshire borderers, and made a series of daring excursions which gave him a prominent place in this hardy byplay of war. In the spring of the present year he raised another company, and was commissioned as its captain, with his brother Richard as his first lieutenant, and the intrepid John Stark as his second. In July still another company was formed, and Richard Rogers was promoted to command it. Before the following spring there were seven such; and more were afterwards added, forming a battalion dispersed on various service, but all under the orders of Robert Rogers, with the rank of major. These rangers wore a sort of woodland uniform, which varied in the different companies, and were armed with smooth-bore guns, loaded with buckshot, bullets, or sometimes both.

The best of them were commonly employed on Lake George; and nothing can surpass the adventurous hardihood of their lives. Summer and winter, day and night, were alike to them. Embarked in whaleboats or birch-canoes, they glided under the silent moon or in the languid glare of a breathless August day, when islands floated in dreamy haze, and the hot air was thick with odors of the pine; or in the bright October, when the jay screamed from the woods, squirrels gathered their winter hoard, and congregated blackbirds chattered farewell to their summer haunts; when gay mountains basked in light, maples dropped leaves of rustling gold, sumachs glowed like rubies under the dark green of the unchanging spruce, and mossed rocks with all their painted plumage lay double in the watery mirror: that festal evening of the year, when jocund Nature disrobes herself, to wake again refreshed in the joy of her undying spring. Or, in the tomb-like silence of the winter forest, with breath frozen on his beard, the ranger strode on snow-shoes over the spotless drifts; and, like Dürer's knight, a ghastly death stalked ever at his side. There were those among them for whom this stern life had a fascination that made all other existence tame.

Rogers and his men had been in active movement since midwinter. In January they skated down Lake George, passed Ticonderoga, hid themselves by the forest-road between that post and Crown Point, intercepted two sledges loaded with provisions, and carried the drivers to Fort William Henry. In February they climbed a hill near Crown Point and made a plan of the works; then lay in ambush by the road from the fort to the neighboring village, captured a prisoner, burned houses and barns, killed fifty cattle, and returned without loss. At the end of the month they went again to Crown Point, burned more houses and barns, and reconnoitred Ticonderoga on the way back. Such excursions were repeated throughout the spring and summer. The reconnoissance of Ticonderoga and the catching of prisoners there for the sake of information were always capital objects. The valley, four miles in extent, that lay between the foot of Lake George and the French fort, was at this time guarded by four distinct outposts or fortified camps. Watched as it was at all points, and ranged incessantly by Indians in the employ of France, Rogers and his men knew every yard of the ground. On a morning in May he lay in ambush with eleven followers on a path between the fort and the nearest camp. A large body of soldiers passed; the rangers counted a hundred and eighteen, and lay close in their hiding-place. Soon after came a party of twenty-two. They fired on them, killed six, captured one, and escaped with him to Fort William Henry. In October Rogers was passing with twenty men in two whaleboats through the seeming solitude of the Narrows when a voice called to them out of the woods. It was that of Captain Shepherd, of the New Hampshire regiment, who had been caprured two months before, and had lately made his escape. He told them that the French had the fullest information of the numbers and movements of the English; that letters often reached them from within the English lines; and that Lydius, a Dutch trader at Albany, was their principal correspondent. Arriving at Ticonderoga, Rogers cautiously approached the fort, till, about noon, he saw a sentinel on the road leading thence to the woods. Followed by five of his men, he walked directly towards him. The man challenged, and Rogers answered in French. Perplexed for a moment, the soldier suffered him to approach; till, seeing his mistake, he called out in amazement, "*Qui êtes vous?*" "Rogers," was the answer; and the sentinel was seized, led in hot haste to the boats, and carried to the English fort, where he gave important information.

An exploit of Rogers towards midsummer greatly perplexed the French. He embarked at the end of June with fifty men in five whaleboats, made light and strong, expressly for this service, rowed about ten miles down Lake George, landed on the east side, carried the boats six miles over a gorge of the mountains, launched them again in South Bay, and rowed down the narrow prolongation of Lake Champlain under cover of darkness. At dawn they were within six miles of Ticonderoga. They landed, hid their boats, and lay close all day. Embarking again in the evening, they rowed with muffled oars under the shadow of the eastern shore, and passed so close to the French fort that they heard the voices of the sentinels calling the watchword. In the morning they had left it five miles behind. Again they hid in the woods; and from their lurking-place saw bateaux passing, some northward, and some southward, along the narrow lake. Crown Point was ten or twelve miles farther on. They tried to pass it after nightfall, but the sky was too clear and the stars too bright; and as they lay hidden the next day, nearly a hundred boats passed before them on the way to Ticonderoga. Some other boats which appeared about noon landed near them, and they watched the soldiers at dinner, within a musket-shot of their lurking-place. The next night was more favorable. They embarked at nine in the evening, passed Crown Point unseen, and hid themselves as before, ten miles below. It was the seventh of July. Thirty boats and a schooner passed them, returning towards Canada. On the next night they rowed fifteen miles farther, and then sent men to reconnoitre, who reported a schooner at anchor about a mile off. They were preparing to board her, when two sloops appeared, coming up the lake at but a short distance from the land. They gave them a volley, and called on them to surrender; but the crews put off in boats and made for the opposite shore. They followed and seized them. Out of twelve men their fire had killed three and wounded two, one of whom, says Rogers in his report, "could not march, therefore we put an end to him, to prevent discovery." They sank the vessels, which were laden with wine, brandy, and flour, hid their boats on the west shore, and returned on foot with their prisoners.

Some weeks after, Rogers returned to the place where he had left the boats, embarked in them, reconnoitred the lake nearly to St. John, hid them again eight miles north of Crown Point, took three prisoners near that post, and carried them to Fort William Henry. In the next month the French found several English boats in a small cove north of Crown Point. Bougainville propounds five different hypotheses to account for their being there; and exploring parties were sent out in the vain attempt to find some water passage by which they could have reached the spot without passing under the guns of two French forts.

The French, on their side, still kept their war-parties in motion, and Vaudreuil faithfully chronicled in his despatches every English scalp they brought in. He believed in Indians, and sent them to Ticonderoga in numbers that were sometimes embarrassing. Even Pottawattamies from Lake Michigan were prowling about Winslow's camp and silently killing his sentinels with arrows, while their "medicine men" remained at Ticonderoga practising sorcery and divination to aid the warriors or learn how it fared with them. Bougainville writes in his Journal on the fifteenth of October: "Yesterday the old Pottawattamies who have stayed here 'made medicine' to get news of their brethren. The lodge trembled, the sorcerer sweated drops of blood, and the devil came at last and told him that the warriors would come back with scalps and prisoners. A sorcerer in the medicine lodge is exactly like the Pythoness on the tripod or the witch Canidia invoking the shades." The diviner was not wholly at fault. Three days after, the warriors came back with a prisoner.

Till November, the hostile forces continued to watch each other from the opposite ends of Lake George. Loudon repeated his orders to Winslow to keep the defensive, and wrote sarcastically to the Colonial Minister: "I think I shall be able to prevent the provincials doing anything very rash, without their having it in their power to talk in the language of this country that they could have taken all Canada if they had not been prevented by the King's servants." Winslow tried to console himself for the failure of the campaign, and wrote in his odd English to Shirley: "Am sorry that this year's performance has not succeeded as was intended; have only to say I pushed things to the utmost of my power to have been sooner in motion, which was the only thing that should have carried us to Crown Point; and though I am sensible that we are doing our duty in acting on the defensive, yet it makes no eclate [sic], and answers to little purpose in the eyes of my constituents."

On the first of the month the French began to move off towards Canada, and before many days Ticonderoga was left in the keeping of five or six companies. Winslow's men followed their example. Major Eyre, with four hundred regulars, took possession of Fort William Henry, and the provincials marched for home, their ranks thinned by camp diseases and small-pox. In Canada the regulars were quartered on the inhabitants, who took the infliction as a matter of course. In the English provinces the question was not so simple. Most of the British troops were assigned to Philadelphia, New York, and Boston; and Loudon demanded free quarters for them, according to usage then prevailing in England during war. Nor was the demand in itself unreasonable, seeing that the troops were sent over to fight the battles of the colonies. In Philadelphia lodgings were given them in the public-houses, which, however, could not hold them all. A long dispute followed between the Governor, who seconded Loudon's demand, and the Assembly, during which about half the soldiers lay on straw in outhouses and sheds till near midwinter, many sickening, and some dying from exposure. Loudon grew furious, and threatened, if shelter were not provided, to send Webb with another regiment and billet the whole on the inhabitants; on which the Assembly yielded, and quarters were found.

In New York the privates were quartered in barracks, but the officers were left to find lodging for themselves. Loudon demanded that provision should be made for them also. The city council hesitated, afraid of incensing the people if they complied. Cruger, the mayor, came to remonstrate. "God damn my blood!" replied the Earl; "if you do not billet my officers upon free quarters this day, I'll order here all the troops in North America, and billet them myself upon this city." Being no respecter of persons, at least in the provinces, he began with Oliver Delancey, brother of the late acting Governor, and sent six soldiers to lodge under his roof. Delancey swore at the unwelcome guests, on which Loudon sent him six more. A subscription was then raised among the citizens, and the required quarters were provided. In Boston there was for the present less trouble. The troops were lodged in the barracks of Castle William, and furnished with blankets, cooking utensils, and other necessaries.

Major Eyre and his soldiers, in their wilderness exile by the borders of Lake George, whiled the winter away with few other excitements than the evening howl of wolves from the frozen mountains, or some nocturnal savage shooting at a sentinel from behind a stump on the moonlit fields of snow. A livelier incident at last broke the monotony of their lives. In the middle of January Rogers came with his rangers from Fort Edward, bound on a scouting party towards Crown Point. They spent two days at Fort William Henry in making snow-shoes and other preparation, and set out on the seventeenth. Captain Spikeman was second in command, with Lieutenants Stark and Kennedy, several other subalterns, and two gentlemen volunteers enamoured of adventure. They marched down the frozen lake and encamped at the Narrows. Some of them, unaccustomed to snow-shoes, had become unfit for travel, and were sent back, thus reducing the number to seventy-four. In the morning they marched again, by icicled rocks and icebound waterfalls, mountains gray with naked woods and fir-trees bowed down with snow. On the nineteenth they reached the west shore, about four miles south of Rogers Rock, marched west of north eight miles, and bivouacked among the mountains. On the next morning they changed their course, marched east of north all day, passed Ticonderoga undiscovered, and stopped at night some five miles beyond it. The weather was changing, and rain was coming on. They scraped away the snow with their snow-shoes, piled it in a bank around them, made beds of spruce-boughs, built fires, and lay down to sleep, while the sentinels kept watch in the outer gloom. In the morning there was a drizzling rain, and the softened snow stuck to their snow-shoes. They marched eastward three miles through the dripping forest, till they reached the banks of

Lake Champlain, near what is now called Five Mile Point, and presently saw a sledge, drawn by horses, moving on the ice from Ticonderoga towards Crown Point. Rogers sent Stark along the shore to the left to head it off, while he with another party, covered by the woods, moved in the opposite direction to stop its retreat. He soon saw eight or ten more sledges following the first, and sent a messenger to prevent Stark from showing himself too soon; but Stark was already on the ice. All the sledges turned back in hot haste. The rangers ran in pursuit and captured three of them, with seven men and six horses, while the rest escaped to Ticonderoga. The prisoners, being separately examined, told an ominous tale. There were three hundred and fifty regulars at Ticonderoga; two hundred Canadians and forty-five Indians had lately arrived there, and more Indians were expected that evening,—all destined to waylay the communications between the English forts, and all prepared to march at a moment's notice. The rangers were now in great peril. The fugitives would give warning of their presence, and the French and Indians, in overwhelming force, would no doubt cut off their retreat.

Rogers at once ordered his men to return to their last night's encampment, rekindle the fires, and dry their guns, which were wet by the rain of the morning. Then they marched southward in single file through the snow-encumbered forest, Rogers and Kennedy in the front, Spikeman in the centre, and Stark in the rear. In this order they moved on over broken and difficult ground till two in the afternoon, when they came upon a valley, or hollow, scarcely a musket-shot wide, which ran across their line of march, and, like all the rest of the country, was buried in thick woods. The front of the line had descended the first hill, and was mounting that on the farther side, when the foremost men heard a low clicking sound, like the cocking of a great number of guns; and in an instant a furious volley blazed out of the bushes on the ridge above them. Kennedy was killed outright, as also was Gardner, one of the volunteers. Rogers was grazed in the head by a bullet, and others were disabled or hurt. The rest returned the fire, while a swarm of French and Indians rushed upon them from the ridge and the slopes on either hand, killing several more, Spikeman among the rest, and capturing others. The rangers fell back across the hollow and regained the hill they had just descended. Stark with the rear, who were at the top when the fray began, now kept the assailants in check by a brisk fire till their comrades joined them. Then the whole party, spreading themselves among the trees that covered the declivity, stubbornly held their ground and beat back the French in repeated attempts to dislodge them. As the assailants were more than two to one, what

Rogers had most to dread was a movement to outflank him and get into his rear. This they tried twice, and were twice repulsed by a party held in reserve for the purpose. The fight lasted several hours, during which there was much talk between the combatants. The French called out that it was a pity so many brave men should be lost, that large reinforcements were expected every moment, and that the rangers would then be cut to pieces without mercy; whereas if they surrendered at once they should be treated with the utmost kindness. They called to Rogers by name, and expressed great esteem for him. Neither threats nor promises had any effect, and the firing went on till darkness stopped it. Towards evening Rogers was shot through the wrist; and one of the men, John Shute, used to tell in his old age how he saw another ranger trying to bind the captain's wound with the ribbon of his own queue.

As Ticonderoga was but three miles off, it was destruction to stay where they were; and they withdrew under cover of night, reduced to forty-eight effective and six wounded men. Fourteen had been killed, and six captured. Those that were left reached Lake George in the morning, and Stark, with two followers, pushed on in advance to bring a sledge for the wounded. The rest made their way to the Narrows, where they encamped, and presently descried a small dark object on the ice far behind them. It proved to be one of their own number, Sergeant Joshua Martin, who had received a severe wound in the fight, and was left for dead; but by desperate efforts had followed on their tracks, and was now brought to camp in a state of exhaustion. He recovered, and lived to an advanced age. The sledge sent by Stark came in the morning, and the whole party soon reached the fort. Abercromby, on hearing of the affair, sent them a letter of thanks for gallant conduct.

Rogers reckons the number of his assailants at about two hundred and fifty in all. Vaudreuil says that they consisted of eighty-nine regulars and ninety Canadians and Indians. With his usual boastful exaggeration, he declares that forty English were left dead on the field, and that only three reached Fort William Henry alive. He says that the fight was extremely hot and obstinate, and admits that the French lost thirty-seven killed and wounded. Rogers makes the number much greater. That it was considerable is certain, as Lusignan, commandant at Ticonderoga, wrote immediately for reinforcements.

The effects of his wound and an attack of small-pox kept Rogers quiet for a time. Meanwhile the winter dragged slowly away, and the ice of Lake George, cracking with change of temperature, uttered its strange cry of agony, heralding that dismal season when winter begins to relax its gripe, but spring still holds aloof; when the sap stirs in the sugar-maples, but the buds refuse to swell, and even the catkins of the willows will not burst their brown integuments; when the forest is patched with snow, though on its sunny slopes one hears in the stillness the whisper of trickling waters that ooze from the half-thawed soil and saturated beds of fallen leaves; when clouds hang low on the darkened mountains, and cold mists entangle themselves in the tops of the pines; now a dull rain, now a sharp morning frost, and now a storm of snow powdering the waste, and wrapping it again in the pall of winter.

In this cheerless season, on St. Patrick's Day, the seventeenth of March, the Irish soldiers who formed a part of the garrison of Fort William Henry were paying homage to their patron saint in libations of heretic rum, the product of New England stills; and it is said that John Stark's rangers forgot theological differences in their zeal to share the festivity. The story adds that they were restrained by their commander, and that their enforced sobriety proved the saving of the fort. This may be doubted; for without counting the English soldiers of the garrison who had no special call to be drunk that day, the fort was in no danger till twenty-four hours after, when the revellers had had time to rally from their pious carouse. Whether rangers or British soldiers, it is certain that watchmen were on the alert during the night between the eighteenth and nineteenth, and that towards one in the morning they heard a sound of axes far down the lake, followed by the faint glow of a distant fire. The inference was plain, that an enemy was there, and that the necessity of warming himself had overcome his caution. Then all was still for some two hours, when, listening in the pitchy darkness, the watchers heard the footsteps of a great body of men approaching on the ice, which at the time was bare of snow. The garrison were at their posts, and all the cannon on the side towards the lake vomited grape and round-shot in the direction of the sound, which thereafter was heard no more.

Those who made it were a detachment, called by Vaudreuil an army, sent by him to seize the English fort. Shirley had planned a similar stroke against Ticonderoga a year before; but the provincial levies had come in so slowly, and the ice had broken up so soon, that the scheme was abandoned. Vaudreuil was more fortunate. The whole force, regulars, Canadians, and Indians, was ready to his hand. No pains were spared in equipping them. Overcoats, blankets, bearskins to sleep on, tarpaulins to sleep under, spare moccasons, spare mittens, kettles, axes, needles, awls, flint and steel, and many miscellaneous articles were provided, to be dragged by the men on light Indian sledges, along with provisions for twelve days. The cost of the expedition is set at a million francs, answering to more than as many dollars of the present time. To the disgust of the officers from France, the Governor named his brother Rigaud for the chief command; and before the end of February the whole party was on its march along the ice of Lake Champlain. They rested nearly a week at Ticonderoga, where no less than three hundred short scaling-ladders, so constructed that two or more could be joined in one, had been made for them; and here, too, they received a reinforcement, which raised their number to sixteen hundred. Then, marching three days along Lake George, they neared the fort on the evening of the eighteenth, and prepared for a general assault before daybreak.

The garrison, including rangers, consisted of three hundred and forty-six effective men. The fort was not strong, and a resolute assault by numbers so superior must, it seems, have overpowered the defenders; but the Canadians and Indians who composed most of the attacking force were not suited for such work; and, disappointed in his hope of a surprise, Rigaud withdrew them at daybreak, after trying in vain to burn the buildings outside. A few hours after, the whole body reappeared, filing off to surround the fort, on which they kept up a brisk but harmless fire of musketry. In the night they were heard again on the ice, approaching as if for an assault; and the cannon, firing towards the sound, again drove them back. There was silence for a while, till tongues of flame lighted up the gloom, and two sloops, ice-bound in the lake, and a large number of bateaux on the shore were seen to be on fire. A party sallied to save them; but it was too late. In the morning they were all consumed, and the enemy had vanished.

It was Sunday, the twentieth. Everything was quiet till noon, when the French filed out of the woods and marched across the ice in procession, ostentatiously carrying their scaling-ladders, and showing themselves to the best effect. They stopped at a safe distance, fronting towards the fort, and several of them advanced, waving a red flag. An officer with a few men went to meet them, and returned bringing Le Mercier, chief of the Canadian artillery, who, being led blindfold into the fort, announced himself as bearer of a message from Rigaud. He was conducted to the room of Major Eyre, where all the British officers were assembled; and, after mutual compliments, he invited them to give up the place peaceably, promising the most favorable terms, and threatening a general assault and massacre in case of refusal. Eyre said that he should defend himself to the last; and the envoy, again blindfolded, was led back to whence he came.

The whole French force now advanced as if to storm the works, and the garrison prepared to receive them. Nothing came of it but a fusillade, to which the British made no reply. At night the French were heard advancing again, and each man nerved himself for the crisis. The real attack, however, was not against the fort, but against the buildings outside, which consisted of several store-houses, a hospital, a saw-mill, and the huts of the rangers, besides a sloop on the stocks and piles of planks and cord-wood. Covered by the night, the assailants crept up with fagots of resinous sticks, placed them against the farther side of the buildings, kindled them, and escaped before the flame rose; while the garri-son, straining their ears in the thick darkness, fired wherever they heard a sound. Before morning all around them was in a blaze, and they had much ado to save the fort barracks from the shower of burning cinders. At ten o'clock the fires had subsided, and a thick fall of snow began, filling the air with a restless chaos of large moist flakes. This lasted all day and all the next night, till the ground and the ice were covered to a depth of three feet and more. The French lay close in their camps till a little before dawn on Tuesday morning, when twenty vol-unteers from the regulars made a bold attempt to burn the sloop on the stocks, with several storehouses and other structures, and several hundred scows and whaleboats which had thus far escaped. They were only in part successful; but they fired the sloop and some buildings near it, and stood far out on the ice watching the flaming vessel, a superb bonfire amid the wilderness of snow. The spectacle cost the volunteers a fourth of their number killed and wounded.

On Wednesday morning the sun rose bright on a scene of wintry splendor, and the frozen lake was dotted with Rigaud's retreating followers toiling towards Canada on snow-shoes. Before they reached it many of them were blinded for a while by the insufferable glare, and their comrades led them homewards by the hand.

CAMPAIGN OF 1778

J. P. MARTIN

As there was no cessation of duty in the army, I must commence another campaign as soon as the succeeding one is ended. There was no going home and spending the winter season among friends and procuring a new recruit of strength and spirits. No, it was one constant drill, summer and winter; like an old horse in a mill, it was a continual routine.

The first expedition I undertook in my new vocation was a foraging cruise. I was ordered off into the country in a party consisting of a corporal and six men. What our success was I do not now remember, but I will remember the transactions of the party in the latter part of the journey. We were returning to our quarters on Christmas afternoon, when we met three ladies, one a young married woman with an infant in her arms, the other two were maidens, for aught I knew then or since, they passed for such. They were all comely, particularly one of them; she was handsome. They immediately fell into familiar discourse with us, were very inquisitive like the rest of the sex, asked us a thousand questions respecting our business, where we had been and where going, &c. After we had satisfied their curiosity, or at least had endeavored to do so, they told us that they (that is, the two youngest) lived a little way on our road in a house which they described, desired us to call in and rest ourselves a few minutes, and said they would return as soon as they had seen their sister and babe safe home.

As for myself, I was very unwell, occasioned by a violent cold I had recently taken, and I was very glad to stop a short time to rest my bones. Accordingly, we stopped at the house described by the young ladies, and in a few minutes they returned as full of chat as they were when we met them in the road. After a little more information respecting our business, they proposed to us to visit one of their neighbors, against whom it seemed they had a grudge and upon whom they wished to wreak their vengeance through our agency. To oblige the ladies we undertook to obey their injunctions. They very readily agreed to be our guides as the way lay across fields and pastures full of bushes. The distance was about half a mile and directly out of our way to our quarters. The girls went with us until we came in sight of the house. We concluded we could do no less than fulfill our engagements with them; so we went into the house, the people of which appeared to be genuine Pennsylvania farmers and very fine folks.

We all now began to relent, and after telling them our business, we concluded that if they would give us a canteen (which held about a quart) full of whiskey and some bread and cheese, we would depart without any further exactions. To get rid of us, doubtless, the man of the house gave us our canteen of whiskey and the good woman gave us a fine loaf of wheaten flour bread and the whole of a small cheese, and we raised the siege and departed. I was several times afterwards at this house and was always well treated. I believe the people did not recollect me and I was glad they did not, for when I saw them I had always a twinge or two of conscience for thus dissembling with them at the instigation of persons who certainly were no better than they should be, or they would not have employed strangers to glut their vengeance upon innocent people, innocent at least as it respected us. But after, it turned much in their favor. It was in our power to take cattle or horses, hay, or any other produce from them, but we felt that we had done wrong in listening to the tattle of malicious neighbors and for that cause we refrained from meddling with any property of theirs ever after. So that good came to them out of intended evil.

After we had received our bread, cheese and whiskey, we struck across the fields into the highway again. It was now nearly sunset, and as soon as we had got into the road, the youngest of the girls, and handsomest and chattiest, overtook us again, riding on horseback with a gallant. As soon as she came up with us, "O here is my little Captain again," said she. (It appeared it was our corporal that attracted her attention.) "I am glad to see you again."

The young man, her sweetheart, did not seem to wish her to be quite so familiar with her "little Captain," and urged on his horse as fast as possible. But female policy is generally too subtle for the male's, and she exhibited a proof of it, for they had scarcely passed us when she slid from the horse upon her feet, into the road, with a shriek as though some frightful accident had happened to her. There was nothing handy to serve as a horse block, so the "little Captain" must take her in his arms and set her upon her horse again, much, I suppose, to their mutual satisfaction, but not so to her gallant, who, as I thought, looked rather glum.

We had now five miles to travel to reach our quarters, and was sick indeed, but we got to our home sometime in the evening, and I soon went to sleep; in the morning I was better.

When I was inoculated with the smallpox I took that delectable disease, the itch; it was given us, we supposed, in the infection. We had no opportunity, or, at least, we had nothing to cure ourselves with during the whole season. All who had the smallpox at Peekskill had it. We often applied to our officers for assistance to clear ourselves from it, but all we could get was, "Bear it as patiently as you can, when we get into winter quarters you will have leisure and means to rid yourselves of it." I had it to such a degree that by the time I got into winter quarters I could scarcely lift my hands to my head. Some of our foraging party had acquaintances in the artillery and by their means we procured sulphur enough to cure all that belonged to our detachment. Accordingly, we made preparations for a general attack upon it.

The first night one half of the party commenced the action by mixing a sufficient quantity, of brimstone and tallow, which was the only grease we could get, at the same time not forgetting to mix a plenty of hot whiskey toddy, making up a hot blazing fire and laying down an oxhide upon the hearth. Thus prepared with arms and ammunition, we began the operation by plying each other's outsides with brimstone and tallow and the inside with hot whiskey sling. Had the animalcule of the itch been endowed with reason they would have quit their entrenchments and taken care of themselves when we had made such a formidable attack upon them, but as it was we had to engage, arms in hand, and we obtained a complete victory, though it had like to have cost some of us our lives. Two of the assailants were so overcome, not by the enemy, but by their too great exertions in the action, that they lay all night naked upon the field. The rest of us got to our berths' somehow, as well as we could; but we killed the itch and we were satisfied, for it had almost killed us. This was a decisive victory, the only one we had achieved lately. The next night the other half of our men took their turn, but, taking warning by our mishaps, they conducted their part of the battle with comparatively little trouble or danger to what we had experienced on our part.

I shall not relate all the minute transactions which passed while I was on this foraging party, as it would swell my narrative to too large a size. I will, however, give the reader a brief account of some of my movements that I may not leave him entirely ignorant how I spent my time. We fared much better than I had ever done in the army before, or ever did afterwards. We had very good provisions all winter and generally enough of them. Some of us were constantly in the country with the wagons; we went out by turns and had no one to control us. Our lieutenant scarcely ever saw us or we him. Our sergeant never went out with us once, all the time we were there, nor our corporal *but* once, and that was when he was the "little Captain." When we were in the country we were pretty sure to fare well, for the inhabitants were remarkably kind to us. We had no guards to keep; our only duty was to help load the wagons with hay, corn, meal, or whatever they were to take off, and when they were thus loaded, to keep them company till they arrived at the commissary's, at Milltown; from thence the articles, whatever they were, were carried to camp in other vehicles under other guards.

I do not remember that during the time I was employed in this business, which was from Christmas to the latter part of April, even to have met with the least resistance from the inhabitants, take what we would from their barns, mills, corncribs, or stalls, but when we came to their stables, then look out for the women. Take what horse you would, it was one or the other's "pony" and they had no other to ride to church. And when we had got possession of a horse we were sure to have half a dozen or more women pressing upon us, until by some means or other, if possible, they would slip the bridle from the horse's head, and then we might catch him again if we could. They would take no more notice of a charged bayonet than a blind horse would of a cocked pistol. It would answer no purpose to threaten to kill them with the bayonet or musket; they knew as well as we did that we would not put our threats in execution, and when they had thus liberated a horse (which happened but seldom) they would laugh at us and ask us why we did not do as we threatened, kill them, and then they would generally ask us into their houses and treat us with as much kindness as though nothing had happened The women of Pennsylvania, taken in general, are certainly very worthy characters. It is but justice, as far as I am concerned, for me to say that I was always well treated both by them and the men, especially the Friends or Quakers, in every part of the state through which I passed, and that was the greater part of what was then inhabited. But the southern ladies had a queer idea of the Yankees (as they always called the New Englanders); they seemed to think that they were a people quite different from themselves, as indeed they were in many respects. I could mention things and ways in which they differed, but it is of no consequence; they were clever and that is sufficient. I will, however, men-tion one little incident, just to show what their conceptions were of us.

I happened once to be with some wagons, one of which was detached from the party. I went with this team as its guard. We stopped at a house, the mistress of which and the wagoner were acquainted. (These foraging teams all belonged in the neighborhood of our quarters.) She had a pretty female child about four years old. The teamster was praising the child, extolling its gentleness and quietness, when the mother observed that it had been quite cross and crying all day. "I have been threatening," said she, "to give her to the Yankees." "Take care," said the wagoner, "how you speak of the Yankees, I have one of them here with me." "La!" said the woman. "Is he a Yankee? I thought he was a Pennsylvanian. I don't see any difference between him and other people."

I have before said that I should not narrate all the little affairs which transpired while I was on this foraging party. But if I pass them all over in silence the reader may perhaps think that I had nothing to do all winter, or at least, that I *did* nothing, when in truth it was quite the reverse. Our duty was hard, but generally not altogether unpleasant. I had to travel far and near, in cold and in storms, by day and by night, and at all times to run the *risk* of abuse, if not of injury, from the inhabitants when *plundering* them of their property, for I could not, while in the very act of taking their cattle, hay, corn and grain from them against their wills, consider it a whit better than plundering—sheer privateering. But I will give them the credit of never receiving the least abuse or injury from an individual during the whole time I was employed in this business. I doubt whether the people of New England would have borne it as patiently, their "steady habits" to the contrary notwithstanding.

Being once in a party among the Welch mountains there came on a tedious rainstorm which continued three or four days. I happened to be at a farmer's house with one or two of the wagon masters. The man of the house was from home and the old lady rather crabbed; she knew our business and was therefore inclined to be *rather* unsociable. The first day she would not give us anything to eat but some scraps of cold victuals, the second day she grew a little more condescending, and on the third day she boiled a potful of good beef, pork, and sauerkraut for us. "Never mind," said one of the wagon masters to me, "mother comes on, she will give us roasted turkeys directly."

There was a little Negro boy belonging to the house, about five or six years of age, who, the whole time I was there, sat upon a stool in the chimney corner; indeed, he looked as if he had sat there ever since he was born. One of the wagon masters said to the landlady one day, "Mother, is that your son that sits in the corner?" "My son!" said she. "Why, don't you see he is a Negro?" "A Negro! Is he?" said the man. "Why I really thought he was your son, only that he had sat there until he was smoke-dried."

While the storm continued, to pass our time several of our party went to a tavern in the neighborhood. We here gambled a little for some liquor by throwing a small dart or stick, armed at one end with a pin, at a mark on the ceiling of the room. While I was at this amusement I found that the landlord and I bore the same name, and upon further discourse I found that he had a son about my age, whose given name was the same as mine. This son was taken prisoner at Fort Lee, on the Hudson River, in the year 1776, and died on his way home. These good people were almost willing to persuade themselves that I was their son. There were two very pretty girls, sisters to the deceased young man, who seemed wonderfully taken up with me, called me "brother," and I fared none the worse for my name. I used often, afterwards, in my cruises to that part of the state, to call in as I passed, and was always well treated by the whole family. The landlord used to fill my canteen with whiskey or peach or cider brandy to enable me, as he said, to climb the Welch mountains. I always went there with pleasure and left with regret. I often wished afterwards that I could find more namesakes.

I was sent one day, with another man of our party, to drive some cattle to the quartermaster general's quarters. It was dark when we arrived there. After we had delivered the cattle, an officer belonging to the quartermaster general's department asked me if I had a canteen. I answered in the negative. I had left mine at my quarters. "A soldier," said he, "should always have a canteen," and I was sorry that I was just then deficient of that article, for he gave us a half-pint tumblerful of genuine old Jamaica spirits, which was, like Boniface's ale, "as smooth as oil." It was too late to return to our quarters that night, so we concluded to go to camp, about three miles distant, and see our old messmates. Ourstomachs being empty, the spirits began to take hold of both belly and brains. I soon became very faint, but, as good luck would have it, my companion happened to have a part of a dried neat's tongue, which he had plundered somewhere in his travels. We fell to work upon that and soon demolished it, refreshed us much and enabled us to reach camp without suffering shipwreck. There was nothing to be had at camp but a little rest and that was all we asked.

In the morning it was necessary to have a pass from the commander of the regiment to enable us to pass the guards on our return to our quarters in the country. My captain gave me one, and then it must be countersigned by the colonel. When I entered the colonel's hut, "Where have you been" (calling me by name) "this winter?" said he. "Why, you are as fat as a pig." I told him I had been foraging in the country. "I think," said he, "you have taken care of yourself; I believe we must keep you here and send another man in your stead, that he may recruit himself a little." I told him that I was sent to camp on *particular* business and with strict orders to return, and that no one else could do so well. Finally, he signed my pass and I soon hunted up the other man when we left the camp in as great a hurry as though the plague had been there.

But the time at length came when we were obliged to go to camp for good and all, whether we chose it or not. An order from headquarters required all stationed parties and guards to be relieved, that all who had not had the smallpox might have an opportunity to have it before the warm weather came on. Accordingly about the last of April we were relieved by a party of southern troops. The commissary, who was a native of Connecticut, although at the commencement of the war he resided in Philadelphia, told us that he was sorry we were going away, for, said he, "I do not much like these men with one eye (alluding to their practice of gouging). I am acquainted with you and if any men are wanted here I should prefer those from my own section of the country to entire strangers." Although we would have very willingly obliged him with Our company, yet it could not be so, we must go to camp at all events. We accordingly marched off and arrived at camp the next day, much to the *seeming* satisfaction of our old messmates, and as much to the real dissatisfaction of ourselves. At least, it was so with me.

Thus far, since the year commenced, "Dame Fortune had been kind," but now "Miss-Fortune" was coming in for *her* set in the reel. I had now to enter again on my old system of starving; there was nothing to eat. I had brought two or three days' rations in my knapsack, and while that lasted I made shift to get along, but that was soon gone and I was then obliged to come to it again, which was sorely against my grain. During the past winter I had had enough to eat and been under no restraint; I had picked up a few articles of comfortable summer clothing among the inhabitants; our lieutenant had never concerned himself about us; we had scarcely seen him during the whole time. When we were off duty we went when and where we pleased "and had none to make us afraid," but now the scene was changed. We must go and come at bidding and suffer hunger besides.

After I had joined my regiment I was kept constantly, when off other duty, engaged in learning the Baron de Steuben's new Prussian exercise. It was a continual drill.

About this time I was sent off from camp in a detachment consisting of about three thousand men, with four field-pieces, under the command of the young General Lafayette. We marched to Barren Hill, about twelve miles from Phila-delphia. There are crossroads upon this hill, a branch of which leads to the city. We halted here, placed our guards, sent off our scouting parties, and waited for—I know not what. A company of about a hundred Indians, from some northern tribe, joined us here. There were three or four young Frenchmen with them. The Indians were stout-looking fellows and remarkably neat for that race of mortals, but they were Indians. There was upon the hill, and just where we were lying, an old church built of stone, entirely divested of all its entrails. The Indians were amusing themselves and the soldiers by shooting with their bows, in and about the church. I observed something in a corner of the roof which did not appear to belong to the building, and desired an Indian who was standing near me to shoot an arrow at it. He did so and it proved to be a cluster of bats; I should think there were nearly a bushel of them, all hanging upon one another. The house was immediately alive with them, and it was likewise instantly full of Indians and soldiers. The poor bats fared hard; it was sport for all hands. They killed I know not how many, but there was a great slaughter among them. I never saw so many bats before nor since, nor indeed in my whole life put all together.

The next day I was one of a guard to protect the horses belonging to the detachment. They were in a meadow of six or eight acres, entirely surrounded by tall trees. It was cloudy and a low fog hung all night upon the meadow, and for several hours during the night there was a jack-o'-lantern cruising in the eddying air. The poor thing seemed to wish to get out of the meadow, but could not, the air circulating within the enclosure of trees would not permit it. Several of the guard endeavored to catch it but did not succeed Just at the dawn of day the officers' waiters came, almost breathless, after the horses. Upon inquiring for the cause of the unusual hurry, we were told that the British were advancing upon us in our rear. How they could get there was to us a mystery, but they *were* there. We helped the waiters to catch their horses and immediately returned to the main body of the detachment. We found the troops all under arms and in motion, preparing for an onset. Those of the troops belonging to our brigade were put into the hurchyard, which was enclosed by a wall of stone and lime about breast high, a good defense against musketry but poor against artillery. I began to think I should soon have some better sport than killing bats. But our commander found that the enemy was too strong to be engaged in the position we then occupied. He therefore wisely ordered a retreat from this place to the Schuylkill, where we might choose any position that we pleased, having ragged woody hills in our rear and the river in front.

It was about three miles to the river. The weather was ex-ceeding warm, and I was in the rear platoon of the detachment except two platoons of General Washington's Guards. The quick motion in front kept the rear on a constant trot. Two pieces of artillery were in front and two in the rear. The enemy had nearly surrounded us by the time our retreat commenced, but the road we were in was very favorable for us, it being for the most part and especially the first part of it through small woods and copses. When I was about halfway to the river, I saw the right wing of the enemy through a lawn about half a mile dis-tant, but they were too late. Besides, they made a blunder here. They saw our rear guard with the two fieldpieces in its front, and thinking it the front of the detachment, they closed in to secure their prey, but when they had sprung their net they found that they had not a single bird under it.

We crossed the Schuylkill in good order, very near the spot where I had crossed it four times in the month of October the preceding autumn. As fast as the troops crossed they formed and prepared for action, and waited for them to attack us; but we saw no more of them that time, for before we had reached the river the alarm guns were fired in our camp and the whole army was imme-diately in motion. The British, fearing that they should be outnumbered in their turn, directly set their faces for Philadelphia and set off in as much or more haste than We had left Barren Hill. They had, during the night, left the city with such silence and secrecy, and by taking what was called the New York road, that they escaped detection by all our parties, and the first knowledge they obtained of the enemy's movements was that he was upon their backs, between them and us on the hill. The Indians, with all their alertness, had like to have "bought the rabbit." They kept coming in all the afternoon, in parties of four or five, whooping and hallooing like wild beasts. After they had got collected they vanished; I never saw any more of them. Our scouting parties all came in safe, but I was afterwards informed by a British deserter that several of the enemy perished by the heat and their exertions to get away from a retreating enemy.

The place that our detachment was now at was the Guif mentioned in the preceding chapter, where we kept the rice and vinegar Thanksgiving of starving memory. We stayed here till nearly night, when, no one coming to visit us, we marched off and took up our lodgings for the night in a wood. The next day we crossed the Schuylkill again and went on to Barren Hill once more. We stayed there a day or two and then returned to camp with keen appetites and empty purses. If anyone asks why we did not stay on Barren Hill till the British came up, and have taken and given a few bloody noses—all I have to say in answer is, that the General well knew what he was about; he was not deficient in either courage or conduct, and that was well known to all the Revolutionary army.

Soon after this affair we left our winter cantonments, crossed the Schuylkill and encamped on the left bank of that river, just opposite to our winter quarters. We had lain here but a few days when we heard that the British army had left Philadelphia and were proceeding to New York, through the Jerseys. We marched immediately in pursuit. We crossed the Delaware at Carroll's Ferry, above Trenton, and encamped a day or two between that town and Princeton. Here I was again detached with a party of one thousand men, as light troops, to get into the enemy's route and follow him close, to favor desertion and pick up stragglers

The day we were drafted [June 24] the sun was eclipsed. Had this happened upon such an occasion in "olden time," it would have been considered ominous either of good or bad fortune, but we took no notice of it. Our detachment marched in the afternoon and towards night we passed through Princeton. Some of the patriotic inhabitants of the town had brought out to the end of the street we passed through some casks of ready-made toddy. It was dealt out to the men as they passed by, which caused the detachment to move slowly at this place. The young ladies of the town, and perhaps of the vicinity, had collected and were sitting in the stoops and at the windows to see the noble exhibition of a thousand half-starved and three-quarters naked soldiers pass in review before them. I chanced to be on the wing of a platoon next to the houses, as they were chiefly on one side of the street, and had a good chance to notice the ladies, and I declare that I never before nor since saw more beauty, considering the numbers, than I saw at that time. They were *all* beautiful. New Jersey and Pennsylvania ladies are, in my opinion, collectively handsome, the most so of any in the United States. But I hope our Yankee ladies will not be jealous at hearing this. I allow that they have as many mental beauties as the others have personal, perhaps more; I know nothing about it. They are all handsome.

We passed through Princeton and encamped on the open fields for the night, the canopy of heaven for our tent. Early next morning we marched again and came up with the rear of the British army. We followed them several days, arriv-ing upon their camping ground within an hour after their, departure from it. We had ample opportunity to see the devastation they made in their rout; cattle killed and lying about the fields and pastures, some just in the position they were in when shot down, others with a small spot of skin taken off their hind quarters and a mess of steak taken out; household furniture hacked and broken to pieces; wells filled up and mechanics' and farmers' tools destroyed. It was in the height of the season of cherries; the innocent industrious creatures could not climb the trees for the fruit, but universally cut them down. Such conduct did not give the Americans any more agreeable feelings toward them than they entertained before.

It was extremely hot weather, and the sandy plains of that part of New Jersey did not cool the air to any great degree, but we still kept close to the rear of the British army. Deserters were almost hourly coming over to us, but of stragglers we took only a few.

My risibility was always pretty easily excited at any innocent ludicrous incident. The following circumstance gave me cause to laugh as well as all the rest who heard it. We halted in a wood for a few minutes in the heat of the day, on the ascent of a hill, and were lolling on the sides of the road, when there passed by two old men, both upon one horse that looked as if the crows had bespoken him. I did not know but Sancho Panza had lost his Dapple and was mounted behind Don Quixote upon Rosinante and bound upon some adventure with the British. However, they had not long been gone past us before another, about the same age and complexion, came stemming by on foot. Just as he had arrived where I was sitting, he stopped short and, looking toward the soldiers, said, "Did you see two old horses riding a Dutchman this road up? Hohl" The soldiers set up a laugh, as well they might, and the poor old Dutchman, finding he had gone "dail foremost" in his question, made the best of his way off out of hearing of us. We, this night turned into a new ploughed field, and I laid down between two furrows and slept as sweet as though I had laid upon bed of down.

The next morning, as soon as the enemy began their march, we were again in motion and came to their last night's encamping ground just after sunrise. Here we halted an hour or two, as we often had to do, to give the enemy time to advance, our orders being not to attack them unless in self-defense. We were marching on as usual, when, about ten or eleven o'clock, we were ordered to halt and then to face to the rightabout. As this order was given by the officers in rather a different way than usual, we began to think something was out of joint somewhere, but what or where our united wisdom could not explain. The general opinion of the soldiers was that some part of the enemy had by some means got into our rear. We, however, retraced our steps till we came to our last night's encamping ground, when we left the route of the enemy and went off a few miles to a place called Englishtown. It was uncommonly hot weather and we put up booths to protect us from the heat of the sun, which was almost insupportable. Whether we lay here one or two nights I do not remember; it matters not which. We were early in the morning mustered out and ordered to leave all our baggage under the care of a guard (our baggage was trifling), taking only our blankets and provisions (our provisions were less), and prepare for immediate march and action.

The officer who commanded the platoon that I belonged to was a captain, belonging to the Rhode Island troops, and a fine brave man he was; he feared nobody nor nothing. When we were paraded,—"Now," said he to us, "you have been wishing for some days past to come up with the British, you have been wanting to fight,—now you shall have fighting enough before night." The men did not need much haranguing to raise their courage, for when the officers came to order the sick and lame to stay behind as guards, they were forced to exercise their authority to the full extent before they could make even the invalids stay behind, and when some of their arms were about to be exchanged with those who were going into the field, they would not part with them. "If their arms went," they said, "*they* would go with them at all events."

After all things were put in order, we marched, but halted a few minutes in the village, where we were joined by a few other troops, and then proceeded on. We now heard a few reports of cannon ahead. We went in a road running through a deep narrow valley, which was for a considerable way covered with thick wood; we were some time in passing this defile. While in the wood we heard a volley or two of musketry, and upon inquiry we found it to be a party of our troops who had fired upon a party of British horse, but there was no fear of horse in the place in which we then were.

It was ten or eleven o'clock before we got through these woods and came into the open fields. The first cleared land we came to was an Indian cornfield, surrounded on the east, west and north sides by thick tall trees. The sun shining full upon the field, the soil of which was sandy, the mouth of a heated oven seemed to me to be but a trifle hotter than this ploughed field; it was almost impossible to breathe. We had to fall back again as soon as we could, into the woods. By the time we had got under the shade of the trees and had taken breath, of which we had been almost deprived, we received orders to retreat, as all the left wing of the army that part being under the command of General [Charles] Lee, were retreating. Grating as this order was to our feelings, we were obliged to comply.

We had not retreated far before we came to a defile, a muddy, sloughy brook. While the artillery were passing this place, we sat down by the roadside. In a few minutes the Commander in Chief and suite crossed the road just where we were sitting. I heard him ask our officers "by whose order the troops were retreating," and being answered, "by General Lee's," he said something, but as he was moving forward all the time this was passing, he was too far off for me to hear it distinctly. Those that were nearer to him said that his words were "d-n him." Whether he did thus express himself or not I do not know. It was certainly very unlike him, but he seemed at the instant to be in a great passion; his looks if not his words seemed to indicate as much. After passing us, he rode on to the plain field and took an observation of the advancing enemy. He remained there some time upon his old English charger, while the shot from the British artillery were rending up the earth ail around him. After he had taken a view of the enemy, he returned and ordered the two Connecticut brigades to make a stand at a fence, in order to keep the enemy in check while the artillery and other troops crossed the before-mentioned defile. (It was the Connecticut and Rhode Island forces which occupied this post, notwithstanding what Dr. [David] Ramsay says to the contrary He seems willing, to say the least, to give the southern troops the credit due to the northern. A historian ought to be sure of the truth of circumstances before he relates them). When we had secured our retreat, the artillery formed a line of pieces upon a long piece of elevated ground. Our detachment formed directly in front of the artillery, as a covering party, so far below on the declivity of the hill that the pieces could play over our heads. And here we waited the approach of the enemy, should he see fit to attack us.

By this time the British had come in contact with the New England forces at the fence, when a sharp conflict ensued. These troops maintained their ground, till the whole force of the enemy that could be brought to bear had charged upon them through the fence, and after being overpowered by numbers and the platoon officers had given orders for their several platoons to leave the fence, they had to force them to retreat, so eager were they to be revenged on the invaders of their country and rights.

As soon as the troops had left this ground the British planted their cannon upon the place and began a violent attack upon the artillery and our detachment, but neither could be routed. The cannonade continued for some time without intermission, when the British pieces being mostly disabled, they reluctantly crawled back from the height which they had occupied and hid themselves from our sight.

Before the cannonade had commenced, a part of the right wing of the British army had advanced across a low meadow and brook and occupied an orchard on our left. The weather was almost too hot to live in, and the British troops in the orchard were forced by the heat to shelter themselves from it under the trees. We had a four-pounder on the left of our pieces which kept a constant fire upon the enemy during the whole contest. After the British artillery had fallen back and the cannonade had mostly ceased in this quarter, and our detachment had an opportunity to look about us, Colonel [Joseph] Cilly of the New Hampshire Line, who was attached to our detachment, passed along in front of our line, inquiring for General Varnum's men, who were the Connecticut and Rhode Island men belonging to our command. We answered, "Here we are." He did not hear us in his hurry, but passed on. In a few minutes he returned, making the same inquiry. We again answered, "Here we are." "Ah!" said he, "you are the boys I want to assist in driving those rascals from yon orchard."

We were immediately ordered from our old detachment and joined another, the whole composing a corps of about five hundred men. We instantly marched towards the enemy's right wing, which was in the orchard, and kept concealed from them as long as possible by keeping behind the bushes. When we could no longer keep ourselves concealed, we marched into the open fields and formed our line. The British immediately formed and began to retreat to the main body of their army. Colonel Cilly, finding that we were not likely to overtake the enemy before they reached the main body of the army, on account of fences and other obstructions, ordered three or four platoons from the right of our corps to pursue and attack them, and thus keep them in play till the rest of the detachment could come up. I was in this party; we pursued without order. As I passed through the orchard I saw a number of the enemy lying under the trees, killed by our fieldpiece, mentioned before. We overtook the enemy just as they were entering upon the meadow, which was rather bushy. When within about five rods of the rear of the retreating foe, I could distinguish everything about them. They were retreating in line, though in some disorder. I singled out a man and took my aim directly between his shoulders. (They were divested of their packs.) He was a good mark, being a broad-shouldered fellow. What became of him I know not; the fire and smoke hid him from my sight. One thing I know, that is, I took as deliberate aim at him as ever I did at any game in my life. But after all, I hope I did not kill him, although I intended to at the time.

By this time our whole party had arrived, and the British had obtained a position that suited them, as I suppose, for they returned our fire in good earnest, and we played the second part of the same tune. They occupied a much higher piece of; ground than we did, and had a small piece of artil lery which the soldiers called a grasshopper. We had no artillery with us. The first shot they gave us from this piece cut off the thigh bone of a captain, just above the knee, and the whole heel of a private in the rear of him. We gave it is poor Sawney (for they were Scotch troops) so hot that he was forced to fall back and leave the ground they occupied. When our commander saw them retreating and nearly joined with their main body, he shouted, "Come, my boys, reload your pieces, and we will give them a set-off." We did so, and gave them the parting salute, and the firing on both sides ceased. We then laid ourselves down under the fences and bushes to take breath, for we had need of it. I presume everyone has heard of the heat of that day, but none can realize it that did not feel it. Fighting is hot work in cool weather, how much more so in such weather as it was on the twenty-eighth of June, 1778.

After the action in our part of the army had ceased, I went to a well, a few rods off, to get some water. Here I found the wounded captain, mentioned before, lying on the ground and begging his sergeant, who pretended to have the care of him, to help him off the field or he should bleed to death. The sergeant and a man or two he had with him were taken up in hunting after plunder. It grieved me to see the poor man in such distress, and I asked the sergeant why he did not carry his officer to the surgeons. He said he would directly. "Directly!" said I, "why he will die directly." I then offered to assist them in carrying him to a meetinghouse a short distance off, where the rest of the wounded men and the surgeons were. At length he condescended to be persuaded to carry him off. I helped him to the place, and tarried a few minutes to see the wounded and two or three limbs amputated, and then returned to my party again, where we remained the rest of the day and the following night, expecting to have another hack at them in the morning, but they gave us the slip.

As soon as our party had ceased firing, it began in the center, and then upon the right, but as I was not in that part of the army, I had no "adventure" in it, but the firing was continued in one part or the other of the field the whole afternoon. Our troops remained on the field all night with the Commander in Chief. A regiment of Connecticut forces were sent to lie as near the enemy as possible and to watch their motions, but they disappointed us all. If my readers wish to know how they escaped so slyly without our knowledge, after such precautions being used to prevent it, I must tell them I know nothing about it. But if they will take the trouble to call upon John Trumbull, Esq., perhaps he will satisfy their curiosity. If he should chance to be out of the way (and ten chances to one if he is not) apply to *McFingal*, Canto 4th.

One little incident happened during the heat of the cannonade, which I was eyewitness to, and which I think would be unpardonable not to mention. A woman whose husband belonged to the artillery and who was then attached to a piece in the engagement, attended with her husband at the piece the whole time. While in the act of reaching a cartridge and having one of her feet as far before the other as she could step, a cannon shot from the enemy passed directly between her legs without doing any other damage than carrying away all the lower part of her petticoat. Looking at it with apparent unconcern, she observed that it was lucky it did not pass a little higher, for in that case it might have carried away something else, and continued her occupation.

The next day after the action each man received a gill of rum, but nothing to eat. We then joined our regiments in the line and marched for Hudson's River. We marched by what was called "easy marches," that is, we struck our tents at three o'clock in the morning, marched ten miles and then encamped, which would be about one or two o'clock in the afternoon. Every third day we rested all day. In this way we went to King's Ferry, where we crossed the Hudson. Each brigade furnished its own ferrymen to carry the troops across. I was one of the men from our brigade; we were still suffering for provisions. Nearly the last trip the batteau that I was in made, while crossing the river empty, a large sturgeon (a fish in which this river abounds) seven or eight feet in length, in his gambolings, sprang directly into the boat, without doing any other damage than breaking down one of the seats of the boat. We crossed and took in our freight and recrossed, landed the men and our prize, gave orders to our several messmates as to the disposal of it, and proceeded on our business till the whole of the brigade had crossed the river, which was not long, we working with new energy in expectation of having something to eat when we had done our job. We then repaired to our messes to partake of the bounty of Providence, which we had so unexpectedly received. I found my share, which was about the seventh part of it, cooked, that is, it was boiled in salt and water, and I fell to it and ate, perhaps, a pound and a half, for I well remember that I was as hungry as a vulture and as empty as a blown bladder. Many of the poor fellows *thought* us happy in beings thus supplied; for my part I *felt* happy.

From King's Ferry the army proceeded to Tarrytown, and from thence to the White Plains. Here we drew some small supplies of summer clothing of which we stood in great need. While we lay here, I, with some of my comrades who were in the battle of the White Plains in the year '76, one day took a ramble on the ground where we were then engaged with the British, and took a survey of the place. We saw a number of the graves of those who fell in that battle. Some of the bodies had been so slightly buried that the dogs or hogs, or both, had dug them out of the ground. The skulls and other bones and hair were scattered about the place. Here were Hessian skulls as thick as a bombshell. Poor fellows! They were left unburied in a foreign land. They had, perhaps, as near and dear friends to lament their sad destiny as the Americans who lay buried near them. But they should have kept at home; we should then never have gone after them to kill them in their own country. But, the reader will say, they were forced to come and be killed here, forced by their rulers who have absolute power of life and death over their subjects. Well then, reader, bless a kind Providence that has made such a distinction between *your* condition and *theirs.* And be careful, too, that you do not allow yourself ever to be brought to such an abject, servile and debased condition.

We lay at the White Plains some time. While here I was transferred to the Light Infantry, when I was immediately marched down to the lines. I had hard duty to perform during the remainder of the campaign. I shall not go into every particular, but only mention a few incidents and accidents which transpired.

There were three regiments of Light Infantry, composed of men from the whole main army. It was a motley group—Yankees, Irishmen, Buckskins and what not. The regiment that I belonged to was made up of about one half New Englanders and the remainder were chiefly Pennsylvanians—two sets of people as opposite in manners and customs as light and darkness. Consequently, there was not much cordiality subsisting between us, for, to tell the sober truth, I had in those days as lief have been incorporated with a tribe of western Indians as with any of the southern troops, especially of those which consisted mostly, as the Pennsylvanians did, of foreigners. But I *was* among them and in the same regiment too, and under their officers (but the officers, in general, were gentlemen) and had to do duty with them. To make a bad matter worse, I was often, when on duty, the only Yankee that happened to be on the same tour for several days together. "The bloody Yankee," or "the d——d Yankee," was the mildest epithets that they would bestow upon me at such times. It often made me think of home, or *it least* of my regiment of fellow Yankees.

Our regiment was commanded by a Colonel [Richard] Butler, a Pennsylvanian, the same, I believe, who was after wards General Butler and was slain by the Indians at the defeat of General [Arthur] St. Clair at the Miamis, but of this I am not certain. He was a brave officer, but a fiery, austere hothead. Whenever he had a dispute with a brother officer, and that was pretty often, he would never resort to pistols and swords, but always to his fists. I have more than once or twice seen him with a "black eye," and have seen other officers that he had honored with the same badge.

As I have said before, I shall, not be very minute in relating my "adventures" during my continuance in this service. The duty of the Light Infantry is the hardest, while in the field, of any troops in the army, if there is any *hardest* about it. During the time the army keeps the field they are always on the lines near the enemy, and consequently always on the alert, constantly on the watch. Marching and guard-keeping, with all the other duties of troops in the field, fall plentifully to *their* share. There is never any great danger of Light Infantry men dying of the scurvy.

We had not been long on the lines when our regiment was sent off, lower down towards the enemy, upon a scouting expedition. We marched all night Just at day-dawn we halted in a field and concealed ourselves in some bushes. We placed our sentinels near the road, lying down behind bushes rocks and stoneheaps. The officers had got wind of a party of the enemy that was near us. A detachment of cavalry which accompanied us had taken the same precaution to prevent being discovered that the infantry had.

We had not been long in our present situation before we discovered a party of Hessian horsemen advancing up the road, directly to where we were lying in ambush for them. When the front of them had arrived "within hail," our colonel rose up from his lurking place and very civilly or dered them to come to him. The party immediately halted, and as they saw but one man of us, the commander seemed to hesitate, and concluded, I suppose, not to be in too much of a hurry in obeying our colonel's command, but that it was the best way for him to retrace his steps. Our colonel then, in a voice like thunder, called out to him, *"Come here, you rascal!"* but he paid very little attention to the colonel's summons and began to endeavor to free himself from what, I suppose, he thought a bad neighborhood. Upon which our colonel ordered the whole regiment to rise from their ambush and fire upon them. The order was quickly obeyed and served to quicken their steps considerably. Our horsemen had, while these transactions were in progress, by going round behind a small wood, got into their rear. We followed the enemy hard up, and when they met our horsemen there was a trifle of clashing. A part forced themselves past our cavalry and escaped; about thirty were taken and a number killed. We had none killed and but two or three of the horsemen slightly wounded. The enemy were armed with short rifles.

There was an Irishman belonging to our infantry, who, after the affray was over, seeing a wounded man belonging to the enemy lying in the road and unable to help himself, took pity on him, as he was in danger of being trodden upon by the horses, and having shouldered him was staggering off with his load, in order to get him to a place of more safety. While crossing a small worn-out bridge over a very muddy brook, he happened to jostle the poor fellow more than usual, who cried out, "Good rebel, don't hurt poor Hushman." "Who do you call a rebel, you scoundrel?" said the Irishman, and tossed him off his shoulders as unceremoniously as though he had been a log of wood. He fell with his head into the mud, and as I passed I saw him struggling for life, but I had other business on my hands than to stop to assist him. I did sincerely pity the poor mortal, but pity him was all I could then do. What became of him after I saw him in the mud, I never knew; most likely he there made his final exit. The infantry marched off with the prisoners, and left the horsemen to keep the field, till we were out of danger with our prize; consequently I never heard anything more of him. But the Irishman reminded me "that the *tender* mercies of the wicked are cruel."

Soon after this I had another fatiguing job to perform. There was a militia officer, a colonel, (his name I have forgotten, though I think it was Jones) who had collected some stores of flour, pork, &c. for the use of the militia in his neighborhood, when any small parties of them were required for actual service. A party of the enemy, denominated "Cowboys" (Refugees) had destroyed his stores. He solicited some men from the Light Infantry, to endeavor to capture some of the gang whom he was personally acquainted with, who belonged to, or were often at, Westchester, a village near King's Bridge. Accordingly, a captain and two subaltern officers and about eighty men, of which I was one, was sent from our regiment, then lying at a village called Bedford, to his assistance.

We marched from our camp in the dusk of the evening and continued our march all night. We heard repeatedly, during the night, the Tories firing on our sentries that belonged to the horse guards, who were stationed on the lines near the enemy. This was often practiced by those villains, not only upon the cavalry but the infantry also, when they thought they could do it with impunity. We arrived at the colonel's early in the morning and stayed there through the day. At night the lieutenant of our detachment with a small party of our men, guided by two or three militia officers, were sent off in pursuit of some of those shooting gentry whom the colonel suspected.

We first went to a house where were a couple of free blacks who were strongly suspected of being of the number. The people of the house denied having any knowledge of such persons, but some of the men inquiring of a small boy belonging to the house, he very innocently told us that there were such men there and that they lay in a loft over the hogsty. We soon found their nest but the birds had flown. Upon further inquiry, however, we found their skulking place and took them both.

We then proceeded to another house, a mile or two distant. Here we could not get any intelligence of the vermin we were in pursuit of. We, however, searched the house but found none. But we (the soldiers) desired the man who attended us with a light to show us into the dairy-house, pretending that the suspected persons might be there, and he accordingly accompanied us there. We found no enemy in this place but we found a friend indeed, because a friend in need. Here was a plenty of good bread, milk and butter. We were as hungry as Indians, and immediately "fell to, and spared not," while the man of the house held the candle and looked at us as we were devouring his eatables. I could not see his heart and of course could not tell what sort of thoughts "harbored there," but I could see his face and that indicated pretty distinctly what passed in his mind. He said *nothing,* but I believe he had as lief his bread and butter had been arsenic as what it was. We cared little for his thoughts or his maledictions; they did not do us half so much hurt as his victuals did us good.

We then returned to our party at the colonel's, where we arrived before daybreak. We stayed here through the day, drew some pork and biscuit, and prepared for our expedition after the Cowboys. At dark we sat off, accompanied by the militia colonel and three or four subaltern militia officers. This was the third night I had been on my feet, the whole time without any sleep, but go we must. We marched but a short way in the road, and then turned into the fields and pastures, over brooks and fences through swamps, mire and woods, endeavoring to keep as clear of the inhabitants as possible. About midnight we crossed a road near a house, the inmates of which, I suppose, were friendly to our cause, as the officers ordered us to stand still and not to speak nor leave our places on any account whatever, while they all entered the house for a few minutes, upon what errand I know not. As soon as the officers joined us again we marched off. One of our sergeants having disobeyed orders and gone round to the back side of the house, unobserved by the rest of us, it being quite dark, upon some occasion best known to himself, we marched off and left him. We had not gone fifty rods before he returned to the place where we were standing when he left us, and not finding us there he hallooed like a brave fellow; but the militia officers said that it would not do to answer, so we marched on and left him to find the way to camp, through what might with propriety be called an enemy's country, as well as he could. He, however, arrived there, with some considerable difficulty, safe and sound.

We kept on still through the fields, avoiding the houses as much as possible. I shall never forget how tired and beat out I was. Every grove of trees or piece of woods I could discern, I hoped would prove a resting place, but there was no rest. About two o'clock we took to the high road when we were between the village of Westchester and King's Bridge. We then came back to the village, where we were separated into small divisions, each led by an officer, either of our own or of the militia, and immediately entered all, the suspected houses at once. What we had to do must be done quickly, as the enemy were so near that they might have been informed of us in less than half an hour. There were several men in the house into which I was led, but one only appeared to be obnoxious to the officer who led us. This man was a Tory Refugee, in green uniform; we immediately secured him. An old man as blind as a bat came out of a bedroom, who appeared to be in great distress for fear there would be murder committed, as he termed it. I told him it was impossible to commit murder with Refugees.

We directly left the house with our prisoner, and joined the other parties and hurried off with all possible speed.

When we had got away and daylight appeared, we found that we had twelve or fourteen prisoners, the most or all of whom had been concerned in the destruction of the colonel's stores. We did not suffer the grass to grow long under our feet until we considered ourselves safe from the enemy that we had left behind us. We then slackened our pace and took to the road, where it was easier getting along than in the fields. Oh! I was so tired and hungry when we arrived at the colonel's, which was not till sundown or after. The most of the fellows we had taken belonged in the neighborhood of this place. As we passed a house, just at night, there stood in the door an elderly woman, who seeing among the prisoners some that she knew, she began to open her batteries of blackguardism upon us for disturbing what she termed the king's peaceable subjects. Upon a little closer inspection, who should her ladyship spy amongst the herd but one of her own sons. Her resentment was then raised to the highest pitch and we had a drenching shower of imprecations let down upon our heads. "Hell for war!" said she, "why, you have got my son Josey, too." Poor old simpleton. She might as well have saved her breath to cool her porridge.

We here procured another day's ration of the good colonel's pork and bread. We stayed through the night, and got some sleep and rest. Early next morning we left our prisoners, blacks and all, to the care of the militia, who could take care of them after we had taken them for them,' and marched off for our encampment, at Bedford, where we arrived at night, sufficiently beat out and in a good condition to add another night's sleep to our stock of rest.

We lay at Bedford till the close of the season. Late in the autumn, the main army lay at New Milford, in the northwestern part of Connecticut; while there, the Connecticut troops drew some winter clothing. The men belonging to that state, who were in the Light Infantry, had none sent them; they, therefore, thought themselves hardly dealt by. Many of them fearing they should lose their share of the clothing (of which they stood in great need), absconded from the camp at Bedford and went to New Milford. This caused our officers to keep patrolling parties around the camp during the night to prevent their going off. In consequence of this, I had one evening nearly obtained a final discharge from the army.

I had been, in the afternoon, at a small brook in the rear of the camp, where the troops mostly got their water, to wash some clothes. Among the rest was a handkerchief, which I laid upon a stone or stump, and when I went to my tent I forgot to take it with me. Missing it after roll call, I went to the place to get it. It was almost dark, and quite so in the bushes, when I got there. I was puzzled for some time to find the place, and longer before I could find the handker chief. After finding it I did not hurry back, but loitered till the patrols were out, for I did not once think of *them*. It had now become quite dark and I had to pass through a place where the soldiers had cut firewood. It was a young growth of wood, and the ground was covered with brush and the stumps about knee-high, quite thick. Just as I entered upon this spot I heard somebody challenge with "Who comes there?" I had no idea of being the person hailed, and kept very orderly on my way, blundering through the brush. I, however, received a second and third invitation to declare myself, but paid no attention to the request.

The next compliment I received was a shot from them. The ball passed very near to me but I still kept advancing, when instantly I had another salute. I then thought, that since I had been thé cause of so much noise and alarm, it would be best for me to get off if possible, for I knew that if I was brought before our hotspur of a colonel I should "buy the rabbit." Accordingly, I put my best foot foremost. The patrol, which consisted of twelve or fifteen men, all had a hack at me, some of the balls passing very near me indeed. One in particular passed so near my head as to cause my ear to ring for some time after. I now sprang to it for dear life, and I was in those days tolerable "light of foot"; but I had not made many leaps before I ran my knee with all my force against a white oak stump, which brought me up so short that I went heels over head over the stumps. I hardly knew whether I was dead or alive. However, I got up and blundered on till I reached my tent, into which I pitched and lay as still as the pain in my knee would allow me. My messmates were all asleep and knew nothing of the affair then, nor did I ever let them or anyone else know of it till after the close of the campaign, when I had joined my regiment in the line and was clear of the southern officers.

But my knee was in a fine pickle; the next morning it was swelled as big as my head, and lame enough. However, it did not long remain so. When I was questioned by the officers or any of the men how I came by my wound, I told them I fell down, and thus far I told the truth; but when anyone asked me how I came to fall down, I was compelled to equivocate a little.

I had often heard of some of the lowbred Europeans, especially Irishmen, boxing with each other in good fellow-ship, as they termed it, but I could not believe it till I was convinced by actual demonstration. While we tarried here, I was one day at a sutler's tent, or hut, where were a number of what we Yankees call "Old Countrymen." Soon after entering the hut, I observed one who was, to appearance, "pretty well over the bay." Directly there came in another who, it appeared, was an old acquaintance of the former's. They seemed exceeding glad to see each other, and so must take a drop of "the cratur" together; they then entered into conversation about former times. The first-mentioned was a stout athletic fellow; the other was a much smaller man. All of a sudden the first says, "Faith, Jammy, will you take a box?" "Aye, and thank ye, too," replied the other.

No sooner said than done, out they went, and all followed to see the sport, as they thought it, I suppose.

It was a cold, frosty day in the month of December; the ground all around the place was ploughed and frozen as hard as a pavement. They immediately stripped to the buff, and a broad ring was directly formed for the combatants (and they needed a broad one), when they prepared for the battle. The first pass they made at each other, their arms drawing their bodies forward, they passed without even touching either. The first that picked them up was the frozen ground, which made the claret, as they called the blood, flow plentifully. They, however, with considerable difficulty, put themselves into a position for a second bout, when they made the same pass-by as at the first. The little fellow, after getting upon his feet again, as well as he could, cried out, "I am too drunk to fight," and crawled off as fast as he was able, to the sutler's hut again; the other . followed, both as bloody as butchers, to drink friends again, where no friendship had been lost. And there I left them. and went to my tent, thankful that Yankees, with all their follies, lacked such a *refined* folly as this.

The main army, about this time, quitted the eastern side of the Hudson River and passed into New Jersey, to winter quarters. The Connecticut and New, Hampshire troops went to Reading and Danbury, in the western part of Connecticut. The Light Infantry, likewise, broke up their encampment at Bedford, and separated to join their respective regiments in the line: On our march to join our regiment, some of our *gentlemen officers*, happening to stop at a tavern, or rather a sort of grogshop, took such a seasoning that two, or three of them became "quite frisky," as the old Indian said of his young squaw. They kept running and chasing each other backward and forward by the troops, as they walked along the road, acting ridiculously. They soon, how ever, broke up the sport, for two of them at last, got by the ears, to the no small diversion of the soldiers, for nothing could please them better than to see the officers quarrel amongst themselves. One of the officers used his sword in the scabbard, the other a cane, and as the song says.

"At every stroke their jackets did smoke/As though they had been all on fire."

Some of the other officers who had not dipped their bills quite so deep, parted them, at the same time representing to them the ridiculous situation they stood in, fighting like blackguards in sight of the soldiers. At length, shame, so far as they had reason to let it operate, beginning to take hold of them, the other officers persuaded them to shake hands in token of future friendship, but they carried wonderful long faces all the rest of the day.

We arrived at Reading about Christmas or a little before, and prepared to build huts for our winter quarters. And now came on the time again between grass and hay, that is, the winter campaign of starving. We had not long been under the command of General Putnam, before the old gentleman heard, or fancied he heard, that a party of the enemy were out somewhere "down below." We were alarmed about midnight, and as cold a night as need be, and marched off to find the enemy, if he could be found. We marched all the remaining part of the night and all the forenoon of the next day, and when we came where they were, they were not there at all at all, as the Irishman said. We now had nothing more to do but to return as we came, which we immediately set about.

We marched back to Bedford, near the encamping ground I had just left. We were conducted into our bed room, a large wood, by our landlords, the officers, and left to our repose, while the officers stowed themselves away snugly in the houses of the village, about half a mile distant. We struck us up fires and lay down to rest our weary bones, all but our jawbones, they had nothing to weary them. About midnight it began to rain, which soon put out all our fires, and by three or four o'clock it came down in torrents. There *we* were, but where our careful officers were, or what had become of them we knew not, nor did we much care. The men began to squib off their pieces in derision of the officers, supposing they were somewhere amongst us, and careless of our condition; but none of them appearing, the men began firing louder and louder, till they had brought it to almost a running fire. At the dawn, the officers, having, I suppose, heard the firing, came running from their warm, dry beds, almost out of breath, exclaiming, "Poor fellows! Are you not almost dead?" We might have been for aught they knew or cared. However, they marched us off to the village, wet as drowned rats, put us into the houses, where we remained till the afternoon and dried ourselves.

It cleared off towards night and about sundown we marched again for camp, which was about twenty miles distant. We marched till sometime in the evening when we were ordered to get into the houses, under the care of the noncommissioned officers, the commissioned officers having again taken care of themselves at an early hour of the night. Myself and ten or fifteen others of our company, being under the charge of our orderly sergeant, could not get any quarters, as the people at every house made some excuse, which he thought all true. We kept pushing on till we had got three or four miles in advance of the troops. We then concluded to try for lodgings no longer, but to make the best of our way to camp, which we did, and arrived there in the latter part of the night.

I had nothing to do but to endeavor to get a little rest, for I had no cooking, although I should have been very glad to have had it to do.

The rest of the troops arrived in the course of the day, and at night, I think, we got a little something to eat, but if we did not, I know what I got by the jaunt, for I got a pleurisy which laid me up for some time. When I got so well as to work I assisted in building our winter huts. We got them in such a state of readiness that we moved into them about New Year's Day. The reader may take my word, if he pleases, when I tell him we had nothing extraordinary, either of eatables or drinkables, to keep a new year or housewarming. And as I have got into winter quarters again, I will here bring my third campaign to a close.

A REARGUARD ACTION

LEO TOLSTOY

Prince Andrey mounted his horse but lingered at the battery, looking at the smoke of the cannon from which the ball had flown. His eyes moved rapidly over the wide plain. He only saw that the previously immobile masses of the French were heaving to and fro, and that it really was a battery on the left. The smoke still clung about it. Two Frenchmen on horseback, doubtless adjutants, were galloping on the hill. A small column of the enemy, distinctly visible, were moving downhill, probably to strengthen the line. The smoke of the first shot had not cleared away, when there was a fresh puff of smoke and another shot. The battle was beginning. Prince Andrey turned his horse and galloped back to Grunte to look for Prince Bagration. Behind him he heard the cannonade becoming louder and more frequent. Our men were evidently beginning to reply. Musket shots could be heard below at the spot where the lines were closest. Lemarrois had only just galloped to Murat with Napoleon's menacing letter, and Murat, abashed and anxious to efface his error, at once moved his forces to the centre and towards both flanks, hoping before evening and the arrival of the Emperor to destroy the insignificant detachment before him.

"It has begun! Here it comes!" thought Prince Andrey, feeling the blood rush to his heart. "But where? What form is my Toulon to take?" he wondered.

Passing between the companies that had been eating porridge and drinking vodka a quarter of an hour before, he saw everywhere nothing but the same rapid movements of soldiers forming in ranks and getting their guns, and on every face he saw the same eagerness that he felt in his heart. "It has begun! Here it comes! Terrible and delightful!" said the face of every private and officer. Before he reached the earthworks that were being thrown up, he saw in the evening light of the dull autumn day men on horseback crossing towards him. The foremost, wearing a cloak and an Astrachan cap, was riding on a white horse. It was Prince Bagration. Prince Andrey stopped and waited for him to come up. Prince Bagration stopped his horse, and recognising Prince

Andrey nodded to him. He still gazed on ahead while Prince Andrey told him what he had been seeing.

The expression: "It has begun! it is coming!" was discernible even on Prince Bagration's strong, brown face, with his half-closed, lustreless, sleepy-looking eyes. Prince Andrey glanced with uneasy curiosity at that impassive face, and he longed to know: Was that man thinking and feeling, and what was he thinking and feeling at that moment? "Is there anything at all there behind that impassive face?" Prince Andrey wondered, looking at him. Prince Bagration nodded in token of his assent to Prince Audrey's words, and said: "Very good," with an expression that seemed to signify that all that happened, and all that was told him, was exacdy what he had foreseen. Prince Andrey, panting from his rapid ride, spoke quickly. Prince Bagration uttered his words in his Oriental accent with peculiar deliberation, as though impressing upon him that there was no need of hurry. He did, however, spur his horse into a gallop in the direction of Tushin's battery. Prince Andrey rode after him with his suite. The party consisted of an officer of the suite, Bagration's private adjutant, Zherkov, an orderly officer, the staff-officer on duty, riding a beautiful horse of English breed, and a civilian official, the auditor, who had asked to be present from curiosity to see the battle. The auditor, a plump man with a plump face, looked about him with a naive smile of amusement, swaying about on his horse, and cutting a queer figure in his cloak on his saddle among the hussars, Cossacks, and adjutants.

"This gendeman wants to see a battle," said Zherkov to Bolkonsky, indicating the auditor, "but has begun to feel queer already."

"Come, leave off," said the auditor, with a beaming smile at once naïve and cunning, as though he were flattered at being the object of Zherkov's jests, and was purposely trying to seem stupider than he was in reality.

"It's very curious, *mon Monsieur Prince,*" said the staff-officer on duty (He vaguely remembered that the title *prince* was translated in some peculiar way in French, but could not get it quite right.) By this time they were all riding up to Tushin's battery, and a ball struck the ground before them.

"What was that falling?" asked the auditor, smiling naively.

"A French pancake," said Zherkov.

"That's what they hit you with, then?" asked the auditor. "How awful!" And he seemed to expand all over with enjoyment. He had hardly uttered the words when again there was a sudden terrible whiz, which ended abrupdy in a thud into something soft, and flop—a Cossack, riding a little behind and to the right of the auditor, dropped from his horse to the ground. Zherkov and the staff-officer bent forward over their saddles and turned their horses away. The auditor stopped facing the Cossack, and looking with curiosity at him. The Cossack was dead, the horse was still struggling.

Prince Bagration dropped his eyelids, looked round, and seeing the cause of the delay, turned away indifferently, seeming to ask, "Why notice these trivial details?" With the ease of a first-rate horseman he stopped his horse, bent over a little and disengaged his sabre, which had caught under his cloak. The sabre was an old-fashioned one, unlike what are worn now. Prince Andrey remembered the story that Suvorov had given his saber to Bagration in Italy, and the recollection was particularly pleasant to him at that moment. They had ridden up to the very battery from which Prince Andrey had surveyed the field of battle.

"Whose company?" Prince Bagration asked of the artilleryman standing at the ammunition boxes.

He asked in words: "Whose company?" but what he was really asking was, "You're not in a panic here?" And the artilleryman understood that.

"Captain Tushin's, your excellency," the redhaired, freckled artilleryman sang out in a cheerful voice, as he ducked forward.

"To be sure, to be sure," said Bagration, pondering something, and he rode by the platforms up to the end cannon. Just as he reached it, a shot boomed from the cannon, deafening him and his suite, and in the smoke that suddenly enveloped the cannon the artillerymen could be seen hauling at the cannon, dragging and rolling it back to its former position. A broad-shouldered, gigantic soldier, gunner number one, with a mop, darted up to the wheel and planted himself, his legs wide apart; while number two, with a shaking hand, put the charge into the cannon's mouth; a small man with stooping shoulders, the officer Tushin, stumbling against the cannon, dashed forward, not noticing the general, and looked out, shading his eyes with his little hand.

"Another two points higher, and it will be just right," he shouted in a shrill voice, to which he tried to give a swaggering note utterly out of keeping with his figure. "Two!" he piped. "Smash away, Medvyedev!"

Bagration called to the officer, and Tushin went up to the general, putting three fingers to the peak of his cap with a timid and awkward gesture, more like a priest blessing some one than a soldier saluting. Though Tushin's guns had been intended to cannonade the valley, he was throwing shells over the village of Schöngraben, in part of which immense masses of French soldiers were moving out.

No one had given Tushin instructions at what or with what to fire, and after consulting his sergeant, Zaharchenko, for whom he had a great respect, he had decided that it would be a good thing to set fire to the village. "Very good!" Bagration said, on the officer's submitting that he had done so, and he began scrutinizing the whole field of battle that lay unfolded before him. He seemed to be considering something. The French had advanced nearest on the right side. In the hollow where the stream flowed, below the eminence on which the Kiev regiment was stationed, could be heard a continual roll and crash of guns, the din of which was overwhelming. And much further to the right, behind the dragoons, the officer of the suite pointed out to Bagration a column of French outflanking our flank. On the left the horizon was bounded by the copse close by. Prince Bagration gave orders for two battalions from the center to go to the right to reinforce the flank. The officer of the suite ventured to observe to the prince that the removal of these battalions would leave the cannon unprotected. Prince Bagration turned to the officer of the suite and stared at him with his lustreless eyes in silence. Prince Andrey thought that the officer's observation was a very just one, and that really there was nothing to be said in reply. But at that instant an adjutant galloped up with a message from the colonel of the regiment in the hollow that immense masses of the French were coming down upon them, that his men were in disorder and retreating upon the Kiev grenadiers, Prince Bagration nodded to signify his assent and approval. He rode at a walking pace to the right, and sent an adjutant to the dragoons with orders to attack the French. But the adjutant returned half an hour later with the news that the colonel of the dragoons had already retired beyond the ravine, as a destructive fire had been opened upon him, and he was losing his men for nothing, and so he had concentrated his men in the wood.

"Very good!" said Bagration.

Just as he was leaving the battery, shots had been heard in the wood on the left too; and as it was too far to the left flank for him to go himself, Prince Bagration despatched Zherkov to tell the senior general—the general whose regiment had been inspected by Kutuzov at Braunau—to retreat as rapidly as possible beyond the ravine, as the right flank would probably not long be able to detain the enemy. Tushin, and the battalion that was to have defended his battery, was forgotten. Prince Andrey listened carefully to Prince Bagration's colloquies with the commanding officers, and to the orders he gave them, and noticed, to his astonishment, that no orders were really given by him at all, but that Prince Bagration confined himself to trying to appear as though everything that was being done of necessity, by chance, or at the will of individual officers, was all done, if not by his orders, at least in accordance with his intentions. Prince Andrey observed, however, that, thanks to the tact shown by Prince Bagration, notwithstanding that what was done was due to chance, and not dependent on the commander's will, his presence was of the greatest value. Commanding officers, who rode up to Bagration looking distraught, regained their composure; soldiers and officers greeted him cheerfully, recovered their spirits in his presence, and were unmistakably anxious to display their pluck before him.

After riding up to the highest point of our right flank, Prince Bagration began to go downhill, where a continuous roll of musketry was heard and nothing could be seen for the smoke. The nearer they got to the hollow the less they could see, and the more distinctly could be felt the nearness of the actual battlefield. They began to meet wounded men. Two soldiers were dragging one along, supporting him on each side. His head was covered with blood; he had no cap, and was coughing and spitting. The bullet had apparently entered his mouth or throat. Another one came towards them, walking pluckily alone without his gun, groaning aloud and wringing his hands from the pain of a wound from which the blood was flowing, as though from a bottle, over his greatcoat. His face looked more frightened than in pain. He had been wounded only a moment before. Crossing the road, they began going down a deep descent, and on the slope they saw several men lying on the ground. They were met by a crowd of soldiers, among them some who were not wounded. The soldiers were hurrying up the hill, gasping for breath, and in spite of the general's presence, they were talking loudly together and gesticulating with their arms. In the smoke ahead of them they could see now rows of grey coats, and the commanding officer, seeing Bagration, ran after the group of retreating soldiers, calling upon them to come back. Bagration rode up to the ranks, along which there was here and there a rapid snapping of shots drowning the talk of the soldiers and the shouts of the officers. The whole air was reeking with smoke. The soldiers' faces were all full of excitement and smudged with powder. Some were plugging with their ramrods, others were putting powder on the touch-pans, and getting charges out of their pouches, others were firing their guns. But it was impossible to see at whom they were firing from the smoke, which the wind did not lift. The pleasant hum and whiz of the bullets was repeated pretty rapidly. "What is it?" wondered Prince Andrey, as he rode up to the crowd of soldiers. "It can't be the line, for they are all crowded together; it can't be an attacking party, for they are not moving; it can't be a square, they are not standing like one."

A thin, weak-looking colonel, apparently an old man, with an amiable smile, and eyelids that half covered his old-looking eyes and gave him a mild air, rode up to Prince Bagration and received him as though he were welcoming an honoured guest into his house. He announced to Prince Bagration that his regiment had had to face a cavalry attack of the French, that though the attack had been repulsed, the regiment had lost more than half of its men. The colonel said that the attack had been repulsed, supposing that to be the proper military term for what had happened; but he did not really know himself what had been taking place during that half hour in the troops under his command, and could not have said with any certainty whether the attack had been repelled or his regiment had been beaten by the attack. All he knew was that at the beginning of the action balls and grenades had begun flying all about his regiment, and killing men, that then some one had shouted "cavalry," and our men had begun firing. And they were firing still, though not now at the cavalry, who had disappeared, but at the French infantry, who had made their appearance in the hollow and were firing at our men. Prince Bagration nodded his head to betoken that all this was exactly what he had desired and expected. Turning to an adjutant, he commanded him to bring down from the hill the two battalions of the Sixth Chasseurs, by whom they had just come. Prince Andrey was struck at that instant by the change that had come over Prince Bagration's face. His face wore the look of concentrated and happy determination, which may be seen in a man who on a hot day takes the final run before a header into the water. The lustreless, sleepy look in the eyes, the affectation of profound thought had gone. The round, hard, eagle eyes looked ecstatically and rather disdainfully before him, obviously not resting on anything, though there was still the same deliberation in his measured movements.

The colonel addressed a protest to Prince Bagration, urging him to go back, as there it was too dangerous for him. "I beg of you, your excellency, for God's sake!" he kept on saying, looking for support to the officer of the suite, who only turned away from him.

"Only look, your excellency!" He called his attention to the bullets which were continually whizzing, singing, and hissing about them. He spoke in the tone of protest and entreaty with which a carpenter speaks to a gentleman who has picked up a hatchet. "We are used to it, but you may blister your fingers." He talked as though these bullets could not kill him, and his half-closed eyes gave a still more persuasive effect to his words. The staff-officer added his protests to the colonel, but Bagration made them no answer. He merely gave the order to cease firing, and to form so as to make room for the two battalions of reinforcements. Just as he was speaking the cloud of smoke covering the hollow was lifted as by an unseen hand and blown by the rising wind from right to left, and the opposite hill came into sight with the French moving across it. All eyes instinctively fastened on that French column moving down upon them and winding in and out over the ups and downs of the ground. Already they could see the fur caps of the soldiers, could distinguish officers from privates, could see their flag flapping against its staff.

"How well they're marching," said some one in Bagration's suite.

The front part of the column was already dipping down into the hollow. The engagement would take place then on the nearer side of the slope . . .

The remnants of the regiment that had already been in action, forming hurriedly, drew off to the right; the two battalions of the Sixth Chasseurs marched up in good order, driving the last stragglers before them. They had not yet reached Bagration, but the heavy, weighty tread could be heard of the whole mass keeping step. On the left flank, nearest of all to Bagration, marched the captain, a roundfaced imposing-looking man, with a foolish and happy expression of face. It was the same infantry officer who had run out of the shanty after Tushin. He was obviously thinking of nothing at the moment, but that he was marching before his commander in fine style. With the complacency of a man on parade, he stepped springing on his muscular legs, drawing himself up without the slightest effort, as though he were swinging, and this easy elasticity was a striking contrast to the heavy tread of the soldiers keeping step with him. He wore hanging by his leg an unsheathed, slender, narrow sword (a small bent sabre, more like a toy than a weapon), and looking about him, now at the commander, now behind, he turned his whole powerful frame round without getting out of step. It looked as though all the force of his soul was directed to marching by his commander in the best style possible. And conscious that he was accomplishing this, he was happy. "Left . . . left . . . left. . ." he seemed to be inwardly repeating at each alternate step. And the wall of soldierly figures, weighed down by their knapsacks and guns, with their faces all grave in different ways, moved by in the same rhythm, as though each of the hundreds of soldiers were repeating mentally at each alternate step, "Left . . . left . . . left . . ." A stout major skirted a bush on the road, puffing and shifting his step. A soldier, who had dropped behind, trotted after the company, looking panic-stricken at his own defection. A cannon ball, whizzing through the air, flew over the heads of Prince Bagration and his suite, and in time to the same rhythm, "Left . . . left . . ." it fell into the column.

"Close the ranks!" rang out the jaunty voice of the captain. The soldiers marched in a half circle round something in the place where the ball had fallen, and an old cavalryman, an under officer, lingered behind near the dead, and overtaking his line, changed feet with a hop, got into step, and looked angrily about him. "Left . . . left . . . left . . ." seemed to echo out of the menacing silence and the monotonous sound of the simultaneous tread of the feet on the ground.

"Well done, lads!" said Prince Bagration.

"For your ex . . . slen, slen, slency!" rang out along the ranks. A surly-looking soldier, marching on the left, turned his eyes on Bagration as he shouted, with an expression that seemed to say, "We know that without telling." Another, opening his mouth wide, shouted without glancing round, and marched on, as though afraid of letting his attention stray. The order was given to halt and take off their knapsacks.

Bagration rode round the ranks of men who had marched by him, and then dismounted from his horse. He gave the reins to a Cossack, took off his cloak and handed it to him, stretched his legs and set his cap straight on his head. The French column with the officers in front came into sight under the hill.

"With God's help!" cried Bagration in a resolute, sonorous voice. He turned for one instant to the front line, and swinging his arms a little with the awkward, lumbering gait of a man always on horseback, he walked forward over the uneven ground. Prince Andrey felt that some unseen force was drawing him forward, and he had a sensation of great happiness.

The French were near. Already Prince Andrey, walking beside Bagration, could distinguish clearly the sashes, the red epaulettes, even the faces of the French. (He saw distinctly one bandy-legged old French officer, wearing Hessian boots, who was getting up the hill with difficulty, taking hold of the bushes.) Prince Bagration gave no new command, and still marched in front of the ranks in the same silence. Suddenly there was the snap of a shot among the French, another and a third . . . and smoke rose and firing rang out in all the broken-up ranks of the enemy. Several of our men fell, among them the round-faced officer, who had been marching so carefully and complacently. But at the very instant of the first shot, Bagration looked round and shouted, "Hurrah!" "Hura . . . a . . . a . . . ah!" rang out along our lines in a prolonged roar, and outstripping Prince Bagration and one another, in no order, but in an eager and joyous crowd, our men ran downhill after the routed French.

The attack of the Sixth Chasseurs covered the retreat of the right flank. In the centre Tushin's forgotten battery had succeeded in setting fire to Schöngraben and delaying the advance of the French. The French stayed to put out the fire, which was fanned by the wind, and this gave time for the Russians to retreat. The retreat of the centre beyond the ravine was hurried and noisy; but the different companies kept apart. But the left flank, which consisted of the Azovsky and Podolsky infantry and the Pavlograd hussars, was simultaneously attacked in front and surrounded by the cream of the French army under Lannes, and was thrown into disorder. Bagration had sent Zherkov to the general in command of the left flank with orders to retreat immediately.

Zherkov, keeping his hand still at his cap, had briskly started his horse and galloped off. But no sooner had he ridden out of Bagration's sight than his courage failed him. He was overtaken by a panic he could not contend against, and he could not bring himself to go where there was danger.

After galloping some distance towards the troops of the left flank, he rode not forward where he heard firing, but off to look for the general and the officers in a direction where they could not by any possibility be; and so it was that he did not deliver the message.

The command of the left flank belonged by right of seniority to the general of the regiment in which Dolohov was serving—the regiment which Kutuzov had inspected before Braunau. But the command of the extreme left flank had been entrusted to the colonel of the Pavlograd hussars, in which Rostov was serving. Hence arose a misunderstanding. Both commanding officers were intensely exasperated with one another, and at a time when fighting had been going on a long while on the right flank, and the French had already begun their advance on the left, these two officers were engaged in negotiations, the sole aim of which was the mortification of one another. The regiments—cavalry and infantry alike were by no means in readiness for the engagement. No one from the common soldier to the general expected a battle; and they were all calmly engaged in peaceful occupations—feeding their horses in the cavalry, gathering wood in the infantry.

"He is my senior in rank, however," said the German colonel of the hussars, growing very red and addressing an adjutant, who had ridden up. "So let him do as he likes. I can't sacrifice my hussars. Bugler! Sound the retreat!"

But things were becoming urgent. The fire of cannon and musketry thundered in unison on the right and in the centre, and the French tunics of Lannes's sharpshooters had already passed over the milldam, and were forming on this side of it hardly out of musket-shot range.

The infantry general walked up to his horse with his quivering strut, and mounting it and drawing himself up very erect and tall, he rode up to the Pavlograd colonel. The two officers met with affable bows and concealed fury in their hearts.

"Again, colonel," the general said, "I cannot leave half my men in the wood. I *beg* you, I *beg* you," he repeated, "to occupy the *position,* and prepare for an attack."

"And I beg you not to meddle in what's not your business," answered the colonel, getting hot. "If you were a cavalry officer . . ."

"I am not a cavalry officer, colonel, but I am a Russian general, and if you are unaware of the fact . . ."

"I am fully aware of it, your excellency," the colonel screamed suddenly, setting his horse in motion and becoming purple in the face. "If you care to come to the front, you will see that this position cannot be held. I don't want to massacre my regiment for your satisfaction."

"You forget yourself, colonel. I am not considering my own satisfaction, and I do not allow such a thing to be said."

Taking the colonel's proposition as a challenge to his courage, the general squared his chest and rode scowling beside him to the front line, as though their whole difference would inevitably be settled there under the enemy's fire. They reached the line, several bullets flew by them, and they stood still without a word. To look at the front line was a useless proceeding, since from the spot where they had been standing before, it was clear that the cavalry could not act, owing to the bushes and the steep and broken character of the ground, and that the French were outflanking the left wing. The general and the colonel glared sternly and significantly at one another, like two cocks preparing for a fight, seeking in vain for a symptom of cowardice. Both stood the test without flinching. Since there was nothing to be said, and neither was willing to give the other grounds for asserting that he was the first to withdraw from under fire, they might have remained a long while standing there, mutually testing each other's pluck, if there had not at that moment been heard in the copse, almost behind them, the snap of musketry and a confused shout of voices. The French were attacking the soldiers gathering wood in the copse. The hussars could not now retreat, nor could the infantry. They were cut off from falling back on the left by the French line. Now, unfavourable as the ground was, they must attack to fight a way through for themselves.

The hussars of the squadron in which Rostov was an ensign had hardly time to mount their horses when they were confronted by the enemy. Again, as on the Enns bridge, there was no one between the squadron and the enemy, and between them lay that terrible border-line of uncertainty and dread, like the line dividing the living from the dead. All the soldiers were conscious of that line, and the question whether they would cross it or not, and how they would cross it, filled them with excitement.

The colonel rode up to the front, made some angry reply to the questions of the officers, and, like a man desperately insisting on his rights, gave some command. No one said anything distinctly, but through the whole squadron there ran a vague rumour of attack. The command to form in order rang out, then there was the clank of sabres being drawn out of their sheaths. But still no one moved. The troops of the left flank, both the infantry and the hussars, felt that their commanders themselves did not know what to do, and the uncertainty of the commanders infected the soldiers.

"Make haste, if only they'd make haste," thought Rostov, feeling that at last the moment had come to taste the joys of the attack, of which he had heard so much from his comrades.

"With God's help, lads," rang out Denisov's voice, "forward, quick, gallop!"

The horses' haunches began moving in the front line. Rook pulled at the reins and set off of himself.

On the right Rostov saw the foremost lines of his own hussars, and still further ahead he could see a dark streak, which he could not distinguish clearly, but assumed to be the enemy. Shots could be heard, but at a distance.

"Quicker!" rang out the word of command, and Rostov felt the drooping of Rook's hindquarters as he broke into a gallop. He felt the joy of the gallop coming, and was more and more lighthearted. He noticed a solitary tree ahead of him. The tree was at first in front of him, in the middle of that borderland that had seemed so terrible. But now they had crossed it and nothing terrible had happened, but he felt more lively and excited every moment. "Ah, won't I slash at him!" thought Rostov, grasping the hilt of his sabre tighdy. "Hur . . . r . . . a . . . a!" roared voices.

"Now, let him come on, whoever it may be," thought Rostov, driving the spurs into Rook, and outstripping the rest, he let him go at full gallop. Already the enemy could be seen in front. Suddenly something swept over the squadron like a broad broom. Rostov lifted his sabre, making ready to deal a blow, but at that instant the soldier Nikitenko galloped ahead and left his side, and Rostov felt as though he were in a dream being carried forward with supernatural swiftness and yet remaining at the same spot. An hussar, Bandartchuk, galloped up from behind close upon him and looked angrily at him. Bandartchuk's horse started aside, and he galloped by.

"What's the matter? I'm not moving? I've fallen, I'm killed . . ." Rostov asked and answered himself all in one instant. He was alone in the middle of the field. Instead of the moving horses and the hussars' backs, he saw around him the motionless earth and stubblefield. There was warm blood under him.

"No, I'm wounded, and my horse is killed." Rook tried to get up on his forelegs, but he sank again, crushing his rider's leg under his leg. Blood was flowing from the horse's head. The horse struggled, but could not get up. Rostov tried to get up, and fell down too. His sabretache had caught in the saddle. Where our men were, where were the French, he did not know. All around him there was no one.

Getting his leg free, he stood up. "Which side, where now was that line that had so sharply divided the two armies?" he asked himself, and could not answer. "Hasn't something gone wrong with me? Do such things happen, and what ought one to do in such cases?" he wondered as he was getting up. But at that instant he felt as though something superfluous was hanging on his benumbed left arm. The wrist seemed not to belong to it. He looked at his hand, carefully searching for blood on it. "Come, here are some men," he thought joyfully, seeing some men running towards him. "They will help me!" In front of these men ran a single figure in a strange shako and a blue coat, with a swarthy sunburnt face and a hooked nose. Then came two men, and many more were running up behind. One of them said some strange words, not Russian. Between some similar figures in similar shakoes behind stood a Russian hussar. He was being held by the arms; behind him they were holding his horse too.

"It must be one of ours taken prisoner. . . . Yes. Surely they couldn't take me too? What sort of men are they?" Rostov was still wondering, unable to believe his own eyes. "Can they be the French?" He gazed at the approaching French, and although only a few seconds before he had been longing to get at these Frenchmen and to cut them down, their being so near seemed to him now so awful that he could not believe his eyes. "Who are they? What are they running for? Can it be to me? Can they be running to me? And what for? To kill me? *Me,* whom every one's so fond of?" He recalled his mother's love, the love of his family and his friends, and the enemy's intention of killing him seemed impossible. "But they may even kill me." For more than ten seconds he stood, not moving from the spot, nor grasping his position. The foremost Frenchman with the hook nose was getting so near that he could see the expression of his face. And the excited, alien countenance of the man, who was running so lightly and breathlessly towards him, with his bayonet lowered, terrified Rostov. He snatched up his pistol, and instead of firing with it, flung it at the Frenchman and ran to the bushes with all his might. Not with the feeling of doubt and conflict with which he had moved at the Enns bridge, did he now run, but with the feeling of a hare fleeing from the dogs. One unmixed feeling of fear for his young, happy life took possession of his whole being. Leaping rapidly over the hedges with the same impetuosity with which he used to run when he played games, he flew over the field, now and then turning his pale, goodnatured, youthful face, and a chill of horror ran down his spine. "No, better not to look," he thought, but as he got near to the bushes he looked round once more. The. French had given it up, and just at the moment when he looked round the foremost man was just dropping from a run into a walk, and turning round to shout something loudly to a comrade behind. Rostov stopped. "There's some mistake," he thought; "it can't be that they meant to kill me." And meanwhile his left arm was as heavy as if a hundred pound weight were hanging on it. He could run no further. The Frenchman stopped too and took aim. Rostov frowned and ducked. One bullet and then another flew hissing by him; he took his left hand in his right, and with a last effort ran as far as the bushes. In the bushes there were Russian sharpshooters.

The infantry, who had been caught unawares in the copse, had run away, and the different companies all confused together had retreated in disorderly crowds. One soldier in a panic had uttered those words—terrible in war and meaningless: "Cut off!" and those words had infected the whole mass with panic.

"Out flanked! Cut off! Lost!" they shouted as they ran.

When their general heard the firing and the shouts in the rear he had grasped at the instant that something awful was happening to his regiment; and the thought that he, an exemplary officer, who had served so many years without ever having been guilty of the slightest shortcoming, might be held responsible by his superiors for negligence or lack of discipline, so affected him that, instandy oblivious of the insubordinate cavalry colonel and his dignity as a general, utterly oblivious even of danger and of the instinct of self-preservation, he clutched at the crupper of his saddle, and spurring his horse, galloped off to the regiment under a perfect hail of bullets that luckily missed him. He was possessed by the one desire to find out what was wrong, and to help and correct the mistake whatever it might be, if it were a mistake on his part, so that after twenty-two years of exemplary service, without incurring a reprimand for anything, he might avoid being responsible for this blunder.

Galloping successfully between the French forces, he reached the field behind the copse across which our men were running downhill, not heeding the word of command. That moment had come of moral vacillation which decides the fate of battles. Would these disorderly crowds of soldiers hear the voice of their commander, or, looking back at him, run on further? In spite of the despairing yell of the commander, who had once been so awe-inspiring to his soldiers, in spite of his infuriated, purple face, distorted out of all likeness to itself, in spite of his brandished sword, the soldiers still ran and talked together, shooting into the air and not listening to the word of command. The moral balance which decides the fate of battle was unmistakably falling on the side of panic.

The general was choked with screaming and gunpowder-smoke, and he stood still in despair. All seemed lost; but at that moment the French, who had been advancing against our men, suddenly, for no apparent reason, ran back, vanished from the edge of the copse, and Russian sharp-shooters appeared in the copse. This was Timohin's division, the only one that had retained its good order in the copse, and hiding in ambush in the ditch behind the copse, had suddenly attacked the French. Timohin had rushed with such a desperate yell upon the French, and with such desperate and drunken energy had he dashed at the enemy with only a sword in his hand, that the French flung down their weapons and fled without pausing to recover themselves. Dolohov, running beside Timohin, killed one French soldier at close quarters, and was the first to seize by the collar an officer who surrendered. The fleeing Russians came back; the battalions were brought together; and the French, who had been on the point of splitting the forces of the left flank into two parts, were for the moment held in check. The reserves had time to join the main forces, and the runaways were stopped. The general stood with Major Ekonomov at the bridge, watching the retreating companies go by, when a soldier ran up to him, caught hold of his stirrup and almost clung on to it. The soldier was wearing a coat of blue fine cloth, he had no knapsack nor shako, his head was bound up, and across his shoulders was slung a French cartridge case. In his hand he held an officer's sword. The soldier was pale, his blue eyes looked impudently into the general's face, but his mouth was smiling. Although the general was engaged in giving instructions to Major Ekonomov, he could not help noticing this soldier.

"Your excellency, here are two trophies," said Dolohov, pointing to the French sword and cartridge case. "An officer was taken prisoner by me. I stopped the company." Dolohov breathed hard from weariness; he spoke in jerks. "The whole company can bear me witness. I beg you to remember me, your excellency!"

"Very good, very good," said the general, and he turned to Major Ekonomov. But Dolohov did not leave him; he undid the bandage, and showed the blood congealed on his head.

"A bayonet wound; I kept my place in the front. Remember me, your excellency."

Tushin's battery had been forgotten, and it was only at the very end of the action that Prince Bagration, still hearing the cannonade in the centre, sent the staff-officer on duty and then Prince Andrey to command the battery to retire as quickly as possible.

The force which had been stationed near Tushin's cannons to protect them had by somebody's orders retreated in the middle of the battle. But the battery still kept up its fire, and was not taken by the French simply because the enemy could not conceive of the reckless daring of firing from four cannons that were quite unprotected. The French supposed, on the contrary, judging from the energetic action of the battery, that the chief forces of the Russians were concentrated here in the centre, and twice attempted to attack that point, and both times were driven back by the grapeshot fired on them from the four cannons which stood in solitude on the heights. Shordy after Prince Bagration's departure, Tushin had succeeded in setting fire to Schöngraben.

"Look, what a fuss they're in! It's flaming! What a smoke! Smardy done! First-rate! The smoke! the smoke!" cried the gunners, their spirits reviving.

All the guns were aimed without instructions in the direction of the conflagration. The soldiers, as though they were urging each other on, shouted at every volley: "Bravo! That's something like now! Go it! . . . First-rate!" The fire, fanned by the wind, soon spread. The French columns, who had marched out beyond the village, went back, but as though in revenge for this mischance, the enemy stationed ten cannons a little to the right of the village, and began firing from them on Tushin.

In their childlike glee at the conflagration of the village, and the excitement of their successful firing on the French, our artillerymen only noticed this battery when two cannon-balls and after them four more fell among their cannons, and one knocked over two horses and another tore off the foot of a gunner. Their spirits, however, once raised, did not flag; their excitement simply found another direction. The horses were replaced by others from the ammunition carriage; the wounded were removed, and the four cannons were turned facing the ten of the enemy's battery. The other officer, Tushin's comrade, was killed at the beginning of the action, and after an hour's time, of the forty gunners of the battery, seventeen were disabled, but they were still as merry and as eager as ever. Twice they noticed the French appearing below close to them, and they sent volleys of grapeshot at them.

The little man with his weak, clumsy movements, was continually asking his orderly *for just one more pipe for that stroke,* as he said, and scattering sparks from it, he kept running out in front and looking from under his little hand at the French.

"Smash away, lads!" he was continually saying, and he clutched at the cannon wheels himself and unscrewed the screws. In the smoke, deafened by the incessant booming of the cannons that made him shudder every time one was fired, Tushin ran from one cannon to the other, his short pipe never out of his mouth. At one moment he was taking aim, then reckoning the charges, then arranging for the changing and unharnessing of the killed and wounded horses, and all the time shouting in his weak, shrill, hesitating voice. His face grew more and more eager. Only when men were killed and wounded he knitted his brows, and turning away from the dead man, shouted angrily to the men, slow, as they always are, to pick up a wounded man or a dead body. The soldiers, for the most part fine, handsome fellows (a couple of heads taller than their officer and twice as broad in the chest, as they mostly are in the artillery), all looked to their commanding officer like children in a difficult position, and the expression they found on his face was invariably reflected at once on their own.

Owing to the fearful uproar and noise and the necessity of attention and activity, Tushin experienced not the slightest unpleasant sensation of fear; and the idea that he might be killed or badly wounded never entered his head. On the contrary, he felt more and more lively. It seemed to him that the moment in which he had first seen the enemy and had fired the first shot was long, long ago, yesterday perhaps, and that the spot of earth on which he stood was a place long familiar to him, in which he was quite at home. Although he thought of everything, considered everything, did everything the very best officer could have done in his position, he was in a state of mind akin to the delirium of fever or the intoxication of a drunken man.

The deafening sound of his own guns on all sides, the hiss and thud of the enemy's shells, the sight of the perspiring, flushed gunners hurrying about the cannons, the sight of the blood of men and horses, and of the puffs of smoke from the enemy on the opposite side (always followed by a cannon-ball that flew across and hit the earth, a man, a horse, or a cannon)—all these images made up for him a fantastic world of his own, in which he found enjoyment at the moment. The enemy's cannons in his fancy were not cannons, but pipes from which an invisible smoker blew puffs of smoke at intervals.

"There he's puffing away again," Tushin murmured to himself as a cloud of smoke rolled downhill, and was borne off by the wind in a wreath to the left. "Now, your ball—throw it back."

"What is it, your honour?" asked a gunner who stood near him, and heard him muttering something.

"Nothing, a grenade . . ." he answered. "Now for it, our Matvyevna," he said to himself. Matvyevna was the name his fancy gave to the big cannon, cast in an old-fashioned mould, that stood at the end.

The French seemed to be ants swarming about their cannons. The handsome, drunken soldier, number one gunner of the second cannon, was in his dreamworld "uncle"; Tushin looked at him more often than at any of the rest, and took delight in every gesture of the man. The sound—dying away, then quickening again—of the musketry fire below the hill seemed to him like the heaving of some creature's breathing. He listened to the ebb and flow of these sounds.

"Ah, she's taking another breath again," he was saying to himself. He himself figured in his imagination as a mighty man of immense stature, who was flinging cannon balls at the French with both hands.

"Come, Matvyevna, old lady, stick by us!" he was saying, moving back from the cannon, when a strange, unfamiliar voice called over his head. "Captain Tushin! Captain!"

Tushin looked round in dismay. It was the same staff-officer who had turned him out of the booth at Grunte. He was shouting to him in a breathless voice:

"I say, are you mad? You've been commanded twice to retreat, and you . . ."

"Now, what are they pitching into me for?" . . . Tushin wondered, looking in alarm at the superior officer.

"I . . . don't . . ." he began, putting two fingers to the peak of his cap. "I . . ."

But the staff-officer did not say all he had meant to. A cannon ball flying near him made him duck down on his horse. He paused, and was just going to say something more, when another ball stopped him. He turned his horse's head and galloped away.

"Retreat! All to retreat!" he shouted from a distance.

The soldiers laughed. A minute later an adjutant arrived with the same message. This was Prince Andrey. The first thing he saw, on reaching the place where Tushin's cannons were stationed, was an unharnessed horse with a broken leg, which was neighing beside the harnessed horses. The blood was flowing in a perfect stream from its leg. Among the platforms lay several dead men. One cannon ball after another flew over him as he rode up, and he felt a nervous shudder running down his spine. But the very idea that he was afraid was enough to rouse him again. "I can't be frightened," he thought, and he deliberately dismounted from his horse between the cannons. He gave his message, but he did not leave the battery. He decided to stay and assist in removing the cannons from the position and getting them away. Stepping over the corpses, under the fearful fire from the French, he helped Tushin in getting the cannons ready.

"The officer that came just now ran off quicker than he came," said a gunner to Prince Andrey, "not like your honour."

Prince Andrey had no conversation with Tushin. They were both so busy that they hardly seemed to see each other. When they had got the two out of the four cannons that were uninjured on to the platforms and were moving downhill (one cannon that had been smashed and a howitzer were left behind), Prince Andrey went up to Tushin.

"Well, good-bye till we meet again," said Prince Andrey, holding out his hand to Tushin.

"Good-bye, my dear fellow," said Tushin, "dear soul! good-bye, my dear fellow," he said with tears, which for some unknown reason started suddenly into his eyes.

The wind had sunk, black storm-clouds hung low over the battlefield, melting on the horizon into the clouds of smoke from the powder. Darkness had come, and the glow of conflagrations showed all the more distinctly in two places. The cannonade had grown feebler, but the snapping of musketry-fire in the rear and on the right was heard nearer and more often. As soon as Tushin with his cannons, continually driving round the wounded and coming upon them, had got out of fire and were descending the ravine, he was met by the staff, among whom was the staff-officer and Zherkov, who had twice been sent to Tushin's battery, but had not once reached it. They all vied with one another in giving him orders, telling him how and where to go, finding fault and making criticisms. Tushin gave no orders, and in silence, afraid to speak because at every word he felt, he could not have said why, ready to burst into tears, he rode behind on his artillery nag. Though orders were given to abandon the wounded, many of them dragged themselves after the troops and begged for a seat on the cannons. The jaunty infantry-officer—the one who had run out of Tushin's shanty just before the battle—was laid on Matvyevna's carriage with a bullet in his stomach. At the bottom of the hill a pale ensign of hussars, holding one arm in the other hand, came up to Tushin and begged for a seat.

"Captain, for God's sake. I've hurt my arm," he said timidly. "For God's sake. I can't walk. For God's sake!" It was evident that this was not the first time the ensign had asked for a lift, and that he had been everywhere refused. He asked in a hesitating and piteous voice. "Tell them to let me get on, for God's sake!"

"Let him get on, let him get on," said Tushin. "Put a coat under him, you, Uncle." He turned to his favourite soldier. "But where's the wounded officer?"

"We took him off; he was dead," answered some one.

"Help him on. Sit down, my dear fellow, sit down. Lay the coat there, Antonov."

The ensign was Rostov. He was holding one hand in the other. He was pale, and his lower jaw was trembling as though in a fever. They put him on Matvyevna, the cannon from which they had just removed the dead officer. There was blood on the coat that was laid under him, and Rostov's riding-breeches and arm were smeared with it.

"What, are you wounded, my dear?" said Tushin, going up to the cannon on which Rostov was sitting.

"No; it's a sprain."

"How is it there's blood on the frame?" asked Tushin.

"That was the officer, your honour, stained it," answered an artillery-man, wiping the blood off with the sleeve of his coat, and as it were apologising for the dirty state of the cannon.

With difficulty, aided by the infantry, they dragged the cannon uphill, and halted on reaching the village of Guntersdorf. It was by now so dark that one could not distinguish the soldiers' uniforms ten paces away, and the firing had begun to subside. All of a sudden there came the sound of firing and shouts again close by on the right side. The flash of the shots could be seen in the darkness. This was the last attack of the French. It was met by the soldiers in ambush in the houses of the village. All rushed out of the village again, but Tushin's cannons could not move, and the artillerymen, Tushin, and the ensign looked at one another in anticipation of their fate. The firing on both sides began to subside, and some soldiers in lively conversation streamed out of a side street.

"Not hurt, Petrov?" inquired one.

"We gave it them hot, lads. They won't meddle with us now," another was saying.

"One couldn't see a thing. Didn't they give it to their own men! No seeing for the darkness, mates. Isn't there something to drink?"

The French had been repulsed for the last time. And again, in the complete darkness, Tushin's cannons moved forward, surrounded by the infantry, who kept up a hum of talk.

In the darkness they flowed on like an unseen, gloomy river always in the same direction, with a buzz of whisper and talk and the thud of hoofs and rumble of wheels. Above all other sounds, in the confused uproar, rose the moans and cries of the wounded, more distinct than anything in the darkness of the night. Their moans seemed to fill all the darkness surrounding the troops. Their moans and the darkness seemed to melt into one. A little later a thrill of emotion passed over the moving crowd.

Some one followed by a suite had ridden by on a white horse, and had said something as he passed.

"What did he say? Where we are going now? To halt, eh? Thanked us, what?" eager questions were heard on all sides, and the whole moving mass began to press back on itself (the foremost, it seemed, had halted), and a rumour passed through that the order had been given to halt. All halted in the muddy road, just where they were.

Fires were lighted and the talk became more audible. Captain Tushin, after giving instructions to his battery, sent some of his soldiers to look for an ambulance or a doctor for the ensign, and sat down by the fire his soldiers had lighted by the roadside. Rostov too dragged himself to the fire. His whole body was trembling with fever from the pain, the cold, and the damp. He was dreadfully sleepy, but he could not go to sleep for the agonising pain in his arm, which ached and would not be easy in any position. He closed his eyes, then opened them to stare at the fire, which seemed to him dazzling red, and then at the stooping, feeble figure of Tushin, squatting in Turkish fashion near him. The big, kindly, and shrewd eyes of Tushin were fixed upon him with sympathy and commiseration. He saw that Tushin wished with all his soul to help him, but could do nothing for him.

On all sides they heard the footsteps and the chatter of the infantry going and coming and settling themselves round them. The sound of voices, of steps, and of horses' hoofs tramping in the mud, the crackling firewood far and near, all melted into one fluctuating roar of sound.

It was not now as before an unseen river flowing in the darkness, but a gloomy sea subsiding and still agitated after a storm. Rostov gazed vacantly and listened to what was passing before him and around him. An infantry soldier came up to the fire, squatted on his heels, held his hands to the fire, and turned his face.

"You don't mind, your honour?" he said, looking inquiringly at Tushin. "Here I've got lost from my company, your honour; I don't know myself where I am. It's dreadful!"

With the soldier an infantry officer approached the fire with a bandaged face. He asked Tushin to have the cannon moved a very little, so as to let a store wagon pass by. After the officer two soldiers ran up to the fire. They were swearing desperately and fighting, trying to pull a boot from one another.

"No fear! you picked it up! that's smart!" one shouted in a husky voice. Then a thin, pale soldier approached, his neck bandaged with a blood-stained rag. With a voice of exasperation he asked the artillerymen for water.

"Why, is one to die like a dog?" he said.

Tushin told them to give him water. Next a goodhumoured soldier ran up, to beg for some red-hot embers for the infantry.

"Some of your fire for the infantry! Glad to halt, lads. Thanks for the loan of the firing; we'll pay it back with interest," he said, carrying some glowing firebrands away into the darkness.

Next four soldiers passed by, carrying something heavy in an overcoat. One of them stumbled.

"Ay, the devils, they've left firewood in the road," grumbled one.

"He's dead; why carry him?" said one of them.

"Come on, you!" And they vanished into the darkness with their burden.

"Does it ache, eh?" Tushin asked Rostov in a whisper.

"Yes, it does ache."

"Your honour's sent for to the general. Here in a cottage he is," said a gunner, coming up to Tushin.

"In a minute, my dear." Tushin got up and walked away from the fire, buttoning up his coat and setting himself straight.

In a cottage that had been prepared for him not far from the artillerymen's fire, Prince Bagration was sitting at dinner, talking with several commanding officers, who had gathered about him. The little old colonel with the half-shut eyes was there, greedily gnawing at a mutton-bone, and the general of twenty-two years' irreproachable service, flushed with a glass of vodka and his dinner, and the staffofficer with the signet ring, and Zherkov, stealing uneasy glances at every one, and Prince Andrey, pale with set lips and feverishly glittering eyes.

In the corner of the cottage room stood a French flag, that had been captured, and the auditor with the naive countenance was feeling the stuff of which the flag was made, and shaking his head with a puzzled air, possibly because looking at the flag really interested him, or possibly because he did not enjoy the sight of the dinner, as he was hungry and no place had been laid for him. In the next cottage there was the French colonel, who had been taken prisoner by the dragoons. Our officers were flocking in to look at him. Prince Bagration thanked the several commanding officers, and inquired into details of the battle and of the losses. The general, whose regiment had been inspected at Braunau, submitted to the prince that as soon as the engagement began, he had fallen back from the copse, mustered the men who were cutting wood, and letting them pass by him, had made a bayonet charge with two battalions and repulsed the French.

"As soon as I saw, your excellency, that the first battalion was thrown into confusion, I stood in the road and thought, 'I'll let them get through and then open fire on them'; and that's what I did."

The general had so longed to do this, he had so regretted not having succeeded in doing it, that it seemed to him now that this was just what had happened. Indeed might it not actually have been so? Who could make out in such confusion what did and what did not happen?

"And by the way I ought to note, your excellency," he continued, recalling Dolohov's conversation with Kutuzov and his own late interview with the degraded officer, "that the private Dolohov, degraded to the ranks, took a French officer prisoner before my eyes and particularly distinguished himself."

"I saw here, your excellency, the attack of the Pavlograd hussars," Zherkov put in, looking uneasily about him. He had not seen the hussars at all that day, but had only heard about them from an infantry officer. "They broke up two squares, your excellency."

When Zherkov began to speak, several officers smiled, as they always did, expecting a joke from him. But as they perceived that what he was saying all redounded to the glory of our arms and of the day, they assumed a serious expression, although many were very well aware that what Zherkov was saying was a lie utterly without foundation. Prince Bagration turned to the old colonel.

"I thank you all, gentlemen; all branches of the service behaved heroically— infantry, cavalry, and artillery. How did two cannons come to be abandoned in the centre?" he inquired, looking about for some one. (Prince Bagration did not ask about the cannons of the left flank; he knew that all of them had been abandoned at the very beginning of the action.) "I think it was you I sent," he added, addressing the staff-officer.

"One had been disabled," answered the staffofHcer, "but the other, I can't explain; I was there all the while myself, giving instructions, and I had scarcely left there. . . . It was pretty hot, it's true," he added modesdy.

Some one said that Captain Tushin was close by here in the village, and that he had already been sent for.

"Oh, but you went there," said Prince Bagration, addressing Prince Andrey.

"To be sure, we rode there almost together," said the staff-officer, smiling affably to Bolkonsky.

"I had not the pleasure of seeing you," said Prince Andrey, coldly and abruptly. Every one was silent.

Tushin appeared in the doorway, timidly edging in behind the generals' backs. Making his way round the generals in the crowded hut, embarrassed as he always was before his superior officers, Tushin did not see the flag-staff and tumbled over it. Several of the officers laughed.

"How was it a cannon was abandoned?" asked Bagration, frowning, not so much at the captain as at the laughing officers, among whom Zherkov's laugh was the loudest. Only now in the presence of the angry-looking commander, Tushin conceived in all its awfulness the crime and disgrace of his being still alive when he had lost two cannons. He had been so excited that till that instant he had not had time to think of that. The officers' laughter had bewildered him still more. He stood before Bagration, his lower jaw quivering, and could scarcely articulate:

"I don't know . . . your excellency . . . I hadn't the men, your excellency."

"You could have got them from the battalions that were covering your position!" That there were no battalions there was what Tushin did not say, though it was the fact. He was afraid of getting another officer into trouble by saying that, and without uttering a word he gazed straight into Bagration's face, as a confused schoolboy gazes at the face of an examiner.

The silence was rather a lengthy one. Prince Bagration, though he had no wish to be severe, apparendy found nothing to say; the others did not venture to intervene. Prince Andrey was looking from under his brows at Tushin and his fingers moved nervously.

"Your excellency," Prince Andrey broke the silence with his abrupt voice, "you sent me to Captain Tushin's battery. I went there and found two thirds of the men and horses killed, two cannons disabled and no forces near to defend them."

Prince Bagration and Tushin looked now with equal intensity at Bolkonsky, as he went on speaking with suppressed emotion.

"And if your excellency will permit me to express my opinion," he went on, "we owe the success of the day more to the action of that battery and the heroic steadiness of Captain Tushin and his men than to anything else," said Prince Andrey, and he got up at once and walked away from the table, without waiting for a reply.

Prince Bagration looked at Tushin and, apparendy loath to express his disbelief in Bolkonsky's offhanded judgment, yet unable to put complete faith in it, he bent his head and said to Tushin that he could go. Prince Andrey walked out after him.

"Thanks, my dear fellow, you got me out of a scrape," Tushin said to him.

Prince Andrey looked at Tushin, and walked away without uttering a word. Prince Andrey felt bitter and melancholy. It was all so strange, so unlike what he had been hoping for.

THE CRIME OF THE BRIGADIER

ARTHUR CONAN DOYLE

Before March 18, clearly, but necessitating time for Gerard to return from official and unofficial hospitality in England after his capture in July 1810. General Sainte-Croix, *beau sabreur* among the dragoons, was killed in October 1810 while reconnoitring English lines (by a gun-boat pot-shot). Since fox-hunting, however inappropriately, formed the subject of many Edwardian English Christmas cards, we may permit ourselves a date in late December. Wellington had withdrawn behind his impregnable lines at Torres Vedras on 8 October; Massena had fallen back on Santarem on 14 November. Modern readers may need to be told that the fox-hunting religion required that the fox be always torn to pieces by the hounds, and that the hounds were sacrosanct.

In all the great hosts of France there was only one officer towards whom the English of Wellington's Army retained a deep, steady, and unchangeable hatred. There were plunderers among the French, and men of violence, gamblers, duellists, and roues. All these could be forgiven, for others of their kidney were to be found among the ranks of the English. But one officer of Massena's force had committed a crime which was unspeakable, unheard of, abominable; only to be alluded to with curses late in the evening, when a second bottle had loosened the tongues of men. The news of it was carried back to England, and country gentlemen who knew little of the details of the war grew crimson with passion when they heard of it, and yeomen of the shires raised freckled fists to Heaven and swore. And yet who should be the doer of this dreadful deed but our friend the Brigadier, Etienne Gerard, of the Hussars of Conflans, gay-riding, plume-tossing, debonnaire, the darling of the ladies and of the six brigades of light cavalry.

But the strange part of it is that this gallant gentleman did this hateful thing, and made himself the most unpopular man in the Peninsula, without ever knowing that he had done a crime for which there is hardly a name amid all the resources of our language. He died of old age, and never once in that imperturbable self-confidence which adorned or disfigured his character knew that so many thousand Englishmen would gladly have hanged him with their own hands. On the contrary, he numbered this adventure among those other exploits which he has given to the world, and many a time he chuckled and hugged himself as he narrated it to the eager circle who gathered round him in that humble cafe where, between his dinner and his dominoes, he would tell, amid tears and laughter, of that inconceivable Napoleonic past when France, like an angel of wrath, rose up, splendid and terrible, before a cowering continent. Let us listen to him as he tells the story in his own way and from his own point of view.

You must know, my friends, said he, that it was towards the end of the year eighteen hundred and ten that I and Massena and the others pushed Wellington backwards until we had hoped to drive him and his army into the Tagus. But when we were still twenty-five miles from Lisbon we found that we were betrayed, for what had this Englishman done but build an enormous line of works and forts at a place called Torres Vedras, so that even we were unable to get through them! They lay across the whole Peninsula, and our army was so far from home that we did not dare to risk a reverse, and we had already learned at Busaco that it was no child's play to fight against these people. What could we do then but sit down in front of these lines and blockade them to the best of our power? There we remained for six months, amid such anxieties that Massena said afterwards that he had not one hair which was not white upon his body. For my own part, I did not worry much about our situation, but I looked after our horses, who were in much need of rest and green fodder. For the rest, we drank the wine of the country and passed the time as best we might. There was a lady at Santarem—but my lips are sealed. It is the part of a gallant man to say nothing, though he may indicate that he could say a great deal.

One day Massena sent for me, and I found him in his tent with a great plan pinned upon the table. He looked at me in silence with that single piercing eye of his, and I felt by his expression that the matter was serious. He was nervous and ill at ease, but my bearing seemed to reassure him. It is good to be in contact with brave men.

'Colonel Etienne Gerard,' said he, 'I have always heard that you are a very gallant and enterprising officer.'

It was not for me to confirm such a report, and yet it would be folly to deny it, so I clinked my spurs together and saluted.

'You are also an excellent rider.'

I admitted it.

'And the best swordsman in the six brigades of light cavalry.'

Massena was famous for the accuracy of his information.

'Now,' said he, 'if you will look at this plan you will have no difficulty in understanding what it is that I wish you to do. These are the lines of Torres Vedras. You will perceive that they cover a vast space, and you will realize that the English can only hold a position here and there. Once through the lines you have twenty-five miles of open country which lie between them and Lisbon. It is very important to me to learn how Wellington's troops are distributed throughout that space, and it is my wish that you should go and ascertain.'

His words turned me cold.

'Sir,' said I, 'it is impossible that a colonel of light cavalry should condescend to act as a spy.'

He laughed and clapped me on the shoulder.

'You would not be a Hussar if you were not a hot-head,' said he. 'If you will listen you will understand that I have not asked you to act as a spy. What do you think of that horse?'

He had conducted me to the opening of his tent, and there was a Chasseur who led up and down a most admirable creature. He was a dapple grey, not very tall, a little over fifteen hands perhaps, but with the short head and splendid arch of the neck which comes with the Arab blood. His shoulders and haunches were so muscular, and yet his legs so fine, that it thrilled me with joy just to gaze upon him. A fine horse or a beautiful woman, I cannot look at them unmoved, even now when seventy winters have chilled my blood. You can think how it was in the year '10.

'This,' said Massena, 'is Voltigeur, the swiftest horse in our army. What I desire is that you should start to-night, ride round the lines upon the flank, make your way across the enemy's rear, and return upon the other flank bringing me news of his dispositions. You will wear a uniform, and will, therefore, if captured, be safe from the death of a spy. It is probable that you will get through the lines unchallenged, for the posts are very scattered. Once through, in daylight you can outride anything which you meet, and if you keep off the roads you may escape entirely unnoticed. If you have not reported yourself by to-morrow night, I will understand that you are taken, and I will offer them Colonel Petrie in exchange.'

Ah, how my heart swelled with pride and joy as I sprang into the saddle and galloped this grand horse up and down to show the Marshal the mastery which I had of him! He was magnificent—we were both magnificent, for Massena clapped his hands and cried out in his delight. It was not I, but he, who said that a gallant beast deserves a gallant rider. Then, when for the third time, with my panache flying and my dolman streaming behind me, I thundered past him, I saw upon his hard old face that he had no longer any doubt that he had chosen the man for his purpose. I drew my sabre, raised the hilt to my lips in salute, and galloped on to my own quarters. Already the news had spread that I had been chosen for a mission, and my little rascals came swarming out of their tents to cheer me. Ah! it brings the tears to my old eyes when I think how proud they were of their Colonel. And I was proud of them also. They deserved a dashing leader.

The night promised to be a stormy one, which was very much to my liking. It was my desire to keep my departure most secret, for it was evident that if the English heard that I had been detached from the army they would naturally conclude that something important was about to happen. My horse was taken, therefore, beyond the picket line, as if for watering, and I followed and mounted him there. I had a map, a compass, and a paper of instructions from the Marshal, and with these in the bosom of my tunic and my sabre at my side I set out upon my adventure.

A thin rain was falling and there was no moon, so you may imagine that it was not very cheerful. But my heart was light at the thought of the honour which had been done me and the glory which awaited me. This exploit should be one more in that brilliant series which was to change my sabre into a baton.

Ah, how we dreamed, we foolish fellows, young, and drunk with success! Could I have foreseen that night as I rode, the chosen man of sixty thousand, that I should spend my life planting cabbages on a hundred francs a month! Oh, my youth, my hopes, my comrades! But the wheel turns and never stops. Forgive me, my friends, for an old man has his weakness.

My route, then, lay across the face of the high ground of Torres Vedras, then over a streamlet, past a farmhouse which had been burned down and was now only a landmark, then through a forest of young cork oaks, and so to the monastery of San Antonio, which marked the left of the English position. Here I turned south and rode quietly over the downs, for it was at this point that Massena thought that it would be most easy for me to find my way unobserved through the position. I went very slowly, for it was so dark that I could not see my hand in front of me. In such cases I leave my bridle loose and let my horse pick its own way. Voltigeur went confidently forward, and I was very content to sit upon his back and to peer about me, avoiding every light. For three hours we advanced in this cautious way, until it seemed to me that I must have left all danger behind me. I then pushed on more briskly, for I wished to be in the rear of the whole army by daybreak. There are many vineyards in these parts which in winter become open plains, and a horseman finds few difficulties in his way.

But Massena had underrated the cunning of these English, for it appears that there was not one line of defence but three, and it was the third, which was the most formidable, through which I was at that instant passing. As I rode, elated at my own success, a lantern flashed suddenly before me, and I saw the glint of polished gun-barrels and the gleam of a red coat.

'Who goes there?' cried a voice—such a voice! I swerved to the right and rode like a madman, but a dozen squirts of fire came out of the darkness, and the bullets whizzed all round my ears. That was no new sound to me, my friends, though I will not talk like a foolish conscript and say that I have ever liked it. But at least it had never kept me from thinking clearly, and so I knew that there was nothing for it but to gallop hard and try my luck elsewhere. I rode round the English picket, and then, as I heard nothing more of them, I concluded rightly that I had at last come through their defences. For five miles I rode south, striking a tinder from time to time to look at my pocket compass. And then in an instant—I feel the pang once more as my memory brings back the moment— my horse, without a sob or stagger, fell stone dead beneath me!

I had never known it, but one of the bullets from that infernal picket had passed through his body. The gallant creature had never winced nor weakened, but had gone while life was in him. One instant I was secure on the swiftest, most graceful horse in Massena's army. The next he lay upon his side, worth only the price of his hide, and I stood there that most helpless, most ungainly of creatures, a dismounted Hussar. What could I do with my boots, my spurs, my trailing sabre? I was far inside the enemy's lines. How could I hope to get back again? I am not ashamed to say that I, Etienne Gerard, sat upon my dead horse and sank my face in my hands in my despair. Already the first streaks were whitening the east. In half an hour it would be light. That I should have won my way past every obstacle and then at this last instant be left at the mercy of my enemies, my mission ruined, and myself a prisoner—was it not enough to break a soldier's heart?

But courage, my friends! We have these moments of weakness, the bravest of us; but I have a spirit like a slip of steel, for the more you bend it the higher it springs. One spasm of despair, and then a brain of ice and a heart of fire. All was not yet lost. I who had come through so many hazards would come through this one also. I rose from my horse and considered what had best be done.

And first of all it was certain that I could not get back. Long before I could pass the lines it would be broad daylight. I must hide myself for the day, and then devote the next night to my escape. I took the saddle, holsters, and bridle from poor Voltigeur, and I concealed them among some bushes, so that no one finding him could know that he was a French horse. Then, leaving him lying there, I wandered on in search of some place where I might be safe for the day. In every direction I could see camp fires upon the sides of the hills, and already figures had begun to move around them. I must hide quickly, or I was lost.

But where was I to hide? It was a vineyard in which I found myself, the poles of the vines still standing, but the plants gone. There was no cover there. Besides, I should want some food and water before another night had come. I hurried wildly onwards through the waning darkness, trusting that chance would be my friend. And I was not disappointed. Chance is a woman, my friends, and she has her eye always upon a gallant Hussar.

Well, then, as I stumbled through the vineyard, something loomed in front of me, and I came upon a great square house with another long, low building upon one side of it. Three roads met there, and it was easy to see that this was the posada, or wine shop. There was no light in the windows, and everything was dark and silent, but, of course, I knew that such comfortable quarters were certainly occupied, and probably by someone of importance. I have learned, however, that the nearer the danger may really be the safer place, and so I was by no means inclined to trust myself away from this shelter. The low building was evidently the stable, and into this I crept, for the door was unlatched. The place was full of bullocks and sheep, gathered there, no doubt, to be out of the clutches of marauders. A ladder led to a loft, and up this I climbed and concealed myself very snugly among some bales of hay upon the top. This loft had a small open window, and I was able to look down upon the front of the inn and also upon the road. There I crouched and waited to see what would happen.

It was soon evident that I had not been mistaken when I had thought that this might be the quarters of some person of importance. Shortly after daybreak an English light dragoon arrived with a despatch, and from then onwards the place was in a turmoil, officers continually riding up and away. Always the same name was upon their lips: 'Sir Stapleton—Sir Stapleton.' It was hard for me to lie there with a dry moustache and watch the great flagons which were brought out by the landlord to these English officers. But it amused me to look at their fresh-coloured, clean-shaven, careless faces, and to wonder what they would think if they knew that so celebrated a person was lying so near to them. And then, as I lay and watched, I saw a sight which filled me with surprise.

It is incredible the insolence of these English! What do you suppose Milord Wellington had done when he found that Massena had blockaded him and that he could not move his army? I might give you many guesses. You might say that he had raged, that he had despaired, that he had brought his troops together and spoken to them about glory and the fatherland before leading them to one last battle. No, Milord did none of these things. But he sent a fleet ship to England to bring him a number of fox-dogs, and he with his officers settled himself down to chase the fox. It is true what I tell you. Behind the lines of Torres Vedras these mad Englishmen made the fox chase three days in the week. We had heard of it in the camp, and now I was myself to see that it was true.

For, along the road which I have described, there came these very dogs, thirty or forty of them, white and brown, each with its tail at the same angle, like the bayonets of the Old Guard. My faith, but it was a pretty sight! And behind and amidst them there rode three men with peaked caps and red coats, whom I understood to be the hunters. After them came many horsemen with uniforms of various kinds, stringing along the roads in twos and threes, talking together and laughing. They did not seem to be going above a trot, and it appeared to me that it must indeed be a slow fox which they hoped to catch. However, it was their affair, not mine, and soon they had all passed my window and were out of sight. I waited and I watched, ready for any chance which might offer.

Presently an officer, in a blue uniform not unlike that of our flying artillery, came cantering down the road—an elderly, stout man he was, with grey side-whiskers. He stopped and began to talk with an orderly officer of dragoons, who waited outside the inn, and it was then that I learned the advantage of the English which had been taught me. I could hear and understand all that was said.

'Where is the meet?' said the officer, and I thought that he was hungering for his bifstek. But the other answered him that it was near Altara, so I saw that it was a place of which he spoke.

'You are late, Sir George,' said the orderly.

'Yes, I had a court-martial. Has Sir Stapleton Cotton gone?'

At this moment a window opened, and a handsome young man in a very splendid uniform looked out of it.

'Halloa, Murray!' said he. 'These cursed papers keep me, but I will be at your heels.'

'Very good, Cotton. I am late already, so I will ride on.'

'You might order my groom to bring round my horse,' said the young General at the window to the orderly below, while the other went on down the road.

The orderly rode away to some outlying stable, and then in a few minutes there came a smart English groom with a cockade in his hat, leading by the bridle a horse—and, oh, my friends, you have never known the perfection to which a horse can attain until you have seen a first-class English hunter. He was superb: tall, broad, strong, and yet as graceful and agile as a deer. Coal black he was in colour, and his neck, and his shoulder, and his quarters, and his fetlocks—how can I describe him all to you? The sun shone upon him as on polished ebony, and he raised his hoofs in a little, playful dance so lightly and prettily, while he tossed his mane and whinnied with impatience. Never have I seen such a mixture of strength and beauty and grace. I had often wondered how the English Hussars had managed to ride over the Chasseurs of the Guards in the affair at Astorga, but I wondered no longer when I saw the English horses.

There was a ring for fastening bridles at the door of the inn, and the groom tied the horse there while he entered the house. In an instant I had seen the chance which Fate had brought to me. Were I in that saddle I should be better off than when I started. Even Voltigeur could not compare with this magnificent creature. To think is to act with me. In one instant I was down the ladder and at the door of the stable. The next I was out and the bridle was in my hand. I bounded into the saddle. Somebody, the master or the man, shouted wildly behind me. What cared I for his shouts! I touched the horse with my spurs and he bounded forward with such a spring that only a rider like myself could have sat him. I gave him his head and let him go—it did not matter to me where, so long as we left this inn far behind us. He thundered away across the vineyards, and in a very few minutes I had placed miles between myself and my pursuers. They could no longer tell in that wild country in which direction I had gone. I knew that I was safe, and so, riding to the top of a small hill, I drew my pencil and note-book from my pocket and proceeded to make plans of those camps which I could see and to draw the outline of the country.

He was a dear creature upon whom I sat, but it was not easy to draw upon his back, for every now and then his two ears would cock, and he would start and quiver with impatience. At first I could not understand this trick of his, but soon I observed that he only did it when a peculiar noise—'yoy, yoy, yoy'—came from somewhere among the oak woods beneath us. And then suddenly this strange cry changed into a most terrible screaming, with the frantic blowing of a horn. Instantly he went mad—this horse. His eyes blazed. His mane bristled. He bounded from the earth and bounded again, twisting and turning in a frenzy. My pencil flew one way and my notebook another. And then, as I looked down into the valley, an extraordinary sight met my eyes. The hunt was streaming down it. The fox I could not see, but the dogs were in full cry, their noses down, their tails up, so close together that they might have been one great yellow and white moving carpet. And behind them rode the horsemen—my faith, what a sight! Consider every type which a great army could show. Some in hunting dress, but the most in uniforms: blue dragoons, red dragoons, red-trousered hussars, green riflemen, artillery men, gold-slashed lancers, and most of all red, red, red, for the infantry officers ride as hard as the cavalry. Such a crowd, some well mounted, some ill, but all flying along as best they might, the subaltern as good as the general, jostling and pushing, spurring and driving, with every thought thrown to the winds save that they should have the blood of this absurd fox! Truly, they are an extraordinary people, the English!

But I had little time to watch the hunt or to marvel at these islanders, for of all these mad creatures the very horse upon which I sat was the maddest. You understand that he was himself a hunter, and that the crying of these dogs was to him what the call of a cavalry trumpet in the street yonder would be to me. It thrilled him. It drove him wild. Again and again he bounded into the air, and then, seizing the bit between his teeth, he plunged down the slope and galloped after the dogs. I swore, and tugged, and pulled, but I was powerless. This English General rode his horse with a snaffle only, and the beast had a mouth of iron. It was useless to pull him back. One might as well try to keep a Grenadier from a wine bottle. I gave it up in despair, and, settling down in the saddle, I prepared for the worst which could befall.

What a creature he was! Never have I felt such a horse between my knees. His great haunches gathered under him with every stride, and he shot forward ever faster and faster, stretched like a greyhound, while the wind beat in my face and whistled past my ears. I was wearing our undress jacket, a uniform simple and dark in itself—though some figures give distinction to any uniform—and I had taken the precaution to remove the long panache from my busby. The result was that, amidst the mixture of costumes in the hunt, there was no reason why mine should attract attention, or why these men, whose thoughts were all with the chase, should give any heed to me. The idea that a French officer might be riding with them was too absurd to enter their minds. I laughed as I rode, for, indeed, amid all the danger, there was something of comic in the situation.

I have said that the hunters were very unequally mounted, and so at the end of a few miles, instead of being one body of men, like a charging regiment, they were scattered over a considerable space, the better riders well up to the dogs and the others trailing away behind. Now, I was as good a rider as any, and my horse was the best of them all, and so you can imagine that it was not long before he carried me to the front. And when I saw the dogs streaming over the open, and the red-coated huntsman behind them, and only seven or eight horsemen between us, then it was that the strangest thing of all happened, for I, too, went mad—I, Etienne Gerard! In a moment it came upon me, this spirit of sport, this desire to excel, this hatred of the fox. Accursed animal, should he then defy us? Vile robber, his hour was come! Ah, it is a great feeling, this feeling of sport, my friends, this desire to trample the fox under the hoofs of your horse. I have made the fox chase with the English. I have also, as I may tell you some day, fought the box-fight with the Bustler, of Bristol. And I say to you that this sport is a wonderful thing—full of interest as well as madness.

The farther we went the faster galloped my horse, and soon there were but three men as near the dogs as I was. All thought of fear of discovery had vanished. My brain throbbed, my blood ran hot—only one thing upon earth seemed worth living for, and that was to overtake this infernal fox. I passed one of the horsemen—a Hussar like myself. There were only two in front of me now: the one in a black coat, the other the blue artilleryman whom I had seen at the inn. His grey whiskers streamed in the wind, but he rode magnificently. For a mile or more we kept in this order, and then, as we galloped up a steep slope, my lighter weight brought me to the front. I passed them both, and when I reached the crown I was riding level with the little, hard-faced English huntsman. In front of us were the dogs, and then, a hundred paces beyond them, was a brown wisp of a thing, the fox itself, stretched to the uttermost. The sight of him fired my blood. 'Aha, we have you then, assassin!' I cried, and shouted my encouragement to the huntsman. I waved my hand to show him that there was one upon whom he could rely.

And now there were only the dogs between me and my prey. These dogs, whose duty it is to point out the game, were now rather a hindrance than a help to us, for it was hard to know how to pass them. The huntsman felt the difficulty as much as I, for he rode behind them, and could make no progress towards the fox. He was a swift rider, but wanting in enterprise. For my part, I felt that it would be unworthy of the Hussars of Conflans if I could not overcome such a difficulty as this. Was Etienne Gerard to be stopped by a herd of fox-dogs? It was absurd. I gave a shout and spurred my horse.

'Hold hard, sir! Hold hard!' cried the huntsman.

He was uneasy for me, this good old man, but I reassured him by a wave and a smile. The dogs opened in front of me. One or two may have been hurt, but what would you have? The egg must be broken for the omelette. I could hear the huntsman shouting his congratulations behind me. One more effort, and the dogs were all behind me. Only the fox was in front.

Ah, the joy and pride of that moment! To know that I had beaten the English at their own sport. Here were three hundred all thirsting for the life of this animal, and yet it was I who was about to take it. I thought of my comrades of the light cavalry brigade, of my mother, of the Emperor, of France. I had brought honour to each and all. Every instant brought me nearer to the fox. The moment for action had arrived, so I unsheathed my sabre. I waved it in the air, and the brave English all shouted behind me.

Only then did I understand how difficult is this fox chase, for one may cut again and again at the creature and never strike him once. He is small, and turns quickly from a blow. At every cut I heard those shouts of encouragement from behind me, and they spurred me to yet another effort. And then at last the supreme moment of my triumph arrived. In the very act of turning I caught him fair with such another back-handed cut as that with which I killed the aide-de-camp of the Emperor of Russia. He flew into two pieces, his head one way and his tail another. I looked back and waved the blood-stained sabre in the air. For the moment I was exalted—superb!

Ah! how I should have loved to have waited to have received the congratulations of these generous enemies. There were fifty of them in sight, and not one who was not waving his hand and shouting. They are not really such a phlegmatic race, the English. A gallant deed in war or in sport will always warm their hearts. As to the old huntsman, he was the nearest to me, and I could see with my own eyes how overcome he was by what he had seen. He was like a man paralyzed, his mouth open, his hand, with outspread fingers, raised in the air. For a moment my inclination was to return and to embrace him. But already the call of duty was sounding in my ears, and these English, in spite of all the fraternity which exists among sportsmen, would certainly have made me prisoner. There was no hope for my mission now, and I had done all that I could do. I could see the lines of Massena's camp no very great distance off, for, by a lucky chance, the chase had taken us in that direction. I turned from the dead fox, saluted with my sabre, and galloped away.

But they would not leave me so easily, these gallant huntsmen. I was the fox now, and the chase swept bravely over the plain. It was only at the moment when I started for the camp that they could have known that I was a Frenchman, and now the whole swarm of them were at my heels. We were within gunshot of our pickets before they would halt, and then they stood in knots and would not go away, but shouted and waved their hands at me. No, I will not think that it was in enmity.

Rather would I fancy that a glow of admiration filled their breasts, and that their one desire was to embrace the stranger who had carried himself so gallantly and well.

THE BLADENSBURG RACES

NEIL SWANSON

I t is twelve and a half o'clock.

The sky is as clean as a scalded plate. The sun is as bright and hot as the polished brass knob of an andiron. Across the gray-drooping, heat-sick tops of the willows, across the stream and the village roofs, at the far east end of the crooked street, the dust cloud over the river road has settled a little, has drifted a little aside. The enemy stands in plain sight.

The enemy looks different. *What's he look different from?* Oh, I don't know . . . nothing in partic'lar . . . only I didn't ex-ex-pect . . . Well, just diff'rent.

The enemy, seen for the first time, always looks different.

Those red-jacketed men over there are no longer a word of contempt in a holiday orator's mouth, no longer an angry phrase in the *Patriot* or the *National Intelligencer.* They are no longer even a false report fetched in by one, of Charlie Ridgley's videttes, no longer a rumor, well yeasted with imagination and kneaded by tongue after tongue until it rises and swells like dough. Those men over there look sort of ordinary, they don't look any bigger than other men. There are a lot of them, though. The column stretches away down the river road as if it went clear to the Old Fields or clear to Marlb'rough or clear to England, maybe. To the cannoneers and the riflemen, left alone in the triangle field, the British column looks as if the most swollen rumors were true. It looks like all the twelve thousand men it was reported to be.

The British, watching the three lines of men on the opposite side of the branch, believe they are facing nine thousand American troops.

There are, on paper, 5,938 Americans. There are, on paper, 4,270 British.

Both those figures are probably high, for neither takes into account the sick and the stragglers. Both armies had suffered attrition,[2] the strength of both had been ground down on the hard, hot grindstone of Maryland's August sun.

There are four good, veteran regiments over there on the river road . . . the 85th . . . the Fourth, the King's Own . . . the 44th, the East Essex Foot . . . the 21st, the Royal North British Fusiliers. Now that the dust has thinned, a man can see that the column is not all red: there are streaks and patches of blue. Besides the four infantry regiments, there are two hundred sailors from the fleet and six hundred royal marines; there is a company of a hundred Negroes "lately armed and disciplined" in Bermuda; there is a detachment of sappers and miners and a detachment of rocket troops. Half the sailors are hauling ammunition and stores, half are dragging the guns by hand . . . one six-pounder and two little grasshoppers taking a three-pound ball. There are two-wheeled powder carts and tumbrils loaded with rockets. There is even a troop of cavalry . . . infantry mounted on Maryland farm nags . . . riding with blanket saddles, with reins and stirrups of rope: The long column waits, silent, solid, closed up, the men six abreast in the road. Where the river road touches the town, a small block of scarlet waits by itself . . . the advance guard . . . fifty men of the 85th.

The waiting is almost over. Little figures go scuttling up the main street, back to the column, back to the cluster of officers on the green slope of Lowndes's hill. The advance guard moves. The column behind it stirs with a sudden flash, with a sudden ripple of light as the bayonets lift, as the muskets go to the carry. Here they come. *Here they come!*

The leading company of the 85th passes out of sight between the farthest houses, it swings left into the street, it is steady and brisk. Behind the raw bank of earth and the wilted camouflage, the Baltimore gunpointers stoop to their guns. They know how the guns are laid; they are sure, but they have to make sure. In the gun corporals' hands, the slow matches smolder and glow. The glow trembles a little. We've never shot at a man, we've never tried to blow a man's insides out with a six-pound chunk of iron. When they get to the corner of that house . . . when the front rank takes six more steps . . . four more . . . Number One . . . *fire!*

The little gun roars and jumps. The trail digs a gouge in the dirt. The embrasure is roily with smoke. Number Two . . . *fire!*

But the neat red block is gone from the village street. It has split apart like a billet of wood when the ax comes down on the block. The two halves are huddled against the walls of the houses on either side of the street. There are only chips left in the street, three chips in scarlet jackets. One lies still, the other two wriggle and squirm. *So that's it. So that's what it's like.*

The second six-pound ball only plows up the empty street, it only throws dirt on the chips.

The advance guard is moving again, it halted for only a moment. But it isn't marching now, it isn't in proper column. The split-apart halves haven't come together, they seem content to stay split. They are two long files on either side of the street, pressed close to the fronts of the houses. The files move in jerks. A man runs, you can see him swerve around the front steps of a house; when he comes to the next house, he drops to his knees and crouches, half hidden behind its steps. Three more men, flattened against a red-brick wall, peel themselves away from the wall and begin to run along the edge of the roadway; they move heavily, their run is a jouncing trot; you can see their knapsacks jounce up and down on their backs. Two of them slip out of sight behind the corner of a house; the third flattens himself again to its wall. Jerkily, in no kind of drill formation, with spurts and pauses, with no neat drill-ground spaces between the men but with irregular gaps, the advance company worms its way down the street toward the elbow-bend of the town. It makes a poor target. It makes no target at all.

Behind it, on the river road, a long section has broken loose from the column halted below Lowndes's hill. The whole, first brigade of the British army is moving into the village. It moves in a strong, steady current . . . the ranks are closed up . . . the men are still six abreast. But the current breaks when it touches the town. It doesn't flow down the street. It turns into, two small rivulets, trickling along the gutters.

The frustrated gunners swear. *What the hell? What in hell are they up to? What kind of fumadiddle is that? The British don't fight like that. They fight in the open; that's how we licked 'em before. God damn it, the British stand up, they don't hide; that's how Braddock got licked. They come ,at you in double ranks . . . in columns of double ranks . . . in thick columns of companies. You can mow 'em down.* But they don't. And you can't.

The Baltimore guns are firing smoothly. The crews are well drilled, they move with a gun-house precision. The six-pound balls are making big splashes of dust in the street, they are knocking bricks out of the houses, they are knocking holes in the walls. But they are doing the enemy almost no damage at all. They can't stop the steady trickle of infantry down through the town.

For this battle was fought hours ago, when Stansbury gave, up Lowndes's hill and the village itself. We are fighting it now with guns, but the guns don't count. This opening phase of the battle was fought when Stansbury picked this position "under cover of the town." Now, one by one, the blunders made in preparing the battle fall on the men who must fight it.

The town is not "cover" for either the guns or the rifles. It is almost perfect cover for the advancing British, filtering through the back yards and between the houses, seeping along the street. The Baltimore guns are hanging away, but "only occasionally" can the crews find "an object" to shoot at. The British infantry is flopping down in the gutters, lying flat in the gardens, squatting behind the big trees. These are hard-bitten men, they have faced flying iron before. They crack jokes when the brick dust showers them. The tough old-campaigner jokes help to steady the few young, recruits who came out from England after the fighting in France was over. But a man is hit, now and then. A six-pound ball strikes a boy stretched out on his belly between two subalterns. It smashes his leg and grinds it completely off. The boy looks at his lieutenant with a "peculiar expression . . . as much as to ask how under such circumstances, he ought to behave." The lieutenant can "not help laughing."

The British have not fired a shot. The battle, so far, belongs to the Baltimore guns. But their fire is slackening; the cartridge chests aren't, too full; they can't afford to waste powder. Major Pihkney stood behind the guns till the second round was fired, but he is down at the end of the open field, now; he has gone forward again to his observation post in front of the batteries, to the top of the bank where the field drops down to the thicketed bottoms. His men—the two companies left here at the apex of the Y, the hundred men of Bill Dyer and Dominic Bader's companies—are sifting down through the bushes, down toward the edge of the stream, toward the bridge. Even then they are still out of range, their rifles still, out of the fight.

But the Baltimore guns have, presently, a target. Just north of the bend of the town, a warehouse juts out from the row of houses. Now, from the warehouse close under the partial concealment of its wall or inside, through a window . . . springs a flash and a noise. The noise is a strange, roaring whoos-shh. The, flash is a stream of flame. A streak of something leaps across the river. It spits fire backwards, it trails fire behind it. It looks a good deal like a comet and it's near of a size with a comet low down in the sky. Only comets don't jump at you out of somebody's yard. They don't come straight at you, either. This thing is coming straight for the guns. It rises, arches, clears the tops of the willows. The wind of it stirs the willows, the fiery sparks drip on the leaves. But it's dropping now, it's curving down toward the field, it's beginning to wobble. You can see a stick, swishing behind it, in and out of the sparks. It hits the ground a good way in front of the guns and kicks up a jet of dirt. It lies there . . . not long, only a second . . . a man can see it quiver. As if it had taken a good deep breath, it wooshes again . . . it darts off to one side with smoke and fire spurting out of its tail . . . it bounces and jumps . . . it darts this way and that . . . it acts like a crazy thing, like a hen with its head chopped off. It leaves a scorched trail in the weeds, a crazily crooked trail with feathers of smoke drift-ing down. When it lies still at last, you can see an eight-foot pole attached to a kind of tube with a pointed nose. The pole, too, is scorched.

Another flash springs from the warehouse . . . another harsh, rushing roar . . . another fire-spitting streak. Then several together, a volley of rockets, a whole skein of fire threads weaving and interweaving. The cannoneers watch them came. Their bodies go tense, they can't help shrinking a little. The rifle-men make themselves small in the bushes, they stare with a fixed fascination. This is the unknown . . . this is the strange new weapon . . . this is the poison gas at Ypres . . . the tanks at Cambrai . . . the flame thrower . . . the incendiary bomb of its day . . . the Stuka . . . the screaming dive bomber . . . the flaming onion . . . the bazooka, the katiusha. Its primary purpose is terror. It can burn ships, explode magazines, set towns on fire. But against living things, it depends more on fear than on fire; its target is minds more than bodies; its flaming trail sets fire to imaginations. It can rout a cavalry charge by stampeding the horses, break up a column of field guns galloping into action; the rocket troops them-selves, when furnished with horses, must leave the teams far to the rear; horses, can become accustomed to gunfire but not to these fiery monsters, not to this tearing sound, half gargle, half strangled whoops-There is something personal about these hurtling, fire-spouting things. You can see them come. They are aimed straight at you . . . at *you*. The truth is that aiming is largely a matter of hope and intention. This new weapon is at least as inaccurate as it is fear-inspiring. What a flight of rockets will do in a little wind is almost beyond prediction; they have been known to turn in mid-r air and plunge down on the troops who discharged them. Even now, in the dead-still calm, they fly every which way. But that is part of their terror: you never can tell: you can't tell what the crazy thing will do when it starts to wobble, you can't guess where it is going; even when it falls and lies still, its nose pointed away, you can't be sure that it's dead, you can't know that it won't gush flame in your face and take three idiotic leaps and come darting back to bury its red-hot metal tip in your guts. It doesn't. Not often, at least. But the thought of it leaves your guts weak.

The volley of rockets falls harmless. The gunners stay at their guns, the riflemen stay in the thicket. They stay, but their nerves are shaken. A man can't help the vibrance of nerves in his knees and the calves of his legs; they aren't really his legs, they are too far away, he isn't too sure they will move when he tells them to move. But they do. The cannoneers go to work: on the warehouse. Their hands may not be quite so deft with the flannel cartridges, they may grip the rammers needlessly tight, but they lay the guns well. "A few well-directed shots" drive the rocketmen out of their nest. The rocket fire stops.

But the infantry, filtering through the village, has already ac-complished the first vital part of its mission. The steady seepage of men has saturated the town, it has had the effect of a flood; the village is filled with almost invisible troops. The whole first brigade has trickled down to the bend of the town and spread northward behind the houses that face the American lines. The lower town has turned into a dam with a thousand men gathered behind it. As if somebody opened a floodgate, a gush of troops bursts from the dam.

It breaks out from the town at the elbow-bend, where the road starts down to the bridge. It is the advance guard again, the leading company of the 85th Foot. It comes down the narrow road in a compact rush, it comes like the small, solid wave in a mill-race when the mill pond gate is opened.

With handspikes and dragropes, with fingers gripping the wheel spokes, with bodies heaving and straining, the Baltimore gunners wrestle the clumsy guns till the muzzles point toward the bridge. A gun sergeant, stooping, his hand raised, sees the head of the running column cross the end of the bridge and the end of the black iron muzzle. His hand drops, he jumps to escape the backward jump of the gun, the number-two gunner presses the match to the vent. The piece recoils, it runs back with its trail kicking dirt, with its matrosses holding it back by the dragropes. A second gun fires and rolls back. On the bridge, the red column recoils . . . not as fast as the guns, but uncertain, a churning of men in confusion, of officers trying to hold the platoons as the gun crews hold to the guns. Then the company breaks and runs. It leaves seven men on the bridge and the road.

But it rallies. It tries again. Not a solid wave, now . . . a succession of little waves . . . little clumps of men running, bent over . . . "small parties at full speed." The Baltimore guns are firing as fast as the gunners can sponge and load and take aim through the hanging smoke. They have help, now. Behind them, on the turnpike, the two six-pounders detached from Captain Ben Burch's Washington battery open fire at long range. Down in the thickets, the rifles begin to crackle. They cut through the grump of the guns like the slash of whips, of whips with a long, thin lash. The shot comes first . . . hard . . . thin . . . then the whine and sting of the echo. The echo draws out like a whiplash being with-drawn, it coils itself in the hollow between the hills. If it weren't for the cannon, a man could think he was standing in Market street, watching the rival stages pulling out from the coachyard of Fountain Inn; he could think he was in, the taproom drinking a tall,-cool drink, hearing the whips go off like shots and making bets on the drivers. *God, I could use a drink!* My throat's like a flannel cartridge. This gun's getting hot . . . my throat's hotter . . . it's drier, too . . . I could swallow that whole damn' sponge. *Handle cartridge! Charge piece! Ram down cartridge! Prime! Take aim!*

Fire!

The six guns behind the embankment are doing the best they can. The two guns on the pike are doing the best they can. But it isn't enough. There are too many motions to make, too many commands. No matter how fast a crew moves, the firing is slow, it takes forever . . . forever. The guns can't keep up: with the blunders made hours ago. Eight muzzle-loading, slow-firing guns, throwing pieces of iron no bigger than a man's fist, might stop the rush of those waves on the narrow bridge . . . they might, if the Baltimore guns had been put where they ought to be, hot behind a barbette meant for bigger, heavier guns . . . if they had been put where their chunks of iron could sweep the bridge from one end clean to the other. But they can't do that, where they are; they can hit the bridge only obliquely, they can only shoot across it from side to side. They might stop those small parties yet, if they only had grapeshot to spray the bridge . . . if they had case shot or canister . . . if they had shells to burst at the feet of those running men or over their heads. But they have only the solid shot.

And the rush is not coming down only that one neat channel, now. The scarlet, steel-white capped waves are still lapping the bridge, they are breaking across it, but there are others as well. The infantry flood dammed up in the town is beginning to leak through the dam. For a moment, the leaks are nothing but drops . . . a man or two, then three or four men, coming through between houses, running down toward the river above the bridge.

The drops multiply and are runlets, the runlets are streams. They gush through the line of houses in strengthening jets. And like jets of water bursting out through a dozen cracks in a dam and flowing down its face, they spread and broaden. The dozen slim streams of red-jacketed soldiers rushing down from among the houses are scattering out, deploying, spreading across the clear ground between the town and the river, flowing together and joining. By the time they reach the east bank of the branch they have formed a line. Not solid. Not thick. Not a drill-ground line. It is loose, uneven; it has sags and bulges. The men are spaced wide apart: this is not Braddock's day, this is not the attack on Breed's Hill: the British soldier has learned a good deal about fighting since then.

This battle line is thick at one end only, the end where" the "small parties" are pressing the bridge, where the small clumps of men are following, one another down the road to the bridge in spite of the furious guns. The guns are excited, now: the iron balls are going wide: each shot sets the guns rolling backward, they must be dragged back again to the bank of dirt and relaid, and the crews are panting and nervous, they don't like the looks of that oncoming line. Except at the bridge, the line is thin, it is only a skirmish line.[16] But it is a line of veteran British infantry with bayonets fixed, it is a line of the Invincibles attacking. And the guns can't even hold back the attack at the bridge, they can't spare a shot for the skirmish line rushing down to the fords.

From the bridge to the mill, upstream, there are eleven hundred men in this attack-the whole 85th is in it, six hundred men. With them are detachments of three other sturdy regiments—the light companies of the King's Own, the East Essex Foot, the Royal North British Fusiliers. With them also are royal marines and the hundred armed Negroes. To meet the attack there are the three Baltimore rifle companies—the Union Yagers, the Sharp Shooters, the Fell's Point Riflemen—a hundred and fifty militia; there are the three infantry companies, another hundred and fifty, perhaps a few more; there are the hundred and fifty gunners and matrosses. In men, this first of the day's three successive engagements is eleven hundred against four hundred and fifty or, at the most, five hundred.

The American batteries change the odds, and the rockets change them also. How much, nobody can say. The guns, in the first few minutes of action, have done more damage than the strange new weapon has done: they have even silenced the rocket fire, temporarily. But both have failed: the rockets have not thrown the weak first line into panic: the guns have not broken up the determined rush for the bridge.

Whatever may be the comparative weight of the guns and the rockets upon the odds of the battle, the blunders outweigh them by far. The results of the long succession of blunders fall with a crushing weight . . . the town abandoned, its houses giving the enemy cover . . . the bridge left standing . . . the guns so placed that they cannot sweep the bridge . . . the guns so placed that they cannot enfilade the river . . . the line of the river itself undefended . . . the enemy furnished again with cover that gives them, now, almost as much protection as they had in the town itself.

Abruptly, the guns have nothing at which to fire. The successive small waves of the advance guard are over the bridge, they are forming in line, the line is plunging into the thickets and out of sight. And the rest of the British line, still on the farther side of the stream, is vanishing too. While it is still advancing across the open ground between the town and the river, the willows and aspens on the west bank begin to conceal it; when it leaps down the east bank and begins to splash through the fords, the trees and brush hide it completely. The guns can do nothing, the gunners can only wait. They cannot even fire blindly into the thickets: the Yagers are down there, somewhere, along with the Fell's Point men, and the infantry company is down there too, on the flank, between the guns and the British infantry coming up from the bridge but still concealed by the brush.

Then the infantry company catches sight of the oncoming bayonets. The men who carry the bayonets are still too far away for smooth-bore muskets to do much harm, but the infantry company fires. It lets off one ragged volley and then it runs. Its captain tries to stop it. Will Pinkney springs down from the top of the bank and runs toward the fleeing men: he shouts, he commands, he threatens: the men rush by him and leave him standing alone.

Abruptly, the odds have changed, they have worsened. The guns cannot fire; the two infantry companies off to the left cannot fire, they are too far away; even Aisquith's Sharp Shooters are out of action, they also are too, far away. For long minutes, the battle belongs to the riflemen down in the thickets . . . to the Fell's Pointers, the Yagers . . . to "somewhat more than a hundred men." The odds are no longer roughly two to one. They are ten to one.

The long skirmish line is across the branch. The two rifle companies fight. The whiplike crack of the rifles is lashing the thickets. The American fire is galling the left the British line, pressing up through the woods from the bridge. The coiling whiplash shots of the rifles pluck men out of the ranks of the 85th. The red-jacketed men go down, they lie still in the yet-green grass of the bottoms or clutch and pluck at the grass. But the rest press on. The British begin to fire.

The Tower muskets are loud, they are blunt. They are more like clubs than whips. They beat at the two small companies. The British infantry drives ahead through the underbrush like a long line of game beaters, threshing the thickets with clubs. And the weight of the blunders continues to fall . . . the first line so weak and so short that there are no men at all to the south of the bridge . . . no troops at all to outflank the enemy when he has crossed the bridge . . . the two companies themselves overlapped and out-flanked as soon as the bridge is crossed . . . the Fifth Maryland Infantry, which Stansbury intended to meet just such a development, now placed far to the rear, far on the opposite flank of Monroe's inexcusable line . . . the nearest troops four hundred yards to the rear and held motionless there . . . these nearest troops of Stansbury's brigade not even visible from where Major Pinkney stands, but hidden from sight by the orchard . . . these nearest available troops not even able to see that the first line has been outflanked and that the guns are in danger.

The rifles are falling back. They can do nothing else; where they are, it would not be useful even to stay and die. Two companies of militia cannot hold back a reinforced regular regiment. Even if they could hold back the men just in front of them, they cannot hold back the two ends of the line that is folding itself around them. The Fell's Point men and the Yagers come running out of the thickets by ones and twos, by scattered bits of platoons. They stop and turn and fire at the first scarlet coats bursting out of the brush behind them. They run, and load as they run, and hang on their heels to fire. They are in wild disorder, but they are still organized troops; all adhesion has not been lost. Even now, in the open field, with the enemy already in force on their right flank, they haven't made up their minds that they ought to quit. Major Pinkney knows they can't "hope to make an effectual stand." They are hopelessly outnumbered; only half of them have bayonets. In a moment, now, he will have to give the command to retreat. But he waits, he looks toward the guns.

The six guns are silent. They have targets now, close, in plain sight. But another blunder is coming home: the guns cannot reach the targets. The embrasures cut in the too-big earthwork keep the gunners from swinging their pieces toward the infantry on the flank. And the impromptu embrasures are still too high: the guns cannot be depressed far enough to fire on the infantry gathering now in the low ground down at the foot of the field.

The British are getting ready to rush the guns. You can hear the officers shouting and see them running along the forming line. The line is straightening out. The men in it are unbuckling the straps of their packs and jerking the straps off their shoulders, they are flinging their knapsacks down on the ground. The line moves, the bayonets start to climb. And still the guns can't touch them; From both the front and the right, the British are closing in. The bayonets cross the point of the Y and climb toward the bank where Major Pinkney is standing; more bayonets cross the pike and come into the field. There was something personal about those rockets, but there is something even more personal about those bayonets; there is something positively intimate about those lean, glinting, knives on the ends of the slanted muskets. Between the guns and the oncoming, curving, enveloping line there are only those two rifle companies . . . only a hundred men or perhaps a few more . . . only those men already driven back once, not broken yet but not in a firm line either . . . milling . . . uncertain.

The gunners, too, are uncertain. *What do we do about this? What are we supposed to do? There's nothing in Duane about this, there's nothing in drill regulations.* The gunners have no weapons, they have only their sponges and rammers, their handspikes. *My God, do we just stand here? Do we just stand here and wait to be killed? Do they want us to throw six-pound balls with our hands? Let's get out . . . let's get out while we've got a chance. They'll take the guns if we don't get out in one hell of a hurry. Fetch the limbers! Tail onto those ropes . . . snatch that piece back here so we can limber up. Where the hell are those drivers? What the hell do they think they're doing? Move, can't you? Move . . .!*

Major Pinkney, watching the guns, watching his own men, watching the enemy's rush, turning again to the guns, sees the gun teams break from the edge of the orchard, the limbers crazily bounding, men clinging to bridles, wrestling the teams around, backing them up to the gun trails. One gun is hooked up. Whips cut at the horses' flanks. The wheel horses squat to the sudden dead weight of the gun, hoofs dig up the dirt in clouds, the horses scramble like cats and plunge into a maddened gallop.

The two rifle companies break, they begin "at the same instant to move towards the artillery." To Will Pinkney, his command for retreat unspoken, it appears that the flight of his men and of the two batteries is a simultaneous movement. He had hoped that his rifles could "venture . . . another fire," but if they had "remained much longer, they must have been taken prisoners or cut to pieces." As it is Captain Bader is taken. And as the guns and the crews and the riflemen stream uphill past the north corner of the orchard, toward the only troops they can see—the Fifth Maryland, with its left flank on the Georgetown road—the last of the guns is in trouble. The horses are out of control, the bayonets only a few yards away. *Leave it! Get that limber away! Spike the gun . . . a file, man . . . stick a file in the vent! Hammer it in! God damn it, use the rammer! Hit it . . . break it off short!* The gun stands forlorn, half in, half out of the embrasure. The last of the gunners run for their lives.

The flight of the guns that got away becomes uncontrollable rout. The terrified gun teams tear up the Georgetown road. The rout pours "in torrents" past the left flank of Stansbury's line, between Burch's three fieldpieces and Laval's cavalry. One team swings off to the right of the road, into a farm lane that runs through the field where the cavalry waits in close order beyond the fence. There is agate in the fence, with dragoons massed behind it. Before the dragoons can clear the gate, the crazed team crashes through into a jumble of rearing, plunging horses. It topples men out of their saddles. It crushes down others, horses and all. The gun, towing behind, swings from one side of, the lane to the- other, ripping the swath through the cavalry wider. One spinning wheel strikes Lieutenant Colonel Lavall on the leg and almost knocks him off his horse.

General Winder, on horseback a few yards behind the Fifth Maryland, watches the headlong retreat. He is calm. He is not alarmed by the dispersal of the first line: he did not, in fact, regard it as a first line but as an advanced force only. His army is intact, his two brigades have not yet been in action. Only the advanced detachment has been driven back, and that defeated force is still available. Already "the stream of the running phalanx" is abating. Lavall is getting his disordered troopers into ranks. The panting riflemen are slowing to a jog, a walk; they are rallying and forming on the left flank of the Fifth. If the excited batteries are given time to pull themselves together, they can be brought into action in a new position.

The commanding general's self-control was not shaken earlier today by the ruin of his first conception of the battle—a determined stand in front of Bladensburg, not here behind it. His self-control is not shaken now: He has in mind a new conception. Sound or un-sound, his new plan is orthodox. It foresees the eventual defeat of Stansbury's regiments and discounts that defeat; it conceives a final and decisive action at the third line, behind the ravine a half mile to the rear; it contemplates the retreat of Stansbury's troops, under pressure but unbroken, to that third line. Which is to say that Winder's new conception is based on the juncture of the two halves of his army: he still intends to bring his whole force into action as one army, on the line established by Beall, Barney, and the Washington brigade.

What he plans looks simple, in the army's printed regulations. It *is* simple, on a drill field. Under fire, it is less, simple; but, for disciplined, tried troops, it is a standard, practical maneuver. What Winder fails to take into consideration is the obvious fact that these troops are neither tried nor disciplined, that they have never practiced any such maneuver, that until yesterday they had never even been a part of a formation larger than a regiment. Even as he watches the stampeding guns and the confused "torrents" of retreating cannoneers and riflemen, he does not foresee confusion.

And he does not see the actual, controlling pattern of the battle. He has overlooked the Y. He has overlooked, too, the first fetal incident of the battle, the first application of the pattern to the combat.

The action at Bladensburg affords an interesting demonstration of the extent to which a single circumstance, a single flaw, can take possession of a battle. Wholly aside from all the rest of the pre-battle errors, the controlling flaw was the neglect of the terrain *below* the bridge. The controlling circumstance was the resulting advance of the British left wing into the copse south of the apex of the Y—an instantaneous advance against so trifling a resistance that the rifle companies and the batteries were swiftly overlapped and outflanked. The defeat of these troops was not in itself important. Retreat from that first line was almost certainly inevitable, even if it had been held by the whole Maryland brigade. But the consequence of the retreat might have been different.

As Stansbury planned the action, the sturdiest regiment he had—the Fifth Maryland Infantry—was on the right flank of the guns, in close support. It was only fifty yards behind the rifles and its right outstretched them: it was on the turnpike if not actually across it. When driven back, the turnpike would have been the natural, convenient line of its retreat. And retreat up the turnpike would have brought the Maryland troops to the position of the Washington brigade: it would have brought about the union of the two halves of the army. All that, of course, is theory. But what happened isn't.

What happened was that the weight of the British left flank—the heaviest part of the attacking line—bore down upon the unprotected right flank of the rifles and the guns. Their retreat is not significant. The *route* of their retreat is vitally significant. The British pressure from the south directed their flight northward and northwestward toward the Georgetown road. The easy ground along the south side of the turnpike, undefended, gave the British left an opportunity for a rapid, undisturbed advance: it gave the enemy a fulcrum from which he could use his left flank as a lever to pry Stansbury's infantry from its position on the slope behind the orchard. Fortuitiously, this swift advance of the British left flank applied pressure to *both* of the first two American positions in a way that took the utmost tactical advantage of the ground and of the direction of the roads.

This pressure tended to push the whole Maryland brigade nothwestward toward the Georgetown road . . . to make that road the natural route of retreat if the brigade gave way. From the very beginning of the action, the. British pressure tended to divide the American army, to drive one half of it toward the upper arm of the Y—the road to Georgetown—and to separate, it from the other half preparing to give, battle in positions drawn across the lower arm of the Y—the Washington turnpike. The Y shape of the roads had set the pattern for the campaign. It had led the invaders and the defenders to collision here at Bladensburg. It had made easier the concentration of the American army. Now it was making easier the division and dispersal of that army.

That is the circumstance Winder fails to see. He rides out now into the Georgetown road and tries to give form to his new conception of the battle . . . to his idea of uniting his brigades at last upon the third line for the ultimate, deciding fight. He orders the captains of the two routed batteries to move on up the road and place their guns "on a rising ground . . . in the rear." He points out the new battery position, a hill "immediately in connection with the positions of General Smith's corps"—the Washington brigade, reinforced by Barney's flotillamen and heavy guns, Scott's regulars, and the militia commands of Beall, Kramer, Waring and Maynard. The batteries trundle off. Winder has taken the first step toward uniting his brigades and toward establishing a'rallying point for Stansbury's troops if they are driven back—as he expects them to be. But he fails to make sure that Stansbury's troops know where the third line is. He fails to point out that the nearest troops, on whom he expects the Maryland brigade to rally if it is compelled to fall back, are almost half a mile south of the Georgetown road. He fails to make sure that Stansbury's colonels even know that there *is* a third line. Instead of specifying a route of retreat that will bring about a junction of the two brigades, he tells John Law, acting commander of Burch's three guns: "When you retreat, take notice that you must retreat by the Georgetown road."

Here, at this point, when the two rifle companies have rallied and the retreat of the Baltimore batteries has been checked and given direction, the first of the day's three actions merges into the second. The first is over, the other just beginning. And it begins, as the first began, with a blow not dealt by the enemy . . . a blow dealt by the weight of Monroe's blunder . . . by the consequences, suspended for more then an hour, but falling now with crushing, invisible weight.

Take time now to glance at the map. Those three neat blocks in a per-pendicular row just to the left of the orchard are Stansbury's three regiments; they aren't as neat on the ground as they look on the map, but they are where, Monroe put them. Now notice the shape of the orchard. It stretches along the Washington turnpike, it spreads at an angle across the American front. At no point along the neat row of blocks can a man see all of the ground ahead, the ground where the enemy is: no matter where a man stands, the orchard hides part of the field: in some places, it hides everything, and in these: places the men in Stansbury's line can see—nothing except the interlaced boughs of the trees.

Winder, trying to see as much of the field as possible, has taken his post at the left of the upper end of the uppermost block in the row of three: he is just behind the flank of the Fifth Maryland. He can see the diagonal sweep of the orchard, he can see the barn, the roof of the mill. He can see all the way down the sloping field to the willows along the river and, over the willows, all the way into the village. But he cannot see through the orchard, he cannot see the open ground southeast of the orchard . . . the long stretch of easy ground leading up from the bridge . . . the ground left undefended when Monroe pulled Stansbury's troops to the rear. Where Winder rides back and forth between the Fifth Maryland and Captain Ben Burch's guns, he can see only half of the battlefield . . . less than half. He does not take time to ride to the other end of the line to see what the situation is there. He knows that his right flank is in the air, but he does not see that the enemy can advance through that unguarded, easy ground with nothing more than a fence to delay the attack. He does not see that the British can come almost up to his flank without being seen by his infantry. He goes into action half blind.

What Winder sees in front, in his less-than-half of the field, seizes his whole attention. The rocket detachment has opened fire again: it is firing on Stansbury's line, but its missiles are wildly erratic: the rockets are flying high over the heads of the men. The ranks squirm. A tremor runs down the line. But the tremor is not fear, yet: it is mostly curiosity: it is caused by men twisting around and craning their necks to look over their shoulders, to watch the fallen rockets darting about in the field behind them like frightened, fiery-tailed liz-ards. Winder puts his horse to a trot; he rides up and down the wriggling ranks, "encouraging the men to disregard the rockets." But he cannot spend much time in steadying the militia. The British infantry is moving to the attack. Red jackets appear at the lower end of the orchard, pressing on in the wake of Will

Pinkney's retreat. They hesitate there, and Ben Burch's three guns open fire. The second combat of the day has begun as the first began, with rocket fire and the racket of field guns.

Patches and flashes of red begin to show in the orchard itself: the skirmishers of the 85th are filtering up the slope through the trees, and the trees give them perfect cover. The British advance, here, is concealed and protected even better than the first rush through the town was concealed by the houses. Thus the second blow of this second, scarcely begun engagement falls on the Mary- land troops . . . the second blow dealt by Monroe . . . the second result of his blundering interference. Monroe placed these troops so that they are completely exposed and the British are almost completely concealed. He made the British a gift of an almost perfect position, and they are making full use of it now. Their infantry, running, crouching under the low-bent limbs, infiltrates the orchard and presses through to the edge; it finds excellent cover there. From the long, oblique front of the orchard, it opens a scat-tering fire.

The orchard begins to bloom. The smoke of the muskets hangs low, it is caught in the trees. The dirty-white smoke gives the apple orchard the shabby look of the morning after a storm in the spring, the blossoms still clinging but no longer fresh, bedraggled and beaten by rain.

But the fire is not heavy yet. The skirmish line is too far away for accurate shooting. The musket balls bury themselves in the dirt or go wailing off overhead. Leaves drift through the smoke of the muskets, lopped branches come flickering down: Burch's guns are pruning the orchard with dull, invisible shears.

At this opening stage of the day's second action, the advantage of numbers is on the American side. On paper, the troops in this second American line muster roughly two thousand men, not counting the crews of the guns and not counting, either, the cavalry off on the flank. Including the cavalrymen (who will take no part in the fight) and the gunners, the maximum paper strength of the Americans is 2,553. Against the eleven hundred of the enemy's first brigade, the odds are little less than two and a half to one.

The enemy is not impressed. To the British regulars, the Yankees drawn up and waiting for their attack on "the brow of a bare green hill" look futile and funny, they present "a very singular and a very awkward appearance." Their order is "tolerably regular," their battle line short and thick; the men are in ranks three deep. They seem to be "sufficiently armed but wretchedly equipped," and most of them "are not dressed in uniform"; they are "clothed part in black coats, others in blue, others in ordinary shooting-jackets and some in round frocks"; they look more like a crowd of spectators than an army. Only a few companies—

"perhaps two or at the most three battalions"—are wearing blue jackets; these, and these only, present "some appearance of regular troops." With complete confidence, with a deft professional skill, Wellington's veterans proceed with the business of moving that rabble of armed civilians out of their way.

The fire from the orchard grows hotter. The skirmish line almost concealed in the fringe of the trees is building up stronger and stronger in spite of the three busy guns. Down the slope, past the end of the orchard, the visible British line is lengthening; it is spreading out to the north, toward the mill; it is matching the American front, reaching out for the American left flank as it already has found and outreached the American right. All the troops of the first British brigade are over the river now. Those who crossed by the upper fords have swept aside the two infantry companies and Captain Aisquith's Sharp Shooters and are re-forming under the partial shelter of the big wooden barn.

Winder rides over to Ben. Burch's guns and gives Butch an order. The three six-pounders begin to batter the barn. They make a fine smashing and crashing. Splinters fly. The broad planks burst into kindling. Burch, watching, is proud of his guns, he is sure that their fire is "very galling to the enemy." But the enemy's line is unshaken; it is straightening; it, is growing steadily stronger as sections and half-platoons, disarranged by their dash through the fords and the thickets, fit themselves into the order of battle. And yonder in Bladensburg, a thick column of reinforcements is moving rapidly down the main street. Winder makes a decision. Now is the time to strike . . . now, before that fresh column can cross the bridge . . . while the enemy's line is still extended and thin. He gallops up to Lieutenant Colonel Joe Sterrett and orders the Fifth to advance.

The Fifth is that mass of blue that has "some, appearance of regular troops;"Mt is the uppermost block in that neat perpendicular row of three little blocks on the map. It is only Baltimore City militia . . . it is nine town companies with high-sounding militia names—the First Baltimore Light Infantry, the Mechanical Volunteers, the Washington Blues, the Baltimore Yeagers, the Independent Company, the Baltimore United Volunteers, the Baltimore Patriots, the. Union Volunteers, the Independent Blues. The Fifth is a kind of town meeting "comprising some of the most substantial businessmen of the city and some distinguished professional men" . . . a highly respectable meeting. Names on the company rosters are the same names you'd expect to see on the list of subscribers to any respectable cause . . . the solid, old-family names: Here and there the names of the sons and the fathers appear on the rosters together. Here and there in the ranks are the leading merchants and lawyers, the owners of ships and ropewalks, the holders of broad estates whose land grants go back a hundred and fifty years to the days of the lords proprietors. Beside them stand men to whom they pay wages . . . shop clerks and wheelwrights and saddlers, watermen, dock hands, prentice boys, millers and tailors, sailmakers, carpenters. The Fifth is a community in itself. It has annexed, now, another cross section of Baltimore-the Union Yagers and the Fell's Point Rifles. Will Pinkney, retreating on foot with his men, has rallied them well. Without orders, he has formed them again on the left of the Fifth. The two rifle companies, beaten and driven in their first meeting with war, have left wounded behind in the triangle field and the thickets; the Yagers have lost their captain; but they are ready to try it again. Will Pinkney has helped himself to somebody's horse. The British officers, watching the American line, are right in deciding, that the body of uniformed troops amounts to "perhaps two or at the most three battalions." It amounts, in fact, to two scant battalions and less than half of a third. It amounts to six hundred men.

Colonel Sterrett is standing up in his stirrups, he has his sword in his hand. The long-drawn command of precaution rings out: "The regiment will advance in line!" The majors repeat it: "Take care to advance in line!" The captains' shouts are echoes. *It surely takes right much talk to get a thing done in the army.* Sterrett raises his sword arm. He raises his voice: "Forwa-ar-rrd . . . "

Again the repeating echoes. The regiment stirs, it marks time. All the helmets jiggle. The pompons and plumes and the curling cock feathers are stirred by the small, rhythmic dance of feet lifting and falling in cadence. The colonel's arm drops. ". . . March!" The Fifth Maryland moves down the slope. The rifles move with it.

Sterrett watches a moment, his back to the enemy. His eyes are sharp, his face is taut with concern. Then the tightness relaxes. Pride touches his face and his eyes. The Fifth is marching as if on parade. Its ranks are as straight as they ever were out on Hampstead Hill, on review. The three solid ranks-almost four solid ranks now, with the subalterns and sergeants marching behind their platoons—are precisely two feet apart. They are moving in short, stiff steps, seventy-six to the minute, each step twenty-four inches long. These men have never been shot at until today, there isn't a man in those ranks who knows anything more about war than what he has read in the paper or what he saw a few minutes ago when the Baltimore guns stampeded or what Will Pinkney's men saw just before they ran. Now the rifles are going back into the fight; they didn't have to, the order didn't include them; but there they are, marching as if they belonged to the Fifth, with their ex-ambassador major riding in front on his borrowed horse. The only nervousness Sterrett can see in the marching lines is the nervous twitching of heads to the right, the nervous care to keep the ranks dressed, the nervous hitch of blue elbows keeping the proper touch in the ranks. Lord . . . Lord . . . it's a handsome regiment. The colonel turns his horse and settles himself to the saddle and rides down the hill toward the blossoming smoke. His staff rides behind him.

For minutes, this is wan as it looks in the pictures, this is a painted battle.

The Fifth is a moving wall . . . a wall topped with sharp, splintery flashes of light. (The bayonets glisten like long, sharp splinters of glass on the top of a garden wall.) The Fifth is a rolling blue wave . . . a long sea-blue wave with bright foam sparkling above it. (The thousand sore feet, tramping together, swash through the susurrant grass with the sound of the surf on the sand.) The Fifth is a broad blue ribbon across the breast of the hill . . . a ribbon edged with steel beads and stitched with the white feather stitching of crossbelts. (The ground is uneven, the ribbon rises and falls, the hill seems to breathe.) The Fifth is five hundred middle-aged men and young men and boys four days out of peaceful homes . . . many from quiet tree-shaded shops where sound is the rustle of India silk on the counter and soft southern voices of women . . . from hot-summer somnolent offices where sound is the scratch of a pen . . . from high-ceilinged courts were sound is the drone of a clerk and the buzz of a fly at the shutters. The Fifth is five hundred civilians in coats that are mostly alike, walking down a long hill in the sun.

It is hot in the sun. *There's a spot in my belly that's cold.* It is noisy here on the hill. Those cannon back there are making a sound that is like empty rum casks being dropped one at a time into the echoing hold of a schooner tied up at Moale's wharf. *They're our guns, they sound good. But only three guns . . . what became of the Baltimore guns?* There's a sound overhead that's silky and soft, it might be silk tearing, it might be sharp scissors shearing through India silk. *It isn't; it's bullets.* There's a sound underfoot that's like a big fly bumping and bumping against the shutters; there's a sound that's like a pen scratching. *It isn't.* It's musket balls bumping the dirt, you can see the dirt jump. It's musket balls whipping the weeds, you can see the dead top of a weed jerk all of a sudden and then lean slowly and fall. *They're shooting at us . . . at me . . . I know it . . . it can't be true.* I'm not here, not really. I'm home. I've just finished dinner at the Fountain. In a minute, now, I'll have to go back to the shop. I'm not being shot at. I'm not scared. God, please don't let me be a scared. It's hot. I'm cold. I got this crossbelt too tight when I put it on again, over there in the orchard. It squeezes my chest. I can't breathe . . . I'm breathing, only it seems like I can't. Christian Keener is breathing, all right. I can hear him, right alongside me. It's funny, with all those guns going off, to be able to hear Chris breathing. I wonder if he can hear me. I wonder if Chris is scared . . . *too.*

This is a battle. It doesn't seem like a battle, it isn't the way I thought it would be. I don't know how I thought it was going to be . . . not like this . . . different somehow . . . strange. This isn't strange. The only thing strange about it is that it seems so ordinary. It's like walking along a strange road, knowing where you're going but not knowing how soon you'll get there or just where you are. It seems like there'd ought to be a sign or a mile-r stone or something to let you know, a sign like "Towson Town,-7 Mi." I don't feel the way I thought I'd feel. I'm not scared exactly . . . I don't think I'm scared . . . it isn't that, mostly . . . I just feel kind of surprised. I've known ever since Sunday that it was going to happen and now it's happening and I feel kind of surr prised. One minute you're standing around and talking and then the next minute you're in a battle. It's like getting up out of bed in the night and walking across the room in the dark and knocking your wind half out on the chest of drawers. The chest was there all the time and you knew it was there and yet you're surprised. That's it . . . I feel like my wind had been about half knocked out. I'm awake but I feel like I can't wake up. My legs are working all right but they don't feel right . . . they feel hollow . . . from the knees down they feel about as weak and thin as a hollow barley straw. I: feel like I'd maybe be sick and have to lie down. I was lying down just a little while ago. We were over there in the orchard and I was lying face dawn in the grass and watching a couple of ants and thinking. It was quiet under the trees, it was so peaceful and still. It was even cool . . . anyway, it was cooler, it was cooler than here; I put my arm around the roll of my blanket and thought about Mary Ellen. *Mary Ellen . . . Mary Ellen . . .*

It isn't quiet there now. It looks cool, though. I know it's too hot for snow, but the smoke piled up all along the edge of the orchard looks like a dirty snowbank. It looks the way snow looks after it's laid on the street two-three days and the chimneys have soiled it, after the walks have been shoveled clear and the snow is banked up along the fronts of the houses and stained with the eavesdrip. The smoke is so thick that it makes a dusk for the muskets. The flashes are plain, as plain as if it was evening and not just a little past noon. When the muskets go off, the quick gusts of red light are like lamplight jumping out into the street across the piled snow from doors thrown suddenly open, and then jumping back when the doors are closed again quickly.

We're not in the orchard now. Why didn't we stay there? Those fellows couldn't see us, if we had stayed . . . they couldn't see us any more than we can see them. We could be shooting at them the way they're shooting at us. We're like pigeons . . . we're like passenger pigeons on a limb, all jam-packed together. I shot into a limbful of pigeons once. Just one shot. It killed seventeen. Seventeen besides those that could still flutter a little and flopped away into the brush. I found some of them, but likely not all. It made me feel kind of sick, the shot tore them so. Am I going to be sick again now? I don't want to be sick.

Don't think about it, think about something else. *Gallia est omnis divisa in partes tres.* Don't think about school. Those delphware dishes on the back shelf might sell if they were set out on the table up toward the front of the shop. Don't think about father's shop. Think about Mary Ellen.

Mary Ellen's so little . . . she has the littlest nose . . . and the littlest hands . . . and she always smiles when she knows I'm going to kiss her . . . and then the smile goes away, like that, just before our lips touch, and she gets all solemn . . . like a judge or a preacher. *Mary Ellen* . . . Those muskets over there in the orchard sound, like the calking hammers, that day we walked down to Harris's Creek to see them building the *Java*. It was hot . . . and you looked so cool. How do girls always manage to look so cool?

Chris . . . Chris . . . you're *out of step. What's the matter with . . .?* Oh God, I'm going to be sick.

"Eyes front! Keep your line dressed!" That's Lieutenant Cooke. That's all right for Lieutenant Cooke. He didn't hear that sound Christian Keener made just before he went down . . . that sudden small *uhhh!* as if he'd been hit by a fist in the pit of his stomach. "Keep your eyes to the front!" My God, do we just leave him there? Are the men behind just going to walk right over him? Can't a man even look to see if he's dead or how badly he's hurt? We do . . . and they are . . . and you can't.

The sag in the line strightens out. The gap closes up. The charge of the Fifth goes on.

Don't think about Christian Keener. Don't think about home. Don't think about Mary Ellen. *Don't think.* Keep in step. Keep your elbow touching the next man's elbow. Keep your eyes fixed to the ground twelve or fifteen paces in front. That's what it says in the drill book.

The ground slopes. You're going downhill. You can't keep from looking at what's ahead . . . the men in red jackets . . . the orchard . . . the smoke.

The Fifth is marching into the obtuse angle formed by the British line that stretches across the open ground between the barn and, the orchard and joins, at the orchard corner, the oblique, invisible line that crouches and fires all along the edge of the trees. The hidden part of the enemy's line is the longer part, it is almost three-fourths of the British front. The Fifth is moving straight down, the slope toward the visible part of the line, it is moving *across* the whole front of the long, concealed line in the orchard. Its right-flank companies come closer at every step to the muskets they cannot see. At every step, the range for the muskets is shortened.

There are new gaps in the ranks of the Volunteers, other sags, other eddies of men confusd by, a sudden blue heap on the ground. With the ranks only two feet apart, you can't stop in time when the man ahead of you stops as if he'd bumped into a tree. You bump into him, you can feel him collapsing against your chest, you can feel him being emptied like a sack that is torn on a nail. You step over the empty blue sack on the ground, you try not to step on the sack. *"Dress . . . dress . . . eyes front!"* The book says if you look to one side you'll pull forward the opposite shoulder, you'll push the whole company out of its proper direction, you'll "occasion a continual waving in the march. The books says "carry the head always upright, the eyes directed to the. ground." It's all down in the book, it's so neat and precise in the book. But it cramps you, it makes your neck stiff, it gives you a crick in the neck. *If you've got to think, think about that.*

The ranks are not quite so straight now, but they are still going ahead. The long sea-blue wave rolls steadily down the hill, breaking a little, unbroken. That sound as of a wave breaking is the long, roaring *whhssshhh* of the rockets rushing across the orchard.

The rockets are not being aimed at the charge. They are aimed at the drab mass of men left behind on the hill . . . at the two so-called regiments hastily pasted together out of the odds and ends of four drafted regiments-on-paper. The enemy's purpose is shrewd: this new weapon's power to strike terror is greatest when it is used against raw, green troops. And those men in their farm clothes and store clothes are obviously as raw and green as a body of "troops" can be. But the rockets are still going wild, they are only dropping sparks on the huddle of paper soldiers before they plunge into the hill and skitter and burn themselves out.

The charge of the Fifth goes on. There is something gallant about it, something pathetic and earnest. Suppose it fails. There is still something gallant about these dressed-up-alike civilians trying so hard to do what the drill book says. (Give them their moment of honor before they are smeared with dishonor to hide the shortcomings of others.) This is no easy thing they are doing . . . marching in rigid silence, in close-packed ranks, across open ground, into the fire of muskets they cannot see, into fire they are not per-mitted to answer. (It isn't easy to walk across a bare field toward a man with a gun in his hands, a man who is trying to kill you. It violates every sensible instinct. It makes you feel naked. It blows a cold wind through your bones.) Only the British are firing. The whole American front is silent, except for Ben Burch's three guns. And now one of the guns falls silent: the advance of the Fifth, down the narrowing slope, has come into its line of fire.[47] Sterrett, looking back over his shoulder, wonders how long his men can endure the strain without cracking. (It isn't easy to let a man shoot at you, time after time, and to do nothing about it except keep on walking toward him.) The Fifth isn't badly hurt. The fire from the hidden line in the orchard isn't the kind of fire that the British faced forty years ago on a hill over Boston harbor.

The British aim is unbelievably bad. In three hundred yards, not a dozen men have been hit. (It isn't easy to keep on walking, erect, toward a man who intends to kill you. The wind sucks the marrow right out of your bones, it sucks the guts out of your belly, your belly's too thin for your pants, your pants want to fall down. You want to fall down on your face on the ground and crawl into the ground and pull the ground over your head.) But there is more to it than being hit or seeing another man hit. The Fifth isn't charging a mere line of men: the Fifth is charging a legend. The troops it can see and the troops it can't see are, by legend, the finest troops in the world. If they are not truly the finest they are at least a part of the armies that broke and defeated the finest who carried Napoleon's eagles. They are regulars . . . veterans . . . British Invincibles. In their own moment of time, they are Caesar's legions and Cromwell's Ironsides, the Grecian phalanx, the Spanish pike-men, the Swedes of Gustavus Adolphus. (In another moment of time there will rise a similar legend—the panzerdivisionen.)

The charge of the Fifth goes on, silent, into the angle formed by the British front. It has covered three-fourths of the open ground. It is less than a hundred yards from the lost barbette. The rallied Rifles on the left flank are close to the splintered barn. The companies at the opposite end of the line are close to the smoking orchard: a few paces more will bring them to grips with the British infantry there. Joe Sterrett, storekeeper-banker leading a charge in his, first five minutes of battle, knows he must make a decision, and make it at once. How far? How far? The shock of six hun-dred men should break that thin line ahead, recapture the earthwork, retake the abandoned gun. But the earthwork is useless, the spiked gun is useless. How far should he take these men? Where is the border that separates duty from error? The Fifth has left its support behind. It is already outflanked on the right. It is marching into a pocket. The enemy's fire is coming from three directions . . . from the trees, from the line in front, from the heavier body of troops being formed for a new attack near the Georgetown road and the lane that leads from the mill and the upper fords. Ben Burch's two guns are still pounding away at the barn but their fire is slow: it takes a long time to sponge and load and prime: it takes a long time to re-lay, after every shot, a gun that weighs almost a ton. And the six-pound balls, when they come, are doing no serious harm; they are keeping the enemy's skirmishers out of the barn but the barn still shields from the gunners' view the gathering troops in the road and the lane.

Let the charge go on? Close with them? Give them the bayonet? Cold steel is the enemy's favorite weapon, he is skilled in its use; to close with a bayonet charge is the object of British infantry tactics. The Fifth Maryland has found bayonets useful as skewers for broiling its beef, it has found they make excellent holders for candles when stuck pointdown in the sod. And half of Will Pinkney's men have no bayonets at all.

Joe Sterrett checks his horse. He turns, and his arm goes up. "Battalions . . . mark time . . . dress . . .!" The six hundred men go into a shuffling dance. They put their right hands on their hips; their knees rise and fall; their feet beat dust out of the ground; their feet beat the ground like a drum. This might be a tribal ceremony, a final appeal to the war-god, an aboriginal war dance. This might all be a part of a savage ritual that prescribes every motion and gesture—the head rigidly turned, the elbow at just such an angle, the foot raised precisely four inches, each foot lifted thirty-six times to the minute. (This is war of another day . . . the day of the flintlock, the slow firing muzzle-loader . . . a day long before machine guns. Marking time under fire is a part of the ritual of close-order battle; it is the device by which regiments straighten their lines. It will go on and on, as unchanging as any tribal ceremony, through many wars yet to be fought. Men will die performing this shuffling, stationary dance on a thousand fields with names such as Bull Run and Sharpsburg and Chancellorsville. Ritual dies hard. It is easier to kill men than to change the rules by which they are killed.) Now, under converging fire that would cut them to pieces if it were not still unbelievably wild, the eleven Baltimore companies straighten their lines as if this were a dress parade.

". . . halt!" The dance ends. But the ceremony goes on. Command of precaution . . . command of preparation . . . command of direction . . . command of execution. Formal, elaborate, ritualistic commands. "The regiment will prepare to fire." "Battalion . . . prepare to fire." The majors, the captains, the lieutenants, the sergeants repeat the elaborate phrases like acolytes. "Battalion . . . company . . . platoon . . . take care to perform the motions of the manual . . ." *My*

God, does it take all that chat to shoot off a gun? You'd play hell, shootin' ducks that-away. The colonel is riding to the rear through the gap between the battalions. There's nothing in front but the enemy now. *If they'd just leave us shoot . . .!* Ready . . ." *Ah . . . now . . . now, by God! All the bay* onets leap straight up, the six hundred men raise their muskets and rifles straight up in front of their faces with "the cock opposite the nipple of the left breast, the barrel perpendicular in front of the left eye, the body quarter faced, to the right." Six hundred thumbs pull the gun locks back. "Aim!" The long barrels swing down; the gleam of the bayonets, suddenly leveled, leaps like a flash of lightning, "Fire!" After the lightning, the thunder.

It makes its own cloud. Smoke smothers the six hundred men. As it rolls, it is torn; the hot blasts that produced it rip through it and tear it apart. Men stare through the rents in the smoke. Their hands, groping for paper cartridges, raising the cartridges up to their mouths, stop in front of their chins; their teeth, ready to bite off the ends of the cartridges, stay wide apart in their wide open mouths. Their mouths fill with sound. Not a cheer. A noise. *A* sound without shape or intention . . . a roar of amazement and triumph and disbelief. *By God . . . by God . . .!* The men in red jackets are going back. The red line is breaking. *We did it! We did it! They're running!* Some of the British are running. Some are walking. Some are shuffling backward and loading and firing and shuffling backward again. Some are sprawled on the ground; they writhe or they try to crawl or they just lie still. The dressed-up-alike civilians are yelling the way the crowd yells when the Liberty Engine Company gets to a fire twenty seconds ahead of the United Hose and Suction Engine Company, they are yelling the way apprentices yell at a game of hot cockles. *That war a dowser! That stung 'em!* The yells are exultant and savage. *Invincibles . . . yea-a-ahhhh!* The yells are, naïve. The red line in front is retreating, but not the red column drawn up in the road nor the invisible line in the orchard.

The yelling is choked by the smoke. The powder fumes turn it to coughing. The high moment passes.

A change comes over the battle and over the Fifth and the Rifles. The six hundred men are firing at will, they are loading and priming and aiming and pulling the tricker as fast as they can. There is ritual still: between one shot and the next, a man with a musket must execute twenty-nine separate motions. But after the opening volley, he must go through the twenty-nine motions alone. It isn't every man for himself, it is every man by himself. Joe Sterrett has struck his blow, he has wielded his men as a weapon for one solid blow. But after the first massed fire the six hundred men ares no longer a single weapon, they are six hundred weapons. Now, when each acts by himself, he loses by ever so little the sense of belonging, of being a part of the whole. By ever so little, the companies lose their cohesion, the men lose the disciplined oneness of will that carried them down the bare slope against every natural instinct. They lose the crowd-comfort, the subconscious counterfeit feeling of being somehow protected by numbers. There is no longer one will, there are six hundred wills. Each man fights his battle alone.

Aim. Vire. Recover. Why the hell do they call it recover? Because the damn' musket kicks your shoulder clear around to the back of your neck? *Port . . . arms. Half cock firelock.* Hook the right thumb over the cock. Full it back to the half. *Open . . . a pan.* Thumb on the hammer, the fingers clenched, the forearm lying along the stock of the musket. Push the thumb hard on the hammer. That's silly. This is a battle . . . I'm in it . . . I guess I'm not scared. If I was scared I wouldn't be thinking of things like that, I wouldn't be thinking about how the army gets everything twisted. Lake calling the hammer a cock and then saying the top of the priming pan is the hammer. It doesn't make sense. *Handle . . . cartridge.* Right elbow thrown back, the right hand to the cartridge box. The book calls it a cartouche box and that's silly too. You'd think we could use our own language, you'd think we could load a musket in English as well as in French. But maybe not: those buggers down there are English: it probably wouldn't be right. *Prime.* Grip the Cartridge between the thumb and the first two fingers. Bring it up, quick, to the mouth. Bite into it . . . not deep, just to the powder. Pfwah. It tastes foul. It tastes like a tarnished brass candlestick smells when Amanda starts scouring it, green tarnish smelt metal smell soap smell all mixed up together and foul. The rough cartridge paper scratches against your tongue. It feels and it tastes like a sock that you've worn till it's stiff. Bring the cartridge down to the pan. Pour powder into the pan . . . *God damn it! It spilled!*

The crash of the big-barreled muskets is more than a sound: it is solid: it falls like a blow: it beats on the ear like a club with a knotty end. The single explosions are harder to bear than a volley. You know when a volley is coming: there's time to take bold of your nerves: you can hold your nerves tight, like reins. But there's no way of knowing when George Golder's musket behind you will blast your left ear or Ben Taylor's explode in the other, After the opening volley the firing is ragged, uneven. Some men load more quickly than others and some men are calmer than others. Some wait for a living target, their faces intent and ab sorbed. Some fire blindly and wild through the smoke in a frenzy of haste, they pant like exhausted runners, they stare in a fixed fasci nation at something they cannot see. Their hands shake as they load, they are shaken by something that is not fear but partakes of the nature of fear and can turn into fear: they are shaken by realization, a kind of naïve suprise. *We knew guns made noise. But not noise like this. Why weren't we told how it would be?* After three or four rounds the crashes begin to collide, they run into each other, they blend into hard, ripping spasms of sound like the flam of a fabulous drum. *This isn't how it should be.* This isn't the long roll of musketry, this noise doesn't roll, it jerks like a man in a fit. The whole earth is a drum and the drummer who beats it is drunks This roar has no pattern nor rhythm; it bursts and subsides and explodes; it breaks but is never quite broken, it never is still. Every now and again you can hear the sticks whack on the rim of the drum—the hard, single shots of the rifles, flat whacks on the rim of the battle.

In the close-packed ranks of the Fifth, one rank firing between the heads of the men in front, the sound is enormous, appalling.[51] It's like all the hammers we heard on the *Java*. It's like being down in the *Java's* hold with the hammers above you, around you. No . . . . no, it's not. A frigate's so big you could get away from the sound, you could crouch in the cavernous hull and the sound couldn't beat on your head. It isn't like hammers: a hammer hits quick, but this roaring is bigger and slower than hammers. It squeezes and grinds like two cannon balls grinding the sides of your head: they squeeze the sound into your head till your head can't hold any more. You can't hear any more.

The appalling sound is a comfort. It covers you, hides you. It shuts the enemy out. Those buggers there in the orchard . . . and down by the earthwork . . . and over there by the barn . . . they're shooting . . . they're trying to kill me. The damned fools, they can't do it. Don't they know they can't do it? Don't they know I can't even hear them? I'm not afraid of those bastards. I'm not afraid any more than I was afraid that time when I was six years old . . . maybe eight . . . and the thundergust beat at the house in the night and I scrooched down deep in the bed with the covers up over my head.

The crashes are woven together, the sound is a thick strong fabric, the smoke is a smothering quilt spread over a blanket of sound, you can pull them up over your head.

You can't see the red lightning flashes: the quilted smoke shuts them out. You can't hear them strike, you can't hear the thunder. You feel it, you feel the house shake. It feels as if giants, with sledges are pounding the walls of the house but you're safe, the blows can't get at you, they only come up through the floor, through the mattress of sound, like a push. . . . Like that. *What was that?* It wasn't a sound: I didn't hear it, I felt it. It felt like the earth had moved underneath of my feet. It felt like somebody pushed me.

The dull shocks of sound that come like a push and a push are two epileptic volleys discharged beyond the right flank or the Fifth and three hundred yards to its rear. The regiments left behind on the slope of the hill when the Fifth advanced have joined in the battle at last . . . first Ragan's, off to the south near the Washington pike, and then Sehutz's holding the center. They are regiments only on paper; even on paper, neither one has so much as its own regimental number. They are a patchwork . . . companies and platoons and detachments from four drafted Baltimore County regiments . . . odds and ends of the Seventh, the 36th, the 15th and the 46th, hastily pasted together. They have never fired volleys before, never stood in a line of battle before. Until last night, when the panicky sentinels turned the whole camp out for nothing, they hadn't known what two regiments looked like in line. And they hadn't seen much, in the dark. Now the volleys they fire are not volleys at all: they are fits and shudders of sound, convulsion after convulsion.

Down the hill where the Fifth is fighting, men turn their heads toward the physical shocks of the sound. They see the smoke of twelve hundred muskets unfold like visible echoes, convulsion after convulsion. It looks like a battle. They yell *Aa-a-aahhh! Yaa-a-a-aaahhh!*

It's like shouting inside of a barrel. Your head is the barrel, the sound can't get out, it is liquid and sticky like rum, it smarts in your throat and your ears.

Men yell without hearing their yells. They don't look like men who are cheering, they look like men who are startled. Their mouths, rounded for shouting, powder-blackened from biting the cartridges, give them a look of enormous surprise. *Denny . . . Denny Magruder . . . you look like a scared pickaninny.* I wish he could hear me. I'd tell him he looks like a nigra boy caught in a melon patch and scared half out of his wits-so scared and surprised he's turned gray all excepting around his mouth. My God, but Magruder looks funny. *I wonder if I look like that.*

The Fifth is excited but, steady. It is still nervous, but not *so* nervous as when it began its advance. It has moved across open ground under fire, against British regulars; it has stopped them dead in their tracks; it has driven part of them back; it is holding its own. With each minute, its confidence grows.

And now, on the left, to the north of the Georgetown road, the infantry company guarding Ben Burch's three guns pushes down toward Will Pinkney's Rifles and joins in the fight. The whole brigade is in action. Four field guns and nearly two thousand muskets are sweeping the space between the two strokes of the Y. On that narrow front they are pinning the light brigade to the ground.

The odds are with them. The odds are about two to one, they are two thousand men to eleven hundred. The two thousand have the four guns; the light brigade had the rockets, at first, but the rocket troop is not in the action now.

The volume of fire from Stansbury's line is impressive and reassuring. It signifies nothing. The reassurance is false.

The two makeshift regiments on the right flank of the Fifth have not stirred from where Monroe put them. They fire where they stand: the only target they have is the orchard: the range is too long for effective shooting: their firing is noisy but harmless. Their own right flank is in the air. The two guns in the turnpike have no flank protection at all. Nobody gives it a thought. Winder is still the piecemeal general: he is completely absorbed in the attack of the Fifth: he is fighting his battle in pieces. Only Will Pinkney is thinking of flank protection, and Pinkney is off at the other end of the line. He is worried about the ford near the mill, he is thinking that enemy troops will be coming from that direction, he has galloped down the mill road to see what is happening there.

What he sees is bad. His own detached rifle company under Ed Aisquith and the two infantry companies that ought to be there have vanished, they have been "withdrawn or driven from their station" which the enemy in the thickets can reach with his shot without being seen. Worse yet, a "sufficiently formidable" force is feeling its way up the mill road and across the adjacent ground. Already the left of Joe Sterrett's line has "nothing to protect it" against the immediate threat of a British attempt to "gain its rear."

He gallops back under fire. The mill road is in plain view of the enemy's skirmishers, the Georgetown road is in plain view of the assault column forming where the shot-splintered barn partially hides it from Burch's gunners. Will Pinkney's right arm is driven backward by a violent blow, then it dangles, his hand flaps on his thigh. He looks at the arm, tries to raise it: the lower half, swings like a pendulum: it is broken above the elbow: a musket ball has gone in at the front, shattered the bone and passed out at the back. He dismounts behind Sterrett's line.

The Fifth is behaving well. Its firing is steady. But it is beginning to suffer. The enemy's fire from the orchard is getting hotter and hotter. The light troops of the British first wave are fighting like Maryland Red Caps, like Pennsylvania Black Boys. They are fighting like Mingoes and Shawnees, taking advantage of all the cover there is they are lying flat on their bellies in the deep orchard grass, they are kneeling behind the gnarled trunks of the old apple trees, they are shooting through the cracks in the walls of the barn, they are crouching behind its corner and in the weeds that grow thick around barns. Their converging fire is raking the ranks of the Fifth with impunity. All along the line, men are going down. The Fifth fires back at the barn, at the weeds, at the trees, at the hanging smoke; only once in a while there are "single men" to shoot at.

The United Volunteers are taking the worst of the galling. George Clarke has been shot, Bill Williams is hit, Sergeant Murray is hit, Acting Sergeant McCulloch is down with a ball-shattered leg. Oh, my Lord . . . the lieutenant's got it! *Denny . . . Denny Magruder . . . did you see that?* They've got Billy Cooke! *Denny, where are you?* Golder . . . George Golder . . . what's happened to Denny? George . . .! They've got you, too. I *swore at George Golder a minute ago. I told him God damn you you mind what you're doing next time you fire over my shoulder you shove that damn' musket two feet out in front of my head. I thought he didn't hear me but maybe he did. 1 wonder if he stepped up closer behind me to do like I said and thai's the reason they hit him.* God damn it . . .!

The United Volunteers have lost thirteen per cent of their men in ten minutes. They are still standing up to the British fire. The whole front is standing. The firing on both sides is heavy, but the Fifth and the Rifles are taking the fire of the enemy's hidden troops "without being able to return [it] with" any probability of effect. And the odds are beginning to change, they are swinging the other way. The whole British second brigade—1,460 bayonets—is over the branch, it has re-formed on this side of the bridge, its column is splitting in two. The 44th, the East Essex regiment, is beginning to move up the Georgetown road. And the rocket troop has found another position, immune from the guns. The rocketmen know their business: they have chosen their target shrewdly—not the "two or at the most three battalions" that wear "the blue jacket" and present "some appearance of regular troops," but the mass of "country people who would have been much more appropriately employed in attending to their agricultural occupations than in standing with muskets in their hands on the brow of a bare green hill" and might pass "very well for a crowd of spectators." They open fire now on Schutz and Ragan's men.

The first rockets go wild, the first "three or four" pass "very high over the heads of the line." The British reduce the angle of fire. The next volley is low, it barely skims over the orchard, it barely misses the white straining faces of Schutz and Ragan's men. Sparks fall on their upturned faces. The sweat on their faces turns cold.

Another sheaf. And another. You can't see a cannon ball coming. You can't hear a musket ball coming: if you hear it, it missed you, you're safe. You see these, things coming. You hear them. They turn your blood cold. It ain't Christian to fight like that . . . it ain't decent a man that way, to burn him alive. It ain't human. *Those things are human!* You can see 'em hang, like, before they drop. You can see 'em lookin' for you. You can see 'em turn an' come at you. My God . . . *oh, my God . . .!* It's like hell-fire. It's judgment an' hell-fire.

The rockets come with a hoarse, whooping roar. They pass close overhead with a roar like storm wind in a chimney . . . the roar of wind across fire . . . the roar of fire pulled by a furious gust. Like wind in a chimney, the rockets suck sparks behind them. They scatter the sparks over the two scraps-of-paper regiments, hastily pasted together.

The paper regiments begin to shrivel. They begin to curl up at the ends and the edges like paper too close to a fire—not on fire yet, not burning, but charring and turning brittle. The two regiments are as brittle as charred paper. Pieces begin to break off. The pieces are blowing away.

Stansbury sees the two regiments going to pieces. He rides down the line, shouting. "Steady! Stand fast! Front . . . face!" His shouts go unheeded. Colonel Schutz, Major Kemp and Stans-bury's aide, Major Woodyear, are trying to rally the men. Stansbury roars at his officers: "Keep them in line! Cut them down if they run! *Cut them down!*" Winder comes galloping up from the rear of the Fifth. He, too, is shouting. The company officers shout, they beg and command, they snatch at men's shoulders and arms. They try to hold pieces of companies with their hands, but the pieces crumble and sift through their fingers and blow away. Colonel Ragan gets forty men together, he forms a piece of a line. Captain Gallaway rallies most of his company. Captain Shower holds part of his. A few of Randall's men stick to their captain. Ensign Brewer's detachment out of the 36th stands fast.

Winder sees the groups of men coming back, he sees fragments of companies still in some kind of order, he thinks the rout has been stopped and he gallops back to the Fifth. He can see the field better down there, be thinks that is the critical place.

It is one of the critical places. The Fifth is in a pocket, the stuff that the pocket is made of is getting stronger, the pocket itself is rapidly getting deeper. The assault column on the left front of the Fifth is beginning to move up the. slope. And the pocket is already deeper than Winder knows: the first wave of the 85th—the company that led the rush over the bridge—is about to burst out of the woods beyond the Washington turnpike, it is almost up to the two lonely guns in the pike, it is almost up to the remnants of Schute and Ragan's line, it is already three hundred yards to the rear of the Fifth's right flank.

Winder looks back. The pieces of line he just left are still there. They are fighting again. A flicker of fire runs along their uneven edges. They smolder and smoke. Then they burst into flame—a brief, desperate outburst of firing. And then they collapse like burned paper consumed and collapsing to ashes. Where the two county regiments stood there are only small swirls of ashes-small, furious struggles where a few of the "country people" who stood to the last are surrounded and overwhelmed by the men of the 85th. Two men in the little group around Ensign Brewer are shot, one dead and one dying; others are taken; Bill Brewer es capes. Colonel Ragan is wounded and taken. Stansbury gets away, "raging profanely." (For years, when it thunders, the country people will say "they hear General Stansbury swearing.") But swearing will not bring back his twelve hundred men. Two-thirds of Winder's front has been swept away. He sees, now, that "a strong column of the enemy" has "passed up the road as high as the right of the Fifth." He must do something and do it at once.

Off to the left and the rear, toward the crest of the rising ground, is a patch of woods. If the Fifth falls back on the woods, it will be out of reach of that hidden firing line, it will draw the enemy out of cover. He gives Colonel Sterrett an order to retire up the hill toward the woods. Then he changes his mind. The Fifth looks steady, it looks as if it can hold on for a little while. If it waits, the British may "issue in a body from the orchard" and risk an attack across open ground into the fire of these still un shaken men. He is afraid that "a movement of retreat" will shake them worse than the enemy's inaccurate muskets. He "instantly" countermands the order and rides over to Burch's guns. But the British aim is improving, their fire is beginning "to annoy the Fifth still more." Winder sees the column "high" on the right deploying to take Sterrett's line "in flank." He changes his mind again. In person, he orders the guns to fall back "to the hill" where he had "directed the Baltimore artillery . . . to halt." He sends the same order to Sterrett.

Ben Burch's gunners are astounded. Not a man in their half-battery has been "touched," they think that the battle is only now "seriously commencing." Burch disobeys the order to limber and retreat. He stays where he is, and his guns continue to fire.

After "two or three rounds," General Winder rides up again and repeats the order "in a peremptory manner." Burch limbers up. The three pieces move off on the Georgetown road. But Winder keeps changing his mind. The guns have gone only "a few yards" when he is at Burch's elbow again. He thinks now that Burch "might venture to unlimber one of [his] pieces and give them another fire." Burch is "in the act of doing so" when Winder countermands that order, too, and hurries the guns to the rear.[100] It is high time, if he wants the guns saved. It is too soon, if he wants the Fifth saved.

The Fifth is obeying his order, it is doing its best to obey. The captains are trying to make themselves heard through the blasts of the muskets, the lieutenants are bawling commands, the sergeants are shouting and swearing. "Cease firing! Cease firing! God damn it, stop! Can you understand that? Stop it, I said! Don't load that piece! Order . . . arms!" *What's happened? Those officers know something. Something's gone, wrong. What? We were doing all right. We were holding 'em. Oh, for God's sake, stop that yelling. What the hell do they want us to do?* Retreat—we've got to retreat.

There are ways to retreat, in the book. There are pictures that show how to do it. There are words . . . there are pages of words . . . words like "column formed upon the rear of the center in motion" . . . words like "battalions in echequier" and "augmentation of sections." There are diagrams . . . they look like geometry . . . they look like a checkerboard, maybe that's what echeqüier means. But they don't look like war. They certainly don't look like this. They have rows of squares . . . rows of little neat squares . . . there is a square for each man and one of the squares is you. *It don't look like me.* Every square has a neat dotted line to show where it should go, in retreat. *I don't see any dotted line on this hill.*

Anyway, we never got that far in the book. We never practiced retreating on dotted lines. All we can do is do it the way we know. "Order . . . arms! Right about . . . face! Carry arms! Mark time! Forward march!" It is not a good way.

Forward? *Forward, hell.* "Eyes front!" *Front, hell.* I was in front before. That's the rear ahead, where we're goin' . . . that hill's the rear, where the guns are . . . *by God . . .! The guns have pulled out!* We're pullin' out too an' I'm in the rear . . . the front rank is the rear rank now an' I'm in it . . .it's still in; front . . . it's closest to the Britishers . . . my behind is the front an' there's ' nothin' between my behind an' those God-damn' muskets . . .those bay'nets. . . . *They're comin'! They're comin' out of the orchard!* "The United Volunteers will keep their eyes to the front." *Who says so?* Ensign John Wilmot says so.

Don't look back . . . don't look to one side . . . the book says if you look to one side you'll pull forward the opposite shoulder, you'll push the whole company out of its proper direction. *That's: what I was thinking a while ago, we were coming down the hill then.* We were advancing then. Now we're running away. *Why in hell don't we run?* Don't look back . . . keep your head up . . . the high collar digs into the back of your neck . . . it burns, the skin is chafed raw . . . the sweat trickles and stings. But that sting lower down . . . that cold sting in the small of your back . . .like a bayonet point. . . . *I don't want to be stuck in the back.*

Don't look back. The enemy's there. The enemy is no longer hidden. You look . . .and he isn't the enemy . . . he is enemies . . . he is personal . . . he is right behind you . . . he's running . . . he has a gun in his hand and a knife on the end of the gun . . . he is coming fast . . . and we're *walking.* To, hell with the proper direction. This isn't drill. To hell with keeping step . . . twenty-four-inch steps. To hell with touching the next man's shoulder . . . the next man was Denny Magruder. I haven't seen Denny since . . . There's the sergeant . . . there's Jim McCulloch . . . he's trying to crawl . . . he's all bloody . . . the ground underneath him is bloody. I don't want to look like that. I *want to get away from here.* The company nearest the orchard breaks first. It has only one officer left. Surgeon Hanson Catlett is with it, he has been tending its wounded. Now he and the ensign rally it quickly. Then the opposite end of the line goes to pieces. What Catlett just helped to do isn't easy: it says so right in the book: it says "no system has laid down a method of accustoming troops to retrieve a sudden charge, or to rally after being broken. The opposite end of the line does not rally. It runs.

Suddenly six hundred men want to get away from there.

Johnny Kennedy lost his Musket. It wasn't his fault. He didn't throw it away, he hadn't meant to lose it. Johnny didn't want to be shot in the back, he didn't want a bayonet shoved through his back, he wanted to go away from there as fast as he could. Or faster. But he saw Sergeant Jim McCulloch trying to crawl, dragging his broken leg.

The enemy was close behind, then. But Johnny stopped running. He laid his musket; down on the ground, he knelt in the bloody grass, he got the sergeant's body Over his shoulder somehow. McCulloch was sick with pain, he wasn't much help. Johnny got his hand on the musket, he managed to get to his feet, he started to walk up the hill. McCulloch was heavy and clumsy, the musket was heavy and clumsy. Private Kennedy's heart battered against his ribs, his breathing ached in his chest, he didn't want to let go of his gun but he had to, he couldn't let go of McCulloch. He saw somebody he knew, he handed the musket over. The enemy was still running but not catching up, the enemy was stopping to shoot at the backs of the running Yankees. The shooting was wild, but a ball found John Kennedy's friend. He dropped his own musket and Johnny's. Henry Fulford lost his courage. He ran with all his might. There was a woods in the rear. If he could reach the woods . . . the lovely, safe, quiet woods . . . But he couldn't. The bullets and grapeshot flew like hailstones around him. Anyway, that was what he thought. There was no grapeshot to fly, there was only Private Fulford's imagination: it turned him away from the woods and chased him into a swamp. He lay there face down, his heart battered against his ribs, his breathing ached in his chest. He was "fatigued almost to death." He didn't say what, became of his musket.

Henry McComas lost the plume off his leather hat. A Britisher shot it right off and left only the stub. Private McComas wasn't too badly upset by his narrow escape from death. But he was right much put out about losing that plume. His annoyance would last for three weeks. Then, in another fight, the British would pay a high price for a curled cock's-feather.

Captain Ben Burch lost his battery. He fell back with his sullen guns but he hadn't eaten for days, he'd been up the most part of three nights, he didn't know what his guns were supposed to do, the heat was making the road go up and down and around. He couldn't keep up with his guns, he tried but he couldn't, he fainted. He lay by the side of the road while the retreat swept around him, over him, past him. When his men missed him they didn't go back, they supposed that he had been captured. John Law, too, lost the guns. He was disgusted and angry. Burch had vanished again, he didn't know what had become of Burch, this was the second time Burch had disappeared in an hour. It looked as if John Law was in command of the half-battery again but he didn't know. He didn't know what to do with it if he was. Nobody gave him orders. They oughtn't to be retreating. The road was a mess. The road was a boiling porridge of half-human beings and dust . . . a blue-corn Indian porridge of militia jackets senselessly churning and bubbling and blundering into each other. The dust was a smothering smoke, the dust was steam from a boiling kettle. You could hear the fire crackle, you could hear dry sticks being broken to feed the fire. Somewhere off yonder there still was a battle of some kind. No body bothered about it. The guns went away from the battle. The dust and the sweat and the sun in his eyes, the disgust in his heart, the senselessly hurrying mob in the Georgetown road got between John Law and his guns. He didn't find them again for three days.

William Winder lost the command of his army—if a man can lose something he never had. The shape of the roads took control. They had interfered before, as Monroe interfered; they could have been overridden. But no longer. Not now. The Y was in full command.

Just as it fixed the pattern of the campaign and of the battle itself, so now the Y fixed the pattern of the retreat. It had brought the two wings of the army together—almost together—but not where Winder chose. Now its convergent force was applying itself in reverse. It became divergent. It split the army apart. Winder could point to a hill, he could tell Joe Myers and Dick Magruder to go there by way of the Georgetown road, he could tell John Law to retreat by that road to that hill. The hill was "immediately in connexion with the positions of General Smith's corps." Smith's corps was the Columbian brigade, reinforced now by Barney's five guns, by Barney's marines and hard-bitten flotilla sailors, by Beall's Anne Arundel men weary but no longer panting, by Maynard and Kramer's militia, by Waring's Prince George's battalion and by Colonel Scott's regular infantry. General Smith's corps was 3,080 men and eleven guns, in order of battle behind the ravines that crossed the Washington turnpike six hundred yards and thirteen hundred yards southwest of the place where Stansbury's men had been. The three thousand-odd men "were not arrayed in line, but posted in advantageous positions in connexion with and supporting each other, according as the nature of the ground admitted and required." Winder's intention to halt his left wing on the hill "immediately in connexion with" these positions was a good intention. His order was not a bad order at all.

But the Georgetown road was not taking orders. It gave them. It carried Magruder's guns and Myers and Burch's "wide" of the place where Winder meant them to be. It threw "the whole mass" of the infantry "off to the right on the retreat toward Montgomery Court House." The "whole of the cavalry, probably from the pressure of the infantry that way, were also thrown wide of the line of retreat" that Winder intended. Winder "had not for a moment, dispersed and disordered as was the whole of Stansbury's command, supposed that their retreat would have taken a different-direction."

Now, pushing his horse through the ruck of the flight, trying vainly to stem it be long current, trying vainly to turn it more toward General Smith's command," he found the bewildered but obedient Baltimore batteries waiting in the road. But between them and Barney's guns on the Washington turnpike stretched three-quarters of a mile of broken and gullied ground. Smith's nearest troops—a flank outpost two companies strong—were eight hundred yards away. It was "impossible" for the batteries "to get across to the turnpike road or unite with General Smith's brigade." At least, Winder thought it was impossible, and his thinking made it so. He didn't ask the Baltimore gunners to try.

The enemy's light troops were in sight down the Georgetown road, they were "pressing the pursuit," they were coming on fast. Winder looked at the shamelessly hurrying mass of his men in the road—half his whole army-flowing heedlessly past the halted guns, cursing the gunners for halting, trying to unhook the traces and steal the horses and running on when they failed. The sickening sight convinced him that it was "impossible to collect any force to support the artillery."

He had the guns in his hand, but he let them go. He made ho attempt to put them into action beside the road, no attempt to check the pursuit with a burst of fire, no attempt to steady and shame and check his own fleeing men with the sight and the sound of their guns. There were fugitives in the fields alongside the road; it would not have occurred to Winder to risk hitting some of them, even to save an army. He directed the artillery to "continue their retreat toward the capital." That was all. No orders to make an attempt to cross the broken ground and join Smith. No orders to find a position from which the guns could cover this flight or cover the retreat of the right wing if Smith, too, should be driven back. No objective, no purpose, no nothing.

The Y had decided what was to happen. All Winder did from now on was to hasten the happening. The Y had broken his army in two. All Winder did from now on was to break up the one strong piece that remained. He kept breaking off little pieces until there was nothing left.

While Winder was hoping and doubting and seeing only imn possibilities, the day's third battle had opened Just as the first battle—Will Pinkney, Joe Myers and Dick Magruder's-had blended into the second, so now Tobias Stansbury and Colonel Joe Sterrett's battle blended into the third. "About half past twelve o'clock," while the troops of Walter Smith's "corps" were going into position, "innumerable rockets thrown from the heights of Bladensburg announced the arrival of the enemy there; and at this period, Commodore Barney's sailors and marines, in quick march, arrived . . . The firing of artillery in front "soon commenced"—Magruder and Myers in action, driving the rocket troop out of its nest, raking the main street of Bladensburg, trying to keep the enemy from crossing the bridge, and failing. Then the right wing heard "musketry, in quick and rapid succession" and "in a few minutes the whole right and centre of the front [second] line, with some small exceptions, were seen retiring in disorder arid confusion." That was the county regiments, breaking under the rockets; the exceptions were the little groups around Ragan and Randall and Shower, around Brewer and Gallaway, fighting it out gallantly. "The firing continued on the extreme left"—the Fifth and the two rifle companies, standing up to converging fire from three sides—"but shortly after" the men who had made that stubborn last stand of the second line began to fall back and then to fall into confusion.

Those were the day's first and second battles as the men of Smith's corps saw them while they waited, to fight the third. They didn't have long to wait, for "mean while, the left of the enemy, in heavy column," was moving up the turnpike. The enemy's left was part of the light brigade. Behind it came half of the second brigade—the Fourth Foot, the King's Own. They came up the same road on which Stansbury's men had made their night march from Lowndes's hill and their countermarch in the morning. They passed through the hot, still woods—the woods blurred again with red dust—and came to the first ravine, to Tournecliffe's bridge and the men who waited beyond it, the last half of the Yankees' army.

"Lieutenant Colonel Scott, with the 36th United States'regiment, was posted in a field on the left of the road, his right resting upon it, and command-ing the road descending into the ravine . . . and the rest of his line commanding the ascent from the ravine." Thus were the men of Smith's corps waiting. This is the where and the how of the waiting. "In the same field, about one hun-dred yards in the rear of the 36th regiment, Colonel Magruder [this is another Magruder] was posted with a part of the 1st regiment of District militia, his right also resting upon the road, the left advanced, pre-Senting a front obliquely to the road, and situated to cover and *to* co-operate with the 36th regiment. Major Peter with his artillery, six six-pounders; Captain Davidson's light infan-try, and Captain Stull's rifle corps, *armed with muskets,* all of the same regiment, were ordered to take possession of the abrupt acclivity . . . terminating the ravine. This was deemed a desirable position, because it commanded completely the ravine and the road crossing it, and a considerable extent of the ground over which the front line would necessarily retire if forced back. But, after a short space of time, report was made [to General Smith] that broken grounds inter-rupted the approach to it with artillery, but by a circuitous route that would consume much time, and that, in case of retreat, the ground in the rear was such as might endanger the safety of the guns. . . . Near to it was a commanding position for artillery, and easy of access from and to the road."

Smith "yielded with reluctance, to the abandonment of the position first ordered, but time did not admit of hesitation." In the "mean while," General Smith had "posted Lieutenant Colonel Kramer, with his battalion of Maryland draughted militia, in the woods, on the right of the road and commanding the ravine which continued in that direction. . . . Upon examining the position taken by Major Peter's battery, it was found that the range of his guns was principally through that part of the field occupied by the 36th regiment. To remove one or the other became necessary, and the difficulty of the ground for moving artillery, and the exigency of the movement, left no alternative. The 36th fell back about one hundred yards, losing, in some measure, the. advantage of its ele vated ground, and leaving the road. The position of the 1st regiment District militia, from this circumstance, was also necessarily changed. It fell back about the same distance, its right still resting on the road, and now formed nearly in line with the 36th."

The Second regiment of the Columbian brigade had been reduced to three hundred and fifty men by the loss of Ben Burch's guns and their infantry escort, sent forward ta Stansbury's line before the first action began. Now the "residue" under its colonel, Brent, was "formed as a reserve a short distance in the rear of Major Peter's battery, and so disposed as to act on the right, or left, or in front, as occasion might require. Near them was posted, in the same manner, Major Waring's Prince George's battalion of militia, about one hundred and fifty." Colonel Beall with his seven hundred and fifty "took a position on the right of the road and nearly fronting it. Beall's post was a low, detached hill; his left flank was two hundred and fifty yards from the turnpike; there was a broad gap between it and Colonel Magruder's First regiment. Is was into this gap that Barney's men came, "in a trot." His five guns wheeled into battery, the two eighteen-pounders side by side in the road, the three twelves to the right, Barney's "infantry"—his sailors turned soldier—deployed to the right of the guns and formed line with the marines commanded by Captain Miller. The gap had been filled, just in time. The 85th was attacking.

The odds, at that moment, favored the Americans. In number of men, they were as three is to two and a half. Brigadier General Walter Smith had not more than 3,080; the enemy had, on the field and in motion, 2,560. Those figures, however, do not take into account the loss of the light brigade in the first two actions-the dead, the wounded, the stragglers: overcome by heat and exhaustion; they do not take into account the men who fell out of Smith's column on its forced march that morning. The stragglers were never counted, the light brigade's killed and wounded were lumped together in the casualty list for the day. Nor do these figures take into account the British reserve—the marine battalion and the 21st Fusiliers—the 1,460 men intact in. the third brigade. Walter Smith had no reserve that he knew of, although the Fairfax militia at last was sweating and swearing its way to the front after having its flints counted twice. But including both the Virginia regiment and the enemy's third brigade, the odds in numbers, of men are not odds at all. The numbers are almost even: 3,880

Americans; 4,020 British. (The figures mean little or nothing; neither reserve fired a shot; they are set down because so many writers have garbled this battle, seizing this figure or that to prove what they wanted to. prove.) Again, the guns weighted the odds. There were eleven guns against one; the British got their six-pounder into this fight, but any of Peter's could match it; three of Barney's were twice its size and two were three times as big. And again, the rockets weighed in the balance against the guns; they did not, in this last engagement, turn the odds as they did in the second.

The first blow of this third battle fell upon Kramer's men, deployed in the woods on the edge of the ravine, to the right of Tournecliffe's bridge. They were "Maryland draughted militia"; there were only two hundred and forty of them; they were six hundred yards out in front of the main positions—six hundred yards out in front of Beall on his hill, six hundred in front of Barhey. They were there for a purpose: to stagger the enemy's first attack if they could, to hurt him as much as they could. They were not expected to hold back an army: before they went out they had been given their orders about retreating: when the pressure became too great they were to retire "through a body of woods" on their right and rally on Colonel Beall's line. Against them now burst the advance of the 85th. They fought well. They hurt the enemy. They were driven back, but not routed; they were still firing as they retreated according to orders. According to orders they slipped through the woods, rallied, and re-formed on the Anne Arundel men.

The "heavy column" on the turnpike had halted while its light troops cleared out the copse on the edge of the ravine; now it began to advance, straight up the road. Barney swung down from his saddle, ran to the nearest gun, aimed it, ran on to the next. When he had laid the guns, he remounted. The leading company of the British advance caught sight of his battery. The column halted. Barney sat waiting, watching, reserving his fire. The head of the column was moving again. Barney spoke to the gun crew beside him. The eighteen-pounder let go. There was no need to fire the other: the road was "completely cleared." But those men down there were Lord Wellington's men: they had stormed three batteries today: they could storm another. They tried. Barney's guns met them with grape shot and swept them away. They re-formed and tried it again, under à flurry of rockets. The murderous fire mowed them down. Barney thought "all were destroyed.

After three attempts, three failures, even the Invincibles had had enough of those frontal attacks. They abandoned the road, deployed through the broken ground of the shallow ravine, came up into the open field in line of battle and drove for Barney's right flank. Barney's twelve-pounders ripped holes through their line, Peter's six smaller guns tore into them with cross fire. They came on, stubborn and gallant. Barney ordered a counterattack. His infantry charged. The light brigade saw them coming, it halted and fired. The marines and flotillamen fired. Four minutes . . . five minues . . . ten . . . fifteen . . . for nobody knows how many minutes . . . this was a stand-up fight, it was two lines of men standing face to face across a few yards of bare ground, slugging it out with ounce balls. "The firing became tremendous" . . . "an unintermitting exchange of tremendous volleys." The ounce balls killed and maimed, they smashed skulls, they broke bones arid tore, flesh. Flotilla Captain John Webster, sailorman fighting on horseback, felt his hat knocked off his head. His horse was shot dead. He looked at the hat and saw a hole through the crown, he left the hat where it lay. A subaltern of the 85th went down, instantly killed, a ball through his windpipe, his spine shot through at the base of his brain. A ball hit Lieutenant Gleig's scabbard and broke it, another laid his arm open. In both of those stubborn lines, the ranking officers were falling. Captain Miller, commanding the American marines, was wounded. Captain Sevier of the marines was wounded. But the British were suffering worse. Lieutenant Colonel Wood, leading the 85th, fell badly hurt. Major Brown, commanding its advance guard, was down with a serious wound. Colonel Thornton of the 85th, commanding the light brigade, was struck and went down with a ball in his thigh, his thigh torn and crippled; he lay on the ground with the musketry crashing above him.

The light brigade wavered. Its senior officers were gone. The guns were making a bloody wreck of its flank. The marines and the sailors ceased firing, they charged with cutlass and bayonet.

The light brigade broke and Streamed down the field. The charge Swept after it surged over a fence, drove the enemy back into the woods where Kramer's militia had fought, to the brink of the ravine. Colonel Thornton rolled over and over down the slope, hoping to escape but expecting "every instant" to be discovered and taken. The charge swept past him. But his brigade had been "totally cut up." The flotillamen and the marines left its "shattered remains" in the ravine and "returned to the guns." The Invincibles' disordered retreat to the woods had drawn Barney's men off to the right of their position; now, returning to it, they angled across the field; they missed Colonel Thornton again.

Four assaults, four bloody repulses. Here, in the right center of the American line, Barney was winning his battle. The rest of the line had not been attacked at all—excepting the two hundred and forty "draughted militia" who had not been a part of the line but an outpost six hundred yards out in front. The rest of the line had not been in action at all—excepting Peter's six field guns which had helped to break up the successive assaults against Barney, and excepting Kramer's battalion. Kramer's men had done what was expected of them: they had fought their delaying action, fired as they fell back, rallied, re-formed: they were ready to fight again. Peter's guns had been served "with great animation." They had not been threatened. They, too, were ready to fight again. As far as the actual fighting had gone, it had gone very well. The situation looked encouraging.

In the meantime, however, a less favorable situation had been developing at the left of the line and beyond it. This situation was compounded of two elements. One was the British East Essex regi-ment, the 44th Foot commanded by Colonel Brooke, the senior among Ross's regimental commanders. The 44th had been pressing the pursuit of Stansbury's routed brigade on the Georgetown road. The other element in the situation was Brigadier General Winder. After giving up all hope of checking the flight of Stansbury's men or of turning them "more toward General Smith's command," and after ordering the Baltimore artillery to continue its retreat without giving it either a purpose or a rallying point, Winder had set out across the broken ground to take command of the right wing, Smith's so-called "corps." He had upwards of half a mile to go and his horse was tired. How soon he started, after he heard the racket of Kramer's fight or the louder uproar of Barney's . . . how fast he rode . . . how long it took him to, cover the thousand yards of uneven ground and reach Smith's left flank, nobody ever knew. Winder himself, in his report, said only that he "turned toward the positions occupied by Lieutenant Colonel, Beall, Commodore Barney and General Smith." (Historians should not pretend to be mind readers. Even with his official report and all the other official reports before me, I cannot read Winder's mind. I can merely form an opinion concerning, his state of mind. The fact is that in his report he listed the positions of Beall, Barney and Smith *in reverse* of the order in which he approached them.)

The situation developed swiftly. Its two elements—the American commanding general and the British East Essex regiment-were active. In combination, they reacted vigorously. So far as the result is concerned, it might be said that they acted in combination. Their mutual reaction did not produce an explosion. It produced a solvent. It dissolved the American army.

The Georgetown road did not lead the East Essex regiment any closer to Smith's positions than it had led the Baltimore guns or Ben Burch's guns. But Colonel Brooke, advancing, was not taking orders from the terrain or the direction of a road. He saw that "the dispersion of the front" that had been composed of Stansbury's regiments had now "caused a dangerous opening" on the left flank of Smith's line. He ordered his regiment to leave the road and strike for the exposed end of that line ahead. The East Essex "ad-vanced rap-idly," wheeled by the left, and "soon gained and was turning" Smith's flank. To meet this "alarming movement," Smith ordered Colonel Brent to shift his regi-ment—the Second of the Columbian brigade—toward the threatened flank. It was a logical countermove: it did not disarrange the troops in combat positions: Brent's regiment had been "formed as a reserve" and had been "so disposed as to act on the right, or left, or in front, as occasion might require." As Brent began to carry out the order, other enemy troops appeared "within long shot" of the center, and Colonel Magruder's First regiment "opened a partial fire, but with-out much effect."

Winder had not yet reached the right wing of his army. He was "not acquainted with the relative position of the different corps composing" General Smith's command and could "not therefore determine who of them engaged the enemy, nor . . . see how they acted." But before he had time to find out, before he was even close to Smith, he had made his estimate of the situation and issued his orders.

This was his estimate as he set it down in his report: "the enemy had advanced up the road [the Washington turnpike], had driven back Lieutenant Colonel Kramer's command. . . . He [the enemy] had come under the destructive fire of Commodore Barney, Which had turned him up the hill towards Lieu-tenant Colonel Beall, whose detachment gave one or two ineffective fires and fled. . . . The enemy, therefore, had gained this commanding position, and was passing our right flank; his force pursuing on the left, had also advanced to a line with our left, and there was nothing there to *oppose him.*"

This was his order: "To preserve Smith's command from being pressed in front by fresh troops of the enemy, who were coming on at the same time, while they were under the certainty of being assailed on both flanks and the rear by the enemy, who respectively gained them; in which circumstances their destruc-tion or surrender would have been inevitable, *I sent to General Smith to retreat.*"

Winder's estimate of the situation looks sound. It has the ring of truth. His order to retreat seems timely.

The estimate was unsound, it rings hollow, the truth is not in it. The obvious fact is that it was not an estimate made on the battlefield: it was made *after* the battle. The revealing flaw in his specious report is the timing of the order to retreat. The flaw runs through his own words: "I sent to General Smith . . ." He was not yet there. He had to "send." When he dispatched the order he did not know many of the details he set down in his report as his reasons for sending it. He could not possibly have known that Colonel Kramer had "well maintained his position and much hurt the enemy, and also continued to fire during his retreat." And his statement that Colonel Beall's men already had fled was flatly contradicted by Barney.

Barney, in his report to the secretary of the navy five days after the battle, described the successful counterattack by which his marines and flotillamen repulsed the light brigade and by which the enemy's assault force "was totally cut up." His next sentence said: "By this time not a vestige of the American army remained, except a body of five or six hundred, posted on a height, on my right, from whom I expected much support, from their fine situation." Barney was on the ground; Barney was no more than two hundred and fifty yards from Beall's position, which was of vital concern to him; Barney said flatly that after the rest of the troops had begun to retreat, Beall's men were still holding their hill.

Winder said that when he "reached the road meaning the Washington turnpike—he "found Commodore Barney's men also retiring on the road, he having been overpowered, by those, who drove off Beall's regiment *about the time I sent the order to retreat.*" In other words, Winder was not on the ground; before he reached the turnpike, the British had had time to organize and deliver two more assaults: they had stormed Beall's hill, they had stormed Barney's battery.

General Smith also bore witness to the revelatory timing of Winder's order. Colonel Brent, he wrote in his official report, was "proceeding in the execution" of Smith's directions to move the reserve regiment to the left to meet the threat of Colonel Brooke's flank attack. When the order to retreat came, he said, the troops of the Columbian brigade had been "but partially engaged, and this principally with light troops and skirmishers, now pressing forward, supported by a column of infantry."

Even the Congressional investigating committee, which took the most excellent care to hurt nobody's feelings, made it clear that General Winder ordered the retreat of a force of more than three thousand men and eleven guns from a position hastily occupied but nevertheless chosen with a fair degree of military skill—a force not yet shaken and most of it not even yet seriously attacked—a force that had stoutly and quickly repelled three of the enemy's attempts to advance, and broken the fourth and strongest attempt into a costly, disorderly flight. "The command of General Smith," the committee reported, "including the Georgetown and city militia, still remained in order, and firm, without any part of them having given way, as well as the command of Lieutenant Colonel Scott of the regulars, and some other corps. The enemy's light troops had, in the meantime, advanced on the left of the road and had gained a line parallel with Smith's command, and, in endeavoring to turn the flank, Colonel Brent was placed in a position calculated to prevent it. . . . At this moment, and in this situation, General Winder ordered the whole of the troops, then stationary, to retreat."

These were not beaten men. Even retreat did not shake them. They fell back, in obedience to orders, over broken and difficult ground, without showing what Winder contemptuously called "the usual incapacity of raw troops to make orderly movements in the face of the enemy." Winder himself admitted that "when he arrived in succession" at the "different corps" of General Smith's troops, as he "did as soon as practicable," he could not recollect to have found any of them that were not in order, and retreating with as little confusion as could have been expected."

Winder accused Beall's Anne Arundel troops of giving "cine or two ineffective fires" and then running. Barney, who was de-pending on them, said they "made no resistance, giving a fire or two, and retired." But there is evidence that Winder was responsible for their failure. Colonel Beall, forthright and blunt, was not the man to higgle and haggle and try to pass blame on to others. "Having marched about sixteen miles that morning," he told the committee of Congress, "my men were fatigued and exhausted. It is not my impression that my command gave way as early as is represented by some." He made, he said, "every exertion to rally the men, and partially succeeded; but they ultimately gave way . . . like the other troops." The other troops fell back under orders. There is another significant sentence in Beall's curt statement: "I have been informed by a gentleman, who acted as one of General Winder's aides, that he brought me an order to retreat; but I do not remember it." The aide who wanted to see justice done to the old Revolutionary colonel and his men was John Eager Howard, Jr., son of another old Revolutionary colonel. He had been a cornet of horse under Captain Henry Thompson, he was a second lieutenant now in Thompson's Independent Company of horse artillery in the Baltimore City brigade. Captain Thompson was in charge of the horse telegraph that kept

Major General Samuel Smith and Brigadier General Stricker in touch with the army in southern Maryland.

If Lieutenant Howard carried Winder's order to Beall, as he said he did, this fact emerges from the confusion: *Not one unit of troops in the American third line at Bladensburg retreated except under orders.* And this fact also emerges: with the exception of three or four detached companies, *the only two units that left their posts without orders, out of the entire American army on the field, were the two so-called "regiments" of ununiformed, undisciplined, untrained draft-men from Baltimore county, without even a regi mental number to make them soldiers-on-paper.* Historians should at least take the trouble to find out what happened, before they sneer at the men who marched out to Bladensburg to offer their lives for their country and who marched away again *under orders.*

Some of them disobeyed orders—Captain Ben Burch and his gunners, fighting on when they had been told to retreat. Some of them couldn't believe the orders—they fell back a little way and then stopped and waited. It couldn't be true. There, must have been some mistake. "The First and Second regiments [of the Columbian brigade] halted and formed, after retreating, five or six hundred paces, but were again ordered by General Winder to retire." They obeyed.

Behind them, Joshua Barney was fighting his last fight.

Others have told that story, they have filled it in with suitably picturesque details, they have told how the gunners stood to their guns till they were "bayoneted with fuses in their hands." Barney did not say that, the authors doubtless know more about writing than he did, they knew what would look well in a book. But it was his fight. Let him tell it:

"They pushed forward their sharp shooters; one of which shot my horse under me; who fell dead between two of my guns. The enemy, who had been kept in check by our fire, for nearly half an hour, now began to out-flank us on the right: our guns were turned that way; he pushed up the hill, about two or three hundred, towards the corps of Americans stationed [there] who, to my great mortification, made no resistance, giving a fire or two, and retired. In this situation we had the whole army of the enemy to contend with. Our ammunition was expended; and, unfortunately, the drivers of my ammunition wagons had gone off in the general panic. At this time, I received a severe wound in my thigh; Captain Miller was wounded; Sailingmaster Warner killed; Acting Sadingmaster Martin killed; and Sailingmaster Martin wounded; but, to the honor of my officers and men, as fast as their companions and messmates fell at the guns, they were instantly replaced from the infantry.

"Finding the enemy now completely in our rear, and no means of defence, I gave orders to my officers and men to retire. Three of my officers assisted me to get off a short distance, but the great loss of blood occasioned such a weakness that I was compelled to lie down. I requested my officers to leave me, which they obstinately refused; hut, upon being *ordered*, they obeyed; one only refrained. In a short time I observed a British soldier, and had him called, and directed him to seek an officer; in a few minutes an officer came, and, on learning who I was, brought General Ross and Admiral Cockburn to me. Those officers behaved to me with the most marked attention, respect and politeness, had a surgeon brought, and my wound dressed immediately. After a few minutes' conversation, the General informed me (after paying me a handsome compliment) that I was paroled, and at liberty to proceed to Washington or Bladensburg; as, also, Mr. Huffington, who had remained, with me, offering me every assistance in his power, giving Orders for a litter to be brought, in which I was carried to Bladensburg. Captain Wainright, first captain to Admiral Cochrane, remained with me, and behaved to me as if I was a brother. During the stay of the enemy at Bladensburg, I received every marked attention possible from the officers of the navy and army.

"My wound is deep, but I flatter myself not dangerous: the ball is not yet extracted. I fondly hope a few weeks will restore me to health, and that an exchange will take place, that I may resume my command, or any other. . . ." On the Washington turnpike, the district militia had halted again. Winder had ordered Smith to "collect the troops, and prepare to make a stand on the heights westward of the turnpike gate. This was done as fast as the troops came up. A front was again presented towards the enemy, consisting principally of the troops of this District, a part of those who had been attached to them in action, and a Virginia regiment of about four hundred men, under Colonel Minor" the Fairfax regiment, its musket flints counted at last. But "whilst the line was yet forming," General Smith "received orders from General Winder to fall back to the capitol, and there form for battle." Smith marched his troops to the Capitol, halted, asked Winder how he wanted the battle line drawn. Winder "gave orders that the whole should retreat through Washington and Georgetown."

Walter Smith, remembering the faces of his men, said that it was "impossible to do justice to the anguish evinced by the troops of Washington and Georgetown on the receiving or this order. The idea of leaving their families, their houses and their homes to the mercy of an enraged enemy was insupportable." Winder's final order of the day accomplished what the sight of the oncoming Invincibles had failed to accomplish. It shook the brigade to pieces. "Some shed tears, others uttered imprecations it was impossible for them to comprehend why troops who were willing to risk an encounter with the enemy should be denied the opportunity."

The still-intact regiments began to disintegrate. "To preserve that order which was maintained during the retreat was now no longer practicable. As they retired through Washington and Georgetown, numbers were obtaining and taking leave to visit their homes, and again rejoining; and with ranks thus broken and scattered, they halted at night on the heights near Tenly-town . . ."

A little before sunset, Ross and Cockburn rode into the aban- doned capital of the United States at the head of a few hundred men, only part of their fresh third brigade. A musket went off behind Robert Sewall's house. The general's horse fell dead. The house was destroyed. For the troops who had missed the battle, it was the beginning of a pleasant evening.

Long after dark the two brigades that had fought and won the battle came slogging down the turnpike. They were tired men, but they marched with heads up: this was too good to miss—the Yankees' "federal city" going up in flames. It was a thing to see. It made a gaudier show than ten king's birthdays and a royal wedding, with fireworks on the Thames. The ammunition in the navy yard was letting go now. The explosions crashed like broadsides, and their gouts of fire made giant set-piece vases from which red and orange flowers sprang upward and unfolded, wilted, drooped and darkened and then bloomed again, still climbing, in a writhing foliage of smoke.

Even the tough Invincibles were awed by the great "sheets of, fire which quivered through the air" and by "the very waving of the flames, heard in the stillness of the night to an extraordinary distance."

They were awed, too, by their own achievement. Less than a week ago they still had been on board their transports. They had been soft from eleven weeks of idleness. They had been miserable and half sick from being packed together like so many salt fish in à barrel, and from being tossed about in ships that rolled like barrels and stank like enormous privies. Without time to recuperate, without cavalry, without artillery, without a supply train, they had cut loose from their base—the fleet—and plunged into a strange, unreconnoitered country. Now they had spent six days inside, that hostile country of eight million people, smashed, its army, taken its capital and senti its rulers flying. It was unbelievable. But it was true.

When the British regiments went into bivouac a quarter of a mile outside the burning city, their boats lay sixty miles behind them. Ahead, closer by twenty miles, lay Baltimore—the hated pirates' nest, the "doomed town" long ago marked down for retribution.

The same storm that drenched Queen Dolly drenched the British camp. To Englishmen unused to the sudden fury of a Maryland thundergust, it was a spectacle almost as stunning as the con-flagration that it partly quenched. "The effect was magnificent beyond the power of language to describe. Flash after flash of vivid lightning displayed not only the bivouac, but the streets, the houses, nay the very windows in the town, with a degree of minuteness far greater than the beams of the noon-day sun would have pro-duced. The storm was over in less than an hour, and then "there was nothing to break in upon the quiet of the night, except an occasional roar as a magazine blew up, or a crash, as a wall or roof fell to the ground." There was another and more violent storm the next day. A little after noon the sky suddenly grew black until "the darkness was as great as if the sun had long set, and the last remains of twilight had come on, occasionally relieved by flashes of lightning streaming through it." The rain, driven by a "prodigious force" of wind, was like "the rushing of a mighty cata-ract" and "the noise of the wind and the thunder, the crash of falling buildings, and the tearing of roofs as they were stript from the walls" and "whisked into the air like sheets of paper" appalled the British demolition parties still intent upon the business of destruction. Soldiers threw themselves flat in the muddy streets or huddled behind undamaged houses or the walls of gutted buildings; but walls toppled, dwellings that had been spared by the troops were wrenched to pieces; thirty men were "buried beneath their ruins." Through the dripping bivouac ran a story that two field guns had been "fairly lifted from the ground and borne several yards to the rear."

The hurricane blew itself out within two hours. While the smoldering debris began to smoke again and the sour stench of wet, charred timber and of hot, soaked ashes overpowered the clean smell of the storm-washed earth, another story spread through the rank and file of the Invincibles. The army was advancing. There would be a night march."

It was more than a mere rumor. With it ran a cautious stir of preparation that had meaning to old soldiers. Sergeants checked equipment. Working parties were turned out to gather firewood—a well-worn trick, that one, but still useful: to slip away in darkness, leaving campfires burning to conceal a new blow. Officers were overheard in sober talk about an important movement that must start before tomorrow morning. Men were detailed to patrols, and when the patrols came back to camp there was no doubt left: they had been sent to warn the Yankee civilians who were still in what was left of Washington to keep themselves indoors from sunset until sunrise or be shot. We're not finished with them yet. We're going after them. Sixty miles in six days . . . and sixteen of them yesterday, with a battle thrown in. They say Baltimore is only forty, miles, they say it's summat of a town. The boats? Ye'll see no boats this while. It's an advance, I tell ye. Why not? What's to stop us? *Them?*

In Baltimore, a man named David Winchester was writing to a relative in Tennessee, he was telling General. James Winchester that the enemy was "in possession of the Capitol of the U.S. and that they did not pay dearly for their temerity is doubly mortifying."

"But to my sorrow," he was writing, "it is not to end here—we expect every instant to hear that they have taken up the line of march for this place and if they do we are gone—we have not a single company of regulars either here or in our vicinity—our own malitia, although brave to a fault, are outnumbered by the mercenaries of our enemy, and you known that any raw malitia we can bring in from the country will afford us no protection—under such discouraging circumstances what is to be done. If the town is ravaged which I solemnly believe we have hot the power to prevent—I shall be totally ruined to a certainty. To me you may be sure this is the most awful moment of my life, not because, if this place is defended, that I shall put my life at hazard in common with my. fellow citizens, but because I am positively sure we shall not succeed. . . . All the valuable goods and women and children are now leaving our city seeking safety in the upper country."

Between the doomed town and the invading army, gathering itself together now for. a night march, there was nothing but the fleeing rabble of "malitia." Those who had fled first and fastest, those who had scrounged rides in baggage wagons or had had cash m their pockets to hire farmers' tigs, were already rattling into Baltimore and bringing panic with them. Private Henry Fulford was among the first to reach home. He was safe, he was whole, he was even reasonably clean. When he ventured from the swamp where he had taken refuge, he had found a farmhouse; he had been "hospitably received and got refreshed," and after dark he had set out "with a guide through woods and by-paths" and had tramped five miles to Ross's tavern where he spent the remainder of the night. His personal retreat had been more comfortable than that of most of the defeated army. But his eyes still stared at bayonets, he could not erase from his mind the terrible calmness of the British troops, the inhuman, machinelike advance of the Invincibles. To him they seemed invincible indeed.

He remembered the fire of the batteries concentrating on the narrow bridge and on the men whose bodies filled the bridge. It had been, he thought, a dreadful thing for flesh and blood to face those chunks of flying iron; but the flesh and blood that had faced the guns' fire and survived it seemed more dreadful yet. He was too tired to rest; the awful memories would nor let him rest, he poured them all into a letter while they were still fresh. "The fire must have been dreadfully galling," he wrote, "but they took no notice of it; their men moved like clockwork; the instant a part of a platoon was cut down it was filled up by the men in the rear without the least noise and confusion whatever, so as to present always a solid column to the mouths of our cannon, they advanced so fast that our artillery had to give way and fall back upon our line, where they commenced again and fired for a short time." Private Fulford was no weakling. He was a successful man, a strong man in the world with which he was familiar. He owned shares in warships—in the *Diamond, the Grampus,* the *Patapsco* and the *Transit*—and the ships that he had helped send out to fight had. burned or taken more than fourteen prizes. Perhaps his state of mind would have been described as shell shock at Soissons or in the Àrgonne. What he said about the Baltimore artillery opening fire again after it was routed from the barbette at Bladensburg is a fair illustration of the confused impressions that men get in battle. Henry Fulford could not have been more than a few hundred feet from the retreating batteries when their flight was finally checked and they were ordered farther to the rear, but he firmly believed that the subsequent cannon fire on the Georgetown road was delivered by those guns; he had no notion that the three fieldpieces which supported the charge of his regiment were Washington guns, not Myers nor Magruder's. In such ways originate many of the errors perpetrated by history.

Private Fulford, in all honesty, proceeded to give bottom to another error. "The British force;" he went on, "was greatly superior in numbers to ours. It is my opinion that not one third of their army came into action at all, any further than by amusing themselves by throwing Congreve rockets at us. They were so strong that We had to give way. I think if we had remained ten minutes longer they would have either killed or taken the whole of us. Now, remembering, he gave up to despair:

"They will be here [in Baltimore] in a few days and we have no force that can face them . . . the only way to save the town and state will be to capitulate."

THE BATTLE OF PALO ALTO, BATTLE OF RESACA DE LA PALMA, MOVEMENT ON CAMARGO

U. S. GRANT

While General Taylor was away with the bulk of his army, the little garrison up the river was besieged [May 3]. As we lay in our tents upon the sea-shore, the artillery at the fort on the Rio Grande could be distinctly heard. The war had begun.

There were no possible means of obtaining news from the garrison, and information from outside could not be otherwise than unfavorable. What General Taylor's feelings were during this suspense I do not know; but for myself, a young second-lieutenant who had never heard a hostile gun before, I felt sorry that I had enlisted. A great many men, when they smell battle afar off, chafe to get into the fray. When they say so themselves they generally fail to convince their hearers that they-are as anxious as they would like to make believe, and as they approach danger they become more subdued. This rule is not universal, for I have known a few men who were always aching for a fight when there was no enemy near, who were as good as their word when the battle did come. But the number of such men is small.

On the 7th of March [May] the wagons were all loaded and General Taylor started on his return, with his army reinforced at Point Isabel, but still less than three thousand strong [2,200], to relieve the garrison on the Rio Grande. The road from Point Isabel to Matamoras is over an open, rolling, treeless prairie, until the timber that borders the bank of the Rio Grande is reached. This river, like the Mississippi, flows through a rich alluvial valley in the most meandering manner, running towards all points of the compass at times within a few miles. Formerly the river ran by Resaca de la Palma, some four or five miles east of the present channel. The old bed of the river at Resaca had become filled at places, leaving a succession of little lakes. The timber that had formerly grown upon both banks, and for a considerable distance out, was still standing. This timber was struck six or eight miles out from the besieged garrison, at a point known as Palo Alto—'Tall trees' or 'woods.'

Early in the forenoon of the 8th of May as Palo Alto was approached, an army [estimated at 6,000], certainly outnumbering our little force, was seen, drawn up in line of battle just in front of the timber. Their bayonets and spear-heads glistened in the sunlight formidably. The force was composed largely of cavalry armed with lances. Where we were the grass was tall, reaching nearly to the shoulders of the men, very stiff, and each stock was pointed at the top, and hard and almost as sharp as a darning-needle. General Taylor halted his army before the head of column came in range of the artillery of the Mexicans. He then formed a line of battle, facing the enemy. His artillery, two batteries and two eighteen-pounder iron guns, drawn by oxen, were placed in position at intervals along the line. A battalion was thrown to the rear, commanded by Lieutenant-Colonel [Thomas] Childs, of the artillery, as reserves. These preparations completed, orders were given for a platoon of each company to stack arms and go to a stream off to the right of the command, to fill their canteens and also those of the rest of their respective companies. When the men were all back in their places in line, the command to advance was given. As I looked down that long line of about three thousand armed men, advancing towards a larger force also armed,

I thought what a fearful responsibility General Taylor must feel, commanding such a host and so far away from friends. The Mexicans immediately opened fire upon us, first with artillery and then with infantry. At first their shots did not reach us, and the advance was continued. As we got nearer, the cannon balls commenced going through the ranks. They hurt no one, however, during this advance, because they would, strike the ground long before they reached our line, and ricochetted through the tall grass so slowly that the men would see them and open ranks and let them pass. When we got to a point where the artillery could be used with effect, a halt was called, and the battle opened on both sides.

The infantry under General Taylor was armed with flint-lock muskets, and paper cartridges charged with powder, buck-shot and ball. At the distance of a few hundred yards a man might fire at you all day without your finding it out. The artillery was generally six-pounder brass guns throwing only solid shot; but General Taylor had with him three or four twelve-pounder howitzers throwing shell, besides his eighteen-pounders before spoken of, that had a long range. This made a powerful armament. The Mexicans were armed about as we were so far as their infantry was concerned, but their artillery only fired solid shot. We had greatly the advantage in this arm.

The artillery was advanced a rod or two in front of the line, and opened fire. The infantry stood at order arms as spectators, watching the effect of our shots upon the enemy, and watching his shots so as to step out of their way. It could be seen that the eighteen-pounders and the howitzers did a great deal of execution. On our side there was little or no loss while we occupied this position. During the battle Major [Samuel] Ringgold, an accomplished and brave artillery officer, was mortally wounded, and Lieutenant Luther, also of the artillery, was struck. During the day several advances were made, and just at dusk it became evident that the Mexicans were falling back. We again advanced, and occupied at the close of the battle substantially the ground held by the enemy at the beginning. In this last move there was a brisk fire upon our troops, and some execution was done. One cannon ball passed through our ranks, not far from me. It took off the head of an enlisted man, and the under jaw of Captain [John] Page of my regiment, while the splinters from the musket of the killed soldier, and his brains and bones, knocked down two or three others, including one officer, Lieutenant [Henry D.] Wallen—hurting them more or less. Our casualties for the day were nine killed and forty-seven wounded.

At the break of day on the 9th, the army under Taylor was ready to renew the battle; but an advance showed that the enemy had entirely left our front during the night. The chaparral before us was impenetrable except where there were roads or trails, with occasionally clear or bare spots of small dimensions. A body of men penetrating it might easily be ambushed. It was better to have a few men caught in this way than the whole army, yet it was necessary that the garrison at the river should be relieved. To get to them the chaparral had to be passed. Thus I assume General Taylor reasoned. He halted the army not far in advance of the ground occupied by the Mexicans the day before, and selected Captain C. F. Smith, of the artillery, and Captain McCall, of my company, to take one hundred and fifty picked men each and find where the enemy had gone. This left me in command of the company, an honor and responsibility I thought very great.

Smith and McCall found no obstruction in the way of their advance until they came up to the succession of ponds, before described, at Resaca. The Mexicans had passed them and formed their lines on the opposite bank. This position they had strengthened a little by throwing up dead trees and brush in their front, and by placing artillery to cover the approaches and open places. Smith and McCall deployed on each side of the road as well as they could, and engaged the enemy at long range. Word was sent back, and the advance of the whole army was at once commenced. As we came up we were deployed in like manner. I was with the right wing, and led my company through the thicket wherever a penetrable place could be found, taking advantage of any clear spot that would carry me towards the enemy. At last I got pretty close up without knowing it. The balls commenced to whistle very thick overhead, cutting the limbs of the chaparral right and left. We could not see the enemy, so I ordered my men to lie down, an order that did not have to be enforced. We kept our position until it became evident that the enemy were not firing at us, and then withdrew to find better ground to advance upon.

By this time some progress had been made on our left. A section of artillery had been captured by the cavalry, and some prisoners had been taken. The Mexicans were giving way all along the line, and many of them had, no doubt, left early. I at last found a clear space separating two ponds. There seemed to be a few men in front and I charged upon them with my company. There was no resistance, and we captured a Mexican colonel, who had been wounded, and a few men. Just as I was sending them to the rear with a guard of two or three men, a private came from the front bringing back one of our officers, who had been badly wounded in advance of where I was. The ground had been charged over before. My exploit was equal to that of the soldier who boasted that he had cut off the leg of one of the enemy. When asked why he did not cut off his head, he replied: 'Some one had done that before.' This left no doubt in my mind but that the battle of Resaca de la Palma would have been won, just as it was, if I had not been there.

There was no further resistance. The evening of the 9th the army was encamped on its old ground near the Fort, and the garrison was relieved. The siege had lasted a number of days, but the casualties were few in number. Major Jacob Brown, of the 7th infantry, the commanding officer, had been killed, and in his honor the fort was named. Since then a town of considerable importance had sprung up on the ground occupied by the fort and troops, which has also taken his name.

The battles of Palo Alto and Resaca de la Palma seemed to us engaged, as pretty important affairs; but we had only a faint conception of their magnitude until they were fought over in the North by the Press and the reports came back to us. At the same time, or about the same time, we learned that war existed between the United States and Mexico, by the acts of the latter country. On learning this fact General Taylor transferred our camps to the south or west bank of the river, and Matamoras was occupied [May 18]. We then became the 'Army of Invasion.'

Up to this time Taylor had none but regular troops in his command; but now that invasion had already taken place, volunteers for one year commenced arriving. The army remained at Matamoras until sufficiently reinforced to warrant a movement into the interior.

General Taylor was not an officer to trouble the administration much with his demands, but was inclined to do the best he could with the means given him. He felt his responsibility as going no further. If he had thought that he was sent to perform an impossibility with the means given him, he would probably have informed the authorities of his opinion and left them to determine what should be done. If the judgment was against him he would have gone on and done the best he could with the means at hand without parading his grievance before the public. No soldier could face either danger or responsibility more calmly than he. These are qualities more rarely found than genius or physical courage.

General Taylor never made any great show or parade, either of uniform or retinue. In dress he was possibly too plain, rarely wearing anything in the field to indicate his rank, or even that he was an officer; but he was known to every soldier in his army, and was respected by all. I can call to mind only one instance when I saw him in uniform, and one other when I heard of his wearing it. On both occasions he was unfortunate. The first was at Corpus Christi. He had concluded to review his army before starting on the march and gave orders accordingly. Colonel Twiggs was then second in rank with the army, and to him was given the command of the review. Colonel and Brevet Brigadier-General [William J.] Worth, a far different soldier from Taylor in the use of the uniform, was next to Twiggs in rank, and claimed superiority by virtue of his brevet rank when the accidents of service threw them where one or the other had to command. Worth declined to attend the review as subordinate to Twiggs until the question was settled by the highest authority. This broke up the review, and the question was referred to Washington for final decision.

General Taylor was himself only a colonel, in real rank, at that time, and a brigadier-general by brevet. He was assigned to duty, however, by the President, with the rank which his brevet gave him. Worth was not so assigned, but by virtue of commanding a division he must, under the army regulations of that day, have drawn the pay of his brevet rank. The question was submitted to Washington, and no response was received until after the army had reached the Rio Grande. It was decided against General Worth, who at once tendered his resignation and left the army, going north, no doubt, by the same vessel that carried it. This kept him out of the battles of Palo Alto and Resaca de la Palma. Either the resignation was not accepted, or General Worth withdrew it before action had been taken.

At all events he returned to the army in time to command his division in the battle of Monterey, and served with it to the end of the war.

The second occasion on which General Taylor was said to have donned his uniform, was in order to receive a visit from the Flag Officer [David Conner] of the naval squadron off the mouth of the Rio Grande. While the army was on that river the Flag Officer sent word that he would call on the General to pay his respects on a certain day. General Taylor, knowing that naval officers habitually wore all the uniform the 'law allowed' on all occasions of ceremony, thought it would be only civil to receive his guest in the same style. His uniform was therefore got out, brushed up, and put on, in advance of the visit. The Flag Officer, knowing General Taylor's aversion to the wearing of the uniform, and feeling that it would be regarded as a compliment should he meet him in civilian's dress, left off his uniform for this occasion. The meeting was said to have been embarrassing to both, and the conversation was principally apologetic.

The time was whiled away pleasantly enough at Matamoras, while we were waiting for volunteers. It is probable that all the most important people of the territory occupied by our army left their homes before we got there, but with those remaining the best of relations apparently existed. It was the policy of the Commanding General to allow no pillaging, no taking of private property for public or individual use without satisfactory compensation, so that a better market was afforded than the people had ever known before.

Among the troops that joined us at Matamoras was an Ohio regiment, of which Thomas L. Hamer, the Member of Congress who had given me my appointment to West Point, was major. He told me then that he could have had the colonelcy, but that as he knew he was to be appointed a brigadier-general, he preferred at first to take the lower grade. I have said before that Hamer was one of the ablest men Ohio ever produced. At that time he was in the prime of life, being less than fifty years of age, and possessed an admirable physique, promising long life. But he was taken sick before Monterey, and died within a few days. I have always believed that had his life been spared, he would have been President of the United States during the term filled by President Pierce. Had Hamer filled that office his partiality for me was such, there is but little doubt I should have been appointed to one of the staff corps of the army—the Pay Department probably—and would therefore now be preparing to retire.

Neither of these speculations is unreasonable, and they are mentioned to show how little men control their own destiny.

Reinforcements having arrived, in the month of August the movement commenced from Matamoras to Camargo, the head of navigation on the Rio Grande. The line of the Rio Grande was all that was necessary to hold, unless it was intended to invade Mexico from the North. In that case the most natural route to take was the one which General Taylor selected. It entered a pass in the Sierra Madre Mountains, at Monterey [now Monterrey], through which the main road runs to the City of Mexico. Monterey itself was a good point to hold, even if the line of the Rio Grande covered all the territory we desired to occupy at that time. It is built on a plain two thousand feet above tide water, where the air is bracing and the situation healthy.

On the 19th of August the army started for Monterey, leaving a small garrison at Matamoras. The. troops, with the exception of the artillery, cavalry, and the brigade to which I belonged, were moved up the river to Camargo on steamers. As there were but two or three of these, the boats had to make a number of trips before the last of the troops were up. Those who marched did so by the south side of the river. Lieutenant-Colonel Garland, of the 4th infantry, was the brigade commander, and on this occasion commanded the entire marching force. One day out convinced him that marching by day in that latitude, in the month of August, was not a beneficial sanitary measure, particularly for Northern men. The order of marching was changed and night marches were substituted with the best results.

When Camargo was reached, we found a city of tents outside the Mexican hamlet. I was detailed to act as quartermaster and commissary to the regiment. The teams that had proven abundantly sufficient to transport all supplies from Corpus Christi to the Rio Grande over the level prairies of Texas, were entirely inadequate to the needs of the reinforced army in a mountainous country. To obviate the deficiency, pack mules were hired, with Mexicans to pack and drive them. I had charge of the few wagons allotted to the 4th infantry and of the pack train to supplement them. There were not men enough in the army to manage that train without the help of Mexicans who had learned how. As it was the difficulty was great enough. The troops would take up their march at an early hour each day. After they had started, the tents and cooking utensils had to be made into packages, so that they could be lashed to the backs of the mules. Sheet-iron kettles, tent-poles and mess chests were inconvenient articles to transport in that way. It took several hours to get ready to start each morning, and by the time we were ready some of the mules first loaded would be tired of standing so long with their loads on their backs. Sometimes one would start to run, bowing his back and kicking up until he scattered his load; others would lie down and try to disarrange their loads by attempting to get on the top of them by rolling on them; other with tent-poles for part of their loads would manage to run a tent-pole on one side of a sapling while they would take the other. I am not aware of ever having used a profane expletive in my life; but I would have the charity of a train of Mexican pack mules at the time.

"LOOK AT JACKSON'S BRIGADE! IT STANDS THERE LIKE A STONE WALL!"

G. T. BEAUREGARD, GENERAL, C. S. A.

S oon after the first conflict between the authorities of the Federal Union and those of the Confederate States had occurred in Charleston Harbor, by the bombardment of Fort Sumter—which, beginning at 4:30 AM on the 12th of April, 1861, forced the surrender of that fortress within thirty hours thereafter into my hands—I was called to Richmond, which by that time had become the Confederate seat of government, and was directed to "assume command of the Confederate troops on the Alexandria line." Arriving at Manassas Junction, I took command on the 2d of June, forty-nine days after the evacuation of Fort Sumter.

Although the position at the time was strategically of commanding importance to the Confederates, the mere *terrain* was not only without natural defensive advantages, but, on the contrary, was absolutely unfavorable. Its strategic value was that, being close to the Federal capital, it held in observation the chief army then being assembled near Arlington by General McDowell, under the immediate eye of the commander-in-chief, General Scott, for an offensive movement against Richmond; and while it had a railway approach in its rear for the easy accumulation of reënforcements and all the necessary munitions of war from the southward, at the same time another (the Manassas Gap) railway, diverging laterally to the left from that point, gave rapid communications with the fertile valley of the Shenandoah, then teeming with live stock and cereal subsistence, as well as with other resources essential to the Confederates. There was this further value in the position to the Confederate army: that during the period of accumulation, seasoning, and training, it might be fed from the fat fields, pastures, and garners of Loudoun, Fauquier, and the Lower Shenandoah Valley counties, which otherwise must have fallen into the hands of the enemy. But, on the other hand, Bull Run, a petty stream, was of little or no defensive strength; for it abounded in fords, and although for the most part its banks were rocky and abrupt, the side from which it would be approached offensively in most places commanded the opposite ground.

At the time of my arrival at Manassas, a Confederate army under General Joseph E. Johnston was in occupation of the Lower Shenandoah Valley, along the line of the Upper Potomac, chiefly at Harper's Ferry, which was regarded as the gateway of the valley and of one of the possible approaches to Richmond; a position from which he was speedily forced to retire, however, by a flank movement of a Federal army, under the veteran General Patterson, thrown across the Potomac at or about Martinsburg. On my other or right flank, so to speak, a Confederate force of some 2500 men under General Holmes occupied the position of Aquia Creek on the lower Potomac, upon the line of approach to Richmond from that direction through Fredericksburg. The other approach, that by way of the James River, was held by Confederate troops under Generals Huger and Magruder. Establishing small outposts at Leesburg to observe the crossings of the Potomac in that quarter, and at Fairfax Court House in observation of Arlington, with other detachments in advance of Manassas toward Alexandria on the south side of the railroad, from the very outset I was anxiously aware that the sole military advantage at the moment to the Confederates was that of holding the *interior lines*. On the Federal or hostile side were all material advantages, including superior numbers, largely drawn from the old militia organizations of the great cities of the North, decidedly better armed and equipped than the troops under me, and strengthened by a small but incomparable body of regular infantry as well as a number of batteries of regular field artillery of the highest class, and a very large and thoroughly organized staff corps, besides a numerous body of professionally educated officers in command of volunteer regiments—all precious military elements at such a juncture.

Happily, through the foresight of Colonel Thomas Jordan—whom General Lee had placed as the adjutant-general of the forces there assembled before my arrival—arrangements were made which enabled me to receive regularly, from private persons at the Federal capital, most accurate information, of which politicians high in council, as well as War Department clerks, were the unconscious ducts. . . .

In these several ways, therefore, I was almost as well advised of the strength of the hostile army in my front as its commander, who, I may mention, had been a classmate of mine at West Point. Under those circumstances I had become satisfied that a well-equipped, well-constituted Federal army at least 50,000 strong, of all arms, confronted me at or about Arlington, ready and on the very eve of an offensive operation against me, and to meet which I could muster 'barely 18,000 men with 29 field-guns.

Previously—indeed, as early as the middle of June—it had become apparent to my mind that through only one course of action could there be a well-grounded hope of ability on the part of the Confederates to encounter successfully the offensive operations for which the Federal authorities were then vigorously preparing in my immediate front, with so consummate a strategist and military administrator as Lieutenant-General Scott in general command at Washington, aided by his accomplished heads of the large General Staff Corps of the United States Army. This course was to make the most enterprising, warlike use of the interior lines which we possessed, for the swift concentration at the critical instant of every available Confederate force upon the menaced position, at the risk, if need were, of sacrificing all minor places to the one clearly of major military value—there to meet our adversary so offensively as to overwhelm him, under circumstances that must assure immediate ability to assume the general offensive even upon his territory, and thus conquer an early peace by a few well-delivered blows.

My views of such import had been already earnestly communicated to the proper authorities; but about the middle of July, satisfied that McDowell was on the eve of taking the offensive against me, I dispatched Colonel James Chestnut, of South Carolina, a volunteer aide-de-camp on my staff who had served on an intimate footing with Mr. Davis in the Senate of the United States, to urge in substance the necessity for the immediate concentration of the larger part of the forces of Johnston and Holmes at Manassas, so that the moment McDowell should be sufficiently far detached from Washington, I would be enabled to move rapidly round his more convenient flank upon his rear and his communications, and attack him in reverse, or get between his forces, then separated, thus cutting off his retreat upon Arlington in the event of his defeat, and insuring as an immediate consequence the crushing of Patterson, the liberation of Maryland, and the capture of Washington.

This plan was rejected by Mr. Davis and his military advisers (Adjutant-General Cooper and General Lee), who characterized it as "brilliant and comprehensive, but essentially impracticable. Furthermore, Colonel Chestnut came back impressed with the views entertained at Richmond—as he communicated at once to my adjutant-general—that should the Federal army soon move offensively upon my position, my best course would be to retire behind the Rappahannock and accept battle there instead of at Manassas. In effect, it was regarded as best to sever communications between the two chief Confederate armies, that of the Potomac and that of the Shenandoah, with the inevitable immediate result that Johnston would be forced to leave Patterson in possession of the Lower Shenandoah Valley, abandoning to the enemy so large a part of the most resourceful sections of Virginia, and to retreat southward by way of the Luray Valley, pass across the Blue Ridge at Thornton's Gap and unite with me after all, but at Fredericksburg, much nearer Richmond than Manassas. These views, however, were not made known to me at the time, and happily my mind was left free to the grave problem imposed upon me by the rejection of my plan for the immediate concentration of a materially larger force—*i.e.,* the problem of placing and using my resources for a successful encounter behind Bull Run with the Federal army, which I was not permitted to doubt was about to take the field against me.

It is almost needless to say that I had caused to be made a thorough reconnoissance of all the ground in my front and flanks, and had made myself personally acquainted with the most material points, including the region of Sudley's Church on my left, where a small detachment was posted in observation. Left now to my own resources, of course the contingency of defeat had to be considered and provided for. Among the measures of precaution for such a result, I ordered the destruction of the railroad bridge across Bull Run at Union Mills, on my right, in order that the enemy, in the event of my defeat, should not have the immediate use of the railroad in following up their movement against Richmond—a railroad which could have had no corresponding value to us eastward beyond Manassas in any operations on our side with Washington as the objective, inasmuch as any such operations must have been made by the way of the Upper Potomac and upon the rear of that city.

Just before Colonel Chestnut was dispatched on the mission of which I have spoken, a former clerk in one of the departments at Washington, well known to him, had volunteered to return thither and bring back the latest information of the military and political situation from our most trusted friends. His loyalty to our cause, his intelligence, and his desire to be of service being vouched for, he was at once sent across the Potomac below Alexandria, merely accredited by a small scrap of paper bearing in Colonel Jordan's cipher the two words, "Trust bearer," with which he was to call at a certain house in Washington within easy rifle-range of the White House, ask for the lady of the house, and present it only to her. This delicate mission was as fortunately as it was deftly executed. In the early morning, as the newsboys were crying in the empty streets of Washington the intelligence that the order was given for the Federal army to move at once upon my position, that scrap of paper reached the hands of the one person in all that city who could extract any meaning from it. With no more delay than was necessary for a hurried breakfast and the writing in cipher by Mrs.

G—of the words, "Order issued for McDowell to march upon Manassas to-night," my agent was placed in communication with another friend, who carried him in a buggy with a relay of horses as swiftly as possible down the eastern shore of the Potomac to our regular ferry across that river. Without untoward incident the momentous dispatch was quickly delivered into the hands of a cavalry courier, and by means of relays it was in my hands between 8 and 9 o'clock that night. Within half an hour my outpost commanders, advised of what was impending, were directed, at the first evidence of the near presence of the enemy in their front, to fall back in the manner and to positions already prescribed in anticipation of such a contingency in an order confidentially communicated to them four weeks before, and the detachment at Leesburg was directed to join me by forced marches. Having thus cleared my decks for action, I next acquainted Mr. Davis with the situation, and ventured once more to suggest that the Army of the Shenandoah, with the brigade at Fredericksburg or Aquia Creek, should be ordered to reënforce me—suggestions that were at once heeded so far that General Holmes was ordered to carry his command to my aid, and General Johnston was given discretion to do likewise. After some telegraphic discussion with me, General Johnston was induced to exercise this discretion in favor of the swift march of the Army of the Shenandoah to my relief; and to facilitate that vital movement, I hastened to accumulate all possible means of railway transport at a designated point on the Manassas Gap railroad at the eastern foot of the Blue Ridge, to which Johnston's troops directed their march. However, at the same time, I had submitted the alternative proposition to General Johnston, that, having passed the Blue Ridge, he should assemble his forces, press forward by way of Aldie, north-west of Manassas, and fall upon McDowell's right rear; while I, prepared for the operation, at the first sound of the conflict, should strenuously assume the offensive in my front. The situation and circumstances specially favored the signal success of such an operation. The march to the point of attack could have been accomplished as soon as the forces were brought ultimately by rail to Manassas Junction; our enemy, thus attacked so nearly simultaneously on his right flank, his rear, and his front, naturally would suppose that I had been able to turn his flank while attacking him in front, and therefore, that I must have an overwhelming superiority of numbers; and his forces, being new troops, most of them under fire for the first time, must have soon fallen into a disastrous panic. Moreover, such an operation must have resuited advantageously to the Confederates, in the event that McDowell should, as might have been anticipated, attempt to strike the Manassas Gap railway to my left, and thus cut off railway communications between Johnston's forces and my own, instead of the mere effort to strike my left flank which he actually essayed.

It seemed, however, as though the deferred attempt at concentration was to go for naught, for on the morning of the 18th the Federal forces were massed around Centreville, but three miles from Mitchell's Ford, and soon were seen advancing upon the roads leading to that and Blackburn's Ford. My order of battle, issued in the night of the 17th, contemplated an offensive return, particularly from the strong brigades on the right and right center. The Federal artillery opened in front of both fords, and the infantry, while demonstrating in front of Mitchell's Ford, endeavored to force a passage at Blackburn's. Their column of attack, Tyler's division, was opposed by Longstreet's forces, to the reënforcement of which Early's brigade, the reserve line at McLean's Ford, was ordered up. The Federals, after several attempts to force a passage, met a final repulse and retreated. After their infantry attack had ceased, about 1 o'clock, the contest lapsed into an artillery duel, in which the Washington Artillery of New Orleans won credit against the renowned batteries of the United States regular army. A comical effect of this artillery fight was the destruction of the dinner of myself and staff by a Federal shell that fell into the fire-place of my headquarters at the McLean House.

Our success in this first limited collision was of special prestige to my army of new troops, and, moreover, of decisive importance by so increasing General McDowell's caution as to give time for the arrival of some of General Johnston's forces. But while on the 19th I was awaiting a renewed and general attack by the Federal army, I received a telegram from the Richmond military authorities, urging me to withdraw my call on General Johnston on account of the supposed impracticability of the concentration—an abiding conviction which had been but momentarily shaken by the alarm caused by McDowell's march upon Richmond. As this was not an order in terms, but an urgency which, notwithstanding its superior source, left me technically free and could define me as responsible for any misevent, I preferred to keep both the situation and the responsibility, and continued every effort for the prompt arrival of the Shenandoah forces, being resolved, should they come before General McDowell again attacked, to take myself the offensive. General McDowell, fortunately for my plans, spent the 19th and 20th in recon-noissances; and, meanwhile, General Johnston brought 8340 men from the Shenandoah Valley, with 20 guns, and General Holmes 1265 rank and file, with 6 pieces of artillery, from Aquia Creek. As these forces arrived (most of them in the afternoon of the 20th) I placed them chiefly so as to strengthen my left center and left, the latter being weak from lack of available troops.

The preparation, in front of an ever-threatening enemy, of a wholly volunteer army, composed of men very few of whom had ever belonged to any military organization, had been a work of many cares not incident to the command of a regular army. These were increased by the insufficiency of my staff organization, an inefficient management of the quartermaster's department at Richmond, and the preposterous mismanagement of the commissary-general, who not only failed to furnish rations, but caused the removal of the army commissaries, who, under my orders, procured food from the country in front of us to keep the army from absolute want—supplies that were otherwise exposed to be gathered by the enemy. . . .

There was much in this decisive conflict about to open, not involved in any after battle, which pervaded the two armies and the people behind them and colored the responsibility of the respective commanders. The political hostilities of a generation were now face to face with weapons instead of words. Defeat to either side would be a deep mortification, but defeat to the South must turn its claim of independence into an empty vaunt; and the defeated commander on either side might expect, though not the personal fate awarded by the Carthaginians to an unfortunate commander, at least a moral fate quite similar. . . .

General Johnston was the ranking officer, and entitled, therefore, to assume command of the united forces; but as the extensive field of operations was one which I had occupied since the beginning of June, and with which I was thoroughly familiar in all its extent and military bearings, while he was wholly unacquainted with it, and, moreover, as I had made my plans and dispositions for the maintenance of the position, General Johnston, in view of the gravity of the impending issue, preferred not to assume the responsibilities of the chief direction of the forces during the battle, but to assist me upon the field. Thereupon, I explained my plans and purposes, to which he agreed.

SUNDAY, July 21st, bearing the fate of the new-born Confederacy, broke brightly over the fields and woods that held the hostile forces. My scouts, thrown out in the night toward Centreville along the Warrenton Turnpike, had reported that the enemy was concentrating along the latter. This fact, together with the failure of the Federals in their attack upon my center at Mitchell's and Blackburn's fords, had caused me to apprehend that they would attempt my left flank at the Stone Bridge, and orders were accordingly issued by half-past 4 o'clock to the brigade commanders to hold their forces in readiness to move at a moment's notice, together with the suggestion that the Federal attack might be expected in that quarter. Shortly afterward the enemy was reported to be advancing from Centreville on the Warrenton Turnpike, and at half-past 5 o'clock as deploying a force in front of Evans. As their movement against my left developed the opportunity I desired, I immediately sent orders to the brigade commanders, both front and reserves, on my right and center to advance and vigorously attack the Federal left flank and rear at Centreville, while my left, under Cocke and Evans with their supports, would sustain the Federal attack in the quarter of the Stone Bridge, which they were directed to do to the last extremity. The center was likewise to advance and engage the enemy in front, and directions were given to the reserves, when without orders, to move toward the sound of the heaviest firing. The ground in our front on the other side of Bull Run afforded particular advantage for these tactics. Centreville was the apex of a triangle—its short side running by the Warrenton Turnpike to Stone Bridge, its base Bull Run, its long side a road that ran from Union Mills along the front of my other Bull Run positions and trended off to the rear of Centreville, where McDowell had massed his main forces; branch roads led up to this one from the fords between Union Mills and Mitchell's. My forces to the right of the latter ford were to advance, pivoting on that position; Bonham was in advance from Mitchell's Ford, Longstreet from Blackburn's, D. R. Jones from McLean's, and Ewell from Union Mills by the Centreville road. Ewell, as having the longest march, was to begin the movement, and each brigade was to be followed by its reserve. In anticipation of this method of attack, and to prevent accidents, the subordinate commanders had been carefully instructed in the movement by me, as they were all new to the responsibilities of command. They were to establish close communication with each other before making the attack. About half-past 8 o'clock I set out with General Johnston for a convenient position—a hill in rear of Mitchell's Ford—where we waited for the opening of the attack on our right, from which I expected a decisive victory by midday, with the result of cutting off the Federal army from retreat upon Washington.

Meanwhile, about half-past 5 o'clock, the peal of a heavy rifled gun was heard in front of the Stone Bridge, its second shot striking through the tent of my signal-officer, Captain E. P. Alexander; and at 6 o'clock a full rifled battery opened against Evans and then against Cocke, to which our artillery remained dumb, as it had not sufficient range to reply. But later, as the Federal skirmish-line advanced, it was engaged by ours, thrown well forward on the other side of the Run. A scattering musketry fire followed, and meanwhile, about 7 o'clock, I ordered Jackson's brigade, with Imboden's and five guns of Walton's battery, to the left, with orders to support Cocke as well as Bonham; and the brigades of Bee and Bartow, under the command of the former, were also sent to the support of the left.

At half-past 8 o'clock Evans, seeing that the Federal attack did not increase in boldness and vigor, and observing a lengthening line of dust above the trees to the left of the Warrenton Turnpike, became satisfied that the attack in his front was but a feint, and that a column of the enemy was moving around through the woods to fall on his flank from the direction of Sudley Ford. Informing his immediate commander, Cocke, of the enemy's movemerit, and of his own dispositions to meet it, he left 4 companies under cover at the Stone Bridge, and led the remainder of his force, 6 companies of Sloan's 4th South Carolina and Wheat's battalion of Louisiana Tigers, with 2 6-pounder howitzers, across the valley of Young's Branch to the high ground beyond it. Resting his left on the

Sudley road, he distributed his troops on each side of a small copse, with such cover as the ground afforded, and looking over the open fields and a reach of the Sudley road which the Federals must cover in their approach. His two howitzers were placed one at each end of his position, and here he silently awaited the enemy now drawing near.

The Federal turning column, about 18,000 strong, with 24 pieces of artillery, had moved down from Centreville by the Warrenton Turnpike, and after passing Cub Run had struck to the right by a forest road to cross Bull Run at Sudley Ford, about 3 miles above the Stone Bridge, moving by a long circuit for the purpose of attacking my left flank. The head of the column, Burnside's brigade of Hunter's division, at about 9:45 AM debouched from the woods into the open fields, in front of Evans. Wheat at once engaged their skirmishers, and as the Second Rhode Island regiment advanced, supported by its splendid battery of 6 rifled guns, the fronting thicket held by Evans's South Carolinians poured forth its sudden volleys, while the 2 howitzers flung their grape-shot upon the attacking line, which was soon shattered and driven back into the woods behind. Major Wheat, after handling his battalion with the utmost determination, had fallen severely wounded in the lungs. Burnside's entire brigade was now sent forward in a second charge, supported by 8 guns; but they encountered again the un-iflinching fire of Evans's line, and were once more driven back to the woods, from the cover of which they continued the attack, reënforced after a time by the arrival of 8 companies of United States regular infantry, under Major Sykes, with 6 pieces of artillery, quickly followed by the remaining regiments of Andrew Porter's brigade of the same division. The contest here lasted fully an hour; meanwhile Wheat's battalion, having lost its leader, had gradually lost its organization, and Evans, though still opposing these heavy odds with undiminished firmness, sought reënforcement from the troops in his rear.

General Bee, of South Carolina, a man of marked character, whose command lay in reserve in rear of Cocke, near the Stone Bridge, intelligently applying the general order given to the reserves, had already moved toward the neighboring point of conflict, and taken a position with his own and Bartow's brigades on the high plateau which stands in rear of Bull Run in the quarter of the Stone Bridge, and overlooking the scene of engagement upon the stretch of high ground from which it was separated by the valley of Young's Branch. This plateau is inclosed on three sides by two small watercourses, which empty into Bull Run within a few yards of each other, a half mile to the south of the Stone Bridge. Rising to an elevation of quite 100 feet above the level of Bull

Run at the bridge, it falls off on three sides to the level of the inclosing streams in gentle slopes, but furrowed by ravines of irregular directions and length, and studded with clumps and patches of young pine and oaks. The general direction of the crest of the plateau is oblique to the course of Bull Run in that quarter and to the Sudley and turnpike roads, which intersect each other at right angles. On the north-western brow, overlooking Young's Branch, and near the Sudley road, as the latter climbs over the plateau, stood the house of the widow Henry, while to its right and forward on a projecting spur stood the house and sheds of the free Negro Robinson, just behind the turnpike, densely embowered in trees and shrubbery and environed by a double row of fences on two sides. Around the eastern and southern brow of the plateau an almost unbroken fringe of second-growth pines gave excellent shelter for our marksmen, who availed themselves of it with the most satisfactory skill. To the west, adjoining the fields that surrounded the houses mentioned, a broad belt of oaks extends directly across the crest on both sides of the Sudley road, in which, during the battle, the hostile forces contended for the mastery. General Bee, with a soldier's eye to the situation, skillfully disposed his forces. His two brigades on either side of Imboden's battery—which he had borrowed from bis neighboring reserve, Jackson's brigade—were placed in a small depression of the plateau in advance of the Henry house, whence he had a full view of the contest on the opposite height across the valley of Young's Branch. Opening with his artillery upon the Federal batteries, he answered Evans's request by advising him to withdraw to his own position on the height; but Evans, full of the spirit that would not retreat, renewed his appeal that the forces in rear would come to help him hold his ground. The newly arrived forces had given the Federals such superiority at this point as to dwarf Evans's means of resistance, and General Bee, generously yielding his own better judgment to Evans's persistence, led the two brigades across the valley under the fire of the enemy's artillery, and threw them into action—1 regiment in the copse held by Colonel Evans, 2 along a fence on the right, and 2 under General Bartow on the prolonged right of this line, but extended forward at a right angle and along the edge of a wood not more than 100 yards from that held by the enemy's left, where the contest at short range became sharp and deadly, bringing many casualties to both sides. The Federal infantry, though still in superior numbers, failed to make any headway against this sturdy van, notwithstanding Bee's whole line was hammered also by the enemy's powerful batteries, until Heintzelman's division of 2 strong brigades, arriving from Sudley Ford, extended the fire on the Federal right, while its battery of 6 10-pounder rifled guns took an immediately effective part from a position behind the Sudley road. Against these odds the Confederate force was still endeavoring to hold its ground, when a new enemy came into the field upon its right. Major Wheat, with characteristic daring and restlessness, had crossed Bull Run alone by a small ford above the Stone Bridge, in order to reconnoiter, when he and Evans had first moved to the left, and, falling on some Federal scouts, had shouted a taunting defiance and withdrawn, not, however, without his place of crossing having been observed. This disclosure was now utilized by Sherman's (W. T.) and Keyes's brigades of Tyler's division; crossing at this point, they appeared over the high bank of the stream and moved into position on the Federal left. There was no choice now for Bee but to retire—a movement, however, to be accomplished under different circumstances than when urged by him upon Evans. The three leaders endeavored to preserve the steadiness of the ranks as they withdrew over the open fields, aided by the fire of Imboden's guns on the plateau and the retiring howitzers; but the troops were thrown into confusion, and the greater part soon fell into rout across Young's Branch and around the base of the height in the rear of the Stone Bridge.

Meanwhile, in rear of Mitchell's Ford, I had been waiting with General Johnston for the sound of conflict to open in the quarter of Centreville upon the Federal left flank and rear (making allowance, however, for the delays possible to commands unused to battle), when I was chagrined to hear from General D. R. Jones that, while he had been long ready for the movement upon Centreville, General Ewell had not come up to form on his right, though he had sent him between 7 and 8 o'clock a copy of his own order which recited that Ewell had been already ordered to begin the movement. I dispatched an immediate order to Ewell to advance; but within a quarter of an hour, just as I received a dispatch from him informing me that he had received no order to advance in the morning, the firing on the left began to increase so intensely as to indicate a severe attack, whereupon General Johnston said that he would go personally to that quarter.

After weighing attentively the firing, which seemed rapidly and heavily increasing, it appeared to me that the troops on the right would be unable to get into position before the Federal offensive should have made too much progress on our left, and that it would be better to abandon it altogether, maintaining only a strong demonstration so as to detain the enemy in front of our right and center, and hurry up all available reënforcements—including the reserves that were to have moved upon Centreville—to our left and fight the battle out in that quarter. Communicating this view to General Johnston, who approved it (giving his advice, as he said, for what it was worth, as he was not acquainted with the country), I ordered Ewell, Jones, and Longstreet to make a strong demonstration all along their front on the other side of the Run, and ordered the reserves below our position, Holmes's brigade with 6 guns, and Early's brigade, also 2 regiments of Bonham's brigade, near at hand, to move swiftly to the left. General Johnston and I now set out at full speed for the point of conflict. We arrived there just as Bee's troops, after giving way, were fleeing in disorder behind the height in rear of the Stone Bridge. They had come around between the base of the hill and the Stone Bridge into a shallow ravine which ran up to a point on the crest where Jackson had already formed his brigade along the edge of the woods. We found the commanders resolutely stemming the further flight of the routed forces, but vainly endeavoring to restore order, and our own efforts were as futile. Every segment of line we succeeded in forming was again dissolved while another was being formed; more than two thousand men were shouting each some suggestion to his neighbor, their voices mingling with the noise of the shells hurtling through the trees overhead, and all word of command drowned in the confusion and uproar. It was at this moment that General Bee used the famous expression, "Look at Jackson's brigade! It stands there like a stone wall"—a name that passed from the brigade to its immortal commander. The disorder seemed irretrievable, but happily the thought came to me that if their colors were planted out to the front the men might rally on them, and I gave the order to carry the standards forward some forty yards, which was promptly executed by the regimental officers, thus drawing the common eye of the troops. They now received easily the orders to advance and form on the line of their colors, which they obeyed with a general movement; and as General Johnston and myself rode forward shortly after with the colors of the 4th Alabama by our side, the line that had fought all morning, and had fled, routed and disordered, now advanced again into position as steadily as veterans. The 4th Alabama had previously lost all its field-officers; and noticing Colonel S. R. Gist, an aide to General Bee, a young man whom I had known as adjutant-general of South Carolina, and whom I greatly esteemed, I presented him as an able and brave commander to the stricken regiment, who cheered their new leader, and maintained under him, to the end of the day, their previous gallant behavior. We had come none too soon, as the enemy's forces, flushed with the belief of accomplished victory, were already advancing across the valley of Young's Branch and up the slope, where they had encountered for a while the fire of the Hampton Legion, which had been led forward toward the Robinson house and the turnpike in front, covering the retreat and helping materially to check the panic of Bee's routed forces.

As soon as order was restored I requested General Johnston to go back to Portici (the Lewis house), and from that point—which I considered most favorable for the purpose—forward me the reënforcements as they would come from the Bull Run lines below and those that were expected to arrive from Manassas, while I should direct the field. General Johnston was disinclined to leave the battle-field for that position. As I had been compelled to leave my chief-of-staff, Colonel Jordan, at Manassas to forward any troops arriving there, I felt it was a necessity that one of us should go to this duty, and that it was his place to do so, as I felt I was responsible for the battle. He considerately yielded to my urgency, and we had the benefit of his energy and sagacity in so directing the reënforcements toward the field, as to be readily and effectively assistant to my pressing needs and insure the success of the day.

As General Johnston departed for Portici, I hastened to form our line of battle against the on-coming enemy. I ordered up the 49th and 8th Virginia regiments from Cocke's neighboring brigade in the Bull Run lines. Gartrell's 7th Georgia I placed in position on the left of Jackson's brigade, along the belt of pines occupied by the latter on the eastern rim of the plateau. As the 49th Virginia rapidly came up, its colonel, ex-Governor William Smith, was encouraging them with cheery word and manner, and, as they approached, indicated to them the immediate presence of the commander. As the regiment raised a loud cheer, the name was caught by some of the troops of Jackson's brigade in the immediate wood, who rushed out, calling for General Beauregard. Hastily acknowledging these happy signs of sympathy and confidence, which reënforce alike the capacity of commander and troops, I placed the 49th Virginia in position on the extreme left next to Gartrell, and as I paused to say a few words to Jackson, while hurrying back to the right, my horse was killed under me by a bursting shell, a fragment of which carried away part of the heel of my boot. The Hampton Legion, which had suffered greatly, was placed on the right of Jackson's brigade, and Hunton's 8th Virginia, as it arrived, upon the right of Hampton; the two latter being drawn somewhat to the rear so as to form with Jackson's right regiment a reserve, and be ready likewise to make defense against any advance from the direction of the Stone Bridge, whence there was imminent peril from the enemy's heavy forces, as I had just stripped that position almost entirely of troops to meet the active crisis on the plateau, leaving this quarter now covered only by a few men, whose defense was otherwise assisted solely by the obstruction of an abatis.

With 6500 men and 13 pieces of artillery, I now awaited the onset of the enemy, who were pressing forward 20,000 strong, with 24 pieces of superior artillery and 7 companies of regular cavalry. They soon appeared over the farther rim of the plateau, seizing the Robinson house on my right and the Henry house opposite my left center. Near the latter they placed in position the two powerful batteries of Ricketts and Griffin of the regular army, and pushed forward up the Sudley road, the slope of which was cut so deep below the adjacent ground as to afford a covered way up to the plateau. Supported by the formidable lines of Federal musketry, these 2 batteries lost no time in making themselves felt, while 3 more batteries in rear on the high ground beyond the Sudley and Warrenton cross-roads swelled the shower of shell that fell among our ranks.

Our own batteries, Imboden's, Stanard's, five of Walton's guns, reënforced later by Pendleton's and Alburtis's (their disadvantage being reduced by the shortness of range), swept the surface of the plateau from their position on the eastern rim. I felt that, after the accidents of the morning, much depended on maintaining the steadiness of the troops against the first heavy onslaught, and rode along the lines encouraging the men to unflinching behavior, meeting, as I passed each command, a cheering response. The steady fire of their musketry told severely on the Federal ranks, and the splendid action of our batteries was a fit preface to the marked skill exhibited by our artillerists during the war. The enemy suffered particularly from the musketry on our left, now further reënforced by the 2d Mississippi—the troops in this quarter confronting each other at very short range. Here two companies of Stuart's cavalry charged through the Federal ranks that filled the Sudley road, increasing the disorder wrought upon that flank of the enemy. But with superior numbers the Federals were pushing on new regiments in the attempt to flank my position, and several guns, in the effort to enfilade ours, were thrust forward so near the 33d Virginia that some of its men sprang forward and captured them, but were driven back by an overpowering force of Federal musketry. Although the enemy were held well at bay, their pressure became so strong that I resolved to take the offensive, and ordered a charge on my right for the purpose of recovering the plateau. The movement, made with alacrity and force by the commands of Bee, Bartow, Evans, and Hampton, thrilled the entire line, Jackson's brigade piercing the enemy's center, and the left of the line under Gartrell and Smith following up the charge, also, in that quarter, so that the whole of the open surface of the plateau was swept clear of the Federals.

Apart from its impressions on the enemy, the effect of this brilliant onset was to give a short breathing-spell to our troops from the immediate strain of conflict, and encourage them in withstanding the still more strenuous offensive that was soon to bear upon them. Reorganizing our line of battle under the unremitting fire of the Federal batteries opposite, I prepared to meet the new attack which the enemy were about to make, largely reënforced by the troops of Howard's brigade, newly arrived on the field. The Federals again pushed up the slope, the face of which partly afforded good cover by the numerous ravines that scored it and the clumps of young pines and oaks with which it was studded, while the sunken Sudley road formed a good ditch and parapet for their aggressive advance upon my left flank and rear. Gradually they pressed our lines back and regained possession of their lost ground and guns. With the Henry and Robinson houses once more in their possession, they resumed the offensive, urged forward by their commanders with conspicuous gallantry.

The conflict now became very severe for the final possession of this position, which was the key to victory. The Federal numbers enabled them so to extend their lines through the woods beyond the Sudley road as to outreach my left flank, which I was compelled partly to throw back, so as to meet the attack from that quarter; meanwhile their numbers equally enabled them to outflank my right in the direction of the Stone Bridge, imposing anxious watchfulness in that direction. I knew that I was safe if I could hold out till the arrival of reënforcements, which was but a matter of time; and, with the full sense of my own responsibility, I was determined to hold the line of the plateau, even if surrounded on all sides, until assistance should come, unless my forces were sooner overtaken by annihilation.

It was now between half-past 2 and 3 o'clock; a scorching sun increased the oppression of the troops, exhausted from incessant fighting, many of them having been engaged since the morning. Fearing lest the Federal offensive should secure too firm a grip, and knowing the fatal result that might spring from any grave infraction of my line, I determined to make another effort for the recovery of the plateau, and ordered a charge of the entire line of battle, including the reserves, which at this crisis I myself led into action. The movement was made with such keeping and dash that the whole plateau was swept clear of the enemy, who were driven down the slope and across the turnpike on our right and the valley of Young's Branch on our left, leaving in our final possession the

Robinson and Henry houses, with most of Ricketts's and Griffin's batteries, the men of which were mostly shot down where they bravely stood by their guns. Fisher's 6th North Carolina, directed to the Lewis house by Colonel Jordan from Manassas, where it had just arrived, and thence to the field by General Johnston, came up in happy time to join in this charge on the left. Withers's 18th Virginia, which I had ordered up from Cocke's brigade, was also on hand in time to follow and give additional effect to the charge, capturing, by aid of the Hampton Legion, several guns, which were immediately turned and served upon the broken ranks of the enemy by some of our officers. . . .

That part of the enemy who occupied the woods beyond our left and across the Sudley road had not been reached by the headlong charge which had swept their comrades from the plateau; but the now arriving reënforcements were led into that quarter. Kemper's battery also came up, preceded by its commander, who, while alone, fell into the hands of a number of the enemy, who took him prisoner, until a few moments later, when he handed them over to some of our own troops accompanying his battery. A small plateau, within the south-west angle of the Sudley and turnpike cross-roads, was still held by a strong Federal brigade—Howard's troops, together with Sykes's battalion of regulars; and while Kershaw and Cash, after passing through the skirts of the oak wood along the Sudley road, engaged this force, Kemper's battery was sent forward by Kershaw along the same road, into position near where a hostile battery had been captured, and whence it played upon the enemy in the open field.

Quickly following these regiments came Preston's 28th Virginia, which, passing through the woods, encountered and drove back some Michigan troops, capturing Brigadier-General Willcox. It was now about 3 o'clock, when another important reënforcement came to our aid—Elzey's brigade, 1700 strong, of the Army of the Shenandoah, which, coming from Piedmont by railroad, had arrived at Manassas station, 6 miles in rear of the battlefield, at noon, and had been without delay directed thence toward the field by Colonel Jordan, aided by Major T. G. Rhett, who that morning had passed from General Bonham's to General Johnston's staff. Upon nearing the vicinity of the Lewis house, the brigade was directed by a staff-officer sent by General Johnston toward the left of the field. As it reached the oak wood, just across the Sudley road, led by General Kirby Smith, the latter fell severely wounded; but the command devolved upon Colonel Elzey, an excellent officer, who was now guided by Captain D. B. Harris of the Engineers, a highly accomplished officer of my staff, still farther to the left and through the woods, so as to form in extension of the line of the preceding reënforcements. Beckham's battery, of the same command, was hurried forward by the Sudley road and around the woods into position near the Chinn house; from a well-selected point of action, in full view of the enemy that filled the open fields west of the Sudley road, it played with deadly and decisive effect upon their ranks, already under the fire of Elzey's brigade. Keyes's Federal brigade, which had made its way across the turnpike in rear of the Stone Bridge, was lurking along under cover of the ridges and a wood in order to turn my line on the right, but was easily repulsed by Latham's battery, already placed in position over that approach by Captain Harris, aided by Alburtis's battery, opportunely sent to Latham's left by General Jackson, and supported by fragments of troops collected by staff-officers. Meanwhile, the enemy had formed a line of battle of formidable proportions on the opposite height, and stretching in crescent outline, with flanks advanced, from the Pittsylvania (Carter) mansion on their left across the Sudley road in rear of Dogan's and reaching toward the Chinn house. They offered a fine spectacle as they threw forward a cloud of skirmishers down the opposite slope, preparatory to a new assault against the line on the plateau. But their right was now severely pressed by the troops that had successively arrived; the force in the south-west angle of the Sudley and Warrenton cross-roads were driven from their position, and, as Early's brigade, which, by direction of General Johnston, had swept around by the rear of the woods through which Elzey had passed, appeared on the field, his line of march bore upon the flank of the enemy, now retiring in that quarter.

This movement by my extreme left was masked by the trend of the woods from many of our forces on the plateau; and bidding those of my staff and escort around me raise a loud cheer, I dispatched the information to the several commands, with orders to go forward in a common charge. Before the full advance of the Confederate ranks the enemy's whole line, whose right was already yielding, irretrievably broke, fleeing across Bull Run by every available direction. Major Sykes's regulars, aided by Sherman's brigade, made a steady and handsome withdrawal, protecting the rear of the routed forces, and enabling many to escape by the Stone Bridge. Having ordered in pursuit all the troops on the field, I went to the Lewis house, and, the battle being ended, turned over the command to General Johnston. Mounting a fresh horse—the fourth on that day—I started to press the pursuit which was being made by our infantry and cavalry, some of the latter having been sent by General Johnston from Lewis's Ford to intercept the enemy on the turnpike. I was soon overtaken, however, by a courier bearing a message from Major T. G. Rhett, General Johnston's chief-of-staff on duty at Manassas railroad station, informing me of a report that a large Federal force, having pierced our lower line on Bull Run, was moving upon Camp Pickens, my depot of supplies near Manassas. I returned, and communicated this important news to General Johnston. Upon consultation it was deemed best that I should take Ewell's and Holmes's brigades, which were hastening up to the battle-field, but too late for the action, and fall on this force of the enemy, while reënforcements should be sent me from the pursuing forces, who were to be recalled for that purpose. To head off the danger and gain time, I hastily mounted a force of infantry behind the cavalrymen then pres-ent, but, on approaching the line of march near McLean's Ford, which the Federals must have taken, I learned that the news was a false alarm caught from the return of General Jones's forces to this side of the Run, the similarity of the uniforms and the direction of their march having convinced some nervous person that they were a force of the enemy. It was now almost dark, and too late to resume the broken pursuit; on my return I met the coming forces, and, as they were very tired, I ordered them to halt and bivouac for the night where they were. After giving such attention as I could to the troops, I started for Manassas, where I arrived about 10 o'clock, and found Mr. Davis at my headquarters with General Johnston. Arriving from Richmond late in the afternoon, Mr. Davis had immediately galloped to the field, accompanied by Colonel Jordan. They had met between Manassas and the battle-field the usual number of stragglers to the rear, whose appearance belied the determined array then sweeping the enemy before it, but Mr. Davis had the happiness to arrive in time to witness the last of the Federals disappearing beyond Bull Run. The next morning I received from his hand at our breakfast-table my commission, dated July 21st, as General in the Army of the Confederate States, and after his return to Richmond the kind congratulations of the Secretary of War and of General Lee, then acting as military adviser to the President.

It was a point made at the time at the North that, just as the Confederate troops were about to break and flee, the Federal troops anticipated them by doing so, being struck into this precipitation by the arrival upon their flank of the Shenandoah forces marching from railroad trains halted *en route* with that aim—errors that have been repeated by a number of writers, and by an ambitious but superficial French author.

There were certain sentiments of a personal character clustering about this first battle, and personal anxiety as to its issue, that gladly accepted this theory. To this may be added the general readiness to accept a sentimental or ultra-dramatic explanation—a sorcery wrought by the delay or arrival of some force, or the death or coming of somebody, or any other single magical event—whereby history is easily caught, rather than to seek an understanding of that which is but the gradual result of the operation of many forces, both of opposing design and actual collision, modified more or less by the falls of chance. The personal sentiment, though natural enough at the time, has no place in any military estimate, or place of any kind at this day. The battle of Manassas was, like any other battle, a progression and development from the deliberate counter-employment of the military resources in hand, affected by accidents, as always, but of a kind very different from those referred to. My line of battle, which twice had not only withstood the enemy's attack, but had taken the offensive and driven him back in disorder, was becoming momentarily stronger from the arrival, at last, of the reënforcements provided for; and if the enemy had remained on the field till the arrival of Ewell and Holmes, they would have been so strongly outflanked that many who escaped would have been destroyed or captured.

Though my adversary's plan of battle was a good one as against a passive defensive opponent, such as he may have deemed I must be from the respective numbers and positions of our forces, it would, in my judgment, have been much better if, with more dash, the flank attack had been made by the Stone Bridge itself and the ford immediately above it. The plan adopted, however, favored above all things the easy execution of the offensive operations I had designed and ordered against his left flank and rear at Centreville. His turning column—18,000 strong, and presumably his best troops—was thrown off by a long ellipse through a narrow forest road to Sudley Ford, from which it moved down upon my left flank, and was thus dislocated from his main body. This severed movement of his forces not only left his exposed left and rear at Centreville weak against the simultaneous offensive of my heaviest forces upon it, which I had ordered, but the movement of his returning column would have been disconcerted and paralyzed by the early sound of this heavy conflict in its rear, and it could not even have made its way back so as to be available for manoeuvre before the Centreville fraction had been thrown back upon it in disorder. A new army is very liable to panic, and, in view of the actual result of the battle, the conclusion can hardly be resisted that the panic which fell on the Federal army would thus have seized it early in the day, and with my forces in such a position as wholly to cut off its retreat upon Washington. But the commander of the front line on my right, who had been ordered to hold himself in readiness to initiate the offensive at a moment's notice, did not make the move expected of him because through accident he failed to receive his own imme-diate order to advance. The Federal commander's flanking movement, being thus uninterrupted by such a counter-movement' as I had projected, was further assisted through the rawness and inadequacy of our staff organization through which I was left unacquainted with the actual state of affairs on my left. The Federal attack, already thus greatly favored, and encouraged, moreover, by the rout of General Bee's advanced line, failed for two reasons: their forces were not handled with concert of masses (a fault often made later on both sides), and the individual action of the Confederate troops was superior, and for a very palpable reason. That one army was fighting for union and the other for disunion is a political expression; the actual fact on the battle-field, in the face of cannon and musket, was that the Federal troops came as invaders, and the Southern troops stood as defenders of their homes, and further than this we need not go. The armies were vastly greater than had ever before fought on this continent, and were the largest volunteer armies ever assembled since the era of regular armies. The personal material on both sides was of exceptionally good character, and collectively superior to that of any subsequent period of the war. The Confed-erate army was filled with generous youths who had answered the first call to arms. For certain kinds of field duty they were not as yet adapted, many of them having at first come with their baggage and servants; these they had to dispense with, but, not to offend their susceptibilities, I then exacted the least work from them, apart from military drills, even to the prejudice of imporant field-works, when I could not get sufficient Negro labor; they "had come to fight, and not to handle the pick and shovel," and their fighting redeemed well their shortcom-ings as intrenchers. Before I left that gallant army, however, it had learned how readily the humbler could aid the nobler duty.

As to immediate results and trophies, we captured a great many stands of arms, batteries, equipments, standards, and flags, one of which was sent to me, through General Longstreet, as a personal compliment by the Texan "crack shot," Colonel B. F. Terry, who lowered it from its mast at Fairfax Court House, by cutting the halyards by means of his unerring rifle, as our troops next morning reoccupied that place. We captured also many prisoners, including a number of surgeons, whom (the first time in war) we treated not as prisoners, but as guests. Calling attention to their brave devotion to their wounded, I recommended to the War Department that they be sent home without exchange, together with some other prisoners, who had shown personal kindness to Colonel Jones, of the 4th Alabama, who had been mortally wounded early in the day.

THE SCOUT TOWARD ALDIE

HERMAN MELVILLE

The cavalry-camp lies on the slope
  Of what was late a vernal hill,
  But now like a pavement bare—
  An outpost in the perilous wilds
  Which ever are lone and still;
  But Mosby's men are there—
  Of Mosby best beware.

Great trees the troopers felled, and leaned
  In antlered walls about their tents;
  Strict watch they kept; 'twas Hark! and Mark!

Unarmed none cared to stir abroad
For berries beyond their forest-fence:
As glides in seas the shark,
Rides Mosby through green dark.

All spake of him, but few had seen
Except the maimed ones or the low;
Yet rumor made him every thing—
A farmer—woodman—refugee—
The man who crossed the field but now;
A spell about his life did cling—
Who to the ground shall Mosby bring?

The morning-bugles lonely play,
Lonely the evening-bugle calls—
Unanswered voices in the wild;
The settled hush of birds in nest
Becharms, and all the wood enthralls:
Memory's self is so beguiled
That Mosby seems a satyr's child.

They lived as in the Eerie Land—
The fire-flies showed with fairy gleam;
And yet from pine-tops one might ken
The Capitol dome—hazy—sublime—
A vision breaking on a dream:
So strange it was that Mosby's men
Should dare to prowl where the Dome was seen.

A scout toward Aldie broke the spell.—
The Leader lies before his tent
Gazing at heaven's all-cheering lamp
Through blandness of a morning rare;
His thoughts on bitter-sweets are bent:
His sunny bride is in the camp—
But Mosby—graves are beds of damp!

The trumpet calls; he goes within;
But none the prayer and sob may know:
Her hero he, but bridegroom too.
Ah, love in a tent is a queenly thing,
And fame, be sure, refines the vow;
But fame fond wives have lived to rue,
And Mosby's men fell deeds can do.

Tan-tara! tan-tara! tan-tara!
Mounted and armed he sits a king;
For pride she smiles if now she peep—
Elate he rides at the head of his men;
He is young, and command is a boyish thing:
They file out into the forest deep—
Do Mosby and his rangers sleep?

The sun is gold, and the world is green,
Opal the vapors of morning roll;
The champing horses lightly prance—
Full of caprice, and the riders too
Curving in many a caricole.
But marshaled soon, by fours advance—
Mosby had checked that airy dance.

By the hospital-tent the cripples stand—
Bandage, and crutch, and cane, and sling,
And palely eye the brave array;
The froth of the cup is gone for them
(Caw! caw! the crows through the blueness wing);
Yet these were late as bold, as gay;
But Mosby—a clip, and grass is hay.

How strong they feel on their horses free,
Tingles the tendoned thigh with life;
Their cavalry-jackets make boys of all—
With golden breasts like the oriole;
The chat, the jest, and laugh are rife.

But word is passed from the front—a call
For order; the wood is Mosby's hall.

To which behest one rider sly
(Spurred, but unarmed) gave little heed—
Of dexterous fun not slow or spare,
He teased his neighbors of touchy mood,
Into plungings he pricked his steed:
A black-eyed man on a coal-black mare,
Alive as Mosby in mountain air.

His limbs were long, and large and round;
He whispered, winked—did all but shout:
A healthy man for the sick to view;
The taste in his mouth was sweet at morn;
Little of care he cared about.
And yet of pains and pangs he knew—
In others, maimed by Mosby's crew.

The Hospital Steward—even he
(Sacred in person as a priest),
And on his coat-sleeve broidered nice
Wore the caduceus, black and green.
No wonder he sat so light on his beast;
This cheery man in suit of price
Not even Mosby dared to slice.

They pass the picket by the pine
And hollow log—a lonesome place;
His horse adroop, and pistol clean;
Tis cocked—kept leveled toward the wood;
Strained vigilance ages his childish face.
Since midnight has that stripling been
Peering for Mosby through the green.

Splashing they cross the freshet-flood,
And up the muddy bank they strain;

A horse at the spectral white-ash shies—
One of the span of the ambulance,
Black as a hearse. They give the rein:
Silent speed on a scout were wise,
Could cunning baffle Mosby's spies.

Rumor had come that a band was lodged
In green retreats of hills that peer
By Aldie (famed for the swordless charge).
Much store they'd heaped of captured arms
And, per adventure, pilfered cheer;

For Mosby's lads oft hearts enlarge
In revelry by some gorge's marge.

"Don't let your sabres rattle and ring;
To his oat-bag let each man give heed—
There now, that fellow's bag's untied,
Sowing the road with the precious grain.
Your carbines swing at hand—you need!
Look to yourselves, and your nags beside.
Men who after Mosby ride."

Picked lads and keen went sharp before—
A guard, though scarce against surprise;
And rearmost rode an answering troop,
But flankers none to right or left.
No bugle peals, no pennon flies:
Silent they sweep, and fain would swoop
On Mosby with an Indian whoop.

On, right on through the forest land,
Nor man, nor maid, nor child was seen—
Not even a dog. The air was still;
The blackened hut they turned to see,
And spied charred benches on the green;
A squirrel sprang from the rotting mill

Whence Mosby sallied late, brave blood to spill.

By worn-out fields they cantered on—
Drear fields amid the woodlands wide;
By cross-roads of some olden time,
In which grew groves; by gate-stones down—
Grassed ruins of secluded pride:
A strange lone land, long past the prime,
Fit land for Mosby or for crime.

The brook in the dell they pass. One peers
Between the leaves: "Ay, there's the place—
There, on the oozy ledge—'twas there
We found the body (Blake's you know);
Such whirlings, gurglings round the face—
Shot drinking! Well, in war all's fair—
So Mosby says. The bough—take care!"

Hard by, a chapel. Flower-pot mould
Danked and decayed the shaded roof;
The porch was punk; the clapboards spanned
With ruffled lichens gray or green;
Red coral-moss was not aloof;
And mid dry leaves green dead-man's-hand
Groped toward that chapel in Mosby-land.

They leave the road and take the wood,
And mark the trace of ridges there—
A wood where once had slept the farm—
A wood where once tobacco grew
Drowsily in the hazy air,
And wrought in all kind things a calm—
Such influence, Mosby! bids disarm.

To ease even yet the place did woo—
To ease which pines unstirring share,
For ease the weary horses sighed:

Halting, and slackening girths, they feed,
Their pipes they light, they loiter there;
Then up, and urging still the Guide,
On, and after Mosby ride.

This Guide in frowzy coat of brown,
And beard of ancient growth and mould,
Bestrode a bony steed and strong,
As suited well with bulk he bore—
A wheezy man with depth of hold
Who jouncing went. A staff he swung—
A wight whom Mosby's wasp had stung.

Burnt out and homeless—hunted long!
That wheeze he caught in autumn-wood
Crouching (a fat man) for his life,
And spied his lean son 'mong the crew
That probed the covert. Ah! black blood
Was his 'gainst even child and wife—
Fast friends to Mosby. Such the strife.

A lad, unhorsed by sliding girths,
Strains hard to readjust his seat
Ere the main body show the gap
'Twixt them and the rear-guard; scrub-oaks near
He sidelong eyes, while hands move fleet;
Then mounts and spurs. One drops his cap—
"Let Mosby find!" nor heeds mishap.

A gable time-stained peeps through trees:
"You mind the fight in the haunted house?
That's it; we clenched them in the room—
An ambuscade of ghosts, we thought,
But proved sly rebels on a bouse!
Luke lies in the yard." The chimneys loom:
Some muse on Mosby—some on doom.

Less nimbly now through brakes they wind,
And ford wild creeks where men have drowned;
They skirt the pool, avoid the fen,
And so till night, when down they lie,
Their steeds still saddled, in wooded ground:
Rein in hand they slumber then,
Dreaming of Mosby's cedarn den.

But Colonel and Major friendly sat
Where boughs deformed low made a seat.
The Young Man talked (all sworded and spurred)
Of the partisan's blade he longed to win,
And frays in which he meant to beat.
The grizzled Major smoked, and heard:
"But what's that—Mosby?" "No, a bird."

A contrast here like sire and son,
Hope and Experience sage did meet;
The Youth was brave, the Senior too;
But through the Seven Days one had served,
And gasped with the rear-guard in retreat:
So he smoked and smoked, and the wreath he blew—
"Any sure news of Mosby's crew?"

He smoked and smoked, eyeing the while
A huge tree hydra-like in growth—
Moon-tinged—with crook'd boughs rent or lopped—
Itself a haggard forest. "Come!"
The Colonel cried, "to talk you're loath;
D'ye hear? I say he must be stopped,
This Mosby—caged, and hair close cropped."

"Of course; but what's that dangling there?"
"Where?" "From the tree—that gallows-bough;
"A bit of frayed bark, is it not?"
"Ay—or a rope; did we hang last?—
Don't like my neckerchief any how;"

He loosened it: "0 ay, we'll stop
This Mosby—but that vile jerk and drop!"

By peep of light they feed and ride,
Gaining a grove's green edge at morn,
And mark the Aldie hills upread
And five gigantic horsemen carved
Clear-cut against the sky withdrawn;
Are more behind? an open snare?
Or Mosby's men but watchmen there?

The ravaged land was miles behind,
And Loudon spread her landscape rare;
Orchards in pleasant lowlands stood,
Cows were feeding, a cock loud crew,
But not a friend at need was there;
The valley-folk were only good
To Mosby and his wandering brood.

What best to do? what mean yon men?
Colonel and Guide their minds compare;
Be sure some looked their Leader through;
Dismounted, on his sword he leaned
As one who feigns an easy air;
And yet perplexed he was they knew—
Perplexed by Mosby's mountain-crew.

The Major hemmed as he would speak,
But checked himself, and left the ring
Of cavalrymen about their Chief—
Young courtiers mute who paid their court
By looking with confidence on their king;
They knew him brave, foresaw no grief—
But Mosby—the time to think is brief.
The Surgeon (sashed in sacred green)
Was glad 'twas not for him to say
What next should be; if a trooper bleeds.

Why he will do his best,as wont,
And his partner in black will aid and pray;
But judgment bides with him who leads,
And Mosby many a problem breeds.

The Surgeon was the kindliest man
That ever a callous trace professed;
He felt for him, that Leader young,
And offered medicine from his flask:
The Colonel took it with marvelous zest.
For such fine medicine good and strong,
Oft Mosby and his foresters long.

A charm of proof. "Ho, Major, come—
Pounce on yon men! Take half your troop,
Through the thickets wind—pray speedy be—
And gain their read. And, Captain Morn,
Picket these roads—all travelers stop;
The rest to the edge of this crest with me,
That Mosby and his scouts may see."

Commanded and done. Ere the sun stood steep,
Back came the Blues, with a troop of Grays,
Ten riding double-luckless ten!—
Five horses gone, and looped hats lost,
And love-locks dancing in a maze—
Certes, but sophomores from the glen
Of Mosby—not his veteran men.

"Colonel," said the Major, touching his cap,
"We've had our ride, and here they are."
"Well done! How many found you there?"
"As many as! bring you here."
"And no one hurt?" "There'll be no scar—
One fool was battered." "Find their lair?"
"Why, Mosby's brood camp everywhere."

He sighed, and slid down from his horse,
And limping went to a spring-head nigh.
"Why, bless me, Major, not hurt, I hope?"
"Battered my knee against a bar
When the rush was made; all right by-and-by.—
Halloa! They gave you too much rope—
Go back to Mosby, eh? elope?"
Brbr>Just by the low-hanging skirt of wood
The guard, remiss, had given a chance
For a sudden sally into the cover—
But foiled the intent, nor fired a shot,
Though the issue was a deadly trance;
For, hurled 'gainst an oak that humped low over,
Mosby's man fell, pale as a lover.

They pulled some grass his head to ease
(Lined with blue shreds a ground-nest stirred).
The Surgeon came—"Here's a to-do!"
"Ah!" cried the Major, darting a glance,
"This fellow's the one that fired and spurred
Downhill, but met reserves below—
My boys, not Mosby's—so we go!"

The Surgeon—bluff, red, goodly man—
Kneeled by the hurt one; like a bee
He toiled the pale young Chaplain too—
(Who went to the wars for cure of souls,
And his own student-ailments)—he
Bent over likewise; spite the two,
Mosby's poor man more pallid grew.

Meanwhile the mounted captives near
Jested; and yet they anxious showed;
Virginians; some of family-pride,
And young, and full of fire, and fine
In open feature and cheek that glowed;
And here thralled vagabonds now they ride—

But list! one speaks for Mosby's side.

"Why, three to one—your horses strong—
Revolvers, rifles, and a surprise—
Surrender we account no shame!
We live, are gay, and life is hope;
We'll fight again when fight is wise.
There are plenty more from where we came;
But go find Mosby—start the game!"

Yet one there was who looked but glum;
In middle-age, a father he,
And this his first experience too:
"They shot at my heart when my hands were up—
This fighting's crazy work, I see!"
But no one is nigh; what next do?
The woods are mute, and Mosby is the foe.

Save what we've got," the Major said;
"Bad plan to make a scout too long;
The tide may turn, and drag them back,
And more beside. These rides I've been,
And every time a mine was sprung.
To rescue, mind, they won't be slack—
Look out for Mosby's rifle-crack."

"We'll welcome it! Give crack for crack!
Peril, old lad, is what I seek."
"O then, there's plenty to be had—
By all means on, and have our fill!"
With that, grotesque, he writhed his neck,
Showing a scar by buck-shot made—
Kind Mosby's Christmas gift, he said.

"But, Colonel, my prisoners—let a guard
Make sure of them, and lead to camp.
That done, we're free for a dark-room fight

If so you say. "The other laughed;
"Trust me, Major, nor throw a damp.
But first to try a little sleight—
Sure news of Mosby would suit me quite."

Herewith he turned—"Reb, have a dram?"
Holding the Surgeon's flask with a smile
To a young scapegrace from the glen.
"O yes!" he eagerly replied,
"And thank you, Colonel, but—any guile?
For if you think we'll blab—why, then
You don't know Mosby or his men."

The Leader's genial air relaxed.
"Best give it up," a whisperer said.
"By heaven, I'll range their rebel den!"
"They'll treat you well," the captive cried;
"They're all like us—handsome—well bred:
In wood or town, with sword or pen,
Polite is Mosby, and his men."

"Where were you, lads, last night?—come, tell!"
"We?—at a wedding in the Vale—
The bridegroom our comrade; by his side
Belisent, my cousin—o, so proud
Of her young love with old wounds pale—
A Virginian girl! God bless her pride—
Of a crippled Mosby-man the bride!"

"Four wall shall mend that saucy mood,
And moping prisons tame him down,
"Said Captain Cloud." God help that day,"
Cried Captain Morn, "and he so young.
But hark, he sings—a madcap one!"
"O we multiply merrily in the May,
The birds and Mosby's men, they say!"

While echoes ran, a wagon old,
Under stout guard of Corporal Chew
Came up; a lame horse, dingy white,
With clouted harness; ropes in hand,
Cringed the humped driver, black in hue;
By him (for Mosby's band a sight)
A sister-rebel sat, her veil held tight.

"I picked them up," the Corporal said,
"Crunching their way over stick and root,
Through yonder wood. The man here—Cuff—
Says they are going to Leesburgtown."
The Colonel's eye took in the group;
The veiled one's hand he spied—enough!
Not Mosby's. Spite the gown's poor stuff,

Off went his hat: "Lady, fear not;
We soldiers do what we deplore—
I must detain you till we march,"
The stranger nodded. Nettled now,
He grew politer than before:—
"'Tis Mosby's fault, this halt and search:"
The lady stiffened in her starch.

"My duty, madam, bids me now
Ask what may seem a little rude.
Pardon—that veil—withdraw it, please
(Corporal! Make every man fall back);
Pray, now I do but what I should;
Bethink you, 'tis in masks like these
That Mosby haunts the villages."

Slowly the stranger drew her veil.
And looked the Soldier in the eye—
A glance of mingled foul and fair;
Sad patience in a proud disdain.
And more than quietude. A sigh

She heaved, and if all unaware,
And far seemed Mosby from her care.

She came from Yewton Place, her home,
So ravaged by the war's wild play—
Campings, and foragings, and fires—
That now she sought an aunt's abode.
Her kinsmen? In Lee's army, they.
The black? A servant, late her sire's.
And Mosby? Vainly he inquires.

He gazed, and sad she met his eye;
"In the wood yonder were you lost?"
No; at the forks they left the road
Because of hoof-prints (thick they were—
Thick as the words in notes thrice crossed),
And fearful, made that episode.
In fear of Mosby? None she showed.

Her poor attire again he scanned:
"Lady, once more; I grieve to jar
On all sweet usage, but must plead
To have what peeps there from your dress;
That letter—'tis justly prize of war."
She started—gave it—she must need.
"Tis not from Mosby? May I read?"

And straight such matter he perused
That with the Guide he went apart.
The Hospital Steward's turn began:
"Must squeeze this darkey; every tap
Of knowledge we are bound to start."
"Garry," she said, "tell all you can
Of Colonel Mosby—that brave man."

"Dun know much, sare; and missis here
Know less dan me. But dis I know—"

"Well, what?" "I dun know what I know."
"A knowing answer!" The hump-back coughed,
Rubbing his yellowish wool-like tow.
"Come—Mosby—tell!" "O dun look so!
My gal nursed missis—let we go."

"Go where?" demanded Captain Cloud;
"Back into bondage? Man, you're free!"
"Well, let we free!" The Captain's brow
Lowered; the Colonel came—had heard:
"Pooh! pooh! His simple heart I see—
A faithful servant.—Lady" (a bow),
"Mosby's abroad—with us you'll go.

"Guard! Look to your prisoners; back to camp!
The man in the grass—can he mount and away?
Why, how he groans!" "Bad inward bruise—
Might lug him along in the ambulance."
"Coals to Newcastle! Let him stay.
Boots and saddles!—our pains we lose,
Nor care I if Mosby hear the news!"

But word was sent to a house at hand,
And a flask was left by the hurt one's side.
They seized in that same house a man,
Neutral by day, by night a foe—
So charged his neighbor late, the Guide.
A grudge? Hate will do what it can;
Along he went for a Mosby-man.

No secrets now; the bugle calls;
The open road they take, nor shun
The hill; retrace the weary way.
But one there was who whispered low,
"This is a feint—we'll back anon;
Young Hair-Brains don't retreat, they say;
A brush with Mosby is the play!"

They rode till eve. Then on a farm
That lay along a hill-side green,
Bivouacked. Fires were made, and then
Coffee was boiled; a cow was coaxed
And killed, and savory roasts were seen;
And under the lee of a cattle-pen
The guard supped freely with Mosby's men.

The ball was bandied to and fro;
Hits were given and hits were met;
"Chickamauga, Feds—take off your hat!"
"But the Fight in the Clouds repaid you, Rebs!"
"Forgotten about Manassas yet?"
Chatting and chaffing, and tit for tat,
Mosby's clan with the troopers sat.

"Here comes the moon!" a captive cried;
"A song! What say? Archy, my lad!"
Hailing are still one of the clan
(A boyish face with girlish hair),
"Give us that thing poor Pansy made
Last year." He brightened, and began;
And this was the song of Mosby's man:

Spring is come; she shows her pass—
Wild violets cool!
South of woods a small close grass—
A vernal wool!
Leaves are a'bud on the sassafras—
They'll soon be full;
Blessings on the friendly screen—
I'm for the South! Says the leafage green.

Robins! fly, and take your fill
Of out-of-doors—
Garden, orchard, meadow, hill,

Barns and bowers;
Take your fill, and have your will—
Virginia's yours!
But, bluebirds! Keep away, and fear
The ambuscade in bushes here.

"A green song that," a sergeant said;
"But where's poor Pansy? Gone, I fear."
"Ay, mustered out at Ashby's Gap."
"I see; now for a live man's song;
Ditty for ditty—prepare to cheer.
My bluebirds, you can fling a cap!
You barehead Mosby-boys—why—clap!"

Nine Blue-coats went a-nutting
Slyly in Tennessee—
Not for chestnuts—better than that—
Hugh, you bumble-bee!
Nutting, nutting—
All through the year there's nutting!

A tree they spied so yellow,
Rustling in motion queer;
In they fired, and down they dropped—
Butternuts, my dear!
Nutting, nutting—
Who'll 'list to go a-nutting?

Ah! Why should good fellows foe men be?
And who would dream that foes they were—
Larking and singing so friendly then—
A family likeness in every face.
But Captain Cloud made sour demur:
"Guard! Keep your prisoners in the pen,
And let none talk with Mosby's men."
That captain was a valorous one
(No irony, but honest truth),

Yet down from his brain cold drops distilled,
Making stalactites in his heart—
A conscientious soul, forsooth;
And with a formal hate was filled
Of Mosby's band; and some he'd killed.

Meantime the lady rueful sat,
Watching the flicker of a fire
Where the Colonel played the outdoor host
In brave old hall of ancient Night.
But ever the dame grew shyer and shyer,
Seeming with private grief engrossed—
Grief far from Mosby, housed or lost.

The ruddy embers showed her pale.
The Soldier did his best devoir:
"Some coffee?—no?—cracker?—one?"
Cared for her servant—sought to cheer:
"I know, I know—a cruel war!
But wait—even Mosby'll eat his bun;
The Old Hearth—back to it anon!"

But cordial words no balm could bring;
She sighed, and kept her inward chafe,
And seemed to hate the voice of glee—
Joyless and tearless. Soon he called
An escort: "See this lady safe
In yonder house.—Madam, you're free.
And now for Mosby.—Guide! With me."

("A night-ride, eh?") "Tighten your girths!
But, buglers! Not a note from you.
Fling more rails on the fires—ablaze!"
("Sergeant, a feint—I told you so—
Toward Aldie again. Bivouac, adieu!")
After the cheery flames they gaze,
Then back for Mosby through the maze.

The moon looked through the trees, and tipped
The scabbards with her elfin beam;
The Leader backward cast his glance.
Proud of the cavalcade that came—
A hundred horses, bay and cream:
"Major! Look how the lads advance—
Mosby we'll have in the ambulance!"

"No doubt, no doubt:—was that a hare?—
First catch, then cook; and cook him brown."
"Trust me to catch," the other cried—
"The lady's letter!—A dance, man, dance
This night is given in Leesburgtown!"
"He'll be there too!" wheezed out the Guide;
"That Mosby loves a dance and ride!"

"The lady, ah!—the lady's letter—
A lady, then, is in the case,"
Muttered the Major. "Ay, her aunt
Writes her to come by Friday eve
(To-night), for people of the place,
At Mosby's last fight jubilant,
A party give, thought able-cheer be scant."

The Major hemmed. "Then this night-ride
We owe to her?—One lighted house
In a town else dark .—The moths, begar!
Are not quite yet all dead!" "How? how?"
"A mute, meek mournful little mouse!—
Mosby has wiles which subtle are—
But woman's wiles in wiles of war!"

"Tut, Major! By what craft or guile—"
"Can't tell! but he'll be found in wait.
Softly we enter, say, the town—
Good! Pickets post, and all so sure—
When—crack! The rifles from every gate,

The Gray-backs fire—dashes up and down—
Each alley unto Mosby known!"

"Now, Major, now—you take dark views
Of a moonlight night." "Well, well, we'll see,"
And smoked as if each whiff were gain.
The other mused; then sudden asked,
"What would you doing rand decree?"
I'd beat, if I could, Lee's armies—then
Send constables after Mosby's men."

"Ay! ay!—you're odd." The moon sailed up;
On through the shadowy land they went.
"Names must be made and printed be!"
Hummed the blithe Colonel. "Doc, your flask!
Major, I drink to your good content.
My pipe is out—enough for me!
One's buttons shine—does Mosby see?

"But what comes here?" A man from the front
Reported a tree athwart the road.
"Go round it, then; no time to bide;
All right—go on! Were one to stay
For each distrust of a nervous mood,
Long miles we'd make in this our ride
Through Mosby-land.—Oh! with the Guide!"

Then sportful to the Surgeon turned:
"Green sashes hardly serve by night!"
"Nor bullets nor bottles," the Major sighed,
"Against these moccasin-snakes—such foes
As seldom come to solid fight:
They kill and vanish; through grass they glide;
Devil take Mosby!"—his horse here shied.
"Hold! look—the tree, like a dragged balloon;
A globe of leaves-some trickery here;
My nag is right—best now be shy."

A movement was made a hubbub and snarl;
Little was plain—they blindly steer.
The Pleiades, as from ambush sly.
Peep out—Mosby's men in the sky!

As restive they turn, how sore they feel,
And cross, and sleepy, and full of spleen,
And curse the war. "Fools, North and South!"
Said one right out. "O for a bed!
O now to drop in this woodland green!"
He drops as the syllables leave his mouth—
Mosby speaks from the undergrowth—

Speaks in a volley! Out jets the flame!
Men fall from their saddles like plums from trees;
Horses take fright, reins tangle and bind;
"Steady—Dismount—form—and into the wood!"
They go, but find what scarce can please:
Their steeds have been tied in the field behind,
And Mosby's men are off like the wind.

Sound the recall! Vain to pursue—
The enemy scatters in wilds he knows,
To reunite in his own good time;
And, to follow, they need divide—
To come lone and lost on crouching foes:
Maple and hemlock, beech and lime,
Are Mosby's confederates, share the crime.

"Major," burst in a bugler small,
"The fellow we left in Loudon grass—
Sir slyboots with the inward bruise,
His voice I heard—the very same—
Some watch word in the ambush pass;
Ay, sir, we had him in his shoes—
We caught him—Mosby—but to lose!"

"Go, go!—these saddle-dreamers! Well,
And here's another.—Cool, sir, cool!"
"Major, I saw them mount and sweep,
And one was humped, or I mistake,
And in the skurry dropped his wool."
"A wig! go fetch it:—the lads need sleep;
They'll next see Mosby in a sheep!

"Come, come, fall back! Reform your ranks—
All's jackstraws here! Where's Captain Morn?—
We've parted like boats in a raging tide!
But stay–the Colonel—did he charge?
And comes he there? Tis streak of dawn;
Mosby is off, the woods are wide—
Hist! there's a groan—this crazy ride!"

As they searched for the fallen, the dawn grew chill;
They lay in the dew: "Ah! Hurt much, Mink?
And—yes—the Colonel! "Dead! but so calm
That death seemed nothing—even death,
The thing we deem everything heart can think;
Amid wilding roses that shed their balm,
Careless of Mosby he lay—in a charm!

The Major took him by the Hand—
Into the friendly clasp it bled
(A ball through heart and hand he rued):
"Good-bye" and gazed with humid glance;
Then in a hollow reverie said
"The weakness thing is lustihood;
But Mosby"—and he checked his mood.

"Where's the advance?—cut off, by heaven!
Come, Surgeon, how with your wounded there?"
"The ambulance will carry all."
"Well, get them in; we go to camp.
Seven prisoners gone? For the rest have care."

Then to himself, "This grief is gall;
That Mosby!—I'll cast a silver ball!"

"Ho!" turning—"Captain Cloud, you mind
The place where the escort went—so shady?
Go search every closet low and high,
And barn, and bin, and hidden bower—
Every covert—find that lady!
And yet I may misjudge her—ay,
Women (like Mosby) mystify.

"We'll see. Ay, Captain, go—with speed!
Surround and search; each living thing
Secure; that done, await us where
We last turned off. Stay! fire the cage
If the birds be flown. "By the cross-road spring
The bands rejoined; no words; the glare
Told all. Had Mosby plotted there?

The weary troop that wended now—
Hardly it seemed the same that pricked
Forth to the forest from the camp:
Foot-sore horses, jaded men;
Every backbone felt as nicked,
Each eye dim as a sick-room lamp,
All faces stamped with Mosby's stamp.

In order due the Major rode—
Chaplain and Surgeon on either hand;
A riderless horse a negro led;
In a wagon the blanketed sleeper went;
Then the ambulance with the bleeding band;
And, an emptied oat-bag on each head,
Went Mosby's men, and marked the dead.

What gloomed them? What so cast them down,
And changed the cheer that late they took,

As double-guarded now they rode
Between the files of moody men?
Some sudden consciousness they brook,
Or dread the sequel. That night's blood
Disturbed even Mosby's brotherhood.

The flagging horses stumbled at roots,
Floundered in mires, or clinked the stones;
No rider spake except aside;
But the wounded cramped in the ambulance,
It was horror to hear their groans—
Jerked along in the woodland ride,
While Mosby's clan their reverie hide.

The Hospital Steward—even he—
Who on the sleeper kept this glance,
Was changed; late bright-black beard and eye
Looked now hearse-black; his heavy heart,
Like his fagged mare, no more could dance;
His grape was now a raisin dry:
Tis Mosby's homily—Man must die.

The amber sunset flushed the camp
As on the hill their eyes they fed;
The picket dumb looks at the wagon dart;
A handkerchief waves from the bannered tent—
As white, alas! The face of the dead:
Who shall the withering news impart?
The bullet of Mosby goes through heart to heart!

They buried him where the lone ones lie
(Lone sentries shot on midnight post)—
A green-wood grave-yard hid from ken,
Where sweet-fern flings an odor nigh—
Yet held in fear for the gleaming ghost!
Though the bride should see threescore and ten,
She will dream of Mosby and his men.

Now halt the verse, and turn aside—
The cypress falls athwart the way;
No joy remains for bard to sing;
And heaviest dole of all is this,
That other hearts shall be as gay
As hers that now no more shall spring:
To Mosby-land the dirges cling.

AN OCCURRENCE AT OWL CREEK BRIDGE

AMBROSE BIERCE

I

A MAN stood upon a railroad bridge in northern Alabama, looking down into the swift water twenty feet below. The man's hands were behind his back, the wrists bound with a cord. A rope closely encircled his neck. It was attached to a stout cross-timber above his head and the slack fell to the level of his knees. Some loose boards laid upon the sleepers supporting the metals of the railway supplied a footing for him and his executioners—two private soldiers of the Federal army, directed by a sergeant who in civil life may have been a deputy sheriff. At a short remove upon the same temporary platform was an officer in the uniform of his rank, armed. He was a captain. A sentinel at each end of the bridge stood with his rifle in the position known as "support," that is to say, vertical in front of the left shoulder, the hammer resting on the forearm thrown straight across the chest—a formal and unnatural position, enforcing an erect carriage of the body. It did not appear to be the duty of these two men to know what was occurring at the centre of the bridge; they merely blockaded the two ends of the foot planking that traversed it.

Beyond one of the sentinels nobody was in sight; the railroad ran straight away into a forest for a hundred yards, then, curving, was lost to view. Doubtless there was an outpost farther along. The other bank of the stream was open ground—a gentle acclivity topped with a stockade of vertical tree trunks, loopholed for rifles, with a single embrasure through which protruded the muzzle of a brass cannon commanding the bridge. Midway of the slope between bridge and fort were the spectators—a single company of infantry in line, at "parade rest," the butts of the rifles on the ground, the barrels inclining slightly backward against the right shoulder, the hands crossed upon the stock. A lieutenant stood at the right of the line, the point of his sword upon the ground, his left hand resting upon his right. Excepting the group of four at the centre of the bridge, not a man moved. The company faced the bridge, staring stonily, motionless. The sentinels, facing the banks of the stream, might have been statues to adorn the bridge. The captain stood with folded arms, silent, observing the work of his subordinates, but making no sign. Death is a dignitary who when he comes announced is to be received with formal manifestations of respect, even by those most familiar with him. In the code of military etiquette silence and fixity are forms of deference.

The man who was engaged in being hanged was apparently about thirty-five years of age. He was a civilian, if one might judge from his habit, which was that of a planter. His features were good—a straight nose, firm mouth, broad forehead, from which his long, dark hair was combed straight back, falling behind his ears to the collar of his well-fitting frock-coat. He wore a mustache and pointed beard, but no whiskers; his eyes were large and dark gray, and had a kindly expression which one would hardly have expected in one whose neck was in the hemp. Evidently this was no vulgar assassin. The liberal military code makes provision for hanging many kinds of persons, and gentlemen are not excluded.

The preparations being complete, the two private soldiers stepped aside and each drew away the plank upon which he had been standing. The sergeant turned to the captain, saluted and placed himself immediately behind that officer, who in turn moved apart one pace. These movements left the condemned man and the sergeant standing on the two ends of the same plank, which spanned three of the cross-ties of the bridge. The end upon which the civilian stood almost, but not quite, reached a fourth. This plank had been held in place by the weight of the captain; it was now held by that of the sergeant. At a signal from the former the latter would step aside, the plank would tilt and the condemned man go down between two ties. The arrangement commended itself to his judgment as simple and effective. His face had not been covered nor his eyes bandaged. He looked a moment at his "unsteadfast footing," then let his gaze wander to the swirling water of the stream racing madly beneath his feet. A piece of dancing driftwood caught his attention and his eyes followed it down the current. How slowly it appeared to move! What a sluggish stream!

He closed his eyes in order to fix his last thoughts upon his wife and children. The water, touched to gold by the early sun, the brooding mists under the banks at some distance down the stream, the fort, the soldiers, the piece of drift—all had distracted him. And now he became conscious of a new disturbance. Striking through the thought of his dear ones was a sound which he could neither ignore nor understand, a sharp, distinct, metallic percussion like the stroke of a blacksmith's hammer upon the anvil; it had the same ringing quality. He wondered what it was, and whether immeasurably distant or near by—it seemed both. Its recurrence was regular, but as slow as the tolling of a death knell. He awaited each stroke with impatience and—he knew not why—apprehension. The intervals of silence grew progressively longer; the delays became maddening. With their greater infrequency the sounds increased in strength and sharpness. They hurt his ear like the thrust of a knife; he feared he would shriek. What he heard was the ticking of his watch.

He unclosed his eyes and saw again the water below him. "If I could free my hands," he thought, "I might throw off the noose and spring into the stream. By diving I could evade the bullets and, swimming vigorously, reach the bank, take to the woods and get away home. My home, thank God, is as yet outside their lines; my wife and little ones are still beyond the invader's farthest advance."

As these thoughts, which have here to be set down in words, were flashed into the doomed man's brain rather than evolved from it the captain nodded to the sergeant. The sergeant stepped aside.

II

Peyton Farquhar was a well-to-do planter, of an old and highly respected Alabama family. Being a slave owner and like other slave owners a politician he was naturally an original secessionist and ardently devoted to the Southern cause. Circumstances of an imperious nature, which it is unnecessary to relate here, had prevented him from taking service with the gallant army that had fought the disastrous campaigns ending with the fall of Corinth, and he chafed under the inglorious restraint, longing for the release of his energies, the larger life of the soldier, the opportunity for distinction. That opportunity, he felt, would come, as it comes to all in war time. Meanwhile he did what he could. No service was too humble for him to perform in aid of the South, no adventure too perilous for him to undertake if consistent with the character of a civilian who was at heart a soldier, and who in good faith and without too much qualification assented to at least a part of the frankly villainous dictum that all is fair in love and war.

One evening while Farquhar and his wife were sitting on a rustic bench near the entrance to his grounds, a gray-clad soldier rode up to the gate and asked for a drink of water. Mrs. Farquhar was only too happy to serve him with her own white hands. While she was fetching the water her husband approached the dusty horseman and inquired eagerly for news from the front.

"The Yanks are repairing the railroads," said the man, "and are getting ready for another advance. They have reached the Owl Creek bridge, put it in order and built a stockade on the north bank. The commandant has issued an order, which is posted everywhere, declaring that any civilian caught interfering with the railroad, its bridges, tunnels or trains will be summarily hanged. I saw the order."

"How far is it to the Owl Creek bridge?" Farquhar asked.

"About thirty miles."

"Is there no force on this side the creek?"

"Only a picket post half a mile out, on the railroad, and a single sentinel at this end of the bridge."

"Suppose a man—a civilian and student of hanging—should elude the picket post and perhaps get the better of the sentinel," said Farquhar, smiling, "what could he accomplish?"

The soldier reflected. "I was there a month ago," he replied. "I observed that the flood of last winter had lodged a great quantity of driftwood against the wooden pier at this end of the bridge. It is now dry and would burn like tow."

The lady had now brought the water, which the soldier drank. He thanked her ceremoniously, bowed to her husband and rode away. An hour later, after nightfall, he repassed the plantation, going northward in the direction from which he had come. He was a Federal scout.

III

As Peyton Farquhar fell straight downward through the bridge he lost consciousness and was as one already dead. From this state he was awakened—ages later, it seemed to him—by the pain of a sharp pressure upon his throat, followed by a sense of suffocation. Keen, poignant agonies seemed to shoot from his neck downward through every fibre of his body and limbs. These pains appeared to flash along well-defined lines of ramification and to beat with an inconceivably rapid periodicity. They seemed like streams of pulsating fire heating him to an intolerable temperature. As to his head, he was conscious of nothing but a feeling of fulness—of congestion. These sensations were unaccompanied by thought. The intellectual part of his nature was already effaced; he had power only to feel, and feeling was torment. He was conscious of motion. Encompassed in a luminous cloud, of which he was now merely the fiery heart, without material substance, he swung through unthinkable arcs of oscillation, like a vast pendulum. Then all at once, with terrible suddenness, the light about him shot upward with the noise of a loud plash; a frightful roaring was in his ears, and all was cold and dark. The power of thought was restored; he knew that the rope had broken and he had fallen into the stream. There was no additional strangulation; the noose about his neck was already suffocating him and kept the water from his lungs. To die of hanging at the bottom of a river!—the idea seemed to him ludicrous. He opened his eyes in the darkness and saw above him a gleam of light, but how distant, how inaccessible! He was still sinking, for the light became fainter and fainter until it was a mere glimmer. Then it began to grow and brighten, and he knew that he was rising toward the surface—knew it with reluctance, for he was now very comfortable. "To be hanged and drowned," he thought, "that is not so bad; but I do not wish to be shot. No; I will not be shot; that is not fair."

He was not conscious of an effort, but a sharp pain in his wrist apprised him that he was trying to free his hands. He gave the struggle his attention, as an idler might observe the feat of a juggler, without interest in the outcome. What splendid effort!—what magnificent, what superhuman strength! Ah, that was a fine endeavor! Bravo! The cord fell away; his arms parted and floated upward, the hands dimly seen on each side in the growing light. He watched them with a new interest as first one and then the other pounced upon the noose at his neck. They tore it away and thrust it fiercely aside, its undulations resembling those of a water-snake. "Put it back, put it back!" He thought he shouted these words to his hands, for the undoing of the noose had been succeeded by the direst pang that he had yet experienced. His neck ached horribly; his brain was on fire; his heart, which had been fluttering faintly, gave a great leap, trying to force itself out at his mouth. His whole body was racked and wrenched with an insupportable anguish! But his disobedient hands gave no heed to the command. They beat the water vigorously with quick, downward strokes, forcing him to the surface. He felt his head emerge; his eyes were blinded by the sunlight; his chest expanded convulsively, and with a supreme and crowning agony his lungs engulfed a great draught of air, which instantly he expelled in a shriek!

He was now in full possession of his physical senses. They were, indeed, preternaturally keen and alert. Something in the awful disturbance of his organic system had so exalted and refined them that they made record of things never before perceived. He felt the ripples upon his face and heard their separate sounds as they struck. He looked at the forest on the bank of the stream, saw the individual trees, the leaves and the veining of each leaf—saw the very insects upon them : the locusts, the brilliant-bodied flies, the gray spiders stretching their webs from twig to twig. He noted the prismatic colors in all the dewdrops upon a million blades of grass. The humming of the gnats that danced above the eddies of the stream, the beating of the dragon-flies' wings, the strokes of the waterspiders' legs, like oars which had lifted their boat—all these made audible music. A fish slid along beneath his eyes and he heard the rush of its body parting the water.

He had come to the surface facing down the stream; in a moment the visible world seemed to wheel slowly round, himself the pivotal point, and he saw the bridge, the fort, the soldiers upon the bridge, the captain, the sergeant, the two privates, his executioners. They were in silhouette against the blue sky. They shouted and gesticulated, pointing at him. The captain had drawn his pistol, but did not fire; the others were unarmed. Their movements were grotesque and horrible, their forms gigantic.

Suddenly he heard a sharp report and something struck the water smartly within a few inches of his head, spattering his face with spray. He heard a second report, and saw one of the sentinels with his rifle at his shoulder, a light cloud of blue smoke rising from the muzzle. The man in the water saw the eye of the man on the bridge gazing into his own through the sights of the rifle. He observed that it was a gray eye and remembered having read that gray eyes were keenest, and that all famous marksmen had them. Nevertheless, this one had missed.

A counter-swirl had caught Farquhar and turned him half round; he was again looking into the forest on the bank opposite the fort. The sound of a clear, high voice in a monotonous singsong now rang out behind him and came across the water with a distinctness that pierced and subdued all other sounds, even the beating of the ripples in his ears. Although no soldier, he had frequented camps enough to know the dread significance of that deliberate, drawling, aspirated chant; the lieutenant on shore was taking a part in the morning's work. How coldly and pitilessly—with what an even, calm intonation, presaging, and enforcing tranquillity in the men—with what accurately measured intervals fell those cruel words:

"Attention, company! . . . Shoulder arms! . . . Ready! . . . Aim! . . . Fire!"

Farquhar dived—dived as deeply as he could. The water roared in his ears like the voice of Niagara, yet he heard the dulled thunder of the volley and, rising again toward the surface, met shining bits of metal, singularly flattened, oscillating slowly downward. Some of them touched him on the face and hands, then fell away, continuing their descent. One lodged between his collar and neck; it was uncomfortably warm and he snatched it out.

As he rose to the surface, gasping for breath, he saw that he had been a long time under water; he was perceptibly farther down stream—nearer to safety. The soldiers had almost finished reloading; the metal ramrods flashed all at once in the sunshine as they were drawn from the barrels, turned in the air, and thrust into their sockets. The two sentinels fired again, independently and ineffectually.

The hunted man saw all this over his shoulder; he was now swimming vigorously with the current. His brain was as energetic as his arms and legs; he thought with the rapidity of lightning.

"The officer," he reasoned, "will not make that martinet's error a second time. It is as easy to dodge a volley as a single shot. He has probably already given the command to fire at will. God help me, I cannot dodge them all!"

An appalling plash within two yards of him was followed by a loud, rushing sound, *diminuendo,* which seemed to travel back through the air to the fort and died in an explosion which stirred the very river to its deeps! A rising sheet of water curved over him, fell down upon him, blinded him, strangled him! The cannon had taken a hand in the game. As he shook his head free from the commotion of the smitten water he heard the deflected shot humming through the air ahead, and in an instant it was cracking and smashing the branches in the forest beyond.

"They will not do that again," he thought; "the next time they will use a charge of grape. I must keep my eye upon the gun; the smoke will apprise me—the report arrives too late; it lags behind the missile. That is a good gun."

Suddenly he felt himself whirled round and round—spinning like a top. The water, the banks, the forests, the now distant bridge, fort and men—all were commingled and blurred. Objects were represented by their colors only; circular horizontal streaks of color—that was all he saw. He had been caught in a vortex and was being whirled on with a velocity of advance and gyration that made him giddy and sick. In a few moments he was flung upon the gravel at the foot of the left bank of the stream—the southern bank—and behind a projecting point which concealed him from his enemies. The sudden arrest of his motion, the abrasion of one of his hands on the gravel, restored him, and he wept with delight. He dug his fingers into the sand, threw it over himself in handfuls and audibly blessed it. It looked like diamonds, rubies, emeralds; he could think of nothing beautiful which it did not resemble. The trees upon the bank were giant garden plants; he noted a definite order in their arrangement, inhaled the fragrance of their blooms. A strange, roseate light shone through the spaces among their trunks and the wind made in their branches the music of æolian harps. He had no wish to perfect his escape—was content to remain in that enchanting spot until retaken.

A whiz and rattle of grapeshot among the branches high above his head roused him from his dream. The baffled cannoneer had fired a random farewell. He sprang to his feet, rushed up the sloping bank, and plunged into the forest.

All that day he traveled, laying his course by the rounding sun. The forest seemed interminable; nowhere did he discover a break in it, not even a wood-man's road. He had not known that he lived in so wild a region. There was something uncanny in the revelation.

By nightfall he was fatigued, footsore, famishing. The thought of his wife and children urged him on. At last he found a road which led him in what he knew to be the right direction. It was as wide and straight as a city street, yet it seemed untraveled. No fields bordered it, no dwelling anywhere. Not so much as the barking of a dog suggested human habitation. The black bodies of the trees formed a straight wall on both sides, terminating on the horizon in a point, like a diagram in a lesson in perspective. Overhead, as he looked up through this rift in the wood, shone great golden stars looking unfamiliar and grouped in strange constellations. He was sure they were arranged in some order which had a secret and malign significance. The wood on either side was full of singular noises, among which—once, twice, and again—he distinctly heard whispers in an unknown tongue.

His neck was in pain and lifting his hand to it he found it horribly swollen. He knew that it had a circle of black where the rope had bruised it. His eyes felt congested; he could no longer close them. His tongue was swollen with thirst; he relieved its fever by thrusting it forward from between his teeth into the cold air. How softly the turf had carpeted the untraveled avenue—he could no longer feel the roadway beneath his feet!

Doubtless, despite his suffering, he had fallen asleep while walking, for now he sees another scene—perhaps he has merely recovered from a delirium. He stands at the gate of his own home. All is as he left it, and all bright and beautiful in the morning sunshine. He must have traveled the entire night. As he pushes open the gate and passes up the wide white walk, he sees a flutter of female garments; his wife, looking fresh and cool and sweet, steps down from the veranda to meet him. At the bottom of the steps she stands waiting, with a smile of ineffable joy, an attitude of matchless grace and dignity. Ah, how beautiful she is! He springs forward with extended arms. As he is about to clasp her he feels a stunning blow upon the back of the neck; a blinding white light blazes all about him with a sound like the shock of a cannon—then all is darkness and silence!

Peyton Farquhar was dead; his body, with a broken neck, swung gently from side to side beneath the timbers of the Owl Creek bridge.

THE *KEARSARGE* SINKS THE *ALABAMA*

LIEUTENANT ARTHUR SINCLAIR CSN

THE ENGAGEMENT

Sunday morning, June 19, 1864, preparations for the fight are made early in the day. At breakfast the officers are advised of the last communication with the shore, and to make their arrangements accordingly. Soon after breakfast the yacht Deerhound, which we had observed to be getting up steam, moved out of the port, passing quite near us. The party on her were watching us with glasses, though no demonstration occurred, even from the ladies. At this time it was unknown to us that the departure was for the purpose of taking up a position of vantage to observe the engagement. We had no communication with the yacht or her people, and did not know but that her owner was continuing his plea-sure-cruise. She passed from sight, and the French ironclad frigate Couronne weighed anchor and stood out of the harbor. We could readily surmise that *her* purpose was to police the channel at the three-mile limit and overlook the fight. She never moved from the league distance during the entire period of the engagement, nor did she offer any assistance at the termination. The neutrality of the Couronne was of the positive, unmistakable kind. It would have occupied a court but a short time to consider and pass upon it.

Between ten and eleven o'clock we got underway, and stood out of the harbor, passing the French liner Napoleon quite near. We were surprised and gratified as she manned the rigging and gave us three rousing cheers, her band at the same time playing a Confederate national air. It must have been an enthusiasm of local birth, a sort of private turn-out of their own. It was much appreciated by us, and no doubt stirred our brave lads to the centre.

Sailors are generous fellows, and always take sides, when allowed, with the little fellow underneath. The scene from the deck of the *Alabama* is one never to be effaced from memory. We are passing out of the harbor through the dense shipping, the bulwarks of all of them crowded with heads watching our exit, and the shores and mole a moving mass of humanity. The day is perfect, scarcely a breath of air stirring, and with but a light cloud here and there in the sky. We soon clear the mole, and shape our course for the offing, to testify by blows and blood the sincerity of our faith in the justice of our cause, and to win, if possible, a crowning triumph for our brave commander.

Our ship as she steams offshore for her antagonist, hull down in the distance and waiting for us, presents a brave appearance. The decks and brass-work shine in the bright morning sunlight from recent holystoning and polishing. The crew are all in muster uniform, as though just awaiting Sunday inspection. They are ordered to lie down at their quarters for rest while we approach the enemy. A beautiful sight—the divisions stripped to the waist, and with bare arms and breasts looking the athletes they are. The decks have been sanded down, tubs of water placed along the spar-deck, and all is ready for the fray. The pipe of the boatswain and mates at length summons all hands aft; and Semmes, mounting a gun-carriage, delivers a stirring address:

"Officers and Seamen of the *Alabama*: You have at length another opportunity of meeting the enemy—the first that has been presented to you since you sunk the Hatteras. In the meantime, you have been all over the world; and it is not too much to say that you have destroyed, and driven for protection under neutral flags, one-half of the enemy's commerce, which at the beginning of the war covered every sea. This is an achievement of which you may well be proud;

and a grateful country will not be unmindful of it. The name of your ship has become a household word wherever civilization extends. Shall that name be tarnished by defeat? The thing is impossible. Remember that you are in the English Channel,—the theatre of so much of the naval glory of our race,—and that the eyes of all Europe are at this moment upon you. The flag that floats over you is that of a young republic, who bids defiance to her enemies whenever and wherever found. Show the world that you know how to uphold it. Go to your quarters."

Again at quarters, and resting "at will." It is the hour of prayer in old England; and many a petition is now going up to the God of battle and of mercy for these brave fellows, many of them now about to embrace their watery winding-sheets. We are soon up with the cavalcade and leave the Couronne, the yacht still steaming seaward, and evidently bent upon witnessing the engagement. She is about two miles distant at the time we "open the ball." The *Kearsarge* suddenly turns her head inshore and steams towards us, both ships being at this time about seven or eight miles from the shore. When at about one mile distant from us, she seems from her sheer-off with helm to have chosen this distance for her attack. We had not yet perceived that the *Kearsarge* had the speed of us. We open the engagement with our entire starboard battery, the writer's thirty-two pounder of the port side having been shifted to the spare port, giving us six guns in broadside; and the shift caused the ship to list to starboard about two feet, by the way, quite an advantage, exposing so much less surface to the enemy, but somewhat retarding our speed. The *Kearsarge* had pivoted to starboard also; and both ships with helms a-port fought out the engagement, circling around a common centre, and gradually approaching each other. The enemy replied soon after our opening; but at the distance her pivot shell-guns were at a disadvantage, not having the long range of our pivot-guns, and hence requiring judgment in guessing the distance and determining the proper elevation. Our pivots could easily reach by ricochet, indeed by point-blank firing, so at this stage of the action, and with a smooth sea, we had the advantage.

The battle is now on in earnest; and after about fifteen minutes' fighting, we lodge a hundred-pound percussion-shell in her quarter near her screw; but it fails to explode, though causing some temporary excitement and anxiety on board the enemy, most likely by the concussion of the blow. We find her soon after seeking closer quarters (which she is fully able to do, having discovered her superiority in speed), finding it judicious to close so that her eleven-inch pivots could do full duty at point-blank range. We now ourselves noted the advantage in speed possessed by our enemy; and Semmes felt her pulse, as to whether *very* close quarters would be agreeable, by sheering towards her to close the distance; but she had evidently reached the point wished for to fight out the remainder of the action, and demonstrated it by sheering off and resuming a parallel to us. Semmes would have chosen to bring about yard-arm quarters, fouling, and boarding, relying upon the superior physique of his crew to overbalance the superiority of numbers; but this was frustrated, though several times attempted, the desire on our part being quite apparent. We had therefore to accept the situation, and make the best of it we could, to this end directing our fire to the midship section of the enemy, and alternating our battery with solid shot and shell, the former to pierce, if possible, the cable chain-armor, the latter for general execution.

Up to the time of shortening the first distance assumed, our ship received no damage of any account, and the enemy none that we could discover, the shot in the quarter working no serious harm to the *Kearsarge*. At the distance we were now fighting (point-blank range), the effects of the eleven-inch guns were severely felt, and he little hurt done the enemy clearly proved the unserviceableness of our powder, observed at the commencement of the action.

The boarding tactics of Semmes having been frustrated, and we unable to pierce the enemy's hull with our fire, nothing can place victory with us but some unforeseen and lucky turn. At this period of the action our spanker-gaff is shot away, bringing our colors to the deck; but apparently this is not observed by the Kearsage, as her fire does not halt at all. We can see the splinters flying off from the armor covering of the enemy; but no penetration occurs, the shot or shell rebounding from her side. Our colors are immediately hoisted to the mizzenmast-head. The enemy having now the range, and being able with her superior speed to hold it at ease, has us well in hand, and the fire from her is deliberate and hot. Our bulwarks are soon shot away in sections; and the after pivot-gun is disabled on its port side, losing, in killed and wounded, all but the compresser-man. The quarter-deck thirty-two pounder of this division is now secured, and the crew sent to man the pivot-gun. The spar-deck is by this time being rapidly torn up by shell bursting on the between-decks, interfering with working our battery; and the compartments below have all been knocked into one. The *Alabama* is making water fast, showing severe punishment; but still the report comes from the engine-room that the ship is being kept free to the safety-point. She also has now become dull in response to her helm, and the sail-trimmers are ordered out to loose the head-sails to pay her head off. We are making a desperate but forlorn resistance, which is soon culminated by the deathblow. An eleven-inch shell enters us at the water-line, in the wake of the writer's gun, and passing on, explodes in the engine-room, in its passage throwing a volume of water on board, hiding for a moment the guns of this division. Our ship trembles from stem to stern from the blow. Semmes at once sends for the engineer on watch, who reports the fires out, and water beyond the control of the pumps. We had previously been aware our ship was whipped, and fore-and-aft sail was set in endeavor to reach the French coast; the enemy then moved in shore of us, but did not attempt to close any nearer, simply steaming to secure the shore-side and await events.

It being now apparent that the *Alabama* could not float longer, the colors are hauled down, and the pipe given, "All hands save yourselves." Our waist-boats had been shot to pieces, leaving us but two quarter-boats, and one of them much damaged. The wounded are despatched in one of them to the enemy in charge of an officer, and this done we await developments. The *Kearsarge* evidently failed to discover at once our surrender, for she continued her fire after our colors were struck. Perhaps from the difficulty of noting the absence of a flag with so much white in it, in the powder smoke. But, be the reason what it may, a naval officer, a gentleman by birth and education, would certainly not be guilty of firing on a surrendered foe; hence we may dismiss the matter as an undoubted accident.

The *Kearsarge* is at this time about three hundred yards from us, screw still and vessel motionless, awaiting our boat with the wounded. The yacht is steaming full power towards us both. In the meantime, the two vessels are slowly parting, the *Alabama* drifting with her fore-and-aft sails set to the light air. The inaction of the *Kearsarge* from the time of the surrender until the last man was picked up by the boats of the two vessels will ever remain a mystery to all who were present, and with whom the writer has since conversed. The fact is, the *Kearsarge* was increasing her distance slowly and surely all the time. Whether the drift of our ship under the sail that was set was accomplishing this alone I am not prepared to say. But both Capt. Jones and Mr. Lancaster noted it, and were under the impression that the fact entitled the yacht to the greater credit in saving life. There really seemed to be more method and judgment displayed by the crews from the yacht than those from the *Kearsarge*. Capt. Jones and Mr. Lancaster both expressed themselves in their communications to the press, that in their opinions but few of the *Alabama*'s men would have been saved but for their presence, so little enterprise was shown by our enemy in looking out for us in the water.

The Deerhound approaches the *Kearsarge*, and is requested by Capt. Winslow to assist in saving life; and then, scarcely coming to a full stop, turns to us, at the same time lowering all her boats, the *Kearsarge* doing the same. The officers and crew of our ship are now leaving at will, discipline and rule being temporarily at an end. The ship is settling to her spar-deck, and her wounded spars are staggering in the "steps," held only by the rigging. The decks present a woful. appearance, torn up in innumerable holes, and air-bubbles rising and bursting, producing a sound as though the boat was in agony. Just before she settled, it was a desolate sight for the three or four men left on her deck.

Engineer O'Brien and self were standing by the forward pivot port, a man from his department near, as his companion for the coming swim, a man from my gun- division to act in the same capacity with me; namely, mutual aid and assistance. We comprised all remaining on board of the late buoyant and self-confident band. The ship had settled by the stern, almost submerging it, and bringing the forward part of the hull, consequently, out of water. We were all stripped for the swim, and watching with catlike intensity the rise of air-bubbles from the hatches, indicating that the ship would yet float. From the wake of the *Alabama*, and far astern, a long, distinct line of wreckage could be seen winding with the tide like a snake, with here and there a human head appearing amongst it. The boats were actively at work, saving first those who were without such assistance.

It has frequently been asked me, and in a recent conversation with engineer O'Brien I found the question had been put to him often, "Why did you remain so long on board?" We both seem to have been actuated by the same motive and impulse, first to avoid the confusion and struggle going on in the efforts to reach the wreckage; but the paramount feeling with me was inability to grasp the fact that the *Alabama* was gone! Our home! around which clustered memories as dear and cherished as attended that first childhood one, and the faculties utterly refused to have the stubborn fact thus ruthlessly thrust upon them. They are rude wrenches these, that scatter shipmate from shipmate in a twinkling, some to death, as in our case, and bury out of sight forever the ship which had come to be the material embodiment of a cause dear almost as life. A happier ship-hold it would be difficult to realize or picture, a sympathetic heart encountered at each turn of mess-room or quarter-deck, and this for two long years. O'Brien broke into the revery or day-dream by unceremoniously pushing the writer overboard, and following in his wake. It need scarcely be added that the bath cooled effectually the heated and disturbed brain, and turned the thoughts of all four of us to the practical question of the moment,—how expert a swimmer are you?

The *Alabama*'s final plunge was a remarkable freak, and witnessed by O'Brien and self about one hundred yards off. She shot up out of the water bow first, and descended on the same line, carrying away with her plunge two of her masts, and making a whirlpool of considerable size and strength.

The *Kearsarge* mounted two eleven-inch Dahlgren shell guns, four thirty-two pounders, and one rifled twenty-eight pounder. The *Alabama* mounted more guns; but the difference in the bore of the pivot-guns of the two ships gave the *Kearsarge* much more weight of metal at a broadside, and made the disparity very great. The complement of the *Kearsarge* was one hundred and sixty five all told, officers and men. The action lasted one hour and a half.

A great deal has been said as to the merits of the fight; and no little feeling has been displayed on both sides, each championing its own, and seeking to evolve from the result so much of credit and praise as the circumstances permit. With the floods of light thrown on the event from time to time by the actors on both sides, assisted by the testimony of reliable and impartial outside lookers on, the reader should without a fear of erring be able to judge for himself the amount of credit to be apportioned to each of the combatants, and also to satisfy himself whether or no Semmes is under all the circumstances to be censured for offering battle, and if blamed at all, to what extent, and in what particulars. Winslow, for protecting his ship with chain-armor, should, in the humble judgment of the writer, submitted with diffidence, be accounted as simply using proper prudence in the direct line of duty. He had not given, accepted, or declined a challenge. But it was his duty to fight if he could, and to win. Semmes knew all about it, and could have adopted the same scheme. It was not his election to do so. Winslow took every means at his disposal to destroy a vessel which had been a scourge to United States commerce, and most likely banished from his thoughts all sentiment of chivalry as out of place.

The writer has already suggested from his own standpoint the motives for seeking the fight which may have moved Semmes; but after all they are mere speculations, simply the sum-up of his own thoughts. No one will know just why he fought, and the reader has as good a right at a guess as any one. Semmes took the chances with the odds against him, and lost all but honor. He could have stayed in port, refitted, and been in good trim to meet any boat of the *Kearsarge* class. But we can look farther, and see that in this case no fight with her would have been probable. The chances are by the time the *Alabama* was ready for sea a fleet of American cruisers would have been off Cherbourg to blockade her. So looking at it, surely it was best to take the bull by the horns, and fight while there was some sort of a chance. Semmes fought his ship with all the skill possible under the circumstances, and displayed throughout the coolness and nerve you would look for from a man who had guided the *Alabama* to such marked success. The career of the ship under him is perhaps the most conspicuous object-lesson of judicious management and forethought in the annals of any navy, and the fact of defeat should weigh not at all against his judgment when we consider the fickle chances of battle.

The courage of the man needs no telling; but the incident of his wounding, and the manner in which he bore it, may be of interest to the reader. He was on the horse-block at the time, and where he remained during the battle; and upon finding his right arm totally disabled by a fragment of shell, he simply called the quartermaster, and having him bind and sling the wounded arm, kept his position, and directed the steering and fighting of his ship up to the surrender. Kell was a devoted friend to him from the moment of his (Semmes) personal misfortune, sticking close by him, entering the water with him, and having the satisfaction of getting with him, safe from all harm, on the deck of the Deerhound. In the state of Semmes's health at this time, considering his age and the wearing cruise he had just wound up, it was fortunate for him that such a strong, athletic fellow as Kell kept near him all the while; and who knows how much Semmes may owe to Kell for that companionship?

The writer had the deck just before getting under way, prior to being relieved, as customary, by the first lieutenant. The commander came up from his breakfast, saluted the deck, and received the usual touch of the hat in return; then he said, "If the bright, beautiful day is shining for our benefit, we should be happy at the omen; "and remarked how well the deck appeared, and that the crew (casting his eye forward) seemed "to enter into the spirit of the fight with bright faces." Finally, he put the direct question, "How do you think it will turn out to-day, Mr. Sinclair?" I was surprised that he should care to have my opinion, or that of any one else; for he rarely addressed any of us off duty, and never asked advice or opinion of his subordinates on weighty matters; at least, not to my knowledge. My reply was necessarily vague: "I cannot answer the question, sir, but can assure you the crew will do their full duty, and follow you to the death."—"Yes," he answered; "that is true." And leaving me, he resumed his usual pacing of the quarter-deck. Most gratifying to Semmes must have been the sympathy and attention of the gallant, generous souls on the yacht; and no doubt it contributed much to ease his sufferings of body and mind.

In England he was warmly received on all sides; and a number of his naval admirers united in a testimonial, which assumed the form of a handsome regulation gold-mounted sword, presented, it was stated, "To replace the one so gallantly worn, defended, and lost."

* * * * *

SOME INCIDENTS OF THE FIGHT

When the order was passed to lower the colors, and the pipe "All hands save yourselves "was given by boatswain Mecaskey and mates, there was at once a rush of men from the gun divisions to protest against surrender. The excitement was great; the men failing to realize that their ship was whipped beyond a shadow of doubt, and able to float but little longer. They demanded to have the honor of sinking with the colors at the peak (or rather at the mizzenmast-head; for the spanker-gaff had long since been shot away). But a few positive words from Semmes and Kell quieted them. The *Kearsarge* was by this time on our quarter, in position for a raking fire, and we were altogether helpless. It was time to stop the useless slaughter, though the lowering of our colors was not apparently seen on the *Kearsarge* for a time, since she did not at once cease firing. No one was hurt on board of us after the act of surrender.

The sad fate of assistant-surgeon Llewellyn has elsewhere been recorded. Late in the fight the writer went below to get a bottle of brandy to sustain Wright of his division, who had been seriously wounded, and came upon Llewellyn, standing deep in water, attending to the injured. "Why, Pills! "I cried, "you had better get yourself and wounded out of this, or you'll soon be drowned!" His reply was, "I must wait for orders, you know." But just then a gang of men came below, and he was enabled to get his injured men off the operating-table, and to the deck. The wounded were immediately placed in the boat, for transfer to the *Kearsarge*. Why Llewellyn did not accompany them it is impossible to say. It is quite likely he did not know the custom in such cases, and he may have waited for orders. The boat with the wounded, under the command of Lieut. Wilson, marine-officer Howell and master's-mate Fulham each taking an oar, was at once cleared from the side. It soon becoming known that Llewellyn could not swim, a couple of empty shell-boxes were procured, and secured on his person, one under each arm, to serve as an improvised life-preserver. He took the water with this arrangement, and when last seen from the ship was making good weather of it, the sea being as calm as a dish. I learned later, on the yacht, that Llewellyn's death was brought about by the shifting of the floats upon his person, which seems most probable. Had he taken a moment's thought for himself, and let it be known that he could not swim earlier, he might easily have been saved. But he was the last man to think of himself in a time of general danger.

Lieutenant of marines Howell was-'known to be no swimmer, and was allowed to take an oar in the boat with the wounded. After the transfer, his dress, or rather undress, not being recognized, and Wilson having gone up the side of the *Kearsarge*, and formally surrendered, he was requested by Capt. Winslow to return with the rest of the boat's crew to the wreckage, and do all he could to save life. It is hardly necessary to say that the request was cheerfully obeyed, or that the boat took all the men it saved to the Deerhound.

During this time I made a second visit between decks. The scene was one of complete wreck. The shot and shell of the enemy had knocked all the compartments into one; and a flush view could be had fore and aft, the water waist-deep, and air-bubbles rising and breaking with a mournful gurgle at the surface. It was a picture to be dwelt upon in memory, but not too long in the reality. I returned hastily to the spar-deck. By this time most of the officers and men had left for the water. The battery was disarranged, some guns run out and secured, some not. The spars were wounded wofully, some of them toppling, and others only held by the wire rigging. The smoke-stack was full of holes, the decks torn up by the bursting of shell, and lumbered with the wreckage of woodwork and rigging and empty shell-boxes. Some sail was set; and the vessel slowly forged ahead, leaving a line of wreckage astern, with the heads of swimmers bobbing up and down amongst it. Toward this the boats from the yacht were rapidly pulling. The *Kearsarge* lay a few hundred yards on our starboard quarter, with her boats apparently free from the davits, and pivot-gun ports not yet closed, nor her guns secured.

I went forward, and with a sailor of my division commenced to strip for the swim, the deep settling of the ship warning us that she was about to go. I was ready first, and sat with my legs dangling in the water, which was now almost flush with the spar-deck, trying to secure a handkerchief containing a lot of English sovereigns about my neck while I waited for my companion. At this moment O'Brien suddenly appeared in our rear, and with a hasty "What are you loafing round here for? Don't you see the ship is settling for a plunge? Over you go!" suited the action to the word, and shoved us both into the sea.

He immediately followed us, and struck out sharply for the boats. But O'Brien's hurry cost me my gold; for it was torn from my neck with the plunge, and went down to enrich the bottom of the Channel. However, we had got away none too soon; for we had hardly cleared her when her bow made a wild leap into the air, and she plunged down on an inclined plane to her grave beneath the waves. As she leaped upward there was a crash, her main-topmast going by the board; and the fore gave way in turn as she took her downward slide. The suction where we were was terribly strong, carrying us all down to a very uncomfortable depth. So deep, indeed, that with my eyes open in perfectly clear water, I found myself in the darkness of midnight. But our struggles soon popped us to the surface, which was by this time quite a luxury; and we kept there very contentedly, swimming in an easy, take-your-time style until picked up. Being rescued, we were deposited, like caught fish, under the thwarts. But my sailor-companion soon discovered that it was a boat from the *Kearsarge* which had done us this favor; and promptly consulting, we arranged to give it the slip, which was successfully accomplished in the confusion, taking again to the sea. The next time we were picked up, it was by a boat from the Deerhound.

It was an incident of note in the fight that nearly all the killed were allotted to Joe Wilson's division. I can recollect of but one in Armstrong's, and in my division we had only one man wounded; and yet the bulk of the enemy's fire was concentrated at the midships of the *Alabama*, and the death-wound was given at the third division, in the wake of the engine-hatch.

Nothing could exceed the cool and thorough attention to details of our first lieutenant on this eventful day. From point to point of the spar-deck in his rapid movement he was directing here, or advising there; now seeing to the transfer of shot, shell, or cartridge; giving his orders to this and that man or officer, as though on dress-muster; occasionally in earnest conversation with Semmes, who occupied the horse-block, glasses in hand, and leaning on the hammock-rail; at times watching earnestly the enemy, and then casting his eye about our ship, as though keeping a careful reckoning of the damage given and received. Nothing seemed to escape his active mind or eye, his commanding figure at all times towering over the heads of those around. How it must have touched him to see the wreck of our gallant boat, of which he was so proud, and which had been for two years his heart's chiefest care! One must be in actual touch with such a life as ours to feel the inspiration.

In the latter part of the engagement Semmes, from the vantage-ground of the horse-block, had observed that the *Alabama* was not answering to her helm promptly, and sent for engineer O'Brien, to ascertain the condition of the water in the lower hold. O'Brien reported it as almost flush with the furnace-fires, and rapidly rising; also that the ship could not possibly float much longer. He was ordered to return to duty. Reaching the engine-room, engineer Pundt interviewed him; and upon learning that the ship's condition was known to Semmes, and the only reply to this statement was, "Return to your duty! "exclaimed excitedly, "Well, I suppose ' Old Beeswax' has made up his mind to drown us like a lot of rats! Here, Matt! take off my boots;" and suiting the action to the word, each assisted the other in removing the wet and soggy boots. But Semmes had made up his mind, from the report of his engineer, to give the order, "All hands save yourselves!" The furnace-fires were soon after flooded, and all hands on duty below ordered to the spar-deck. Nor was the order given any too soon.

Said engineer O'Brien, after the landing of the rescued party at Southampton, "I think for Spartan coolness and nerve these two German messmates of ours (Meulnier and Schroeder) surpass anything in my observation and reading. I was on duty close to them, a few yards only separating us. They had command of the shot-and-shell passing division, and were stationed at the shell-room hatch, tending the "whip-tackle." A shell entered, and brought up a few yards from them. It must have been a five-second fuse, from the distance of the *Kearsarge* from us at this stage of the action, for it exploded almost immediately. I protected myself as well as I could from the fragments. So soon as the smoke and dust cleared away, I looked, intending to go to their assistance, expecting to find them wounded, or perhaps dead; when, to my amazement, there they stood hauling on the tackle as though attending an exercise drill. They were the calmest men I ever saw; the most phlegmatic lot it was ever my privilege to fight alongside of."

A most remarkable case of desperate wounding. and after-tenacity of life was noted by the writer in the latter part of the fight. It was imperative to get the ship's head off if possible, the vessel not answering to her helm as quickly as desired, and the danger imminent. The *Kearsarge* would soon be in a position to rake us; and though the wind was light, and the manoeuvre not likely to be of much practical benefit, a sail-trimmer and forecastle-man, John Roberts, was ordered out by Kell to loose the jib. He had executed the order, and was returning, when he was struck by a solid shot or shell, which completely disembowelled him. Roberts in this desperate plight clung to the jib-boom, and working along the foot-rope, reached the top-gallant-forecastle, thence climbed down the ladder to the spar-deck, and with shrieks of agony, and his hands over his head, beating the air convulsively, reached the port gangway, where he fell and expired. He was a man of commanding stature, five or six and twenty years of age, of unusual physical strength, an able seaman, and as well behaved at all times as would be expected of an officer. An Englishman by birth, and a typical English man-of-war's man.

It was a touching scene, the transfer of our wounded men as prisoners to the *Kearsarge*, in our only boat left seaworthy at the davits. Among them was James King 2d, an Irishman, and a man of powerful frame. He had been made quite a "butt" by all our crew, quizzed on all occasions, not being an educated "sailor-man," but what we designated on shipboard a "landsman." "Conne-mara" was the nickname attached to him, suggested by the county in which he was born. King, who was of a hot, quick temper, had constantly resented the practical jokes of the men at his expense, causing the vexed first lieutenant to wonder if it was practical to keep Connemara out of the "brig." He was for all this a generous, open-hearted Irishman; and his attachment was strong for officers and ship. He was mortally wounded; and just as his comrades were about to lift him into the boat destined for the *Kearsarge*, he sent for Kell, and stretching out his feeble hand to him, remarked, "I have sent for you, Mr. Kell, to ask your forgiveness for all the trouble I've caused you since my enlistment on the ship. Please forgive poor Connemara now he is going to his long home." Kell, kneeling by his side, supporting and stroking his head, said, "My poor, dear boy, I have nothing to forgive; nothing against you, my brave lad; and I trust you will be in better trim soon."—"No," was the reply; "Connemara is going fast. Good-by, Mr. Kell. God bless you, Mr. Kell!" He died on the *Kearsarge*.

Michael Mars was another son of Erin, a splendid type of the English man-of-war's man, and appropriately named. He was in many ways the most remarkable figure among our crew, and trustworthy to the uttermost. Still, strange to say, constantly in the "brig" for minor offences, such as playing practical jokes on his messmates, and even at times including the younger officers, if the field was clear for the exercise of his pranks. Nothing vicious or of serious moment happened among his offences, making it therefore a worry to Kell to report and Semmes to punish him. An admirable part of his composition was his indifference to rum. Mars distinguished himself in this memorable fight. He was compresser-man of the after pivot-gun, commanded by Lieut. Joseph D. Wilson, manned by twenty-two men, ten on each side, and two captains, first and second, in the rear. The gun, a very heavy one, eight-inch solid shot or shell weapon, had just been loaded and run out to fire, and Mars had stooped on his knees to compress (to retard recoil), when an eleven-inch shell from the enemy struck full in the middle of the first man on the port side of the gun, passing through the entire lot, killing or wounding them, and piling up on the deck a mass of human fragments. Such a ghastly sight the writer never saw before, and hopes never to see again. Mars at once rose to his feet uninjured, seized a shovel from the bulwarks, and soon had the mass of flesh overboard, and the deck resanded. To have observed the man, you would have supposed him engaged in the ordinary morning-watch cleaning of decks. The pivot-gun had a picked crew, selected principally from the coal-heavers and firemen, they being heavy, powerful men. At this stage the quarter-deck thirty-two pounder of Wilson's division, and commanded in person by Midshipman Anderson, was "secured," and the crew sent to man the more important gun, depleted of half its crew. Later in the action, when the *Alabama* had settled with her spar-deck flush with the water, and all hope was abandoned, the order was given, "All hands save yourselves!" through the boatswain and his mates. Semmes, who, with Kell, was stripping for the swim, seated on the quarter-deck, sent for Mars and Free-mantle, and telling them that he (Semmes) was unable to save his diary and ship-papers, his right arm being wounded by a fragment of shell, asked if they could take care of them. The seamen accepted the trust; and Bartelli, wading into the cabin, returned with them. Easing themselves down in the sea, Mars swam with one arm to the boat of the Deerhound, holding the documents above the water, and Freemantle to a French boat. Semmes and Kell followed suit; and the former had the gratification of knowing his notes were safe and once more in his possession. Mars would deliver the precious papers to none other on the yacht, though told Semmes was safe in the cabin. He wished to deliver them in person, and succeeded. This latter fact was learned by the writer from Capt. Jones of the Deerhound.

We were soon steaming in the yacht to Southampton, which port we reached without further adventure. Here Mars left us, sailor-like, for another cruise. As the years roll by the writer often thinks of Mars, and wonders what is his fate; whether he who did such gallant deeds was at last swallowed by insatiable old ocean, or whether we shall meet again, and tell each other of our later pilgrimage through life. If toiling here yet, may God, as in the past, keep watch and ward over the jovial, generous, and brave Irishman!

Capt. Jones narrates a pleasing instance of noble self-sacrifice on the part of our captain of the forecastle. In coming up to a number of men struggling in the water, he observed an old gray-haired seaman swimming along contentedly, and while engaged pulling some others into his boat, called out to the old fellow, "Come this way, and get on board." To which the old fellow replied, "Oh, I can keep up for a while longer! Save those other lads; they need your services more than I do. Your boat can't carry all of us."

THE BATTLE OF MANILA BAY

ADMIRAL GEORGE DEWEY

Manila Bay is a spacious body of water opening out from a narrow entrance between high headlands and expanding toward a low-lying country until it has a navigable breadth of over twenty miles. On either side of the inlet are high volcanic peaks densely covered with tropical foliage, while in the passage itself lie several islands. The principal islands, Cor-regidor and Caballo, divide this entrance into two channels, known as Boca Grande, the great mouth, and Boca Chica, the little mouth.

Boca Chica has a width of two miles, while Boca Grande would have double this if it were not for the small island of El Fraile. This, being some distance off the main-land, practically reduces the breadth of Boca Grande to about three miles. Corregidor and Caballo are high and rocky, effectually commanding both entrances, while El Fraile, though smaller, is large enough to be well fortified and to aid in the defence of the broader channel.

No doubt the position is a strong one for defensive batteries, but the Spaniards, in keeping with their weakness for procrastination, had delayed fortifying the three islands until war appeared inevitable. Then they succeeded in mounting sufficient guns to have given our squadron a very unpleasant quarter of an hour before it met the Spanish squadron, provided the gunners had been enterprising and watchful.

Examination of these batteries after their surrender on May 2 showed that there were three 5.9-inch breech-loading rifles on Caballo Island, three 4.7-inch breech-loading rifles on El Fraile rock, and three 6.3-inch muzzle-loading rifles at Punta Restinga, commanding the Boca Grande entrance, which our squadron was to use; three 8-inch muzzle-loading rifles on Corregidor, three 7-inch muzzle-loading rifles at Punta Gorda, and two 6.3-inch breech-loading rifles at Punta Lasisi, commanding the Boca Chica entrance. The complement manning these batteries, as given by the official papers found in the commandant's office at Cavite Arsenal, was thirteen officers and two hundred and forty-six men. While the muzzle-loaders were relatively unimportant, the six modern rifles commanding the Boca Grande, at a range of a mile and a half, if accurately served, could deliver a telling fire.

A cable received from our consul-general at Singapore the day before we left Mirs Bay stated that the Boca Grande channel had been mined. His information was from the steamer *Isla de Panay,* which had just arrivec at Singapore from Manila. This agreed with the accounts of Consul Williams, and with those of merchant-captains from Manila who had recently arrived in Hong Kong.

This subject of mines had been fully discussed in the conferences of myself and staff and the captains of our ships. We decided that submarine mines in Boca Grande might safely be considered a negligible quantity First, the depth of water rendered the planting of submarine mines in Boca Grande, except by experts of much experience, a matter of great difficulty; secondly, either contact or electrical mines would deteriorate so rapidly in tropical waters as to become ineffective in a short time after being placed; and, thirdly, all agreed that the many reports of warnings to vessels, of notices that the passage was dangerous, of compulsory pilotage and of spectacular zigzag courses appeared suspiciously like a cry of "wolf," intended to have its due effect upon a presumptuous enemy.

It was a similar course of reasoning, I recalled, that opened the Suez Canal during the Arabi Pasha rebellion. Hundreds of merchant-steamers had been blocked at the entrance to the canal in the fear of mines said to have been planted by the Egyptians, when an Italian man-of-war under the command of a torpedo expert (late Vice-Admiral Morin, minister of marine) appeared. He said that the Egyptians had hardly skill enough to lay mines properly, and if these had been laid as long as reported they were probably innocuous. So he steamed through the canal in spite of warning, and thus raised a blockade that had lasted for weeks.

The city of Manila lies upon the eastern side of Manila Bay, some twenty-five miles from the entrance, with the headland of Sangley Point and the naval station of Cavite five miles nearer. At all these places there were shore batteries, which added materially to the problem that our squadron had to solve. The batteries on the water-front of the city had thirty-nine heavy guns, four 9.4, four 5.5, two 5.9, two 4.7 breech-loading rifles; nine 8.3 muzzle-loading mortars; eighteen 6.3 muzzle-loading rifles; and eight breech-loading Krupp field pieces. At Sangley Point was a battery with two 5.9 breech-loading rifles and at Canacao one 4.7 breech-loading rifle. These three guns and three of the Manila batteries fired on our ships during the engagement. It will be noted that four guns of the Manila batteries being over 9-inch were larger calibre than any on board our ships.

Before reaching the entrance to Manila Bay there is another bay which might be made an invaluable aid to the protection of the capital and its harbor from naval attack. This is Subig Bay, situated thirty miles to the northward of Corregidor and directly upon the flank of any enemy threatening Manila. With this strategic point effectively occupied, no hostile commander-in-chief would think of passing it and leaving it as a menace to his lines of communication. But with it unoccupied the way was clear,

The Spaniards had inaugurated a small naval reservation at Olongapo, the port of Subig, and at various times appointed boards of officers to report upon the strategic advantages of the situation. So emphatic were the recommendations of these boards in favor of Subig as a naval station in place of Cavite that the change might have been made except for the strong social and official opposition, which preferred life in the capital to comparative exile in a provincial port. Therefore, the fortification of the bay had been neglected; and although at the last moment there was a nervous attempt to improvise defences, so little was done that when, on April 26, the Spanish admiral finally realized that Subig Bay was the strongest point for the defence of his fleet and of Manila, and accordingly sailed from Cavite for Subig, he found, upon arrival, that comparatively nothing had been accomplished and that the position was untenable.

Only twenty-four hours before the arrival of our scouts he got under way and steamed back to Cavite. In his official report he writes feelingly of his disgust that no guns had been mounted and that the entrance had not been mined. He was in error about the mines, however. A Spanish officer assured the executive officer of the *Concord* that eighty mines had been planted in the entrance of Subig Bay. Some fifteen others which the Spaniards had neglected to plant were found later by our officers in the Spanish storehouse at the Subig Bay naval station. In order to get their powder the insurgents had pulled up many of the eighty that had been planted.

So far as our Squadron is concerned, no doubt if we had entered Subig Bay we should have found the mines there as negligible a quantity as those which had undoubtedly been planted in Manila Bay and its entrance. I simply mention their existence to show the state of misinformation in the Spanish admiral's mind about his own resources. He naively adds, in continuing his report, that under the circumstances his vessels could not only have been destroyed if found in Subig Bay, but that, owing to the great depth of water, they would have been unable to save their crews in case of being sunk. What a singular lack of morale and what a strange conclusion for a naval officer!

A comparison of the relative strength of the two squadrons about to be engaged may easily be made (which, however, does not mention some twenty-five small gunboats not brought into action, but which might have been transformed into torpedo-launches for night attack or defence of the entrance to the bay).

In action we had six ships to the Spaniards' seven, but we were superior in class of vessel and in armaments. We had fifty-three guns above the 4-inch calibre and the Spaniards thirty-one; fifty-six guns under 4-inch to the Spaniards' forty-four; eight torpedo-tubes to the Spaniards' thirteen; officers and men, 1,456 to the Spaniards' 1,447. It will be seen that, in keeping with American naval precedent, we were much more heavily armed in ratio to our personnel than the enemy. Neither side had any armored ships and both fought with brown powder. The fact that we were not armored made the heavy guns of the Spanish batteries, if they were brought to bear on us, a serious consideration.

As for the batteries noted in the *Olympia's* official log as having fired on us during the battle and verified after the surrender, they were two 6.3-inch muzzle-loaders and three 9.4-inch from the Manila batteries; two 5.9-inch from the Sangley Point battery; and one 4.7-inch from the Canacao battery. All except the two muzzle-loaders mentioned were modern breech-loading rifles.

As we cruised southward after leaving Mirs Bay, the weather was such that we could continue the preparation of crews and ships for action by drilling the men again in battle drills and their stations in case of fire, and for repairing injuries to the ships by shell-fire, while we built barricades of canvas and iron to shield the gun crews, protected the sides and ammunition hoists with lengths of heavy sheet chain faked up and down over a buffer of awnings, and threw overboard much extra wood-work which, while essential to comfort in time of peace, might become ignited in an engagement. Had the Spaniards disposed of their wood-work their ships would have burned less fiercely both at Manila and at Santiago. At night all lights were extinguished except one on the taffrail to denote position, and even this was so carefully screened as to be visible only from directly astern. The presence of the squadron on the waters was denoted alone by the dark forms of the ships and the breaking of phosphorescence at their bows and in the wake of their propellers.

Now, Consul Williams, when he came on board just before our departure from Mirs Bay, had brought news which was anything but encouraging. It upset my preconceived ideas, as I had counted upon fighting in Manila Bay. Just as the consul was leaving Manila he had learned of the sailing of the Spanish squadron for Subig Bay. Thus Admiral Montojo at the last moment seemed to have realized the strategic advantage of Subig over Manila, which we had hoped he would fail to do. When we sighted land near Cape Bolinao early on the morning of May 30, the *Boston* and *Concord* were signalled to proceed at full speed to reconnoitre Subig Bay.

Later, some of our officers declared that they heard the sound of heavy guns firing in the direction which the *Boston* and *Concord* had taken. Though I could not hear any firing myself, I sent the *Baltimore* to support the two scouts if necessary, and to await the rest of the squadron at the entrance to the bay.

As the day broke the coast of Luzon, which had been indefinitely seen on the horizon, appeared clearly in outline. We kept at a distance of three or four miles as we cruised slowly, keeping our speed to that of our slowest vessel, the collier *Nanshan*. In the hope of obtaining news we overhauled some of the fishing-boats in our path, but they knew nothing of the movements of the Spanish squadron. At 3.30 in the afternoon the three ships which had been sent ahead as scouts were sighted at the entrance to the bay. I waited very anxiously for their signal. When it came, saying that no enemy had been found, I was deeply relieved. I remember that I said to Lamberton, "Now we have them."

The distance from Subig Bay to Corregidor was only thirty miles. As we had decided to run past the batteries at the entrance to Manila Bay under cover of darkness, we slowed down and finally stopped. All the commanding officers were signalled to come on board the flag-ship. When they were in my cabin, and Wildes, of the *Boston,* and Walker, of the *Concord,* had corroborated in person the import of their signals that there were no Spanish vessels in the vicinity, I said:

"We shall enter Manila Bay to-night and you will follow the motions and movements of the flag-ship, which will lead."

There was no discussion and no written order and no further particulars as to preparation. For every preparation that had occurred to us in our councils had already been made. I knew that I could depend upon my captains and that they understood my purposes. My position in relation to my captains and to all my officers and crews was happy, indeed, by contrast with that of the unfortunate Montojo, who tells in his official report of how, upon arriving at Subig Bay on the night of April 25 with six of his ships, he found that none of his orders for the defence of the bay had been executed. The four 5.9-inch guns which should have been mounted a month previously were lying on the shore; yet in landing-drill our men have often mounted guns of equal calibre on shore in twenty-four hours. Aside from the planting of the mines which have been mentioned and the sinking of three old hulks at the eastern entrance of the bay, nothing had been done.

Soon after his arrival at Subig on the 28th Admiral Montojo received the following cable from the Spanish consul at Hong Kong:

"The enemy's squadron sailed at 2 PM from Mirs Bay, and according to reliable accounts they sailed for Subig to destroy our squadron and then will go to Manila."

A council of war was held, and the captains of the Spanish ships unanimously voted to return to Manila rather than, as their own consul had expressed it, be destroyed where they were. So on the morning of the 29th the Spanish squadron steamed back to Cavite. The attitude of the commanding officers must have been the attitude of the personnel. Any force in such a state of mind is already half beaten. The morale of his squadron, as revealed by Montojo's report after the battle, bore out my reasoning before the war had begun, that everywhere the Spaniards would stand upon the defensive. This must mean defeat in the end, and the more aggressive and prompt our action the smaller would be our losses and the sooner peace would come.

When my captains, after receiving their final orders on board the flagship, had returned to their own ships, the squadron resumed its course to Corregidor. As the gloom of night gradually shut out the details of the coast, the squadron steamed quietly on toward the entrance of Manila Bay with all lights masked and the gun crews at the guns. By degrees the high land on either side loomed up out of the darkness, while the flag-ship headed for Boca Grande, which was the wider but comparatively little used channel. A light shower passed over about eleven o'clock and heavy, cumulus clouds drifting across the sky from time to time obscured the new moon. The landmarks and islands were, however, fairly visible, while compass bearings for regulating our course could readily be observed.

It was thirty-six years since, as executive officer of the *Mississippi,* I was first under fire in the passage of Forts Jackson and St. Philip under Farragut, and thirty-five years since, as executive officer, I had lost my ship in the attempted passage of the batteries of Port Hudson. Then, as now, we were dependent upon the screen of darkness to get by successfully, but then I was a subordinate and now the supreme responsibility was mine.

If the guns commanding the entrance were well served, there was danger of damage to my squadron before it engaged the enemy's squadron. If the Spaniards had shown enterprise in the use of the materials which they possessed, then we might have expected a heavy fire from the shore batteries. One who had military knowledge did not have to wait for the developments of the Russo-Japanese War to know how quickly modern guns of high velocity and low trajectory may be emplaced and how effective they may be, when fired from a stationary position, against so large a target as a ship. Had the batteries search-lights they could easily locate us, while we could locate them only by the flash of their guns.

When we were ten miles from Boca Grande we judged, as we saw signal lights flash, that we had already been sighted either by small vessels acting as scouts or by land lookouts. El Fraile was passed by the flag-ship at a distance of half a mile and was utilized as a point of departure for the course up the bay clear of the San Nicolas Shoals. When El Fraile bore due south (magnetic) the course was changed to northeast by north. We were not surprised to find the usual lights on Corregidor and Caballo Islands and the San Nicolas Shoals extinguished, as this was only a natural precaution on the part of the Spaniards.

There were no vessels, so far as we could see, cruising off the entrance, no dash of torpedo-launches which might have been expected, no sign of life beyond the signalling on shore until the rear of the column, steaming at full speed, was between Corregidor and El Fraile.

As we watched the walls of darkness for the first gun-flash, every moment of our progress brought its relief, and now we began to hope that we should get by without being fired on at all. But about ten minutes after midnight, when all except our rear ships had cleared it, the El Fraile battery opened with a shot that passed between the *Petrel* and the *Raleigh*. The *Boston, Concord, Raleigh,* and *McCulloch* returned the fire with a few shots. One 8-inch shell from the *Boston* seemed to be effective. After firing three times El Fraile was silent. There was no demonstration whatever from the Caballo battery, with its three 6-inch modern rifles, no explosion of mines, and no other resistance. We were safely within the bay. The next step was to locate the Spanish squadron and engage it.

Afterward we heard various explanations of why we were not given a warmer reception as we passed through. Some of the officers in the El Fraile battery said that their dilatoriness in opening fire was due to the fact that their men were ashore at Punta Lasisi and could not get off to their guns in time after they heard of the squadron's approach. An eye-witness on Corregidor informed me that our squadron was perfectly visible as it was passing through the entrance, but for some extraordinary reason the commanding officer gave no orders to the batteries to open fire.

Perhaps the enemy thought that he had done all that was necessary by cutting off the usual lights on Corregidor and Caballo Islands and San Nicolas Shoals for guiding mariners, and he expected that without pilots and without any knowledge of the waters we would not be guilty of such a foolhardy attempt as entering an unlighted channel at midnight.

Once through the entrance, as I deemed it wise to keep moving in order not to be taken by surprise when the ships had no headway, and as, at the same time, I did not wish to reach our destination before we had sufficient daylight to show us the position of the Spanish ships, the speed of the squadron was reduced to four knots, while we headed toward the city of Manila. In the meantime the men were allowed to snatch a little sleep at their guns; but at four o'clock coffee was served to them, and so eager were they that there was no need of any orders to insure readiness for the work to come.

Signal lights, rockets, and beacon lights along the shore, now that we were sure of grappling with the enemy, no longer concerned us. We waited for dawn and the first sight of the Spanish squadron, which I had rather expected would be at the anchorage off the city of Manila. This seemed naturally the strong position for Admiral Montojo to take up, as he would then have the powerful

Manila battery, mounting the guns which have already been enumerated, to support him. But the admiral stated in his report that he had avoided this position on account of the resultant injury which the city might have received if the battle had been fought in close proximity to it.

The *Nanshan* and *Zafiro*, as there was no reserve ammunition for either to carry, had been sent, with the *McCulloch*, into an unfrequented part of the bay in order that they should sustain no injury and that they might not hamper the movements of the fighting-ships. When we saw that there were only merchantmen at the Manila anchorage, the squadron, led by the flag-ship, gradually changed its course, swinging around on the arc of a large circle leading toward the city and making a kind of countermarch, as it were, until headed in the direction of Cavite. This brought the ships within two or three miles of shore, with a distance of four hundred yards between ships, in the following order: *Olympia* (flag), *Baltimore, Raleigh, Petrel, Concord,* and *Boston.*

About 5.05 the Luneta and two other Manila batteries opened fire. Their shots passed well over the vessels. It was estimated that some had a range of seven miles. Only the *Boston* and *Concord* replied. Each sent two shells at the Luneta battery. The other vessels reserved their fire, having in mind my caution that, in the absence of a full supply of ammunition, the amount we had was too precious to be wasted when we were seven thousand miles from our base. My captains understood that the Spanish ships were our objective and not the shore fortifications of a city that would be virtually ours as soon as our squadron had control of Manila Bay.

With the coming of broad daylight we finally sighted the Spanish vessels formed in an irregular crescent in front of Cavite. The *Olympia* headed toward them, and in answer to her signal to close up, the distance between our ships was reduced to two hundred yards. The western flank of the Spanish squadron was protected by Cavite Peninsula and the Sangley Point battery, while its eastern flank rested in the shoal water off Las Pinas.

The Spanish line of battle was formed by the *Reina Cristina* (flag), *Castilla, Don Juan de Austria, Don Antonio de Ulloa, Isla de Luzón, Isla de Cuba,* and *Marqués del Deuro.*

The *Velasco* and *Lezo* were on the other (southern) side of Cavite Point, and it is claimed by the Spaniards that they took no part in the action.-Some of the vessels in the Spanish battle-line were under way, and others were moored so as to bring their broadside batteries to bear to the best advantage. The *Castilla* was protected by heavy iron lighters filled with stone.

Before me now was the object for which we had made our arduous preparations, and which, indeed, must ever be the supreme test of a naval officer's career. I felt confident of the outcome, though I had no thought that victory would be won at so slight a cost to our own side. Confidence was expressed in the very precision with which the dun, war-colored hulls of the squadron followed in column behind the flag-ship, keeping their distance excellently. All the guns were pointed constantly at the enemy, while the men were at their stations waiting the word. There was no break in the monotone of the engines save the mechanical voice of the leadsman or an occasional low-toned command by the quartermaster at the conn, or the roar of a Spanish shell. The Manila batteries continued their inaccurate fire, to which we paid no attention.

The misty haze of the tropical dawn had hardly risen when at 5.15, at long range, the Cavite forts and Spanish squadron opened fire. Our course was not one leading directly toward the enemy, but a converging one, keeping him on our starboard bow. Our speed was eight knots and our converging course and ever-varying position must have confused the Spanish gunners. My assumption that the Spanish fire would be hasty and inaccurate proved correct.

So far as I could see, none of our ships was suffering any damage, while, in view of my limited ammunition supply, it was my plan not to open fire until we were within effective range, and then to fire as rapidly as possible with all of our guns.

At 5.40, when we were within a distance of 5,000 yards (two and one-half miles), I turned to Captain Gridley and said:

"You may fire when you are ready, Gridley."

While I remained on the bridge with Lamberton, Brumby, and Stickney, Gridley took his station in the conning-tower and gave the order to the battery. The very first gun to speak was an 8-inch from the forward turret of the *Olympia,* and this was the signal for all the other ships to join the action.

At about the time that the Spanish ships were first sighted, 5.06, two submarine mines were exploded between our squadron and Cavite, some two miles ahead of our column. On account of the distance, I remarked to Lamberton:

"Evidently the Spaniards are already rattled."

However, they explained afterward that the premature explosions were due to a desire to clear a space in which their ships might manoeuvre.

At one time a torpedo-launch made an attempt to reach the *Olympia,* but she was sunk by the guns of the secondary battery and went down bow first, and another yellow-colored launch flying the Spanish colors ran out, heading for the *Olympia,* but after being disabled she was beached to prevent her sinking.

When the flag-ship neared the five-fathom curve off Cavite she turned to the westward, bringing her port batteries to bear on the enemy, and, followed by the squadron, passed along the Spanish line until north of and only some fifteen hundred yards distant from the Sangley Point battery, when she again turned and headed back to the eastward, thus giving the squadron an opportunity to use their port and starboard batteries alternately and to cover with their fire all the Spanish ships, as well as the Cavite and Sangley Point batteries. While I was regulating the course of the squadron, Lieutenant Calkins was verifying our position by cross-bearings and by the lead.

Three runs were thus made from the eastward and two from the westward, the length of each run averaging two miles and the ships being turned each time with port helm. Calkins found that there was in reality deeper water than shown on the chart, and when he reported the fact to me, inasmuch as my object was to get as near as possible to the enemy without grounding our own vessels, the fifth run past the Spaniards was farther inshore than any preceding run. At the nearest point to the enemy our range was only two thousand yards.

There had been no cessation in the rapidity of fire maintained by our whole squadron, and the effect of its concentration, owing to the fact that our ships were kept so close together, was smothering, particularly upon the two largest ships, the *Reina Cristina* and *Castilla*. The *Don Juan de Austria* first and then the *Reina Cristina* made brave and desperate attempts to charge the *Olympia,* but becoming the target for all our batteries they turned and ran back. In this sortie the *Reina Cristina* was raked by an 8-inch shell, which is said to have put out of action some twenty men and to have completely destroyed her steering-gear. Another shell in her forecastle killed or wounded all the members of the crews of four rapid-fire guns; another set fire to her after orlop; another killed or disabled nine men on her poop; another carried away her mizzen-mast, bringing down the ensign and the admiral's flag, both of which were replaced; another exploded in the after ammunition-room; and still another exploded in the sick-bay, which was already filled with wounded.

When she was raised from her muddy bed, five years later, eighty skeletons were found in the sick-bay and fifteen shot holes in the hull; while the many hits mentioned in Admiral Montojo's report, and his harrowing description of the shambles that his flag-ship had become when he was finally obliged to leave her, shows what execution was done to her upper works. Her loss was one hundred and fifty killed and ninety wounded, seven of these being officers. Among the killed was her valiant captain, Don Luis Cadarso, who, already wounded, finally met his death while bravely directing the rescue of his men from the burning and sinking vessel.

Though in the early part of the action our firing was not what I should have liked it to be, it soon steadied down, and by the time the *Reina Cristina* steamed toward us it was satisfactorily accurate. The *Castilla* fared little better than the *Reina Cristina*. All except one of her guns was disabled, she was set on fire by our shells, and finally abandoned by her crew after they had sustained a loss of twenty-three killed and eighty wounded. The *Don Juan de Austria* was badly damaged and on fire, the *Isla de Luzón* had three guns dismounted, and the *Marqués del Duero* was also in a bad way. Admiral Montojo, finding his flag-ship no longer manageable, half her people dead or wounded, her guns useless and the ship on fire, gave the order to abandon and sink her, and transferred his flag to the *Isla de Cuba* shortly after seven o'clock.

Victory was already ours, though we did not know it. Owing to the smoke over the Spanish squadron there were no visible signs of the execution wrought by our guns when we started upon our fifth run past the enemy. We were keeping up our rapid fire, and the flag-ship was opposite the centre of the Spanish line, when, at 7.35, the captain of the *Olympia* made a report to me which was as startling as it was unexpected. This was to the effect that on board the *Olympia* there remained only fifteen rounds per gun for the 5-inch battery.

It was a most anxious moment for me. So far as I could see, the Spanish squadron was as intact as ours. I had reason to believe that their supply of ammunition was as ample as ours was limited.

Therefore, I decided to withdraw temporarily from action for a redistribution of ammunition if necessary. For I knew that fifteen rounds of 5-inch ammunition could be shot away in five minutes. But even as we were steaming out of range the distress of the Spanish ships became evident. Some of them were perceived to be on fire and others were seeking protection behind Cavite Point. The *Don Antonio de Ulloa*, however, still retained her position at Sangley Point, where she had been moored. Moreover, the Spanish fire, with the exception of the Manila batteries, to which we had paid little attention, had ceased entirely. It was clear that we did not need a very large supply of ammunition to finish our morning's task; and happily it was found that the report about the *Olympia's* 5-inch ammunition had been incorrectly transmitted. It was that fifteen rounds had been fired per gun, not that only fifteen rounds remained.

Feeling confident of the outcome, I now signalled that the crews, who had had only a cup of coffee at 4 AM, should have their breakfast. The public at home, on account of this signal, to which was attributed a nonchalance that had never occurred to me, reasoned that breakfast was the real reason for our withdrawing from action. Meanwhile, I improved the opportunity to have the commanding officers report on board the flag-ship.

There had been such a heavy flight of shells over us that each captain, when he arrived, was convinced that no other ship had had such good luck as his own in being missed by the enemy's fire, and expected the others to have both casualties and damages to their ships to report. But fortune was as pronouncedly in our favor at Manila as it was later at Santiago. To my gratification not a single life had been lost, and considering that we would rather measure the importance of an action by the scale of its conduct than by the number of casualties we were immensely happy. The concentration of our fire immediately we were within telling range had given us an early advantage in demoralizing the enemy, which has ever been the prime factor in naval battles. In the War of 1812 the losses of the *Constitution* were slight when she overwhelmed the *Guerrière* and in the Civil War the losses of the *Kearsarge* were slight when she made a shambles of the *Alabama*. On the *Baltimore* two officers (Lieutenant F. W. Kellogg and Ensign N. E. Irwin) and six men were slightly wounded. None of our ships had been seriously hit, and every one was still ready for immediate action.

In detail the injuries which we had received from the Spanish fire were as follows:

The *Olympia* was hulled five times and her rigging was cut in several places. One six-pound projectile struck immediately under the position where I was standing. The *Baltimore* was hit five times. The projectile which wounded two officers and six men pursued a most erratic course. It entered the ship's side forward of the starboard gangway, and just above the line of the main deck, passed through the hammock-netting, down through the deck planks and steel deck, bending the deck beam in a wardroom state-room, thence upward through the after engine-room coaming, over against the cylinder of a 6-inch gun, disabling the gun, struck and exploded a box of three-pounder ammunition, hit an iron ladder, and finally, spent, dropped on deck. The *Boston* had four unimportant hits, one causing a fire which was soon extinguished, and the *Petrel* was struck once.

At 11.16 AM we stood in to complete our work. There remained to oppose us, however, only the batteries and the gallant little *Ulloa*. Both opened fire as we advanced. But the contest was too unequal to last more than a few minutes. Soon the *Ulloa*, under our concentrated fire, went down valiantly with her colors flying.

The battery at Sangley Point was well served, and several times reopened fire before being finally silenced. Had this battery possessed i1 four other 6-inch guns which Admiral Montojo had found uselessly lyin on the beach at Subig, our ships would have had many more casualties t report. Happily for us, the guns of this battery had been so mounted tha they could be laid only for objects beyond the range of two thousand yard: As the course of our ships led each time within this range, the shots passe over and beyond them. Evidently the artillerists, who had so constructe their carriages that the muzzles of the guns took against the sill of th embrasure for any range under two thousand yards, thought it out of th question that an enemy would venture within this distance.

The *Concord* was sent to destroy a large transport, the *Mindanao*, whic had been beached near Bacoor, and the *Petrel*, whose light draught woul permit her to move in shallower water than the other vessels of the squad ron, was sent into the harbor of Cavite to destroy any ships that had taken refuge there. The *Mindanao* was set on fire and her valuable carge destroyed. Meanwhile, the *Petrel* gallantly performed her duty, and after a few shots from her 6-inch guns the Spanish flag on the government build ing was hauled down and a white flag hoisted. Admiral Montojo had beer wounded, and had taken refuge on shore with his remaining officers and men; his loss was three hundred and eighty-one of his officers and crew and there was no possibility of further resistance.

At 12.30 the *Petrel* signalled the fact of the surrender, and the firing ceased. But the Spanish vessels were not yet fully destroyed. Therefore the executive officer of the *Petrel*, Lieutenant E. M. Hughes, with a whale boat and a crew of only seven men, boarded and set fire to the *Don Juar de Austria, Isla de Cuba, Isla de Luzón, General Lezo, Coreo*, and *Marqué del Duero*, all of which had been abandoned in shallow water and left scuttled by their deserting crews. This was a courageous undertaking, a: shese vessels were supposed to have been left with trains to their magazines and were not far from the shore, where there were hundreds of Spanish soldiers and sailors, all armed and greatly excited. The *Manila*, an armed transport, which was found uninjured after having been beached by the Spaniards, was therefore spared. Two days later she was easily floated, and or many years did good service as a gunboat. The little *Petrel* continued her work until 5.20 PM, when she rejoined the squadron, towing a long string of tugs and launches, to be greeted by volleys of cheers from every ship.

The order to capture or destroy the Spanish squadron had been executed :o the letter. Not one of its fighting-vessels remained afloat. That night wrote in my diary: "Reached Manila at daylight. Immediately engaged;he Spanish ships and batteries at Cavite. Destroyed eight of the former, including the *Reina Cristina* and *Castilla*. Anchored at noon off Manila."

As soon as we had sunk the U*lloa* and silenced the batteries at Sangley Point, the *Olympia*, followed by the *Baltimore* and *Raleigh*, while the *Concord* and *Petrel* were carrying out their orders, started for the anchorage)ff the city. The Manila batteries, which had kept up such a persistent though impotent firing all the early part of the day, were now silent and made no attempt to reopen as our ships approached the city. Consul Williams was sent on board a British ship moored close inshore near the mouth of the Pasig River, with instructions to request her captain to be the bearer of a message to the Spanish captain-general. This message was taken ashore at 2 PM, in the form of a note to the British consul, Mr. E. H. Rawson-Walker, who, after the departure of Mr. Williams, had assumed charge of our archives and interests, requesting him to see the captain-general, and to say to him, on my behalf, that if another shot were fired at our ships from the Manila batteries we should destroy the city. Moreover, if there were any torpedo-boats in the Pasig River they must be surrendered, and if we were allowed to transmit messages by the cable to Hong Kong the captain-general would also be permitted to use it. Assurance came promptly that the forts would not fire at our squadron unless it was evident that a disposition of our ships to bombard the city was being made. This assurance, which was kept even during the land attack upon the city, some three months later, led me to drop anchor for the first time since we had entered the bay. From the moment that the captain-general accepted my terms the city was virtually surrendered, and;I was in control of the situation, subject to my government's orders for the future. I had established a base seven thousand miles from home which I might occupy indefinitely. As I informed the secretary of the navy in my cable of May 4, our squadron controlled the bay and could take the city at any time. The only reason for awaiting the arrival of troops before demanding its surrender was the lack of sufficient force to occupy it.

In answer to the other points of my message, the captain-general, Don Basilio Augustin Davila, said that he knew of no torpedo-boats in the river, but that if there were any his honor would not allow him to surrender them. As there were none, he was quite safe in making this reservation, which did not affect the main fact, that his capital was under our guns. He refused my request about the cable. As a result he found himself cut off from all telegraphic communication with the outside world on the next morning, because I directed the *Zafiro* to cut the cable.

As the sun set on the evening of May 1, crowds of people gathered along the water-front, gazing at the American squadron. They climbed on the ramparts of the very battery that had fired on us in the morning. The *Olympia's* band, for their benefit, played "La Paloma" and other Spanish airs, and while the sea-breeze wafted the strains to their ears the poor colonel of artillery who had commanded the battery, feeling himself dishonored by his disgraceful failure, shot himself through the head.

During the mid-watch that night a steam-launch was discovered coming off from Manila. The crews went to quarters and search-lights and guns were trained upon her until she approached the *Olympia,* when she was allowed to come alongside. A Spanish official was on board. He desired permission to proceed to Corregidor to instruct the commanding officer that none of the batteries at the entrance to the bay were to fire on our ships when passing in or out. Permission was granted and he was told to return the following morning. When he came he was put on board the *Raleigh,* which was sent, with the *Baltimore* as escort, to demand the surrender of all the defences at the entrance to the bay. The surrender was made and the garrisons disarmed. The next day I had the *Boston* and *Concord* land parties, who disabled the guns and brought their breech-plugs off to the ships. All the ammunition found, as it was of a calibre unsuited to any of our guns, was destroyed.

Meanwhile, to my surprise, on the morning of May 2, the Spanish flag was seen to be again flying over the Cavite arsenal. Captain Lamberton was sent at once to inquire what it meant, and to demand a formal surrender. He went over to Cavite in the *Petrel,* and upon leaving her to go on shore gave instructions that in case he did not return within an hour she was to open fire on the arsenal. Upon landing he found the Spanish soldiers and sailors under arms, and in answer to his inquiry, what was meant by this and by the hoisting of the Spanish colors, he was informed by the Spanish commandant, Captain Sostoa, that the colors had been lowered the day before only as token of a temporary truce. Captain Lamberton's reply to this evasive excuse was an ultimatum that if the white flag were not hoisted by noon he would open fire.

Captain Sostoa then asked for time in which to refer the matter to Madrid, and this being refused, for time to refer it to the authorities at Manila. But he was informed that only an unconditional surrender of officers, men, and arms would be considered. Captain Lamberton then returned to the *Petrel,* and at 11.35 the white flag was hoisted by the order of Admiral Montojo; and it was this order, peculiarly enough, and not the loss of his squadron, that led to his court-martial upon his return to Spain. Shortly afterward all the Spanish officers and men evacuated the place. Possibly imperfect knowledge of each other's language by Captain Lamberton and Captain Sostoa led to a misunderstanding of our terms by the Spaniards. In a way this was fortunate for us, as we were in no position to take care of prisoners. We had what we needed: possession of the arsenal, with its machinery, workshops, and supplies, as a base for future operations.

To us it seems almost incomprehensible that the guns of Caballo and Corregidor and Punta Restinga failed to fire on our ships; that when our vessels were hampered by the narrow waters of the entrance there was no night attack by the many small vessels possessed by the Spaniards; and that during the action neither the *Isla de Cuba* nor the *Isla de Luzón,* each of them protected by an armored deck and fitted with two torpedo-tubes, made any attempt to torpedo our ships.

Naturally, the Spanish government attempted to make a scapegoat of poor Admiral Montojo, the victim of their own shortcomings and maladministration, and he was soon afterward ordered home and brought before a court-martial. It was some satisfaction to know that a factor in influencing the court in concluding that he had fulfilled his duty in a courageous manner was a letter from me testifying to his gallantry in the action, which I was glad to give in response to his request.

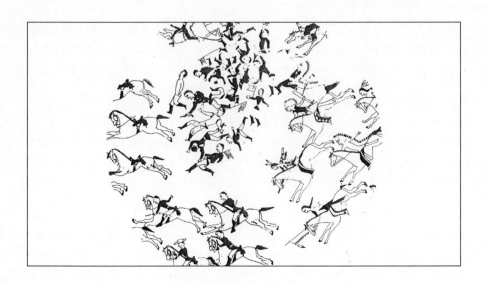

THE BATTLE OF THE LITTLE BIG HORN

SITTING BULL'S VERSION

Through the intercession of Major Walsh, Sitting Bull was persuaded at nightfall to hold a special conference with me. It was explained to him that I was not his enemy, but that I was his good friend. He was told by Major Walsh that I was a great paper chief; one who talked with a million tongues to all the people in the world. Said the Major : "This man is a man of wonderful medicine; he speaks, and the people on this side and across the great water open their ears and hear him. He tells the truth; he does not lie. He wishes to make the world know what a great tribe is encamped here on the land owned by the White Mother. [This interview took place at Fort Walsh, on British Territory, and the "White Mother" here mentioned is Queen Victoria.] He wants it understood that her guests are mighty warriors. The Long-Haired Chief (alluding to General Custer) was his friend. He wants to hear from you how he fought and whether he met death like a brave."

"Agh-howgh *I*" (It is well) said Sitting Bull.

He finally agreed to come, after dark, to the quarters which had been assigned to me, on the condition that nobody should be present except myself, his interlocutor, Major Walsh, two interpreters, and the stenographer I had employed for the occasion.

At the appointed time, half-past eight, the lamps were lighted, and the most mysterious Indian Chieftain who ever flourished in North America was ushered in by Major Walsh, who locked the door behind him. This was the first time that Sitting Bull had condescended, not merely to visit but to address a white man from the United States. During the long years of his domination he had withstood, with his hands, every attempt on the part of the United States government at a compromise of interests. He had refused all proffers, declined any treaty. He had never been beaten in a battle with United States troops; on the con-trary, his warriors had been victorious over the pride of our army. Pressed hard, he had retreated, scorning the factions of his bands who accepted the terms offered them, with the same bitterness with which he scorned his white enemies.

Here he stood, his blanket rolled back, his head upreared, his right moc-casin put forward, his right hand thrown across his chest.

I arose and approached him, holding out both hands. He grasped them cordially. "How!" said he. "How!"

And now let me attempt a better portrait of Sitting Bull. He is about five feet, ten inches high. He was clad in a black and white calico shirt, black cloth leggings and moccasins, magnificently embroidered with beads and porcupine quills. He held in his left hand a fox-skin cap, its brush drooping to his feet; with the dignity and grace of a natural gentleman he had removed it from his head at the threshold. His long, black hair hung far down his back, athwart his cheeks and in front of his shoulders. His eyes gleamed like black diamonds. His visage, devoid of paint, was noble and commanding; nay, it was something more. Besides the Indian character given to it by high cheek-bones, a broad, retreating forehead, a prominent, aquiline nose, and a jaw like a bull dog's, there was about the mouth something of beauty, but more of an expression of exquisite, cruel irony. Such a mouth and such eyes as this Indian's, if seen in the countenance of a white man, would appear to denote qualities similar to those which animated the career of Mazarin and inspired the pen of Machiaevelli.

Yet there was something fearfully sweet in his smile as he extended to me his hands.

Such hands! They felt as small and soft as a maiden's, but when I pressed them I could feel the sinews beneath the flesh quivering hard, like a wild animal's. I led him to a seat, a lounge set against the wall, on which he sank with indolent grace. Major Walsh, brilliant in red uniform, sat beside him, and a port- able table was brought near. Two interpreters brought chairsand seated themselves, and at a neighboring desk the stenographer took his place.

I turned to the interpreter and said:—

"Explain again to Sitting Bull that he is with a friend."

The interpreter explained.

"Banee!" said the chief, holding out his hand again and pressing mine.

Major Walsh here said: "Sitting Bull is in the best mood now that you could possibly wish. Proceed with your questions, and make them as logical as you can. I will assist you, and trip you up occasionally if you are likely to irritate him."

Then the dialogue went on. I give it literally

"You are a great chief," said I to Sitting Bull, "but you live behind a cloud. Your face is dark, my people do not see it. Tell me, do you hate the Americans very much?"

A gleam as of fire shot across his face.

"I am no chief."

This was precisely what I expected. It will dissipate at once the erroneous idea which has prevailed, that Sitting Bull is either a chief or a warrior.

"What are you?"

"I am," said he, crossing both hands upon his chest, slightly nodding, and smiling satirically, "a man."

"What does he mean?"I inquired, turning to Major Walsh. "He means," responded the Major, "to keep you in ignorance of his secret if he can. His position among his bands is anomalous. His own tribes, the Uncpapas, are not all in fealty to him. Parts of nearly twenty different tribes of Sioux, besides a remnant of the Uncpapas, abide with him. So far as I have learned, he rules over these fragments of tribes, which compose his camp of twenty-five hundred, including between eight hundred and nine hundred warriors, by sheer compelling force of intellect and will. I believe that he understands nothing particularly of war or military tactics, at least not enough to give him the skill or the right to command warriors in battle. He is supposed to have guided the fortunes of several battles, including the fight in which Custer fell. That supposition, as you will presently find, is partially erroneous. His word was always potent in the camp or in the field, but he has usually left to the war chiefs the duties appertaining to engagements. When the crisis came he gave his opinion, which was accepted as law."

"What was he then?"I inquired, continuing this momentary dialogue with Major Walsh. "Was he, is he, a mere medicine man?"

"Don't for the world," replied the Major, "intimate to him, in the questions you are about to ask him, that you have derived the idea from me, or from any one, that he is a mere medicine man. He would deem that to be a profound insult. In point of fact he is a medicine man, but a far greater, more influential medicine man than any savage I have ever known. He has constituted himself a ruler. He is a unique power among the Indians.

He does not interfere with the rights or duties of others. His power consists in the universal confidence which is given to his judgment, which he seldom denotes until he is asked for an expression of it. It has been, so far, so accurate, it has guided his people so well, he has been caught in so few mistakes and he has saved even his ablest and oldest chiefs from so many evil consequences of their own misjudgment, that to-day his word among them all, is worth more than the united voices of the rest of the camp. He speaks. They listen and they obey. Now let us hear what his explanation will be."

"You say you are no chief?" No! "with considerable hauteur.

"Are you a head soldier?"

"I am nothing—neither a chief nor a soldier."

"What? Nothing?"

"Nothing."

"What, then, makes the wariors of your camp, the great chiefs who are here along with you, look up to you so? Why do they think so much of you?"

Sitting Bull's lips curled with a proud smile.

"Oh, I used to be a kind of a chief; but the Americans made me go away from my father's hunting ground."

"You do not love the Americans?"

You should have seen this savage's lips.

"I saw to-day that all the warriors around you clapped their hands and cried out when you spoke. What you said appeared to please them. They liked you. They seemed to think that what you said was right for them to say. If you are not a great chief, why do these men think so much of you?

At this Sitting Bull, who had in the meantime been leaning back against the wall, assumed a posture of mingled toleration and disdain.

"Your people look up to men because they are rich; because they have much land, many lodges, many squaws?" "Yes."

"Well, I suppose my people look up to me because I am poor.

That is the difference"

What is your feeling toward the Americans now?"

He did not even deign an answer. He touched his hip, where his knife was. I asked the interpreter to insist on an answer.

"Listen," said Sitting Bull, not changing his posture, but putting his right hand out upon my knee. "I told them to-day what my notions were—that I did not want to go back there.

Every time that I had any difficulty with them they struck me first. I want to live in peace."

"Have you an implacable enmity to the Americans? Would you live with them in peace if they allowed you to do so; or do you think that you can only obtain peace here?"

"The White Mother is good."

"Better than the Great Father?" "Howgh!"

And then after a pause, Sitting Bull continued. "They asked me to-day to give them my horses. I bought my horses, and they are mine. I bought them from men who came up the Missouri in mackinaws. They do not belong to the Government, neither do the rifles. The rifles are also mine. I bought them; I paid for them. Why I should give them up I do not know. I will not give them up."

"Do you really think, do your people believe, that it is wise to reject the proffers that have been made to you by the United States Commissioners? Do not some of you feel as if you were destined to lose your old hunting grounds? Don't you see that you will probably have the same difficulty in Canada that you have had in the United States?"

"The White Mother does not lie."

"Do you expect to live here by hunting? Are there buffaloes enough? Can your people subsist on the game here?" "I don't know; I hope so."

"If not, are any part of your people disposed to take up agriculture? Would any of them raise steers and go to farming?"

"I don't know."

"What will they do, then?"

"As long as there are buffaloes that is the way we will live."

"But the time will come when there will be no more buffaloes."

"Those are the words or an American."

"How long do you think the buffaloes will last?"

Sitting Bull arose. "We know," said he, extending his right hand with an impressive gesture, "that on the other side the buffaloes will not last very long. Why? Because the country there is poisoned with blood—a poison that kills all the buffaloes or drives them away. It is strange," he continued, with his peculiar smile, "that the Americans should complain that the Indians kill buffaloes. We kill buffaloes, as we kill other animals, for food and clothing, and to make our lodges warm. They kill buffaloes—for what? Go through your country. Seethe thousands of carcasses rotting on the Plains. Your young men shoot for pleasure. All they take from a dead buffalo is his tail, or his head, or his horns, perhaps, to show they have killed a buffalo. What is this? Is it robbery? You call us savages. What are they? The buffaloes have come North. We have come North to find them, and to get away from a place where the people tell lies."

To gain time, and not to dwell importunately on a single point, I asked Sitting Bull to tell me something of his early life. In the first place, where he was born?

"I was born on the Missouri Eiver; at least I recollect that somebody told me so—I don't know who told me or where I was told of it."

"Of what tribe are you?"

"I am an Uncpapa."

"Of the Sioux?"

"Yes; of the great Sioux Nation."

"Who was your father?"

"My father is dead."

" Is your mother living?"

"My mother lives with me in my lodge."

"Great lies are told about you. White men say that you lived among them when you were young; that you went to school; that you learned to write and read from books; that you speak English; that you know how to talk French?"

"It is a lie."

"You are an Indian?"

(Proudly) "lama Sioux."

Then, suddenly relaxing from his hauteur, Sitting Bull began to laugh. "I have heard," he said "of some of these stories. They are all strange lies. What I am I am," and here he leaned back and resumed his attitude and expression of barbaric grandeur.

"I am a man. I see. I know. I began to see when I was not yet born; when I was not in my mother's arms. It was then I began to study about my people. I studied about many things. I studied about the small-pox, that was killing my people—the great sickness that was killing the women and children. I was so interested that I turned over on mv side. The God Almiabt.v must have told me at that time [and here Sitting Bull unconsciously revealed his secret], that I would be the man to be the judge of all the other Indians—a big man, to decide for them in all their ways."

"And you have since decided for them?"

"I speak. It is enough."

"Could not your people, whom you love so well, get on with the Americans?" "No!" "Why?"

"I never taught my people to trust Americans. I have told them the truth—that the Americans are great liars. I have never dealt with the Americans. Why should I? The land belonged to my people. I say I never dealt with them—I mean I never treated them in a way to surrender my people's rights. I traded with them, but I always gave full value for what I got. I never asked the United States Government to make me presents of blankets or cloth, or anything of that kind. The most I did was to ask them to send me an honest trader that I could trade with, and I proposed to give him buffalo robes and elk skins, and other hides in exchange for what we wanted. I told every trader who came to our camps that I did not want any favors from him—that I wanted to trade with him fairly and equally, giving him full value for what I got, but the traders wanted me to trade with them on no such terms. They wanted to give little and get much. They told me if I did not accept what they give me in trade they would get the government to fight me. I told them I did not want to fight."

"But you fought?"

"At last, yes; but not until I had tried hard to prevent a fight. At first my young men, when they began to talk bad, stole five American horses. I took the horses away from them and gave them back to the Americans. It did no good. By and by we had to fight."

It was at this juncture that I began to question the great savage before me in regard to the most disastrous, most mysterious Indian battle of the century,—Custer's encounter with the Sioux on the Big Horn—the Thermopylae of the plains. Sitting Bull, the chief genius of his bands, has been supposed to have commanded the Sioux forces when Custer fell.

That the reader may understand Sitting Bull's statements, it will be necessary for him to read the following preliminary sketch.

Custer, on the 22d of June, started up the Rosebud, with the following order from General Terry in his pocket:—

"Lieutenant-Colonel Custer, Seventh Cavalry.

"Colonel : The brigadier-general commanding directs that as soon as your regiment can be made ready for the march, you proceed up the Rosebud in pursuit of the Indians whose trail was discovered by Major Reno a few days since. It is, of course, impossible to give any definite instructions in regard to this movement, and, were it not impossible to do so, the department commander places too much confidence in your zeal, energy and ability, to wish to impose upon you precise orders which might hamper your action when nearly in contact with the enemy. He will, however, indicate to you his own views of what your action should be, and he desires that you should conform to them unless- you shall see sufficient reason for departing from them. He thinks that you should proceed up the Rosebud until you ascertain definitely the direction in which the trail above spoken of leads. Should it be found, as it appears to be almost certain that it will be to turn toward the Little Big Horn, he thinks that you should still proceed southward, perhaps as far as the headquarters of the Tongue, and then turn toward the Little Big Horn, feeling constantly, however, toward your left, so as to preclude the possibility of the escape of the Indians to the south or southeast by passing around your left flank. The column of Colonel Gibbon is now in motion for the mouth of the Big Horn. As soon as it reaches that point it will cross the Yellowstone and move up at least as far as the parks of the Big and Little Big Horn. Of course, its future movements must be controlled by circumstances as they arise; but it is hoped that the Indians, if upon the Little Big Horn, may be so nearly inclosed by two columns that their escape will be impossible. The department commander desires that on your way up the Rosebud you should thoroughly examine the upper part of Tulloch's Creek, and that you should endeavor to send a scout through to Colonel Gibbon's column with information of the result of your examination. The lower part of this creek will be examined by a detachment of Colonel Gibbon's command. The supply steamer will be pushed up the Big Horn as far as the forks of the river are found to be navigable for that space, and the department commander, who will accompany the column of Colonel Gibbon, desires you to report to him there not later than the expiration of the time for which your troops are rationed, unless in the meantime you receive further orders. Respectfully,

"E. W. Smith,

Captain Eighteenth Infantry, Acting Assistant Adjutant-General."

With these tentative instructions, General Custer proceeded on his way. Hearing of the Indians, he found that he had a great opportunity to strike them. He touched their trail and followed it. He laid his plans, with what lack of success we know. But shall we not also inquire what was the real cause of his untimely, unnecessary failure?

General Custer had been chided for a division of his troops. In point of fact he never attacked an Indian camp when he had more than a company, without so separating his command as to encompass, bewilder and capture it. We shall presently see whether it was the fault of his dispositions on this occasion which lost him his last battle. Here is Reno's account of the way in which the commands respectively, under Custer, himself and Benteen, started into action:—

"The regiment left the camp at the mouth of Rosebud River, after passing in review before the department commander, under command of Brevet Major General G. A. Custer, Lieutenant-Colonel, on the afternoon of the 22d of June, and marched up the Rosebud twelve miles and encamped. On the 23d, marched up the Rosebud, passing many old Indian camps, and following a very large lodge-pole trail, but not fresh, making thirty-three miles. On the 24th, the march was continued up the Rosebud, the trail and signs freshening with every mile, until we had made twenty-eight miles, and we then encamped and waited for information from the scouts. At 9: 25 PM Custer called the officers together and informed us that, beyond a doubt, the village was in the valley of the Little Big Horn, and that to reach it it was necessary to cross the divide between the Rose bud and Little Big Horn, and that it would be impossible to do so in the daytime without discovering our march to the Indian; that we would prepare to move at eleven PM This was done the line of march turning from the Rosebud to the right, one of its branches, which headed near the summit at the divide

"About two PM of the 25th, the scouts told him that he could not cross the divide before daylight. We then made coffee and rested three hours, at the expiration of which time the march was resumed, the divide crossed, and about eight AM, the com mand was in the valley of one of the branches of the Little Big Horn. By this time the Indians had been seen, and it was Cer tain that we could not surprise them, and it was determined to move at once to the attack.

"Previous to this no division of the regiment had been made] since the order was issued on the Yellowstone annulling wingj and battalion organizations. General Custer informed me he would assign commands on the march. I was ordered by Lieut W. W. Cook, adjutant, to assume command of Companies M, A, and G, Capt. Benteen of Companies H, D, and K, Custer raj taining C, E, F, I and L under his immediate command, and Company B, Capt. McDougall, in rear of the pack train. I assumed command of the companies assigned to me, and without any definite orders moved forward with the rest of the colum and well to its left. I saw Benteen moving further to the left, and as they passed he told me he had orders to move well to the left and sweep everything before him. I did not see him again until about half-past two PM The command moved down the creek toward the Little Big Horn Valley, Custer, and five companies, on the right bank, myself and three companies on the left bank, and Benteen further to the left and out of sight."

It appears to have been about the middle of the forenoon when: Custer thus subdivided his column. Reno goes on to say that at half-past twelve Lieut. Cook, Custer's adjutant, came to him,told him that the village was only two miles away, and ordered him to: move forward rapidly and charge it. Other evidence likewise shows that this order was given about that time, and that Reno was urged not to let up on the Indians. The Indian village, consisting of camps of Cheyennes, Ogallalas, Minneconjous and Uncpapas, was nearly three miles long. Reno crossed the Little

Big Horn, formed his first line just south of the crossing and charged, He says :—

"I deployed, and, with the Ree scouts at my left charged down the valley with great ease for about two and a half miles." Reno, instead of holding the ground thus gained, retreated, being hard pressed. He made a temporary stand in a bunch of timber, but finally retreated back over the valley, and across the Little Big Horn and up the bluffs, on the summit of which he intrenched himself late in the afternoon.

Custer's march to the ford, where he attempted to cross the Little Big Horn and attack the Indians in their rear, was much longer than Reno's march, consequently Custer's assault was not made until after Reno's. Custer's intention was to sandwich, as it were, the main body of the Indians between Reno's and his own forces. He hoped by thus pressing them on two sides—Reno constantly fighting them and he himself constantly fighting them—to disconcert them an crush them at last. His plan is thus seen to have been that of a general. It relieves him from the aspersion of rashness. It must, in this connection, be remembered that Custer had fought Indians many times and had never been beaten by them, although on several occasions he had encountered more than three times the number of his own troops. He trusted in this instance to the fealty of his own officers, the bravery of his soldiers and his own genius to overcome the mere weight of numbers, as he had so often done before.

"Did you know the Long Haired Chief? I asked Sitting "No."

"What! Had you never seen him?" "No. Many of the chiefs knew him." "What do they think of him?" "He was a great warrior."

"Was he brave?"

"He was a mighty chief."

:Now, tell me. Here is something that I wish to know. Big lies are told about the fight in which the Long Haired Chief was killed. He was my friend. No one has come back to tell the truth about him, or about that fight. You were there; you know. Your chiefs know. I want to hear something that forked tongues do not tell—the truth."

"It is well."

Here I drew forth a map of the battle-field and spread it out across Sitting Bull's knees and explained to him the names and situations as represented on it, and he smiled.

"We thought we were whipped," he said.

"Ah! Did you think the soldiers were too many for you?"

"Not at first; but by-and-by,yes. Afterwards, no."

"Tell me about the battle. Where was the Indian camp first attacked?"

"Here" (pointing to Reno's crossing on the map).

"About what time in the day was that?"

"It was some two hours past the time when the sun is in the centre of the sky."

"What white chief was it who came over there against your warriors?"

"The Long Hair."

"Are you sure?"

"The Long Hair commanded."

"But you did not see him?"

"I have said that I never saw him."

"Did any of the chiefs see him?"

"Not here, but there," pointing to the place where Custer charged and was repulsed, on the north bank to the Little Big Horn.

"Why do you think it was the Long Hair who crossed first and charged you here at the right side of the map?" "A chief leads his warriors."

"Was there a good fight here, on the right side of the map? Explain it to me?"

"It was so," said Sitting Bull, raising his hands. "I was lying in my lodge. Some young men ran into me and said: ' The Long Hair is in the camp. Get up. They are firing in the camp.' I said, all right, and jumped up and stepped out of my lodge."

"Where was your lodge." "Here, with my people," answered Sitting Bull, pointing to the group of Uncpapa lodges, designated as "abandoned lodges "on the map.

"So the first attack was made, then, on the right side of the map, and upon the lodges of the Uncpapas?" "Yes."

"Here the lodges are said to have been deserted?" "The old men, the squaws, and the children were hurried away."

"Toward the other end of the camp?"

"Yes. Some of the Minneconjou women and children also left their lodges when the attack began." "Did you retreat at first?" "Do you mean the warriors?" "Yes, the fighting men."

"Oh, we fell back, but it was not what warriors call a retreat; it was to gain time. It was the Long Hair who retreated. My people fought him here in the brush (designating the timber behind which the Indians pressed Reno) and he fell back across here (placing his finger on the line of Reno's retreat to the northern bluffs)

"So you think that was the Long Hair whom your people fought in that timber and who fell back afterwards to those heights?"

"Of course."

"What occurred afterward? Was there any heavy fighting after the retreat of the soldiers to the bluffs?" "Not then; not there." "Where, then?"

"Why, down here; "and Sitting Bull indicated with his finger the place where Custer approached and touched the river. "That," said he, "was where the big fight was fought a little later. After the Long Hair was driven back to the bluffs he took this road (tracing with his finger the line of Custer's march on the map), and went down to see if he could not beat us there." "

[Here the reader should pause to discern the extent of Sitting Bull's error, and to anticipate what will presently appear to be Reno's misconception or mistake. Sitting Bull, not identifying

Reno in the whole of this engagement, makes it seem that it was Custer who attacked, when Reno attacked in the first place, and afterward moved down to resume the assault from a new position] "When the fight commenced here," I asked, pointing to the spot where Custer advanced behind the Little Big Horn, "what happened?"

"Hell!"

"You mean, I suppose, a fierce battle?" "I mean a thousand devils."

"The village was by this time thoroughly aroused?"

"The squaws were like flying birds; the bullets were like humming bees."

"You say that when the first attack was made off here on the right of the map, the old men and squaws and children ran down the valley toward the left. What did they do when this second attack came from up here toward the left?"

"They ran back again to the right, here and there," answered Sitting Bull, placing his swarthy fingers on the words "Abandoned Lodges."

"And where did the warriors run?"

"They ran to the fight—the big fight."

"So that in the afternoon, after the first fight, on the right hand side of the map, was over, and after the big fight on the left hand side began, you say the squaws and children all re -turned to the right hand side, and that the warriors, the fighting men of all the Indian camps, ran to the place where the big fight was going on?"

"Yes."

"Why was that? Were not some of the warriors left in front of these intrenchments on the bluffs, near the right side of the map? Did not you think it necessary,—did not your war chiefs think it necessary,—to keep some of your young men there to fight the troops who had retreated to these intrenchments?"

"No."

"Why?"

"You have forgotten." "How?"

"You forget that only a few soldiers were left by the Long Hair on those bluffs. He took the main body of his soldiers with him to make the big fight down here on the left."

"So there were no soldiers to make a fight left in the in-trenchments on the right hand bluff?"

"I have spoken. It is enough. The squaws could deal with "them. There were none but squaws and pappooses in front of them that afternoon."

This startling assertion of Sitting Bull involves the most terrible charge which has been brought against Reno. It amounts to an assertion, that Reno, having made his assault, been beaten and retreated, stayed thereon the bluffs without renewing the attack for which Gen. Custer, who had by this time come down with his horsemen on the rear of the Sioux camp from the north, vainly awaited—how hopelessly!

"Well, then," I inquired of Sitting Bull, "did the cavalry, who came down and made the big fight, fight?"

Again Sitting Bull smiled.

"They fought. Many young men are missing from our lodges. But is there an American squaw who has her husband left? Were there any Americans left to tell the story of that day?"

"No" "How did they come on to the attack?"

"I have heard that there are trees which tremble.

"Do you mean the trees with trembling leaves?"

"Yes."

"They call them in some parts of the Western country Quaking Asps; in the eastern part of the country they call them Silver Aspens."

"Hah? A great white chief, whom I met once, spoke these words, ' Silver Aspens,' trees that shake; these were the Long Hair's soldiers."

"You do not mean that they trembled before your people because they were afraid?"

"They were brave men. They were tired. They were too tired."

"How did they act? How did they behave themselves?" At this Sitting Bull again arose. I also arose from my seat, as did the other persons in the room, except the stenographer

"Your people," said Sitting Bull, extending his right hand, "were killed. I tell no lies about dead men. These men who came with the Long Hair were as good men as ever fought. When they rode up their horses were tired and they were tired. When they got off from their horses they could not stand firmly on their feet, They swayed to and fro—so my young" men have told me—like the limbs of cypresses in a great wind. Some of them staggered under the weight of their guns. But they begun to fight at once; but by this time, as I have said, our camps were aroused, and there were plenty of warriors to meet them. The;, fired with needle guns. We replied with magazine guns—repeating rifles. It was so (and here Sitting Bull illustrated by patting his palms together with the rapidity of a fusillade). Our young men rained lead across the river and drove the white braves back."

"And then?"

"And then they rushed across themselves." "And then?"

"And then they found that they had a good deal to do."

"Was there at that time some doubt about the issue of the battle, whether you would whip the Long Hair or not?"

"There was so much doubt about it that I started down there (here again, pointing to the map) to tell the squaws to pack up the lodges and get ready to move away."

"You were on that expedition, then, after the big fight had fairly begun?"

"Yes."

"You did not personally witness the rest of the big fight? You were not engaged in it?"

"No; I have heard of it from the warriors."

When the great crowds of your young men crossed the river in front of the Long Hair, what did they do? Did they attempt to assault him directly in his front?"

"At first they did, but afterward they found it better to try and get around him. They formed themselves on all sides of him, except just at his back."

"How long did it take them to put themselves around his flanks?"

"As long as it takes the sun to travel from here to here "(indicating some marks upon his arm, with which, apparently, he is used to gauge the progress of the shadow of his lodge across his arm, and probably meaning half an hour. "The trouble was with the soldiers," he continued; "they were so exhausted, and their horses bothered them so much, that they could not take good aim. Some of their horses broke away from them and left them to stand and drop and die. When the Long Hair, the General, found that he was so outnumbered and threatened on his flanks, he took the best course he could have taken. The bugle blew. It was an order to fall back. All the men fell back fighting and dropping. They could not fire fast enough, though. But from our side it was so," said Sitting Bull, and here he clapped his hands rapidly, twice a second, to express with what quickness and continuance the balls flew from the Henry and Winchester rifles wielded by the Indians. "They could not stand up under such a fire," he added.

"Were any military tactics shown? Did the Long Haired Chief make any disposition of his soldiers, or did it seem as though they retreated altogether, helter-skelter, fighting for their lives?"

"They kept in pretty good order. Some great chief must have commanded them all the while. They would fall back across a *coulie*, and make a fresh stand beyond, on higher ground. The map is pretty nearly right. It shows where the white men stopped and fought before they were all killed. I think that is right— down there to the left, just above the Little Big Horn. There was one party driven out there, away from the rest, and there a great many men were killed. The places marked on the map are pretty nearly the places where all were killed."

"Did the whole command keep on fighting until the last?"

"Every man, so far as my people could see. There were no cowards on either side."

I inquired of Sitting Bull: "How long did this big fight continue?"

"The sun was there," he answered, pointing to within two hours of from the western horizon.

"This big fight, then, extended through three hours?"

"Through most of the going forward of the sun."

"Where was the Long Hair the most of the time?"

"I have talked with my people; I cannot find one who saw the Long Hair until just before he died. He did not wear his hair long as he used to wear it. His hair was like yours," said Sitting Bull, playfully touching my forehead with his fingers. "It was short, but it was of the color of the grass when the frost comes."

' Did you hear from your people how he died? Did he die on horseback" "No; none of them died on horseback." "All were dismounted?" "Yes."

"And Custer, the Long Hair?"

"Well, I have understood that there were a great many brave men in that fight, and that from time to time, while it was going on, they were shot down like pigs. They could not help themselves. One by one the officers fell.

Any way it was said that up there where the last fight took place, where the last stand was made, the Long Hair stood like a sheaf of corn with all the ears fallen around him."

"Not wounded?"

"No."

"How many stood by him?" "A few."

"When did he fall?"

"He killed a man when he fell. He laughed."

"You mean he cried out?"

"No, he laughed; he had fired his last shot.

"From a carbine?"

"No, a pistol."

"Did he stand up after he first fell?"

"He rose up on his hands and tried another shot, but his pistol would not go off,"

"Was any one else standing up when he fell down?"

"One man was kneeling, that was all. But he died before the Long Hair. All this was far up on the bluffs, far away from the Sioux encampment. I did not see it. It was told to me. But it is true."

"The Long Hair was not scalped?'

"No; my people did not want his scalp."

"Why?"

"I have said he was a great chief."

"Did you at any time," I persisted, "during the progress of the fight, believe that your people would get the worst of it?"

"At one time, as I have told you, I started down to tell the squaws to strike the lodges. I was then on my way up to the right end of the camp, where the first attack was made upon us But before I reached that end of the camp, where the Minnecon jou and Uncpapa squaws and children were, and where some of-the other squaws—Cheyennes and Ogallalas—had gone, T was overtaken by one of the young warriors, who had just come from the fight. He called out to me. He said: ' No use to leave camp; every white man is killed.' So I stopped and went no further. I turned back, and by-and-by I met the warriors returning."

"But in the meantime," I asked," were there no warriors occupied up here at the right end of the camp? Was nobody left, except the squaws and the children and the old men, to take care of that end of the camp? Was nobody ready to defend it against the soldiers in those intrenchments up there?"

Oh," replied Sitting Bull again, "there was no need to waste warriors in that direction. There were only a few soldiers in those intrenchments, and we knew they wouldn't dare to come out."

This finished the interview, and with a few more How! Hows', the wily chieftain withdrew.

THE SERGEANT'S
PRIVATE MAD HOUSE

STEPHEN CRANE

The moonlight was almost steady blue flame and all this radiance was lavished out upon a still lifeless wilderness of stunted trees and cactus plants. The shadows lay upon the ground, pools of black and sharply outlined, resembling substances, fabrics, and not shadows at all. From afar came the sound of the sea coughing among the hollows in the coral rock.

The land was very empty; one could easily imagine that Cuba was a simple vast solitude; one could wonder at the moon taking all the trouble of this splendid illumination. There was no wind; nothing seemed to live.

But in a particular large group of shadows lay an outpost of some forty United States marines. If it had been possible to approach them from any direction without encountering one of their sentries, one could have gone stumbling among sleeping men and men who sat waiting, their blankets tented over their heads; one would have been in among them before one's mind could have decided whether they were men or devils. If a marine moved, he took the care and the time of one who walks across a death-chamber. The lieutenant in command reached for his watch and the nickel chain gave forth the faintest tinkling sound. He could see the glistening five or six pairs of eyes that slowly turned to regard him. His sergeant lay near him and he bent his face down to whisper. "Who's on post behind the big cactus plant? "

"Dryden," rejoined the sergeant just over his breath.

After a pause the lieutenant murmured: "He's got too many nerves. I shouldn't have put him there." The sergeant asked if he should crawl down and look into affairs at Dryden's post. The young officer nodded assent and the sergeant, softly cocking his rifle, went away on his hands and knees. The lieutenant with his back to a dwarf tree, sat watching the sergeant's progress for the few moments that he could see him moving from one shadow to another. Afterward, the officer waited to hear Dryden's quick but low-voiced challenge, but time passed and no sound came from the direction of the post behind the cactus bush.

The sergeant, as he came nearer and nearer to this cactus bush—a number of peculiarly dignified columns throwing shadows of inky darkness-had slowed his pace, for he did not wish to trifle with the feelings of the sentry, and he was expecting the stern hail and was ready with the immediate answer which, turns away wrath. He was not made anxious by the fact that he could not yet see Dryden, for he knew that the man would be hidden in a way practised by sentry marines since the time when two men had been killed by a disease of excessive confidence on picket. Indeed, as the sergeant went still nearer, he became more and more angry. Dryden was evidently a most proper sentry.

Finally he arrived at a point where he could see Dryden seated in the shadow, staring into the bushes ahead of him, his rifle ready on his knee. The sergeant in his rage longed for the peaceful precincts of the Washington Marine Barracks where there would have been no situation to prevent the most complete non-commissioned oratory. He felt indecent in his capacity of a man able to creep up to the back of a G Company member on guard duty. Never mind; in the morning back at camp—

But, suddenly, he felt afraid. There was something wrong with Dryden. He remembered old tales of comrades creeping out to find a picket seated against a tree perhaps, upright enough but stone dead. The sergeant paused and gave the inscrutable back of the sentry a long stare. Dubious he again moved forward. At three paces, he hissed like a little snake. Dryden did not show a sign of hearing.

At last, the sergeant was in a position from which he was able to reach out and touch Dryden on the arm. Whereupon was turned to him the face of a man livid with mad fright. The sergeant grabbed him by the wrist and with discreet fury shook him. "Here! Pull yourself together! "

Dryden paid no heed but turned his wild face from the newcomer to the ground in front. Don't you see 'em, sergeant? Don't you see 'em? "

"Where? "whispered the sergeant.

"Ahead, and a little on the right flank. A reg'lar skirmish line. Don't you see 'em?"

"Naw," whispered the sergeant. Dryden began to shake. He began moving one hand from his head to his knee and from his knee to his head rapidly, in away that is without explanation. "I don't dare fire," he wept. "If I do they'll see me, and oh, how they'll pepper me! "

The sergeant lying on his belly, understood one thing. Dryden had gone mad. Dryden was the March Hare. The old man gulped down his uproarious emotions as well as he was able and used the most simple device. "Go," he said, "and tell the lieutenant while I cover your post for you."

"No! They'd see me! They'd see me! And then they'd pepper me! O, how they'd pepper me!"

The sergeant was face to face with the biggest situation of his life. In the first place he knew that at night a large or small force of Spanish guerillas was never more than easy rifle range from any marine outpost, both sides maintaining a secrecy as absolute as possible in regard to their real position and strength. Everything was on a watch-spring foundation. A loud word might be paid for by a night-attack which would involve five hundred men who needed their earned sleep, not to speak of some of them who would need their lives. The slip of a foot and the rolling of a pint of gravel might go from consequence to consequence until various crews went to general quarters on their ships in the harbour, their batteries booming as the swift search-light flashes tore through the foliage. Men would get killed—notably the sergeant and Dryden—and outposts would be cut off and the whole night would be one pitiless turmoil. And so Sergeant George

H. Peasley began to run his private madhouse behind the cactus-bush.

"Dryden," said the sergeant, "you do as I tell you and go tell the lieutenant."

"I don't dare move," shivered the man. "They'll see me if I move. They'll see me. They're almost up now. Let's hide-"

"Well, then you stay here a moment and I'll go and-"

Dryden turned upon him a look so tigerish that the old man felt his hair move. "Don't you stir," he hissed. "You want to give me away. You want them to see me. Don't you stir." The sergeant decided not to stir.

He became aware of the slow wheeling of eternity, its majestic incomprehensibility of movement. Seconds, minutes, were quaint little things, tangible as toys, and there were billions of them, all alike. "Dryden," he whispered at the end of a century in which, curiously, he had never joined the marine corps at all but had taken to another walk of life and prospered greatly in it. "Dryden, this is all foolishness." He thought of the expedient of smashing the man over the head with his rifle, but Dryden was so superna-turally alert that there surely would issue some small scuffle and there could be not even the fraction of a scuffle. The sergeant relapsed into the contemplation of another century.

His patient had one fine virtue. He was in such terror of the phantom skirmish line that his voice never went above a whisper, whereas his delusion might have expressed itself in hyena yells and shots from his rifle. The sergeant, shuddering, had visions of how it might have been—the mad private leaping into the air and howling and shooting at his friends and making them the centre of the enemy's eager attention. This, to his mind, would have been conventional conduct for a maniac. The trembling victim of an idea was somewhat puzzling. The sergeant decided that from time to time he would reason with his patient. "Look here, Dryden, you don't see any real Spaniards. You've been drinking or—something. Now—"

But Dryden only glared him into silence. Dryden was inspired with such a profound contempt of him that it was become hatred. "Don't you stir! "And it was clear that if the sergeant did stir, the mad private would introduce calamity. "Now," said Peasley to himself, "if those guerillas *should* take a crack at us to-night, they'd find a lunatic asylum right in the front and it would be astonishing."

The silence of the night was broken by the quick low voice of a sentry to the left some distance. The breathless stillness brought an effect to the words as if they had been spoken in one's ear.

"Halt—who's there—halt or I'll fire! "Bang!

At the moment of sudden attack particularly at night, it is improbable that a man registers much detail of either thought or action. He may afterward say: "I was here." He may say: "I was there." "I did this." "I did that." But there remains a great incoherency because of the tumultuous thought which seethes through the head. "Is this defeat? "At night in a wilderness and against skilful foes half-seen, one does not trouble to ask if it is also Death. Defeat is Death, then, save for the miraculous. But the exaggerating magnifying first thought subsides in the ordered mind of the soldier and he knows, soon, what he is doing and how much of it. The sergeant's immediate impulse had been to squeeze close to the ground and listen—listen—above all else, listen. But the next moment he grabbed his private asylum by the scruff of its neck, jerked it to its feet and started to retreat upon the main outpost. To the left, rifle-flashes were bursting from the shadows. To the rear, the lieutenant was giving 10 some hoarse order or admonition. Through the air swept some Spanish bullets, very high, as if they had been fired at a man in a tree. The private asylum came on so hastily that the sergeant found he could remove his grip, and soon they were in the midst of the men of the outpost. Here there was no occasion for enlightening the lieutenant. In the first place such surprises required statement, question and answer. It is impossible to get a grossly original and fantastic idea through a man's head in less than one minute of rapid talk, and the sergeant knew the lieutenant could not spare the minute. He himself had no minutes to devote to anything but the business of the outpost. And the madman disappeared from his pen and he forgot about him.

It was a long night and the little fight was as long as the night. It was a heart-breaking work. The forty marines lay in an irregular oval. From all sides, the Mauser bullets sang low and hard. Their occupation was to prevent a rush, and to this end they potted carefully at the flash of a Mauser—save when they got excited for a moment, in which case their magazines rattled like a great Waterbury watch. Then they settled again to a systematic potting.

The enemy were not of the regular Spanish forces. They were of a corps of guerillas, native-born Cubans, who preferred the flag of Spain. They were all men who knew the craft of the woods and were all recruited from the district. They fought more like red Indians than any people but the red Indians themselves. Each seemed to possess an individuality, a fighting individuality, which is only found in the highest order of irregular soldiers. Personally they were as distinct as possible, but through equality of knowledge and experience, they arrived at concert of action. So long as they operated in the wilderness, they were formidable troops. It mattered little whether it was daylight or dark; they were mainly invisible. They had schooled from the Cubans insurgent to Spain. As the Cubans fought the Spanish troops, so would these particular Spanish troops fight the Americans. It was wisdom.

The marines thoroughly understood the game. They must lie close and fight until daylight when the guerillas promptly would go away. They had withstood other nights of this kind, and now their principal emotion was probably a sort of frantic annoyance.

Back at the main camp, whenever the roaring volleys lulled, the men in the trenches could hear their comrades of the outpost, and the guerillas pattering away interminably. The moonlight faded and left an equal darkness upon the wilderness. A man could barely see the comrade at his side. Sometimes guerillas crept so close that the flame from their rifles seemed to scorch the faces of the marines, and the reports sounded as if from two or three inches of their very noses. If a pause came, one could hear the guerillas gabbling to each other in a kind of drunken delirium. The lieutenant was praying that the ammunition would last. Everybody was praying for daybreak.

A black hour came finally, when the men were not fit to have their troubles increased. The enemy made a wild attack on one portion of the oval, which was held by about fifteen men. The remainder of the force was busy enough, and the fifteen were naturally left to their devices. Amid the whirl of it, a loud voice suddenly broke out in song:

"When shepherds guard their flocks by night, All seated on the ground, An angel of the Lord came *down* And glory shone around."

"Who the hell is that? "demanded the lieutenant from a throat full of smoke. There was almost a full stop of the firing. The Americans were somewhat puzzled. Practical ones muttered that the fool should have a bayonet-hilt shoved down his throat. Others felt a thrill at the strangeness of the thing. Perhaps it was a sign!

"The minstrel boy to the war has gone, In the ranks of death you'll find him, His father's sword he has girded on And his wild harp slung behind him."

This croak was as lugubrious as a coffin. "Who is it? Who is it? "snapped the lieutenant. "Stop him, somebody."

"It's Dryden, sir," said old Sergeant Peasley, as he felt around in the darkness for his madhouse. "I can't find him—yet."

"Please, O, please, O, do not let me fall; You're—gurgh-ugh——"

The sergeant had pounced upon him.

This singing had had an effect upon the Spaniards. At first they had fired frenziedly at the voice, but they soon ceased, perhaps from sheer amazement. Both sides took a spell of meditation.

The sergeant was having some difficulty with his charge. "Here, you, grab 'im. Take 'im by the throat. Be quiet, you devil."

One of the fifteen men, who had been hard-pressed, called out, "We've only got about one clip a-piece, Lieutenant. If they come again—"

The lieutenant crawled to and fro among his men, taking clips of cartridges from those who had many. He came upon the sergeant and his madhouse. He felt Dryden's belt and found it simply stuffed with ammunition. He examined Dryden's rifle and found in it a full clip. The madhouse had not fired a shot. The lieutenant distributed these valuable prizes among the fifteen men. As the men gratefully took them, one said: "If they had come again hard enough, they would have had us, sir,—maybe."

But the Spaniards did not come again. At the first indication of daybreak, they fired their customary good-bye volley. The marines lay tight while the slow dawn crept over the land. Finally the lieutenant arose among them, and he was a bewildered man, but very angry. "Now where is that idiot, Sergeant?"

"Here he is, sir," said the old man cheerfully. He was seated on the ground beside the recumbent Dryden who, with an innocent smile on his face, was sound asleep.

"Wake him up," said the lieutenant briefly.

The sergeant shook the sleeper. "Here, Minstrel Boy, turn out. The lieutenant wants you."

Dryden climbed' to his feet and saluted the officer with a dazed and childish air. "Yes, sir."

The lieutenant was obviously having difficulty in governing his feelings, but he managed to say with calmness, "You seem to be fond of singing, Dryden? Sergeant, see if he has any whisky on him."

"Sir? "said the madhouse stupefied. "Singing—fond of singing? "

Here the sergeant interposed gently, and he and the lieutenant held palaver apart from the others. The marines, hitching more comfortably their almost empty belts, spoke with grins of the madhouse. "Well, the Minstrel Boy made 'em clear out. They couldn't stand it. But—I wouldn't want to be in his boots. He'll see fireworks when the old man interviews him on the uses of grand opera in modern warfare. How do you think he managed to smuggle a bottle along without us finding it out? "

When the weary outpost was relieved and marched back to camp, the men could not rest until they had told a tale of the voice in the wilderness. In the meantime the sergeant took Dryden aboard a ship, and to those who took charge of the man, he defined him as "the most useful—crazy man in the service of the United States."

WITH THE FIFTH CORPS
IN CUBA

FREDERIC REMINGTON

I approach this subject of the Santiago campaign with awe, since the ablest correspondents in the country were all there, and they wore out lead-pencils most industriously. I know I cannot add to the facts, but I remember my own emotions, which were numerous, interesting, and, on the whole, not pleasant. I am as yet unable to decide whether sleeping in a mud-puddle, the confinement of a troop-ship, or being shot at is the worst. They are all irritating, and when done on an empty stomach, with the object of improving one's mind, they are extravagantly expensive. However, they satisfied a life of longing to see men do the greatest thing which men are called on to do.

The creation of things by men in time of peace is of every consequence, but it does not bring forth the tumultuous energy which accompanies the destruction of things by men in war. He who has not seen war only half comprehends the possibilities of his race. Having thought of this thing before, I got a correspondent's pass, and ensconced myself with General Shafter's army at Tampa.

When Hobson put the cork in Cervera's bottle, it became necessary to send the troops at once, and then came the first shock of the war to me. It was in the form of an order to dismount two squadrons of each regiment of cavalry and send them on foot. This misuse of cavalry was compelled by the national necessities, for there was not at that time sufficient volunteer infantry equipped and in readiness for the field. It is without doubt that our ten regiments of cavalry are the most perfect things of all Uncle Sam's public institutions. More good honest work has gone into them, more enthusiasm, more intelligence, and they have shown more results, not excepting the new navy or the postal system.

The fires of hatred burned within me. I was nearly overcome by a desire to "go off the reservation." I wanted to damn some official, or all officialism, or so much thereof as might be necessary. I knew that the cavalry officers were to a man disgusted, and thought they had been misused and abused. They recognized it as a blow at their arm, a jealous, wicked, and ignorant stab. Besides, the interest of my own art required a cavalry charge.

General Miles appeared at Tampa about that time, and I edged around towards him, and threw out my "point." It is necessary to attack General Miles with great care and understanding, if one expects any success. "General, I wonder who is responsible for this order dismounting the cavalry?" I ventured.

I think the "old man" could almost see me coming, for he looked up from the reading of a note, and in a quiet manner, which is habitual with him, said, "Why, don't they want to go?" and he had me flat on the ground.

"Oh yes, of course! They are crazy to go! They would go if they had to walk on their hands!" I said, and departed. A soldier who did not want to go to Cuba would be like a fire which would not burn—useless entirely. So no one got cursed for that business; but it is a pity that our nation finds it necessary to send cavalry to war on foot. It would be no worse if some day it should conclude to mount "bluejackets" for cavalry purposes, though doubtless the "bluejackets" would "sit tight." But where is the use of specialization? One might as well ask the nurse-girl to curry the family horse.

So the transports gathered to Port Tampa, and the troops got on board, and the correspondents sallied down to their quarters, and then came a wait. A Spanish warship had loomed across the night of some watch-on-deck down off the Cuban coast. Telegrams flew from Washington to "stop where you are." The mules and the correspondents were unloaded, and the whole enterprise waited.

Here I might mention a series of events which were amusing. The exigencies of the service left many young officers behind, and these all wanted, very naturally, to go to Cuba and get properly shot, as all good soldiers should. They used their influence with the general officers in command; they begged, they implored, and they explained deviously and ingeniously why the expedition needed their particular services to insure success. The old generals, who appreciated the proper spirit which underlay this enthusiasm, smiled grimly as they turned "the young scamps" down. I used to laugh to myself when I overheard these interviews, for one could think of nothing so much as the school-boy days, when he used to beg off going to school for all sorts of reasons but the real one, which was a ball-game or a little shooting-trip.

Presently the officials got the Spanish warship off their nerves, and the transports sailed. Now it is so arranged in the world that I hate a ship in a compound, triple-expansion, forced-draught way. Barring the disgrace, give me "ten days on the island." Do anything to me, but do not have me entered on the list of a ship. It does not matter if I am to be the lordly proprietor of the finest yacht afloat, make me a feather in a sick chicken's tail on shore, and I will thank you. So it came about that I did an unusual amount of real suffering in consequence of living on the *Segurança* during the long voyage to Cuba. I used to sit out on the afterdeck and wonder why, at my time of life, I could not so arrange that I could keep off ships. I used to consider seriously if it would not be a good thing to jump overboard and let the leopard-sharks eat me, and have done with a miserable existence which I did not seem to be able to control.

When the first landing was made, General Shatter kept all the correspondents and the foreign military attachés in his closed fist, and we all hated him mightily. We shall probably forgive him, but it will take some time. He did allow us to go ashore and see the famous interview which he and Admiral Sampson held with Garcia, and for the first time to behold the long lines of ragged Cuban patriots, and I was convinced that it was no mean or common impulse which kept up the determination of these ragged, hungry souls.

Then on the morning of the landing at Daiquiri the soldiers put on their blanket rolls, the navy boats and launches lay by the transports, and the light ships of Sampson's fleet ran slowly into the little bay and "turned everything loose" on the quiet, palm-thatched village. A few fires were burning in the town, but otherwise it was quiet. After severely pounding the coast, the launches towed in the long lines of boats deep laden with soldiery, and the correspondents and foreigners saw them go into the overhanging smoke. We held our breath. We expected a most desperate fight for the landing. After a time the smoke rolled away, and our people were on the beach, and not long after some men climbed the steep hill on which stood a block-house, and we saw presently the Stars and Stripes break from the flag-staff. "They are Chinamen!" said a distinguished foreign soldier; and he went to the other side of the boat, and sat heavily down to his reading of our artillery drill regulations.

We watched the horses and mules being thrown overboard, we saw the last soldiers going ashore, and we bothered General Shafter's aid, the gallant Miley, until he put us all on shore in order to abate the awful nuisance of our presence.

No one had any transportation in the campaign, not even colonels of regiments, except their good strong backs. It was for every man to personally carry all his own hotel accommodations; so we correspondents laid out our possessions on the deck, and for the third time sorted out what little we could take. I weighed a silver pocket-flask for some time, undecided as to the possibility of carriage. It is now in the woods of Cuba, or in the ragged pack of some Cuban soldier. We had finally three days of crackers, coffee, and pork in our haversacks, our canteens, rubber ponchos, cameras, and six-shooter—or practically what a soldier has.

I moved out with the Sixth Cavalry a mile or so, and as it was late afternoon, we were ordered to bivouac. I sat on a hill, and down in the road below saw the long lines of troops pressing up the valley towards Siboney. When our troops got on the sand beach, each old soldier adjusted his roll, shouldered his rifle, and started for Santiago, apparently by individual intuition.

The troops started, and kept marching just as fast as they could. They ran the Spaniards out of Siboney, and the cavalry brigade regularly marched down their retreating columns at Las Guasimas, fought them up a defile, out-flanked, and sent them flying into Santiago. I think our army would never have stopped until it cracked into the doomed city in column formation, if Shafter had not discovered this unlooked-for enterprise, and sent his personal aide on a fast horse with positive orders to halt until the "cracker-line" could be fixed up behind them.

In the morning I sat on the hill, and still along the road swung the hard-marching columns. The scales dropped from my eyes. I could feel the impulse, and still the Sixth was held by orders. I put on my "little hotel equipment," bade my friends good-bye, and "hit the road." The sides of it were blue with cast-off uniforms. Coats and overcoats were strewn about, while the gray blankets lay in the camps just where the soldiers had gotten up from them after the night's rest. This I knew would happen. Men will not carry what they can get along without unless they are made to; and it is a bad thing to "make" American soldiers, because they know what is good for them better than any one who sits in a roller-chair. In the tropics mid-day marching under heavy kits kills more men than damp sleeping at night. I used to think the biggest thing in Shaffer's army was my pack.

It was all so strange, this lonely tropic forest, and so hot. I fell in with a little bunch of headquarters cavalry orderlies, some with headquarters horses, and one with a mule dragging two wheels, which I cannot call a cart, on which General Young's stuff was tied. We met Cubans loitering along, their ponies loaded with abandoned soldier-clothes. Staff-officers on horseback came back and said that there had been a fight on beyond, and that Colonel Wood was killed and young Fish shot dead—that the Rough Riders were all done to pieces. There would be more fighting, and we pushed forward, sweating under the stifling heat of the jungle-choked road. We stopped and cracked cocoanuts to drink the milk. Once, in a sort of savanna, my companions halted and threw cartridges into their carbines. I saw two or three Spanish soldiers on ahead in some hills and brush. We pressed on; but as the Spanish soldiers did not seem to be concerned as to our presence, I allowed they were probably Cubans who had taken clothes from dead Spanish soldiers, and so it turned out. The Cubans seem to know each other by scent, but it bothered the Northern men to make a distinction between Spanish and Cuban, even when shown Spanish prisoners in order that they might recognize their enemy by sight. If a simple Cuban who stole Spanish soldier clothes could only know how nervous it made the trigger fingers of our regulars, he would have died of fright. He created the same feeling that a bear would, and the impulse to "pull up and let go" was so instinctive and sudden with our men that I marvel more mistakes were not made.

At night I lay up beside the road outside of Siboney, and cooked my supper by a soldier fire, and lay down under a mango-tree on my rubber, with my haversack for a pillow. I could hear the shuffling of the marching troops, and see by the light of the fire near the road the white blanket-rolls glint past its flame—tired, sweaty men, mysterious and silent too but for the clank of tin cups and the monotonous shuffle of feet.

In the early morning the field near me was covered with the cook-fires of infantry, which had come in during the night. Presently a battery came dragging up, and was greeted with wild cheers from the infantry, who crowded up to the road. It was a great tribute to the guns; for here in the face of war the various arms realized their interdependence. It is a solace for cavalry to know that there is some good steady infantry in their rear, and it is a vast comfort for infantry to feel that their front and flanks are covered, and both of them like to have the shrapnel travelling their way when they "go in."

At Siboney I saw the first wounded Rough Riders, and heard how they had behaved. From this time people began to know who this army doctor was, this Colonel Wood. Soldiers and residents in the Southwest had known him ten years back. They knew Leonard Ward was a soldier, skin, bones, and brain, who travelled under the disguise of a doctor, and now they know more than this.

Then I met a fellow-correspondent, Mr. John Fox, and we communed deeply. We had not seen this fight of the cavalry brigade, and this was because we were not at the front. We would not let it happen again. We slung our packs and most industriously plodded up the Via del Rey until we got to within hailing distance of the picket posts, and he said: "Now, Frederic, we will stay here. They will pull off no more fights of which we are not a party of the first part." And stay we did. If General Lawton moved ahead, we went up and cultivated Lawton; but if General Chaffee got ahead, we were his friends, and gathered at his mess fire. To be popular with us it was necessary for a general to have command of the advance.

But what satisfying soldiers Lawton and Chaffee are! Both seasoned, professional military types. Lawton, big and long, forceful, and with iron determination. Chaffee, who never dismounts but for a little sleep during the darkest hours of the night, and whose head might have been presented to him by one of William's Norman barons. Such a head! We used to sit around and study that head. It does not belong to the period; it is remote, when the race was young and strong; and it has "warrior" sculptured in every line. It may seem trivial to you, but I must have people "look their part." That so many do not in this age is probably because men are so complicated; but "war is a primitive art," and that is the one objection I had to von Moltke, with his simple, student face. He might have been anything. Chaffee is a soldier.

The troops came pouring up the road, reeking under their packs, dusty, and with their eyes on the ground. Their faces were deeply lined, their beards stubby, but their minds were set on "the front"—"on Santiago." There was a suggestion of remorseless striving in their dogged stepping along, and it came to me that to turn them around would require some enterprise. I thought at the time that the Spanish commander would do well to assume the offensive, and marching down our flank, pierce the centre of the straggling column; but I have since changed my mind, because of the superior fighting ability which our men showed. It must be carefully remembered that, with the exception of three regiments of Shafter's army, and even these were "picked volunteers," the whole command was our regular army—trained men, physically superior to any in the world, as any one will know who understands the requirements of our enlistment as against that of conscript troops; and they were expecting attack, and praying devoutly for it. Besides, at Las Guasimas we got the *moral* on the Spanish.

Then came the "cracker problem." The gallant Cabanais pushed his mules day and night. I thought they would go to pieces under the strain, and I think every "packer" who worked on the Santiago line will never forget it. Too much credit cannot be given fhem. The command was sent into the field without its proper ratio of pack-mules, and I hope the blame of that will come home to some one some day. That was the *direct* and *only* cause of all the privation and delay which became so notable in Shaffer's operations. I cannot imagine a man who would recommend wagons for a tropical country during the rainy season. Such a one should not be censured or reprimanded; he should be spanked with a slipper.

So while the engineers built bridges, and the troops made roads behind them, and until we got *"three days' crackers ahead"* for the whole command, things stopped. The men were on half-rations, were out of tobacco, and it rained, rained, rained. We were very miserable.

Mr. John Fox and I had no cover to keep the rain out, and our determination to stay up in front hindered us from making friends with any one who had. Even the private soldiers had their dog-tents, but we had nothing except our two rubber ponchos. At evening, after we had "bummed" some crackers and coffee from some good-natured officer, we repaired to our neck of woods, and stood gazing at our mushy beds. It was good, soft, soggy mud, and on it, or rather in it, we laid one poncho, and over that we spread the other.

"Say, Frederic, that means my death; I am subject to malaria."

"Exactly so, John. This cold of mine will end in congestion of the lungs, or possibly bronchial consumption. Can you suggest any remedy?"

"The fare to New York," said John, as we turned into our wallow.

At last I had the good fortune to buy a horse from an invalided officer. It seemed great fortune, but it had its drawback. I was ostracized by my fellow-correspondents.

All this time the reconnoissance of the works of Santiago and the outlying post of Caney was in progress. It was rumored that the forward movement would come, and being awakened by the bustle, I got up in the dark, and went gliding around until I managed to steal a good feed of oats for my horse. This is an important truth as showing the demoralization of war. In the pale light I saw a staff-officer who was going to

Caney, and I followed him. We overtook others, and finally came to a hill overlooking the ground which had been fought over so hard during the day. Capron's battery was laying its guns, and back of the battery were staff-officers and correspondents eagerly scanning the country with field-glasses. In the rear of these stood the hardy First Infantry, picturesquely eager and dirty, while behind the hill were the battery horses, out of harm's way.

The battery opened and knocked holes in the stone fort, but the fire did not appear to depress the rifle-pits. Infantry in the jungle below us fired, and were briskly answered from the trenches.

I had lost my canteen and wanted a drink of water, so I slowly rode back to a creek. I was thinking, when along came another correspondent. We discussed things, and thought Caney would easily fall before Lawton's advance, but we had noticed a big movement of our troops towards Santiago, and we decided that we would return to the main road and see which promised best. Sure enough, the road was jammed with horses of Grimes's battery under whip and spur. Around El Poso ranch stood Cubans, and along the road the Rough Riders—Roosevelt's now, for Wood was a brigadier.

The battery took position, and behind it gathered the foreigners, naval and military, with staff-officers and correspondents. It was a picture such as may be seen at a manœuvre. Grimes fired a few shells towards Santiago, and directly came a shrill screaming shrapnel from the Spanish lines. It burst over the Rough Riders, and the manœuvre picture on the hill underwent a lively change. It was thoroughly evident that the Spaniards had the range of everything in the country. They had studied it out. For myself, I fled, dragging my horse up the hill, out of range of Grimes's inviting guns. Some as gallant soldiers and some as daring correspondents as it is my pleasure to know did their legs proud there. The tall form of a staff-major moved in my front in jack-rabbit bounds. Prussian, English, and Japanese, correspondents, artists, all the news, and much high-class art and literature, were flushed, and went straddling up the hill before the first barrel of the Dons. Directly came the warning scream of No. 2, and we dropped and hugged the ground like starfish. Bang! right over us it exploded. I was dividing a small hollow with a distinguished colonel of the staff.

"Is this thing allowed, colonel?"

"Oh yes, indeed!" he said. "I don't think we could stop those shrapnel."

And the next shell went into the battery, killing and doing damage. Following shell were going into the helpless troops down in the road, and Grimes withdrew his battery for this cause. He had been premature. All this time no one's glass could locate the fire of the Spanish guns, and we could see Capron's smoke miles away on our right. Smoky powder belongs with arbalists and stone axes and United States ordnance officers, which things all belong in museums, with other dusty rust.

Then I got far up on the hill, walking over the prostrate bodies of my old friends the Tenth Cavalry, who were hugging the hot ground to get away from the hotter shrapnel. There I met a clubmate from New York, and sundry good foreigners, notably the Prussian (von Goetzen), and that lovely "old British salt" Paget, and the Japanese major, whose name I could never remember. We sat there. I listened to much expert artillery talk, though the talk was not quite so impressive as the practice of that art.

But the heat—let no man ever attempt that after Kipling's "and the heat would make your blooming eyebrows crawl."

This hill was the point of vantage; it overlooked the flat jungle, San Juan hills, Santiago, and Caney, the whole vast country to the mountains which walled in the whole scene. I heard the experts talk, and I love military science, but I slowly thought to myself this is not my art—neither the science of troop movement nor the whole landscape. My art requires me to go down in the road where the human beings are who do these things which science dictates, in the landscape which to me is overshadowed by their presence. I rode slowly, on account of the awful sun. Troops were standing everywhere, lying all about, moving regularly up the jungle road towards Santiago, and I wound my way along with them, saying, "Gangway, please."

War is productive of so many results, things happen so awfully fast, men do such strange things, pictures make themselves at every turn, the emotions are so tremendously strained, that what knowledge I had fled away from my brain, and I was in a trance; and do you know, cheerful reader, I am not going to describe a battle to you.

War, storms at sea, mountains, deserts, pests, and public calamities leave me without words. I simply said, "Gangway" as I wormed my way up the fateful road to Santiago. Fellows I knew out West and up North and down South passed their word to me, and I felt that I was not alone. A shrapnel came shieking down the road, and I got a drink of water and a cracker from Colonel Garlington. The soldiers were lying alongside and the staff-officers were dismounted, also stopping quietly in the shade of the nearest bush. The column of troops was working its way into the battle line.

"I must be going," I said, and I mounted my good old mare—the colonel's horse. It was a tender, hand-raised trotting-horse, which came from Colorado, and Was perfectly mannered. We were in love.

The long columns of men on the road had never seen this condition before. It was their first baby. Oh, a few of the old soldiers had, but it was so long ago that this must have come to them almost as a new sensation. Battles are like other things in nature—no two the same.

I could hear noises such as you can make if you strike quickly with a small walking-stick at a very few green leaves. Some of them were very near and others more faint. They were the Mausers, and out in front through the jungle I could hear what sounded like a Fourth of July morning, when the boys are setting off their crackers. It struck me as new, strange, almost uncanny, because I wanted the roar of battle, which same I never did find. These long-range, smokeless bolts are so far-reaching, and there is so little fuss, that a soldier is. for hours under fire getting into the battle proper, and he has time to think. That is hard when you consider the seriousness of what he is thinking about. The modern soldier must have moral quality; the gorrilla is out of date. This new man may go through a war, be in a dozen battles, and survive a dozen wounds without seeing an enemy. This would be unusual, but easily might happen. All our soldiers of San Juan were for the most part of a day under fire, subject to wounds and death, before they had even a chance to know where the enemy was whom they were opposing. To all appearance they were apathetic, standing or marching through the heat of the jungle. They flattened themselves before the warning scream of the shrapnel, but that is the proper thing to do. Some good-natured fellow led the regimental mascot, which was a fice, or a fox-terrier. Really, the dog of war is a fox-terrier. Stanley took one through Africa. He is in all English regiments, and he is gradually getting into ours. His flag is short, but it sticks up straight on all occasions, and he is a vagabond. Local ties must set lightly on soldiers and fox-terriers.

Then came the light as I passed out of the jungle and forded San Juan River. The clicking in the leaves continued, and the fire-crackers rattled out in front. "Get down, old man; you'll catch one!" said an old alkali friend, and I got down, sitting there with the officers of the cavalry brigade. But promptly some surgeons came along, saying that it was the only safe place, and they began to dig the sand to level it. We, in consequence, moved out into the crackle, and I tied my horse with some others.

"Too bad, old fellow," I thought. "I should have left you behind. Modern rifle fire is rough on horses. They can't lie down. But, you dear thing, you will have to take your chances." And then I looked at the preparation for the field hospital. It was altogether too suggestive. A man came, stooping over, with his arms drawn up, and hands flapping downward at the wrists. That is the way with all people when they are shot through the body, because they want to hold the torso steady, because if they don't it hurts. Then the oncoming troops poured through the hole in the jungle which led to the San Juan River, which was our line of battle, as I supposed. I knew nothing of the plan of battle, and I have an odd conceit that no one else did, but most all the line-officers were schooled men, and they were able to put two and two together mighty fast, and in most instances faster than headquarters. When educated-soldiers are thrown into a battle without understanding, they understand themselves.

As the troops came pouring across the ford they stooped as low as they anatomically could, and their faces were wild with excitement. The older officers stood up as straight as if on parade. They may have done it through pride, or they may have known that it is better to be "drilled clean" than to have a long, ranging wound. It was probably both ideas which stiffened them up so.

Then came the curious old tube drawn by a big mule, and Borrowe with his squad of the Rough Riders. It was the dynamite-gun. The mule was unhooked and turned loose. The gun was trundled up the road and laid for a shot, but the cartridge stuck, and for a moment the cheerful grin left the red face of Borrowe. Only for a moment; for back he came, and he and his men scraped and whittled away at the thing until they got it fixed. The poor old mule lay down with a grunt and slowly died. The fire was now incessant. The bullets came like the rain. The horses lay down one after another as the Mausers found their billets. I tried to take mine to a place of safety, but a sharpshooter potted at me, and I gave it up. There was no place of safety. For a long time our people did not understand these sharp-shooters in their rear, and I heard many men murmur that their own comrades were shooting from behind. It was very demoralizing to us, and on the Spaniards' part a very desperate enterprise to lie deliberately back of our line; but of course, with bullets coming in to the front by the bucketful, no one could stop for the few tailing shots. The Spaniards were hidden in the mango-trees, and had smokeless powder.

Now men came walking or were carried into the temporary hospital in a string. One beautiful boy was brought in by two tough, stringy, hairy old soldiers, his head hanging down behind. His shirt was off, and a big red spot shone brilliantly against his marble-like skin. They laid him tenderly down, and the surgeon stooped over him. His breath came in gasps. The doctor laid his arms across his breast, and shaking his head, turned to a man who held a wounded foot up to him, dumbly imploring aid, as a dog might. It made my nerves jump, looking at that grewsome hospital, sand-covered, with bleeding men, and yet it seemed to have fascinated me; but I gathered myself and stole away. I went down the creek, keeping under the bank, and then out into the "scrub," hunting for our line; but I could not find our line. The bullets cut and clicked around, and a sharp-shooter nearly did for me. The thought came to me, what if I am hit out here in the bush while all alone? I shall never be found. I would go back to the road, where I should be discovered in such case; and I ran so quickly across a space that my sharp-shooting Spanish friend did not see me. After that I stuck to the road. As I passed along it through an open space I saw a half-dozen soldiers sitting under a tree. "Look out—sharp-shooters!" they sang out. "Wheet!" came a Mauser, and it was right next to my ear, and two more. I dropped in the tall guinea-grass, and crawled to the soldiers, and they studied the mango-trees; but we could see nothing. I think that episode cost me my sketch-book. I believe I lost it during the crawl, and our friend the Spaniard shot so well I wouldn't trust him again.

From the vantage of a little bank under a big tree I had my first glimpse of San Juan Hill, and the bullets whistled about. One would "tumble" on a tree or ricochet from the earth, and then they shrieked. Our men out in front were firing, but I could not see them. I had no idea that our people were to assault that hill—I thought at the time such an attempt would be unsuccessful. I could see with my powerful glass the white lines of the Spanish intrenchments. I did not understand how our men could stay out there under that, gruelling, and got back into the safety of a low bank.

A soldier said, while his stricken companions were grunting around him, "Boys, I have got to go one way or the other, pretty damn quick." Directly I heard our line yelling, and even then did not suppose it was an assault.

Then the Mausers came in a continuous whistle. I crawled along to a new place, and finally got sight of the fort, and just then I could distinguish our blue soldiers on the hill-top, and I also noticed that the Mauser bullets rained no more. Then I started after. The country was alive with wounded men—some to die in the dreary jungle, some to get their happy-home draft, but all to be miserable. Only a handful of men got to the top, where they broke out a flag and cheered. "Cheer" is the word for that sound. You have got to hear it once where it means so much, and ever after you will grin when Americans make that noise.

San Juan was taken by infantry and dismounted cavalry of the United States regular army without the aid of artillery. It was the most glorious feat of arms I ever heard of, considering every condition. It was done without grub, without reserves of either ammunition or men, under tropical conditions. It was a storm of intrenched heights, held by veteran troops armed with modern guns, supported by artillery, and no other troops on the earth would have even thought they could take San Juan heights, let alone doing it.

I followed on and up the hill. Our men sat about in little bunches in the pea-green guinea-grass, exhausted. A young officer of the Twenty-fourth, who was very much excited, threw his arms about me, and pointing to twenty-five big negro infantrymen sitting near, said, "That's all—that is all that is left of the Twenty-fourth Infantry," and the tears ran off his mustache.

Farther on another officer sat with his arms around his knees. I-knew him for one of these analytical chaps—a bit of a philosopher—too highly organized—so as to be morose. "I don't know whether I am brave or not. Now there is S—; he don't mind this sort of thing. I think—"

"Oh, blow your philosophy!" I interrupted. "If you were not brave, you would not be here."

The Spanish trenches were full of dead men in the most curious attitudes, while about on the ground lay others, mostly on their backs, and nearly all shot in the head. Their set teeth shone through their parted lips, and they were horrible. The life never runs so high in a man as it does when he is charging on the field of battle; death never seems so still and positive.

Troops were moving over to the right, where there was firing. A battery came up and went into position, but was driven back by rifle fire. Our batteries with their smoky powder could not keep guns manned in the face of the Mausers. Then, with gestures much the same as a woman makes when she is herding chickens, the officers pushed the men over the hill. They went crawling. The Spanish were trying to retake the hill. We were short of ammunition. I threw off my hat and crawled forward to have a look through my glass at the beyond. I could hardly see our troops crouching in the grass beside me, though many officers stood up. The air was absolutely crowded with Spanish bullets. There was a continuous whistle. The shrapnel came screaming over. A ball struck in front of me, and filled my hair and face with sand, some of which I did not get out for days. It jolted my glass and my nerves, and I beat a masterly retreat, crawling rapidly backwards, for a reason which I will let you guess. The small-arms rattled; now and then a wounded man came back and started for the rear, some of them shot in the face, bleeding hideously.

"How goes it?" I asked one.

"Ammunition! ammunition!" said the man, forgetful of his wound.

I helped a man to the field hospital, and got my horse. The lucky mare was untouched. She was one of three animals not hit out of a dozen tied or left at the hospital. One of these was an enormous mule, loaded down with what was probably officers' blanket rolls, which stood sidewise quietly as only a mule can all day, and the last I saw of him he was alive. Two fine officers' chargers lay at his feet, one dead and the other unable to rise, and suffering pathetically. The mule was in such an exposed position that I did not care to unpack him, and Captain Miley would not let any one shoot a horse, for fear of the demoralizing effect of fire in the rear.

A trumpeter brought in a fine officer's horse, which staggered around in a circle. I saw an English sabre on the saddle, and recognized it as Lieutenant Short's, and indeed I knew the horse too. He was the fine thoroughbred which that officer rode in Madison Square military tournament last winter, when drilling the Sixth Cavalry. The trumpeter got the saddle off, and the poor brute staggered around with a bewildered look in his eager eyes, shot in the stifle-joint, I thought; and then he sat down in the creek as a dog would on a hot day. The suffering of animals on a battle-field is most impressive to one who cares for them.

I again started out to the hill, along with a pack-train loaded with ammunition. A mule went down, and bullets and shell were coming over the hill aplenty. The wounded going to the rear cheered the ammunition, and when it was unpacked at the front, the soldiers seized it like gold. They lifted a box in the air and dropped it on one corner, which smashed it open.

"Now we can hold San Juan Hill against them garlics—hey, son!" yelled a happy cavalryman to a doughboy.

"You bet—until we starve to death."

"Starve nothing'—we'll eat them gun-teams."

Well, well, I said, I have no receipt for licking the kind of troops these boys represent. And yet some of the generals wanted to retreat.

Having had nothing to eat this day, I thought to go back to headquarters camp and rustle something. Besides, I was sick. But beyond the hill, down the road, it was very dangerous, while on the hill we were safe. "Wait for a lull; one will come soon," advised an old soldier. It is a curious thing that battle firing comes like a big wind, and has its lulls. Now it was getting dark, and during a lull I went back. I gave a wounded man a ride to the field hospital, but I found I was too weak myself to walk far. I had been ill during the whole campaign, and latterly had fever, which, taken together with the heat, sleeping in the mud, marching, and insufficient food, had done for me.

The sight of that road as I wound my way down it was something I cannot describe. The rear of a battle. All the broken spirits, bloody bodies, hopeless, helpless suffering which drags its weary length to the rear, are so much more appalling than anything else in the world that words won't mean anything to one who has not seen it. Men half naked, men sitting down on the road-side utterly spent, men hopping on one foot with a rifle for a crutch, men out of their minds from sunstroke, men dead, and men dying. Officers came by white as this paper, carried on rude litters made by their devoted soldiers, or borne on their backs. I got some food about ten o'clock and lay down. I was in the rear at headquarters, and there were no bullets and shells cracking about my ears, but I found I had discovered no particular nervousness in myself, quite contrary to my expectations, since I am a nervous man, but there in the comparative quiet of the woods the reaction came. Other fellows felt the same, and we compared notes. Art and literature under Mauser fire is a jerky business; it cannot be properly systematized. I declared that I would in the future paint "set pieces for dining-rooms." Dining-rooms are so much more amusing than camps. The novelist allowed that he would be forced to go home and complete "The Romance of a Quart Bottle." The explorer declared that his treatise on the "Flora of Bar Harbor" was promised to his publishers.

Soldiers always joke after a battle. They have to loosen the strings, or they will snap. There was a dropping fire in the front, and we understood our fellows were intrenching. Though I had gotten up that morning at half past three, it was nearly that time again before I went to sleep. The fever and the strong soldier-coffee banished sleep; then, again, I could not get the white bodies which lay in the moonlight, with the dark spots on them, out of my mind. Most of the dead on modern battle-fields are half naked, because of the "first-aid bandage." They take their shirts off, or their pantaloons, put on the dressing, and die that way.

It is well to bear in mind the difference in the point of view of an artist or a correspondent, and a soldier. One has his duties, his responsibilities, or his gun, and he is on the firing-line under great excitement, with his reputation at stake. The other stalks through the middle distance, seeing the fight and its immediate results, the wounded; lying down by a dead body, mayhap, when the bullets come quickly; he will share no glory; he has only the responsibility of seeing clearly what he must tell; and he must keep his nerve. I think the soldier sleeps better nights.

The next day I started again for the front, dismounted, but I only got to El Poso Hill. I lay down under a bank by the creek. I had the fever. I only got up to drink deeply of the dirty water. The heat was intense. The re-enforcing troops marched slowly up the road. The shells came railroading down through the jungle, but these troops went on, calm, steady, like true Americans. I made my way back to our camp, and lay there until nightfall, making up my mind and unmaking it as to my physical condition, until I concluded that I had "finished."

VIRTUE IN WAR

STEPHEN CRANE

I

Gates had left the regular army in 1890, those parts of him which had not been frozen having been well fried. He took with him nothing but an oaken constitution and a knowledge of the plains and the best wishes of his fellow-officers. The Standard Oil Company differs from the United States Government in that it understands the value of the loyal and intelligent services of good men and is almost certain to reward them at the expense of incapable men. This curious practice emanates from no beneficent emotion of the Standard Oil Company, on whose feelings you could not make a scar with a hammer and chisel. It is simply that the Standard Oil Company knows more than the United States Government and makes use of virtue whenever virtue is to its advantage. In 1890 Gates really felt in his bones that, if he lived a rigorously correct life and several score of his class-mates and intimate friends died off, he would get command of a troop of horse by the time he was unfitted by age to be an active cavalry leader. He left the service of the United States and entered the service of the Standard Oil Company. In the course of time he knew that, if he lived a rigorously correct life, his position and income would develop strictly in parallel with the worth of his wisdom and experience, and he would not have to walk on the corpses of his friends.

But he was not happier. Part of his heart was in a barracks, and it was not enough to discourse of the old regiment over the port and cigars to ears which were polite enough to betray a languid ignorance. Finally came the year 1898, and Gates dropped the Standard Oil Company as if it were hot. He hit the steel trail to Washington and there fought the first serious action of the war. Like most Americans, he had a native State, and one morning he found himself major in a volunteer infantry regiment whose voice had a peculiar sharp twang to it which he could remember from childhood. The colonel welcomed the West Pointer with loud cries of joy; the lieutenant-colonel looked at him with the pebbly eye of distrust; and the senior major, having had up to this time the best battalion in the regiment, strongly disapproved of him. There were only two majors, so the lieutenant-colonel commanded the first battalion, which gave him an occupation. Lieutenant-colonels under the new rules do not always have occupations. Gates got the third battalion—four companies commanded by intelligent officers who could gauge the opinions of their men at two thousand yards and govern themselves accordingly. The battalion was immensely interested in the new major. It thought it ought to develop views about him. It thought it was its blankety-blank business to find out immediately if it liked him personally. In the company streets the talk was nothing else. Among the non-commissioned officers there were eleven old soldiers of the regular army, and they knew—and cared—that Gates had held commission in the "Sixteenth Cavalry "—as Harper s Weekly says. Over this fact they rejoiced and were glad, and they stood by to jump lively when he took command. He would know his work and he would know their work, and then in battle there would be killed only what men were absolutely necessary and the sick list would be comparatively free of fools.

The commander of the second battalion had been called by an Atlanta paper, "Major Rickets C. Carmony, the commander of the second battalion of the 307th—, is when at home one of thebiggest wholesale hardware dealers in his State. Last evening he had ice-cream, at his own expense, served out at the regular mess of the battalion, and after dinner the men gathered about his tent where three hearty cheers for the popular major were given." Carmony had bought twelve copies of this newspaper and mailed them home to his friends.

In Gates's battalion there were more kicks than ice-cream, and there was no ice-cream at all. Indignation ran high at the rapid manner in which he proceeded to make soldiers of them. Some of his officers hinted finally that the men wouldn't stand it. They were saying that they had enlisted to fight for their country—yes, but they weren't going to be bullied day in and day out by a perfect stranger. They were patriots, they were, and just as good men as ever stepped—just as good as Gates or anybody like him. But, gradually, despite itself, the battalion progressed. The men were not altogether conscious of it. They evolved rather blindly. Presently there were fights with Carmony's crowd as to which was the better battalion at drills, and at last there was no argument. It was generally admitted that Gates commanded the crack battalion. The men, believing that the beginning and the end of all soldiering was in these drills of precision, were somewhat reconciled to their major when they began to understand more of what he was trying to do for them, but they were still fiery untamed patriots of lofty pride and they resented his manner toward them. It was abrupt and sharp.

The time came when everybody knew that the Fifth Army Corps was the corps designated for the first active service in Cuba. The officers and men of the 307th observed with despair that their regiment was not in the Fifth Army Corps. The colonel was a strategist. He understood everything in a flash. Without a moment's hesitation he obtained leave and mounted the night express for Washington. There he drove Senators and Congressmen in span, tandem and four-in-hand. With the telegraph he stirred so deeply the governor, the people and the newspapers of his State that whenever on a quiet night the President put his head out of the White House he could hear the distant vast commonwealth humming with indignation. And as it is well known that the Chief Executive listens to the voice of the people, the 307th was transferred to the Fifth Army Corps. It was sent at once to Tampa, where it was brigaded with two dusty regiments of regulars, who looked at it calmly and said nothing. The brigade commander happened to be no less a person than Gates's old colonel in the "Sixteenth Cavalry "—as Harper's Weekly says—and Gates was cheered. The old man's rather solemn look brightened when he saw Gates in the 307th. There was a great deal of battering and pounding and banging for the 307th at Tampa, but the men stood it more in wonder than in anger. The two regular regiments carried them along when they could, and when they couldn't waited impatiently for them to come up. Undoubtedly the regulars wished the volunteers were in garrison at Sitka, but they said practically nothing. They minded their own regiments. The colonel was an invaluable man in a telegraph office. When came the scramble for transports the colonel retired to a telegraph office and talked so ably to Washington that the authorities pushed a number of corps aside and made way for the 307th, as if on it depended everything. The regiment got one of the best transports, and after a series of delays and some starts, and an equal number of returns, they finally sailed for Cuba.

II

Now Gates had a singular adventure on the second morning after his arrival at Atlanta to take his post as a major in the 307th.

He was in his tent, writing, when suddenly the flap was flung away and a tall young private stepped inside.

"Well, Maje," said the newcomer, genially, "how goes it? "

The major's head flashed up, but he spoke without heat.

"Come to attention and salute."

"Huh! "said the private.

"Come to attention and salute."

The private looked at him in resentful amazement, and then inquired:

"Ye ain't mad, are ye? Ain't nothin' to get huffy about, is there? "

"I—Come to attention and salute."

"Well," drawled the private, as he stared, "seein' as ye are so darn perticular, I don't care if I do—if it'll make yer meals set on yer stomick any better."

Drawing a long breath and grinning ironically, he lazily pulled his heels together and saluted with a flourish.

"There," he said, with a return to his earlier genial manner. "How's that suit ye, Maje? "

There was a silence which to an impartial observer would have seemed pregnant with dynamite and bloody death. Then the major cleared his throat and coldly said:

"And now, what is your business?"

"Who—me? "asked the private. "Oh, I just sorter dropped in." With a deeper meaning he added: "Sorter dropped in in a friendly way, thinkin' ye was mebbe a different kind of a feller from what ye be."

The inference was clearly marked.

It was now Gates's turn to stare, and stare he unfeignedly did.

"Go back to your quarters," he said at length.

The volunteer became very angry.

"Oh, ye needn't be so up-in-th'-air, need ye? Don't know's I'm dead anxious to inflict my company on yer since I've had a good look at ye. There may be men in this here battalion what's had just as much edjewcation as you have, and I'm damned if they ain't got better manners. Good-mornin'," he said, with dignity; and, passing out of the tent, he flung the flap back in place with an air of slamming it as if it had been a door. He made his way back to his company street, striding high. He was furious. He met a large crowd of his comrades.

"What's the matter, Lige? "asked one, who noted his temper.

"Oh, nothin'," answered Lige, with terrible feeling. "Nothin'. I jest been lookin' over the new major—that's all."

"What's he like? "asked another.

"Like? "cried Lige. "He's like nothin'. He ain't out'n the same kittle as us. No. Gawd made him all by himself—sep'rate. He's a speshul produc', he is, an' he won't have no truck with jest common—men, like you be."

He made a venomous gesture which included them all.

"Did he set on ye? "asked a soldier.

"Set on me? No," replied Lige, with contempt. "I set on him. I sized 'im up in a minute. ' Oh, I don't know,' I says, as I was comin' out; ' guess you ain't the only man in the world,' I says."

For a time Lige Wigram was quite a hero. He endlessly repeated the tale of his adventure, and men admired him for so soon taking the conceit out of the new officer. Lige was proud to think of himself as a plain and simple patriot who had refused to endure any high-soaring nonsense.

But he came to believe that he had not disturbed the singular composure of the major, and this concreted his hatred. He hated Gates, not as a soldier sometimes hates an officer, a hatred half of fear. Lige hated as man to man. And he was enraged to see that so far from gaining any hatred in return, he seemed incapable of making Gates have any thought of him save as a unit in a body of three hundred men. Lige might just as well have gone and grimaced at the obelisk in Central Park.

When the battalion became the best in the regiment he had no part in the pride of the companies. He was sorry when men began to speak well of Gates. He was really a very consistent hater.

III

The transport occupied by the 307th was commanded by some sort of a Scandinavian, who was afraid of the shadows of his own topmasts. He would have run his steamer away from a floating Gainsborough hat, and, in fact, he ran her away from less on some occasions. The officers, wishing to arrive with the other transports, sometimes remonstrated, and to them he talked of his owners.

Every officer in the convoying warships loathed 11 him, for in case any hostile vessel should appear they did not see how they were going to protect this rabbit, who would probably manage during a fight to be in about a hundred places on the broad, broad sea, and all of them offensive to the navy's plan. When he was not talking of his owners he was remarking to the officers of the regiment that a steamer really was not like a valise, and that he was unable to take his ship under his arm and climb trees with it. He further said that "them naval fellows "were not near so smart as they thought they were.

From an indigo sea arose the lonely shore of Cuba. Ultimately, the fleet was near Santiago, and most of the transports were bidden to wait a minute while the leaders found out their minds. The skipper, to whom the 307th were prisoners, waited for thirty hours half way between Jamaica and Cuba. He explained that the Spanish fleet might emerge from Santiago Harbour at any time, and he did not propose to be caught. His owners—Whereupon the colonel arose as one having nine hundred men at his back, and he passed up to the bridge and he spake with the captain. He explained indirectly that each individual of his nine hundred men had decided to be the first American soldier to land for this campaign, and that in order to accomplish the marvel it was necessary for the transport to be nearer than forty-five miles from the Cuban coast. If the skipper would only land the regiment the colonel would consent to his then taking his interesting old ship and going to h—with it.

And the skipper spake with the colonel. He pointed out that as far as he officially was concerned, the United States Government did not exist. He was responsible solely to his owners. The colonel pondered these sayings. He perceived that the skipper meant that he was running his ship as he deemed best, in consideration of the capital invested by his owners, and that he was not at all concerned with the feelings of a certain American military expedition to Cuba. He was a free son of the sea—he was a sovereign citizen of the republic of the waves. He was like Lige.

However, the skipper ultimately incurred the danger of taking his ship under the terrible guns of the New York, Iowa, Oregon, Massachusetts, Indiana, Brooklyn, Texas and a score of cruisers and gunboats. It was a brave act for the captain of a United States transport, and he was visibly nervous until he could again get to sea, where he offered praises that the accursed 307th was no longer sitting on his head. For almost a week he rambled at his cheerful will over the adjacent high seas, having in his hold a great quantity of military stores as successfully secreted as if they had been buried in a copper box in the cornerstone of a new public building in Boston. He had had his master's certificate for twenty-one years, and those people couldn't tell a marlin-spike from the starboard side of the ship.

The 307th was landed in Cuba, but to their disgust they found that about ten thousand regulars were ahead of them. They got immediate orders to move out from the base on the road to Santiago. Gates was interested to note that the only delay was caused by the fact that many men of the other battalions strayed off sight-seeing. In time the long regiment wound slowly among hills that shut them from sight of the sea.

For the men to admire, there were palm-trees, little brown huts, passive, uninterested Cuban soldiers much worn from carrying American rations inside and outside. The weather was not oppressively warm, and the journey was said to be only about seven miles. There were no rumours save that there had been one short fight and the army had advanced to within sight of Santiago. Having a peculiar faculty for the derision of the romantic, the 307th began to laugh. Actually there was not anything in the world which turned out to be as books describe it. Here they had landed from the transport expecting to be at once flung into line of battle and sent on some kind of furious charge, and now they were trudging along a quiet trail lined with somnolent trees and grass. The whole business so far struck them as being a highly tedious burlesque.

After a time they came to where the camps of regular regiments marked the sides of the road—little villages of tents no higher than a man's waist. The colonel found his brigade commander and the 307th was sent off into a field of long grass, where the men grew suddenly solemn with the importance of getting their supper.

In the early evening some regulars told one of Gates's companies that at daybreak this division would move to an attack upon something.

"How d'you know?" said the company, deeply awed.

"Heard it."

"Well, what are we to attack?" "Dunno."

The 307th was not at all afraid, but each man began to imagine the morrow. The regulars seemed to have as much interest in the morrow as they did in the last Christmas. It was none of their affair, apparently.

"Look here," said Lige Wigram, to a man in the 17th Regular Infantry, "whereabouts are we goin' ter-morrow an' who do we run up against—do ye know? "

The 17th soldier replied, truculently: "If I ketch th'—what stole my terbaccer,

I'll whirl in an' break every—bone in his body."

Gates's friends in the regular regiments asked him numerous questions as to the reliability of his organisation. Would the 307th stand the racket? They were certainly not contemptuous; they simply did not seem to consider it important whether the 307th would or whether it would not.

"Well," said Gates, "they won't run the length of a tent-peg if they can gain any idea of what they're fighting; they won't bunch if they've about six acres of open ground to move in; they won't get rattled at all if they see you fellows taking it easy, and they'll fight like the devil as long as they thoroughly, completely, absolutely, satisfactorily, exhaustively understand what the business is. They're lawyers. All excepting my battalion."

IV

Lige awakened into a world obscured by blue fog. Somebody was gently shaking him. "Git up; we're going to move." The regiment was buckling up itself. From the trail came the loud creak of a light battery moving ahead. The tones of all men were low; the faces of the officers were composed, serious. The regiment found itself moving along behind the battery before it had time to ask itself more than a hundred questions. The trail wound through a dense tall jungle, dark, heavy with dew.

The battle broke with a snap—far ahead. Presently Lige heard from the air above him a faint low note as if somebody were blowing softly in the mouth of a bottle. It was a stray bullet which had wandered a mile to tell him that war was before him. He nearly broke his neck looking upward. "Did ye hear that? "But the men were fretting to get out of this gloomy jungle. They wanted to see something. The faint rup-rup-rrrrup-rup on in the front told them that the fight had begun; death was abroad, and so the mystery of this wilderness excited them. This wilderness was portentously still and dark.

They passed the battery aligned on a hill above the trail, and they had not gone far when the gruff guns began to roar and they could hear the rocket-like swish of the flying shells. Presently everybody must have called out for the assistance of the 307th. Aides and couriers came flying back to them.

"Is this the 307th? Hurry up your men, please, Colonel. You're needed more every minute."

Oh, they were, were they? Then the regulars were not going to do all the fighting? The old 307th was bitterly proud or proudly bitter. They left their blanket rolls under the guard of God and pushed on, which is one of the reasons why the Cubans of th3t part of the country were, later, so well equipped. There began to appear fields, hot, golden-green in the sun. On some palm-dotted knolls before them they could see little lines of black dots—the American advance. A few men fell, struck down by other men who, perhaps half a mile away, were aiming at somebody else. The loss was wholly in Carmony's battalion, which immediately bunched and backed away, coming with a shock against Gates's advance company. This shock sent a tremor through all of Gates's battalion until men in the very last files cried out nervously, "Well, what in hell is up now? "There came an order to deploy and ad. vance. An occasional hoarse yell from the regulars could be heard. The deploying made Gates's heart bleed for the colonel. The old man stood there directing the movement, straight, fearless, sombrely defiant of—everything. Carmony's four companies were like four herds. And all the time the bullets from no living man knows where kept pecking at them and pecking at them. Gates, the excellent Gates, the highly educated and strictly military Gates, grew rankly insubordinate. He knew that the regiment was suffering from nothing but the deadly range and oversweep of the modern rifle, of which many proud and confident nations know nothing save that they have killed savages with it, which is the least of all informations.

Gates rushed upon Carmony.

"—it, man, if you can't get your people to deploy, for-sake give me a chance! I'm stuck in the woods!"

Carmony gave nothing, but Gates took all he could get and his battalion deployed and advanced like men. The old colonel almost burst into tears, and he cast one quick glance of gratitude at Gates, which the younger officer wore on his heart like a secret decoration.

There was a wild scramble up hill, down dale, through thorny thickets. Death smote them with a kind of slow rhythm, leisurely taking a man now here, now there, but. the cat-spit sound of the bullets was always. A large number of the men of Carmony's battalion came on with Gates. They were willing to do anything, anything. They had no real fault, unless it was that early conclusion that any brave high-minded youth was necessarily a good soldier immediately, from the beginning. In them had been born a swift feeling that the unpopular Gates knew everything, and they followed the trained soldier.

If they followed him, he certainly took them into it. As they swung heavily up one steep hill, like so many wind-blown horses, they came suddenly out into the real advance. Little blue groups of men were making frantic rushes forward and then flopping down on their bellies to fire volleys while other groups made rushes. Ahead they could see a heavy house-like fort which was inadequate to explain from whence came the myriad bullets. The remainder of the scene was landscape. Pale men, yellow men, blue men came out of this landscape quiet and sad-eyed with wounds. Often they were grimly facetious. There is nothing in the American regulars so amazing as his conduct when he is wounded—his apologetic limp, his deprecatory arm-sling, his embarrassed and ashamed shot-hole through the lungs. The men of the 307th looked at calm creatures who had divers punctures and they were made better. These men told them that it was only necessary to keep a-going. They of the 307th lay on their bellies, red, sweating and panting, and heeded the voice of the elder brother.

Gates walked back of his line, very white of face, but hard and stern past anything his men knew of him. After they had violently adjured him to lie down and he had given weak backs a cold, stiff touch, the 307th charged by rushes. The hatless colonel made frenzied speech, but the man of the time was Gates. The men seemed to feel that this was his business. Some of the regular officers said afterward that the advance of the 307th was very respectable indeed. They were rather surprised, they said. At least five of the crack regiments of the regular army were in this division, and the 307th could win no more than a feeling of kindly appreciation.

Yes, it was very good, very good indeed, but did you notice what was being done at the same moment by the 12th, the 17th, the 7th, the 8th, the 25 th, the—

Gates felt that his charge was being a success. He was carrying out a successful function. Two captains fell bang on the grass and a lieutenant slumped quietly down with a death wound. Many men sprawled suddenly. Gates was keeping his men almost even with the regulars, who were charging on his flanks. Suddenly he thought that he must have come close to the fort and that a Spaniard had tumbled a great stone block down upon his leg. Twelve hands reached out to help him, but he cried:

"No—d-—your souls—go on—go on!"

He closed his eyes for a moment, and it really was only for a moment. When he opened them he found himself alone with Lige Wigram, who lay on the ground near him.

"Maje," said Lige, "yer a good man. I've been a-follerin' ye all day an' I want to say yer a good man."

The major turned a coldly scornful eye upon the private.

"Where are you wounded? Can you walk? Well, if you can, go to the rear and leave me alone. I'm bleeding to death, and you bother me."

Lige, despite the pain in his wounded shoulder, grew indignant.

"Well," he mumbled, "you and me have been on th' outs fer a long time, an' I only wanted to tell ye that what I seen of ye t'day has made me feel mighty different."

"Go to the rear—if you can walk," said the major.

"Now, Maje, look here. A little thing like
that-"

"Go to the rear." Lige gulped with sobs.

"Maje, I know I didn't understand ye at first, but ruther'n let a little thing like that come between us, I'd—I'd——"

"Go to the rear."

In this reiteration Lige discovered a resemblance to that first old offensive phrase, "Come to attention and salute." He pondered over the resemblance and he saw that nothing had changed. The man bleeding to death was the same man to whom he had once paid a friendly visit with unfriendly results. He thought now that he perceived a certain hopeless gulf, a gulf which is real or unreal, according to circumstances. Sometimes all men are equal; occasionally they are not. If Gates had ever criticised Lige's manipulation of a hay fork on the farm at home, Lige would have furiously disdained his hate or blame.

He saw now that he must not openly approve the major's conduct in war. The major's pride was in his business, and his, Lige's congratulations, were beyond all enduring.

The place where they were lying suddenly fell under a new heavy rain of bullets. They sputtered about the men, making the noise of large grasshoppers.

"Major! "cried Lige. "Major Gates! It won't do for ye to be left here, sir. Ye'll be killed."

"But you can't help it, lad. You take care of yourself."

"I'm damned if I do," said the private, vehemently. "If I can't git you out, I'll stay and wait."

The officer gazed at his man with that same icy, contemptuous gaze.

"I'm—I'm a dead man anyhow. You go to the rear, do you hear? "

"No."

The dying major drew his revolver, cocked it and aimed it unsteadily at Lige's head. "Will you obey orders? ""No." "One?" "No."

"Two?" "No."

Gates weakly dropped his revolver.

"Go to the devil, then. You're no soldier, but—" He tried to add something, "But——" He heaved a long moan. "But—you—you—oh, I'm so-o-o tired."

* * * * *

V

After the battle, three correspondents happened to meet on the trail. They were hot, dusty, weary, hungry and thirsty, and they repaired to the shade of a mango tree and sprawled luxuriously. Among them they mustered twoscore friends who on that day had gone to the far shore of the hereafter, but their senses were no longer resonant. Shackles was babbling plaintively about mint-juleps, and the others were bidding him to have done.

"By-the-way," said one, at last, "it's too bad about poor old Gates of the 307th. He bled to death. His men were crazy. They were blubbering and cursing around there like wild people. It seems that when they got back there to look for him they found him just about gone, and another wounded man was trying to stop the flow with his hat! His hat, mind you. Poor old Gatesie!"

"Oh, no, Shackles! "said the third man of the party. "Oh, no, you're wrong. The best mint-juleps in the world are made right in New York, Philadelphia or Boston. That Kentucky idea is only a tradition."

A wounded man approached them. He had been shot through the shoulder and his shirt had been diagonally cut away, leaving much bare skin. Over the bullet's point of entry there was a kind of a white spider, shaped from pieces of adhesive plaster. Over the point of departure there was a bloody bulb of cotton strapped to the flesh by other pieces of adhesive plaster. His eyes were dreamy, wistful, sad. "Say, gents, have any of ye got a bottle? "he asked.

A correspondent raised himself suddenly and looked with bright eyes at the soldier.

"Well, you have got a nerve," he said grinning. "Have we got a bottle, eh! Who in h—do you think we are? If we had a bottle of good licker, do you suppose we could let the whole army drink out of it? You have too much faith in the generosity of men, my friend! "

The soldier stared, ox-like, and finally said, "Huh?"

"I say," continued the correspondent, somewhat more loudly, "that if we had had a bottle we would have probably finished it ourselves by this time."

"But," said the other, dazed, "I meant an empty bottle. I didn't mean no full bottle."

The correspondent was humorously irascible.

"An empty bottle! You must be crazy! Who ever heard of a man looking for an empty bottle? It isn't sense! I've seen a million men looking for full bottles, but you're the first man I ever saw who insisted on the bottle's being empty. What in the world do you want it for? "

"Well, ye see, mister," explained Lige, slowly, "our major he was killed this mornin' an' we're jes' goin' to bury him, an' I thought I'd jest take a look 'round an' see if I couldn't borry an empty bottle, an' then I'd take an' write his name an' reg'ment on a paper an' put it in th' bottle an' bury it with him, so's when they come fer to dig him up sometime an' take him home, there sure wouldn't be no mistake."

"Oh! "

THE TAKING OF LUNGTUNGPEN

RUDYARD KIPLING

So we loosed a bloomin'volley,
An'we made the beggars cut.
An'when our pouch was emptied out,
We used the bloomin'butt,
Ho! My!
Don't yer come anigh,
When Tommy is a playin'with the
bayonit an'the butt.

Barrack Roam Ballad

My friend Private Mulvaney told me this, sitting on the parapet of the road to Dagshai, when we were hunting butterflies together. He had theories about the Army, and coloured clay pipes perfectly. He said that the young soldier is the best to work with, "on account av the surpassing innocinse av the child."

"Now, listen! "said Mulvaney, throwing himself full length on the wall in the sun. "I'm a born scutt av the barrick room! The Army's mate an'dhrink to me, bekaze I'm wan av the few that can't quit ut. I've put in sivinteen years, an'the pipeclay's in the marrow av me. Av I cud have kept out av wan big 'dhrink a month, I wud have been a Hon'ry Lift'nint by this time—a nuisance to my betthers, a laughin'shtock to my equils, an'a curse to meself. Bein'fwhat I am, I'm Privit Mulvaney, wid no good-conduc'pay an'a devourin'thirst. Always barrin'me little frind Bobs Bahadur, I know as much about the Army as most men."

I said something here.

"Wolseley be shot! Betune you an'me an'that butterfly net, he's a ramblin', incoherent sort av a divil, wid wan oi on the Quane an'the Coort, an'the other on his blessed silf—everlastin'ly playing Saysar an'Alexandrier rowled into a lump. Now Bobs is a sinsible little man. Wid Bobs an'a few three-year-olds, I'd swape any army av the earth into a towel, an'throw it away af therward. Faith, I'm not jokin'! 'Tis the bhoys—the raw bhoys—that don't know fwhat a bullet manes, an'wudn't care av they did—that dhu the work. They're crammed wid bull-mate till they fairly ramps wid good livin'; and thin, av they don't fight, they blow each other's hids off. 'Tis the trut'I'm tellin'you. They shud be kept on water an'rice in the hot weather; but there'd be a mut'ny av 'twas done.

"Did ye iver hear how Privit Mulvaney tuk the town av Lungtungpen? I thought not! 'Twas the Lift'nint got the credit; but 'twas me planned the schame. A little before I was inviladed from Burma, me an'four-an'-twenty young wans undher a Lift'nint Brazenose, was ruinin'our dijeshins thryin'to catch dacoits. An'such double-ended divils I niver knew! 'Tis only a dah an'a Snider that makes a dacoit. Widout thim, he's a paceful cultivator, an'felony for to shoot. We hunted, an'we hunted, an'tuk fever an'elephints now an'again; but no dacoits. Evenshually, we puckarowed wan man. 'Trate him tinderly,'sez the Lift'nint. So I tuk him away into the jungle, wid the Burmese Interprut'r an'my clanin'-rod. Sez I to the man, 'My paceful squireen,'sez I, 'you shquot on your hungers an'dimonstrate to my frind here, where your frinds are whin they're at home?'Wid that I introjuced him to the clanin'-rod, an'he comminst to jabber; the Interprut'r interprutin'in betweens, an'me helpin'the Intilligence Departmint wid my clanin'-rod whin the man misremembered.

"Prisintly, I learn that, acrost the river, about nine miles away, was a town just dhrippin'wid dahs, an'bohs an'arrows, an'dacoits, an'elephints, an'jingles, 'Good! 'sez I; 'this office will now close! '

"That night, I went to the Lift'nint an'communicates my information. I never thought much of Lift'nint Brazenose till that night. He was shtiff wid books an'the-ouries, an'all manner av thrimmin's no manner av use. 'Town did ye say?'sez he.'Accordin'to the the-ouries av War, we shud wait for reinforcemints.'—'Faith! 'thinks I, 'we'd betther dig our graves thin ;'for the nearest throops was up to their shtocks in the marshes out Mimbu way. 'But,'says the Lift'nint, 'since 'tis a speshil case, I'll make an excepshin. We'll visit this Lungtungpen tonight.'

"The bhoys was fairly woild wid deloight whin I tould 'em; an', by this an'that, they wint through the jungle like buck-rabbits. About midnight we come to the shtrame which

I had clane forgot to minshin to my orficer. I was on, ahead, wid four bhoys, an'I thought that the Lift'nint might want to the-ourise. 'Shtrip bhoys! 'sez I. 'Shtrip to the buff, an'shwim in where glory waits! '—'But I can't shwim! 'sez two of thim. 'To think I should live to hear that from a bhoy wid a board-school edukashin! 'sez I. 'Take a lump av timber, an'me an'Conolly here will ferry ye over, ye young ladies!'

"We got an ould tree-trunk, an'pushed off wid the kits an'the rifles on it. The night was chokin'dhark, an'just as we was fairly embarked, I heard the Lift'nint behind av me callin'out. 'There's a bit av a nullah here, sorr,'sez I, 'but I can feel the bottom already.'So I cud, for I was not a yard from the bank.

"'Bit av a nullah! Bit av an eshtuary! 'sez the Liftn'int. 'Go on, ye mad Irish-man! Shtrip bhoys! 'I heard him laugh; an'the bhoys begun shtrippin'an'rollin'a log into the wather to put their kits on. So me an'Conolly shtruck out through the warm wather wid our log, an'the rest come on behind.

"That shtrame was miles woide! Orth'ris, on the rear-rank log, whispers we had got into the Thames below Sheerness by mistake. 'Kape on shwimmin', ye little blayguard,'sez I, 'an'Irriwaddy.'—'Silence, men! 'sings out the Lift'nint. So we shwum on into the black dhark, wid our chests on the logs, trustin'in the Saints an'the luck av the British Army.

"Evenshually, we hit ground—a bit av sand—an'a man. I put my heel on the back av him. He skreeched an'ran.

"'Now we've done it! 'sez Lift'nint Brazenose. 'Where the Divil is Lungtungpen?'There was about a minute and a half to wait. The bhoys laid a hould av their rifles an'some thried to put their belts on; we was marchin'wid fixed baynits av coorse. Thin we knew where Lungtungpen was ; for we had hit the river-wall av it in the dhark, an'the whole town blazed wid thim messin'jingles an'Sniders like a cat's back on a frosty night. They was firm'all ways at wanst; but over our heads into the shtrame.

"'Have you got your rifles?'sez Brazenose. 'Got 'em!'sez Orth'ris. 'I've got that thief Mulvaney's for all my backpay, an'she'll kick my heart sick wid that blunderin'long shtock av hers.'—'Go on! 'yells Brazenose, whippin'his sword out. 'Go on an'take the town! An'the Lord have mercy on our sowls! "

"Thin the bhoys gave wan divastatin'howl, an'pranced into the dhark, feelin'for the town, an'blindin'an'stiffin'like Cavalry Ridin'Masters whin the grass pricked their bare legs. I hammered wid the butt at some bamboo-thing that felt wake, an'the rest come an'hammered contagious, while the jingles was jingling, an'feroshus yells from inside was shplittin'our ears. We was too close under the wall for thim to hurt us.

"Evenshually, the thing, whatever ut was, bruk ; an'the six-an'-twenty av us tumbled, wan after the other, naked as we was borrun, into the town of Lungtungpen. There was a melly av a sumpshus kind for a whoile; but whether they tuk us, all white an'wet, for a new breed av divil, or a new kind of dacoit, I don't know. They ran as though we was both, an'we wint into thim, baynit an'butt, shriekin'wid laughin'. There was torches in the shtreets, an'I saw little Orth'ris rubbin'his showlther ivry time he loosed my long-shtock Martini; an'Brazenose walkin'into the gang wid his sword, like Diarmid av the Gowlden Collar—barring he hadn't a stitch av clothin'on him. We diskivered elephints wid dacoits under their bellies, an', what wid wan thing an'other, we was busy till mornin'takin'possession av the town of Lungtungpen.

"Then we halted an'formed up, the wimmen howlin'in the houses an'the Lift'nint blushin'pink in the light av the mornin'sun. 'Twas the most ondasint p'rade I iver tuk a hand in. Foive-an'-twinty privits an'a orficer av"the Line in review ordher, an'not as much as wud dust a fife betune 'em all in the way of clothin'! Eight av us had their belts an'pouches on; but the rest had gone in wid a handful av cartridges an'the skin God gave them. They was as nakid as Vanus.

"'Number off from the right! 'sez the Lift'nint. 'Odd numbers fall out to dress; even numbers pathrol the town till relieved by the dressing party.'Let me tell you, pathrollin'a town wid nothin'on is an expeyrience. I pathrolled for tin minutes, an'begad, before 'twas over, I blushed. The women laughed so. I niver blushed before or since; but I blushed all over my carkiss thin. Orth'ris didn't pathrol. He sez only, 'Portsmouth Barricks an'the 'Ard av a Sunday! 'Thin he lay down an'rolled any ways wid laughin'.

"Whin we was all dhressed, we counted the dead—sivinty-foive dacoits besides the wounded. We tuk five elephints, a hunder'an'sivinty Sniders, two hunder'dahs, and a lot of other burglarious thruck. Not a man av us was hurt— excep'maybe the Lift'nint, an'he from the shock of his dasincy.

"The Headman av Lungtungpen, who surrinder'd himself asked the Interprut'r—'Av the English fight like that wid their clo'es off, what in the wurruld do they do wid their clo'es on?'Orth'ris began rowlin'his eyes an'crackin'his fingers an'dancin'a step-dance for to impress the Headman. He ran to his house; an'we spint the rest av the day carryin'the Lift'nint on our showlthers round the town, an'playin'wid the Burmese babies—fat, little, brown little divils, as pretty as picturs.

"Whin I was inviladed for the dysent'ry to India, I sez to the Lift'nint, 'Sorr,'sez I, 'you've the makin'in you av a great man; but, av you'll let an ould sodger spake, you're too fond of the-ourisin'.'He shuk hands wid me and sez, 'Hit high, hit low, there's no plazin'you, Mulvaney. You've seen me waltzin'through Lungtungpen like a Red Injin widout the warpaint, an'you say I'm too fond av the-ourisin'?'—'Sorr,'sez I, for I loved the bhoy; 'I wud waltz wid you in that condishin through Hell, an'so wud the rest av the men!'Thin I went downsh-trame in the flat an'left him my blessin'. May the Saints carry ut where ut shud go, for he was a fine upstandin'young orficer.

"To rcshume. Fwhat I've said jist shows the use av three-year-olds. Wud fifty seasoned sodgers have taken Lungtungpen in the dhark that way? No! They'd know the risk av fever an'chill. Let alone the shootin'. Two hunder'might have done ut. But the three-year-olds know little an'care less; an'where there's no fear, there's no danger. Catch thim young, feed thim high, an'by the honour av that great, little man Bobs, behind a good orficer, 'tisn't only dacoits they'd smash wid their clo'es off—'tis Con-ti-nental Ar-r-r-mies! They tuk Lungtung-pen nakid; an'they'd take St. Petersburg in their dhrawers! Begad, they would that!"

So saying, Mulvaney took up his butterfly-net, and returned to the barracks.

ONE OFFICER, ONE MAN

AMBROSE BIERCE

Captain Graffenreid stood at the head of his company. The regiment was not engaged. It formed a part of the front line-of-battle, which stretched away to the right with a visible length of nearly two miles through the open ground. The left flank was veiled by woods; to the right also the line was lost to sight, but it extended many miles. A hundred yards in rear was a second line; behind this, the reserve brigades and divisions in column. Batteries of artillery occupied the spaces between and crowned the low hills. Groups of horsemen—generals with their staffs and escorts, and field officers of regiments behind the colors—broke the regularity of the lines and columns. Numbers of these figures of interest had field-glasses at their eyes and sat motionless, stolidly scanning the country in front; others came and went at a slow canter, bearing orders. There were squads of stretcher-bearers, ambulances, wagon-trains with ammunition and officers' servants in rear of all—of all that was visible—for still in rear of these, along the roads, extended for many miles all that vast multitude of non-combatants who with their various impedimenta are assigned to the inglorious but important duty of supplying the fighters' many needs.

An army in üne-of-battle awaiting attack, or preparing to deliver it, presents strange contrasts. At the front are precision, formality, fixity and silence. Toward the rear these characteristics are less and less conspicuous, and finally, in point of space, are lost altogether in confusion, motion and noise. The homogeneous becomes heterogeneous. Definition is lacking; repose is replaced by an apparently purposeless activity; harmony vanishes in hubbub, form in disorder. Commotion everywhere and ceaseless unrest. The men who do not fight are never ready.

From his position at the right of his company in the front rank, Captain Graffenreid had an unobstructed outlook toward the enemy. A half-mile of open and nearly level ground lay before him, and beyond it an irregular wood, covering a slight acclivity; not a human being anywhere visible. He could imagine nothing more peaceful than the appearance of that pleasant landscape with its long stretches of brown fields Over which the atmosphere was beginning to quiver in the heat of the morning sun. Not a sound came from forest or field—not even the barking of a dog or the crowing of a cock at the half-seen plantation house on the crest among the trees. Yet every man in those miles of men knew that he and death were face to face.

Captain Graffenreid had never in his life seen an armed enemy, and the war in which his regiment was one of the first to take the field was two years old. He had had the rare advantage of a military education, and when his comrades had marched to the front he had been detached for administrative service at the capital of his State, where it was thought that he could be most useful. Like a bad soldier he protested, and like a good one obeyed. In close official and personal relations with the governor of his State, and enjoying his confidence and favor, he had firmly refused promotion and seen his juniors elevated above him. Death had been busy in his distant regiment; vacancies among the field officers had occurred again and again; but from a chivalrous feeling that war's rewards belonged of right to those who bore the storm and stress of battle he had held his humble rank and generously advanced the fortunes of others. His silent devotion to principle had conquered at last: he had been relieved of his hateful duties and ordered to the front, and now, untried by fire, stood in the van of battle in command of a company of hardy veterans, to whom he had been only a name, and that name a by-word. By none—not even by those of his brother officers in whose favor he had waived his rights—was his devotion to duty understood. They were too busy to be just; he was looked upon as one who had shirked his duty, until forced unwillingly into the field. Too proud to explain, yet not too insensible to feel, he could only endure and hope.

Of all the Federal Army on that summer morning none had accepted battle more joyously than Anderton Graffenreid. His spirit was buoyant, his faculties were riotous. He was in a state of mental exaltation and scarcely could endure the enemy's tardiness in advancing to the attack. To him this was opportunity—for the result he cared nothing. Victory or defeat, as God might will; in one or in the other he should prove himself a soldier and a hero; he should vindicate his right to the respect of his men and the companionship of his brother officers—to the consideration of his superiors. How his heart leaped in his breast as the bugle sounded the stirring notes of the "assembly"!' With what a light tread, scarcely conscious of the earth beneath his feet, he strode forward at the head of his company, and how exultingly he noted the tactical dispositions which placed his regiment in the front line! And if perchance some memory came to him of a pair of dark eyes that might take on a tenderer light in reading the account of that day's doings, who shall blame him for the unmartial thought or count it a debasement of soldierly ardor?

Suddenly, from the forest a half-mile in front—apparently from among the upper branches of the trees, but really from the ridge beyond—rose a tall column of white smoke. A moment later came a deep, jarring explosion, followed—almost attended—by a hideous rushing sound that seemed to leap forward across the intervening space with inconceivable rapidity, rising from whisper to roar with too quick a gradation for attention to note the successive stages of its horrible progression! A visible tremor ran along the lines of men; all were startled into motion. Captain Graffenreid dodged and threw up his hands to one side of his head, palms outward. As he did so he heard a keen, ringing report, and saw on a hillside behind the line a fierce roll of smoke and dust—the shell's explosion. It had passed a hundred feet to his left! He heard, or fancied he heard, a low, mocking laugh and turning in the direction whence it came saw the eyes of his first lieutenant fixed upon him with an unmistakable look of amusement. He looked along the line of faces in the front ranks. The men were laughing. At him? The thought restored the color to his bloodless face—restored too much of it. His cheeks burned with a fever of shame.

The enemy's shot was not answered: the officer in command at that exposed part of the line had evidently no desire to provoke a cannonade. For the forbearance Captain Graffenreid was conscious of a sense of gratitude. He had not known that the flight of a projectile was a phenomenon of so appalling character. His conception of war had already undergone a profound change, and he was conscious that his new feeling was manifesting itself in visible perturbation. His blood was boiling in his veins; he had a choking sensation and felt that if he had a command to give it would be inaudible, or at least unintelligible. The hand in which he held his sword trembled; the other moved automatically, clutching at various parts of his clothing. He found a difficulty in standing still and fancied that his men observed it. Was it fear? He feared it was.

From somewhere away to the right came, as the wind served, a low, intermittent murmur like that of ocean in a storm—like that of a distant railway train—like that of wind among the pines—three sounds so nearly alike that the ear, unaided by the judgment, cannot distinguish them one from another. The eyes of the troops were drawn in that direction; the mounted officers turned their field-glasses that way. Mingled with the sound was an irregular throbbing. He thought it, at first, the beating of his fevered blood in his ears; next, the distant tapping of a bass drum.

"The ball is opened on the right flank," said an officer.

Captain Graffenreid understood: the sounds were musketry and artillery. He nodded and tried to smile. There was apparently nothing infectious in the smile.

Presently a light line of blue smoke-puffs broke out along the edge of the wood in front, succeeded by a crackle of rifles. There were keen, sharp hissings in the air, terminating abruptly with a thump near by. The man at Captain Graffenreid's side dropped his rifle; his knees gave way and he pitched awkwardly forward, falling upon his face. Somebody shouted "Lie down!" and the dead man was hardly distinguishable from the living. It looked as if those few rifle-shots had slain ten thousand men. Only the field officers remained erect; their concession to the emergency consisted in dismounting and sending their horses to the shelter of the low hills immediately in rear.

Captain Graffenreid lay alongside the dead man, from beneath whose breast flowed a little rill of blood. It had a faint, sweetish odor that sickened him. The face was crushed into the earth and flattened. It looked yellow already, and was repulsive. Nothing suggested the glory of a soldier's death nor mitigated the loathsomeness of the incident. He could not turn his back upon the body without facing away from his company.

He fixed his eyes upon the forest, where all again was silent. He tried to imagine what was going on there—the lines of troops forming to attack, the guns being pushed forward by hand to the edge of the open. He fancied he could see their black muzzles protruding from the undergrowth, ready to deliver their storm of missiles—such missiles as the one whose shriek had so unsettled his nerves. The distension of his eyes became painful; a mist seemed to gather before them; he could no longer see across the field, yet would not withdraw his gaze lest he see the dead man at his side.

The fire of battle was not now burning very brightly in this warrior's soul. From inaction had come introspection. He sought rather to analyze his feelings than distinguish himself by courage and devotion. The result was profoundly disappointing. He covered his face with his hands and groaned aloud.

The hoarse murmur of battle grew more and more distinct upon the right; the murmur had, indeed, become a roar, the throbbing, a thunder. The sounds had worked round obliquely to the front; evidently the enemy's left was being driven back, and the propitious moment to move against the salient angle of his line would soon arrive. The silence and mystery in front were ominous; all felt that they evil to the assailants.

Behind the prostrate lines sounded the hoof-beats of galloping horses; the men turned to look. A dozen staff officers were riding to the various brigade and regimental commanders, who had remounted. A moment more and there was a chorus of voices, all uttering out of time the same words—"Attention, battalion!" The men sprang to their feet and were aligned by the company commanders. They awaited the word "forward"—awaited, too, with beating hearts and set teeth the gusts of lead and iron that were to smite them at their first movement in obedience to that word. The word was not given; the tempest did not break out. The delay was hideous, maddening! It unnerved like a respite at the guillotine.

Captain Graffenreid stood at the head of his company, the dead man at his feet. He heard the battle on the right—rattle and crash of musketry, ceaseless thunder of cannon, desultory cheers of invisible combatants. He marked ascending clouds of smoke from distant forests. He noted the sinister silence of the forest in front. These contrasting extremes affected the whole range of his sensibilities. The strain upon his nervous organization was insupportable. He grew hot and cold by turns. He panted like a dog, and then forgot to breathe until reminded by vertigo.

Suddenly he grew calm. Glancing downward, his eyes had fallen upon his naked sword, as he held it, point to earth. Foreshortened to his view, it resembled somewhat, he thought, the short heavy blade of the ancient Roman. The fancy was full of suggestion, malign, fateful, heroic!

The sergeant in the rear rank, immediately behind Captain Graffenreid, now observed a strange sight. His attention drawn by an uncommon movement made by the captain—a sudden reaching forward of the hands and their energetic withdrawal, throwing the elbows out, as in pulling an oar—he saw spring from between the officer's shoulders a bright point of metal which prolonged itself outward, nearly a half-arm's length—a blade! It was faintly streaked with crimson, and its point approached so near to the sergeant's breast, and with so quick a movement, that he shrank backward in alarm. That moment Captain Graffenreid pitched heavily forward upon the dead man and died.

A week later the major-general commanding the left corps of the Federal Army submitted the following official report:

"SIR: I have the honor to report, with regard to the action of the 19th inst., that owing to the enemy's withdrawal from my front to reinforce his beaten left, my command was not seriously engaged. My loss was as follows: Killed, one officer, one man."

IN THE TRENCHES

ALDEN BROOKS

It was a terribly dark night, wet and piercing cold. The pavements were slippery with a muddy slush. They tramped along in silence; not a word; each man his own thoughts, yet each man's thoughts the same. Slowly, however, their blood warmed a little, and their shoulderstraps settled into place. The trenches were five kilometres away to the north. By the time they reached the field kitchens, the night was a little less dark; dawn was coming. There was a wee light burning. They halted beside it and wondered what was going to happen next. One or two went and knocked on the rough huts where the cooks slept. Perhaps there might be some chance of getting a little coffee.

"Coffee for us? You're crazy. Do you think they'd waste coffee on us?"

But it so happened that they had halted for just that reason. From the wee light there came a man with great buckets of hot coffee. They gathered about him and held out their tin cups. The man told them not to crowd around so, he could not see what he was doing, and there was plenty for everybody. Standing up, they gulped it down. It was hot. It warmed. Shortly afterward they were filing along the channels through the earth—the third trenches, the second trenches, then slowly into the first trenches. The watchers there rose stiffly and made room for them. A blue rocket shot up from the Germans opposite. It lit up the landscape with a weird light. The earth seemed to grow colder. Then the artillery began intermittently. Then it got to work in earnest, and for half an hour or more it tore the sky above into shreds. They became impatient. They wanted to know what they were waiting for. It was the captain.

"What in the hell is he fussing about now?"

"Oh, he's fussing about the machine-guns!"

"Oh, he's always fussing about something or other!"

"Hell, that's his business!"

Presently the captain came creeping along. He spoke in a low whisper to the young lieutenant in charge of De Barsac's section.

"Are your men ready?"

"Yes, all ready"

"You've placed your machine-guns the way I told you?"

"Yes."

"Good. Then, you understand, you attack right after us. Give me a few minutes, then come out and dash right up"

There was silence again. The captain moved off. Presently George snickered.

"That's all. Dash right up. Well, I'll promise you one thing, old whiskers," he murmured to a watcher by his side, "if I've got to rot and stink out here for the next month, I'll try and carry my carcass as near as I can to their nostrils rather than to yours"

"Shut up," growled Jules.

George looked around.

"God! you're not funking it, are you?"

"Oh, what do you lose? Nothing. Eh! What do you leave behind?"

"Old man, I leave behind more wives than you"

"Yes, I guess you do—yes, I guess you do—yes, I guess that's about it"

"Stop that noise," whispered the lieutenant.

The artillery fire ceased. A minute later they heard the shouts of the other company over to the left, and above the shouting, the rapid, deadly, pank-pank-pank of the German machine-guns. They stood up instinctively; they swung on their knapsacks; they drew out their bayonets and fixed them on their rifles, and while they did so, their breath steamed upon the cold, damp air. Then, standing there in a profound silence, they looked across at each other through that murky morning light and gave up now definitely everything life had brought them. It was a bitter task, much harder for some than for others; but when the lieutenant suddenly said, "At'em, boys!" all were ready. A low, angry snarl shot from their lips. Like hunted beasts, ready to tear the first thing they met to pieces in a last death-struggle, they scrambled out of the trench. Creeping through the barbed wire, they advanced stealthily until a hail of bullets was turned upon them, then they leaped up with a mighty yell, ran some twenty paces, fell flat upon the ground, and leaped up once more. Head bent down, De Barsac plunged forward. Bullets sang and hissed about him. Every instant he expected death to strike him. He stumbled on, trying to offer it the brain and nothing else. He fell headlong over shell holes, but each time picked himself up and staggered on and on. Hours seemed to pass. He remembered George's words. Not rot here—nor here nor here—but carry one's carcass higher and higher. Finally, he heard the young lieutenant yelling, "Come on, boys, come on, we're almost there." He looked up. Clouds of smoke, bullets ripping up the earth, comrades falling about him, a few hurrying on, all huddled up like men in a terrible rainstorm. Of a sudden he found himself among barbed wire and pit holes. The white bleached face of a man, dead weeks ago, leered at him. He stepped over the putrid body and flung himself through the wire. It tore his clothes, but failed to hold him. Bullets whizzed around his head, but they all seemed to be too high. Then, of a sudden, he realized that he was actually going to reach the trench. He started up. He gripped his rifle in both hands and let out a terrible yell. He became livid with rage. Up out of the ground rose a wave of Germans. He saw George drive his bayonet into the foremost; and as the bayonet snapped off, heard him shout: "Keep it and give it to your sweetheart for a hatpin!" A tall, haggard German charged full at him. He stood his ground, parried the thrust. The German's rifle swung off to one side and exposed his body. With a savage snort he drove his bayonet into the muddy uniform. He felt it go in and in, and instinctively plunged it farther and twisted it around, then heard the wretch scream, and saw him drop his rifle and grasp at life with extended arms, and watched him fall off the bayonet and sink down, bloody hands clasped over his stomach, and a golden ring upon the fourth finger. He stood there weak and flabby. His head began to whirl. Only just in time did he ward off the vicious lunge of a sweating bearded monster. Both rifles rose up locked together into the air. Between their upstretched arms the two men glared at each other.

"Schwein!" hissed the German.

With an adroit twist, De Barsac threw the other off and brought the butt of his rifle down smack upon the moist red forehead. The fellow sank to his knees with a grunt and, eyes closed, vaguely lifted his hand toward his face. De Barsac half fell over him, turned about, and clubbed the exposed neck as hard as he could with his rifle. Bang! went the rifle almost in his sleeve. He swore angrily. But the bullet had only grazed his arm. He leaped on with a loud shout. Within a crater-like opening in the earth a wild, uproarious fight was going on. He caught one glimpse of George swinging the broken leg of a machine-gun and battering in heads right and left, then was engulfed in the melee.

A furious struggle took place—a score of Frenchmen against a score of Germans—in a cockpit of poisoned, shell-tossed earth. None thought of victory, honor. It was merely a wild, frenzied survival of the fittest, wherein each man strove to tear off, rid himself of this fiendish thing against him. Insane with fury, his senses steeped in gore, De Barsac stabbed and clubbed and stabbed; while close by his side a tall Breton, mouth ripped open with a bayonet point, lip flapping down, bellowed horribly: "Kill! Kill! Kill!"

They killed and they killed; then as the contest began to turn rapidly in their favor, their yells became short, swift exclamations of barbaric triumph; then, unexpectedly, it was all over, and the handful of them that remained understood that, by God and by Heaven, they ten, relic though they were of two hundred better men, had actually come through it all alive and on top. The lieutenant, covered with blood, his sword swinging idly from his wrist, staggered over and leaned upon De Barsac's shoulder. In his other hand he held the bespattered broken leg of the machine-gun. So George must be dead. De Barsac burst out laughing nervously. The lieutenant laughed until he had to double up with a fit of coughing. What a picnic! Others sat down, breathing heavily, and told the whole damned German army to come along and see what was waiting for them. But a bullet flew out of the heap of fallen. It burned the skin on De Barsac's forehead like a hot poker. In a twinkling all ten were on their feet again glaring like savages. The lieutenant reached the offender first. The broken leg of the machine-gun came down with an angry thud; then the rest of them turned about and swarmed over the sloping sides of the pit and exterminated, exterminated.

"He's only playing dead. Give him one just the same. Hell! Don't waste a bullet. Here let me. There, take that, sausage!"

The lieutenant climbed up and took a cautious peep over the top of the crater. There was nothing to see. A dull morning sky over a flat rising field. A bit of communicating trench blown in. Way over to the left, like something far off and unreal, the pank-pank-pank of machine-guns and the uproar of desperate fighting. Behind, on the other side, a field littered with fallen figures in light blue, many crawling slowly away.

"What's happening?" asked De Barsac, still out of breath.

"Can't see. The fighting's all over to the left. Everybody seems to have forgotten us. As far as I can judge, this was an outpost, not a real trench"

"Well, whatever it was, it's ours now," said someone.

"Well, why don't they follow us up?"

"Yes, by God, right away, or else—"

"Oh, they will soon!" said the lieutenant, "so get busy—no time to waste. Block up that opening, and fill your sand-bags, all the sand-bags you can find, and dig yourselves in."

But they stood there astonished, irritated. Yes, where were the reinforcements? If reinforcements did not come up, they were as good as rats trapped in a cage. The lieutenant had to repeat his command. Angrily they shoved the dead out of their way and dug themselves in and filled up the sand-bags and built a rampart with them along the top of the hoilow. They swore darkly. No reinforcements! Not a man sent to help them! So it was death, after all. By chance they uncovered a cement trough covered with boards and earth, a sort of shelter; and down there were a great number of cartridge-bands for a machine-gun. The sight of them inspired the lieutenant. He went and busied himself over the captured machine-gun, still half buried in the dirt. Only one leg was broken off; that was all. Hurriedly he cleaned the gun and propped it up between the bags. Then he stood back and rubbed his hands together and laughed boyishly and seemed very pleased. The sun came up in the distance; it glittered upon the frost in the fields. But with it came the shells. Cursing furiously, the ten ducked down into the trough, and for an hour or more hooted at the marksmanship. Only one shell exploded in the crater. Though it shrivelled them all up, it merely tossed about a few dead bodies and left a nasty trail of gas. They became desperate savages again. Then the firing ceased, and the lieutenant scrambled out and peered through the sand-bags. He turned back quickly, eyes flashing. "Here they come, boys!"

They jumped up like madmen and pushed their rifles through the sandbags. The lieutenant sat down at the machine-gun. De Barsac fed the bands. Over the field came a drove of gray-coated men. Their bayonets sparkled wonderfully in the new morning light; yet they ran along all doubled up like men doing some

Swedish drill. They seemed to be a vast multitude until the machine-gun began to shoot. Then the ten saw that they were not so many after all.

"Take care she doesn't jam, old man," said the lieutenant to De Barsac.

"Oh, don't worry, she isn't going to jam!"

They were both very cool.

"Ah! now she's getting into them beautifully," said the lieutenant; "look at them fall. There we go. Spit, little lady, spit; that's the way—steady, old man."

As if by some miracle the gray line of a sudden began to break up. Many less came rushing on. They were singing some guttural song. The rifles between the sand-bags answered them like tongues aflame with hate; but the machine-gun answered them even faster still, a remorseless stream of fire. Finally, there were only some seven or eight left. The lieutenant did not seem to notice them.

"You see how idiotic it all is," he said nonchalantly. "These attacks with a company or two? Why, our little friend here could have taken care of a whole battalion!"

Only one man remained. He was yelling fiercely at the top of his lungs. He looked like some devil escaped from hell. He came tearing on. Bullets would not hit him. Then he was right upon them. But he saw now he was alone and his whole expression changed. Across his eyes glistened the light film of fear. The man with the torn lip jumped up.

"Here you are," he spluttered hideously, "all yours!"

A loud report in De Barsac's ears, smoke and the muddy soles of a pair of hobnailed boots trembling against the nozzle of the machine-gun.

"Do you see what I mean?" continued the lieutenant, "What is the use of it? Did I say a battalion? Why we could have managed a whole regiment—now, then, somebody shove those pig feet out of the way, so that I can finish off the whole lot properly."

The sun came up now in earnest and warmed them; but though they sat back in their little caves and ate some of the food they had brought and then rolled cigarettes and smoked them, they were very nervous and impatient. Every so often one of them would go up the other side of the pit and look back. Always the same sight through the tangle of barbed wire—a foreground heaped with dead, a field sprinkled with fallen blue figures, and three or four hundred yards away the trenches they had come from; otherwise, not a soul. Once they waved a handkerchief on a bayonet. It only brought a shower of bullets. So that was it. After they had accomplished the impossible, they were going to be left here to die like this. A little later the shells once more began to explode about them. The aim once more was very poor, but they knew it was the prelude to another attack. Death was again angling for them—and this time—

"Here they come!" shouted the lieutenant.

They stood up and, pushing their rifles well out through the sand-bags, glanced along the barrels. They swore furiously at what they saw—twice as many of the pig-eaters as before. De Barsac anxiously fed the bands to the vibrating machine before him. The lieutenant's face was very stern and set. It had lost its boyish look. Suddenly there was a terrific explosion, clouds of smoke, and a strange new pungent odor of gas. A man left his post and, eyes closed, turned round and round and went staggering down the slope and stumbled over a dead man and lay where he fell. They stopped firing and huddled against their caves until the lieutenant shouted out something and the machine-gun trembled again. Then there were two more frightful explosions right over their heads. Great God! It was their own artillery!

Through the fog of smoke De Barsac could only see the lieutenant, cringed up over the machine. His face became purple with rage as he hissed into De Barsac's ear his whole opinion of the matter. If he had not said anything before, it was because it was not fit that he should; but before dying now he wanted to tell one man, one other Frenchman, what he thought of a general staff who could first send men out stupidly to their slaughter, then abandon them in positions won, and finally kill them off with their own artillery. But De Barsac, now that the smoke had rolled away a little, was hypnotized by the huge gray wave roaring toward them nearer and nearer. The machine-gun seemed to be helpless among them. However many fell, others came rushing on. Then, unexpectedly, a shell skimmed just over the heads of the nine and exploded full among the advancing throngs. It was the most beautiful sight any of the nine had ever seen. The gray figures were not simply knocked over, but blown into pieces. And in quick succession came explosion after explosion. Priceless vengeance! The field seemed to be a mass of volcanoes. The ranks faltered, broke, plunged about blindly in the smoke, turned, and fled. Only a few came charging wildly on. But the trembling little machine-gun lowered its head angrily. One by one the figures went sprawling, just as if each in turn had of a sudden walked on to slippery ice. So ended the second attack. The third attack, following right after, was a fiasco. The artillery now had their measure to a yard. The shells blew up among them before they were half started. The nine along the crater top did not fire a shot. Shortly afterward they heard the roar of an aeroplane overhead. It must have been there all the time, head in the wind. Under the wings were concentric circles of red and white about a blue dot. The mere sight of it intoxicated them like champagne. And when it was all over for the moment, and the distant figure, moving off, waved his hand, they gave him a cheer it was a great pity he could not hear.

"You see, boys," said the lieutenant gayly, "he's telling us that it's all right now. Reinforcements will be up after dark."

They sat back once more and scraped the blood and muck off their uniforms and smoked and found another meal, and for want of a suitable oath mumbled abstractedly to themselves. Long, tedious hours followed. Little by little it grew colder; then, at last, the sun began to go down. A dreary, desolate landscape stretched out all around. But the thought that reinforcements would soon be coming cheered them. They rose up and got ready to go, then stood about impatiently. The lieutenant had to tell them to never mind what was going on behind them, but stick to their posts. It grew darker, and darker still. Now help would be here any minute. They heard voices; but they were mistaken. It became quite dark, night, half an hour, an hour, two hours, and still no one came, only an ever-increasing cannon fire all around them, shells whistling and screaming to and fro over their heads, red and blue rockets, cataclysms of sound ceaselessly belched into the hollow. At last they threw their knapsacks off in disgust and sat down and cursed and swore as they had never cursed or sworn before.

The night air became painfully cold. They had to stand up again and stamp about to keep warm and not fall asleep. The lieutenant told them to fire off their rifles from time to time. Jules came nearer to De Barsac.

"Ah!" grumbled De Barsac, "they're making monkeys of us"

"Yes—or else they don't know we've taken this place"

"Oh, they know that well enough. Look at the artillery. No; they don't want this hole. They never wanted it. We were never meant to get here."

"Yes," said a voice in the darkness, "it's like this: They went to Joffre and said:" General, some damned fools have gone and taken an outpost over there.

"The hell they have!' says Joffre." Why, the damned fools! Well, give them all the military medal.

"Very well, General," says the Johnny who brought the message, "but they are rather hard to reach."

"Oh, in that case," says Joffre, "just finish the poor devils off with a couple of shells."

"Look here, boys," said the lieutenant, "cut that talk out. You know, as well as I do, that Joffre had nothing to do with this—"

"Well, why the devil then doesn't he send someone up to reinforce us?"

"Well," said the lieutenant after a pause, "look at all those fireworks. There's enough iron in the air to kill ten army corps. They don't dare come up."

"Don't dare? Christ! we dared, didn't we?"

"Well, they may come up by and by."

But no one came; just the furious interchange of shells all night long. So dawn appeared once more and found them stiff, weary, half frozen, and in their dull, hollow eyes no longer a ray of hope. And soon the shells began to fall again upon the hollow. Heedlessly the young lieutenant stood up and took a long look back at those trenches from which help should come. A shell broke just above him. He was still standing upright; but the top of his head was gone, only the lower jaw remained. Blood welled up for a second, then the figure slowly sank into a heap. De Barsac took the revolver out of the clinched hand and removed the cartridge-belt. He went back and sat down at the machine-gun.

"Feed the bands, will you, when the time comes?" he said to Jules.

"Look here," said a man, "it's sure death hanging on here any longer. I'm going to make a dash back for it before it is too light."

"Stay where you are," growled De Barsac.

"No, I'm going to take my chance."

"Do you hear what I say? Get back where you belong, or I'll blow your brains out."

More shells exploded over them. They were caught unawares. They had barely time to crawl into the trough. In fact, some of them had not. The man, who at last wanted to run away, doubled himself up grotesquely and coughed blood until he slowly rolled down toward the bottom of the pit. And there amidst the smoke was the man with the torn lip, lying on one elbow, and both legs smashed off above the knees. De Barsac and Jules tried to haul him under cover.

"Don't bother, boys; no, don't bother—I'm done for now—my mouth was nothing—but this finishes me—no, you can't stop it bleeding—so get back quick—and I'm not frightened of death—I like it—really, I do—I've been waiting for it for a long time."

The bombardment continued. It soon became a tremendous affair. It was the worst bombardment any of them had ever experienced. It was as if they were trying to hide in the mouth of a volcano. They never could have imagined such a thing possible. Then it grew even worse still. The very inside of hell was torn loose and hurled at them. Sheltered though they were in the cement trough, they were slowly buried under earth and stones and wood and dead flesh. And so, while they lay there thus, suffocated by gas and smoke, blind, deaf, senseless, the bombardment went on hour after hour. In fact, it was a great wonder that any of them lived on. But they were only six. And it is always difficult to kill the last six among a crowd of dead; the very dead themselves rise up and offer protection. At last the French artillery once more began to gain the master hand, and the bombardment gradually weakened, and finally it ceased altogether. Slowly, very slowly, the six unravelled themselves. They did not recognize their surroundings. Most of the dead had disappeared, just morsels of flesh and bone and uniform, here and there. They did not recognize themselves. As for rifles, knapsacks, machine-gun, ammunition, they had no idea where any of these were. Should an attack come now, they were defenseless. But that was just the point. They had not come out to live, but to die. The bottom of the pit was more or less empty now. One by one they went and sat down there and stared stupidly at the ground. If another shell came into the crater, they would all be killed outright. But no shell came—just a nice, warm midday sun ahead. So, presently, for want of something better to do, they gathered about a blood-soaked loaf of bread, a box of sardines, a canteen full of wine, and in this cockpit of poisonous, shell-tossed earth, with only a blue sky overhead and a few distant melodious shells singing past, they ate their last meal together. As they ate they slowly decided several things.

First of all, they decided they were cursed; but that, such being the case and since it was their fate to die like this, forgotten in this bloodstained hole, they would die like men, like Frenchmen. Then they decided that this hole was their property. Back of them lay France and her millions of acres and her millions of men; but right here in the very forefront of the fighting was this sanguinary pit; it belonged to them, all six of them, and they would die defending it. Then, finally, as soldiers of experience, they decided many things about modern warfare that all the thousand and one generals and ministers did not know. They decided that knapsacks were useless, and rifles also. What one wanted was a knife, a long knife—look, about as long as that, well, perhaps a little longer—a revolver, bombs, and endless machine-guns, light and easy to carry. They agreed it was a pity none of them would survive to give these valuable conclusions to the others back there.

But after the six had finished their meal and had smoked up all the tobacco of the only man who had any left, they decided that death was not so hard upon them as they first thought. They could still meet it as it should be met. They rose stiffly and found here a spade, there a rifle, and eventually the machine-gun. Under De Barsac's direction they threw up once more a semblance of a bulwark along the top of the hollow, and to show that there was still some fight left in them, fired a few volleys at the Germans, that is to say, all the cartridges they had left, save a full magazine for that last minute when one goes under, killing as many as one can. But whether because the Germans had grown to be a trifle frightened of them, or for some other reason, they received no reply to their taunts beyond an occasional bullet—just a sweet little afternoon when people in cities flock about, straighten their shoulders, sniff the soft atmosphere, and inform each other that Spring is coming. After a time they slumped down where they were, all of them, and stretching out their wet, mud-soaked legs, fell asleep like tired children, and slept on and on until they were awakened in the dark by scores of mysterious figures who patted them on the back, told them they were all heroes, and explained how each time the German artillery had driven them back, and how all they had to do now was to take hold of the rope there and go home to Bray.

So they got up slowly and, hands upon the rope, wandered off. Once they stopped. They heard men digging away busily toward them. They said nothing. They wandered on.

But before the six could reach even the men digging toward them, the darkness was suddenly rent with stupefying explosions, and shell fragments slashed among them. They fell apart, tumbled into shell holes, rose up, fell down again, lost touch with each other, and what became of them all no one will ever know. One or two must have been killed outright; the others must have crawled about in the dark until Fate decided what she wished to do with them. It was rather a sad end; for they deserved better than this, and the Germans did not prevent reinforcements from coming up. But thus ended the six; who they were and what became of them the world will never know.

De Barsac fell flat upon his stomach and put his hands over his head. The ground shook under him. The darkness was a bedlam of endless explosions and death hisses. He rose up again and made a dash for it, a wild, frenzied dash for life and safety. But though he ran on some distance, it was blind work and the ground was littered with obstacles, and suddenly he was lying half buried under a pile of earth. He was in great pain; such that he moaned and moaned; yet he could not move, and now it was less cold and it was morning. Slowly he extricated his right arm, but his left he could not move, and he had to take the dirt away handful by handful, until the sun made his head ache. When his arm was at last uncovered, he could not move it. His whole sleeve was a mass of blood, and the sun had gone of a sudden and it was raining, and the wet ground was tossing him about again like a man in a blanket, and his leg was broken and blood was trickling into his eyes. He moaned upon his arm until the sun again made his head ache, and Jules and his father had disappeared. He asked them to stay there a little longer, but the man next him was so repulsive he could not die thus beside him. Leaning on his right elbow and pushing with his left foot, he moved away inch by inch; only the dead man followed him, or it was his brother, and he was repelled as before, so he took the canteen away from the dead man across his path and drank the stuff down. Then he began to shout at the top of his lungs. A race of bullets swished by over his head. He fell back again on his side and cried weakly into his arm. But presently he crawled on, inch by inch, until even the sun got tired watching him, and he fell down into a sort of trench. There were a lot of dead men there, but all their canteens were empty except one, and he had a great loaf of bread strapped on his knapsack. It was very good inside under the crust.

He sat up and looked around slowly. Just an empty trench, not a living soul, just the dead. How he had got here he could not remember, except that it had taken days, weeks. If his leg were not broken, he might get up now and walk away somewhere. Ah, what dirty luck! As if his arm were not enough! He judged it was late afternoon. He wondered what had happened to the others—well, he would get the machine-gun into place all by himself and kill, kill, right up to the end. Then he remembered that, of course, that was over. Yes, of course, I'm out of my head.

He took some more cognac out of the canteen. He found his knife and his emergency roll. Slowly he cut off his sleeve, and slowly over the great bloody hole in his arm he wound the bandage; then he emptied the iodine bottle over it, and yelled and moaned with pain. But by and by he felt better. Some one spoke to him. It was a white face among the black dead men. He gave the fellow cognac. They sat up together and ate bread and drank cognac. They talked together. All the friend had was a bullet through his chest, just a little hole, but he said it hurt him every time he tried to breathe. He belonged to the 45th. The trench here had been taken by the Germans, only the Germans had to abandon it because they had lost a trench over there to the left.

"Yes," said De Barsac. "That was us"

By and by De Barsac asked the friend if he could get up and walk. The friend said he thought he could now. So he got up and fell down, and got up and fell down, until the third time he did not fall.

"Wait," said De Barsac, "my leg's broken"

They helped each other. They went along scraping the sides of the channel. De Barsac moaned in constant agony. But they saw two men with a stretcher in the fields above. De Barsac halloed feebly. The men turned around with a start; then one of them said, with a scowl: "All right, wait a minute." Then there was the ordinary explosion overhead. They saw nothing more of the two men. just a bit of broken stretcher and canvas sticking up out of the ground and a large cloud of dark smoke rolling away fainter and fainter. The trench was muddy. The trench smelled. The whole land smelled. The earth about was all burned yellow. The clay was red. There were boards in the bottom of the trench, but the boards wabbled and one could not hop along them. They slopped and twisted about.

"Here," said the friend, "lean on me some more."

But he only fainted. So they both lay huddled up in the mud of the channel, and death came down very near them both. But De Barsac's face was lying against a tin can in the mud, and he lifted himself up and saw that it was nearly dark and he shivered with cold. He remembered the cognac. He gulped it all down. It hurt his arm, made it throb, throb, throb; but it somehow also made him feel Hke laughing. So he laughed; then he cried; then he laughed; all because the friend at his side was dead and he loved him. He had not known him very long, but he loved him. He turned the head up and the friend's eyes opened. He was not dead, after all. Quickly De Barsac hunted for the cognac and at last he found it. He was horrified. He had drunk it all and not left the friend any. But there were just a few drops.

"Thanks, old camel," said the friend.

De Barsac slowly got up and, after he had got up, he helped the friend up. "Come on."

"All right."

"Here, you get on my back."

"No, you get on mine."

But they both fell again. So they decided to crawl along. Only it was growing colder and colder, and the waits were awful. Finally, the white face said:

"I'm—I'm going to sleep a little—you go on—you see—then you call me—then I'll come along."

De Barsac wondered why they had not thought of doing it that way before. He crawled on and on. At last he stopped and called back. The friend did not come the way he said he would. He was asleep of course. De Barsac started back to fetch him, only some men came along and stepped on him until they suddenly stepped off.

"Yes, he's alive"

De Barsac pointed feebly up the channel"He's back there," he said. "Who?" "The friend."

"He's delirious," said a voice.

"Well, pass him back to the stretcher-bearers and look lively with those machine-guns."

The dressing-station was all under ground and lined with straw. It was very warm, only it was also very crowded. They gave him some hot soup with vegetables in it. He lay back on the stretcher and perspired; and though he was now in very great pain, he said nothing, because he had nothing to say. The surgeon, sleeves rolled up, bent over him. He set his leg and slapped plaster about. He swabbed his head and made him nearly scream. Then he unwound the bandage on his arm and swore and stood up and said: "Too late. Put on the tag, 'Operate at once.'"

It was cold between the two wheels under the open stars amid the cigarette smoke, but the ambulances in Bray made a powerful noise, and through the darkness a sergeant looked at him under a lantern and said impatiently:

"Well, I don't give a damn, there isn't an inch of space left. Fire him along to Villers-Bretonneux with that convoy that's starting."

The ambulance rocked and bounced over the roads, and it was twice as cold as before. He had not enough blankets. The ambulance smelled so he knew the man to his left must be dead; yes, the man to his left, not the man above, for the man above from time to time dripped hot blood upon him, now upon his neck, now upon his face. In the big shed at Villers-Bretonneux it was warm again, and he lay there upon the straw with the others while crowds of peasant people stared at them. One woman came up and offered him half an orange. He did not take it. Another woman said: "He's out of his head, poor fellow." He said: "No, I'm not."

After the man on the stretcher next to him had told him he was wounded in the stomach, left shoulder, and both legs, the man on the stretcher next him asked him where he came from and how things were getting on there. He said: "All right."

Then the man on the stretcher next him said weakly: "Well, you seem to have picked up all the mud there is up there." So he said: "Oh, there's plenty left!" and a neat little man in black, with a red ribbon in his buttonhole, shook his head and said to a large man staring with a heavy scowl: "They're all that way, you know; a joke on their lips up to the end."

They carried him out through the crowd, and when he was opposite the bloody table under the great arc-light, the men carrying him had to stop a second and the doctor said to the man holding the end of the leg: "Bend down, idiot, haven't you ever sawed wood?" And he saw that there were beads of perspiration upon the doctor's forehead, and he wondered why. In the train it was very, very warm, only it smelled dreadfully—that same smell. He knew now it was the man in the bunk next to him that was dead, and he wanted to tell the attendant so, only the shadows on the wooden ceiling danced about as the train rushed along over bridges and through tunnels. The shadows danced about, and sometimes they were horsemen on chargers and sometimes they were just great clouds flying out across the ocean, and all the time that the shadows danced about and the train rushed on and on a man in the other end of the compartment yelled and swore. But although he called the attendants all the names a man has ever called another, the attendants did not move. One said:

"Well, if they do shunt us over on to that other service, that'll mean we'll get down to Paris now and then."

And the first man answered:

"Oh, well, anything for a change—pass me the morphine again, will you, if you're through with it."

The train stopped, and every one wanted to know where they were. One of the attendants told them, "Amiens" He was taken out slowly and carried before a man with a glossy, black beard, smoking a pipe, who read the tag on his buttonhole and wrote something on a sheet of paper. They took him out into the cold, biting wind of a railway yard and carried him across railway tracks and set the stretcher down in pools of black mud, and argued whose turn it was, while a long freight-train rolled slowly by and a man blew a whistle. The ambulance bobbed lightly over cobbles amid the clang of street-cars and the thousand noises of a city. This ambulance also smelled that same smell; but it could not be the man next to him, for he was all alone. Then the ambulance ran along a smooth drive and stopped, and the flaps were opened and he was lifted out and carried into a long hallway, where a small man in red slippers scampered about and told others to come, and a white-hooded woman bent over him.

"What's the matter with him?"

"Operation."

"Yes—his left arm—the smell is sufficient indication. George, tell the doctor not to go away."

The white-hooded woman again leaned over him. Her face was wrinkled and tired, but her eyes were very beautiful—they were so gentle and so sad.

"How do you feel?"

"Yes," he mumbled.

"Poor boy! What's your name?"

"Pierre De Barsac."

She took his hand gently and held it.

"Well, Pierre, don't worry. We are going to take care of you."

A little later she said:

"Poor fellow! Are you suffering?"

Tears came into his eyes and he nodded his head.

They carried him up-stairs. They went up slowly, very carefully, and as they turned the corners of the staircase the eyes of the little man with the red slippers glittered and strained over the end of the stretcher. They undressed him. They washed him. They put him to bed. They unwound his arm. Then they stood away and stopped talking. They left him alone with a great wad of damp cotton upon his arm until the doctor came and said:

"My boy, we've got to amputate your left arm at the shoulder."

"At the shoulder," he repeated mechanically.

"Yes, it's the only thing that will save you. What's your profession?"

"Lawyer."

The doctor smiled pleasantly.

"Oh, then you are all right! An arm the less will be a distinction."

They went away. He turned over a little and looked at his arm. He realized that this was the dead thing he had so often smelled. The arm was all brown. It crackled under his finger; then came the large cotton wad where there were strips of black flesh. The hand was crumpled up like a fallen leaf. He saw the scar on his forefinger where, as a little boy, he had cut through the orange too swiftly. What a scene that was, and his mother was dead now, and his father was very old, and the hand now was going to be taken away from him! He turned his head back and cried weakly, not on account of his hand, but because he was in such pain, his arm, his leg, his head, everything. They rolled him into another room. They fussed about him. They hurt him dreadfully; but he said nothing, because he had nothing to say. Then he was back there again, beside the lieutenant, only the machine-gun jammed and he had to break the leg off and use it against the hordes of pig-eaters, and smoke, more smoke, down one's nostrils, and then it was awful, awful, never like this, and he clutched the pig-eater by the throat and swore, swore, until now more smoke came rolling into his nostrils, and the white-hooded nurse was standing by his bed.

She went away; and when he woke up again, he was all alone. There was a bandage upon his left arm; no, his left shoulder. His arm hurt much less; he felt much better. By and by he moved his right hand over. The sleeve of the nightgown was empty.

He lay there quietly a long time and looked up into the sky through some pine boughs swaying in the wind. They reminded him of other trees he knew of—trees way back there in Brittany.

A little later she said:

"Poor fellow! Are you suffering?"

Tears came into his eyes and he nodded his head.

They carried him up-stairs. They went up slowly, very carefully, and as they turned the corners of the staircase the eyes of the little man with the red slippers glittered and strained over the end of the stretcher. They undressed him. They washed him. They put him to bed. They unwound his arm. Then they stood away and stopped talking. They left him alone with a great wad of damp cotton upon his arm until the doctor came and said:

"My boy, we've got to amputate your left arm at the shoulder."

"At the shoulder," he repeated mechanically.

"Yes, it's the only thing that will save you. What's your profession?"

"Lawyer."

The doctor smiled pleasantly.

"Oh, then you are all right! An arm the less will be a distinction."

They went away. He turned over a little and looked at his arm. He realized that this was the dead thing he had so often smelled. The arm was all brown. It crackled under his finger; then came the large cotton wad where there were strips of black flesh. The hand was crumpled up like a fallen leaf. He saw the scar on his forefinger where, as a little boy, he had cut through the orange too swiftly. What a scene that was, and his mother was dead now, and his father was very old, and the hand now was going to be taken away from him! He turned his head back and cried weakly, not on account of his hand, but because he was in such pain, his arm, his leg, his head, everything. They rolled him into another room. They fussed about him. They hurt him dreadfully; but he said nothing, because he had nothing to say. Then he was back there again, beside the lieutenant, only the machine-gun jammed and he had to break the leg off and use it against the hordes of pig-eaters, and smoke, more smoke, down one's nostrils, and then it was awful, awful, never like this, and he clutched the pig-eater by the throat and swore, swore, until now more smoke came rolling into his nostrils, and the white-hooded nurse was standing by his bed.

She went away; and when he woke up again, he was all alone. There was a bandage upon his left arm; no, his left shoulder. His arm hurt much less; he felt much better. By and by he moved his right hand over. The sleeve of the nightgown was empty.

He lay there quietly a long time and looked up into the sky through some pine boughs swaying in the wind. They reminded him of other trees he knew of—trees way back there in Brittany by the seaside where he was born. They swayed beautifully to and fro, and every so often they bent over and swished against the window-pane.

Presently he smiled, smiled quietly, happily. Life, when one can live it, is such a really wonderful thing.

BLOWING UP A TRAIN

T. E. LAWRENCE

Blowing up trains was an exact science when done deliberately, by a sufficient party, with machine-guns in position. If scrambled at it might become dangerous. The difficulty this time was that the available gunners were Indians; who, though good men fed, were only half-men in cold and hunger. I did not propose to drag them off without rations on an adventure which might take a week. There was no cruelty in starving Arabs; they would not die of a few days' fasting, and would fight as well as ever on empty stomachs; while, if things got too difficult, there were the riding camels to kill and eat; but the Indians, though Moslems, refused camel-flesh on principle.

I explained these delicacies of diet. Ali at once said that it would be enough for me to blow up the train, leaving him and the Arabs with him to do their best to carry its wreck without machine-gun support. As, in this unsuspecting district, we might well happen on a supply train, with civilians or only a small guard of reservists aboard, I agreed to risk it. The decision having been applauded, we sat down in a cloaked circle, to finish our remaining food in a very late and cold supper (the rain had sodden the fuel and made fire not possible) our hearts somewhat comforted by the chance of another effort.

At dawn, with the unfit of the Arabs, the Indians moved away for Azrak miserably. They had started up country with me in hope of a really military enterprise and first had seen the muddled bridge and now were losing this prospective train. It was hard on them; and to soften the blow with honour I asked Wood to accompany them. He agreed, after argument, for their sakes; but it proved a wise move for himself, as a sickness which had been troubling him began to show the early signs of pneumonia.

The balance of us, some sixty men, turned back towards the railway. None of them knew the country so I led them to Minifir, where, with Zaal, we had made havoc in the spring. The re-curved hill-top was an excellent observation-post, camp, grazing ground and way of retreat, and we sat there in our old place till sunset, shivering and staring out over the immense plain which stretched map-like to the clouded peaks of Jebel Druse, with Um el Jemal and her sister-villages like ink-smudges through the rain.

In the first dusk we walked down to lay the mine. The rebuilt culvert of kilometre 172 seemed still the fittest place. While we stood by it there came a rumbling and through the gathering darkness and mist a train suddenly appeared round the northern curve, only two hundred yards away. We scurried under the long arch and heard it roll overhead. This was annoying; but when the course was clear again, we fell to burying the charge. The evening was bitterly cold with drifts of rain blowing down the valley.

The arch was solid masonry, of four metres span, and stood over a shingle water-bed which took its rise on our hill-top. The winter rains had cut this into a channel four feet deep, narrow and winding, which served us as an admirable approach till within three hundred yards of the line. There the gully widened out and ran straight towards the culvert, open to the sight of anyone upon the rails.

We hid the explosive carefully on the crown of the arch, deeper than usual, beneath a tie, so that the patrols could not feel its jelly softness under their feet. The wires were taken down the bank into the shingle bed of the watercourse, where concealment was quick; and up it as far as they could reach. Unfortunately, this was only sixty yards, for there had been difficulty in Egypt over insulated cable and no more had been available when our expedition started.

Sixty yards was plenty for the bridge, but little for a train: however, the ends happened to coincide with a little bush about ten inches high, on the edge of the watercourse, and we buried them beside this very convenient mark. It was impossible to leave them joined up to the exploder in the proper way, since the spot was evident to the permanent way-patrols as they made their rounds.

Owing to the mud the job took longer than usual, and it was very nearly dawn before we finished. I waited under the draughty arch till day broke, wet and dismal, and then I went over the whole area of disturbance, spending another half-hour in effacing its every mark, scattering leaves and dead grass over it, and watering down the broken mud from a shallow rain-pool near. Then they waved to me that the first patrol was coming and I went up to join the others.

Before I had reached them they came tearing down into their prearranged places, lining the watercourse and spurs each side. A train was corning from the north. Hamud, Feisal's long slave, had the exploder; but before he reached me a short train of closed box-wagons rushed by at speed. The rainstorms on the plain and the thick morning had hidden it from the eyes of our watchman until too late. This second failure saddened us further and Ali began to say that nothing would come right this trip. Such a statement held risks as prelude of the discovery of an evil eye present; so, to divert attention, I suggested new watching posts be sent far out, one to the ruins on the north, one to the great cairn of the southern crest.

The rest, having no breakfast, were to pretend not to be hungry. They all enjoyed doing this and for a while we sat cheerfully in the rain huddled against one another for warmth behind a breastwork of our streaming camels. The moisture made the animals' hair curl up like a fleece so that they looked queerly dishevelled. When the rain paused, which it did frequently, a cold moaning wind searched out the unprotected parts of us very thoroughly. After a time we found our wetted shirts clammy and comfortless things. We had nothing to eat, nothing to do and nowhere to sit except on wet rock, wet grass or mud. However, this persistent weather kept reminding me that it would delay Allenby's advance on Jerusalem and rob him of his great possibility. So large a misfortune to our lion was a half-encouragement for the mice. We would be partners into next year.

In the best circumstances, waiting for action was hard. Today it was beastly. Even enemy patrols stumbled along without care, perfunctorily, against the rain. At last near noon, in a snatch of fine weather, the watchmen on the south peak flagged their cloaks wildly in signal of a train. We reached our positions in an instant, for we had squatted the late hours on our heels in a streaming ditch near the line so as not to miss another chance. The Arabs took cover properly. I looked back at their ambush from my firing point and saw nothing but the grey hillsides.

I could not hear the train coming but trusted, and knelt ready for perhaps half an hour when the suspense became intolerable, and I signalled to know what was up. They sent down to say it was coming very slowly and was an enormously long train. Our appetites stiffened. The longer it was the more would be the loot. Then came word that it had stopped. It moved again.

Finally, near one o'clock, I heard it panting. The locomotive was evidently defective, (all these wood-fired trains were bad), and the heavy load on the up-gradient was proving too much for its capacity. I crouched behind my bush while it crawled slowly into view past the south cutting and along the bank above my head towards the culvert. The first ten trucks were open trucks, crowded with troops. However, once again it was too late to choose, so when the engine was squarely over the mine I pushed down the handle of the exploder. Nothing happened. I sawed it up and down four times.

Still nothing happened; and I realised that it had gone out of order and that I was kneeling on a naked bank, with a Turkish troop train crawling past fifty yards away. The bush, which had seemed a foot high, shrank smaller than a figleaf; and I felt myself the most distinct object in the countryside. Behind me was an open valley for two hundred yards to the cover where my Arabs were waiting, and wondering what I was at. It was impossible to make a bolt for it or the Turks would step off the train and finish us. If I sat still, there might be just a hope of my being ignored as a casual Bedouin.

So there I sat, counting for sheer life, while eighteen open trucks, three box-wagons, and three officers' coaches dragged by. The engine panted slower and slower and I thought every moment that it would break down. The troops took no great notice of me but the officers were interested, and they came out to the little platforms at the ends of their carriages, pointing and staring. I waved back at them, grinning nervously and feeling an improbable shepherd in my Meccan dress with its twisted golden circlet about my head. Perhaps the mud-stains, the wet and their ignorance made me accepted. The end of the brake van slowly disappeared into the cutting on the north.

As it went, I jumped up, buried my wires, snatched hold of the wretched exploder, and went like a rabbit uphill into safety. There I took breath and looked back to see that the train had finally stuck. It waited, about five hundred yards beyond the mine, for nearly an hour to get up a head of steam, while an officers' patrol came back and searched, very carefully, the ground where I had been seen sitting. However the wires were properly hidden: they found nothing: the engine plucked up heart again and away they went.

Mifleh was past tears, thinking I had intentionally let the train through; and when the Serahin had been told the real cause they said "bad luck is with us." Historically they were right; but they meant it for a prophecy so I made sarcastic reference to their courage at the bridge the week before, hinting that it might be a tribal preference to sit on came guard. At once there was uproar, the Serahin attacking more furiously, the Beni Sakhr defending. Ali heard the trouble and came running.

When we had made it up the original despondency was half forgotten. Ali backed me nobly, though the wretched boy was blue with cold and shivering in an attack of fever. He gasped that their ancestor the Prophet had given to Sherifs the faculty of "sight," and by it he knew that our luck was turning. This was comfort for them: my first instalment of good fortune came when in the wet, without other tool than my dagger, I got the box of the exploder open and persuaded its electrical gear to work properly once more.

We returned to our vigil by the wires, but nothing happened, and evening drew down with more squalls and beastliness, everybody full of grumbles. There was no train; it was too wet to light a cooking fire; our only potential food was camel. Raw meat did not tempt anyone that night and so our beasts survived to the morrow.

Ali lay down on his belly, which position lessened the hunger-ache, trying to sleep off his fever. Khazen, Ali's servant, lent him his cloak for extra covering. For a spell I took Khazen under mine, but soon found it becoming crowded. So I left it to him and went downhill to connect up the exploder. Afterwards I spent the night there alone by the singing telegraph wires, hardly wishing to sleep, so painful was the cold. Nothing came all the long hours, and dawn, which broke wet looked even uglier than usual. We were sick to death of Minifir, of railways, of train watching and wrecking, by now. I climbed up to the main body while the early patrol searched the railway. Then the day cleared a little. Ali awoke much refreshed and his new spirit cheered up. Hamud, the slave, produced some sticks which he had kept under his clothes by his skin all night. They were nearly dry. We shaved down some blasting gelatine and with its hot flame got a fire going while the Sukhar hurriedly killed a mangy camel, the best spared of our riding-beasts, and began with entrenching tools to hack it into handy joints.

Just at that moment the watchman on the north cried, "A train." We left the fire and made a breathless race of the six hundred yards downhill to our old position. Round the bend, whistling its loudest, came the train, a splendid two-engined thing of twelve passenger coaches travelling at top speed on the favouring grade. I touched off under the first driving wheel of the first locomotive, and the explosion was terrific. The ground spouted blackly into my face and I was sent spinning, to sit up with the shirt torn to my shoulder and the blood dripping from long, ragged scratches on my left arm. Between my knees lay the exploder, crushed under a twisted sheet of sooty iron. In front of me was the scalded and smoking upper half of a man. When I peered through the dust and steam of the explosion the whole boiler of the first engine seemed to be missing.

I dully felt that it was time to get away to support but when I moved, I learnt that there was a great pain in my right foot because of which I could only limp along with my head swinging from the shock. Movement began to clear away this confusion as I hobbled towards the upper valley, whence the Arabs were now shooting fast into the crowded coaches. Dizzily I cheered myself by repeating aloud in English, "Oh, I wish this hadn't happened."

When the enemy began to return our fire, I found myself much between the two. Ali saw me fall and, thinking that I was hard hit, ran out with Turki and about twenty men of his servants and the Beni Sakhr to help me. The Turks found their range and got seven of them in a few seconds. The others, in a rush, were about me—fit models, after their activity, for a sculptor. Their full white cotton drawers drawn in, belllike, round their slender waists and ankles; their hairless brown bodies, and the love-locks plaited tightly over each temple in long horns; made them look like Russians dancers.

We scrambled back into cover together and there, secretly, I felt myself over, to find I had not once been really hurt; though besides the bruises and cuts of the boiler-plate and a broken toe, I had five different bullet-grazes on me (some of them uncomfortably deep) and my clothes ripped to pieces.

From the watercourse we could, look about. The explosion had destroyed the arched head of the culvert and the frame of the first engine was lying beyond it at the near foot of the embankment down which it had rolled. The second locomotive had toppled into the gap and was lying across the ruined tender of the first. Its bed was twisted. I judged them both beyond repair. The second tender had disappeared over the further side and the first three wagons had telescoped and were smashed in pieces.

The rest of the train was badly derailed, with the listing coaches butted end to end at all angles zigzagged along the track. One of them was a saloon decorated with flags. In it had been Mehmed Jemal Pasha, commanding the Eighth Army Corps, hurrying down to defend Jerusalem against Allenby.

His chargers had been in the first wagon; his motor-car was on the end of the train and we shot it up. Of his staff we noticed a fat ecclesiastic, whom we thought to be Assad Shukair, Imam to Ahmed Jemal Pasha and a notorious pro-Turk pimp. So we blazed at him till he dropped.

It was all long bowls. We could see that our chance of carrying the wreck was slight. There had been some four hundred men on board and the survivors, now recovered from the shock, were under shelter and shooting hard at us. At the first moment our party on the north spur had closed and nearly won the game. Mifleh on his mare chased the officers from the saloon into the lower ditch. He was too excited to stop and shoot and so they got away scathless. The Arabs following him had turned to pick up some of the rifles and medals littering the ground and then to drag bags and boxes from the train. If we had had a machine-gun posted to cover the far side, according to my mining practice, not a Turk would have escaped.

Mifleh and Adhub rejoined us on the hill and asked after Fahad. One of the Serahin told how he had led the first rush, while I lay knocked out beside the exploder, and had been killed near it. They showed his belt and rifle as proof that he was dead and that they had tried to save him. Adhub said not a word but leaped out of the gully and raced downhill. We caught our breaths till our lungs hurt us watching him, but the Turks seemed not to see. A minute later he was dragging a body behind the left-hand bank.

Mifleh went back to his mare, mounted, and took her down behind a spur. Together they lifted the inert figure on to the pommel and returned. A bullet had passed through Fahad's face, knocking out four teeth and gashing the tongue. He had fallen unconscious but had revived just before Adhub reached him and was trying on hands and knees, blinded with blood, to crawl away. He now recovered poise enough to cling to a saddle. So they changed him to the first camel they found and led him off at once.

The Turks, seeing us so quiet, began to advance up the slope. We let them come half-way and then poured in volleys which killed some twenty and drove the others back. The ground about the train was strewn with dead, and the broken coaches had been crowded but they were fighting under the eye of their Corps Commander and, undaunted began to work round the spurs to outflank us.

We were now only about, forty left and obviously could do no good against them. So we ran in batches up the little stream-bed, turning at each sheltered angle to delay them by pot-shots. Little Turki much distinguished himself by quick coolness, though his straight-stocked Turkish cavalry carbine made him so exposed his head that he got four bullets through his head-cloth. Ali was angry with me for retiring slowly. In reality my raw hurts crippled me but to hide from him this real reason I pretended to be easy, interested in and studying the Turks. Such successive rests while I gained courage for a new run kept him and Turki far behind the rest.

At last we reached the hill-top. Each man there jumped on the nearest camel and made away at full speed eastward into the desert for an hour. Then in safety we sorted our animals. The excellent Rahail, despite the ruling excitement, had brought off with him, tied to his saddle-girth, a huge haunch of the camel slaughtered just as the train arrived. He gave us the motive for a proper halt, five miles farther on, as a little party of four camels appeared marching in the same direction. It was our companion, Matar, coming back from his home village to Azrak with loads of raisins and peasant delicacies.

So we stopped at once, under a large rock in Wadi Dhuleil, where there was a barren fig-tree, and cooked our first meal for three days. There, also, we bandaged up Fahad, who was sleepy with the lassitude of his severe hurt. Adhub, seeing this, took one of Matar's new carpets and, doubling it across the camel-saddle, stitched the ends into great pockets. In one they laid Fahad while Adhub crawled into the other as makeweight and the camel was led off southward towards their tribal tents.

The other wounded men were seen to at the same time. Mifleh brought up the youngest lads of the party and had them spray the wounds with their piss as a rude antiseptic. Meanwhile we whole ones refreshed ourselves. I bought another mangy camel for extra meat, paid rewards, compensated the relatives of the killed and gave prize-money for the sixty or seventy rifles we had taken. It was small booty but not to be despised. Some Serahin, who had gone into the action without rifles able only to throw unavailing stones, had now two guns apiece. Next day we moved into Azrak, having a great welcome and boasting—God forgive us—that we were victors.

AIR BATTLE

CHARLES NORDHOFF AND JAMES NORMAN HALL

O ne early morning in November, Harvey McKail, Golasse, and I were loafing around the messroom stove. The other members of Spad 597, with the exception of Captain Clermont, were out on an eight to ten o'clock patrol. A new motor was being installed in the captain's Spad, so he was doubtless having as luxurious a morning in his own barrack as we were in ours. The other three squadrons of Group 31 had gone off at eight-thirty to furnish protection to a lot of Brequet bombing planes sent out to drop huge bombs on ammunition dumps near Metz. McKail, Golasse and I were to go up at ten-fifteen for a high patrol so we had slept till nine, and now, a quarter of an hour later, still dressed in pyjamas, we were crunching buttered toast and drinking chocolate. McKail was reading Henry James' Gabrielle de Bergerac, and Golasse and I were exchanging boyhood reminiscences. Our lives up to the war had been as different as possible. His had been spent wholly in Paris; he had never been farther from the boulevards than to St. Cloud, and it was hard for him to understand what ranch life in California could be like. Still less could he picture the South Seas.

"Do you mean to say you really enjoyed being there?" he asked incredulously.

"Enjoyed it! That's a mild way of stating it," I replied. "Fro going back after the war; Forbes and I are going together if we get through."

Golasse shook his head. "You Americans are a queer lot. Well, you can have your South Sea island. Give me Paris. Give me the Café Maxeville on a fine summer evening, with a glass of porto on the table beside me, plenty of money to buy more when it's gone, and nothing to do til to-morrow. Give me—"

He didn't finish the sentence. Just then Old Felix came in and his beard fairly bristled with excitement. "Gentlemen! I don't like to disturb you, but there's a Boche coming this way! I thought you might like to see him."

We rushed outside, and heard at once the far-off brisk detonations of anti-aircraft fire. It was a windless, cloudless morning; eight or ten miles away to the southeast the sky was dotted with the tiny white smoke blossoms of French seventy-fives. The smoke from the French anti-aircraft shells was always white and that of the Germans black, so we knew at once that the plane was a Boche. He was still too far away to be seen, but we could follow his course by the shell bursts, and he was evidently coming our way.

"Another of those photographic buses," said Golasse. "Seiden, there's some cold meat for us. Let's go after it. What do you say, McKail?"

I looked at my watch—a quarter to ten. "Haven't time," I said. "We're due for high patrol in half an hour."

Just then an orderly from Group headquarters scorched across the field on a motor-cycle. It was Flingot, the chauffeur who had met me at Chalons the night I joined the squadron.

"Now then! Now then!" he said. "Don't stand there looking at him. That won't win the war. Hop along, you two! Captain's orders."

He handed Golasse a pencilled note which read:

Golasse. You and Seiden take off at once after that two-seater. Never mind the ten-fifteen patrol. McKail will wait for the scheduled information. Good luck!

There was no time to dress, of course. We sprinted down the field, bearskin coats over our pyjamas. Orders had already been sent to hangars; the mechanics had trundled out our Spads and were warming up the motors by the time we had arrived. We jumped into our flying suits and were ready for the take-off within three minutes. At least I was, but Golasse's mechanics were having trouble with his motor. It spluttered and back-fired, and refused to turn up more than a thousand revolutions. Golasse was cursing and waving his arms, "Go on!" he yelled. "I'll be along in a minute." So I waved and started off alone.

My little ship had never climbed more beautifully. I took height over the aerodrome, watching it shrink and shrink until the great field with its rows of barracks and hangars looked no larger than a playing card. The horizons rolled back; soon I could see for miles in every direction, and above me, but still off to the right, the sky sparkled every little while with points of intense light where the French anti-aircraft shells were bursting. The minute puffs of smoke were climbing the sky in my direction. It looked as though the German meant to make a long sweep across the Salient and reenter his own territory somewhere to the northwest.

I turned northeast and climbed in a wide circle so that I could have the sun at my back when high enough to attack, at the same time keeping a sharp lookout for other Germans. There were none to be seen, however, but far to the eastward the sky, at about three thousand metres, was plentifully sprinkled with shell bursts, both black and white. There was no lack of aerial activity over the lines. Apparently the two-seater, taking altitude over his own territory, had sailed serenely across the front at a great height.

Presently I could make him out, a minute speck moving jauntily among the smoke blossoms. Every anti-aircraft battery along the sector seemed to be blazing away at him, and some of them were making good practice. They were putting them very close, in groups of three and four, but he moved in a leisurely fashion, flying in wide detours and circles. As I watched him I was convinced that Golasse was right in thinking it a photographic plane, sent out to take long range pictures with one of those marvellous high-altitude cameras the Germans had. The two men went about their business as calmly and methodically as though anti-aircraft fire was nothing to them and the possibility of pursuit by hostile planes had not crossed their minds.

I wondered whether they saw my Spad on their trail, climbing steadily up the sky. I could see them plainly enough now, not more than two miles away and about a thousand metres over me. "They must see me," I thought, "but it doesn't appear to worry them." Now and then they would make a wide turn, very slowly, as though they had throttled down for picture-taking, and then move leisurely on. I felt a little uneasy at their apparent disregard for me, and scrutinised the air below me, hoping to see Golasse. The sight of his Spad would have been a welcome one, but I was not to be granted it. No Golasse—no anybody save myself and the two Germans, who looked bigger and more sinister every moment.

While making a turn I was astonished to find that we were almost over the Senard aerodrome, which now appeared to be about the size of a postage stamp. I had been looking overhead constantly and had paid little attention to direction except to follow the Germans. We had turned west without knowing it, and were flying parallel to the front and about ten miles inside our lines. "Lord!" I thought. "Now's my time! What luck if I could bring down a German right over my field!" He was almost directly above me now, but still a good five hundred metres higher. Useless to pull up and fire a burst at that distance, but I was rather surprised that the observer didn't spray a few bullets in my direction. He didn't, however, at least I saw no pencilled lines of smoke from tracers. They still flew in the most leisurely manner, as though they thought me not worth bothering about; and somehow their manner of flying told me that they were old pilots who knew their business thoroughly. Their ship, with its silvered undersurface and the huge black crosses on the wings, looked like a veteran too, long accustomed to making flights deep into enemy territory. By that time I had made it out to be a Rumpler.

I didn't like the way they ignored my little Spud, and felt a welcome flush of anger surging through me. "Just wait a minute, you two!" I thought. "You may be old hands at this game, and you maybe know that I'm a young one. Just the same you'll have to notice me."

I crept up, crept up, turning off from their course as I gained my last three hundred metres of altitude, and taking care to keep the sun at my back. "Now, my boy," I said, "Go to it!"

I made a half turn to the left, at the same time crooking my forefinger around the machine-gun trigger on the joy-stick, and started toward what I considered my prey. I had made my calculations with the utmost care, so that I could attack directly from behind and a little below the two-seater, approach-ing him under cover of his blind spot. The only mistake I made was in forgetting, momentarily, that the two Germans might do some calculating as well. As I have said, I started toward my prey, and to my great astonishment he wasn't there.

Then I heard a sound as peculiar as it was uncomfortable—flac! flac-flac! flac! I knew what that meant: bullets were going through the fabric of my bus. I made a steep turn and found that the German pilot had dived suddenly about fifty metres and levelled off again so that his observer could have me in full view.

And so he did have me, and was giving me a full dose with both guns. I thought certainly I was lost; the muzzles of his two guns were pointing straight at me and my Spad seemed to be hanging motionless. But he didn't have me in his sights for long. I made a diving turn and had him broadside on a little above me again. I pulled the trigger. My gun popped once and jammed.

Of all the exasperating things that could happen in the air, a jammed gun was assuredly the worst, and it seemed always to occur at the most critical moment possible. It was by no means easy to clear a stoppage; and in order to do so it was necessary to withdraw from a fight for several moments, and a pilot was lucky if his opponent permitted him to withdraw. I was grateful to those Germans for allowing me to do so in this case. They flew steadily on, I was following at a safe distance, all the while hammering on my crank handle with the little wooden mallet we carried for such emergencies. I knew from the position of my crank handle that I had a bulged cartridge to deal with, but I got rid of it at last and went on again, full motor.

The two-seater was about half a mile in front of me now, flying at the same altitude. I gained on him rapidly, and in my excitement opened fire when still one hundred and fifty metres distant. My tracers appeared to be going directly into the plane, and yet, to my astonishment, and disgust, it showed no signs of being damaged. I must have fired between fifty and seventy-five rounds when all of a sudden the Rumpler loomed up directly in front of me. I had not realised how much faster I was going, and as a result I nearly got him by running into him. He turned just as I zoomed over him and I had a vivid glimpse of my opponents. The observer was sighting down through his camera but looked up just as I passed and seized the handle of his guns with an air of annoyance and surprise as much as to say, "Oh—!! Here's that pest back again!" The pilot turned his head over his shoulder, and I had a fleeting view of the vacant stare of his goggles and a flowing blond moustache. I did an Immelmann turn to come back at them and, unfortunately, in making it, passed directly above them whereupon the observer gave me another burst. I heard a loud whang-g-g and knew that something had been hit, but it was not till several minutes later that I saw that one of my bracing wires had been cut through.

One of the most surprising things to me, in an air battle, was the rapidity with which two planes could separate. At one second you were close enough to see the colour of your opponent's moustache and the kind of flying clothes he wore; a few seconds later, as you turned to come back, you found that he was a half a mile or even three-quarters of a mile away. Two planes flying at a combined speed of perhaps two hundred and fifty miles per hour are soon separated when going in opposite directions.

So it went for another ten or fifteen minutes. After leaving Rheims, the Rumpler made another wide sweep into French territory, all the way from five to eight or nine miles behind the trenches. I had a map from the Verdun Sector in my map case, but we had long since flown out of that, over country I had never before seen from the air. The German pilot showed me everything worth seeing, from the military stand-point behind our lines: aerodromes, hospitals, ammunition and supply dumps and the like, all quite unknown to me. I wondered why I was not joined by some other friendly plane until it occurred to me that other Spads below, seeing me, would refrain from joining up. Pilots would think: "That Rumpler is his victim. I'll not horn in on his victory. Hope he gets the blighter. Awful crust he's got, that Boche, coming all this way back." The anti-aircraft batteries, too, had ceased firing, doubtless from the fear of hitting the wrong ship; for all this while I was trailing along very close behind, vainly trying to coax my Spad up the last short slope of sky that would give me another chance to attack. It was damnable to think that A-A battery commanders were perhaps watching me through binoculars, counting on me to do something and wondering why I didn't.

"I will!" I said. "I will! Don't worry. If he gives me half a chance." I had forgotten to be afraid, or even in the least uneasy about my own skin. I had forgotten my severed bracing wire and my coughing motor. I had forgotten what time it was, how long I had been flying, how much gas I had left—everything but my intense longing to knock down the cheeky Rumpler that had already flown with impunity across seventy-five miles of French territory.

And then my chance came, more quickly than I had bargained for. The Germans had just made a circle over a flying field I was later to know very well, deep in our territory, at the village of Fareen-Tardenois. It was not an aerodrome, but a small aviation-supply depot furnished only with two hangars. The Rumpler circled over it, so I circled too, as I had already done a score of times while they took their photographs. Then, their mission over apparently, they headed due north to cross their own lines. But they held that course for no longer than a minute. Suddenly the pilot went down in a steep turn and I saw the observer seize his guns and swing them around to fire at me.

This time I was not caught napping, and I wasted no precious seconds trying to get under his tail. I turned left as the Rumpler did, and got in a beautiful burst of about thirty rounds, again broadside on, and from a distance of not more than fifty yards. The observer repaid me with a shorter burst, but a murderously accurate one. Again I heard the ominous flac! flac-flac-flac! flac-flac! but it was only for a second. My Spad flopped over in a half turn and came back in the opposite direction so prettily that the thought, "Did I do that?" flashed through my mind. So it was always in the air: the manœuvres one made instinctively were always better than those made with deliberation. It was from that moment that I began to learn how to take care of myself in the air. Every old war-time pilot must have had some such illuminating experience which taught him more in three seconds than his flying instructions could do in five months. Thereafter, when I met a German ship, I kept my eye on that and let my Spad do its own manœuvring.

Turning, I found the Rumpler coming for me from a distance of two hundred yards—straight for me this time, the pilot firing the guns mounted on his motor hood. So I made for him, my guns crackling steadily. Our motors seemed to be eating each other's bullets; in fact they were, as I discovered later, but we flashed past each other, both seemingly intact. I made a vertical turn to the right and then saw something that made me shout for joy. The Rumpler was going off, and his propeller was standing stock-still. He had a "dead-stick," as we used to say. I thought for a second or two I had imagined this, for not infrequently pilots thought they saw what they hoped to see. It was true, however. The propeller was standing vertically, motionless. What a thrill it gave me to see it! "Now I've got them!" I thought. "I'll force them down in our lines!"

But the Germans had other plans about where they meant to land. They were planing very flatly, making a straight course for their own territory. I glanced at my altimeter. Forty-eight hundred metres. They had sufficient altitude to enable them to land behind their own lines if they were careful not to lose height unnecessarily. My motor was coughing and spitting as though at its last gasp, but I quickly over-took them. The rear gunner was waiting for me; I could see him turning his guns this way and that, trying to get a line on me; but his pilot was afraid of losing altitude which he could not regain, so I had little difficulty in keeping the observer guessing. He fired two or three bursts, but they went wide of the mark. "I'll have to shoot them," I thought. "These men are old hands. They can't be frightened into landing." So I went after them again, hoping that my marksmanship would be good enough to wing them both but not good enough to kill either. I had a wonderful chance now. They were planing all the while, of course, tail up at such an angle that I could see the surface of the underbody. I pressed the triggered. My gun fired twice and stopped. This time it wasn't a missfire or a bulged shell casing. I had run out through my entire belt of cartridges.

I didn't know what to do then. I had never thought of such an emergency as this. I confess that what I felt like doing was crying with vexation and disappointment, I had tried hard for that Rumpler, and to have him escape me at the last moment, when victory was all but in my hand—it was too much for me. And all the while the wide belt of desolate country that marked the trench lines was drawing nearer, Soon they would be sailing over it safely, I made a feint at an attack from the side so that both pilot and observer could see me, but that didn't frighten them in the least. The observer swung his guns round and gave me a dose of lead in the tail just as I passed under him. Had he been half a second quicker the chances are that I shouldn't be telling this story.

Help came in histrionic eleventh-hour fashion. Greased lightning decorated with tricolour cocardes streaked down the sky, turned left and fired, turned right and fired, flipped upside down, fired again, and vanished. I saw the German observer drop his guns and collapse in his seat as though he had been pushed down by strong, invisible hands. The little friendly plane flashed into view again; it was precisely as though it had the power of being everywhere at once, and visible or invisible as it chose. This time it came down from the side in plain view of the German pilot, but keeping well above him. The Frenchman, or whoever it was, did a barrel turn, at the same time cutting his motor down to come down on the Rumpler, but the German didn't wait for him to fire again. He turned away from his lines—slowly, and I could feel as well as see with what reluctance—and planed down into France.

We were right at his tail, the Frenchman on one side, I on the other. He was flying a Nieuport, type 27, and on the side of his fuselage was painted a black dragon, and another insignia which I made out to be a skull-and-crossbones design against a black background. I waved and he waved back, then reached out and went through the motions of shaking hands. He pulled up till he was opposite the German pilot's cockpit and I followed to the same position on the other side. The Frenchman yelled something at the Boche and pointed down. The German looked over the side and waved his hand as much as to say, "All right." I looked, too, and saw the hangars of an aerodrome off to our left front. We were all three so close together that we could see each other's faces. It gave me a curious feeling to be flying wing to wing with a Rumpler. The pilot's yellow moustache was even longer than it had seemed when I had my first fleeting view of it. The ends fluttered back in the wind around the sides of his flying helmet. The observer was crumpled down in his cockpit, his head hanging to one side. We weren't long in coming down. Two or three minutes later the German landed with his "dead-stick." The Rumpler rolled a little way and stopped, and I saw a crowd of mechanics rushing out to it. The Frenchman and I followed him down.

ALWIN YORK OR
THE SWORD OF THE
LORD AND OF GIDEON

THEODORE ROOSEVELT

A scant hundred and fifty years ago the United States was but a fringe of settlements that clung to the skirts of the Atlantic. A few miles inland from the seaboard the "backwoods" stretched unbroken from north to south. The restless pioneer spirit that built our country was astir, and hardy men and brave women were pushing westward, ever westward. The rush was starting over trackless mountain and tangled forest, turbulent river and wide, shimmering plain, which never faltered until the covered wagons jolted over a crest and the broad Pacific stretched horizon-far.

To the north the stream westward flowed along the lakeshore by the Wilderness Trail. By the wagons walked the men. When there was a halt for the night children tumbled out over the tailboard like mud-turtles from a log in a pond. The families carried their scant household goods. At Oyster Bay, we have in our library a Windsor rockingchair that went with my wife's great-great-grandparents over this trail from Vermont to the settlement of Ohio.

To the south the pioneers struck the Appalachian Mountains as the first great barrier to their advance. These ranges stretch like a bulwark down the mid-eastern part of our country. Though not high, they are rugged and very beautiful. In spring they are cloaked in green, save where some gray shoulder of rock has thrust through. In autumn they are painted by the purple pomp of changing foliage gorgeous as a columbine.

Into these mountains tramped the wilderness hunters. They were lean, silent men, clad in coonskin caps and homespun. Around their necks were slung powderhorns. They carried the heavy, smoothbore flintlock guns. Such men were Daniel Boone and Sinnon Kenton.

These lone hunters carried more than their rifles over their shoulders; they carried the destiny of a nation. They were stout fighting men. Under Braddock they were all that stood between the British regulars and massacre. During the Revolutionary War they fought notably for the colonies and independence. Morgan's rifles were composed of them. Under General Clarke they beat the Indians time and again, and won Kentucky and Ohio for the colonists.

In the closing years of the eighteenth century one of these wilderness hunters worked his way over the Cumberland Mountains. He wandered south along the western slope until he came to the lovely little valley now known as the "Three Forks of the Wolf." The country looked so friendly and fertile that he settled there, cleared his fields, and travelled no more. His name was Conrad Pile.

The land attracted other settlers, and soon a little community was nestling between the rugged slopes of the mountains. It was christened Pall Mall, though no one knows why. After many years of uncertainty it was assigned to the State of Tennessee.

Like most of the other settlements in these hills the people were isolated, and had but little contact with the men and women of the lowlands. They were poor, for the valley yielded a scanty living. Most of them left but rarely the mountains that surrounded their log and board cabins. Schools were almost unknown. Children worked, not as training for life, but because it was necessary to work to live. The fiery spirit still flamed, and it was from the men of the Tennessee and Kentucky Mountains that "Old Hickory" drew the raw levees that beat the pick of the veteran British regulars at New Orleans.

Perhaps the strongest force in shaping these men and women was their religion. Their faith was of the deep-rooted, zealous type that carried the Roundheads to victory under Cromwell. Their ministers were circuit-riders, who travelled weary miles to carry the gospel to their widely scattered flocks. It was the religion of the Bible, hard and narrow at times but living, and was brought into the occurrences of everyday life, not kept as a thing apart. It was not merely for Sunday consumption in a padded pew. The citizens were the spiritual as well as probably the physical descendants of the Covenanters. For their general, when forming them for battle, to ride down their lines with a sword in one hand and a Bible in the other, would not have struck them as strange but as natural.

Next to their religion they were perhaps most influenced by the wilds. Hunting or trapping in the wooded hills was the recreation of the men. The youth of the mountains were learned in woodcraft. They could shoot rapidly and accurately and were toughened by life in the open.

During the Civil War these mountains formed an isolated island of loyalty to the Union in a sea of secession. Though the majority of the people were Federals some were Confederate sympathizers, and bitter bloody feuds tore the little hill settlements.

At the dawn of the twentieth century more than a hundred years had passed since old Conrad Pile halted from his wandering in the valley of the Three Forks of the Wolf, but Pall Mall was not greatly changed. The men wore homespun, the women calico. The houses were but little improved. Indeed, the log cabin Conrad built was still in use. The people spoke a language which was not, as many believe, a corruption of English, but an old form. They used "hit" for "it," which is the old neuter form of he or him. They spoke of "you'uns," which is an old colloquial plural of you. Over their sewing the girls sang early English, ballads, long forgotten by the rest of the world. Their recreations were husking-bees and log-rolling parties. This little valley in the mountains seemed a changeless back-eddy in the march of progress. The Reverend Rosier Pile, the great-great-grand-son of Conrad, was preacher. Full eighty per cent of the people were descend-ants of the first half-dozen settlers.

Among these were William York and his wife. They had eleven children, one of whom was a strapping, red-headed young mountaineer named Alvin. The family lived in a little tworoom board cabin. William York was a blacksmith by profession, but loved hunting and spent much of his time wandering over the hills.

Alvin was much like the boys of his acquaintance. His education was scant. The little mountain school he attended was open only for three months during the summer. For the rest of the year it was closed, because the children had to work, or were winter-bound in their scattered homes on the hillsides. All young York got of "book-l'arnin'" was a foundation in the "three Rs." There was other training, however, that stood him in good stead. When he was not working on the farm or at the school, he was hunting. At an early age he had been given a rifle and it was his most valued possession.

The men of Pall Mall had cleared a rough rifle-range for themselves and had competitions on Saturdays. They used the Old muzzle-loading, ball-powder-and-patch rifles handed down by their forefathers. Such rifles are very accurate for perhaps seventy-five yards. Turkeys and beeves were the usual prizes. In a turkey contest they did not use a target, but the turkey itself. In one competition the turkey was tethered by its foot to a stake some hundred and forty yards from the competitors. In another it was tied behind a log forty yards distant in such fashion that only its head showed. In both instances the turkey was given freedom of action, so that the target was constantly on the move. A turkey's head is not large, and a man who can hit it when it is bobbing about is a real marksman.

John Sowders, young York's principal rival at these matches, used to "limber up" by sticking carpet-tacks in a board and driving them home with his bullets at a range of twenty-five yards.

When Alvin York and two of his brothers were well grown, their father died. The mother, however, with their aid and the small farm, managed to keep the family together. There was no money for trimmings, but everyone had enough to eat. Her tall, red-headed son for a time had a mild "fling"—drank his corn whiskey and went on parties with his contemporaries among the boys. In the mid-twenties his stern religion gripped him and he stopped drinking. He took a deeper interest in church affairs and became an elder.

Early in the spring of 1917, word came to the little mountain community that the United States had declared war on Germany. They were such a back-eddy of the country that they had heard very little of the cumulative causes. Indeed, I have been told that the men who came to enlist in the army from some of the more isolated spots in these mountains believed that we were again at war with England, and were deeply suspicious when told we were her ally. At the Three Forks of the Wolf the War was not popular. Memories of the Civil War, with its bitter interfamily feuds, were still alive in the community. Few of the young fellows volunteered. At last the draft came.

Alvin York was a husky six-footer nearly thirty years old. He did not believe in war. He felt that the New Testament definitely stood against the killing of man by man. "For all they that take the sword shall perish with the sword." He was engaged to be married and was the principal support of his mother. Pastor Pile, of whose church he was a member, firmly believed that the tenets of his church forbade war. All York had to do was to state his case. He had clear grounds on which to claim exemption, but he was made of sterner stuff. Though he believed it wrong to kill, he believed it necessary to serve his country. He refused to claim exemption or let any one make such application in his behalf.

Down to Jamestown, the county-seat, he rode on one of his two mules. He registered, was examined and passed. Back at Pall Mall he told his womenfolk the news. They grieved bitterly, but they knew that a man must seek his happiness by following what he believes to be right.

His blue card reached him in November. In a few hours he said good-by and drove in a buggy to Jamestown. He was sent to Camp Gordon near Atlanta, Ga. It was the first time he had ever been out of sight of his beloved mountains. In his diary he wrote: "I was the homesickest boy you ever seen."

After nearly three months' training he was assigned in February, 1918, to Company G, 328th Infantry, 82nd Division. This division was really a cross-section of the country. Its men were drawn from every State of the Union. They were of every racial stock that goes to make up our nation, from the descendants of colonial English to the children of lately arrived Italian immigrants. Every trade and occupation was represented among its personnel.

Now began his battle with himself as to what course it was right for him to follow. His mother had weakened at the thought that he might be killed, and together with Pastor Pile had written to the officers stating that York's religion forbade war. York himself was deeply troubled, for Pastor Pile in letters pleaded with him not to jeopardize his eternal salvation by killing man.

He turned, in his distress, to his immediate superiors, Major G. E. Buxton and Captain E. C. B. Danforth, Jr. Fortunately both were men of high principle and broad vision. They realized at once that here was no yellow-streaked malingerer but a sincere man seeking guidance.

Late one evening the three men met in the little tarpaper shack that served Buxton for quarters. There, in the hard light of the single unshaded electric bulb that dangled from the ceiling, the officers reasoned with the lanky, red-headed private. The causes that led to the War were explained in detail. Then they turned to the Bible, and by text and teaching showed that while peace was desirable it must not be a peace at any price. Though we are in the world to strive for righteousness, justice, and peace, if one of these has to be sacrificed in order to obtain the other two, it must be peace.

They read him the thirty-third chapter of Ezekiel, and told him that he and all Americans were as "the watchman" in the Bible. On them was laid the charge of guarding humanity. To fail in the task would be traitorous.

York was absolutely honest. He strove for light. Gradually he became convinced, as had his spiritual ancestors the Covenanters, that right and war were bedfellows in this instance. Once his mind was clear, there was no faltering or hesitation. If it was right to fight at all, then it was right to fight with all your might. He flung himself into the drill and training with every ounce of energy he possessed. He soon showed that his days of shooting at the Three Forks of the Wolf were not ill spent. The Enfield rifle with which the division was equipped was the best firearm he had ever used. In rapid firing at moving targets he easily outdistanced the other men.

Some months passed. The American troops had reached Europe. Instead of a division or two scattered through the line that stretched like a dike across the north of France, the Americans now had over two million men. The United States had an army in the field and was prepared to carry her share of the battle. The tide had turned, and the Allies were crushing the gray lines back. The Germans had lost the initiative.

Our army was attacking as a unit. The battle of the Argonne was raging. Through the shell-torn woods and fields, over hills and valleys, the American troops were fighting their way forward. Then came a check. The 1st Division had gone through, but the divisions on its right and left had en-countered severe resistance. As a result the Regulars were thrust out in the enemies' lines, and were swept with fire from three sides. It was impera-tive that the lines on the right and left be advanced. The 82nd Division was selected for this mission. On October 6th they were assigned a position on the left of the First Division, with orders to attack on Chatel Chehery Hills.

All day on October seventh the 328th Infantry lay in shell-holes and ditches, on the slopes of Hill 223, and along the road that stretched to its rear. All day long the German shrapnel and high explosive burst along their lines. Behind them and in front were the wooded slopes of the rough Argonne hills. The ground was heavy with rain, the soldiers were mud-caked and sodden with wet.

Beyond Hill 223, the farthest point of their advance, was an open valley about five hundred yards wide. On the other side of this valley rose three hills, the central one steep and rugged, the other two gently sloping. The crest of the ridge formed by these was held by a division of veteran German troops, hard-schooled by years of war.

The position was of great importance, for behind these hills lay the narrow-gauge railroad, which supplied the Germans in the forest where they had checked the advance of the American battle line.

Late in the afternoon of October eighth York's battalion, the Second, received its orders. It was to relieve the 1st which had seized the hill, and then to thrust due west into the German flank. The attack was to start at six next morning from Hill 223, and the final objective was the railroad.

Through the black of the night the troops stumbled up the wooded slopes and took their position. Dawn came with gray reluctance; a heavy mist drifted through the treetops and choked the valley below. Gradually it lifted and shredded off. Zero hour had come.

The Americans started down through the tangled undergrowth. The sun rose and swallowed the last remnants of mist, giving the Germans a fair view of the attacking troops. Immediately from all sides the hostile fire burst. High explosives shrieked through the trees, filling the air with scraps of iron and flying splinters. Shrapnel exploded in puffs of smoke and rained down its bullets on the advancing men. Through it all machine-guns spattered our advance with a rattling hurricane of lead.

When they had descended the long wooded slope they started across the open country. The flanking fire was so ferocious that the American lines melted like snow in a spring thaw. To advance was impossible. The companies lay frozen to the ground while bullets whipped over them like sleet in a northeaster.

Lieutenant Stewart, a splendid young giant from Florida, commanded a platoon in York's company. He jumped to his feet and called to his men to follow. So great was their confidence in him that they struggled up and started ahead, though it looked certain death. He had not gone ten yards before a bullet struck him shattering his right thigh, and he crashed to the ground. Though his leg was shattered his manhood was not. By a supreme effort he shoved himself erect on the one leg left, and started to hop for-ward. A couple of yards farther he pitched on his face. A bullet had struck him in the head and his gallant spirit had joined the hero-dead of the nation.

The platoon dropped to the ground again and lay flat. It was clear that no advance could be attempted until the guns that were sweeping the plain with flanking fire were silenced. Captain Danforth decided to send a detachment from York's platoon on this mission.

Raising his head from the ground he turned to the platoon. Sergeant Harry Parsons, an ex-vaudeville actor from New York, was commanding it. Like a well-trained soldier he was watching his company commander for orders.

The roar of the artillery drowned all sound of his voice, so Danforth pointed to the hill on the left and motioned in its direction. Parsons understood at once. Quietly but quickly he chose three squads of his platoon. The German fire had taken its toll, a third of the men were wounded or dead. Of the twenty-four who had composed these squads when they left the hill-crest half an hour ago, only sixteen remained.

The make-up of this detachment was in itself a mute comment on our country and our army. Of the sixteen soldiers, eight had English names; the other eight were men whose parents had come from Ireland, Italy, Poland, Germany, and Sweden. One of the members of this patrol was Alvin York of Tennessee, lately promoted corporal.

Sergeant Early was placed in command. He was told to outflank in any fashion possible the machineguns that were causing the damage, and beat down their fire or destroy them.

On their bellies the men wormed their way to the woods, hitching themselves along below the bullets that swept scythelike across the field.

When they reached the cover of the trees they rose and, crouching, threaded their way to the left. Stealing from stump to stump, taking cover wherever possible, they reached the far end of the valley without casualties. Here fortune favored them, for they found a thicket that concealed them until they were nearly half-way across.

Suddenly bullets began to rattle around them, passing with the crack of a whip. They were under fire from the right flank. They must either retreat and abandon their mission or quickly pass on. Sergeant Early's decision was made without hesitation. They moved forward. In a few seconds they were clambering up the steep hillside beyond the valley. The boldness of this move protected them. The Germans were watching the hills opposite and the valley, but not the slopes on which their own guns rested. For a moment the Americans were sheltered. The soul-satisfying relief that comes to a soldier when he finds himself defiladed from fire is like waking after a severe illness to find the pain gone.

Stumbling through the brush and dead leaves they came to a wood path that led in rear of the crest. Here they halted for a moment to get their bearings and decide on the next move. To their left stretched unbroken woodlands from which no sound of firing came. To their right crackled the machineguns they were to silence. They had succeeded in reaching a position in rear of the Germans.

While they were standing breathless, listening for any sound that might give a further clew, they caught faintly the guttural sound of Germans talking in the valley on the reverse slope of the hill. Just at this moment a twig snapped, and right ahead of them they saw two German stretcher-bearers. There was no time to be lost, for these men might give the alarm to the machineguns, and the Americans opened fire at once. Both Germans escaped into the woods, though one was wounded. The time for discussion had passed. It was now or never. Quick as a flash Early called: "As skirmishers, forward!"

Down the bank of a small stream they plunged, and up the other side. Here the woods were thinner. Suddenly they saw just above them about fifty Germans gathered near a small board hut. The surprise of the Americans was nothing to that of the Germans, who knew themselves to be well in rear of their own lines. They had been getting their orders for a counter-attack when out of the bush had burst the Americans, ragged, unshaven, with fierce eyes and gleaming bayonets.

A couple of Boches tried to reach for their rifles, but the crack of the Enfields halted them. Up went their hands, and "Kamerad!" echoed through the grove.

It was the battalion headquarters of the machineguns. Among the group were a major and two junior officers. The Americans formed a crescent and moved toward their prisoners, who were on high ground just above them. On the left flank was Alvin York. As he approached the group the bushes became sparser. Right above him, not forty yards away, he saw German machine-guns. The Boche gunners had got the alarm. They were trying frantically to turn their guns to the rear. A few of them picked up rifles and fired at York, who stood in plain sight. The bullets burnt his face.

A command in German was shouted. At once the prisoners dropped flat on their faces. York and six of his comrades, who were now close to the Germans, did the same. Sergeant Early, with the other Americans, did not understand what was happening and remained standing. A burst of fire swept the grove.

Six of our patrol fell dead and three were wounded, including the sergeant. The surviving Americans were now among their prisoners. Probably on this account the hail of bullets was held two or three feet above the ground. There were no more casualties.

York was a comparatively green soldier. He was fighting not for the love of fighting, but for a firm conviction of the righteousness and justice of our cause. The shadows of the men who fought at Naseby and Marston Moor stood at his elbow. The spirit that inspired Cromwell and Ireton, Hampden and Vane, stirred in him. He saw "enfranchised insult" in the persons of the German soldiers, and, like the Covenanters, with a cold fury he "smote them hip and thigh."

He was in the open. Calling to his comrades, who were cloaked by the bushes and could neither see nor be seen, to stay where they were and guard the prisoners, he prepared to take the offensive. Crawling to the left through some weeds, he reached a point from which he got a clear view of the German emplacements. Just as the got there the German fire ceased. Several rose and started down the slope in the direction of the Americans to investigate. Quick as a flash York's rifle spoke. One pitched forward on his face and the rest scuttled back. Again a hail of bullets swept through the grove.

In a few minutes it slackened. York sat up and took the position used by hunters since rifles were first invented. The range to the gun-pits was that at which he had so often shot in those seemingly distant days, in his far-off home in the Tennessee mountains. This time, however, he was not shooting for sport but "battling for the Lord." He saw several German heads peering cautiously over the emplacements. He swung his rifle toward one and fired; the helmet flew up and the head disappeared. Four times more he fired before the Germans realized what was happening and ducked back.

Bullets spattered around him, splintering the tree at his elbow and covering him with slivers of wood and dust. Heedless of the danger, he watched the ridge until another head appeared. Again his rifle cracked and again the head disappeared. Hitting German heads at forty yards was easy for a man who had hit turkey heads at the same range, and whose nerves were of iron because of his belief in his cause.

The battle rested entirely on his shoulders, for the rest of the Americans were so screened by the brush that they were only able to fire a few scattered shots.

The Germans could not aim at this lone rifleman, for whenever a head appeared it was met with a bullet from the mountaineer. York was not fighting from a passion for slaughter. He would kill any one without compunction who stood in the way of victory; but it was not killing but victory for which he strove. He began calling: "Come down, you-all, and give up."

The battle went on.

At times the Boche riflemen would creep out of their emplacements, take cover behind some tree, and try to get the American. The hunter from the Cumberland Mountains was trained to note the slightest movement. The man who could see a squirrel in the tree-top could not fail to observe a German when he moved. Every time he found them and fired before they found him. That ended the story.

The Germans by this time knew that the brunt of the battle was being borne by one American. They realized they were not quick enough to kill him by frontal attack, so they sent an officer and seven men around his left flank to rush him. These crawled carefully through the brush until they were within twenty yards of him. Then with a yell they sprang up and came at him on a dead run, their fixed bayonets flashing in the sun.

The clip of cartridges in York's rifle was nearly exhausted and he had no time to reload. Dropping his Enfield he seized his automatic pistol. As they came lunging forward through the undergrowth he fired. One after another the Germans pitched forward and lay where they fell, huddled gray heaps in the tangled woods. Not only had York killed them all, but each time he had shot at the man in rear in order that the others might not halt and fire a volley on seeing their comrade fall. The machine-gun fire had slackened during the charge. Again it burst forth and again York stilled it with his rifle.

The grim, red-headed mountaineer was invincible. Almost unaided he had already killed some twenty of his opponents. The German major's nerve was shaken. He could speak English. Slowly he wriggled on his stomach to where the American sat and offered to tell the machine-gunners to surrender. "Do it and I'll treat ye white," said York.

At this moment a lone German crawled close, jumped to his feet, and hurled a grenade. It went wide, but when the Enfield spoke its bullet did not. The German pitched forward on his face, groaning. The Boche major then rose to his knees and blew his whistle shrilly. All firing ceased. He called an order to his men. Instantly they began scrambling to their feet, throwing down belts and side-arms.

The American was alert for treachery. When they were half-way down the hill, with their hands held high over their heads, he halted them. With the eyes of a backwoodsman he scanned each for weapons. There were none. The surrender was genuine.

Corporal York stood up and called to his comrades. They answered him from where they had been guarding their first prisoners. The thick grove had prevented them from taking an active part in the fighting, but they had protected York from attacks by the prisoners who would otherwise have taken him from the rear.

Sergeant Early, the leader of the patrol, was lying in the brush desperately wounded in the abdomen. York called: "Early, are you alive?"

"I am all through," groaned the sergeant. "You take command. You'll need a compass. Turn me over. You'll find mine in my pocket. Get our men back as soon as you can, and leave me here."

York had well over a hundred prisoners, as sixty had come from the machine-gun emplacements. Some of the Americans doubted the possibility of getting them back to the lines. York paid no attention to this. He formed the Germans in column of twos, placing our wounded at the rear, with prisoners to carry Sergeant Early, who could not walk. Along the flanks he stationed his surviving comrades, with instructions to keep the column closed up and to watch for treachery. He himself led, with the German major in front of him and a German officer on each side.

Before they started York had had the major explain to the men that at any sign of hostility he would shoot to kill, and the major would be the first to die. They had seen enough of the deadly prowess of the mountaineer. Not one made the attempt. He marched his column around the hill to a point from which he could probably have taken them back safely, but his mission was to clear the hill of machine-guns. He knew that some still remained on the front slope.

Turning the column to the left, he advanced on the Boche garrisons. As he approached he had the German major call to each in turn to surrender. When they did he disarmed them and added them to his train of prisoners. In only one instance did a man attempt to resist. He went to join the long roll of German dead.

York's troubles were not over. Though he had cleaned up and destroyed the machineguns, he still had to get back to our lines with the men he had captured. To do this he had to be very careful, for so large a body of Ger-mans marching toward our lines might well be taken for a counter-attack and mowed down with rifle-fire. Bringing all his woodcraft into play he led his long column of gray-clad prisoners over the ridge and down through the brush, until he reached the foot of the slope up which his patrol had climbed earlier in the day.

Suddenly from the brush on the other side the command "Halt!" rang out. York jumped to the front to show his uniform, and called out that he was bringing in prisoners. He was just in time to prevent casualties. The lines of our infantry opened to let the party through. As the doughboys from left and right looked between the tree-trunks they saw gray form after gray form pass. A yell of approval rang out. Some one shouted: "Are you bringing in the whole German Army?" The lines closed behind the column. Corporal York had fulfilled his mission.

In a few minutes he reported at battalion headquarters. The prisoners were counted. There were one hundred and thirty-two, including three officers, one a major. With less than a year's military training a red-headed mountaineer, practically single-handed, had fought a veteran battalion of German troops, taken thirty-five guns, killed twenty men, captured one hundred and thirty-two and the battalion commander.

For three weeks more the Division hammered its way forward. The stubborn German defense was beaten back, the Allies drove on to Sedan. Even among the fighting troops rumors of peace became more persistent. One morning word came to the front lines where the tired men stood, ankle-deep in mud—an armistice had been signed.

York had become a sergeant. He was with his company. His feat, as he saw it, was merely a part of the day's work. The officers and men of the 82nd Division, however, were very proud of him. They had. reported the facts to General Headquarters. The story had spread like wild-fire, and Alvin York was famous.

During his simple country life York had never met any of the great of the world. His nearest approach to a general had been when he stood stiffly at attention while the general inspected the ranks. Now he found himself honored of all, because physical courage, especially when backed by moral worth, commands universal admiration. General Headquarters ordered him from place to place in France. A brigade review was held in his honor. He was decorated not only by the United States but also by the Allies. At Paris Poincaré, the president of the French Republic, pinned the highest decorations to his coat.

In May, 1919, he came back with his regiment to our country. Here enthusiasm ran even higher. The streets of New York were jammed with people who cheered themselves hoarse. He went to see the Stock Exchange, where no visitors are allowed on the floor. Not only was he permitted to visit the floor but business was suspended and the stockbrokers carried him around on their shoulders.

In Washington, when he went to the gallery of the House of Representatives, the congressmen stopped debate and cheered him to the echo. Great banquets were given for him, which were attended by the highest ranking civil, military, and naval officials.

In his olive-drab uniform, with his medals and shock of red hair, he was a marked man. When he walked the streets enthusiastic crowds gathered. There were men and women to greet him at the railroad-stations as he travelled back to Tennessee to be mustered out.

He was offered a contract for $75,000 to appear in a moving-picture play on the War. He was approached by vaudeville firms, who suggested tours on which they agreed to give him a salary of $1,000 a week. Newspapers were willing to pay fabulous sums for articles by him.

He was taken up on a mountain and shown the kingdoms of the world. Ninety-nine men out of a hundred would have cracked under the adulation. Ninety-nine men out of a hundred who can bear the famine worthily will lose their heads at the feast. York did not. Though his twelve months in the army had greatly broadened him, his character was still as strong and unshaken as the rock of his own hills. He refused the offers of money or position, saying rightly that these were made him only because of his feat in the Argonne. To sell his war record would be putting a price on patriotism.

As soon as he could he made his way back to his home in the mountains, his family, and his friends. There he was met by his mother in her calico bonnet, his sisters and brothers, and Grace Williams, the mountain girl to whom he was betrothed.

In a few days there was an open-air wedding at Pall Mall. It was held on the hillside. A gray ledge of rock served as altar. The new leaves of spring danced in the sunlight, casting flickering shadows on the white starched "Sunday-go-to-meeting" dresses and blue serge "store clothes" of the mountain folk, who had driven in from the surrounding country. The governor of the State officiated, assisted by Pastor Pile. The bride and groom were Grace Williams and Sergeant Alvin York, late of the United States Army.

Though York refused to sell his service record, he knew his Bible far too well to have forgotten the parable of the talents. That which it would be wrong to use for his own benefit, it would be wrong not to use for the benefit of others. His experience in the world had made him bitterly conscious of his scanty education. He realized that "wisdom excelleth folly as far as light excelleth darkness." He decided to bend his efforts toward establishing proper schools for the children of the hills.

The people of Tennessee had been collecting an Alvin York Fund. He asked them to turn it into a foundation for building schools in the mountains. All he would accept for himself was a small farm.

BRIDGE ON THE RIVER KWAI

ALISTAIR URQUHART

The Japanese put us straight to work. This section of railway, further north, would eventually join up with that of our earlier handiwork at Hellfire Pass. We began clearing jungle, just as we had at the first Kanyu cutting. The work was certainly easier than gouging our way through the rocks and boulders of Hellfire Pass but it was still horrendous. With the same guards and Japanese officers hovering around us it was the same torment. Brutality, disease, starvation and death stalked our every step.

On the first evening of our arrival, still barefoot and naked except for our Jap-happies, we did some remedial work on the huts, some of which leaned at crazy angles like jungle versions of the Leaning Tower of Pisa. The roofs all needed replacing with fresh atap leaves. Whether by design or otherwise, we reverted to the same sleeping arrangements as at the first camp, taking up the same places. Men took a lot of comfort from routine and familiarities, no matter how fickle or fleeting they may have been.

After a few weeks of steady progress we were nearing the river Kwai, across which the Japanese intended us to build two bridges, the first to be made of wood and bamboo, the second to be of steel and concrete. It was going to be a major engineering operation and I doubted that we would manage it in our state and with the pathetic tools we had to hand.

We carried on clearing the path for the track of the railway, while work parties went into the jungle felling trees for the bridge and bamboo for the scaffolding.

Then disaster struck. One night I awoke with dysentery calling. Holding my aching stomach I raced to the latrines in the dark but on the way back to my hut a Korean guard stopped me. He had come out of the darkness and caught me by surprise. He yammered in my face. I had no idea what he was on about. At first I thought he was admonishing me for failing to salute him but I had never noticed the bugger. He was still talking frantically and pointing down at my midriff. To my horror I realised he was becoming frisky.

'Jiggy, jiggy,' he was saying, trying to grab me.

'No!' I shouted at him.

'Jiggy. You me, jiggy.'

I told him 'No' again, firmly. He carried on trying to grab me so without hesitating I kicked him as hard as I could, barefooted, square between his legs. He collapsed, groaning in agony.

I bolted for my hut but his roaring had summoned hordes of other guards. Unfortunately I ran slap bang into one of them. He seized on to me and before I knew it they were coming at me from all quarters. Rifle butts and fists sent me to the ground. Someone stabbed me in the backside with a bayonet. Boots and fists flailed into my body before they hauled me up and dragged me to the front of the Japanese officers' hut. Bleeding from the blows to the head and face, I waited for the interpreter, who had been summoned. As I swayed an NCO kept beating me, knocking me to the ground. Each time I fell he made me stand up again. Eventually the interpreter was raised, along with the camp commandant, the dreaded Black Prince. This was a moment of absolute terror. Throughout my captivity I had tried at all times to stay out of range of the brutal Japanese guards and now here I was receiving the personal attentions of the camp's sadist-in-chief. The guards all stood to attention as the commandant asked the Korean for his side of the story. No doubt he left out the bit about making sexual advances towards me.

When he was done the commandant asked why I had assaulted the guard. I told them the truth. The interpreter relayed my story and when he had finished the Black Prince started screaming at all and sundry. I had no idea what was going on. I just knew I was in serious trouble. They took the Korean guard away and marched me to the front of the guardhouse, where I was forced to stand to attention. Racked with pain and suffering from broken toes, I wobbled and wilted. Any sign of slumping over brought a flurry of rifle butts to the kidneys to straighten me up again. Every minute of every hour throughout the night was pure torture. On top of the pain came the constant buzzing and biting from the camp's abundant insect life.

At sunrise the men assembled for breakfast and roll-call before going out to slave on the railway. The guards kept me behind. As day broke I was a hopeless mess. The rising sun bore down on my defenceless body and when I lost consciousness my personal minders threw buckets of water over me and kicked me to attention.

And so it went on hour after endless hour. It was relentless. My bashed eyes had now closed and my face felt swollen as blood seeped from my head, body and feet. My body burned in the unforgiving sun and the only water I got was sloshed from the bucket as they revived me after I collapsed from heat exhaustion. I prayed that it would end, prayed for a bullet through the brain. But no, they continued to play out their game of torture like a cat with a mouse.

Sunset came. The men returned and averted their eyes a sure sign that my predicament was serious. Nobody showed any signs of sympathy or concern, to do so was to risk reprisals on themselves. The rest of the chilly night passed in a blur of kicks and beatings. I hallucinated and felt as if I were going insane. Those bastards did not deserve to live not in my book. Throughout the night I was more often on the ground and being sloshed with river water than I was at attention.

Come morning my officer went to the Black Prince to protest on my behalf. He was a very brave man and predictably got slapped savagely for his troubles. After the men left for work the Black Prince instructed two guards to haul me off to the black hole. My heart sank. I knew that most men kept in there, usually for three or four weeks, did not come out alive. And if they did they had been reduced to crippled wrecks who never fully recovered. The guards threw me into one of the bamboo cages. With bent knees, I leant with my back raised and arms at my sides as they squeezed its door shut. Darkness and the filth of the previous occupants engulfed me. I knelt and sobbed, falling in and out of consciousness.

The corrugated iron covering the semi-submerged cage intensified the stifling heat. In the darkness the sense of isolation was devastating and I became half out of my mind with pain and exhaustion.

Days came and went, the only notion of time provided by the arrival of a watery bowl of rice once a day. The next few days were the worst I had experienced on the railway, like a culmination of the extremes of temperature from the steel carriages on the way up to the railway, along with the death march and every other ounce of suffering endured since, all crammed into that tiny, backbreaking black hole. Malaria struck me down, causing uncontrollable shivers and pain that was diverted only when tropical ulcers and kidney stones reared to the fore. My hair matted, dirty and unshaven, lice crawling all over me, no soap or water, no drugs or hope, my degradation was complete.

I had counted six or seven bowls of rice by the time they allowed me out. As I crawled out of the dark cell and back to my hut, I deemed myself lucky to have spent such a short period in the black hole. I had been in for a week and it could easily have been a month. To me it felt like a century.

I reached my hut on all fours and Dr Mathieson and his orderlies got to work on me. Slowly they brought me back to life with lime juice, water and scavenged food scraps, a little milk and some duck eggs. Within a week, even in my feeble condition, I was passed as fit and sent back to work on the first railway bridge over the river Kwai. Happily I never saw that Korean guard again.

We marched back along the track we had been clearing until it opened up at the river. What I saw stunned me. During the fortnight of my imprisonment and convalescence the outline of a bridge had grown out of the water. It was a truly amazing sight. The bridge stood encased in a great bamboo cage of scaffolding and hundreds of prisoners teemed all over it like ants. It was astonishing to think that this had been built with little more than bare hands and primitive technology. The general opinion among us men had been that the undertaking was impossible. But then again we had thought the same of Hellfire Pass and we somehow managed to do that too.

Two Japanese engineers, who were always officers, stayed on site at all times. Though many were English-educated, most of them dictated their orders through interpreters. Their working methods were haphazard to say the least. Where we would have used tapes to measure distances, they guessed. It didn't seem to bother them if some railway sleepers jutted out a foot more than others. But they were very demanding and prone to strike out with the four-foot iron bars that they carried. No doubt they were under enormous pressures themselves to get the bridge done but the way they treated the men, like animal slavers, was unforgivable.

The men used an antiquated rope-and-pulley system to drive teak piles deep into the river floor. The pile driver had a huge rock on the top of it and the prisoners raising it heaved on the ropes as if in a game of tug o' war, while a Nippon engineer would keep them in time with a rhythmic count of 'Ichi, ni, san, shi'. On his command they would suddenly all let go of the rope sending the rock crashing down on the pile below. Simple but effective, I thought. The laboured chanting and heaving, which went on for up to eighteen hours a day, made me think of the ancient Pharaohs and how their slaves had achieved the seemingly impossible by constructing the pyramids. There was certainly something biblical about our plight.

For those working in the muddied river, sometimes up to their necks, life could be much more difficult. The filthy water infected cuts and sores. It was also impossible to see where you were treading and many more injuries occurred that way. The additional danger of falling objects, including logs and struts, meant that mortality rates among these men were extremely high. Making the most of my climbing skills and head for heights, I tried to work as high up the structure as possible. Some men hated working aloft but for me it meant I could work at a more sedate pace to recover from the black hole and I was out of reach of the guards and their flailing sticks.

While the piles were driven into the river bed, prisoners made sections of the bridge on land, mostly from bamboo and teak, in a basic fabrication yard. Once they had finished a twenty-foot section elephants manoeuvred it down to the river and men built it on to the piles. After a stint on the bridge I moved to the yard and spent most of my time drilling holes, using an awl. It was a real production line: against a backdrop of shouting and hammering from the river, the logs were rolled in and hoisted on to trestles for me to drill holes into. Most of the time the logs would be too thick for the awl and I would have to drill halfway through the log, turn it over and drill in from the other side, hoping that the holes met in the middle. The metal bolts destined for the holes were already rusting and I doubted whether they would last very long. It was tough, tiring work boring into those hard jungle woods but at least I could work on my own. It also meant that I could slack off a bit and do very little, whereas those working in a group found themselves watched constantly and could not afford that luxury. When I went down to the river it was a marvel to watch the men working. To see the bridge rising from the Kwai, being built in the midst of the jungle, with no machinery or sense of civilisation, was unreal.

Building the bridge was probably the easiest time I experienced on the railway. The work was more about craft and guile than brute strength and physical labour. But it never stopped the guards from making us work at double time or administering beatings for little or no reason whatsoever. On one occasion I received a severe beating after failing to drill a half-inch hole through a twelve-inch-diameter log. It sounded like a simple job but the awl I had been given reached only halfway through the log. Once I had drilled as far as I could I turned the log around and started drilling from the other side, hoping that it would join in the middle. But of course this time that was too much to ask. Even though I had been given an almost impossible task, a rotund Korean guard, whom we nicknamed 'Musso' because of his similarity to the Italian fascist dictator, noticed and went berserk. He screamed in my face, telling me what I had done wrong as if I had failed to notice.

'Do it your bloody self then!' I snapped. I regretted those words almost immediately. Musso was a nasty piece of work and slammed his rifle butt into my face. It floored me and knocked out one of my front teeth. The tooth had snapped off at an angle, painfully exposing raw nerves. After several more blows and kicks I quickly recovered and scrambled back to work, just thankful not to have been beaten to death.

The broken tooth was agonising and hours later, after we finished work, I paid another visit to the medical hut. The orderlies breezily set about me with a pair of pliers as if they were a pair of mechanics working on a rusty old tractor. One held my head tightly while the other tugged and tugged, eventually managing to wrench out the offending incisor. It was excruciating but the orderlies had evidently become quite proficient as dentists and it was all over pretty quickly.

The building of the bridge on the river Kwai took a terrible toll on us and the depiction of our sufferings in the film of the same name was a very, very sanitised version of events. Unlike the well-fed extras in the movie, we did not whistle the 'Colonel Bogey' tune. Nor did we work alongside Americans, nor did we have any semblance of uniform. We were naked, barefoot slaves. And there were certainly no pretty and scantily clad local girls wandering through the jungle.

And contrary to the film, our real-life commander Colonel Philip Toosey did not collaborate with the Japanese. I was not alone in doing as little work as possible without blatantly shirking, which resulted in sadistic beatings. Energy, every ounce of it, bad to be conserved for survival. To bust a gut on starvation rations was absolute suicide. We had long lost our dignity and working faster certainly would not have brought any back. In fact it would have resulted in the opposite with even more of us dying.

Instead we made constant attempts at sabotage. Men whispered orders to impair the construction of the bridge wherever possible. Some charged with making up concrete mixtures deliberately added too much sand or not enough, which would later have disastrous effects. We collected huge numbers of termites and white ants and deposited them into the grooves and joints of load-bearing trunks.

Out of sight of the guards I furtively sawed halfway through wooden bolts wherever possible, hoping they would snap whenever any serious weight, like a train, was placed upon them.

We slogged on, starving and diseased, believing that things just could not get any worse and then, in June, the monsoon arrived. For months the land mass of the Indian subcontinent had been heating up, creating an area of low pressure that now drew in mighty moisture-laden winds from the Indian Ocean. The rains flooded our huts, with rivers running through them complete with small brown fish that some of the starving men succeeded in catching. We became permanently sodden. The camp ground transformed into a sea of mud and conditions around the latrines became unspeakable. Work on the bridge and railway turned even more hazardous, magnifying our misery, yet we were unprepared for the horror about to be unleashed upon us by the monsoon.

For the river Kwai and its tributaries harboured a killer even more lethal than the Japanese and our starvation diet. As an inevitable consequence of the lack of sanitation and the tens of thousands of bodies buried in shallow graves or dumped in the jungle, the river system was loaded with cholera bacteria and the monsoon season became cholera season. As the heightened waters of the Kwai flushed Vibrio cholerae throughout the land, this fearful disease cast a black shadow over the camp. Cholera arrived unseen and unheard but soon had us in its grip. I was slow to hear about it. But I sensed something terrible in the camp. More men were falling ill than usual and the Japanese kept their distance, leaving us alone. They were scared to death of catching cholera themselves. The Japanese Imperial Army had experienced the devastating impact of cholera among its troops in China in 1937 and again in 1940-1, and feared its swift progress like the Black Death.

Cholera outbreaks are related to standards of hygiene, food preparation and the quality of drinking water all of which were undeniably horrific on the railway. Rats were also rife and had muscled into our lives to such an extent that we hardly shooed them away any more, and they are also carriers of the cholera bacteria, another parallel with the plague.

One of our officers gathered us together for an extraordinary general meeting. As serious-looking as I had ever seen him, he said, 'A cholera epidemic is threatening us all. We have set up a quarantine area and you are advised to avoid it wherever possible. Need I remind you all not to drink unboiled water? If you are unsure of its origins, find out or leave it. Understood? This is our biggest test yet.'

Cholera had infected a stream that ran past our camp. The Japanese had refused to build a bridge across it to stop it from spreading, so we had to use contaminated boats to cross the water. By the end of it all we would lose thousands on the railway quite needlessly to cholera. The conditions in the coolie camps were even worse and tens of thousands of native labourers, sometimes entire camps, were wiped out.

Overnight cholera struck me down. I woke up with explosive diarrhoea and violent, projectile vomiting. My ears were ringing and I felt dizzy. Cramps started in my bowels and soon spread all over my body as it rapidly dehydrated. I was drying from the inside out, shrivelling like a picked grape left out in the sun. The cholera bacteria burrowed into the walls of my small intestine producing toxins that sucked the vital salts and every ounce of water out of my body. I was unsure what was wrong but I knew it was serious -I did not want to finish up with the life drained out of me. I had always been extremely careful to drink only boiled water so at first I was doubtful that it was cholera. I did not know much about it but I knew that the first twenty-four hours were crucial. If you see through a day and a night, you would probably survive. Most men who succumbed did so in the first few hours, a horrible death and so quick. Men who threw the bodies of cholera victims on to funeral pyres in the morning could easily contract the disease, die and be thrown on the pyre themselves in the evening. They died in agony like crazed animals and it was dreadful to see.

I lay in my bed, unable to rise for the work party. By then I was semiconscious and I thought this was the end. I was hallucinating. Vivid red flashes stormed my eyelids. I knew I had to seek help. After psyching myself up I managed to rise and wobble to Dr Mathieson's hut. As soon as I walked in he knew that I had cholera. It was a death sentence and he was reluctant to tell me. Instead he simply said, 'You'll have to be isolated. You'll be looked after.'

His orderlies led me to a cream-coloured bell tent, like we had used in the Scouts. As they peeled back the tent's front flap, a deathly stench leaped out. Unknown to me this was the 'death tent' and I was the unlucky thirteenth occupant of a dimly lit space already full of men. When I saw their state, their eyes rolled back, rasping, unintelligible voices, raised legs with knees bent the bizarre telltale sign of a cholera sufferer -I knew that my number was up. The orderlies were putting me in here to die. The fight was fading from me and I lay down on the canvas floor with a sense of of complete and utter desolation.

I have no idea how long I lay there. I was no longer aware of those around me or if anyone came and tended to me. My mind drifted. I allowed myself some thoughts of home, even though they were jumbled and vague. I became upset when I couldn't picture the faces of my mum, dad and Aunt Dossie. I even struggled to remember what Hazel looked like. Feverish dreams rampaged terrifyingly through my mind. The walls of the tent seemed to move and expand like an inflated balloon, only to pop and come crashing back on top of me. A sudden death seemed as inviting as a warm bath.

Eventually, on what must have been the following day, some orderlies carried me out of the tent and back to the hospital hut. Out of the thirteen men in that tent, Dr Mathieson told me months later, I was the only survivor. His medical staff tried to keep me alive by giving me as many sips of sterilised water as possible. They also forced some coconut milk puree down my throat, as water alone was not enough. While treatment should have been relatively simple, the lost fluids needing to be replaced with a liquid mixture of sugar and salts, the Japanese refused to give us any extra supplies, even though progress on the railway had dropped off and the outbreak threatened to wipe out the whole camp them included. I was only half compos mentis and just wanted to sleep. But the orderlies kept tapping my cheeks to keep me awake and engaged me in conversation to keep my mind and soul engaged. They found the dog-eared black-and-white photographs in my bed-space and asked about my family. I rambled on about Aberdeen and playing practical jokes on Dossie. They asked who the pretty blonde girl was the photo more worn than others. The lovely Hazel. I thought of her and how we used to dance at the Palais de Dance, how she was the only girl who could keep up with my twinkling toes, now reduced to bloodied and mangled stumps. The orderlies tried to make me laugh, asking how far I got with Hazel, and I told them about our long walks through the dandelions of Duthie Park, how I would try to get her alone, those piercing blue eyes all to myself.

Florence Nightingale could not have faulted their patience and unwavering care. If I had given up hope, they never did. And by this time I had very little hope left in me. The idea of suicide was a constant threat, not just for me but for many men. Some gave in and threw themselves from the bridge or head first down the latrines. There was no doubt that clinical depression had muddied most of our minds.

I could have lain there for days or weeks. It was hard to be certain. A Japanese doctor visited the camp and inspected me. Eventually the medical officers persuaded him, along with the Black Prince, that I was of no further use. My days working on the railway were over, at least while in the condition I was. Permission came through for me to be sent down river to the mass hospital camp at Chungkai.

I was leaving a camp that had reduced us to animals, starved half-dead beasts of burden. It had brought out the best and the worst in us. My carers showed endless compassion but the camp was also full of men who would steal food from the sick and dying.

The next thing I knew I was being carried down to the river on a stretcher and loaded on to a forty-foot barge with a dozen or so other 'heavy sick', many with gaping tropical ulcers or recovering from cholera. As we were towed by a tugboat down the river, I was still so weak that I ignored everything around me and could not even bring myself to respond to the others making idle chit-chat on the peaceful journey downstream. Calmly scything through the jungle I knew I was leaving the hell of camp life.

After an overnight stop, where we slept in a cutting on the riverbank, we arrived at Chungkai hospital camp. It was then that I realised how lucky I was. A massive place, it was located in a jungle clearing beside the Meelong River, near where the railway commenced and about a hundred kilometres from Bangkok. To think that all of the men in that square mile were either sick or recovering from illness and injury really tells a tale in itself. There were nearly ten thousand survivors gathered in the camp in various states of decay. It was the first time that I could grasp the vast, industrial scale of the railway.

On arrival at Chungkai British orderlies met us at the riverbank. Our state horrified them. They carried me by stretcher to a hospital hut, where they categorised me and left me alone. Lying on a short bamboo cot with no bedding, I looked around. In the long, bright hut lay about thirty others all in much the same decrepit state. Cholera had been the final straw for my health and I could no longer walk. Dysentery, malaria, beriberi and gaping tropical ulcers that engulfed both ankles and lower calves had been enough but cholera finished me off. Mentally, losing control of my legs was too much. Either I was too damned weak or they were irreparably damaged, because no matter what my brain instructed them to do I could no longer even move my legs.

I was so devastated that I thought I may as well be dead. Having led such a full, active and sporting life, losing my legs was worse than going blind for me.

I had real fears that I would never walk again and so depression set in. I could not see a glimmer of light at the end of tunnel only blackness.

Some orderlies came into the hut and gave us all a liquid meal, which had some egg in it and milk either goat or coconut, I could not be sure. If I tasted it now, it would probably be foul but at the time it was wonderful. The best thing I had tasted in over a year.

I lay in that hut for over a week with the black dog of depression nipping at my sorry heels. The cheery orderlies and doctors tried talking to me to lift my spirits but my mind was unresponsive. I could see that they were not trying to help me walk again so I felt that they were just pacifying me. Like all of the patients I dreaded the nightly agonising round of the orderlies who scraped out our suppurating ulcers with a sharpened dessert spoon. The only highlight of my day was food. I was definitely a difficult and moody patient.

One of the doctors was a very tall Australian medical officer, and he conducted my general examination. I was greatly impressed by him during my brief consultation. A striking figure with an aura of authority and leadership, he seemed never to waste his words or actions as if every single minute were utterly necessary and priceless. The orderlies all worshipped him.

They told me his name was 'Weary' Dunlop. He worked miracles at Chungkai and enjoyed the adulation of his men for taking numerous beatings from the Japanese to prevent sick men from being sent to work.

Shortly after his capture on Java in March 1942 he had personally saved the lives of four patients. The Japanese had stormed into the prison hospital and demanded that it be broken up. Their commanding officer ordered that four of the boys two paraplegics and two blind lads should be bayoneted. Colonel Dunlop put himself between the Japanese bayonets and a young British serviceman, Billy Griffiths, who had been blinded and lost both hands when he walked into a booby trap. In the tense stand-off that followed the Japanese backed down. (After the war Griffiths became a leading figure in the development of disabled sport in the UK and both men were reunited on the This Is Your Life television programme.)

Dunlop set a shining example of how officers ought to conduct themselves and gave all too many a showing up. He was twice threatened with execution but intervened constantly on behalf of the sick men. He introduced order, fairness, record-keeping and above all hope to Chungkai.

Dunlop became a legendary figure both during and after the war, and was knighted for his amazing bravery and for saving countless lives. When Sir

Edward 'Weary' Dunlop died in 1993, he was rightly given a full state funeral in Melbourne.

After a couple of weeks of feeding and rest they decided I was ready for rehabilitation. I took some amount of convincing but once they hoisted me out of bed and started carrying me from the hut, my protests were futile.

My admiration and respect for the medical staff would only increase with every day at Chungkai. Despite their mammoth task and the flood of sick men dumped at the camp every day, their dedication and patience were aweinspiring. They had built parallel bars outside with a canopy over the bamboo apparatus for shade. Men used the gymnastic-type equipment to learn to walk again, holding themselves upright with their arms and upper body and retraining their legs. On my first visit the staff sat me down on a stool beside the bars and I watched a man struggle and strain, with beads of sweat streaming down his forehead, to walk the length of the bars, helpers waiting to catch him if he fell. I thought to myself, I'll never be able to do that.

But that was to come. First the orderlies had much simpler, allegedly more achievable tasks for me to tackle. As I sat there on the three-legged stool they attached to my right foot a small bag with some sand or dirt in it.

'Try and lift your foot off the ground. Even an inch will do.'

I tried but nothing happened. My brain was willing but my foot refused to budge.

'Keep trying,' they encouraged. But no matter what I tried it wasn't moving. Within minutes I was exhausted and they told me to rest. They left me alone, stewing in self-loathing, and came back half an hour later.

'Try again. But this time I want you to concentrate with all your might from brain to foot. It's all about mind over matter.'

From an early age I had relished a challenge and I hated being beaten. I focused my eyes on the hairs on my foot and willed it to move. After a while the orderlies shouted, 'Yes, you did it!' Although I never saw it I must have raised my foot half an inch and for the next couple of hours I sat there trying to repeat it. I was sweating like a pig, the frustration oozing out of me as I made incremental progress. The old stubborn Alistair was returning. By the end of the session I could lift both feet an inch off the ground.

The staff carried me back to my hut, where I fell asleep exhausted. The next day they took me back and sitting on that stool I managed to raise my leg two or three inches. I felt ready for the parallel bars and the orderlies agreed. They lifted me up and held my shrunken backside as I dangled my useless legs.

Being on my feet felt surreal, as if I had never walked before. They pushed me to try to move a leg.

'You moved your leg when you were sitting down so you can do it now.'

Try as I might, I couldn't get my legs to move.

'Don't worry about it if you can't. We'll try again tomorrow.'

I went back to the stool and tried again. Once I had mastered lifting one bag of weights I went on to the next heaviest. I gave up only when completely knackered, and they carried me back to the hut.

On the way back a young chap was walking towards me when he stopped suddenly and said excitedly, 'It's not you, is it? Is it you? Is it?'

I recognised him straight away. 'Yes, it's me, Freddie.'

'Awright mucker! It's been a while.'

Indeed it had. It was the first time I had smiled in months. Freddie Brind looked remarkably fit and well, considering. I was not surprised he struggled to recognise me, however. I had lost three or four stone and most of my dignity and self-respect.

One of the medical officers carrying me told Freddie, 'Alistair here has been learning to walk again. He's doing very well.'

As they carried me Freddie trailed alongside, talking at a million miles a minute. It was as if we had never been parted. At the hut the orderlies left and we were alone. We were so pleased to see each other. For me he was a breath of fresh air. I had constantly worried about him, his brother Jim and the other lad, John Scott. I still felt like I had let them down, abandoning them at Changi all those months ago. It seemed like a lifetime ago. I wanted to know everything but I struggled to get a word in. He told me he had been at Chungkai for almost twelve months, having arrived with his brother. He did not know what had happened to John, who became separated from them at Changi. But Freddie was more interested in telling me what I should be doing. He might only have been aged fifteen then but he was a truly inspirational figure.

Lying in my bed I must have looked a pathetic, sorry soul. He told me in no uncertain terms, 'This isn't you, Alistair. You need to pull yourself together. You can do it.'

He must have noticed the deep-rooted scepticism that lay behind my watery eyes.

'You can do it all right, mucker. I'll see to it. In fact I'll have you swimming across that river before you know it. I swim across it every day to collect dead bamboo for the cooks' fires and you can come with me, it's a breeze.'

'No way,' I said. I couldn't even walk I couldn't see how I could ever possibly swim again.

'You wait and see,' he beamed. 'Wait there.'

He dashed off. Good old Freddie, I smiled. He had made it. The senior Gordon Highlanders officers must have pleaded with the Japanese not to send the boys to the railway and instead to the relative safety of Chungkai. I was surprised, though, that they had not been kept at Changi, which may have been safer. Still Freddie looked healthy and the glint in his eyes registered that he remained as cheeky as ever.

Freddie soon returned with some cake and his brother Jim. It was great to see him too. He had lost some weight but still looked quite healthy. He was the same old Jim; it was impossible to get a word out of him. Instead I devoured the cake, which he called 'Gula Malacca' and told me was made from the sap of a palm tree. It was extremely sweet and tasty the first amount of sugar to pass my lips in two years. It was possibly not the best thing for me, as I had some bowel problems after that but it was so delicious that it was worth it. I stopped short of asking Freddie where he got it from; I didn't want to know. And if Freddie had been in Chungkai for a year without my supervision to rein in his unbridled curiosity and enthusiasm, he no doubt knew every nook and cranny of the place.

From then on I saw Freddie daily. He swam across the river every day to collect firewood for the cooks. All of the wood around the camp had already been pilfered so the best pickings were across the 150-yard-wide stretch of fast-flowing brown water. He would dash across, bundle together a load and haul it back behind him. For his efforts the cooks gave him extra food. The Japanese knew of his exploits but never stopped him. He was doing no harm and he always returned. Even they found it difficult to be mad with Freddie.

He was also embroiled with the Australians and their clandestine cigarette production and distribution racket. All of these activities were done at night and were so well concealed that the Japanese never shut them down as long as I was there. Freddie told me how they made the cigarettes. They used a flat wooden board, which had a thick parchment attached to it that rolled around a thin piece of bamboo glued through it. The tobacco, which must have been smuggled inside the camp through the wire, was placed on the parchment. Paper came from books usually the Bible, which was the preferred choice as it best kept alight and it was rolled around the bamboo stick, wrapping itself around the tobacco. Once licked and sealed it formed a perfect smoke. I was amazed at how professional the cigarettes looked. The Dutch, who mainly kept to themselves, had their own operation.

Freddie was the Australians' top salesman. A natural barrow boy he could sell fish to the sea. He sneaked from hut to hut, group to group he was never caught and flogged his illicit wares. After some time, he told me, he had established a large clientele and everyone knew him as the boy in the know. He was paid a cut from the earnings and always had dollars in his pocket. While I never approved of his occupation, I was always grateful for the food he purchased for me from the sanctioned canteen. The supplements to my diet, which included two-egg omelettes, molasses, coconut and papaya, assisted in my recovery and probably later helped save my life.

Meanwhile the medical orderlies told Freddie in no uncertain terms which were often the only terms he fully responded to not to interfere with my rehab. But after Freddie's arrival on the scene I approached my physical exercises with a renewed vigour. Through sheer hard toil I slowly started to make headway. Day by day my movement returned. I lifted all of the weights attached to my foot and progressed to the parallel bars. Once I could struggle from one end to the other with help from my arms, they gave me a pair of crutches. After a few weeks on them I graduated to just one crutch and eventually was walking unaided, albeit with a pronounced rolling, John Wayne-like gait.

Despite my weeping tropical ulcers and still faltering walk, I was recovering well. In the evenings Freddie and I would talk for hours, much like we did on top of the hill at Changi. I even took in several theatrical shows, which the men had organised themselves. They were always outrageous burlesque affairs, held on a rickety stage and with an improvised orchestra. There was a piano, trumpet, saxophone and drums, and always plenty of laughs. It was a real boost to the spirits.

Compared with the other camps this truly was a holiday camp. I hardly ever saw a guard, let alone a coordinated or even random beating or punishment. Men walked about freely, traded, smoked cigarettes, sang songs and even played sports.

Reading between the lines and picking up on snippets of overheard conversations, I soon realised just how unlucky I had been. The Kanyu camps, under the sadistic rule of the Black Prince, were by far the worst camps I heard about. Other men talked of earning weekly pay for their work on the railway, which they saved and spent in canteens in their camps or when they got to Chungkai. Others enjoyed days off and long weekends. Some Japanese allowed men to sing rousing songs as they worked. Other prisoners had chatted with native lassies as they strolled past and traded with locals.

As I ventured further from my hut, exploring the vast camp, I saw dozens of blokes hopping around with legs lopped off. They were mainly victims of gangrene brought on by tropical ulcers. A couple of the senior doctors at Chungkai had been doing an incredible number of amputations and with rudimentary equipment and no anaesthetics, had attained amazingly high success rates. One of these doctors, a Canadian called Captain Marko, had performed 120 amputations.

As my condition improved I was able to take in the amazing hospital camp operation. Artisans and tradesmen among the prisoners had made an astonishing array of medical equipment, adapting old Ovaltine cans, Japanese beer bottles and mess tins to become retractors, saline drips and anaesthetic masks. They employed bamboo to make shunts, false legs, a dentist's chair and even an orthopaedic bed. They set up stills to produce surgical alcohol and distilled water. Drugs were bought on the black market and smuggled in to the camp, I would later learn, by the heroes of the secret 'V organisation interned British businessmen in Bangkok, who also alerted the neutral authorities to our plight.

Chungkai was about rebuilding minds as well as bodies. Many of us had to relearn how to socialise and to overcome the trauma of the railway. Accordingly there were plenty of organised activities to keep my mind occupied in the evenings. We had so many talented and professional people in our ranks to give classes and talks. There were professors and lecturers in all manner of disciplines but one of the most popular speakers was a cockney burglar, who regularly entertained audiences with tales of how he had robbed his way across London. Chungkai had a great theatre too, a massive and fantastically well-organised place with concerts every Friday and Saturday night. These were of classical, jazz and popular music, along with cabaret shows of a professional level. The one I enjoyed most was called 'Wonderbar'. It included a can-can routine and the prisoners' favourite drag queen Bobby Spong.

One afternoon when I was at the Thai-run canteen buying a coconut with some dollars Freddie had generously insisted that I take, I saw a notice on the message board that caught my eye. I recognised the name immediately.

The handwritten notice proclaimed, 'E. W. Swanton renowned cricket commentator and observer to give talk on Test match cricket this evening after dinner at the hut beside the officers' mess.'

I went on my own, as cricket and especially talk of cricket was too boring an activity for restless Freddie. I had always admired the sport and enjoyed tussling with my brother Douglas on the green down from our house. Ernest William Swanton had been one of Britain's leading cricket writers and commentators before the war and even claimed to have been taken in his pram to watch the great W. G. Grace batting for London County. The hut was already crammed full when I entered, and pitched in darkness. Once the murmurs subsided a voice at the front began. I knew it was Swanton he had a very distinguished voice and I recognised his impeccable accent from listening to Test matches on the wireless back in Aberdeen. Swanton, who had joined the Bedfordshires, was wounded during the battle for Singapore and was in hospital when the Japanese overran us. At Chungkai he could often be seen cradling his beloved 1939 copy of cricket bible Wisden, which he had convinced a Japanese censor to mark as 'Not subversive'.

He introduced himself with his own blend of pomposity and gregarious-ness and began talking on Test cricket. We stood in reverential silence. Such were his descriptive powers that you could almost hear the compelling crack of leather on willow. Listening to him I was surprised to hear that he was full of praise and admiration for the Australians. He was envious of their hardened attitude and the way they played without fear of reputations. To the harrumph-ing of some English chaps who stood near me, he proclaimed the Australian great, Don Bradman, as the best player he had ever seen. Bradman's powers of concentration, he said, distinguished him from his English counterparts, includ-ing Denis Compton. 'It's the blazing fire in their bellies,' Swanton recalled. He went on to describe a century that he had witnessed Bradman score, 'all along the ground, hardly a shot in anger, or an ounce of effort'.

Swanton had us lapping up every word he said. He told of his disappoint-ment at being overlooked by his newspaper, the London Evening Standard, for the 1932-3 Ashes tour of Australia, which would become infamous as the 'Bodyline' tour. But he dismissed the furore over the series, in which English bowlers perfected a brutal and uncompromising tactical move of aiming deliv-eries at the head and body of the opposing batsmen, to thwart Bradman in particular, as media 'hype'. Despite some men offering their views on Bodyline and questions flying at Swanton from all quarters, he swerved the topic. Instead he spoke on the English greats he had seen, including the prolific Wally Ham-mond, Len Hutton and Mr Bodyline himself, Harold Larwood.

After a mesmerising ninety minutes Swanton wrapped up his talk and the men retreated to their huts. Some stayed behind to speak to him, no doubt raising their contrary views on Bodyline, and I hovered around for a while. I thought of shaking his hand and thanking him for one of the most enjoyable moments I had had in captivity but he seemed well tied up, so I wandered into the warm night air. I took a walk around the camp to stretch my legs that had been aching standing there listening for so long. My 'happy feet' were buzzing and so was my mind. The talk had enlivened me.

While it lifted my spirits, it was a stark reminder that there was a world outside this rotten jungle. Chungkai was proving an almost enjoyable period. The only downside for me was that I knew it wouldn't last. Always looming in the back of my mind was the notion that after my recovery I would be sent back to the railway. I knew that the Japanese periodically asked British commanders for so many men to go back to work on the railway. Obviously the fittest went first. If the required numbers were not provided, the Japanese stormed in and took men at random. Walking back to my hut from the Swanton talk finally feeling weary, I decided to stay put as long as possible. I would fake the state of my health, make it out to be worse than it was, lie to the doctors and avoid seeing them wherever I could. At least my ulcers were taking some time to heal and while they gaped open, surely I would be safe.

After six months or so, once my waddling walk had been ironed out, Freddie decided I was ready to swim across the river with him. I had my doubts but I wasn't going to let him know that, so I agreed.

Having once been a strong swimmer one of the best at Bon Accord Swimming Club I had to have faith in myself. I knew that I could at least keep myself afloat. Freddie reassured me that he was there to save me. 'I've got my lifesaving badge young fellow.' I'm more likely to save you,' I grumbled, as I eased myself down the riverbank and into the water. I stayed by the bank and floundered around with some easy breaststroke until I realised I could float. Not having had a proper bath or shower for more than two years, being submerged in the water was so heavenly. It was amazingly refreshing and I splashed the water over my face as Freddie dog-paddled in circles around me.

'How does it feel?' he asked.

'Like I'm on holiday.'

'Ready to cross the river?'

'Maybe tomorrow,' I said. 'I'm happy enough here for now. Let me enjoy it.'

The next day we returned. We ventured upstream slightly so that the current of the river would be with us as we swam. I soon trailed behind Freddie, who was an excellent swimmer, and he treaded water until I caught up again. I reckoned it was about four lengths of an Olympic-sized swimming pool–two hundred metres. However far it was, I was completely knackered when I got to the other side. I got my puff back while Freddie gathered some dry wood, and we swam back.

After that I joined Freddie in the river crossings almost every day. I enjoyed the task and it no doubt helped my rehabilitation. I also hoped that I was improving my stock and the wood-collecting duties would prevent me from being sent back to the railway. The thought of returning sent shudders down my spine and I tried not to dwell on it.

But of course I was right. One day the dreadful news came -I was being sent back to work.

An officer found me in the hut and said, 'Collect your things. You leave in the morning.'

'Where to?'I asked, already knowing the answer.

'Who knows? May God be with you.'

I told Freddie, who outwardly took it rather well. He shook my hand and vowed to keep in touch no matter what. I think I took the departure worse than he did, fearing for the both of us. What was next? I prayed to be spared from another railway camp even one with a canteen.

In the morning I gathered on the parade square with a few hundred other men. After much waiting around with no information to chew over, we were marched into the jungle. Within a few hours along a narrow path we arrived at another camp. This was known as Tamarkan and was much smaller than Chungkai it was more like a railway camp, although cleaner and, since it was a recuperation camp, more sanitary. Fears of being sent to work were soothed when the interpreter told us that we would be here only temporarily, before being sent 'somewhere else'. So for the next few days we kicked our heels. I walked about a lot, trying to keep my fitness levels up for whatever lay before me. It was extremely depressing to be there, especially after Chungkai. An air of resignation hung among us and after a few days we were almost glad to be moving again.

The guards loaded us on to trucks and drove us back to Bam Pong, where I had started my jungle trek all those months and tears ago. It took all day to get there, and we arrived choking with dust and thirst. I did not need to be told what to do when we stopped by a train: the steel carriages looked sickeningly familiar. My mind spinning, stomach churning, I was pushed inside, again with thirty or forty others. Thoughts of being disposed of returned, even though I knew they didn't need to take us far to do that.

The Korean guard was trying to close the door but desperate men blocked it with their bare feet. They pleaded with him, 'Leave the door open, please! Please!'

He looked confused, as if he were considering our frantic pleas. This ray of hope spurred the men on.

'We won't jump!'

'We'll close it at sidings and stops,' another said.

Unbelievably the guard allowed the door to remain open. It made a hell of a difference. As we got moving it provided an almost pleasant breeze. We could also hang each other outside bum first to do our business in a more sanitary, albeit more hazardous manner. I could not get over the fact of the guard allowing the door to stay open, about the first act of kindness or sympathy I had received from one of them. We all agreed to roll the doors shut when we came to stops so other guards wouldn't get wind of it and question why it was open. We still had some common sense left in us.

While the breeze helped, it was still a torturous journey. There was nothing to do but stand and wait it out. By now I could shut down my mind more easily than before and ignore terrible thoughts or happenings. But knowing that we had five days to go to get back to Singapore only made the journey longer. At least on the way up to the railway we always thought that the next siding, or next stop, would be our final destination. Now we just knew that it would go on and on, and on . . .

SITTANG BEND

GEORGE MACDONALD FRASER

I parted company with Nine Section on coming back from leave. It would have happened anyway, with the battalion reorganisation, for they were mostly old soldiers due for repatriation and demob, and I was not, but there was a more immediate reason. My application to go before a War Office Selection Board to see if I was fit for officer training had been granted by the colonel, and when the next board assembled, in a few weeks' time, I would be sent up to Meiktila to be flown out to face the examiners. Splendid news which put the wind right up me, for while if I passed I would go straight on to one of the Indian military academies, failure would mean returning to the battalion with my tail between my legs.

In the meantime I was not to be attached to a platoon, but to company H.Q., where I was to make myself generally useful.

So I packed up my traps in the section billet, to cries of "Bloody 'ell, w'at's the Army comin' to?", "Wiv my permish you'll get a commish!", "If ye think Ah'll ivver gi'e you a salute, ye're arse is oot the winder!" and trudged across to company H.Q., not feeling a wrench, exactly, but suddenly lonely. We'd been together, a close-knit, interdependent unit, for six months of war, and now I would never march with them again, or stand stags with them, or look round for them in action. The bond that had formed wasn't quite one of friendship, although I'd liked them, Forster excepted—no one could like Foshie, for all the sterling qualities among his less agreeable traits. (The Duke had been right: he was a good soldier, sour, carnaptious, and derisive, but when you hesitated at the bunker entrance or the branch in the track, and glanced sideways, he would be there, sucking his teeth and looking wicked, on the balls of his feet, sniffing for Jap.)

The others I had learned to respect and admire and be thankful for, but it had been trust more than affection. Sometimes, in a field game, you find a player with whom you fit like hand in glove; you've never seen or spoken to him before, but you have an instant understanding and work together almost by instinct, and when you shake hands at the end you're surprised to find that you don't really know each other at all, except in one narrow field, and part company. Liking doesn't really come into it; you just remember, With occasional regret, how well you combined. That was how it was with Nine Section; if there was an emotional tie, it was one of gratitude.

I would have felt the parting more if it had been absolute, but they were just down the road, and I found myself dropping in at their basha to cadge a pialla of tea and listen to them beefing about their new section leader, a full corporal, and Irish at that; I felt an unworthy glow on discovering that they didn't like him.

"Regimental Paddy!" was Nick's verdict. "Mind you, there's summat tae be said for the booger—at least 'e's full growed an' auld enoof tae vote, nut like soom that ye git parked on ye—knaw w'at Ah mean, Jock?"

"Aye, yoong lance-jacks, an' the like o' them," said Grandarse. "Scotch lance-jacks is the woorst, Ah always say. Clivver boogers, full o' bullshit."

"Haggis-bashin' bastards," agreed Wattie. "Burgoo-belters."

"Scotchies, Ah've shit 'em," said Forster. "Aye gittin' aboov theresels, wantin' commissions, don't-ye-know-old-boy. One thing, we've bin gittin' a decent brew-up since we got rid o' you, Jock."

"Lying sod," I said. "Who's taken over?"

"Genera) Slim sends us doon a dixie ivvery day frae Meiktila," said Nick. "Wid a note on't lid: 'Drink oop, lads, ye'll a' git killed'." He emptied the contents of his pialla in disgust. "Wee's bin pishin' in't brew-tin, for Christ's sek?"

"W'at they got ye on these days, Jock?" asked Morton. "Ablutions?"

"Ablutions orficer, that's wot 'e's gonna be," said Parker. "Right, Jockie boy? Wiv my permish you can 'ave two pips an' a latrine bucket, an' spend the duration diggin' shitahses for the Pioneers. You won't know the difference from Nine Section -semper in excreta."

In fact, what they had me on at Company H.Q. was filling in wherever a spare lance-corporal was needed, and I was kept fairly active in an irritatingly piecemeal way. Unknown to anybody, the war was into its last month, although there was no sign of this along the Rangoon road. Jap's final effort to break across to the east was at its height; they were coming out of the Pegu Yomas like gang-busters, and there was action all the way from Pegu to Penwegon and beyond. Patrols and ambushes were being stepped up, his attacks were being driven back or fought to a standstill, and apart from the main thrusts the country was crawling, literally, with stragglers, many of them half-dead with disease and starvation. They were wandering in the jungle, drifting down the rivers, lying in the chaungs, too spent to do anything but wait to die or be captured; even the "comfort girls" who marched with the Jap armies were being rounded up. But the remnants of z8th Army who were still on their feet were not giving up; their casualties were mounting into thousands, but they were making Fourteenth Army fight right down to the wire.

So while Nine Section were operating with their new corporal, I found myself going out in strange company, and missing them damnably. I was only out two or three times with different sections, and we accounted for the odd enemy, killed or captured, including the one I mentioned in the foreword who came screaming at us with a home-made spear, one against a dozen and he should have been dead weeks ago by the look of him.

"An' after this, it'll be Malaya," I heard a sergeant say. "God knaws 'oo many divisions Jap's still got doon theer—joongle a' the way tae Singapore, be Christ! They say we'll be gittin' mules again. Wrap oop an' roll on!"

Malaya, mules, and more Japanese—well, it wouldn't be my indaba, unless I failed wosbie. Although even if I passed, what were the odds that I wouldn't be back as a second-lieutenant, commanding a platoon in Borneo or Sumatra, nine months hence? On VE Day it had seemed that our war, too, must soon be over, but now if anything it was hotting up, and people were talking of another campaign. With mules. And if anyone had told us that thousands of miles away in the Pacific an aircraft called Enola Gay was preparing to load up, it wouldn't have meant a thing.

Meanwhile, the war still had novelties in store, and as I recall them they seem quite apart from anything that had gone before; it's almost as though they took place in a different world, and I was a different person. That can only be because they happened away from the enclosed regular military life to which I had grown so accustomed; they were, in the proper sense of the word, eccentric, a curious detached interlude of my time in Burma.

It began with a summons to the company basha where I was ordered to hand in my pay-book, that AB 64 Part I which is the documentary proof of your military existence, and which you part with only in unusual circumstances. My new company commander, an abrupt but good-natured veteran, explained.

"There's a selection board meeting in two weeks' time, at Chittagong, so you'll be going up to Meiktila in a week or so. Nervous?" He grinned sympathetically. "I've heard they pass about one in three nowadays, but don't let that worry you—most of 'em probably never saw an angry Jap and haven't any qualifications except School Cert and three years' service in the stores." Which wasn't true, but was a fair reflection of a 17th Div infantry major's view of the rest of the military scene. "Got your AB 64? It'll have to go to your old company commander so that he can give you your character in writing. Leave it with the clerk."

That was enough to set the adrenalin pumping. I hadn't seen Long John for weeks, since he was with one of the other companies. It hadn't occurred to me that he would have to pass judgment on my general fitness, recording it forever in my pay-book, where it would be scrutinised by those cold, fish-like examiners. What would he say? Well, he was the one who'd promoted me—and on my first outing my section had looted half an air-drop, and on the second I'd fallen down a well. Was he aware of these things? I could hear the selection board president: "In a word, corporal, you showed your talent for leadership by failing to restrain your men from pillaging, and in the attack on Pyawbwe you hid underwater. H'm . . ." Common sense told me that Long John would confine himself to general observations . . . but what would they be? Sins of omission and commission rose up to confront me . . . dear God, the best he could say was "Average", or at a pinch "Satisfactory", and what could be more damning than that?

"By the way," said the major, "d'you know anything about this anti-tank gun, the Piat?"

1 said I did; I'd been trained in its use in England, although I'd never fired it.

"At least you'll know one end from t'other," he said, "which is more than anyone else does. We've had one in store for a bit, but no one's mentioned it until now. Corporal, give us that file marked Piat. Yes . . . there's been a request for one from—." He mentioned an unpronounceable village which I'd never heard of. "About twenty miles up the road, small unit near the river. They also want an instructor. Let's see, you've still got a week in hand . . . well, why not? Take it up, show 'em how it works, and either bring it back yourself or leave it with them and fetch a receipt. But make it clear that you've to be back here inside a week—here, I'll give you a chit for their O.C." He squinted at the file and gave a barking laugh. "A captain whose name, to judge from his bloody awful writing, is Grief. Well, he should know . . ."

Pleased at the prospect of change, and escaping from the orbit of a company sergeant-major who had proved himself a dab hand at finding work for idle lance-corporals to do, I went off to renew acquaintance with the projector, infantry, anti-tank, commonly called the Piat. It was the British counterpart of the American bazooka, and might have been designed by Heath Robinson after a drunken dinner of lobster au gratin. It's not easy to describe, and I may have forgotten some of its finer points, such as its exact measurements, but I'll do my best.

From memory, then, it consisted of about four feet of six-inch steel pipe, one end of which was partly cut out to leave a semi-cylindrical cradle about a foot long, in which you laid the bomb. Ar the other end of the pipe was a thick butt pad which fitted into your shoulder when you lay on the ground in a firing position, the body of the pipe being supported on a single expanding leg. The bomb, a sinister black object fifteen or so inches overall, had a circular tail fin containing a propellant cartridge, a bulging black body packed with high explosive, and a long spiked nose with a tiny cap which, when removed, revealed a gleaming detonator.

Within the body of the pipe was a gigantic spring which had to be cocked after each shot: you lay on your back and dragged the Piat on top of you, braced your feet against the projecting edges of the butt pad, and heaved like hell at something or other which I've forgotten. After immense creaking the spring clicked into place, and you crawled out from under, gamely ignoring your hernia, laid an uncapped bomb gently in the front cradle, resumed the lying firing position, aligned the barleycorn sight with the gleaming nose of the bomb, pressed the massive metal trigger beneath the pipe, thus releasing the coiled spring which drove a long steel plunger up the tail fin of the bomb, detonating the propellant cartridge, you and the Piat went ploughing backwards with the recoil, and the bomb went soaring away—about a hundred yards, 1 think, but it may have been farther. The whole contraption weighed about a ton, and the bombs came in cases of three; if you were Goliath you might have carried the Piat and two cases.

Like many British inventions, it looked improbable, unwieldy, and unsafe—and it worked. The principle was that when the bomb hita tank, the long spiked nose penetrated the armour, and all the concentrated explosive in the bulging body rushed through into the tank's interior, brewing up everyone within. Where a Piat had hit, the only visible exterior damage was a small, neat hole, or so they tell me. I never fired it at a tank.

I drew it from the stores with four cases of bombs—all they had—refreshed my memory by stripping and reassembling it, and hopped a truck next morning. I also took my rifle and fifty rounds, as per regulations, plus my kukri and a couple of grenades; if there was trouble I wanted some real weaponry handy.

The monsoon had eased by now, and it was a pleasant hour's drive to the village where there was a battered jeep waiting, with a Burmese driver. We loaded the Piat aboard and bounced away along a sunlit track past paddy-fields which were calm silver lakes fringed by scrub and jungle, and another hour brought us to a little collection of huts half-hidden by undergrowth on the edge of nowhere, which was the operational base of the officer 1 always think of as "Captain Grief"—and I call him that now because he may still be about, and I don't want him suing me or trying to kill me or, even worse, seeking me out for a jovial reunion.

Civilian readers may think my description of him, especially his conversation, exaggerated. It is not, and any old soldier will bear me out, for he was a prize specimen of a type in which the British Army has always been rich—I've no doubt he was at Hastings, and will be there, eccentric as ever, when Gabriel sounds the last rally: a genuine, guaranteed, paid-up head-case. Which is not to say that he was clinically mad, just that he behaved as though he was. You have heard of them: when touched with genius they become Chinese Gordon or Lord Cochrane or, in the last war, Wingate, that gifted guerrilla who revived the military beard, carried an alarm clock to remind everyone what time it was, scrubbed himself with a toothbrush, quoted Holy Writ, and was an authority on Donald Duck–or so I have been reliably informed. Splendid men, especially to keep away from.

Captain Grief may have been less gifted, but he had all the Deolali hallmarks. He was driven apparently by some high-octane spirit, full of restless energy and strange cries like: "Bags o' panic!" and "Bash on regardless!" and even "Aha, Ermintrude, at last we meet–over the bridge you go!", uttered with a glittering eye as he paced up and down, clapping his hands. He was tall, rangy, lantern-jawed, and eager as an unleashed hound. His dress consisted of an old tweed fishing cap, a dilapidated bush shirt, corduroy trousers, and brothel-creeper boots, and my heart sank at the sight of him, for I could read the signs: this was one who would probably want the Piat mounted on a jeep, with me manning it in the passenger seat and himself at the wheel, roaring with laughter at top speed and changing gear with his foot.

To be fair, he did have tranquil moments, in which he sat brooding, sighing frequently and talking to himself. But he was in full cry when we drew up outside his basha.

"Come on, come on, come on!" he shouted, rubbing his hands and beaming. "Let's get weaving! Is this the old iskermoffit?* Let's have a dekko!" Before I could get out he was ferreting in the back

A corruption, I believe, of iskar mafit (Arabic), signifying in Army slang, "the thing". "Yagger", of unknown origin, was synonymous. for the Piat. "Stone me! Who's been robbing the Titanic's engine room? Got bags of ammo for it, have you, corporal? Bang on, good show! All right, stand at ease, stand easy, come in, have a pew, let's get to it! Tea, Sarn't Jones! Tea and your most welcoming smile for our friend here, Lance-corporal Whatsit–you don't mind if I call you Whatsit? It was my mother's name." He threw himself into a canvas chair, put his dreadful boots on the rickety table, and beamed at me. "So that thing's a tank-buster, is it? Right, put me in the picture! Take a refreshing sip, and shoot!"

I did, and he hung on every word, interrupting only occasionally with exclamations like "Spot on!" and "Just the old boot!". Then I lay on the floor and cocked it, showed him how the trigger worked, and demonstrated the sight, and he promptly tried for himself, recocking it with one swift jerk and whipping into a firing position in almost the same movement. 1 impressed on him that the bombs were sensitive, and he cried: "Piece o' cake!", untwirled the cap, and regarded the gleaming copper nose as though it were a rare gem.

"Bloody marvellous! Look at this, Jones—breathe on it and reach for your harp! Right, corporal, let's recap—this little isker pierces the target and all the good news rushes through, causing alarm and despondency to those on the other side? Great -woomf!" He flourished the bomb spear-fashion, while I made mewing noises and Jones, a stout little Welshman, watched resignedly. "Not to panic, people! Everything's under control! We replace the dinky little cap, so—gad, the skill in these two hands! Take it and press it between the leaves of your diary." He handed me the bomb. "What's the effective range?"

"I'm not sure, sir. A hundred yards, thereabouts."

"Tis not so wide as a church door, but 'tis enough, 'twill serve!" said Grief happily. "Now, corporal, eyes down, look in—we can't use it against tanks, 'cos Jap hasn't any—and I wouldn't fancy it against low-flying aircraft, but since he hasn't got any of those left either, we're quids in! How about boats?"

"Boats, sir?"

"The very word I was looking for! Note it down, Jones. Yes, good ancient—boats! Floating vehicles, and I don't mean the Queen Mary. Wooden jobs, sampans, lifeboats, rafts, once-roundthe-lighthouse-in-the-ruddy-Skylark things." He cupped a hand to his ear, expectantly. "Take your time, writing on one side of the paper only."

The line between affected eccentricity and jungle-happiness is a fine one, but I was sure by now that this was your normal wild man, and not permanently tap. Apart from his three pips he wore no insignia, and I wondered if he was a Sapper, which would account for a lot. The reckless confidence with which he handled H.E. was right in character—I once knew a Sapper who corrected a wobbly table by shoving a land-mine under one leg, and it was weeks before we discovered the thing was armed and ready to blow.

I said it should sink any small craft, but that if it burst in the open rather than a confined space its explosive force would be dissipated. He nodded gravely and said, in a heavy Deep South drawl: "Naow, ain't that a goddam sha-ame . . . In other words, not much of an anti-personnel job. Be honest, hold nothing back!"

I said it ought to do as much damage as a 36 grenade, perhaps more, and he brightened.

"You wouldn't want to be within fifteen yards, wearing your best battle-dress?"

"Not even wearing denims, sir," I said, entering into the spirit of the thing, and he regarded me with alarm.

"I doubt if there's a suit of denim this side of Cox's Bazaar," he said in a hushed voice. "Oh, well, it can't be helped." He gave a sudden explosive laugh, slapped his hands on the table, and was off again. "Right–Sarn't Jones, this is the form! We'll have a practice shoot, with good old Whatsit here pressing the doodah and shouting 'Fore!' Everyone on parade, no exceptions, summon 'em from the four corners–every man in the unit must be thoroughly clued up on this supreme example of the ballistic engineer's art, so that if our young friend should cop his lot, which—" he flashed me a cheerful smile and assumed another American accent "- which we shall do all in our power to ensure is a calamity that does not eventuate—" he became British again "-some other poor bugger will be able to fire the thing." He gave me a sad stare. "But we shall miss you, corporal. Yes . . . yes, we shall."

Jones asked when he wanted the parade, and Grief resumed his seat. "In one hour, neither more nor less! All mustered, Mr Colman, everybody out, bags o' bull, bags o' panic, tallest on the right, shortest on the left, and heigh-ho for the governor's gouty foot!" He waved in dismissal. "Find the good corporal a modest lodging, give him his fill of meat and drink, and put a sentry on his beastly bombs, twenty-four hours a day or longer if need be. Away, avaunt!"

You may have noticed that for all his idiotic persiflage, Captain Grief had mastered the basics of the Piat, handled it like an expert, asked sensible questions, and was wasting no time in having it demonstrated to his men, all of which was reassuring. True, as I gathered up the Piat and Jones collected the bomb-cases, he was lying back in his canvas seat, doing physical jerks with his arms and crooning, to the tune of "Mairsie doats":

Liberty boats and Carley floats And little rubber dinghies Paddle your own canoe Up your flue . . . but then, as I saluted before withdrawing, he suddenly sat upright and took me flat aback by saying, in a normal, quiet voice, and with a smile that was both sane and friendly:

"Hold on a minute—don't know what I've been thinking of. Corporal, I haven't even asked your name."

Relieved, I told him, and handed over the chit from my company commander, explaining that I had to be back at my unit within the week. He nodded and promised to see to it, shook hands, and said he was glad to have me on the strength. Then he glanced at the note, frowned, turned it over, and said:

"That's strange . . . no, your company commander doesn't seem to have mentioned it . . . I wonder why? Still, you can tell me." He looked at me, clear-eyed and rational: "Are you a lurkin' firkin or a peepin' gremlin?"

Just when I'd started believing he was all there. I glanced at Jones, but he was gazing stolidly at the wall.

"I beg your pardon, sir?" I said, and Grief repeated the question, with just a hint of suspicion. "I'm afraid I don't know, sir."

"You–don't–know?" He seemed stunned. "Well," he said severely, "you'll have to find out by tomorrow, you know! Oh, yes! Dammit all, d'you think you can just walk in here off the street, without proper classification or even a note from Miss Tempest the games mistress? We have to know who we're dealing with, for heaven's sake! You find out, jildi,* or there'll be fire and sword along Banana Ridge, I can tell you! Understand? Right, fall out!"

He sat down abruptly, seized a map, gave me a dirty look, peered at the map intently, and gave a violent start: "'Here be dragons', by God! But stay—can it be a minute shred of mosquito dung? Let us read on . . .'"

When we were safely outside I turned helplessly to Jones: "Which are you–a lurkin' firkin or a peepin' gremlin?" He gave me a look.

"Me? I'm a tricksy pixie. An' that's not all, boyo. Soon's he found out I was Welsh he wanted me to sing the Hallelujah Chorus. I told 'im I can't sing a note, an' 'e says: 'You're no more Welsh than I am. You're prob'ly a bloody spy. Spell Llandudno, or it'll be the worse for you!' Straight up, it's what 'e said. Oh, aye, some mothers do 'ave 'em."

"But . . . it's just an act–isn't it? I mean, for a minute he sounded perfectly normal. Or is he really cocoa?"

"Don't look at me, boy," said Jones wearily. "Oh, 'e's all right, like . . . well, 'e's daft as a badger, but 'e knows what 'e's doin' -most o' the time. Between you an' me, I reckon 'e's due for leave, know what 1 mean? Aye, about two years' leave. Come on, an' we'll get you settled."

He had a little hut of his own, and I dumped my gear while he brewed up and got out the bully and biscuits and put me in the picture. The unit, which was only of platoon strength, was composed entirely of Shan scouts, friendly hillmen from beyond the Salween; it was one of those little temporary groups which

"quickly spring up on the fringes of most armies in the field and fade away when no longer needed. This one, Jones believed, was Grief's personal creation.

"'E's an I-man, see—an Intelligence wallah—well, you can tell from 'is patter, can't you?—but 'e was with the Bombay Sappers an' Miners, accordin' to what 'e told me -"

"I'm not surprised. You're not an Engineer or an I-man, are you?"

"No bloody fears, I'm Signals, me. But I speak Burmese, see, an' Grief doesn't. Boy, you should try translatin' 'is sort o' chat to a bunch o' Shans! Yeah, I been out yere since '37. Puttin' up telegraph lines for the bleedin' elephants to pull down. Aye, well, roll on demob!"

"But what d'you do—the unit, I mean?"

"Watchin' the river, layin' ambushes, at night, mostly, 'cos that's when Jap tries to slip past. ☒ 'ad two armies up yonder, you know, 15th an' 33rd-"

"I'm aware."

"Oh, at Meiktila, was you? An' Pyawbwe? Well, you seen 'em for yourself, then. They been swarmin' down this way lately, kee-pin' as far east as they can, see, but plenty of 'em uses the river, too, an' we've 'ad three or four duffies, an' shot up their boats an' rafts. A lot of 'em got by, mind you -"

"So that's why he was on about boats! God, he must be harpie—what does he think a Piat can do against open boats that grenade launchers and two-inch mortars can't?"

"Oh, we got mortars an' launchers, but I s'pose 'e figured a Piat would be more accurate, bein' a tank-buster .. . Look, boyo, if 'e 'eard somebody 'ad invented a gun for firm' Rugby balls under water, 'e'd want it! An' 'e'd find a use for it, an' all. You wait an' see."

The demonstration firing of the Piat took place on a paddy close to the camp. Grief, bursting with excitement, strode up and down before his platoon, sturdy Burmans in khaki shorts and head scarves who listened with no trace of expression on their flat, sinister faces while I named the parts and explained the mechanism with Jones translating. Then I cocked the thing, nipping my fingers in my nervousness, trying to ignore Grief's barks of encouragement. "Take the strain—heave! Bags of action, bags o' swank, Strang the Terrible pits his muscles against the machine, can he do it, can he hell, yes he can! Got it, corporal! Smashing, good show! Spinach wins the day!"

The target chosen was an old Jap bunker, a good solid construction, and 1 wondered if the Piat would even dent it—assuming I hit it, for never having fired the weapon it was with no confidence that I uncapped a bomb, laid it carefully in place, and took up the firing position.

"Range–eighty yards!" bawled Grief, standing over me. "Well, eighty or eighty-two, we won't niggle!" Silly bastard. "Wind backing nor-nor-east, visibility good, scattered showers in western districts! On your marks, take your time, and may God defend the right!" He flourished his hands and placed his forefingers in his ears. I had adjusted the supporting leg to what I hoped was the correct elevation, took a firm grip, lined up the sight, and pulled. There was an ear-splitting crack, the pad hit me a smashing blow, and as Piat and I were shunted violently back there was a great crump from up ahead. I looked, and approximately halfway to the target a large cloud of smoke was hanging over a tiny crater.

"Jesus McGonigal!" roared Grief. "Ranging shot! Up fifty, direction, spot on, elevation—well, nobody's perfect! Try again, corporal, remember the spider, we're all with you, man and beast! Bags 1 be number two on the gun!"

He recocked the Piat himself, and by the time I had another bomb ready he was fiddling with the sight, adjusting the elevating leg, and squinting towards the target. "Gravity, muzzle velocity, density, intensity, one for his nob, and bullshit baffles brains! There–into the breach, old Whatsit, and if all else fails we'll fix a bayonet on the bloody thing and charge! Fire at Will, he's hiding in the cellar, the cowardly sod!"

1 lined up the sight, held on like grim death, pulled the trigger, and being ready this time for the recoil was able to watch the bomb's flight. It arced slowly up, dipped, and descended, there was a brilliant orange flash and a roar, a billowing black cloud, and beneath it–nothing. The bunker had vanished.

"Take that, you jerry-built abomination! Flaunt your roof at me, would you? I'll huff and I'll puff and you've had your chips!"

Grief was off like an electric hare, with his platoon chattering and laughing at his heels. Well pleased, I followed more slowly, pacing out the range: it was exactly seventy-nine yards.

"He'd measured it, had he?" I said to Jones.

"Don't you believe it, boyo," he said. "He didn't need to."

Grief and his gang were standing round the wreckage-filled pit in which beams and thatch were tangled in the fallen earth of the roof. As we joined him he heaved a deep sigh and looked solemn.

"Alas, poor Will, everybody's target, I fear he's been fired at for the last time. He's down there somewhere with his ears ringing and his arse full of shrapnel." He shook his head and then was off again, sixteen to the dozen. "Not a bad bomb, corporal, not bad at all–and you can tell the manufacturers I said so, you unregenerate gremlin, you! Or was it firkin? Not that 1 give two hoots, I couldn't care less, but I don't want you wandering about in a state of uncertainty. Right, Sarn't Jones, dismiss the parade, depart and take your ease, and if anyone rings tell 'em the redskins have cut the wires. I'm going for a kip."

He strode off to his basha, humming "Any Old Iron", and I didn't see him again for twenty-four hours, which was a nuisance, because I wanted to suggest that I give two of his scouts a thorough course on the Piat and return to my unit without delay; I felt I'd had just about my ration of Captain Grief. But he had attached his own version of a "Do Not Disturb" sign to his basha door (it read "Wake Me At Your Peril"), so I turned in early and was lulled to sleep by Sergeant Jones, who had the Welsh gift of talking perfect English in a musical monotone, on and on and on. He lay on his charpoy, staring at the roof, telling me how he and his unit had once mounted guard at Caernarvon Castle, or it may have been the Naafi at Catterick, and so help me he did it down to the smallest detail.

"... it was full ceremonial, Jock, see, an' we was fell in in greatcoats with belts an' bay'nets, bags o' bull, an' a luvvly sight we were. 'You're a luvvly sight, lads', says the R.S.M., Williams 'is name was, played in the back row, was it, for Neath, big strong fellow, built like a slag-heap, played a trial once, I think, anyway 'e fell us in an' inspected us, an' then it was 'Atten-shun!, slope arms, as-you-were, slope arms, that's better, move to the right in threes, right turn, by the left quick march, 'eft-'ight-'eft-'ight, pick 'em up, bags o' swank ...'"

You have to make allowances for a man who's had nobody but Grief to talk to for weeks, but I was astonished, on waking some time towards dawn, to hear a hoarse murmur from the other side of the hut: "... an' then for the last time it was present arms, one-two-three, an' the general salute, an' all the top brass at attention, see, and the band playin' the Luvvly Ash Grove, an' slope arms, one-two-three, an' march off by comp'nies, sarn't-major, an' platoon move to the left in threes, left turn, by the right quick march, an' we marched off, bags o' swank, 'eft-'ight-'eft-'ight an' the band playin' Men of Harlech in the hollow, do ye hear like rushin' billow, an' Williams sayin' keep the dressin', don't go spoilin' it now ..."

Grief was absent next morning, and Jones, possibly exhausted by his nocturnal filibuster, or sulky because I'd dropped off in the middle of it, was withdrawn and edgy. With his help I got two of the Shan scouts proficient on the Piat, but firmly refused their request to be allowed to fire it; with only ten bombs in hand we couldn't afford it.

It was dusk when Grief reappeared, emerging from the jungly fringe of the paddy with his long loping stride, two of his Shans trotting behind. They'd been travelling; Grief's bush-shirt was badly torn, and all three were caked in mud to the thighs, breathing hard and soaked in sweat. Grief flourished his carbine and shouted "Sarn't Jones!", and for the next half-hour the two of them were in closed conference while I kicked my heels, feeling out of it and wondering what was up, and how it would concern me. I brewed up, and presently Jones emerged, issuing instructions to the Shan sergeant and his section leaders; they scampered away, and Jones came across to my fire, filled his pialla, and asked how I fancied night marching.

"Jap's comin' down-river tonight, see, a big bunch. Some of 'em in boats, mebbe rafts, wi' the main body marchin' on the far bank to cover 'em. It's paddy that side, see, an' they'll 'ave scouted to make sure it's clear. But this yere bank's jungly, an' we got West Yorks an' Gurkhas farther up, an' no sign o' Jap this side o' the river. 'E'll try to slip past on the water an' the far bank, an' we won't let 'im. Grief wants you on the Piat."

It was no time to suggest that one of the Burmans I'd instructed should take over. I asked how far.

"Near eight miles to the ambush point, an' gotta be there by midnight." That was less than four hours away.

"Over wet paddy and jungle? That's shifting. I'll need two men to take turns with me toting the Piat. And two for the bombs. How many Japanni?"

"Hundred, maybe two, Grief thinks." He shook his head in admiration. "'E's a bugger, 'e is. Been scoutin' em 'alf the day, up to 'is neck in river. The comes back at the double, bitten rotten with leeches, 'e is. There's a Gurkha platoon rendezvousin' with us at the ambush, so we'll 'ave plenty support. Right." He emptied his pialla on to the fire. "Let's earn our Jap campaign pay."

I'd say that when you've done one night march through scrub and paddy you've done them all, except that this one was a bastard. Three miles an hour on hard level is the Army norm, but you can't do that through ankle-deep water and undergrowth, not by starlight you can't, so we were forced marching whenever the ground permitted. Luckily silence didn't matter, or we'd not have got half-way in time. The Piat was a monster, heavy as sin and snagging on everything, and we had to change carriers every few minutes, except on the open ground, where we could carry it two at a time, one on either end. Jones and another scout carried the bomb cases and our rifles, and since we were at the rear of the little column I cannot report on Captain Grief's deportment at the head. If he had breath enough to natter, even to himself, he was a fitter man than I. Within twenty minutes I was streaming sweat, and the Piat was wearing burning grooves on either shoulder; after two hours I was seriously wondering if I'd make it. My back and leg muscles were one great ache, the skin seemed to have been worn off my shoulders, I'd been whipped stupid by foliage, and I could only hope that the mud which plastered my legs was suffocating the leeches. In the last hour, by the time the whisper for silence came down the line, I was tottering, and too beat to take consolation from the fact that Jones and even the Shans didn't seem any better.

Then we were lying in rank grass among bushes, with the jungly screen behind us, and dimly seen in front the pale sheen of river water. Overhead a few stars were out in the pale night sky, but the far bank was lost in darkness, as if anybody cared by that time. It was positive pleasure just to lie there on the soggy ground, letting the aches drain away, muscles fluttering with tiredness. A couple of yards to my left there was a Shan mortar team in the lee of a bamboo thicket; Jones was to my right with the bomb-cases.

I must have dozed, rotten soldier that I was, for it was with a start that I was aware of movement behind, and heard Grief's voice and another English one: the Gurkha subaltern. There was rustling in the undergrowth, whispering of orders, as the Gurkhas took up their positions along the bank to our right; then the sound of their stealthy movement died away, and there was only the soft jungle chorus of chirps and croaks against the background murmur of the heavy Burmese night, and a voice at my ear inquiring: "Ever had an invite to Viceregal Lodge, corporal? Course you haven't, neither have I, so we can compare notes, tear their characters to pieces, mean bastards. Bugger these night-glasses, show you nothing but war movies, no cartoons, not even an organ interlude . . ."

He was alongside, prone in the grass, and although his face was nothing but a pale blur I could imagine the manic gleam in his eye. He went on, in a conversational whisper:

"Right, this is the form! There's one bloody great boat, sampan type, full of paying passengers, and she'll be as close in under the far bank as she can get—unless some dopey Samurai has run her aground first, in which case we'll demand our money back. Wait for the mortar flares, and then sink me the ship, master gunner, sink her, split her in twain—or thrain, if you feel like it. Don't bother about anything else; she's your bird. The range'll be about eighty yards—is the figure familiar? Spot on! Jones! Jones, are ye there, Morriarity? Slither over here to the mortar—no, never mind his bloody bombs, I'll look after 'em! Come on, jildi!"

Jones wriggled past me, and there was more whispering beside the bamboo thicket as Grief issued instructions for the mortar. "Two flares, and then the H.E. iskers, as fast as you can—and make sure the buggers put 'em in right way up, or they'll find your bollocks on a nearby tree . . ."

Then he was away into the dark, and the Shan who had been with Jones crawled up beside me, opening a bomb case, and I realised with a shock that I hadn't cocked the Piat. I rolled over, pulled the heavy tube on top of me, heaved until it clicked, checked that the elevating leg was where it had been for the successful practice shot, and took a bomb from the case, fingers over the safety cap. I could hear Jones busy with the little two-inch mortar, and to my right there was the snap of a Bren magazine being pushed home, and the oily sliding click as the gun was cocked. No sound from far out in the darkness ahead; as we lay waiting I became aware for the first time of clouds of voracious mosquitos, but you daren't slap or do anything except keep rubbing your face and cursing inwardly.

A silent, sweating fifteen minutes, and Grief was kneeling beside me again. "There's someone at the door," he whispered. "Two minutes, about." Without being told I uncapped the bomb and laid it in place. "All set, Jones? On the whistle, let there be light, and we'll be able to see for bleeding miles!"

I suppose I must have been on edge with excitement, but I don't remember it. I know 1 was straining eyes and ears—was there sound or movement far out in the murk, where the far bank must be, or was it my imagination? I cuddled the butt-pad, left hand up and across to grip the barrel, felt in the dark for the trigger, touched it, and took my hand away, which was just as well, for when the whistle came with a piercing unexpected shriek I gave a violent twitch which would certainly have sent the bomb winging away prematurely. Jones's mortar exploded with a metallic whang, echoed twice along the bank, there was a second's pause and then three soft pops far overhead—and the darkness lifted in a great blaze of silver light as the three tiny parachutes with their burning flares hung over the river.

It all registered in an instant: the broad surface of the water shining with the reflected glare, the far bank lined with little dark figures caught like rabbits in headlights, standing, running, dropping to earth, a raft halfway across crowded with men, and beyond it, near the far bank, the dark outline of a big unwieldy-looking craft about twice the size of a ship's lifeboat and high out of the water, and even as 1 took it in the Brens were stuttering along the bank, the rifles cracking in rapid fire, and I lined the barleycorn sight on the gleaming copper nose and pulled the trigger, shuddered with the recoil, rolled on my back dragging the Piat on top of me, and I was counting, one-thousand-two-thousand-three-thousand . . . up to six, waiting for the blast that would mean a hit, but it didn't come. Snarling, 1 dumped the Piat down, rolled in behind it, and Grief was slipping another bomb into the cradle while all around the rattle of Brens and rifles was deafening, and the air was heavy with cordite smoke, and the scene ahead was changing eerily as the flares drifted down to the water even as other flares broke out overhead, and a crimson Verey light arced away with a trail of smoke, passing over the raft and plumping into the water—an instant's glimpse of the raft suddenly bare as the Brens raked it and ploughed up the bright water in which heads were bobbing. Beyond it the boat was drifting slowly, and now there were men visible on her stern. I lined up the sight, aiming just behind the bow, squeezed, took a terrific glancing blow on the chin from the recoil, and was on my back again, feet slipping on the rest—strange that I should remember that, and the Piat twisting in my grip like a live thing—and then the firing position again, and Grief slipping in another bomb and leaning towards me to shout above the noise:

"Near miss, just short! Keep her as she is!"

Just short . . . I tried to snuggle the butt just that bit lower, squeezed, absorbed the recoil, rolled over dragging at the Piat and thinking, Jesus the things you do for eighteen rupees a week . . . and the next few seconds live in my memory like nothing else in my life. It seems now to have gone on forever, but it can have been only a few heart-beats, a tiny piece of time in which I thought this is the end, china, and you're going to find the Great Perhaps.

The light was beating down on the group by the bamboo thicket, almost close enough to touch—my frantic rollings had brought me right beside them. Jones was lying on the mortar base-plate, one hand steadying the upright tube of the barrel, the other on the firing-wheel. A kneeling Shan was shoving an uncapped high explosive shell into the muzzle, and he was doing what Grief had warned against, what every mortar instructor has nightmares about— inserting the gold-gleaming nose first! Upside bloody down, and when he let it go it would slide down the eighteen-inch tube with that metallic slither which would be the last thing that anyone within ten feet of the mortar would ever hear.

The phrase "my heart stood still" isn't really adequate, because it didn't have time. Even if I hadn't been pinned under the Piat like a blasted beetle I couldn't have done anything, nor could Jones for the simple reason that he hadn't noticed, and why Grief, who should have been watching my bomb's flight, should have glanced aside, God alone knows, instinct, telepathy, search me, but in that split instant he was suddenly hurtling over me in a flat dive, yelling "Jesus!", one hand outflung to drive the mortar barrel sideways, knocking the Shan arse over tip so that he and Grief hit the bamboo stalks in a tangle of limbs–and the bomb rolled gently over the wet grass, stopped, and lay there winking at us.

Grief sat up, adjusted his hat, picked up the bomb, helped Jones to resurrect the mortar, took the goggling Shan gently by the ear, said: "Oh, you clumsyclumsy!", and carefully showed him how the bomb should go in, fins first. Then he said: "See? No sweat, no panic, tik hai?" and patted the Shan on the head before scrambling forward to look at the river. I snapped into action as one is liable to do after a moment's immobilising panic, cocking the Piat and rolling back into a firing position, but Grief wasn't bothering with a bomb, and the Shan scout beside me was pointing and shouting in excitement.

I'd heard no explosion from my last shot, my attention being elsewhere, and it was a moment before I took in the significance of the small black cloud over by the far bank. Half-hidden by it, the boat had swung away from us and was lying at an odd angle, bow submerged, there were men in the water–and suddenly the last flare must have died in the river and there was pitch blackness with the red tracers flying and criss-crossing through it, two streams of them converging where the boat had been. Two more flares went up, in quick succession, illuminating river and far bank, and the boat was gone, heads bobbing in the broken water, the raft had split into chunks of bamboo debris, and shots were whipping overhead—the Japs on the far bank were firing back at the Bren flashes, but after a while the shots became sporadic and then stopped altogether, and Grief came scrambling back. "Cease fire!" sounded along the bank as the flares went out again, and I heard Grief telling Jones to put up another. The mortar whanged, the flare burst, and now the river was empty except for a few shreds of the raft drifting away to the right. Nothing was moving on the far bank; you couldn't see if there was anything hidden in the narrow shadow beneath its overhang, but either Grief or the Gurkha officer was taking no chances, for presently three of the Brens opened up again, raking the shallows and the face of the bank. The flare vanished, the firing stopped, the command came to ease springs, the stench of cordite began to clear, the Gurkhas were getting to their feet, and I pressed the trigger of the empty Piat which clanged resoundingly as the spring was released. Bad practice, 1 should have released it gradually, but I was too damned tired and shaken by the memory of that mortar bomb.

So, I gathered, was Jones, for he held me spellbound with his description of how that bloody daft Shan, look you, had been puttin' an effin' H.E. down the spout the WRONG WAY for Chrissake, an' Jones hadn't seen nuthin', see, till Grief came flyin' an' knocked the silly bugger endways in the nick o' time, see, or we'd all have been blown to buggery, of all the stupid bloody wog tricks it would turn your hair white, bigod. Thanks to him 1 caught only snatches of what Grief and the Gurkha were saying . . . "None got over this side, any-way . . . about twenty on the raft . . . can't say about the boat . . . write 'em off, sick and wounded probably . . . God knows about those on the bank . . . Baluch'll take care of 'em."

From which I deduced that the fugitives on the far side could expect another ambush farther down, but how many were accounted for, by us or any-one else, I don't know. It was a not untypical operation for that time, fairly messy and of minor importance in military terms. It was the last time 1 ever heard a shot fired in war. For the rest, I'm not ashamed to admit that my most lasting memory of the night's work is of that dully gleaming bomb-nose poised at the muzzle of Jones's mortar with the thin brown fingers about to let it go—and if, considering what else happened in that faraway forgotten ambush, that seems unreasonably egoistic, I can only quote Macaulay on the folly of supposing that a man cares for his fellow-creatures as much as he cares for himself.

The return journey I hardly remember, except that we reached the camp in broad daylight, knackered to a man, and I steeped my feet in hot salt water before collapsing on my blanket. After that it's vague: 1 think I was there for another day, possibly two, before being jeeped to the main road and hopping a truck to the battalion, but I certainly recall stripping, cleaning, and reassembling the Piat, handing it over to two grinning Shans and getting a receipt for it and its remaining bombs from Jones, and Grief sitting back in his canvas chair with his hands behind his head, holding forth:

"There's a nasty secretive streak in you, Whatsit, and I take a pretty dim view of it—fact, I can hardly bloody see it, through a glass darkly. You knew dam' well you weren't a peepin' gremlin or a lurkin' firkin, didn't you, but did you let on, did you hell, and don't tell me you'd forgotten, either! Good God, one look in the mirror, plain as a pikestaff, even Jones can see it, can't you, Jones? Yes, blush, Whatsit, the murder's out—evil weevil written all over you! Can't think how I didn't spot it, got weevils in my own family, both sides, incestuous business, don't talk about it. So, you're going—well, so long, mind the step, don't lift anything on the way out, and keep an eye open for the roamin' gnomes, the bastards are everywhere! Who knows, we may meet at Philippi . . ."

Thus far, I'm happy to say, we haven't.

SHOULDER TO SHOULDER
WITH GURKHAS

TIM NEWARK

There is a remarkable black-and-white photograph in the Gurkha Museum in Winchester. It shows Gordon Highlanders and Gurkha soldiers standing and sitting next to each other shoulder-to-shoulder, alternating Highlander with Gurkha in five sturdy rows. Straight-faced, they pose against a bleak, stone-strewn landscape of mountains on the North-West Frontier of India. At a time when European soldiers looked down on anyone beyond the Mediterranean as a 'nigger' or a 'wog', this display of inter-racial kinship is astounding. The photograph was taken shortly after the soldiers had fought together at the battle of Dargai in October 1897 and testifies for ever to their mutual respect for each other's fighting skills.

The Highlanders and the Gurkhas have a special relationship within the British Army. Both originate in the highlands of their countries–the Gurkhas coming from the mountains of Nepal -and both have fierce reputations for hand-to-hand combat. The Gurkhas have adopted many of the traits of Highland regiments, including pipe bands and the wearing of tartan and glengarries. Although coming from completely different cultures, there is a wordless understanding between them that was captured perfectly in an encounter described by John Masters in Bugles and a Tiger, his memoir of life on campaign in the North-West Frontier in the 1930s.

An officer in the 4th Gurkha Rifles, Masters noticed an Argyll and Sutherland Highlander sit down for a chat with one of his riflemen. The Gurkha showed him his kukri, the famous curved knife of Nepal, and denied that it could be thrown as a boomerang. Masters was puzzled as to how the two soldiers managed to communicate for the best part of an hour as neither of them spoke each other's language. He crept close to them to overhear their conversation.

> Each soldier was speaking his own language and using few gestures—it was too hot on the rocks for violent arm-waving. I could understand both sides of the conversation, the Gurkhali better than the 'English', and it made sense. Questions were asked, points taken, opinions exchanged, heads nodded and lips sagely pursed. When [they] moved on, the two shook hands, and the Jock said, 'Abyssinia, Johnny!'1

John Masters also received a lesson on the importance of the kilt from a Highland major leaning against a urinal with his kilt raised: 'Join a Highland regiment, me boy. The kilt is an unrivalled garment for fornication and diarrhoea.'

The Gurkhas were first recruited to the East India Company's army in 1816, following their defeat in a war with the company. It was in 1857 during the Indian Mutiny that they proved their loyalty and the Highland regiments got the full measure of them. They were at Lucknow when the Highlanders stormed the rebel strongholds. 'Jung Bahadoor and his Goorkhas had also done good service,' noted Captain Douglas Wimberley of the 79th Cameron Highlanders. 'They advanced from the Charbagh Bridge over the canal on the south side of the city towards the Residency, seizing the enemy's positions one by one, and so covered the left of Sir Colin's own advance.'3

The Gurkhas were not the only native troops to impress the Highlanders during the Indian Mutiny. The Sikhs of the Punjabi regiments raced the Scots to attack the rebels and on one occasion stepped in to save the life of Sir Colin Campbell. The Times journalist William Russell observed the incident:

Campbell was inspecting his troops towards the end of the fighting at Lucknow when he noticed a half-dead Gazee rebel rising to slash at him with his sword. 'Bayonet that man!' he ordered.

The Highlander made a thrust at him, but the point would not enter the thick cotton quilting of the Gazee's tunic; and the dead man was rising to his legs, when a Sikh who happened to be near, with a whistling stroke of his sabre cut off the Gazee's head at one blow, as if it had been the bulb of a poppy!

Gurkhas and Sikhs joined with the 72nd and 92nd Highlanders when they marched out of Kabul to avenge the British massacre at Maiwand in Afghanistan in 1880. In a gruelling march to relieve British forces trapped at Kandahar, they crossed over 280 miles of treacherous terrain in just three weeks. To avoid the 110-degree heat, they began each day at 2.45 a.m. and had to contend with a shortage of water, sandstorms and raiding Afghans. The Seaforths and Gordons formed the rear guard and frequently did not get into camp until long after dark. Once they got to Kandahar, the Highlanders, Gurkhas and Sikhs immediately went into action, routed the Afghans and recaptured some of the guns lost at Maiwand. Their commander, Major-General Frederick Roberts, was mightily impressed by all his soldiers. 'I looked upon them all as my valued friends,' he later wrote, 'all were eager to close with the enemy, no matter how great the odds against them.' But it was at Dargai that the fighting talents of the Gurkhas and Highlanders came together most brilliantly.

* * * * *

The mountainous North-West Frontier between Afghanistan and British India has always been a hot spot for rebellion and banditry. In August 1897, Afridi tribesmen captured forts along the strategically important Khyber Pass. This success encouraged another tribe, the Orakzais, and soon the entire border region was ablaze. Sikh soldiers of the British Indian Army did their best to hold their positions, but were overwhelmed and slaughtered. Gathering their forces, the British administration decided to punish the tribesmen by invading their summer homeland in the Tirah Maidan valley.

The task force was led by Lieutenant-General Sir William Lock-hart and numbered nearly 12,000 British and 22,000 Gurkha and Indian troops. It was formed into two divisions of two brigades each, in which two British battalions were paired with two Gurkha or Sikh battalions. The Gurkhas and Sikhs had already been in action against the Afridi while the 1st Gordon Highlanders had become acclimatized to hill climbing in previous operations. The rest of the English battalions found the rugged terrain very hard going and many succumbed to cholera and dysentery. The Tirah Maidan had never been penetrated by British forces and the rebel tribesmen presumed they would be safe behind its high valleys and narrow passes.

The British concentrated their forces at the railhead of Kushul-garh. To reach enemy territory from there would require a week-long eighty-mile march through a desolate land largely devoid of water and food. To supply Lockhart's two divisions required an enormous baggage train of over 40,000 mules and camels. The advance began in October 1897 and the ground became rougher and rougher and the tracks more precipitous until the narrow paths rose so steeply that the Gurkhas in front looked 'like flies crawling on a wall'. Abruptly, their procession was halted by enemy fire coming from the village of Dargai, perched on top of a cliff one thousand feet above a track leading along a mountain ridge. The Orakzai snipers hid among the huge boulders and it was clear that the position would have to be taken before the British column could move on.

On 18 October, the l/3rd Gurkhas and the 2nd King's Own Scottish Borderers were charged with taking the heights at Dargai. It was a formidable physical objective, involving climbing a steep rock-strewn slope in full view of the enemy. Light 2.5-inch mountain guns were used to provide cover. The Gurkhas fired their .303 Lee-Metford rifles in two volleys and then climbed in single file to a ridge–beyond that they faced a sprint across dead ground. With enough men gathered, they took a deep breath and bolted over the crest into a hail of fire. Seeing the Gurkhas hurtling towards them, the Orakzais hastily withdrew and left them to take the Dargai Heights.

It seemed a straightforward operation to allow the British column to advance unhindered, but it depended on the Gurkhas and Borderers holding on to the heights. There was not water enough for this and they had to evacuate their hard-won position. Thousands of gathering Afridis had heard the earlier gunfire and rallied to the Orakzais who now flooded back to the mountain top, knocking the British back to square one. Falling back, they came under heavy gunfire and the 1st Gordon Highlanders and 15th Sikhs were called in to help cover them.

Soon, they were under fire themselves and their Major Jennings-Bramly was killed. But the Highlanders stood steady until nightfall, repelling an attack within just a few yards of their fixed bayonets, and then carried their dead and wounded over rocks to their camp eight miles away at Shinawari. 'I walked beside one poor fellow who was badly hit,' said an officer of the Gordons. 'He grasped my hand as firmly as he could, but never complained, though the jolting of the stretcher must have been agony.' To help their Scots comrades, men of the King's Own Scottish Borderers came out a mile from their camp to bring them water.

It was a disheartening action and all the worse because the British commanders decided they had no alternative but to take the Dargai Heights again on the 20th. The 3rd Gurkha Scouts and the 1/2nd Goorkhas (the traditional spelling of their unit name) were to lead the attack, with the 1st Dorsets, 2nd Derbyshire, and 1st Gordons in support and reserve. The march up the narrow path towards Dargai began early in the morning at 5.00 a.m. It demanded a zigzag climb for half a mile up the side of a valley protected from enemy fire. Yet it was demanding work and the combat-fit men had to pause every so often to catch their breath. By 11.00 a.m., the Gurkhas were huddled behind the ridge that had protected them two days earlier. The Gordons offered covering fire from the boulders beneath them.

When ordered, the Gurkhas charged over the crest into the dead ground between them and the base of the cliff beneath Dargai. This time, there were even more rebel tribesmen firing at them from behind stone sangars (fortifications). In ten minutes, the Gurkhas suffered sixty-seven casualties and their brave attack faltered. Next, the Dorsets ran into the storm of bullets. Only two of their officers and a handful of soldiers reached the halfway mark across the open ground, lying down among the bodies of wounded and dead men all round them. Captain AK Slessor of the 2nd Battalion the Derbyshire Regiment was waiting on the slope beneath the fighting but soon saw the effects of it.

> Presently wounded men, chiefly Gurkhas at first, began to come down past us, some supported by their comrades, some borne on blood-stained stretchers; then a dhoolie [cart] containing a Gurkha officer, dead; and still we sat waiting. Before long dead men were being dragged down the steep slope by the legs with scant ceremony. After all, it did not hurt them, and the path had to be cleared.

When a group from the 2nd Derbyshires went over the top to join the fighting, all but one were dropped by the enemy. After three hours of combat, Gurkhas, Dorsets and Derbys were all huddled behind the ridge. They could make no headway against the Afridi and Orakzai sharpshooters, hidden among the rocks above them. The British could barely poke their head above the ridge without receiving bullets through their sun helmets. To make matters worse, the lead mule bringing more ammunition for the British up the slope stumbled and fell backwards, carried over the precipice by the weight of the ammunition boxes, followed by two more mules. The situation was dire.

It was then that the Gordons were ordered into action, supported by the 3rd Sikhs. On the precipitous mountainside, their commander, Lieutenant-Colonel HH Mathias, made a laconic speech -'Highlanders, the General says the position must be taken at all costs. The Gordons will take it.'

They had just climbed the steep side of the valley to bring themselves level with the other soldiers, but with hardly a pause for breath they scrambled over the ledge towards the rebel tribesmen. Slessor and his men were told to move aside to let the Highlanders through.

> Roused to fierce enthusiasm by their trusted leader's stirring speech, and by the familiar skirl of the pipes, the Highlanders leapt to the assault. Up they came, a long thin string of men with stern, set faces, stumbling, scrambling up the steep in a frenzy of courage not to be gainsaid, amidst spasmodic gasps from the pipes, and cheers from any who had breath to utter, a sight for those who witnessed it to remember all their lives.

Everyone was impressed by their fearless determination, especially the campaign commander Sir William Lockhart, who praised the initial rush of the Gordons in his dispatch from the battlefield.10 Slessor felt the Gordons had the slight advantage over his men in that they had fought over the same ground two days before and knew it could be taken. Also, a fusillade from eighteen British mountain guns exploded over the cliff top just at the moment the Highlanders crested the ridge; but they still faced thousands of rebel rifles directed at them as they ran across the killing zone.

Colonel Mathias personally led the next stage of the advance. Rather than attacking in small rushes, he ordered his men to press forward in full battalion strength, so hundreds of Highlanders surged across the open ground. Even then, five leading officers and forty-one soldiers went down almost straight away. Major Macbean was shot in the groin but dragged himself to a boulder and cheered on his men. The pipers played Cocko' the North. One of them, George Findlater, was shot through both feet and fell to the ground. He crawled to a rock, propped himself up and carried on playing his pipes. For that act, he won the Victoria Cross.

Colonel Mathias—a veteran of the Nile campaign of 1884—made it across the exposed slope, but was feeling his age when he paused for a rest. 'Stiff climb,' he gasped to his Colour-Sergeant. 'Not quite . . . so young . . . as I was . . . you know.' The younger man slapped him on the back cheerily, knocking any remaining wind out of him. 'Never mind, sir! Ye're gaun verra strong for an auld man!'

The Gurkhas watched the Highlanders with open-mouthed admiration—taking a position they had sacrificed so many of their men for. Lieutenant Tillard of the Gurkha Scouts later recorded their wonder at the kilted warriors.

> Then followed a scene it is hard for me to describe, it makes me shake with excitement even now. The Gordons advanced at once without any hesitation, each man trying to get in front of everyone else, the pipes playing and men cheering. They were greeted by the same deadly fire as before but they never stopped or wavered although many of them were down. It was one wild continuous rush of men all eager to get at the enemy. The sight was magnificent and the excitement so intense that I for one, although I was shouting at the top of my voice felt the tears springing up into my eyes and could not keep them back.

Seeing the Gordon Highlanders rush fearlessly towards the cliff beneath Dargai, the Gurkhas, Sikhs, Dorsets and Derbys joined in the attack. The Highlanders climbed up the rock face and when they reached the summit of their target, the Afridis and Orakzais had fled. The Dargai Heights were theirs, and what a victory it was—celebrated across Britain as yet another display of the fierce bravery of the Highlander. Four Victoria Crosses were awarded in total, one of them to Gordon Private Edward Lawson, a Northumbrian, who carried his wounded Lieutenant to cover and then, despite being shot twice, continued to rescue another soldier. Colonel Mathias was recommended for a VC, but was debarred because he was a commanding officer. Seven Distinguished Conduct Medals were awarded.

Exhilarated by their triumph, the Gordons were not slow to recognize the contribution of their fellow soldiers and volunteered to carry down the wounded and dead of the Gurkhas. It was a gesture never forgotten and explains the warmth of the joint photograph taken shortly afterwards. The Gurkhas had lost the most men in the battle, with two officers and sixteen men killed and forty-nine wounded. The Gordons lost one officer and two men killed, six officers and thirty-five men wounded.

The victory at Dargai captured the imagination of the public in Britain in the year of Queen Victoria's Diamond Jubilee. Two heroic paintings showing the Highlanders and Gurkhas in action were exhibited at the Royal Academy in 1898 and both featured Piper Findlater, wounded but playing his pipes against a boulder. One of the paintings, entitled The Cock o' the North, by Richard Caton Woodville, was turned into a popular Christmas print. Two more Dargai paintings were exhibited in that year, also featuring Find-later, and it was no surprise when he was invited to play at the Royal Tournament. Colonel Mathias's words became a catchphrase and a note appeared on an umbrella stand at the Army and Navy Club in London, reading: 'Do not leave your umbrella in this club. The Gordons will take it!'

Findlater caused controversy when, because he could find no work thanks to his injuries, he took up an offer to play at the Alhambra Music Hall. His regiment was furious but the scandal provoked the government into raising the pension associated with winning the VC from £10 to £50 per annum. Although he was said to have played the regimental march throughout the fighting, he later confessed he had no recollection of what he played.

Best-selling Flashman author George MacDonald Fraser was an officer in the Gordon Highlanders just after the Second World War and he remembered a lively conversation in the sergeants' mess in which everyone had a different opinion of the tune played at Dargai. In the end, it was accepted that the Regimental Sergeant Major at the time was asked by Findlater's Colonel what he played at Dargai. The RSM was absolutely certain it was the regimental march. But 'it was only later that it occurred to [the Colonel] that the RSM had not been within half a mile of Findlater during the battle, and couldn't know at all. But Cock o' the North the RSM had said, and Cock o' the North it has been ever since, and always will be.'

· · · · ·

The daring deeds of Highlanders on the North-West Frontier were performed in some of the last old-style Victorian campaigns of empire that provided a British audience with reasons to be proud of their fighting men. As the twentieth century approached, technology changed the way war was conducted. A new intensity of firepower was unleashed and warfare became far more costly and far less glorious. This was already to be seen in colonial warfare, with machine guns and repeating rifles inflicting tremendous casualties. The introduction of high-velocity rifles with a considerably extended flat trajectory meant that gunfire became more accurate and deadly over a longer range. The British were to be on the receiving end of this in the Boer War in South Africa in 1899, and it came as a shock that revived bitter memories of the kind of losses last sustained in the Crimean War.

As in that war, several Scottish battalions were organized into Highland Brigades. In Lord Methuen's advance on Kimberley in November 1899, the 3rd (Highland) Brigade consisted of the 1st Gordon Highlanders, 2nd Royal Highlanders (Black Watch), 1st Argyll and Sutherland Highlanders, 2nd Seaforth Highlanders and 1st Highland Light Infantry. For Lord Roberts's offensive against Bloemfontein in February 1900, the 3rd (Highland) Brigade, under the charismatic leadership of Major-General Sir Hector Macdonald, included the 1st Argyll and Sutherland Highlanders, 1st Highland Light Infantry, 2nd Seaforth Highlanders, and 2nd Royal Highlanders (Black Watch). Highland battalions were also attached to other mixed brigades.

In their battles against the Boers, the Highlanders faced an enemy different to their usual colonial adversaries. The Boers were skilled sharpshooters, armed with high-velocity rifles such as the German-supplied magazine-fed Mauser. When shooting from well concealed trenches, these riflemen could make mincemeat of the traditional volley-and-bayonet tactics of the Highlanders.

The terrible impact of this modern warfare was described by Corporal James H Noble of the 1st Argyll and Sutherland Highlanders at the battle of Magersfontein on 11 December 1899. It was one of three defeats in a few days that made up the notorious 'Black Week' for the British forces. Part of Lord Methuen's advance to relieve Kimberley, the combat was intended to deliver a knockout blow against the Boers positioned in the Magersfontein hills before the town. The Boers dug into trenches at the foot of the hills and commanded the flat ground approaching them. Barbed wire, traditionally used by farmers to fence off their land, was fixed up before the trenches. On the 10th, Methuen, assuming the Boers were on the hills, subjected the hill tops to a fierce artillery bombardment; but the shells had little effect on the Boers sheltering below and gave them good warning of the coming attack.

The 1st Argyll and Sutherland Highlanders, part of the 3rd Highland Brigade, commanded by Major-General Andrew Wau-chope, were ordered to their attacking positions at dusk. Around 9.00 p.m., a storm crackled above the soldiers, drenching them in rain as they lay down on the flat terrain. At half-past midnight, the Highlanders were told to move off towards the enemy lines. So as not to get lost in the darkness, they were told to advance in Quarter Column formation, which meant that a mass of 3,400 men moved forward in a dense column. They had little idea of the location of the hidden trenches before them and by 4.00 a.m. they were only 400 yards away from the Boers—that is, within easy range of their deadly Mausers.

'It was just commencing to break daylight,' recalled Corporal Noble, 'when Colonel Goff was giving us orders (in a whisper) to extend when one shot was fired by the Boers followed immediately by an incessant storm of bullets, for a time all was confusion till some person (unknown) gave the order to retire.'16 The Highlanders were caught in their close formation and every bullet struck home. 'The blow was so unexpected,' said Noble, 'that the whole Brigade staggered and fell back.'

The 2nd Black Watch fixed bayonets and charged at the Boer trenches. Private James Williamson was among them. He and his mates pulled up the barbed-wire fence in front of them and rushed on to the trenches but the weight of fire was too much.

> The bullets were coming down on us like hailstones, so we had to stick there, about 30 yards from the trenches, as soon as I lay down I got a Mauser bullet through my left foot which made me wilder so I started firing back but my luck was out that day, for they peppered at me as if I was the only man firing at them.

A second bullet severed a muscle in his left leg, a third thudded into his back, but he kept on firing. A fourth bullet struck his right shoulder, making him drop his rifle. He picked it up, but got a fifth bullet in his right leg and then a sixth that broke his right arm. Williamson could do nothing more but lie on the ground a helpless spectator of the fighting around him.

Brigade commander Wauchope was killed almost immediately as he desperately ordered his men to spread out. The majority of the Highlanders withdrew, shocked by the hail of bullets but determined to rally and attack again. 'By firing volleys and advancing by rushes,' said Noble, '[we] managed to get within about 900 yards of the position, but could make very little impression on the enemy who were so cunningly entrenched.'

British artillery helped out by sending a barrage of shells into the Boer trenches, having finally worked out where they were, but this fire also hit the few Highlanders who attempted to break through the enemy lines. By midday, the majority of Highlanders were helplessly pinned down in the open ground beneath a baking sun. Wearing kilts beneath their khaki jackets, their legs were exposed and got burned by the sun, leaving them to blister the next day. They remained in this position until 4.00 p.m. when the assembly was sounded and the Highlanders retreated from the battlefield. At least one observer claimed that some of the Highlanders were so panicked that their officers had to threaten them at gunpoint, but other first-hand accounts tell of an orderly withdrawal.

The next day, the Boers signalled a truce, allowing the British to remove their wounded and dead. Wauchope was buried first, followed by his officers and other ranks. The pipers played The Flowers of the Forest and Noble recorded the funeral service was 'a very impressive one, many giving way to tears'. The Highlanders had suffered a heavy toll, with 202 men killed and 496 wounded, although Noble reported a higher figure of 870 casualties for the brigade, with 98 coming from the Argyll and Sutherland battalion.

Lord Methuen expressed his regret for their losses to the Highlanders in a speech, declaring their advance was carried out perfectly but was betrayed by someone shouting the word 'retire' when the order 'charge' would have seen the Boer lines taken. He made no mention of his catastrophic failure to locate the position of the enemy trenches, which led directly to so many deaths.

Methuen's evasion of responsibility for the defeat infuriated Corporal WT Bevan of the Argyll and Sutherland Highlanders. 'Why did the Brigade advance in quarter-column formation?' he asked. 'It was not fighting, it was simply suicide. Men were hung on the wire like crows, and were simply riddled with bullets. We hear that our brave general [Wauchope] remonstrated with Lord Methuen before we left camp about the plans, but Methuen only told him to obey orders.' Bevan's criticism was later published as a letter in a London newspaper and reflected a growing discontent among British soldiers at the incompetence of their commanders. The disasters of 'Black Week' and the consequent uproar in British newspapers led to the replacement of Sir Redvers Buller as Commander-in-Chief by Lord Roberts, but Methuen kept his job.

Many letters appeared in Scottish newspapers detailing the realities of the war. 'We were under fire about fifteen hours,' wrote one Highlander to his parents about fighting on the Modder River. "The whistling of the rifle bullets all around you, and the crack, crack, crack of the Maxim all day long was a strain on the nervous system. It makes one a bit nervous when you hear the least crack of anything. I hope I won't have to go up again because I will be very nervous after getting shot once.' The arrival of this letter was a relief to the soldier's family as he had been presumed killed.

Other men described the desperate tactics they faced. "The Boers threw all their dead horses in the river,' wrote one private. 'Thousands of them came floating down, and we had to drink it, and it did stink, but we were glad to get it.' Some men just got angry. 'One chap of ours was shot dead whilst assisting a wounded comrade, and the dirty beggars even shelled our ambulances. I saw it myself, so I know it is true.'

Despite the grim truth of modern warfare appearing throughout the national press, there was still room for heroic moments involving tough Highlanders with an old-fashioned approach to fighting. Nine Victoria Crosses were won by Highland regiments in the Boer War, one of them by Lance-Corporal John Frederick Mackay of the 1st Gordon Highlanders, who nearly became the first man to win two VCs.

Under fire at Doorncop near Johannesburg, on 20 May 1900, Mackay rushed forward several times to help his wounded comrades, despite putting himself at risk of being shot. He carried one man to cover and it was a miracle he survived unscathed. He was recommended for the VC by Lord Roberts in June, but in the meantime he had acted heroically in combat at Wolverkrantz in July and was recommended for a Bar to his medal. Unfortunately, the rules stipulated that a Bar could only be added if the award of the initial VC had already been approved, which it had not. Mackay got his VC without Bar and ended his career in the army as a Lieutenant-Colonel.

With its soldiers in khaki exposed to rapid fire from modern weapons, the Boer War gave a taste of the conflicts to come in the rest of the twentieth century. As Highlander Private Chonlarton put it in a letter to a friend, 'It is pure warfare we are having now.'

TRAGEDY IN VIETNAM
The French Foreign Legion in Viet NAM

ADRIAN D. GILBERT

Following the defeat of Japan in 1945, the British and Chinese initially took control of Indochina before handing it back to France. But when the French returned to Vietnam in early 1946 they were opposed by a well-organised, communist-inspired national liberation movement under the leadership of Ho Chi Minh and his military planner, Vo Nguyen Giap.

The Vietnamese communists (Viet Minh) instigated a guerrilla war against the French. At first this consisted of little more than a series of minor skirmishes, but all the while the Viet Minh were building up their strength in the remote mountainous region of north-east Vietnam and the Red River Delta. From 1948 onwards the fighting increased in intensity, followed by a full-scale offensive against the French in 1950.

As French conscripts were forbidden to serve outside metropolitan France, the bulk of the French forces stationed in Indochina came from colonial units and the Foreign Legion. The 2nd Foreign Legion Regiment came ashore at Haiphong Harbour in February, to be joined by three other infantry regiments: the cavalry regiment and two newly raised paratroop battalions (with a third acting as a depot battalion).

To counter the Viet Minh, the French adopted a containment strategy by building strong-points across the country, often dotted along a major highway (Route Colonial or RC). The Viet Minh began to attack the more remote outposts in earnest during 1948, beginning with the assault on Phu-Tong-Hoa (along RC 3) on the evening of 25 July. The post was held by 104 legionnaires commanded by Captain Cardinal, along with Lieutenant Charlotton and Second Lieutenant Bevalot. The attack began at 1930 hours with a bombardment from 75mm field guns and mortars that destroyed much of the post's defences, mortally wounding both Cardinal and Charlotton. This was followed by a series of human-wave attacks from Viet Minh infantry that breached the post's outer defences. The fort was set to be overrun. Legionnaire X described the fight for survival:

The south-east bastion, Second Lieutenant Bevalot himself directing the defence, held. The moon came through the clouds dispersing a feeble light, but enough to enable our men to see what they were doing. The rebels were subjected to a violent fusillade. The 81mm mortar managed to land a bomb just outside the breach. In the northern angle, Sergeant Guillemand hung on with a few survivors, showering grenades into the courtyard. Near the main gate, Corporals Huegen and Polain were killed, the latter being bayoneted after a most courageous fight. It was nearly 22 hours.

From this moment, however, the balance of the combat began to swing in our favour. Sergeant Andry and Sergeant Fissler, with three legionnaires, advanced, firing their automatics from the hip at point-blank range, and cleared the central buildings of the enemy. Corporal Camilleri and two legionnaires crawled through the breach and slaughtered the Viets who had occupied the northwest bastion.

By 23 hours, the post was entirely in our hands and trumpets could be heard sounding the retreat. Though no further attacks were launched, the enemy kept up a sporadic bombardment.

Lieutenant Charlotton asked a legionnaire to sit beside him and talk about the Legion; he died just after one o'clock. Captain Cardinal died about four, happy in the knowledge that the post was held.

A bloody dawn broke on the 26th over the post of Phu-Tong-Hoa. Within the walls lay over forty Viet Minh dead. There were bodies strewn outside the walls, in the gaps in the bamboo; we counted more than 200 of them.

During the attack the post had radioed to nearby Bac-Kan for help. Major Paul Grauwin, a senior medical officer who would win fame at Dien Bien Phu, was in Bac-Kan at the time:

A relief column set out from Bac-Kan; it ran into a terrible ambush and had to return to Bac-Kan with a great number of wounded.

Another relief column set out from Cao-Bang, under Colonel Simon, who was in command of the regiment. After two days of difficult and dangerous progress, Colonel Simon and his column came within sight of Phu-Tong-Hoa, thinking to find nothing but ruins and corpses. They were received at the entrance to the shattered outpost by the forty [unwounded] legionnaires, drawn up in perfect order, wearing their superb parade uniforms.

The successful defence of Phu-Tong-Hoa did not prevent the Viet Minh from continuing their attacks on isolated outposts and the convoys that connected them. RC 4 ran parallel to the Chinese border, from Lang Son in the south to Cao Bang in the north, through the remote mountainous region of the Viet Bac that had become a Viet Minh stronghold. The battle to hold open RC 4 would become one of the toughest engagements ever fought by the Legion.

Elements of the Legion were deployed along RC 4 to act as patrouilles d'overture (opening patrols); these cleared mines and booby traps and defended the convoys from Viet Minh ambushes. The French journalist Lucien Bodard accompanied a convoy driving northwards up RC 4:

In the green darkness I could not even see the soldiers who were supposed to be protecting us. I asked the radio sergeant whether the covering force had in fact been posted there. It had. At dawn men had left all the posts and they had climbed and marched for hours, taking up their positions in all the dangerous places. Perhaps during this taking up of positions all over the countryside there had been skirmishes and men killed—I did not know and I never shall know; this was merely everyday routine. And when we were gone by they would leave their positions, march for hours and hours and then shut themselves in their posts. Perhaps they would not have fired a single shot; perhaps they would have had to fight to save their lives or to guard the convoy. They were the world's most extraordinary traffic police.

We were beginning to rise to the Luong Phai Pass. This was the most blood-drenched area in the whole of Indochina. The road climbed the sheer mountainside like a winding ladder, turning its dizzy hairpin bends: and there was not one of these corners that had not been used for an ambush and which had not seen the most savage hand-to-hand fighting.

I sensed the convoy's intense apprehension from the automatic head movements, all swinging together. Far away from here, right down in Cochinchina on the Camau road, I had seen men's eyes all turn together at the same second, staring, searching, first on the right and then on the left. But then there were only a score or two of them. Here on the RC 4 there were hundreds of us, perhaps a thousand, and we were all swinging our heads with the same automatic reflex. It was extraordinarily comic, and at the same time extraordinarily dramatic. And the weapons which bristled from every vehicle followed the heads and eyes that were searching for the signs of danger.

The convoy arrived safely, yet the strain of those travelling with it was clearly apparent, as Bodard recalled: 'That night the whole convoy got drunk. It was a tradition: the military authorities allowed it. This time it was nothing extraordinary. But if there had been men killed or wounded the survivors would have drunk until they reached oblivion–until they had lost all recollection, all awareness.'

Leslie Aparvary, a soldier in the newly formed 1st BEP (Bataillon Étranger de Parachutiste), had fled the post-war communist regime in Hungary to join the Legion. He recalled an attack on a convoy that he and his paratroopers were guarding near the outpost of Dong Khe on RC 4:

We climbed up the hill to secure a vantage point from which we could scan the road. The advance guard appeared around noon, and the convoy was almost past us when all hell broke loose. The Viet Minhs, hiding in the hills facing Dong Khe, had waited until most of the convoy had shifted into firing range, and then they had opened fire from all sides. We hastened to assist the others just as fast as we could. We succeeded in running perhaps one kilometre before their shots bogged us down. It was possible to make headway only by creeping and crawling, darting about, and taking cover if we could find it behind trees and bushes. By this time we could see the enemy clearly. There were so many of them!

There was not time to take aim. All we could do was shoot in their general direction. 'Douze-septs' [12.7mm (0.5ins) heavy machine guns], mortars and small cannon spread death everywhere. The vehicles in the convoy ignited one after the other. We tried to force our way through to reach the central point of the attack. The number of defenders had already diminished to half the original number and the cry for assistance was great. The rattle of firearms was deafening. Movement of any sort was treacherously difficult on the steep mountainside. We tried to carve a path upwards, while our opponents were shielded and fired at us from the comfort of their trenches. It was thanks to our 'douze-sept' and the small cannon on our tanks that we gained ground step-by-step and eventually were able to send the enemy flying.

Every now and then a man senses that the end is near. Never in my life had the wings of death loomed so close ess well-defended convoys could face disaster, however. A veteran gionnaire sergeant described a Viet Minh ambush on RC 4:

Technically it was far and away the best—really scientific, with everything synchronised. And you can believe me when I say so, because I was there. To begin with the Viets paralysed the convoy. Mines went off behind the armoured cars at the head of the column, cutting them off from the trucks. Immediately after that a dozen un-attackable machine guns in those limestone cliffs opened up, raking the whole line. Then came a hail of grenades. These [came from] regulars lying close-packed along the embankment over the road and they dropped them just so, tossing a dozen at each vehicle. There were flames everywhere. Anywhere you looked there were burning trucks, and they completely blocked the road. All this took only a minute.

Then there was a terrific shouting. It was the charge. Thousands of naked bodies leaped up from the sides of the road, just by us, and hurled themselves at the convoy. We were still inside. But before this tide broke over us we jumped out and forced our way through the current. Our idea was to climb the embankment and regroup into little fighting units. We shouted to one another to keep in touch, but the Viets shouted louder still. We could see mobs of Viets below us, attacking our comrades who had not been able to follow us and regroup. They went under in a few seconds.

The Viets were very methodical. Regulars went from truck to truck, gathering the weapons and the goods that had been left behind; then they set fire to the vehicles. Other regulars attacked the French who were still fighting on the embankments. Coolies with jungle knives finished off the wounded who had fallen onto the roadway or into the ditches. It was hand-to-hand fighting everywhere. There were hundreds of single combats, hundreds of pairs of men killing each other. In the middle of all this mess the political commissars very calmly supervised the work in hand, giving orders to the regulars and the coolies—orders that were carried out at once.

The middle of the convoy was wiped out. The armoured cars at the tail end began firing their guns point-blank into the trucks the Viets has taken. There were Red officers hurrying about in the midst of the fighting calling out 'Where is the colonel? Where is the colonel?' in French. They meant Colonel Simon, the CO of the 3rd Étranger, the man with a bullet in his head–it had been there for years; he got it long before the war in Indochina. He was in the convoy and Giap had ordered that he should be taken alive.

I was in the part of the convoy that was destroyed. I found myself on the embankment together with a few legionnaires, and we fought furiously for half an hour: then we were overwhelmed. I escaped into the forest and hid in some undergrowth about fifty yards from the road. Just next to me I heard some shots. It was the legionnaires blowing their brains out–the Viets had discovered them. As for me, I was not discovered.

I don't know how the whole nightmare ended. They say that Colonel Simon managed to gather a hundred of his men around him and form them up in squares that thrust back the waves of Viets with grenades for hours on end. Three hours later the reinforcements came up–the heavy armour. A few minutes before the sound of the tracks was heard the Viets had disengaged. At the very beginning when they attacked, they had sounded the charge on the trumpet. Now there was another trumpet call for the retreat and they vanished into the jungle in perfect order, unit by unit. Special formations of coolies carried off their killed and wounded, as well as all the loot they had taken.

We remained on the battlefield. The road was a graveyard, a charnel-house. Nothing was left of the convoy but a heap of ripped-open bodies and blackened engines. It was already beginning to stink. The survivors gathered on the road-way; we cleared it and picked up the corpses and the wounded. And what was left of the convoy set off again.

Despite the fact that the defence of RC 4 and its outposts was clearly intenable, the French refused to give it up to the Viet Minh. It was only in 1950–when the Viet Minh had been massively reinforced by the new communist regime in China–that the French made plans to evacuate the route. By then, however, it was too late. On 8 September an overwhelming force of 16 Viet Minh battalions, supported by artillery, was unleashed against the outpost at Dong Che–held by two companies from the 3rd Legion Regiment, just 160-men strong. The result was inevitable. Lucien Bodard described he disaster, as those on the outside anxiously awaited news of the outpost's fate:

One Saturday at noon came the first message from Dong Khe, the one that said that Giap had set things in motion, that he had begun his 'general counter-offensive'.

On the first day, however, the outcome was not clear. The messages from Dong Khe said the losses were very small, and even that the garrison's artillery had silenced two Viet guns. But the second day, a long drawn-out Sunday, the messages became progressively fewer and shorter, and they contained all the formulas of a 'deteriorating situation': by twilight on that Sunday more than half the legionnaires had been killed or wounded. There was one last but not entirely desperate message, but the coming of night brought an unbroken silence–Dong Khe no longer answered.

There was still silence on Monday morning and the sky was so low that Upper Tonkin was nothing but a grey sheet, the mountains entirely lost in the clouds. Nevertheless a jankers (Ju-52 aircraft] was ordered to go and look at Dong Khe–an almost impossible flight through the monsoon and among the mountain tops. And the Junkers, when it had last pushed through, when it was circling over the Dong Khe basin, knew what the news was. The French flag had disappeared from the shattered mast; great blackish flames were still rising from the post; there was nothing but ruin and desolation.

The dying of the post, held by the finest troops in the Legion, had lasted sixty hours. The death throes were known only by a few radio messages; then came the great silence of the end. For that was what the war in Indochina was like–the fighting men died alone and the high command did not even know the manner of their death.

The French were finally convinced that RC 4 must be abandoned, but the loss of Dong Khe meant that the most northerly outpost, Cao Bang, was now dangerously isolated. Under the command of the tough Colonel Charton, the legionnaires stationed in Cao Bang prepared to evacuate the position. Meanwhile, a column of North African troops under Colonel Marcel Le Page was to march northward from That Khe, recapture Dong Khe and then rendezvous with Charton's force, before they both moved southward along RC 4 to Lang Son.

On leaving That Khe, Le Page's column was strengthened by the 1st BEP. On 30 September, with the paras in the lead, the French fought their way directly towards Dong Khe, but were repulsed by mass Viet Minh attacks and then pinned down in the shattered limestone jungle gorges to the west of Dong Khe. On 3 October, Charton's force–which included wounded and Vietnamese civilians–left Cao Bang. Initially all went well until Charton's progress down RC 4 was blocked by the Viet Minh; he was then instructed to march along a jungle trail skirting Dong Khe to meet up with Le Page's increasingly beleaguered force. The Viet Minh now concentrated on Charton's troops, and although the French fought their way to a rendezvous with Le Page, casualties were enormous and the situation desperate.

One of Charton's Legion officers witnessed the meeting with Le Page's North Africans: 'In a matter of seconds, when I saw what was coming from the Le Page column, I realised that we were already on the beaten side–that the Viets were stronger than we were. These broken men were afraid; they spread fear all around them among our people.'

He went on to describe the final hours of the French trapped in the jungle defiles:

A little after four we began to march towards That Khe, about twenty miles off. The column was very long; and in the rear there were still some Cao Bang civilians! Charton was wounded by a grenade thrown from a thicket and he disappeared. When the column came up close to a pass the ambush opened fire–it was all over very quickly. Tens of thousands of Viets rushed at us. It was a sudden storming operation with no precautions or manoeuvres, to get it over and done with–liquidation. An execution. For a few minutes the column fought back furiously, waving to and fro and breaking into thousands of separate personal battles in the midst of this wild tumble of rocks and greenery.

We were attacked with everything that could kill–there were still shells coming in, but now they were reaching us at point-blank range. And then it was the grenade and the knife; and above all there was this huge number of Viets rushing at us–they kept coming out of the jungle, little smooth men with green leaves on their helmets. Yet there was still time for some bitter unhappiness. Just next to me I saw a captain collapse, weeping; and a little farther off a sergeant was wandering about, careless of the bullet that would kill him, waiting for it. There were officers who got their men to shoot them. Some completely surrounded Moroccans charged, singing a battle chant until they were all killed. There were a few last words of farewell between friends; then everything stopped.

There was a silence over the destroyed column; and a smell. That silence, you know, with groaning in it; and that smell of bodies that comes with a great slaughter–they are the first realities of defeat. Then presently there was another reality, and a far more surprising one–that of Viet Minh discipline. I had expected barbarity; but within a few moments after the last shot what I saw was an extraordinary scrupulousness–the establishment of exact order. Viet officers moved all over the battlefield, not at all as conquerors–merely as though one operation had been finished and another one was beginning. I could make no vanity in them–no triumph.

The men of 1st BEP and the 3rd Legion Regiment fought to the end. After Charton had been wounded and captured by the Viet Minh, Le Page instructed the remnants of his command to break up into small groups and fight their way back to That Khe; just 23 Legion paras from an entire battalion managed to escape the Viet Minh. But even as the survivors staggered back to the relative safety of That Khe, they found that they had already been outflanked. A general panic ensued and the French shamefully evacuated the garrison of Lang Son without a fight, scrambling back to the Red River Delta and leaving vast amounts of munitions and equipment to the enemy.

Fortunately for the French, Giap and the Viet Minh overreached themselves and they suffered repeated setbacks as they tried to breach the defences surrounding the Red River Delta. This bought the French in Tonkin a much-needed, if temporary, respite.

Although Tonkin was the main theatre of war in Vietnam, Cochin China in the south of the country was also an important area of operations, as the Viet Minh fought to gain control of the low-lying paddy fields around the city of Saigon. Viet Minh activity in the south tended to be on a smaller scale than in Tonkin, their fighters infiltrating villages and conducting small-scale raids and assassinations before slipping away into jungle and marshland. Fighting this 'invisible enemy' was virtually impossible. Even when there was good intelligence, the Viet Minh were adept at avoiding contact. A young officer in the Legion's 13th DBLE (Demi-Brigade de Légion Étrangère) recalled an attempt to pin down the enemy:

My objective was a Viet Minh 'factory' on a little island in the Plain of Reeds [close to Saigon]. Usually I put my men into sampans and we'd go up the canals, whose banks are lined with water palms so that they can hem you in like the walls of a prison. You can't see anything, but you can be seen. This time, so as not to be picked up, we went on foot through the shit, as we call it–the stinking marsh covered with reeds and lotus that stretches out for ever.

The approach lasted for hours, and all the time we were up to our waists in the muck. We had started at midnight: by dawn we had still not been seen. We were only a few hundred yards from the factory. Then came the horn sounding the alarm. I looked through my field glasses. The little island was like an ant hill that had been stirred up. I heard explosions and saw flames. I knew what that meant. The Viets were taking their heavy equipment away in boats and they were carrying out their scorched-earth policy with the rest. It always happens that way.

It took us another half hour to get ashore, to struggle up onto firm ground. There was nothing but destruction and emptiness. Some frantic buffaloes by the remains of the burning huts. We killed them. The stocks of rice had been soaked in gasoline and now they were only smouldering heaps. We found little in the way of machinery, all smashed with hammers. But all the truly valuable equipment, the lathes for making shells and electric motors, had been carried off, in spite of its weight.

We did not see a single man, either. There were certainly hundreds of Viets still there, but so hidden there was no hope in finding them. Some would have turned into bushes. Others would be right down in the mud, breathing through hollow bamboos. Most would be in carefully prepared burrows. It was like being surrounded by a crowd of ghosts: they would stay for hours on end, waiting for us to go.

The officer went on to describe the frustration of these operations in the wetlands of the Plain of Reeds, between Saigon and the Mekong River:

It is unbelievably monotonous. There are the ambushes—the ones you set and above all the ones you fall into. Suddenly men you can't see, amphibious creatures in the water and the mud, start firing: you don't even know where the shots are coming from. Then there is the chasing. Sometimes it is we who are after the Viets and sometimes the other way about, but it is always the same business. Men sunk deep into the mud, the gluey mud, slowly forcing their legs through it to catch other men who are bogged down in the same way. You only see their heads, and the Plain of Reeds is so flat that you might think they were dots stuck to its surface. When you come to the open space of a canal or an irrigation ditch you swim under water, so as not to present a target: all that you see of a man is one hand holding up a tommy gun or the part of a mortar that must never get wet. Often some of my men are drowned.

In an attempt to provide mechanised support to the hard-pressed infantry, the French deployed two US amphibious vehicles of Second World War vintage: the armoured Alligator vehicle, equipped with heavy machine guns and a recoilless rifle, and the lighter Crab. British legionnaire Adrian Liddell Hart was assigned to a Crab, first as a machine-gunner and then a driver, and he outlined operations in and around the Mekong Delta:

Here and there we came across long strips of thick jungle forest often fringed with irrigated banana plantations and other evidences of human cultivation. Occasionally a radio aerial could be seen protruding from the foliage—a sign of military as well as human habitation. After the Crabs had nosed up like half submerged dinosaurs to provide covering power, some of us would scramble through the clearing to investigate. Sometimes there were already groups of infantry in evidence, slowly working through the forest in the hope of flushing out the rebels.

Here and there we rooted round for dumps of arms or other supplies which might be concealed, overturning heavy bowls of rice and peering under floorboards. Several times I came across little notebooks with Chinese characters neatly and methodically inscribed in then. Then once more we pressed forward against a receding vista or reeking forest.

But the enemy? He was everywhere–and nowhere. Inevitably warned by spies, by sympathetic or fearful inhabitants of our approach, possibly before we had even left the camp, he had vanished into the vast wilderness which he knew so much better than we. For hours, for days, we scanned the horizon in vain. Beyond the still grass, deep in the menacing woods, far up the muddy swollen tributaries, lay the enemy . . . We might make wide sweeps but our net had wide meshes.

Just as it was possible get used to the bizarre conditions on operations, so I became acclimatised to the daily life and atmosphere of the camp, with its characteristic confusion and suspicion and grind. Indeed, this whole existence of fighting and working had a single rhythm–slogging work in the camp, hectic days of preparation for an operation, hours of uneasy relaxation as the legionnaires drank on the landing craft, days and nights of strenuous, marauding sweeps as we heaved and dug and churned our way through swamp and jungle, songs over forest fires, and then once more, without a break, the work of cleaning and repairing the Crabs, maintaining and guarding the camp, with snatched moments, often late at night, of drinking from the upturned bottle in the foyer. 'En Avant!'

The Legion had its successes, however, as the DBLE officer explained:

Not long ago we got three hundred at one go. An informer guided our legionnaires to a Viet meeting that was being held on the banks of the Saigon River. The meeting was camouflaged in a field of maize. But we knew where it was a going on, and we charged right for the spot. The Viets flung themselves into the river, sinking into the water and the mud of the submerged forest and wriggling in among the mangrove roots. But the Saigon River is a tidal stream and the tide was on the ebb. We only had to wait. Two hours later the first Viets, stark naked, were in sight. They tried very hard to bury themselves deeper, digging down in the drying mud with their hands. We shot them like so many rabbits. The water ebbed further and further, and as it retreated every yard of mud had its quarry in it.

As the officer was quick to concede, however, simply killing Viet Minh was not enough–'there's an inexhaustible supply'–and, worse still, the French were indiscriminate in their methods: 'It's not only the full-blown Viet that we kill. We only know afterwards, and not always then. Often they are just villagers, people's militia, half or even only a quarter Viet.'

The French attitude to the Vietnamese population was, at best, indifferent. Little or no attempt was made to distinguish between civilians and combatants, and atrocities were commonplace. Lacking popular support, the French used extreme methods to gain intelligence of Viet Minh activities, further alienating the ordinary Vietnamese farmers and their families. Henry Ainley–a legionnaire sent to his battalion headquarters north of Saigon while working alongside the intelligence section–was sickened by French methods in Vietnam:

Torture and brutality were routine matters in the questioning of suspects, and frequently I was obliged to be an unwilling and disgusted witness, powerless to intervene. Unfortunately, brutality and bestiality were not exclusively reserved for official suspects. Rape, beating, burning, torturing on entirely harmless peasants and villagers were of common occurrence in the course of punitive patrols and operations by French troops, throughout the length and breadth of Indochina; the same measure evidently being applied to bona fide Viet Minh as well. Not only were these measures exclusively applied by the men; officers and NCOs assumed an active and frequently dominating role.

It was not an infrequent occurrence to hear these men bragging of the number of murders or rapes they had committed or the means of torture they had applied or the cash, jewels or possessions they had stolen. If one queried the morality of their actions the immediate reflection was 'Well, hell they are only "bounyouls" [natives]. Who the devil cares, anyway?' Before such a widespread and generally accepted practice there was nothing to do but look, listen and say nothing.

The fundamental counter-insurgency principle that 'the people are the prize' was lost on the French. And this failure only hurried the French ejection from Indochina.

By 1953 the French were losing control of Tonkin outside the defensive lines of the Red River Delta. This allowed the Viet Minh to push into neighbouring Laos with little opposition. In order to inhibit these Viet Minh operations the French decided to seize and hold Dien Bien Phu, a village that lay astride the main Viet Minh route into Laos. Two French airborne battle groups (including the Legion's 1st BEP) parachuted into Dien Bien Phu in November 1953, fortifying the area and constructing two air strips.

The apparent success of this move encouraged the French to extend their plan to include the possibility of waging a set-piece battle against the Viet Minh, where, it was believed, French superiority in artillery and air power would prove decisive. Giap seemed to have taken up the challenge when the French discovered that he had sent two of his best divisions towards Dien Bien Phu. The French flew in reinforcements and hurriedly began to improve the site's defences. Dien Bien Phu lay in a bowl-shaped valley, surrounded by densely wooded hills. The French lacked the time and resources to defend the hills, but instead contented themselves in building a series of mutually supporting strong-points in the valley, each one reputedly named after the mistresses of the garrison commander, Colonel (later General) Christian de Castries. Of the 13 fighting battalions at Dien Bien Phu, seven would be supplied by the Legion.

Sergeant Bleyer was assigned to the strongpoint called Beatrice, where he and his platoon began to dig in:

We immediately went to work clearing brush, cutting trees and building the most solid blockhouses possible, each platoon competing with that intensity particular to the Legion. I could only encourage my men. Having had a little experience during the Russian campaign [1941-5], I knew the damage that could be done by artillery. My legionnaires–terrific lads–were also well aware of the risks we were running.

Bleyer and his comrades, were, in fact, being dangerously complacent. Once again, the French underestimated the Viet Minh's military capabilities. An army of coolies had dragged 75mm field artillery and 120mm mortars to the hills surrounding the French positions.

Meticulously camouflaged–and well dug-in–the Viet Minh artillery would prove decisive. The French, by contrast, had not built the reinforced-concrete bunkers necessary to withstand Viet Minh shells, relying on relatively flimsy timber-and-dirt defences.

The bombardment of Dien Bien Phu opened on 31 January 1954, and after steady probing and the digging of assault trenches, Giap launched attacks on 13 March against the more exposed French positions. Among these was Beatrice, whose defenders included the 3rd Battalion of the DBLE. Captain Nicolas of the 10th Company described the beginning of the attack:

On 13 March the Viet Minh artillery preparation began. The entire day had been spent trying to fill in the Viet Minh approach trenches. During this extremely violent preparation the Viet Minh reopened their trenches and pushed them up to the wire under cover of the thick dust raised by the explosions that surrounded the centre of resistance with a veritable smoke screen.

Sergeant Kubiak, of the 1st Battalion, saw the attack on Beatrice from the main position:

The day began just like any other, digging fatigues, working on our defences . . . Towards 16.55 hours, I was having a drink with a friend. Then suddenly, without warning, it was what I imagine the end of the world will be like. The post Beatrice just went up in smoke, reduced to rubble . . . Blockhouse by blockhouse, trench by trench, everything collapsed, burying men and weapons under the debris.

Bleyer, meanwhile, was in the thick of the bombardment and subsequent Viet Minh attack:

Heavy artillery fire smashed everything, and it had barely stopped when the Viets were already in our wire. I went to get my orders, but the blockhouse of Lieutenant Carriere had collapsed under direct fire from bazookas and recoilless rifles. The lieutenant himself had been killed, and the controls of the defensive charges weren't working. I tried in vain to make contact with Lieutenant Jego. Then I found myself facing the Viets, who I welcomed with shots from my Colt. A grenade exploded between my legs.

Although wounded, Bleyer rallied other legionnaires before the whole position was taken. Only a few men got back to friendly lines. Major Paul Grauwin, one of the senior medical officers at Dien Bien Phu, treated some of the wounded survivors:

I returned to the field hospital, where some men with minor wounds had just arrived, having managed to escape from Beatrice. Their eyes were round with terror as they told of their experiences. 'If you could have seen them, Major, thousands and thousands of them, jumping over each other, over the ones who were already dead, mown down by our fire. Then the thousands of shells—when they had finished falling, half our shelters had collapsed.'

Gabrielle, another outer strong-point, then came under intense pressure. The 1st BEP was ordered to launch a counter-attack in support of Gabrielle's hard-pressed defenders. Almost immediately the Legion paratroopers came under intense fire from a Viet Minh blocking force along the Nam Ou River. According to Lieutenant Desmaizieres, of the battalion's 3rd Company:

The fighting began brutally; the 4th [Company] suffered serious losses. Norbert [the company commander] was wounded by a bullet in the thigh that made him howl with rage and pain. Standing under fire, he dropped his pants to apply a dressing while his orderly provided cover. Lieutenants Boisbouvier and Bertrand had crossed the ford, but they were pinned down with their legionnaires. Manoeuvring to the left of the trail, the source of the main firing, and supported by the tanks, the 3rd Company succeeded in breaking through and proceeded towards the objective.

But to the consternation of the paras, they saw the defenders beginning to withdraw from Gabrielle. The legionnaires of 1st BEP then began to retire as well, their efforts in vain. Desmaizieres concluded: 'a few [Algerian] riflemen held on till dusk before being overrun. The withdrawal of what was left of the BEP's companies was carried out under fire from the Viet cannons. They seemed to be celebrating their victory.'

The fall of Beatrice and Gabrielle was followed by the loss of Anne-Marie on the night of 17-18 March. The main airstrip was now vulnerable to Viet Minh artillery fire, and after the loss of several aircraft on the runway it was closed; the only assistance that could be provided to the garrison would have to come from parachute drops.

Despite this blow, the French fought on stubbornly, repulsing a series of Viet Minh offensives at the end of March and beginning of April. Casualties were heavy, however, and the garrison's medical organisation began to buckle under the strain, especially now that the seriously wounded could not be evacuated by air. Major Paul Grauwin left this graphic account of the conditions he was forced to work under:

Next came paratroopers from the Eighth Assault and the First Battalion of the Foreign, North African sappers, Senegalese gunners, Vietnamese, Thai's. A leg torn off, a wheezing thorax, an open stomach, a bloody hole in place of an eye, with the eye, smashed, hanging down on the cheek. An artery spurting up a jet of warm blood, abrupt and relentless; another leg torn off, a shoulder gaping open . . .

I had Major Martinelli put into Lieutenant Gindrey's shelter. But still they came, more and more of them, a lieutenant, a captain, a string of coolies helping one another along. Shells were whistling, ten or more at a time, exploding all at once. The shelters were full and fresh arrivals no longer even had room to lie down.

'Put them in the X-ray room—we can get four in there.' The next order was, 'Put them in the resuscitation ward—we can squeeze a few more in there.' Ten minutes later I found myself wedged between the phone and Lachamp's desk. A Vietnamese with the upper jaw broken had collapsed at my feet and was grasping my legs with his arms. Each time he breathed he spat blood and his eyes reflected his terror.

The next order was, 'Use the operating theatre.' I had to put a stop to operations. God help us. The first thing was to protect the wounded from the shells which were falling worse than ever. The operating theatre was soon full up. Howls, cries, groans and the ringing of the phone all mingled with the unholy din outside, filling my ears so that I could no longer think. From that moment I was no longer aware whether it was day or night, whether I was hungry or thirsty, whether I was a living human being or only a character in a nightmare.

I remember having heard someone say: 'Gabrielle has fallen. Anne-Marie has been abandoned.' Is that important? What does strategy or the number of Viets killed in the barbed wire around Gabrielle matter to me? Because this little fellow from Montpelier lying on a stretcher in the X-ray room is going to die; because there is blood spurting up into my face from a hole in this thorax and I can't stop it; because this abdomen, which is as hard as stone, belongs to a legionnaire who tells me, 'Ich bin fertig, ich weiss [I'm ready, I know]'; because this Vietnamese's dark eyes are full of reproach as he asks me why I have cut his leg off.

During April the Viet Minh steadily encroached on what remained of the French positions, digging trenches and building up supplies in preparation for the final assault. The French, meanwhile, were reinforced from the air by four paratroop battalions (two from the Legion), which provided much-needed practical support, as well as improving morale. But the defenders were even more impressed by a further parachute drop, as Grauwin explained:

Towards the middle of April, a special order of the day, signed by General de Castries, informed us that, in response to a request from the commander-in-chief, thousands of men in all branches of the service had volunteered to drop on Dien Bien Phu, without making any preliminary drops or having any previous training.

It was unbelievable, unprecedented; we could hardly believe our eyes as we read. Our hearts were filled with relief; around me I could hear the soldiers, visitors and wounded expressing their joy and enthusiasm. Now they were convinced that everything would be done for Dien Bien Phu, that the higher command had decided to hold on to the end—until victory.

There could be no doubting the heroism of these novice paratroops, especially as many knew only too well–unlike Grauwin–the real hopelessness of the situation. French aircraft were operating towards the end of their range, and were unable to supply the garrison with sufficient supplies and munitions. They had also failed to make much impression on the Viet Minh artillery that was pounding the French positions into oblivion. As the French got weaker, so Giap's forces grew stronger. Matters were made worse by the coming of the monsoon on 22 April, leaving the French defences waterlogged; the more battered simply collapsed into a sea of mud.

Oh 1 May the Viet Minh threw all their forces at the remaining French positions. Sergeant Kubiak recorded the final days of Dien Bien Phu in his diary:

5 May 1954

We've been fighting for fifty days. Sheer hell!

The Viets are bombarding us with their 'orgues de Staline'–twelve-barrelled rocket launchers–and my sector is having particular attention paid to it. Again I feel it's the end of the world, and I'm not the only one who feels that way. In the dark I cross myself. It's extraordinary how intensely one believes when death is roaming around. I got a splinter in my face. It gave me a lovely pair of black eyes. Blood spurted and I was almost knocked out.

But I realised that if I could still keep on my feet, things weren't too bad. I got my automatic well sited. About time. Another wave of Viets was coming at us. Independent fire. Death spitting from every corner. Men falling like flies on both sides.

Today is the 6 May.

The heat is killing as soon as the sun rises. The piles of fly-covered corpses are decomposing rapidly. The air we breathe is scarcely perfumed with attar of roses!

On 7 May the Viet Minh overran the main French position, but the legionnaires–including the wounded–were determined to fight on, as Kubiak explained:

Legionnaire S. was by my side. He'd been hit several times in the belly and walked doubled up. He was in agony . . . Suddenly firing broke out from a blockhouse and I saw Viets falling. I ran across, went in, and could hardly believe my eyes. It was a couple of wounded men who were firing the machine gun. They grinned when they saw me. 'I've got the odd hole in me,' said one, 'but

I can still fight.' He had a huge bandage round his belly and, as he staggered to his feet, blood began to ooze through. As for the other, who had been acting as leader, he had only one arm and a shell splinter in the lung.

Suddenly I heard the battalion commander swearing like a trooper. I turned in the direction he was looking and saw a white flag fluttering over the General's HQ. It was difficult to guess his reactions.

We opened on the Viets with everything we'd got and it wasn't long before they were answering back in no mean manner, the whole mass of their artillery concentrating on us. For me the last few minutes are hazy. A shell spat under my nose and I collapsed in the mud, hit in the right leg. Suddenly a Viet jumped into the trench, saw me and I'd had it. He came slowly towards me, and I couldn't move. He cocked his sub-machine, aimed deliberately and fired. I don't know what happened, but suddenly he collapsed on top of me and I passed out.

I learnt afterwards that a legionnaire had killed him just as he fired and the shot had missed me by a millimetre. It was his corpse falling on me that protected me from the other Viets.

It was the 7 May. For me the battle was over, my life as a prisoner beginning.

Following de Castries' decision to surrender, a few determined defenders tried to fight their way out, but almost all were either killed or captured. Some 11,000 men—many of them wounded—were led away into what would become a prolonged and cruel captivity. Pierre Schoendoerffer remembers feeling 'rage and bitterness at being abandoned' and seeing the enemy at close hand:

We left the putrefaction of the battlefield, and suddenly saw grass, trees, and inhaled good odour. There was a clear sunset, and high in the sky the last [French] Dakota [supply plane] was dropping a cargo of medicine. The Viet Minh were tense and very young. Despite their heavy losses, there was no brutality. We climbed a hill, and, reaching the crest, we could see an entire valley filled with Viet Minh troops ready to attack. They watched us intently as we passed.

The defeat had destroyed the elite of the French army, and France had little alternative but to withdraw from Indochina. On 21 July 1954 the French signed a negotiated settlement: Laos and Cambodia received their independence while Vietnam was divided at the 17th parallel into a communist North and a US-sponsored South. More than 10,000 soldiers and officers of the Foreign Legion had been killed in a hopeless bid to hang on to this colonial possession thousands of miles from France.